Praise for these n̶[...]rs:

JAYNE ANN KRENTZ

"A master of the genre...nobody does it better!"
—*Romantic Times*

"Each and every Krentz book is to be savored
over and over again."
—*Rave Reviews*

BARBARA DELINSKY

"Barbara Delinsky knows the human heart
and its immense capacity to love and to believe."
—*Washington PA Observer-Reporter*

An author..."of sensitivity and style."
—*Publishers Weekly*

TESS GERRITSEN

"Readers will learn to expect the unexpected
from this dynamic and innovative author."
—*Gothic Journal*

"Tess Gerritsen brings us action,
adventure and compelling romance."
—*Romantic Times*

JAYNE ANN KRENTZ

is one of today's best-loved authors of women's fiction. With multiple *New York Times* bestselling novels to her credit, she is a prolific and innovative writer. She has delved into psychic elements, intrigue, fantasy, historicals and even futuristic romances. Jayne lives in Seattle with her husband.

BARBARA DELINSKY

was born and raised in suburban Boston. She worked as a researcher, photographer and reporter before turning to writing full-time in 1980. With more than fifty novels to her credit, she is truly one of the shining stars in contemporary romance fiction. This talented writer has received numerous awards and honors, and her involving stories have made her a *New York Times* bestselling author. There are over 12 million copies of her books in print worldwide—a testament to Barbara's universal appeal.

TESS GERRITSEN

is an accomplished woman with an interesting history. Once a practicing physician, she has chosen instead to write full-time, using her medical knowledge to add to her intricate and dramatic stories. Tess has co-written *Adrift*, a CBS screenplay, and has several other screenplays optioned by HBO. A *New York Times* bestselling author, she is also writing mainstream medical thrillers with much success. Having lived in Hawaii, she now resides in Camden, Maine, with her physician husband and two sons.

JAYNE ANN KRENTZ
BARBARA DELINSKY
TESS GERRITSEN

Family Passions

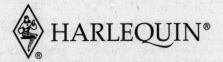

HARLEQUIN®

TORONTO • NEW YORK • LONDON
AMSTERDAM • PARIS • SYDNEY • HAMBURG
STOCKHOLM • ATHENS • TOKYO • MILAN • MADRID
PRAGUE • WARSAW • BUDAPEST • AUCKLAND

ISBN 0-373-83525-6

FAMILY PASSIONS

CONTENTS

THE FAMILY WAY   9
Jayne Ann Krentz

CHANCES ARE   183
Barbara Delinsky

PRESUMED GUILTY   377
Tess Gerritsen

THE FAMILY WAY
Jayne Ann Krentz

CHAPTER ONE

HE KNEW SOMETHING WAS wrong the instant he turned the silver Ferrari into the curving drive. Case McCord felt his stomach tighten in a cold knot. Pru's snappy little candy-red Ford stood in front of the steps that led up to the wide open doors of the house. There was another familiar car in the drive, an impossibly long, aging, white Cadillac El Dorado, its chrome gleaming in the late afternoon sun. McCord ignored it.

It was the red Ford that alarmed him. The trunk of the car was open, and Steve Graham, the young handyman-gardener McCord had hired a few months ago, was busy trying to fit one of Pru's huge suitcases into the minuscule space.

She meant to go through with her threat, McCord thought in astonishment. She was going to walk out, just as she had said. He couldn't believe it. She wouldn't dare.

McCord slammed the Ferrari to a halt behind the little Ford and wrenched open his car door. Steve Graham paused in his task of trying to wedge the suitcase into the trunk and glanced over his shoulder. The worried expression on his young surf-and-sun-tanned face turned into one of welcoming relief.

"Boy, am I glad to see you, Mr. McCord. Caught an early flight, huh? I was afraid you wouldn't get here in time. It's all a big mess. Pru says she's leaving. For good, she says. Martha's having a fit, and Mr. Arlington is going through your whiskey like there was no tomorrow. The caterers arrived an hour ago, and they're all wandering around looking confused. Pru refuses to talk to 'em and get them organized. Your guests will be here in another couple of hours or so, and Pru says she wants to be long gone by then."

"I have a feeling," McCord said through ominously set teeth, "that Pru isn't worried about leaving before the guests arrive. More likely she intended to get out of here before I got home. She knows there's going to be hell to pay."

Some of the boyish relief disappeared from Steve's expression. He blinked a little nervously at his employer and coughed to clear his throat. "She said you weren't due back until later this evening."

"She made a mistake," McCord informed the younger man. "A big one." He swung around, heading for the steps. His booted feet made a crunching sound as he strode across the graveled drive. He took the steps two at a time and halted for an instant on the top one, turning back momentarily to snap at Steve, "Take that suitcase out of the trunk. Pru's not going anywhere."

"But she said she wanted to be out of here in the next fifteen minutes."

"Take the damned suitcase out of the car, Graham, or you're fired."

Steve Graham had been working for Case McCord long enough to respect the dangerously soft tone of voice, even if he hadn't believed the threat. McCord's voice never rose when he got angry. Instead it went the other direction—low, controlled and ice cold.

In his hurry to remove the luggage from the tiny trunk, Steve scraped the side of the suitcase. He stared down at the scratch in dismay. Then he sighed philosophically. Better to have to replace one of Pru's suitcases than risk McCord's fury.

And there was no doubt that Case McCord was furious.

Prudence Kenyon was in the kitchen trying to soothe Martha Hewett, the housekeeper, when she heard McCord's footsteps in the hall. Pru closed her eyes in a brief moment of profound irritation and regret. She should have moved more quickly today. She shouldn't have allowed herself to get distracted first by J.P.'s arrival and then by Martha's anxiety attack. Most of all, she should have guessed that something would go wrong at the last minute.

Something certainly had gone wrong. McCord had obviously

caught an earlier flight than the one on which he had been scheduled to return to San Diego.

"Oh, thank goodness, there's Mr. McCord now." Martha Hewett's tight breathing miraculously began to ease as she relaxed. She put away the small bottle of tablets without taking one of the little blue pills inside. Her eyes brightened with relief and hope. "He'll take care of everything, Pru, you'll see." She patted Pru's arm, instantly reversing the roles of caretaker and patient.

Pru had time for a quick glare at the beaming Martha. The anxiety attack seemed to have completely disappeared in the wink of an eye, leaving the short, stout fifty-year-old woman with a serene smile and a relieved expression in her bright hazel eyes.

"Congratulations on the quick recovery, Martha," Pru observed brusquely just as the kitchen's swinging door was opened with enough force to make the china rattle in a nearby cupboard. The two servers who had arrived with the caterer jumped. Pru didn't bother to turn around. She knew who had just entered the huge, gleaming kitchen. "Perhaps you don't really need that prescription, after all," she said to the housekeeper.

But Martha wasn't paying any attention to Pru. She was staring past her at the big man who was standing in the kitchen doorway, filling the whole room with the force of his presence. "You got home early, Mr. McCord. I'm so glad. We've got something of a crisis on our hands here. Nothing that can't be handled by the time your guests arrive," she added hastily. "If you could just talk to Pru, I'm sure everything will work out fine. She's a little upset."

"Is that right, Pru? Are you a *little upset?*"

Pru heard the ruthless softness in his voice and raised her eyes briefly toward the ceiling in silent supplication before forcing herself to swing around with a cool smile. "Not in the least, McCord. Everything's under control as far as I'm concerned. I thought Martha was having one of her attacks but it seems I was mistaken. If you both will excuse me, I'll be on my way."

Boldly she started forward, mentally crossing her fingers in the hope that he would automatically step out of her way. She should have known better. McCord didn't move. He blocked the door as effectively as an armored tank, saying nothing at all until she was forced to halt a few paces from her goal. His dark, hooded gaze swept her from head to toe, taking in the narrow green pullover, snug-fitting jeans and sandals she was wearing. It was very obvious she was not dressed for entertaining the VIPs who were due later that evening.

"So," McCord murmured much too gently as he folded his arms across his broad chest and leaned negligently against the doorjamb, "you meant it. You were really planning to leave."

Pru drew a breath and prayed that only she knew how shaky it was. "Of course, I meant it. We have that much in common, McCord. Neither of us makes false threats. I just left things a bit late, that's all. You weren't due back for another hour."

"You left things much too late." McCord straightened away from the door, his gaze raking Martha and the two nervous men in the catering uniforms. "I have no intention of finishing this conversation in front of an audience. Let's go." He turned to stride back down the hall, clearly expecting her to follow dutifully.

Pru shook her head over the massive arrogance of the man. "I'm afraid I haven't got time for an extended discussion, McCord," she called down the hall after him. "I've got to be on my way. And you'd better see about getting everything organized for your party tonight. There's a lot to be done before your guests arrive."

McCord was already at the open door to the study. He turned to look at her. "To hell with the party. If you've got the nerve to try walking out on me, you can damn well find the nerve to have an extended discussion on the subject. Get in here, Pru, unless you want to have this conversation in the middle of the hall."

"You're not going to find any privacy in the study," Pru warned as she reluctantly started toward him. "J.P.'s in there."

McCord glanced inside the comfortable, book-lined room.

"Hello, J.P. Didn't anyone ever tell you it's dangerous to get involved in a domestic quarrel?" He walked into the room.

Pru groaned. This was going to be every bit as bad as she had imagined. It would have been so much simpler if she'd got away before McCord had arrived. Now she was stuck having to go through a major scene, one the entire household, assorted caterers and J.P. Arlington himself would witness. Nothing was ever easy when you were dealing with Case McCord.

But, then, she had known that from the beginning.

Pru walked down the hall toward the study as though she were marching toward a court-martial. She told herself she had to remember that it was McCord who had been tried and convicted and that she was judge and jury, not him. McCord had a way of turning the tables in a situation such as this. If she wasn't careful, she would find herself caving in, surrendering, giving up and generally turning into mush.

No one who hadn't been forced to confront McCord could possibly understand just how intimidating and arrogantly forceful he could be, Pru thought. There were a number of factors that contributed to this ability, not the least of which was his sheer size.

McCord was tall, a couple of inches over six feet. He was also hard and lean and strongly, smoothly muscled. His hair was almost as dark as his eyes and closely trimmed in an effort to control a faint wave. It was his eyes that held the key to Case McCord, Pru had often thought. They dominated the blunt, harsh lines of his face.

Those dark eyes held both a razor-sharp intelligence and a simmering passion that was never far below the surface. Intelligence and passion could be a volatile combination in a man, a *lethal* combination. Fury, arrogance and sheer masculine stubbornness were all forces that could be honed to fine degrees by such a mixture. So, too, could sensuality, loyalty, and protectiveness.

At times such as this when he was angry, those brilliant, passionate eyes were fathomless pools of cryptic danger. Only a fool would ignore the warning.

But, then, she had been ignoring the warnings that emanated from Case McCord since she had first met him, Pru reminded herself bracingly. That had been six months ago when she had come to work for the Arlington Foundation for Agricultural Research and Development. It was too late to start exercising caution this afternoon.

An observer who knew nothing about Case McCord might have guessed immediately that the man spent a lot of his time outdoors working the land. This afternoon McCord was dressed in a silk tie, gray slacks and a white shirt, but that was only because he'd just returned from an Arlington Foundation meeting in Washington, D.C. The boots he wore were a better clue to his usual clothing style. When McCord wasn't dressed to deal with the scientists, research experts and officials of foreign governments, he generally wore jeans and a casual open-throated shirt. When he was in one of the foundation's experimental fields, he frequently wore a classic Stetson hat.

No, it wouldn't have been hard for an outside observer to guess that Case McCord was at home in rich fertile fields and sundrenched acres of growing crops. What such an observer might not have understood was that McCord had more than just an intuitive feel for crops and soil and weather. He also had a scientist's extensive training in those subjects.

Case McCord was one of the many research experts employed by the Arlington Foundation. He had joined the foundation staff three years ago, rising rapidly to his present high-level position because, in addition to his scientific training, McCord had a natural talent for leadership. The Arlington Foundation was committed to the improvement of agricultural techniques in developing countries. As its founder, J.P. Arlington, was fond of saying in his Texas drawl, people couldn't learn to enjoy the wonders of democracy until they had first discovered the wonders of a full stomach.

At the request of foreign governments and private enterprise, the foundation sent its experts all over the globe. McCord had originally been hired for his knowledge of soil, but his responsibilities now extended into the realm of management and organization. Old J.P. was sharp enough to recognize and make use of the talents he discovered in his staff. Old J.P. was fairly sharp in a number of ways, Pru had discovered during the six months she had been working in the publishing department of the foundation. In his own way, the old man was as smart and dangerous as McCord. The thought of having to enter the study and face both of them was daunting.

She should have said to heck with the evening's social preparations and left McCord's home yesterday, Pru decided. She had been a fool to let her sense of professional responsibility get in the way of her sense of responsibility to herself. Well, the sooner this little scene was over, the better.

Taking a firm grip on her emotions, Pru entered the study. McCord was standing, feet braced slightly apart, in front of his desk, eyeing J.P. Arlington with a cold gaze.

J.P. was, as usual, quite a sight. He was dressed to complement the big, flashy El Dorado parked in the drive. The silver-trimmed, peach-colored western-style suit he wore was not the least bit effeminate on his big frame. He had removed his matching Stetson, displaying his wealth of silver hair. His eyes were gray, and there were a thousand tiny lines radiating out from the corners. Those lines had been induced by years spent under a hot Texas sun. J.P. had inherited land, but forty years ago he'd found the oil under it all by himself.

Arlington was sprawled in McCord's chair, his lizard-skin boots propped on the polished desktop. He had a bottle of whiskey open on the low table beside the chair and a glass in his hand. He grinned broadly at Pru as she walked into the room.

"Well, now, maybe we can finally get this little mess sorted out 'fore it goes any farther. I told you to wait till McCord got home, didn't I, girl? Everything's gonna be just fine and dandy now. Nothing like a little communication to work out the problems, I always say. Dealing with McCord can be like dealing with a mule. First you got to whamp him up 'longside the head with a two-by-four just to get his attention. But once that part's done, you'll find he can be right reasonable.'' J.P. shot a suddenly narrowed glance at the man standing on the other side of the desk. ''Talk to her, McCord. I want this little matter worked out as soon as possible. We've got those ten honchos due here in—'' he glanced at the big chunk of gold on his wrist ''—less then two hours.''

''I'll talk to her,'' McCord vowed, ''but not with you sitting there interrupting every three minutes. Get out, J.P. This is between Pru and myself. It doesn't involve you.''

''The hell it doesn't, boy. I need her. She's a damn good journal editor and an even better hostess. If I find myself having to hire someone else to do her job, I'm gonna hold you personally responsible. Now *do* something.''

''Get out of my study, J.P.'' McCord repeated.

Arlington glowered at him and then looked at Pru. ''You think you can handle him all by yourself, Pru?''

''Oh, yes,'' Pru said with a confidence she was far from feeling. ''I can handle him.''

J.P. hauled himself up out of the chair. ''All right. I'll give you two a while to work this out on your own.'' He glared at McCord. ''But I expect results. Don't let Pru here get away, hear me? Blow this, McCord, and I'll have your hide nailed to the hood of my El Dorado.'' Glass in hand, Arlington stomped out of the room, slamming the door behind him.

Pru watched him go and then resolutely turned back to face McCord. She summoned up a bright, determined smile. ''This conversation is a waste of time. I want to be on my way and you're going to have your hands full getting ready for your guests this evening. Martha has full instructions, and all the caterers need is some general guidance, but there's still a certain amount of organizing to be done. I suggest you have Steve set up the bar and tend it. He's getting quite good at that sort of thing. Make sure he puts on a clean white shirt first. Also, when the guests arrive don't let J.P. start telling his stories about his days in the oil fields. You know how he is when he gets on that subject. Be sure to tell Martha to serve the French brandy. This crowd will expect it. Other than that, I'm sure you'll be fine.''

McCord leaned back against his desk, his big hands planted solidly on either side of his powerful thighs. His dark eyes were narrowed and grim. ''Stop it, Pru. We both know you're not going anywhere.''

Pru shook her head sadly. ''You're wrong,'' she said gently. ''I really am going to leave, McCord. I told you before you left for Washington that I would be gone by the time you returned.''

''You were upset when I left. You didn't mean what you were saying.''

''I meant every word,'' Pru told him. ''You just didn't pay any attention.''

''I never pay much attention to ultimatums. That's what you were trying to do before I left, wasn't it, Pru? You tried to make me think you were delivering an ultimatum. You should know me well enough by now to know I'd call your bluff.''

''It's no bluff. My suitcases are packed. I'm ready to go.''

McCord's mouth tightened. ''I should let you walk right out that door. It might teach you a lesson.''

''I've already learned my lesson, McCord.''

''Is that right?'' His gaze was mocking. ''Which lesson was that? I seem to recall teaching you a number of interesting things during the past few months.''

As the warm, embarrassed color blazed in her face, his eyes moved slowly and possessively over her, taking in the sweep of bronzed brown hair that curved just about her shoulders and the clear golden-green of her eyes. He examined the delicate shape of her soft mouth and then went on to the gentle curves of her small breasts. Then his gaze went lower, gliding over the full curve of her hips. There was no doubt about what he was thinking. There was also no denying the memories he was deliberately evoking.

Pru was realistic enough to know that she was not a beautiful woman. She was reasonably attractive in an open, honest sort of way, but she was far from being a riveting beauty. In McCord's arms, though, she had learned what it meant to feel beautiful.

She felt the heat intensify in her cheeks. The past few months with Case McCord had been a passionate interlude unlike anything Pru had ever known in her life. McCord had been smart enough to guess almost at once just how limited her previous sexual experience had been, and he had capitalized on that fact. He had taken great pleasure in teaching her to respond to him. His teaching had been so good that Pru had actually convinced herself that he was in love with her—as in love with her as she was with him. She'd finally had to admit to herself that she'd been wrong.

She held on to her dignity and her self-control as the heated memories flickered in her mind, well aware of the alert, assessing expression in McCord's eyes. She mustn't show any weakness. Not now. McCord would see it and use it.

Determinedly she held McCord's gaze. "The real lesson I learned from you is one my Aunt Wilhelmina spent years trying to teach my sister and me back when we were growing up in Spot, Texas. It's a lesson mothers have tried to teach their daughters since the world began."

"Is that right?" he mocked. "What is this great gem of feminine wisdom?"

"'Give a man free whiskey and he'll get used to the notion of not having to pay for it. It's tough to collect after he's drunk his fill,'" Pru quoted grimly. Aunt Wilhelmina's words echoed in her ears.

McCord's head came up angrily. For an instant his simmering temper threatened to rage out of control. "That's a stupid, juvenile thing to say."

"I tried being very adult and sophisticated about moving in with you, McCord, but it didn't work. Three months ago when you invited, or rather informed me that I was to come and live with you, I told myself that you could be domesticated, that somehow you'd see the wonders of having a good home life and a woman who cared for you. But the more I gave, the more you took. Last week I finally admitted to myself that the situation is hopeless. You're never going to change. You don't want marriage and commitment. You just want all the convenience and advantages of having a woman in your home and in your bed without having to give up anything in return."

"You seemed to be getting something you wanted out of the arrangement," he tossed back. "Why the complaints now?"

"I told you before you left on your trip," she reminded him in a clear, gentle voice. "I came to live with you because I believed our arrangement, as you call it, was going somewhere important. I thought we were building a future together. But after three months under your roof, I realize I was deluding myself." She had deluded herself into thinking he loved her. "As Aunt Wilhelmina would say, 'Weaving daydreams around a man like you is about as useless as putting shoes on a goose.'"

"You're right about one thing. If there was any deluding being done, you were doing it to yourself. You knew I wasn't interested in marriage," he reminded her harshly. "I've never pretended otherwise."

"No," she agreed with forced lightness, "you certainly haven't. Unfortunately, I've decided I do want marriage. And you've made it quite clear I won't ever get that kind of commitment from you."

"So you decided to try to force my hand, didn't you? But it won't work, Pru. I told you that before I left for Washington. There's not a chance in hell I'd let any woman, you included, manipulate me to that extent."

Pru nodded, gazing down at her entwined hands for a moment as she absorbed the pain of his words. "I understand. You've been very honest with me. I was only misleading myself."

"Don't give me that self-deprecating martyr act." McCord came away from the desk and stalked past her to the wide bay window that overlooked the lush garden. "It's not going to work any better than the ultimatum did."

Pru's mouth tightened. "Then I'd better stop wasting your time and mine. I've got a long drive ahead of me. Goodbye, McCord. The past few months have been interesting.'' She whirled around and headed for the door.

McCord tore away from the window as he realized she really was going to walk out. He caught her arm just as she reached for the doorknob. Yanking her back to face him, he stared down into her composed features.

"You're not going anywhere and you know it. Don't try to play games with me, Pru. You don't stand a chance."

"How many times do I have to explain? I'm not playing a game. I'm leaving. Just as I said I would. Your mistake, McCord, is in thinking I'm trying to manipulate you. I'm not. I'm cutting my losses and getting out. There's no future with you."

"Because I won't put a ring on your finger?"

"Because you're either too much of a coward or you're simply too selfish to make a genuine commitment. I haven't been able to decide which reason applies, but in the end it doesn't matter. Either way I want out."

"You think I'm going to get down on my knees and beg you to stay? You think that by threatening to leave you can get a promise of marriage out of me? Is that it?"

She shook her head wearily and glanced pointedly down to where his fingers were clenched around her arm. "You don't understand, McCord. What's more, I don't think you ever will. You're brilliant when it comes to figuring out how to grow wheat in a desert, but you're just plain dumb when it comes to understanding what it takes to have a real relationship. Please let me go. I told you, I have a long drive ahead of me."

He didn't remove his fingers from her arm. His eyes blazed down at her. "Where is this long drive going to take you? Into some other man's arms? Is that it, Pru? Have you got another man on your string? Someone you've been keeping in reserve in case you couldn't manipulate me into marrying you? Who is he? Does he know about the past few months? Does he know what you've been learning in my arms? How you tremble when I touch you in the middle of the night? Do you think you'll find with just any man what you've found with me?''

"I've got news for you, McCord. You may be good in bed, but that's not enough. Not for me. Now kindly let go of my arm. You're hurting me.'' For the first time that day she was getting angry. It was risky to let any strong emotion intrude on the composure she had imposed on herself. McCord would seize the opening and use it to his own advantage.

"You're not walking out of here,'' McCord told her, each word spoken with dangerous emphasis. He glanced down at his hand on her arm and with obvious effort released her. "You can't do it.''

"Why not?'' She flung open the door. Her self-control was slipping rapidly now. She had to get out of the house.

"You know why not.'' McCord was striding after her as Pru hurried down the hall toward the front door. *"You can't leave me because you're in love with me and you know it.''*

Pru caught her breath but she didn't pause. He knew. She had hoped to be able to salvage that much in the way of pride, but apparently she wasn't to be so lucky. It shouldn't have surprised her to discover that Case McCord was well aware of the extent of her emotional involvement with him. The man was too damn smart for any woman's good.

There was nothing she could say in response to his challenge. It was the truth, and it was unbearably obvious that they both knew it. Pru saw no reason to add to her humiliation by acknowledging the fact. She went out the front door, aware of McCord hard on her heels.

Steve Graham was standing next to her car, her suitcase beside him on the graveled drive. He looked up anxiously as Pru came through the doorway. His eyes went from her face to the grimly furious expression of the man behind her.

"Haven't you got those suitcases in the trunk yet, Steve?'' Pru started down the steps.

"Mr. McCord said not to load them. He said you weren't leaving."

"He was wrong. I'm leaving. If you won't put them in the car, I will."

Steve bent to hoist one of the suitcases. "I'll do it, if that's what you really want, Pru." He cast a defiant glance at McCord, who ignored him.

"If you think I'll come after you on my hands and knees, you're crazy, woman." McCord stood braced on the top step as if he was ready for battle. "This game isn't going to work. Face it and stop behaving like a melodramatic teenager threatening to run away from home because she can't get her own way."

Pru said nothing as Steve slammed the trunk on her suitcases. There was nothing left to say. Without a word she climbed into the Ford, fastened the seat belt and turned the key in the ignition. A moment later she was speeding down the drive.

A glance in her rearview mirror showed J.P., Martha and Steve all hovering around the solid rock of masculine fury that was Case McCord. After that one look, she didn't glance back again.

McCord watched the little red Ford until it disappeared from sight. No one around him said a word. When he finally turned to stalk back into the house he found himself confronting three accusing faces.

For an instant no one spoke and then Martha said in a forlorn voice, "She's gone.

"That's obvious, isn't it?" McCord snapped. "I suggest you get busy, Martha. Apparently there are a lot of things to be done before our guests arrive. You haven't got time for one of your anxiety attacks. Steve, I understand you're going to handle the bar this evening. Go set it up. Try not to leave bottles and glasses lying around tonight the way you leave the gardening tools scattered around the grounds. Why are you three looking at me like that? This isn't my fault, you know. It was Pru who threw the temper tantrum and walked out two hours before a party."

"Don't put the blame on her," J.P. muttered. "She didn't want anything more than what any nice young lady from Texas has got a right to expect from her man. You've been as happy as a bull in clover for the past few months. Got everything you wanted, didn't you? But you never noticed that sweet little Pru was hurtin' inside. It was only a matter of time before she upped and left. Surprised it took this long. Don't know what I'm gonna do for a hostess, let alone a good journal editor now.''

''I'm going to miss her,'' Steve remarked wistfully. ''We were just getting the garden into shape. She won't be here to see how the tomatoes turn out.''

Martha sniffed and reached for a handkerchief. ''She was certainly a very understanding person.'' She blew into the scrap of linen. ''Not everyone understands what it's like to have anxiety attacks.''

McCord's eyes glittered with frustrated fury. ''Kindly ash-can the maudlin postmortems. I don't want to hear them. We've got a lot to do in the next two hours. Get moving, all of you.'' He forged through the small group on the steps and strode down the hall into the study. Not even J.P. tried to stop him.

Once inside he slammed the door closed, walked over to his desk and picked up the bottle of whiskey J.P. had left behind. There was a spare glass sitting on the small shelf beside the desk. McCord splashed the amber liquid into it and then moved to the window.

She was gone. Afternoon sunlight still streamed through the windows, but the place already seemed empty and dark. It was as though she'd walked out of the house and turned off all the lights behind her.

McCord's hand tightened into a fist around the glass of whiskey.

CHAPTER TWO

A WEEK AFTER her grand exit from Case McCord's home, Pru found herself stretched out on a lounger beside her sister's pool in Pasadena. A large table umbrella sheltered her from the direct glare of the sun. The entire Los Angeles basin was simmering in the warmth of the early summer heat, and Pru found herself thinking of how pleasant the gardens in McCord's home would be on a day like this. His lovely house on a hillside in La Jolla just north of San Diego had a cooling view of the ocean. She was going to miss it on days such as this.

The view from McCord's gardens wasn't the only thing she was going to miss, she reflected as she watched her small niece and nephew splashing happily in the cool crystal water of the pool. Even as the thought went through her mind she was inundated with another small wave of pool water. Pru was already so damp from the children's exuberant actions that she was considering bestirring herself for another dip.

Before she could make up her mind on the matter, Annie Gates stuck her attractive blond head around the kitchen door and called out to her sister. "Hey, Pru. Want a glass of lemonade?"

"I do," seven-year-old Katy yelled from the pool.

Not to be outdone, her brother, Dave, echoed the appeal. "So do I."

Annie wrinkled her nose in affectionate admonishment. "Are these the same two kids who didn't have room for brussels sprouts at lunch?"

"I'm hungry now," Katy assured her mother.

"Me, too," Dave repeated predictably. He was almost two years younger than his sister, but he was quick to pick up on her lead. By watching Katy, he was rapidly learning that assertiveness pays in this world.

Pru grinned at her older sister. "If you're making lemonade, you'd better make it in quantity."

"Heck, if the response is this good, I might just start charging for it." Annie disappeared back into her gleaming modern kitchen. When she came outside a few minutes later, she was carrying a large plastic pitcher of lemonade and four plastic glasses. "Okay, everyone, come and get it."

Katy and Dave needed no second invitation. They bounced out of the pool to collect their glasses and then went over to their child-sized lounge chairs to drink the lemonade.

"Just what I needed," Pru told her sister as she reached for a glass.

"You're not the only one." Annie sat back in a webbed chair and propped her sandaled feet on the end of Pru's lounger. "Somebody turned the heat on early this year. Almost reminds me of summer in Spot, Texas. Almost, but not quite. How are you feeling?"

Pru smiled and sipped lemonade. "Fine. Any reason why I shouldn't?"

"No, of course not." Annie sighed. "Sorry if I'm being over-protective. It's just that since you don't have a husband to fuss over you, I feel obliged to fill the gap."

"I appreciate it," Pru said gently, "but it's not necessary. I really am okay."

Annie eyed her shrewdly. "Or at least as okay as any woman can be when she finds herself unmarried and pregnant?"

"I'm twenty-seven years old, Annie. I'm not some naive teen-ager who's got herself into trouble."

"No, you're a rather naive twenty-seven-year-old who's got herself into trouble. That bastard."

Pru shook her head. There wasn't much she could say. Annie had formed her own opinion of Case McCord. She was a protective older sister, and she was not inclined to take an understanding or charitable view of the man who had got Pru pregnant. "I've told you, Annie. He doesn't know I'm pregnant."

"Would it have made any difference?" Annie challenged.

Pru hesitated. "I don't know. I didn't put it to the test. If he wasn't interested in marrying me for myself, I certainly didn't want him marrying me because of the baby."

"You're too proud for your own good, Pru."

"I can handle this on my own. Lots of women do."

"That doesn't make it right!"

"I know." Pru shrugged. "But these things happen."

"You should never have got involved with him." It wasn't the first time Annie had made the observation. "The day you phoned to tell me you were moving in with him I knew you were headed for trouble. He used you."

"At the time," Pru said reflectively, "I thought he needed me. I know he wanted me. I hoped he loved me."

"Well, of course he *wanted* you. You fell right into his palm, didn't you? Men are always willing to take what's available, especially if they don't have to pay for it."

Pru's eyes widened and then her smile turned into outright laughter. "You sound just like Aunt Wilhelmina."

"Be grateful Aunt Wilhelmina doesn't know about this situation yet. When she finds out she's going to have hysterics."

"No, she won't. She'll simply come to the conclusion that there's bad blood in the family. She won't be surprised. She undoubtedly suspected it all along," Pru said humorously, thinking of the iron-spined, rigidly upright aunt who had raised her and her sister.

"She always meant well. And she tried hard to make up for mother's, uh, shortcomings." Having lived away from Aunt Wilhelmina for several years now, Annie was willing to be broadminded on the subject. "Someday she'll reap whatever heavenly reward exists for martyred spinsters who wind up having to raise their sister's illegitimate children," Annie added dryly. "When are you going to tell her you not only lived with a man for a few months, but you also went and got yourself pregnant by him?''

"Not until I have to," Pru said bluntly. "Aunt Wilhelmina hasn't mellowed much with age, and you know it. I'd just as soon not listen to all her lectures on men drinking their fill of free whiskey and milk without feeling obliged to pay for the booze or buy the cow.''

"I'll tell you something," Annie said quietly, her eyes going to her daughter. "Every time I think of Katy growing up and starting to date, I find myself inclining toward Aunt Wilhelmina's point of view. I know it sounds old-fashioned and cynical, but I want to tell her not to risk giving herself to a man until she's very, very sure of him.''

"Until he's proven himself by putting a ring on her finger, you mean.''

"Face it, Pru. You wouldn't be in the situation you're in today if you'd followed Aunt Wilhelmina's advice.''

Pru regarded her sister evenly. "Are you going to tell me you didn't sleep with Tony until you were married? Because I won't believe you. You were head over heels in love with him and he couldn't keep his hands off you.''

Annie had the grace to blush and then she smiled. "Well, at least I was reasonably sure of our feelings for each other before we made love. That's more than you can say, isn't it, Pru? You knew from the beginning that you were taking a huge risk when you got involved with Case McCord.''

"At least he was honest with me," Pru said quietly. "He told me from the start he had no intention of getting married.''

"You didn't believe him?''

"I thought," Pru murmured, "that I could change his mind. I thought that deep down he had the makings of a good family man. He's very much a homebody, you know. The only evenings he didn't spend at home with me were the ones he spent traveling for the foundation. I would swear that during our time together McCord was totally faithful to me.''

"You weren't together all that long. Maybe the novelty hadn't had a chance to wear off."

"You're turning very cynical these days, Annie."

"I get more than cynical every time I think about what he's done to you. I get furious."

"I knew what I was doing and I knew the risk I was taking," Pru pointed out. "I also knew when I told him I wanted to make serious plans about our future that he would probably explode."

"When did you confront him?"

"The day I got home from the clinic after finding out for certain I was pregnant. I handled it all wrong. I know that now. But I was feeling a little emotional at the time."

"I'll bet you were," Annie said with great feeling. "So you gave him an ultimatum?"

"McCord doesn't respond well to ultimatums. He was due to leave the next day on a trip to Washington, D.C. I told him that if he wouldn't agree to settle our future, I wouldn't be around when he got back. I guess I managed to convince myself that he really did love me and he would realize it when faced with the prospect of losing me."

"You figured wrong."

Pru shrugged. "He assumed I was trying to manipulate him, to force his hand. And in a sense I suppose I was."

"As long as you were trying to force his hand, you should have pulled out all the stops," Annie said candidly. "You should have told him you were pregnant."

Pru closed her eyes, remembering the stormy scene in the study before she'd left McCord's house for the last time. "I couldn't do it. I wanted him to want me. I didn't want him offering marriage out of a sense of obligation. I think he might have done it. He's got a rather eccentric but quite rigid code of honor. But everyone knows that a marriage that takes place solely because of an unplanned pregnancy doesn't have much chance of lasting. The truth is, he meant what he said in the beginning. He doesn't want to get married. He doesn't want a long-term commitment. I should have taken him at his word.''

"How much longer could you have stayed with him on his terms if you hadn't got pregnant?''

Pru's mouth tightened. "I don't know, Annie. I wanted more from him than he was willing to give. I wanted it long before I discovered I was pregnant. I longed for a commitment right from the start. I guess Aunt Wilhelmina's teachings went deeper than I thought.''

"It's not the fault of Aunt Wilhelmina,'' Annie declared roundly. "It's just the way you are. You're the kind of woman who would give herself completely in a relationship. You're generous, warmhearted and utterly loyal. Some part of you wants the same kind of response in exchange. You tried to force that response from a man who has no intention of ever giving it. That was your first mistake. Getting pregnant was your second. How did it happen, anyway?''

"The usual way.''

"This isn't a joke, Pru. What went wrong? Did your contraceptive fail?''

Pru took another long sip of lemonade. "Not exactly. There was one night when we didn't use anything. I was unlucky.''

"But why did you take the chance?''

Pru's brows climbed as she regarded her sister over the rim of the glass. "You want a blow-by-blow account?''

Annie smiled wryly. "Of course not. I just wondered how you could have forgotten when it's obvious neither you nor McCord wanted any unexpected events.''

"McCord had been out of the country for ten days.''

"Ah.'' Annie nodded sagely. "Ten days of abstinence made him careless, hmm?''

"No,'' Pru said thoughtfully. "Ten days of surveying the problems of the drought in Africa got to him. You can only imagine what it's like over there, Annie. McCord had to witness it firsthand. The Arlington Foundation is setting up programs in a couple of African countries to teach basic agricultural skills to the farm-ers. It's also designing some more sophisticated training programs for researchers and scientists over there. But McCord didn't stay in the cities. He went out into the country to see the land for himself. The land…and the people who are dying on it.''

Pru broke off, remembering the weary, bleak expression on McCord's face the night he had returned. The grim reality of what he had seen had taken its toll. McCord might not be capable of making a commitment to a woman, but he was very committed to his work.

''I think I'm beginning to get the picture. He was worn out and probably feeling rather helpless in the face of such an overwhelm-ing problem. Add to that a good case of jet lag and you have a man who is not thinking as clear as he should about certain things,'' Annie concluded with the first trace of understanding she had yet shown for McCord.

''He went straight to bed. So did I.'' Pru took a deep breath. ''But he woke up in the middle of the night and he, well, things just happened.'' She didn't try to explain the rest. There was no way to describe the urgent, primitive hunger that had blazed in McCord's eyes in the shadows of the big bed that night. No way to explain her own awareness of his need.

After ten days of looking at death, McCord had been reaching out for life. He had reached for Pru, and she had gone into his arms without a moment's hesitation.

''I see,'' Annie said softly. She was silent for a long moment, her eyes on her two healthy, well-fed children who were highly unlikely to ever know the meaning of drought and famine. Then she reached for the lemonade pitcher. ''And so your whole life is suddenly changed.''

''Yes.''

''Well, as Aunt Wilhelmina always says, 'It's not the big things in life that generally do you in, it's the little stuff. You're more likely to get bitten by a tick than by a rattlesnake.'''

''I'm not sure McCord would like being compared to a tick,

but I can understand what Aunt Wilhelmina was trying to say," Pru murmured.

There was silence under the umbrella for a long while as both women watched the children scramble back into the pool. Pru relaxed again and leaned back in the lounger. Her hand went unconsciously to her still-flat stomach. She indulged herself by trying to decide if her baby would have McCord's dark hair and fathomless eyes.

"You can stay here as long as you like, Pru," Annie finally said sincerely. "Tony won't mind."

"You've both been very generous, but I won't be imposing on you much longer. I think I'll take the apartment we looked at yesterday."

"The one near CalTech?" Annie nodded. "It's a good area. If you get that job on campus that you applied for on Monday, everything will be perfect. Or just about perfect," she amended practically.

"Speaking of Tony," Pru ventured.

"Umm?"

"You haven't told him yet about my, er, condition have you?"

"No, of course not. I promised I wouldn't, didn't I?"

"Yes. Sorry."

Annie smiled wryly. "You won't be able to keep it a secret for long, Pru."

"I know. It's just that it's all so new. The whole idea of being pregnant is very strange. I need time to adjust."

"I understand." Annie was about to add something else when she was interrupted by the distant sound of the doorbell. "Sounds like we've got visitors. I'll be right back. Keep an eye on the kids for me."

"Sure." Pru watched her sister slip back into the house and then turned her attention to Katy and Dave who were busy playing king of the mountain with an inflated plastic raft.

"Aren't you coming back into the pool, Aunt Pru?" Katy demanded from her precarious perch on top of the bright blue raft. Dave was busily trying to bounce his sister off into the water.

"In a few minutes," Pru called back. She folded her bare legs and sat forward so that she would have a better view of the children's active play. Both kids were at home in the pool, but they were still small and vulnerable in so many ways. Annie and Tony were very protective of them.

She would protect her own baby, Pru reflected, feeling wise and maternal, but she wouldn't overprotect him or her. Children needed room to test themselves. Room to grow and make their own mistakes.

Up to a point.

Pru decided that if she had a daughter she would do her level best to keep the young woman from making the kind of mistake Pru herself had made, just as Aunt Wilhelmina had tried to keep Pru and Annie from making the kind of mistake their mother had made. Women were probably fated to pass the warning along from one generation to the next forever. And there would always be a few who would ignore it to their cost.

Pru was pulled out of her philosophical reflections by the sound of her sister's voice. Annie was agitated about something. Pru couldn't hear the words, but she caught the tone. Automatically she glanced toward the kitchen door in time to see it swing abruptly open.

It wasn't Annie who came through the door first. It was Case McCord.

Pru's glass of lemonade tilted precariously in her hand, spilling a couple of sweet, sticky drops onto her bare thigh. She was hardly aware of the small splash of coolness on her sun-warmed skin. Her whole attention was riveted on the man coming toward her.

A dangerous, deceptive flare of hope suddenly came alive somewhere deep inside Pru in that moment, and she realized that it had never really died. A part of her had been nourishing that reckless hope since the day she had walked out of McCord's La Jolla home.

His eyes went to her face instantly, and Pru was jolted by the impact of his dark, assessing gaze. She sat very still on the lounger, not quite daring to move. The reality of McCord's presence was almost more than she could accept. The strength and will and driving determination of the man were palpable forces surrounding him.

With a searching hunger that she hoped didn't show in her eyes, Pru examined him. He was dressed in his usual casual style: jeans and a long-sleeved shirt, the cuffs of which had been rolled up on his forearms to reveal the strong, sinewy muscles. His near-black hair was slightly tousled, as if he'd recently run his fingers through it in an impatient gesture. His boots sounded loud on the tiled patio that edged the pool. He headed toward Pru with long, ground-eating strides.

Pru was dimly aware of Annie hastening along in McCord's wake, snapping at him in an infuriated voice rather like a small, enraged terrier. "Damn it, you have no business barging in here like this. My sister has a right to decide whether or not she wants to see you. I won't have you harassing her, do you hear me?"

"Mommy? What's wrong?" Katy stopped her rough-and-tumble pool play to glance curiously at the newcomer. Beside her, Dave, too, went still. His blue eyes took in the stranger with a great deal of interest.

"Nothing's wrong," Annie declared forcefully. "This man says he wants to see your aunt, that's all. Go back to your game." Annie called ahead to Pru. "I didn't know who he was, Pru, until he was inside the house. I'm sorry about this. You don't have to speak to him if you don't want to, you know."

McCord spoke for the first time as he came to a halt in front of Pru. "She'll talk to me," he announced in his soft, even voice. "Won't you, Pru?"

Slowly Pru unfolded her legs and sat up on the edge of the lounger. Her eyes never left his face. "What are you doing here, McCord?"

His smile was wry, rueful and strangely gentle. His dark eyes were shadowed and deep. "You know the answer to that, don't you, Pru? I came to find you."

Her pulse was beating a little too fast, a little too strong. "Why?"

He crouched in front of her so that his gaze was on a level with hers. "I think you know the answer to that, too. I've come to take you home with me. It's where you want to be and it's where I want you to be."

She shook her head, feeling dazed. She couldn't believe he was here. Case McCord was not the kind of man to run after a woman, any woman. "I don't know what to say," she whispered.

He reached out and caught hold of her, his strong fingers closing warmly around her small hand. "You're not usually at a loss for words. You certainly weren't the day you left." He stood up and tugged her to her feet in front of him. "Why do you look so shocked, honey? Didn't you expect to see me one of these days?"

"No," she blurted honestly as her mind began to clear itself of the strange, disoriented sensation. "I assumed you meant what you said when you made it plain you had no intention of coming after me. You always mean what you say, McCord."

"I can make mistakes like anyone else."

She heard the faint, familiar arrogance behind the words. "Oh, I don't doubt that for a minute. I just wouldn't expect you to admit those mistakes. At least not so quickly."

He chuckled softly and tugged at her hand. "Let's go someplace where we can talk. It's almost five-thirty. Go change your clothes and I'll take you out for drinks and dinner. We don't need an audience." He indicated the two children and Annie, all of whom were watching the encounter with great attention.

His words jarred Annie out of her unwilling silence. She looked at her sister. "You don't have to go anywhere with him, Pru."

"I know." Pru looked at McCord. "Give me a reason, McCord."

"To come with me?" The hint of arrogance was stronger now. It was evident in the tilt of his brows and the hardening edge of his smile. He wasn't accustomed to having to justify his actions. "Do I need to give you a reason? Don't you want to come with me, Pru?"

"Not if you're under the impression that everything between us can be put back the way it was. I wasn't having hysterics the day I left. And I didn't walk out in a rage. I left because it was the best thing for me to do under the circumstances. I haven't changed my mind."

"I have," he told her simply.

She stared at him. "You've changed your mind?"

"You've made it clear you won't settle for anything except marriage. I want you back. If the only way I can have you is to marry you, then there's nothing left to argue about. Go change your clothes, Pru. We'll go somewhere private and discuss marriage."

Her mouth trembled when she tried to find a response. No words came into her head. Pru turned to look at her sister, seeking some hint of how to handle the bizarre situation. But Annie was looking distinctly thoughtful.

"Go get dressed, Pru," she said quietly. "McCord is right. You can't hold a private discussion with this kind of audience hanging around."

Pru glanced at McCord. There was a steady, watchful expression on his face, as if he were afraid she would panic and run.

The knowledge that he half expected her to react in such a ridiculous manner sent a shot of adrenaline-inspired strength through Pru's system. With a cool little nod, she excused herself and walked across the patio toward the sliding glass doors that opened onto the living room. A moment later she vanished inside.

McCord watched her go, aware that his body was already tightening just at the sight of her sweetly rounded bottom outlined by the red bikini she was wearing. God, he had missed her. This past week had been one of the most frustrating and miserable he had ever spent.

"She was quite sure you wouldn't come after her," Annie remarked, interrupting McCord's reverie.

He snapped his attention back from the sliding glass doors and turned to look at Pru's sister. She didn't look much like Pru, he decided. Annie was a sassy-haired blonde with blue eyes while Pru's hair was much longer and darkened into a warm shade of bronzed brown. He liked the golden-green of Pru's eyes better, too, McCord thought. He saw the protective hostility in Annie's gaze and sighed inwardly. He wasn't surprised.

"I didn't properly introduce myself earlier, Ms. Gates."

"Don't worry about it. I've figured out who you are. Are you serious about marrying Pru, or is this just a trick to get her back to San Diego with you?"

McCord felt a brief rush of fury at the clear sisterly skepticism so visible in Annie's face. Coolly, he repressed it. "I'm serious about it. I wouldn't have mentioned it otherwise."

"When?"

He looked at her blankly. "When what?"

"When are you going to marry her?" Annie asked impatiently.

"As soon as possible." He challenged her silently and was briefly startled when Annie merely nodded.

"Good," she said, "I think it's for the best." She turned back to the pool. "All right, kids. Time to get out and get ready for dinner."

Katy and her brother moved reluctantly to the steps and clambered out. "Is he going to have dinner with us?" the little girl asked, her eyes on McCord.

"No," her mother said briskly. "He's going to take Aunt Pru out to dinner. Run along now." She turned back to McCord. "Have a seat, Mr. McCord. My sister will be out in a minute." She started toward the house but halted abruptly when McCord spoke behind her.

"I'll take care of your sister, Annie," he said quietly.

Annie's gaze flickered over him in quick assessment. "It's not going to be as easy as you think, McCord."

"What won't be easy?"

"Convincing her to marry you. You've already done too good a job convincing her you don't want to marry her." She turned away again and continued on into the house.

McCord stood by the rippling pool and thought about the problem. Annie was right. He'd done a hell of a job convincing Pru he would never marry her. He'd been honest about his feelings on the subject of marriage right from the start, even though at the time he'd worried about losing her because of it. But she'd eventually come into his arms with all the honeyed, passionate generosity of her nature. And then she'd moved in with him and proceeded to turn his house into a home.

As far as McCord had been concerned, the arrangement between himself and Pru had had a more solid foundation than did most marriages. He'd been angry and stunned when she'd suddenly insisted on discussing their future. Having his sweet, generous-hearted, passionate Prudence turn into a willful, demanding woman who dared to threaten him with an ultimatum had infuriated him. He had immediately decided that the most effective way of teaching her that he would not be manipulated by a woman was to call her bluff.

But she'd meant every word of her ultimatum.

For the first full day after Pru had walked out, McCord had told himself she would be back. She loved him—he was sure of it. When the burst of feminine temperament had died away, he was certain she would come flying back to him.

He'd still been reeling from the shock of having her carry out her threat when the bill from the women's clinic had arrived. The moment he'd torn it open and examined the contents, a great deal had suddenly become excruciatingly clear. On her own, Pru might very well have come back to her lover. But she was no longer on her own. She was pregnant.

She was carrying McCord's baby; the baby of a man who had arrogantly claimed he had no interest in marriage. Belatedly McCord had realized exactly what was behind Pru's decision to leave. She'd been forced to assume that if he couldn't abide the thought of marriage, he would be even more unwilling to accept the fact that he was a father. Still, she'd gathered her nerve and taken the risk of pushing for marriage. When he'd rejected her, she'd done the only thing she'd thought she could do under the circumstances. She'd left.

Tonight he would have to woo her all over again, soothe her uncertainties and fears until she felt safe in surrendering to him once more. Because there really was no option now. The instant he had realized she was pregnant, McCord's whole world had realigned itself.

No longer could he allow his past to shape his present.

McCord stood alone on the sun-warmed tiles of the patio and thought of the past. For three years now he had cut himself off from everything and everyone he had known from cradle to young manhood. He had told himself he could live without those things and those people, even pretend they didn't exist. He had walked away from the stubborn, proud man who was his father, from the raw memories of his dead fiancée and the unborn child who had died with her. He'd also walked away from his inheritance.

But now he was going to marry and have a baby. Everything had changed.

CHAPTER THREE

PRU ORDERED FRUIT JUICE instead of her customary glass of wine when the cocktail waitress came by to take the order. McCord glanced at her with an amused expression.

"Have you decided to live up to your name tonight? Afraid to let your brain get cluttered with alcohol?"

"Under the circumstances, I think a measure of prudence makes sense." She had recovered her equilibrium now. As she sat across from him in the cozy bar that adjoined the dining room of the expensive restaurant McCord had chosen, Pru felt she was finally able to regard him in a rational, cautious manner.

It was much too soon to confess that she was pregnant and that she was avoiding alcohol for that reason only. She had to take this slowly and carefully. McCord, as usual, was moving very fast. The last time he had moved this fast, she had found herself agreeing to live with him.

McCord reached across the small table and covered her hand with his own. His eyes were hooded in the shadows, but the dark fire in them was quite evident to someone who knew him as well as Pru thought she did.

"You don't have to worry, honey. If we wind up in bed tonight, it will be because you want to be there, not because I got you drunk and seduced you. Give me some credit. I've never used that tactic on you."

"You never had to," she heard herself admit ruefully. The fruit juice and McCord's whiskey arrived before he could respond. When the waitress left, Pru studied her drink.

"Does that bother you, Pru?" McCord asked softly. "The fact that you wanted me as much as I wanted you?"

Her head came up, her eyes serious and a little troubled. "I'm not ashamed of the way I felt about you, but I think it made things easy for you and difficult for me."

"You're in love with me, aren't you, Pru?" His gaze was very direct, allowing no room for maneuvering. "That's the bottom line. It's the reason you went to bed with me the first time and it's the reason you finally agreed to come and live with me."

She forced a small shrug. "You always seem to have all the answers, don't you, McCord?"

"Are you going to deny it?"

"No. There's not much point. It doesn't matter, anyway. You'll believe what you want to believe. The real question is how you feel about me."

He blinked at the cool way she had turned the tables on him. A reluctant smile of admiration edged his mouth for a few seconds. "I want you back. I want you in my bed and in my home. I realize you need the security of marriage in order to be happy. I'm willing to give you that security."

She pushed her glass of fruit juice aside and leaned forward to ask the only question that mattered. "Do you love me, McCord?"

He was silent for a moment. "I don't know," he finally said with blunt honesty. "What do you think?"

She shivered. "I think you do, but for some reason you're going to have a hard time admitting it. I wish I knew what the reason is. It's been driving me crazy ever since I first met you."

It took a lot to startle McCord, but he definitely looked surprised by her thoughtful words. "What the hell are you talking about?"

She smiled and sat back in her chair, studying him. The scooped neck of her narrow white cotton knit dress slipped slightly to one side, revealing the delicate hollows and curves of her shoulder. The candlelight gleamed on the thin gold chain she wore around her neck. In the soft light her eyes were almost gold. "Don't you realize how little I or anyone else for that matter knows about you, McCord? Oh, J.P. knows you're brilliant in your area of expertise and that you have a talent for getting things done in the field. Martha knows you like peanut butter pie and that you detest sweet after-dinner liqueurs. Steve knows you like gardens and lots of healthy growing things around your home.''

"What about you, Pru? What do you know about me?"

She made a small movement with her hand. ''I know you went to good schools, that you're committed to the work of the foundation, that you've been faithful to me since we've met.''

He smiled faintly. ''What makes you so sure of that?''

"I don't know. I just am.''

He nodded. "Go on with your list.''

"Well, I've learned a hundred little things about you—"

"Including how to please me in bed.''

She tried to ignore the deliberate look in his eyes. "You're a good teacher. That's not the point, McCord. What I was about to say is that while I know a lot of small, inconsequential things about you, there are a lot of important things I don't yet understand.''

"Such as?''

"Why you were so adamantly against marriage, for one thing.'' There was a heartbeat of silence before Pru asked the next question. "Have you ever been married before, McCord?''

"No. I was engaged three years ago.''

She chewed on her lower lip, considering the cryptic response. "And things went wrong?''

"Very wrong.''

"You're…you're not still carrying a torch for her, are you?''

"She's dead, Pru. She was killed in a car accident. No, I am definitely not carrying a torch for her.'' The tone of his voice made it clear that that was all he intended to say on the subject.

Pru absorbed the implications of the abrupt words. "Is that why you didn't want to marry? Too much trauma left over from your first engagement?''

He lifted his whiskey glass and took a slow swallow. "What happened in the past doesn't concern you, Pru.''

"Maybe not, but I'm entitled to know why you've suddenly changed your mind about marrying me," she tossed back.

He lowered his glass. "I've told you why I've changed my mind. I want you back and you've made it clear marriage is your price."

Pru shuddered, closing her eyes in pain. She sat very still. "This isn't going to work, is it? I'm sorry, McCord. Please believe me, I never intended to set a price on myself and demand you meet it. I never wanted this kind of situation to develop between us. I wish I could make things easy for both of us. Unfortunately I can't live with you. Not any longer. But now I know I can't marry you, either. Not as long as you view the whole thing as a business transaction. I refuse to sell myself to you in exchange for a ring."

"Pru…"

She ignored him, getting to her feet in a swift movement and reaching for her small purse. "You don't have to worry about me, McCord. I'll call a cab."

"Damn it, Pru, sit down." He was on his feet before she could get around her chair. His hand closed over her wrist, exerting just enough pressure to force her gently but firmly back down into her seat. His eyes blazed with masculine irritation. "You've already walked out on me once in front of an audience. I'm not going to let you do it a second time. You've shredded my ego and my pride pretty thoroughly, lady. I don't need another dose of your feminine temperament. Isn't it enough for you that I'm here on my hands and knees trying to offer marriage?"

She stared at him, straining against the hold on her wrist. When she realized it wasn't going to slacken she settled back in her chair. He released her and sprawled into his own seat, glaring at her.

There was a measure of tense silence before Pru's sense of humor finally surfaced. "On your hands and knees, McCord? Please excuse me, I hadn't realized you were actually groveling. I had the distinct impression you were here to order me to marry you."

His mouth twisted wryly. "It would certainly make my life simpler if I could. Do you know what I've been through in the past week? From the moment you left, Martha and Steve have barely spoken to me. J.P. has delivered at least one lecture a day on how to treat a good woman. You'd think I'd had you chained to my bed, forced to live in sin for the past three months from the way everyone acts. Even if I could convince you to come back and live with me without the benefit of marriage, I'm damn sure J.P., Martha and Steve wouldn't allow it. They all think I've had my wicked way with you long enough. Now that you've escaped my clutches, they hope you'll stay out of my reach until you've forced me to do the right thing."

"I had no idea," Pru murmured dryly, "just how many people in this world still harbored the same sentiments as my Aunt Wilhelmina when it came to such things as living with a man versus marrying him."

McCord groaned. "This is the famous aunt who gave you the lectures on not sleeping with a man until you'd got him to the altar?"

"That's her." For some reason Pru was suddenly feeling more cheerful. A certain tension between herself and McCord had just been broken, she realized. A large measure of the ease they usually experienced in each other's company had been restored. She began to relax for the first time that evening.

"It occurs to me," McCord observed slowly, "that there are a few things I don't know about you. I hadn't even met your sister until today. Is there anyone else in your family?"

"Just Aunt Wilhelmina. She lives in Spot, Texas."

"Your parents?" he prompted gently.

"My mother is dead," Pru said quietly. "She was killed shortly after I was born. She was in a car with a man who was very drunk at the wheel. He might have been my father. They were on their way to Mexico. I like to think they were going to get married over the border. A childhood fantasy of mine."

"Lord, Pru, I didn't realize—"

"It's all right. I never really knew her. Annie suffered more than I did. She was five years older than me, and she still has a few memories of our mother."

"And her father?"

"A trucker. He was long gone by the time Annie was born. My mother was apparently a very reckless young woman when it came to choosing her male companions. She was also very desperate to get out of Spot, Texas. Apparently she hoped some man would help her. Two illegitimate children were the result. My aunt is very much afraid there's bad blood somewhere in the family."

"What do you and your sister believe?"

Pru smiled gently. "That my mother was born dirt-poor and that on two occasions she tried desperately to escape her poverty by getting involved with men she hoped would marry her. She guessed wrong both times."

"So it was your aunt who raised you?"

Pru nodded. "My aunt was always very proud of the fact that she didn't take the low road out of poverty. She got herself an education. Eventually became a grade-school teacher. She wound up supporting two young children on that salary." Pru paused and then said slowly, "It's very difficult growing up under the care of someone who makes no secret of the fact that she was forced to make great sacrifices for you. Frankly, there were times when I wished she'd just let the state take Annie and me." Pru smiled. "But of course Aunt Wilhelmina would never have done that. She is an honorable woman who always knows her duty and does it."

"While making sure that everyone around her knows she's doing it?"

"Exactly."

"I know the type." McCord's mouth lifted in amusement.

"Well, I can hardly complain. Aunt Wilhelmina is a good woman. She devoted her life to making certain neither Annie nor I followed in our mother's footsteps. She was very strict with us, but she got us both through school and college. And she understood when the first thing we wanted to do after graduation was shake the dirt of Spot, Texas, from our feet. She had a few doubts about the wisdom of first Annie and then me going to California, but she figured she'd done her best to instill basic values. Now it was up to us to keep our own lives in order. She was thrilled when Annie married Tony Gates. She could stop worrying about one of us, at least. She comes out to see them frequently. I think she's mellowing a bit as she grows older. She seems to enjoy Annie's kids.''

"I take it you never told your aunt about your relationship with me?'' McCord held up a hand before Pru could respond. "Forget I asked. It's obvious you wouldn't let her know you were living with a man without benefit of a wedding ceremony unless you absolutely had to. I imagine she's the type who would go through the roof?''

"More likely she would just decide bad blood will out,'' Pru corrected him.

McCord shook his head in chagrined wonder. "I knew it wasn't easy for you to make the decision to move in with me, but I had no idea just how much you had to overcome in your own mind to do it.''

Pru thought about that. "It was something of an unstable situation right from the start. But I might have been able to make it work, if only—'' She broke off abruptly.

"If only what, honey?'' McCord held the verbal door open, trying to coax her inside. Perhaps now she would tell him about the baby. But she shied away from mentioning it. He wondered why, but he said nothing. It was, after all, her surprise. She had a right to spring it on him.

"Never mind. McCord, what are we going to do?''

"Get married.''

"I'm not sure. I just don't know. There are so many things to be considered. So many things I've realized I don't know about you.''

"Don't worry about it, Pru. You love me, and I don't want any other woman except you. It has recently been brought home to

me in no uncertain terms that you need a marriage licence in order
to be content. I'll see that you get one.''

She was right about some elements of the situation. There were
a lot of things she should know about him, McCord decided, but
tonight wasn't the time to tell her. She was still feeling tense and
uncertain in spite of the more relaxed atmosphere between them.
He didn't want to try and explain his family situation at the moment. That could come later. Right now he had to concentrate on
gentling her back into his life. ''Honey, you know me as well as
anyone else in the world does. Better, if you want the truth. You
know I've never lied to you. You have to believe me when I tell
you that I want you with me.''

''But marriage?''

He saw the undisguised longing and hope that lighted her eyes.
She really did love him, he thought. She was just afraid to admit
it aloud. He was touched by the fact that she hadn't tried to use
the baby to force his hand. It made him realize how deep her pride
ran.

During the past week he'd begun to acknowledge to himself
that marriage might not be such a bad idea after all. The notion
had been growing on him, he realized. Like a fungus, as J.P.
Arlington would have said. McCord discovered he rather liked the
idea of having Pru tied to him legally as well as emotionally.
Something about the concept suited the possessive side of his nature. He wondered why the realization hadn't occurred to him
earlier. Probably, he admitted silently, because there had been no
need to think about it. J.P. was right. McCord had been as happy
as a bull in clover. There had been no reason to think about al-
tering a situation that had suited him perfectly.

''Yes, Pru. Marriage. It's what you want, and I'm willing to go
along.''

She didn't seem thrilled with the way he had phrased it, but
she didn't bounce out of her chair and run out the door, either.
She was silent for a long moment. When she spoke, her voice was
very soft and tentative.

"Have you ever..." Pru stopped, cleared her throat and tried again. "Have you ever thought about having children?"

McCord smiled with all the reassurance at his command. "I figure if we're going to get married, we might as well go the whole route. And the sooner the better. We're not getting any younger, are we? I think we'd make good parents, don't you?"

"Yes," she said happily, "I think we would."

There was a trace of relief in her eyes, but she said nothing. McCord didn't push.

He concentrated on letting the evening flow gently after that. Deliberately he turned the conversation toward more general topics, filling her in on news of the foundation and giving her Steve Graham's report on the garden.

"One of these days I'm going to find a way to teach him to put away his tools," McCord said with a grimace as he finished describing the progress of the tomatoes.

"He loves gardening and he's learning so much from you. You know you enjoy teaching him," Pru pointed out. "Why make such a fuss about a minor bad habit?"

"It's hard on the tools and someone could get hurt, that's why," McCord growled.

Pru grinned. "It's such a small thing. Don't worry about it."

"See if you're still saying that after you step on a rake," McCord said.

Because it was his nature to settle matters in a clean, straightforward fashion instead of letting them stay muddled, McCord would have preferred to keep up the pressure on Pru. Now that his own decision had been made, he was impatient with Pru's uncertainty. But he was increasingly aware that she was teetering on the brink, and he was equally sure he knew which way she would fall when the time came.

As the meal drew to a close, McCord forced himself to consider his immediate options. He had a simple choice to make. He could either try to coax her back to his hotel room or he could take her to her sister's house and leave her with a chaste, gentlemanly kiss.

There was no question which option he favored. He had spent the evening in an uncomfortable, tantalizing state of semiarousal. One touch was all it would have taken to bring him to that explosive point. It was obvious Pru was being very cautious about touching him. He wondered if that meant she was as close to flash point as he was. He thought she might be. After all, he had spent several months getting to know her intimately, learning exactly what it took to make her shiver with excitement and in the process developing a sixth sense for reading her responses.

She was his woman, McCord thought, and he knew her well. If he pushed just a bit tonight he could push her right back into his bed. It was where he wanted her, and he had a hunch that, even though she wasn't quite prepared to admit it yet, it was where she wanted to be.

As they rose to leave the restaurant, his eyes rested for a moment on the delicate curve of her breasts beneath the narrow cotton knit dress. When she walked ahead of him toward the door, he was vividly conscious of the subtly provocative sway of her hips. It was going to be fascinating to watch the changes her slender body went though during pregnancy.

He suddenly discovered that the thought of his babe curled safely now in its warm nest was more intensely exciting than he would have believed possible. McCord ached to make love to the woman who was carrying his child. The fierce, possessive sensation jolted him, making him catch his breath. As if she sensed something was wrong, Pru glanced back with a small frown.

"McCord? Is something the matter?"

"No," he said tightly, knowing now which option he had to choose. "There's nothing wrong. At least, nothing I can do anything about tonight." He caught her arm as they moved out onto the sidewalk. The silver Ferrari was parked half a block down the street. "It's time I got you back to your sister's place. It's getting late."

Pru inhaled the warm, balmy air, aware of the comforting

strength in McCord's arm as he guided her down the street. "You're going to take me straight home?"

"I didn't say that. I said I'm going to take you straight back to Annie's. Your sister's place isn't home for you, Pru. Your home is with me."

"You sound very sure of that."

"I am sure," he said as he stopped beside the Ferrari and opened the car door. "And when you're sure, too, I'll take you home. Until then, I'll just take you back to Annie's house."

She looked up at him warily as she slid into the seat. He smiled faintly at the shielded expression in her eyes and then closed the car door very firmly before she could decide what to say in response. As she watched him walk around the front of the Ferrari, Pru felt a sharp pang of longing. She wanted to touch him when he folded himself gracefully into the driver's seat, but she didn't quite dare. Surreptitiously she touched her still-flat stomach instead.

Without a word McCord guided the Ferrari down the palm-lined street that wound through Annie's affluent neighborhood. It wasn't until he parked the car in front of the Southwestern-style house that he finally spoke.

"I'll come by for you in the morning. We can spend the day at the beach." He studied her, one arm draped over the wheel as he waited for her response.

Pru tried to force herself to think clearly and logically but couldn't. "All right," she heard herself say. "That would be nice."

He nodded once and climbed out of the car. When he got her to the front door he stopped. She knew at once he was going to turn around and leave immediately. For the first time that evening Pru reached out to touch him.

"McCord?"

"What is it, Pru?"

"I... Don't you want to come inside? You haven't met Tony."

"I can wait until I know for certain I'm going to be a member of the family." He leaned down to brush his mouth against hers. The kiss was fleeting and rigidly restrained.

Pru made a small sound, a combination of protest and longing that was almost lost in the soft sounds of the night. If McCord heard it, he gave no sign. He lifted his head almost at once, as if the touch of her lips burned him.

"The doorbell," he prompted.

Pru blinked. "What?"

"Ring the doorbell."

"Oh." She fumbled in her purse. "It's all right. I have a key."

He took it from her and inserted it into the lock. When she was over the threshold, he nodded good-night and turned to go back down the walk toward the Ferrari.

Pru was torn between wanting to scream and wanting to laugh. Slowly she closed the door and leaned back against it. Annie appeared in the hallway, her concerned eyes full of questions.

"Somehow," Annie said calmly, "I wasn't expecting you home tonight."

"Ah, that's because you don't know Case McCord very well." Pru came away from the door. "The man is smart. Smart enough to know when to push and when to let his victim fumble her own way right into the trap."

"You don't seem too upset about his tactics."

Pru smiled secretly. "I'm not too upset because I think he really means it, Annie. I think he really does want to marry me."

Annie grinned. "I think you're right. How long are you going to keep him dangling?"

Pru touched her stomach. "Not long. I just want enough time to be sure." She sighed in soft wonder. "I didn't think he'd come after me, Annie. I honestly thought I'd never see him again."

"Then you don't know him as well as you think you do. I took one glance at his face this afternoon when he forced his way through the front door and I knew immediately he wasn't leaving here without you."

SHE KEPT HIM WAITING two more days. They spent one of those days on the beach and another at Disneyland. It was fun doing frivolous things with McCord again, she thought on the drive back from Disneyland. The realization made her glance at McCord who was negotiating the intricacies of the Los Angeles freeway system.

"How much time do you have, McCord? Won't J.P. be needing you?"

McCord grinned, but he didn't take his eyes off the traffic. "J.P. gave me strict instructions not to come back without you."

Her eyes widened. "I didn't know he was that concerned about losing one little journal editor."

"I think it's your hostessing abilities he misses most. He's accustomed to having you organize the cocktail parties and brunches and dinners the foundation gives. He dreads having to figure out how to do it on his own. You've spoiled him. With the first annual foundation ball coming up in a couple of weeks, he's desperate. You were the one who talked him into it, don't forgot. Remember how you assured him he'd get a fortune in contributions to the foundation if he put on a first-class charity ball? You've been taking care of everything up to this point, and the thought of putting the affair on without you around to supervise is enough to traumatize him. The only thing J.P. knows how to do is barbecue a steak. He's overwhelmed by the idea of caviar and canapés."

"He could find another hostess."

"He wants you back." McCord paused a fraction of a heartbeat and added, "So do I." Then he smiled. "J.P. says that without you, I'm about as useful to him as, uh…"

Pru kept her gaze on his hard profile and asked sweetly, "About as useful as mammary glands on a bull?"

"Something like that. J.P. was a bit more graphic."

"I'll bet. That's the sort of thing J.P. or my aunt would say." She sat quietly for a few more minutes, staring out the window. Then she nodded to herself. "All right."

McCord risked a quick glance, his eyes rapidly searching her face. "All right? You're accepting my proposal?"

"Yes." She smiled. "If you're sure you want to marry me, McCord, then, yes, I accept."

He snapped his attention back to the freeway traffic. "You picked a fine time to tell me."

"Any complaints?"

"No, ma'am," he assured her fervently. "I'll take what I can get."

"You are sure, aren't you, McCord?" she asked quietly. "I couldn't stand it if you…if you changed your mind or came to regret marrying me. I truly don't want to force you into this."

"I know that, Pru. Stop worrying. I'm very sure I want to marry you."

That evening Pru and McCord told their news to Annie and Tony. Annie laughed and hugged her sister. Tony, a slender, good-looking man in his early thirties, shook McCord's hand and offered him a drink.

"You'll need one before you talk to Aunt Wilhelmina," he informed McCord.

"I didn't know I was scheduled to meet her." McCord accepted the whiskey and settled onto the sofa next to Pru. He eyed his fiancée quizzically. "Don't tell me she's in the neighborhood. I thought she lived in Texas."

It was Annie who responded. "She does. But we'll have to call her later and tell her Pru's getting married. She'd never forgive Pru otherwise."

Pru made a face. "No loss."

"Now, Pru, you know you don't mean that." Annie grinned. "What's the matter? Afraid McCord might change his mind after he's dealt with Aunt Wilhelmina?"

"It's a distinct possibility."

Tony chuckled. "You'll survive, McCord."

"How bad is she?" McCord asked dubiously, but there was laughter in his eyes when he glanced at Pru.

"Just imagine every battle-ax of a teacher you ever had in grade school all rolled into one. All those teachers who kept you after class to finish your work and all those who sent you to the principal whenever you put one little finger out of line. And don't forget all the ones who made you feel like an absolute idiot whenever you blew a math test or a spelling exam. Then there were those whose idea of sex education was to warn you that you get a girl pregnant by dancing too close to her. You get the picture?" Tony took a swallow of his drink. "But I made it through the inquisition, so I expect you to pull yourself together like a man and do the same."

"Inquisition?" McCord asked blandly.

"Sure." Tony enlightened him. "She'll ask you how much money you make, if you own your own home, what your future prospects are, and whether or not you have health insurance and a pension plan. Then she'll want to know if you're marrying Pru because you've got her in trouble."

Pru went utterly still, aware of the fierce warmth leaping into her cheeks. She shot a quick, painful glance at her sister. Annie shook her head very slightly, silently reassuring Pru that she hadn't told Tony about the baby. Pru drew a long breath of relief. Then she looked at McCord. He seemed oblivious of her tension. He was laughing ruefully at what Tony had just said.

"Has anybody ever tried telling Aunt Wilhelmina that the answers to all those questions are none of her business?" McCord asked.

"Are you kidding? Tell Aunt Wilhelmina to mind her own business? What a mind-boggling thought." Tony managed an expression of stunned amazement.

Annie held up a hand to stop her husband. "Enough. You'll scare him off before he even talks to her. Don't worry, McCord. Tony is exaggerating. He has a weird sense of humor."

"I'm glad to hear it," McCord said. "Why don't we make the call and get this over with?"

Pru spoke up, glancing at her watch. "It's almost nine o'clock back in Texas. Why don't we wait until tomorrow?"

"Nervous, honey?" McCord was laughing at her. "Afraid I'll chicken out after I've talked to Aunt Wilhelmina?"

"Well, no, it's just that I—"

"Don't worry," he said softly, some of the amusement fading from his eyes. It was replaced by a suggestion of grimness. "Whatever problems you've got with Aunt Wilhelmina are nothing compared to the problems I've got with my family. At least you're still speaking to your aunt."

"What are you talking about?" Pru stared at him in astonishment. "What family? You've never mentioned anyone, McCord."

He picked up the small designer telephone that was sitting on a nearby end table and handed it to Pru. "Call your aunt."

"But what about your family?" she demanded.

"I'll take you to meet them after the wedding. I'm not fool enough to let you meet them ahead of time."

"But, McCord—"

"One gauntlet at a time, Pru. Call your aunt."

Pru's fingers felt cold and numb as she dialed her aunt's number in Texas. Something was very wrong. It occurred to her that there were still too many things she didn't know about Case McCord.

CHAPTER FOUR

THREE NIGHTS LATER Pru stood in front of the expanse of mirror that lined one wall of the elegant inn bathroom and wondered why she was feeling so nervous. It was McCord who waited for her out in the bedroom. The same McCord with whom she had lived for three months. The McCord who had taught her the wonders of her own sensuality. The McCord who could make her feel incredibly beautiful in bed.

The McCord who had got her pregnant.

It wasn't as if he were a stranger. He had been her lover and now he was her husband. Soon he'd be the father of her child. Her attack of bridal jitters didn't make sense.

They had been married that afternoon in a small, simple ceremony with only Annie and Tony present. Considering the questions and uncertainty and the painful emotions Pru had been through during the two weeks leading up to the wedding, the ceremony itself was something of an anticlimax. She had been aware of McCord's strong, steady voice as he made his vows, heard her own soft words and then, quite quickly, it was all over.

McCord had settled her into the Ferrari afterward and turned to say farewell to his new brother-in-law. Annie had leaned down to speak to her sister through the window.

"You still haven't told him about the baby, have you?" Annie had whispered.

Pru had shaken her head, smiling. "No. This is a special time. The wedding and the honeymoon are for us, McCord and me. I want us to be able to concentrate on each other for a day or two. Then I'll tell him."

"I understand," Annie had said, grinning. "I think I like your husband, Pru. He certainly handled Aunt Wilhelmina well the other night. I thought I'd collapse laughing when she started grilling him on the phone and he just listened and smiled and said he'd have his banker write her a letter of reference. Poor Wilhelmina. I can just imagine her expression. There she was asking all those pointed questions and McCord just brushed past them.''

''He can be very good at ignoring what he doesn't consider important.''

''The best part was when she asked him if he'd got you in trouble,'' Annie had said with a rueful grimace. ''Tony was right. Aunt Wilhelmina really did ask that. I couldn't believe it.''

Pru had flushed slightly, remembering McCord's response. Although she and the others hadn't been able to hear the question, they had all known when it had come because McCord, phone to his ear, had rested his amused gaze on Pru's scarlet cheeks.

''Don't worry about it, Aunt Wilhelmina,'' he'd advised. ''If there's trouble, it's nothing I can't handle.''

For just an instant Pru had wondered if McCord knew about the pregnancy. The intensity of his gaze had almost burned her. But then she had told herself that he couldn't possibly know.

Aunt Wilhelmina had been almost too outraged to respond for several seconds. In the end, however, when the phone had been handed back to Pru, she'd pronounced herself reasonably satisfied with McCord.

''Sounds like he's got both feet on the ground, Pru,'' Aunt Wilhelmina had declared. ''Bold as brass and proud as the devil, but that's not altogether bad in a man. He also sounds slicker than a greased hog on ice. Be grateful he's marrying you. He's the type who could have talked you right into bed without bothering with the ring. Call me when you get back from your honeymoon.''

''Well?'' McCord had asked, not appearing overly concerned. ''What's the verdict?''

Pru had cleared her throat. ''She says you sound slicker than a greased hog on ice and that I should be grateful you're marrying me because otherwise you might easily have ruined me.''

McCord had winced. "Ouch. The woman does have a narrow view of the world, doesn't she?" Then he'd grinned wickedly. "Are you grateful that I'm marrying you, Pru?"

She'd batted her eyes in mock admiration. "Oh, yes, terribly grateful. Words can't begin to express my gratitude."

McCord had laughed and wrapped one large hand around the nape of her neck. He'd pulled her toward him and dropped a kiss on her nose. "As if I had a choice."

She hadn't known how to take that comment, but decided he'd meant it as a joke.

After the ceremony, McCord had driven her up the coast past Ventura. They'd checked into a beautiful, rambling inn near the ocean and Pru had been delighted with the fireplace, the huge bath and the luxurious furnishings of the small suite. The perfect honeymoon hotel, she'd decided exuberantly.

But now she was unaccountably nervous, and she didn't know why. One thing was for sure—the longer she delayed going out into the bedroom, the more anxious she got.

She took one last look at the flowing lines of the pale yellow, low-necked negligee she had bought for her honeymoon and then straightened her shoulders and opened the connecting door.

McCord was standing in front of the window, gazing out over the darkened sea. He was stripped to the waist, and he had taken off his shoes. The jeans he'd put on after dinner rode low on his hips, and his broad, smoothly muscled shoulders gleamed a faint gold in the dim light of the bedside lamp.

He'd opened the bottle of champagne he'd ordered earlier from room service, and two fluted glasses stood on the table beside him. When he heard the sound of the bathroom door being opened, he turned to confront his bride. His eyes were endlessly dark and unfathomably deep, but the shimmer of possessiveness in them was unmistakable. Pru halted in the doorway, a little disconcerted by the directness of his gaze.

McCord smiled faintly and reached for the bottle of champagne. He filled the two glasses, picked them up and came deliberately across the room to offer one to Pru. She took it with fingers that trembled ever so slightly and managed to return his smile.

"I know," McCord said with a soft reassurance as he stood looking down at her. "I'm a little nervous, too."

"I suppose that's one of the advantages to having lived with a man before you marry him," Pru murmured. "He knows you well enough by the wedding night to guess how you're feeling when you come out of the bathroom."

"There is a certain comfort in familiarity, isn't there?" McCord tipped the champagne to her lips and urged her to take a sip.

Pru thought of all the current advice that encouraged pregnant mothers not to drink and contented herself with barely wetting her tongue. Then she wrinkled her nose as she realized she really didn't care for the taste. Odd. Normally she enjoyed good champagne.

"If we're so familiar to each other, why are we feeling nervous?" Pru asked, looking up at McCord.

He shrugged. "Probably because, when all is said and done, it's different being married."

Pru felt a wave of unease go through her. Her eyes widened in the soft light, the underlying anxiety plain in them. "McCord, are you very, very sure this is what you wanted?"

He took the unfinished glass from her fingers, set it down beside his own and then wrapped his strong hands around her shoulders. She was fascinated by the masculine certainty that blazed out at her from his eyes.

"Oh, yes, my sweet Prudence, this is what I wanted. It just took me a while to realize it." He brushed his mouth lightly over hers, and then his grip on her shoulders tightened.

Pru's smile was tremulous with relief as he pulled her up against his hard chest. Overwhelmed by the depth of her feelings for him and the tremendous relief she felt at finally being with McCord again, Pru clung to him. Her head rested against his bare shoulder, and she closed her eyes as the warm, musky scent of him washed through her senses.

"I never thought I'd see you again," she whispered.

"You should have known better." He dropped the softest of kisses into her hair.

"You said you wouldn't come after me."

"I was madder than hell at the time. Besides, I thought you were bluffing. I couldn't believe you'd really leave me."

Pru felt suddenly guilty. Her arms tightened around his waist. "I'm sorry. I thought I had to leave."

"I know," he said gently. "After getting to know you all these months, and after talking to your Aunt Wilhelmina, I can only conclude it's a miracle you stayed with me as long as you did before you demanded a more settled arrangement. You're the kind of woman who wants to make a commitment. And you want the same thing in return. I should have realized that months ago. I should have guessed what would happen as soon as I knew you were in love with me."

She turned her face toward his shoulder and astonished both of them by nipping his skin with her small white teeth. "Beast. What makes you so sure I'm in love with you?"

"I don't know. Since the first time I took you to bed, I've felt very sure of you." His hold on her tightened as she started to protest. "I know that sounds arrogant, but it's your own fault, you know. You never tried to hide your responses from me. That's why I didn't pay any attention when you threatened to leave. I thought you loved me too much to carry out the threat."

"I didn't think I had any choice."

His hands moved slowly and luxuriously along her slender back as he gentled the tension in her. "I know, sweetheart. For what it's worth, I think you were right. We couldn't have gone on much longer the way we were. It was time to settle the future." His dark voice was a whisper of midnight velvet against her skin as he cradled her chin in one palm and lifted her face for his kiss.

The last of Pru's uncertainty left her in a soft soundless sigh as she felt the reassuring touch of his mouth. The hunger and the need in him rippled through her, touching all of her senses.

McCord wanted her with the same limitless desire she had always sensed in him.

His desire wasn't really unlimited, she thought with womanly anticipation. It only seemed like that in the beginning because the sensual demand emanating from him was so huge. When McCord took her in his arms, Pru felt as though she had been swept into a deep, torrential waterfall of masculine need. But she knew from past experience that she could turn the thundering cascade into a slow, lazy river of contentment.

His mouth moved heavily on hers until she made a tiny sound of pleasure and opened her lips. McCord was inside at once, tasting her, provoking her, exciting her as only he could. Pru shivered in his grasp.

"It's been so long," McCord muttered against her mouth.

"Only a couple of weeks."

"Seems like forever." He deepened the kiss again until she was leaning into his strength. When he felt her fingers clenching and unclenching on his shoulders, he groaned and scooped her up in his arms.

"McCord?" She looked up at him with wide, trusting eyes that were luminous with her love.

"I told myself I was going to make tonight very special. If you look at me like that before I've even got you to the bed, I won't be able to last long enough to do this right." He put her down on the turned-back sheets of the wide bed and stood gazing at her for a long moment.

Pru smiled. "Don't you know it's always special with you? You always seem to be able to last long enough to do things right."

He grinned abruptly, a slanting, teasing, excitingly wicked grin of pure masculine anticipation. His hands went to the snaps of his jeans. "I guess that's another wedding night advantage we've got, isn't it, honey? We don't have to worry about whether we'll be able to please each other." The jeans landed on the floor, and McCord stepped closer to the bed.

Pru's pulse quickened at the sight of his lean, hard body. She had seen him aroused before, of course, but the sight of his strong, heavy manhood never failed to send a shudder of excitement through her. "I should be used to seeing you naked." Her fingertips glided softly over his hard thigh as he came slowly down beside her. "But somehow I don't think I'll ever get completely accustomed to sharing a bedroom with you."

McCord chuckled, a deep, sexy, richly amused sound. "I know. I like the way you always blink and stare for a couple of seconds whenever you see me nude. Does unmentionable things to my ego." He leaned over to kiss the hollow of her throat. "Don't worry. You should get over that particular hang-up sometime during the next sixty years or so."

Pru sank her fingertips into the thickness of his hair and looked up at him with a sudden, earnest intensity. "You think we'll be together that long?"

His eyes blazed. "We both made a promise and a commitment today, Pru. Now that the deed is done, there's no turning back for either of us. I don't make promises or commitments lightly, and neither do you. We're going to make this marriage work."

The words were a vow and Pru accepted them as such. With a soft, throaty sound she put her arms around his neck and pulled his head back down to hers. She felt his fingers at the laces of her nightgown even as his mouth urged her lips apart once more.

The shimmering fabric of the gown was pushed aside until McCord had freed Pru's small, full breasts. When his palm grazed lightly over one nipple, drawing it into a hard peak, Pru gasped. He drank the small sound of desire from her lips and then he slid his warm hand to the other rosy crest. By the time he was finished with the light, teasing touch, Pru's breasts were exquisitely sensitive.

She moaned into his mouth and sought the hard contours of his body with impatient hands. Her fingertips laced through the mat of curling hair on his chest, sliding across the flat, male nipples until McCord was the one who was making the soft sounds of need. His hand slipped down to her stomach, and he spread his fingers possessively over her.

"You're so sweet and sexy and honest with your loving," he murmured. "You always give yourself to me completely, nothing held back."

She trembled, deeply aware of the warmth of his palm. It occurred to her that she hadn't been completely honest with him recently. He still didn't know about the baby. "I doubt if you were exactly overwhelmed with my generosity two weeks ago when I walked out," she whispered.

"There was nothing ungenerous about your actions. You did what you felt you had to do. You were feeling desperate. I understand that now." He trailed a string of hot, damp kisses over the curves of her breast and then he started working his way down to her navel.

"Oh, McCord," Pru heard herself say as she lifted herself against his hand, "I'm so glad you decided you wanted to marry me, after all. It could never be this good with anyone else. I would have been so lonely...."

"So would I." His fingers went lower, moving to the place that shielded her most exotic secrets. With unerring expertise he explored the flowering heart of her desire. His fingers glided through the flowing warmth there.

Pru clung more tightly to the strong, reassuring bulk of his shoulders as she felt the deliciously familiar, yet ever new sensations that were starting to flood her body. McCord's hands had always held magic, she thought. It was such an indescribable relief to know she wouldn't have to live without that magic now.

With a gentle assertiveness that would not be denied, McCord probed farther, urging her thighs apart until he could tease and tantalize every hidden fold. When his rough fingertips found the source of the dampening heat between her legs, Pru cried out softly. Then she turned her head into his shoulders and used her teeth against his skin with sweet, feminine savagery.

"Ah!" McCord's response was tight with his barely leashed

need. "Every time I start thinking you're all sweetness and light, you manage to remind me that there's a healthy dose of she-cat in you."

"You should know. You're the one who brought her out into the open." She heard his sexy laughter as she ran her hand down his body to find the waiting shaft of his manhood. When she touched the throbbing, rock-hard evidence of his desire, he groaned and murmured hot, dark words in her ear.

The sensual demand in his voice was as enthralling and as exciting as his touch. Pru stirred restlessly, opening herself more invitingly.

"That's the way I like to see you, sweetheart. Hot and wet and needing me."

She tightened her intimate hold on him, teasing him as he was teasing her. "I do need you, McCord. So very much." She was aching with the longing he had elicited. When she moved against him, tightening her arm around his neck, she caught a fleeting glimpse of gold. It was the ring he had put on her hand that morning. She loved him, she thought. She loved him so much that she could never leave him again.

"It's only been two weeks and I feel like I'm going to explode." McCord sounded wryly annoyed as his control rapidly slipped away from him. "I shouldn't be surprised. You've had this effect on me since the first moment I met you. I think I'm going to like being married. It's going to be good to know that you really do belong to me, legally as well as every other way. I wonder why I didn't realize it before?"

She couldn't answer that question for him. Pru could only be glad that he had asked it. "Love me, McCord," she begged, wrapping her arms around him and drawing him closer. "Please love me."

He said nothing, but his thigh slid aggressively between her legs. McCord found her throat with his lips as he lowered himself along the quivering length of her. She felt his solid male shaft touch the smooth, silky skin of her inner thigh and then his hand was clasping her rounded bottom, lifting her. Now she could feel the waiting, blunt hardness of him, but he didn't push himself into her.

Pru was suddenly aware of the stillness in him and opened her lashes to see a waiting fire in his eyes. She had never known him to hesitate before. His body was shuddering with the force of his need. But he was holding himself in check.

"McCord?"

"You do it, Pru. Guide me. Take me inside, sweetheart. Let me know you want me and show me exactly how you want me. I'll be as slow and careful and gentle as you want me to be. I promise."

She shook her head once in wondering confusion. This was a new side of the McCord she thought she knew so well. His consideration touched her deeply. She sank her fingers into his hair and smiled. "I want you to be the way you always are with me. You've never, ever hurt me, McCord."

He closed his eyes for an instant. When he opened them again, the dark gaze burned her. "Sometimes I'm a little rough with you."

She didn't understand. "Only in a very exciting way. Have I ever complained?" Her smile was unconsciously provocative.

"No." His voice was uneven. "You always respond to me so beautifully. I'm addicted to your responses, don't you know that? But I thought that now you…that is, I figured you'd want to take things a little slower, a little more gently than we usually do."

Her smile deepened. "Because this is my wedding night? Don't worry, McCord. All I want tonight is what I've always had with you. But if you'd like a little direction…" She slid one hand down his body, found the poised weight of him and gave him the guidance he said he wanted.

McCord realized he'd made a mistake when he nearly exploded in her hand. The touch of her fingers on his pulsing, throbbing manhood was almost more than he could stand at that moment.

"That's enough," he gasped. He reached down to pull her hand out of the way. "Forget it. Bad idea. I'll never last if you don't let go." He caught her hand and cradled it in his own as he kissed the center of her palm. Then he released her wrist and gripped her shoulders. He had waited long enough. She said there was no need to be extra careful or gentle tonight. He'd trust her to know what was best under the circumstances. She wouldn't do anything that might put the pregnancy at risk.

The image of Pru starting to grow round and full with his baby filled his mind even as he drove into her with all the pent-up hunger that had been gnawing at him for the past two weeks. It was an unbearably exciting picture that threatened to shred what was left of his self-control.

As if she sensed the powerful need coursing through him, Pru responded in kind. Her body shivered and trembled in his grasp. Her eyes were tightly closed against the waves of sensation that were steadily tightening her slender softness. McCord craved the feeling of her body when she was vibrating with sensual reaction the way she was tonight. The effect on him was stronger than that of any drug. It filled his senses and sent ripples of pleasure and power through him.

He could never get enough of her, he thought dazedly as he surged into her. He slid one hand back down beneath her to hold her hips and then pushed himself so deeply into her that he felt as though he were a part of her.

"Yes, McCord. Yes, my love. Please, please, oh, yes, *please.*"

He heard the breathless, squeezed way the last *please* sounded as it hovered on her lips and then he felt her body lock convulsively around his. She was beyond herself, her senses spinning out of control and, as always happened, she pulled him into the whirlwind with her.

"Oh, God, *Pru.*" Whatever else he said after that was lost as a shuddering release whipped through him. McCord held on to Pru with a grip that couldn't have been shaken loose by dynamite. He held her to him with violent strength as together they shared the moment of exquisitely wordless communion and shimmering passion.

They stayed wrapped together in the depths of the wide bed as long moments passed and their bodies slowly spiraled back to reality. McCord waited until he felt his breath return to normal before he reluctantly eased himself away from Pru's warm, soft body. Her hand moved in a vague, languid gesture, and he saw the flare of gold on her finger.

"My wife," he said quietly. The strange sense of possessiveness and satisfaction he had been experiencing since he'd put that ring on her finger this morning welled up in him again. He looked down at her love-gentled face. "You're my wife now."

"You're my husband." Her eyes were filled with a dreamy wonder. She snuggled closer. He could feel the sleepy trust in her as she nestled in his arms.

"I'm glad," McCord said with crystal-clear realization, "that it's all settled this time. You won't run away from me again."

It was a statement, not a question, but Pru didn't seem to notice or care. She dropped a tiny kiss on his damp chest and shook her head resolutely. "Never again."

As she fell asleep in his arms, McCord wondered in affectionate amusement just how much longer she was going to wait before she told him about the baby.

Pru awoke the next morning with a distinctly queasy feeling in her stomach. She felt momentarily disoriented, and then the full impact of her vague nausea hit her.

She had thought she was going to be one of the lucky ones who didn't suffer from morning sickness. Apparently she had been wrong.

"Oh, Lord." She lay very still, staring at the ceiling, and hoped the feeling would pass.

At the sound of her softly muttered words, McCord stirred sleepily. His heavy arm was resting on her stomach. Pru wished badly that he would remove it. Normally she loved the intimate way he cradled her while they slept. But this morning the weight on her stomach seemed to be contributing toward her unpleasant queasiness.

"Are you awake already?" McCord turned onto his side and lazily threw one foot over her ankle. His hand on her stomach moved deliberately.

The small movement was enough to turn the queasiness into a definite feeling of sickness. Pru was suddenly sure that just lying very still and hoping was not going to save her.

She hadn't even told McCord. What a way to break the news to him.

"Honey?" McCord studied her through narrowed eyes. "Are you okay?"

"I have to go to the bathroom," Pru explained urgently. She was already shoving back the covers and swinging her feet over the edge of the bed.

"I see." His words were dry, tinged with a faint trace of humor.

But he spoke to empty air. Pru was already through the bathroom door, slamming and locking it shut behind her. She dashed for the porcelain bowl.

The next few minutes constituted a very unpleasant time. It was made even more unpleasant for Pru because she couldn't decide which was worse, the morning sickness or the knowledge that this was a stupid way to tell McCord she was pregnant. She'd planned to do it in a much more dignified, romantic style. Perhaps over a candlelit dinner or while she was undressing for bed.

She flushed the toilet just as McCord started pounding on the door.

"Pru? Are you sick? What's the matter? Open the door, honey."

It occurred to her that she had never been sick around him. She was generally as healthy as a horse. Aunt Wilhelmina hadn't raised any weaklings.

"I'm okay, McCord. I'll be out in a few minutes."

"Open the door now, Pru." Indulgence and concern were rapidly being replaced by firm command in McCord's voice.

Pru knew that voice. She also knew she wasn't up to defying him this morning. The nausea had passed, but she still felt weak. It wasn't a good idea to argue with McCord unless you were feeling in top form. It was difficult enough to do it even then. Wearily Pru unlocked the door.

It swung open immediately. McCord stood on the threshold, hands on hips, glaring at her with fierce concern. "What's going on?"

"I just woke up feeling a little nauseous, that's all."

He examined her pale, wan face. "I can see that. Feeling any better now?"

"I'll live. I think."

He appeared to be about to say something more and then changed his mind. His voice softened. "Go lie down for a while, honey. I'll take my shower and we can talk about it when I get out. You should be feeling better by then."

Talk about what? she wondered. How did he know she wanted to talk about something important? She couldn't quite make sense of the words, but she didn't feel like contradicting him. A few minutes more in bed might be enough to get her through this lingering unpleasantness. She could spend the time figuring out how to tell him he was about to become a father.

He guided her gently to the bed and tucked her back in. Then he smiled enigmatically down at her. "I'll be out in fifteen minutes." He leaned down and kissed her forehead and then he sauntered into the bathroom.

Pru stared after him, perplexed. He was being altogether too casual about finding his new wife sick in the bathroom first thing in the morning. She wondered how long it would be before he began to put two and two together. McCord wasn't a stupid man. In fact, he was generally alarmingly smart.

She assimilated that bit of data and light began to dawn. Pru began to wonder which of them had been dismayingly slow recently.

He knew.

The realization went through her mind like wildfire. Pru shoved back the covers again and sat bolt upright. "It's impossible," she breathed. He couldn't know. No one knew except her sister, and she trusted Annie not to have betrayed her secret.

There was only one other source for the information. The clinic must have called for some reason. Or perhaps a letter had been sent.

The bill. Of course. She'd forgotten all about the bill that would have arrived in the mail. McCord must have had the shock of his life when he opened it.

Shaking a little, this time from agitation, not nausea, Pru stood up and looked frantically around the room. The odds were he would have left the paperwork at home unless he'd arrived prepared to confront her with his knowledge.

McCord was always prepared. He would have brought the bill with him as proof in case she attempted to deny her pregnancy. Pru rushed across the room and flung open the closet door. She heard the shower pounding in the distance as she quickly went through the pockets of McCord's lightweight sport coat. Then she knelt to unzip the battered leather flight bag that McCord always used when he traveled.

Inside the bag she found fresh underwear, fresh shirts, a couple of silk ties and a buff-colored envelope bearing the return address of a women's health clinic in San Diego.

She straightened slowly, clutching the envelope in her hand as the door to the bathroom opened. She turned to see McCord standing in the doorway with a towel wrapped around his waist. He was watching her with those fathomless dark eyes.

"What's the matter now, Pru?"

Her fingers clenched around the envelope. "You knew, didn't you? You found out I was pregnant. That's why you insisted on marrying me. *You knew.*"

CHAPTER FIVE

"I KNEW," McCord said very quietly.

"Damn it, why didn't you say anything?" Pru wailed.

"Why didn't *you* say anything," he countered.

"I didn't want you to marry me just because I was pregnant!"

"Oh, hell," McCord said grimly. "I should have guessed. I wondered why you didn't tell me. I thought maybe you were just too proud to use the baby to get what you wanted." He frowned. "Come to think of it, I guess that was part of the reason, wasn't it?"

She ignored his logic. "How could you do this to me, McCord? You've ruined everything." Pru felt her shaky emotions slipping out of control. She threw the incriminating envelope toward the trash container. It missed and fluttered lightly to the rug.

McCord folded his arms and lounged against the doorframe. He was good at that, Pru thought resentfully. On the rare occasions they had got involved in a serious argument, he'd usually spent a lot of the time propped in a doorway watching her with those bottomless dark eyes.

"You're getting emotional, Pru. I suppose that's only natural, given your present condition, but I think you'd better calm down and take a rational look at the situation."

"A rational look?" she stormed. "Meaning, my aunt was right? I should just shut up and be grateful you decided to marry me? Well, I've got news for both of you. I'm not my mother. I'm not some dirt-poor small-town girl who thinks the only way to escape poverty is by getting some man to marry her. I'm not poor, re-member? I have a good education, my own car, money in the bank and excellent job prospects. What's more, I'm living in sunny California where anything goes. I won't be shunned or ostracized. I can afford to have this baby and raise it alone. Lots of women are doing it these days.''

"But you're not going to have this baby and raise it alone, are you, Pru? You're married now." McCord's gaze went deliberately to the region of her stomach and then lifted back to her face. "I'm the father of your child. If I hadn't come after you, you would never have told me, would you? Why not, Pru? Afraid that if I knew you were pregnant, I'd throw you out or demand that you get an abortion?''

She stared at him in shock. It was the coldness of his voice that startled her more than the words. Never in all the months she'd known him had he sounded quite this chilled and remote. "Of course not. I was afraid you'd probably marry me if you found out I was pregnant. That's why I didn't tell you. Can't you understand?''

He came away from the door, moving toward her with long, pacing strides. Pru tried to step back, but there was no place to retreat. The closet was directly behind her. When his hands closed over her shoulders, she flinched, not because he had hurt her, but because of the expression in his eyes.

"No, I don't understand," he stated through set teeth. "You wanted to get married. If you thought I'd marry you if I knew you were pregnant, *why didn't you use that as a weapon to get what you wanted?* Tell me, Pru. That's the one thing I haven't been able to figure out.''

"Forcing you to marry me because of the baby is hardly a solid foundation on which to build a marriage." Pru moved one hand in a helpless little gesture. "I gave you my ultimatum, as you called it, because I thought it might bring you to your senses and make you see that what we had was good enough to warrant a…a more permanent arrangement. I thought if I could just shake you out of your state of smug, male satisfaction, you'd realize you really did want me. When you followed me to Annie's in Pasadena, I just assumed you'd finally come to the right conclusion about us and that you had decided you wanted to marry me after all.''

He gave her a small shake. "Pru, listen to me, I did want to marry you."

"Because you found out I was pregnant."

"I won't deny that was a factor, but I would have come after you even if that bill hadn't arrived from the clinic."

She glared up at him. "Just answer one question, McCord."

His mouth tightened ominously. "What question?"

"Did the clinic bill arrive before or after you made up your mind to follow me to Pasadena?"

There was a short pause that gave Pru her answer before McCord even opened his mouth. She gave a resigned sigh as he said carefully, "Pru, the clinic bill came in the mail the day after you left. I was still in a rage because you'd dared to walk out on me."

She nodded her head forlornly, accepting the unalterable fact. "So it was knowing that I was pregnant that made you decide to act. You showed up in Pasadena a few days after that. Took you a while to figure out where I'd gone, I suppose."

"Yes, it did, damn it. I finally had to force J.P. to give me your personnel file. You never bothered to tell me your sister lived in Pasadena. You barely even mentioned that you had a sister. Come to think of it, you barely mentioned your Aunt Wilhelmina in Texas, either. It wasn't easy locating you. Why didn't you tell me more about your family, Pru?"

She tried a small shrug. It wasn't easy because he was still gripping her shoulders. "Why didn't you ever tell me about yours? Let's face it, McCord. Married people share information on families. Couples involved in a convenient no-strings-attached affair don't have any reason to discuss such things."

"I don't know why not. We talked about everything else under the sun." He released her and stalked across the room to the window. "You didn't make any effort to involve me with your family because you were embarrassed about the fact that you were living with me. That's it, isn't it, Pru?''

"Be grateful," she muttered. "Aunt Wilhelmina would have been down on you like a pile of rocks if she knew I was living with you."

"And your sister?"

"I told her when I moved in with you. She understood," Pru said quietly.

"But she didn't approve?"

"She worried about me. I think she thought I was taking a risk."

"And when you showed up pregnant and alone on her doorstep, she knew for certain you'd been taking a risk." McCord glanced back over his shoulder, his eyes hard.

Pru walked slowly over to the bed and sank down on it with her back to McCord. "I should have taken better precautions. I should have been more careful."

There was silence behind her and then McCord said quietly, "It was my fault. It happened that night I got back from Africa, didn't it?"

Pru nodded. "Yes."

He rubbed the back of his neck with a reflective, massaging action, as though trying to ease some inner tension. "I've never been so exhausted and angry and depressed in my life as I was the night I got back from that trip. I'd never seen such endless, unrelenting death. It's overwhelming. Trying to believe in a future for those people is almost impossible. Everything the foundation is trying to do represents such a small amount of assistance compared to what the land and nature and the various governments are doing to the people trying to stay alive."

"I understand," Pru said softly, hearing the depths of the carefully concealed emotion in his voice.

"When I woke up in the middle of the night and realized I was home and that you were with me, I didn't stop to think about taking precautions. All I wanted to do was confirm the fact that we were both still alive and that there was a future. The next morning I thought about how careless I had been. Then I forgot about it because you never said anything. I figured everything must be all right. It never occurred to me that you'd keep quiet if you discovered you were pregnant.''

He didn't have to spell it out, she thought. She knew how that trip to Africa had affected him. When he'd awakened in the middle of the night, she hadn't given much thought to precautions, either. All her womanly instincts had been to offer comfort and warmth and confirmation of life.

For the first time since she'd awakened that morning, a small dart of wry amusement went through her. ''I guess we got fairly irrefutable evidence of just how determined life is to go on,'' she murmured.

She sensed that her brief burst of humor had startled him. He came back from the window and sat down on the bed beside her. Pru felt the strength of his arm as he put it around her shoulder.

''I know this isn't starting out like the fairy-tale marriage you probably always wanted, Pru,'' McCord said quietly. ''It's easy to see that I'm not exactly your idea of a knight in shining armor. But we're going to make things work. I told you last night that we've both made promises and a commitment.''

''And now we're stuck with those promises and the commitment?'' she challenged.

''You know the answer to that.'' His gaze was watchful and shadowed as he studied her face.

Pru thought of how much she loved this man and then she thought about the baby she was carrying. The child had a right to know his or her father, especially since the father was determined to shoulder his responsibilities. Slowly and deliberately Pru took hold of her frazzled emotions. McCord was right, of course. He usually was when it came to the practical, rational side of life.

''Under the circumstances, marriage appears to be the best option,'' she finally said very formally.

"It's the only option, and we've already exercised it. There's no going back."

She smiled wearily. "You don't have to beat me over the head with it any longer. I was feeling a little emotional earlier, but I'm back under control now."

"I'm glad to hear it." He didn't look as though he quite believed her, however.

"I suppose," Pru continued thoughtfully, "that Aunt Wilhelmina is right. I really should be grateful to you for tracking me down and demanding marriage. A lot of men wouldn't have bothered."

His jaw hardened. "Damn it, Pru, I don't want your gratitude. We created this situation together and we'll work through it together."

Her mouth curved slightly as she slid out from under the shelter of his arm and got to her feet. "You mean I don't have to grovel three times a day and kiss your toes on Fridays?"

He stood up beside her, his hands moving possessively around the nape of her neck. "You can kiss my toes," he said deliberately, "any time you feel like it."

"Be still, my beating heart." She wrinkled her nose. "I'm not sure that kind of excitement is good for the baby."

His eyes softened, and he pulled her close, burying his face in her hair. "It's going to be all right, honey. Everything's going to work out just fine. We may have got off to a somewhat rocky start, but the going will get smoother once we make up our minds to stop snapping at each other."

"You mean once I make up my mind to stop snapping at you, don't you, McCord? The truth is, you've been very good-natured and generous about this whole thing right from the start. I see that now. Earlier I was being selfish and emotional. It won't happen again."

He looked down into her earnest face and smiled faintly. "Is that right?"

She nodded determinedly. "Yes, it is. Don't laugh at me,

McCord. I've been through enough lately. I don't need you laughing at me.''

He groaned and squeezed her gently. ''I'm not laughing at you, sweetheart.'' Her soft breasts were crushed against his chest, and a curling tendril of her hair wrapped itself around the hard muscle of his upper arm. ''I'm just relieved there's not going to be any more argument on the subject of our marriage.''

''I rarely argue with you, McCord.''

''I know. But when you do, I feel like I'm in the middle of a lightning storm. You're unpredictable. I don't know which way to move for fear of provoking you further.''

''That doesn't seem to stop you from trying to respond,'' she observed dryly.

''A man's got to do something when his woman's going up in flames.'' He started to lower his head so that he could kiss her, but she slipped out of his arms. ''Pru?''

''It's getting late. I'd better take my shower.'' She was already walking into the bathroom. The satiny nightgown flowed around her slim ankles. ''My appetite seems to be returning with a vengeance. I can't wait for breakfast. I'll be out in a few minutes, McCord.''

The door slammed shut with some force. McCord stood looking at it for a long, thoughtful moment. He wanted to believe the resolute edict he'd just handed down to his new wife. He wanted to convince himself that everything really was straightened out and that there would be smooth sailing from now on between them.

But there was no point trying to kid himself. Pru had accepted the marriage, but she wasn't truly happy or content with her situation. She'd wanted to be married for what she thought of as all the right reasons. Instead, she was convinced McCord had married her out of a sense of duty and responsibility.

He didn't have any means of proving otherwise.

McCord spent some time dwelling on the irony of her conclusions. She assumed he had married her because he felt responsible for the baby. He wondered what his family would think if they knew how firmly she believed her own analysis of his actions. It made an amusing picture.

He pushed the thought aside as he walked to the closet and pulled out his jeans and a long-sleeved white shirt. For the first time he gave serious consideration to how he had reacted when he'd seen the bill from the clinic. It would have been nice if he could have at least offered Pru the reassurance of knowing he'd already made up his mind to come after her before the bill arrived.

But the truth was, he'd been both outraged and enraged the day following her departure. He'd felt betrayed in a way he'd never experienced before in his life, not even after he'd discovered three years ago that Laura Reynolds, his fiancée, was pregnant. The emotions that had been eating at him since the moment Pru had walked out the door had been unnerving and frightening in their intensity.

He'd spent some time assuring himself Pru would come crawling back on her hands and knees. He'd even fantasized about how he would react when she did. His fantasies had been greatly aided by the large quantity of whiskey he'd consumed after J.P.'s interminable, boring dinner party had finally ended. Such parties were always a bore when Pru wasn't around to manage things. She had a knack for putting people at ease and keeping a conversation going. As J.P. was fond of saying, people responded to Pru the way flies did to potato salad.

The fantasies he'd concocted the night after the party and had perfected while dawn broke over the California coast were brilliantly, satisfyingly vivid. In his mind he'd worked out an elaborate reconciliation scene in which Pru would cry and apologize and promise never to leave again.

He, on the other hand, would have been remote and distant at first, then politely condescending, and finally, generously forgiving. The little scene had quite naturally ended with a vision of taking Pru to bed where she could properly make up for all she'd put him through.

Before he'd worked out all the details of his fantasy, the morning mail had arrived, bringing with it the bill from the clinic. The moment he'd opened it, everything had changed.

No, that wasn't true. Nothing had changed. McCord fastened the snaps of his jeans with a brisk, savage efficiency. The end result was the same. One way or another he would have found a means of bringing Pru back where she belonged. Her place, whether she knew it or not, was in his home and in his bed.

PRU WAS AMAZED by her own hunger at breakfast. She wolfed down four slices of whole wheat toast, two poached eggs, a pile of hash browns and a large glass of orange juice before she even realized what she was doing. As she polished off the last of the toast, she saw McCord watching her with amusement in his eyes. She flushed and put down the scrap of toast, uneaten.

"If I'm not careful, I'm going to gain a ton," she muttered.

He picked up the bit of toast and held it to her lips. "Don't worry about it. You're going to look cute plump."

"Thanks a lot," she said, annoyed. But as soon as she opened her mouth he pushed the toast inside, and she had no other recourse except to eat it. It tasted delicious. She could have eaten three more slices, but she was careful not to say so. "Are we going back to La Jolla today?"

McCord hesitated and then shook his head. "No."

Pru glanced around at the elegant dining room. "You want to stay here longer?" She wasn't sure how she felt about that. Her feeling of being on a real honeymoon had ended this morning when she'd found the clinic envelope.

"I'd like to stay here a while longer," McCord said, watching her closely, "but we can come back another time. We should be heading back to La Jolla as soon as possible, but there's something I want to do first."

Pru nodded, realizing she wanted to return home. It was strange how she'd thought of McCord's house as her home from the moment she'd moved in with him. "Fine." There was no disguising the sense of relief she felt. The honeymoon was definitely over. It had been over before it had begun.

McCord saw her reaction, and his dark brows came together in a severe expression. "An overnight trip isn't much of a honeymoon."

Pru lifted one shoulder with studied negligence. "It's perfectly adequate under the circumstances."

He looked as if he wanted to argue, but he didn't. Instead, he said calmly, "There's something we have to do before we go home."

She eyed him inquiringly. "So you said. What is it?"

He cradled his coffee cup in two hands and took a deep swallow. "I want to introduce you to my family."

Pru considered that. "You make it sound as though you'll be introducing me to the Spanish Inquisition. Have you got a bunch of Aunt Wilhelminas in your family?"

"Believe me," McCord said bluntly, "Aunt Wilhelmina is a pussycat compared to my relatives. At least your aunt never actually disinherited you and informed you she thought you were dishonorable, disloyal and disgusting."

"I'm not sure I like the alliteration. That's a lot of dises. Disinherited, dishonorable, disloyal and disgusting." Pru was amazed. "What kind of family have you got, anyway?"

"A very proud, very stubborn, very unforgiving one. Also, a very wealthy one. My father made his money early on in California real estate. I grew up on a farm that just happened to be in the middle of Orange County. Twenty years ago my father sold the land to real-estate developers for a fortune. My father is a very shrewd man. As it happened, he had a natural flair for making money with land. He converted the profits from the farm into a very successful real-estate development company, which promptly invested in more land. After that, there was no stopping him. Officially he's still president of McCord Enterprises, but he's turned the day-to-day running of the operation over to my younger brother, Kyle. Kyle is shaping up to be even shrewder and more successful than my father. McCord Enterprises is growing by leaps and bounds.''

Pru's eyes widened. "Are both your parents alive?''

"Very much alive." McCord took another sip of coffee. "So is my brother Kyle and his wife Carrie. Kyle is doing the McCords proud.''

The way he said that caught Pru's attention. "Was that supposed to be your job? Before you got, uh, disinherited?''

"I'm the oldest son," McCord said without any inflection. "My father always assumed I'd step into his shoes. Even after I insisted on majoring in agricultural sciences, he still had hopes. I...tried to please him for a few years.''

Pru tipped her head to one side and tapped one fingernail lightly on the tablecloth. "Lucky for you, you got kicked out of the family fold, hmm?''

It was McCord's turn to look surprised. "Why do you say that?''

"It saved you from having to become a full-time corporate executive and follow in your father's footsteps. I can't imagine a worse fate for you, McCord. You need to be able to deal with more fundamental things." She smiled faintly. "You're a farmer at heart. It's hard enough for you and J.P. to do the kind of socializing and entertaining required for Arlington Foundation business as it is. I can't imagine you trapped behind a desk all day, too. If you'd taken over the reins of your dad's firm, you would have been stuck in a fancy corporate office. The closest you would have got to the land was going out on a golf course.''

McCord continued to stare at her for a long moment, and then a slow grin appeared on his face. "You're right, you know. It would have been a disaster. I didn't realize it myself until after I was banished.''

"Were you actually banished, McCord?''

"Not officially. My parents just made it clear I was a grave disappointment to them and unworthy of my name and heritage. I seem to recall saying something at the time to the effect that people who had been growing beans for a living less than twenty years ago didn't have to be overly concerned about names and heritages. The argument deteriorated rapidly after that. It ended with me walking out of their lives. I took the Ferrari and what I had in the bank and that was it.''

"What on earth did you do to alienate your family so completely?" Pru couldn't imagine any father being less than proud of a son like Case McCord.

"It's a long, dull story, Pru." McCord withdrew emotionally from the conversation. It was as though a shutter had been lowered to conceal his eyes. Once again they were dark and fathomless. "Let's just say I didn't marry the right woman."

Pru's mouth fell open in shock. "You were supposed to marry a certain woman?" she asked weakly.

"It was three years ago, Pru. I've already told you. She's dead now."

"The fiancée you mentioned the other night at dinner?" Pru asked tightly.

"That's right. Her father was my father's best friend and a partner in many of his deals. Laura was supposed to inherit a fair-sized chunk of McCord Enterprises. Shortly before he died, her father asked my father to look after Laura. My parents thought of her as the daughter they never had. Laura's mother disappeared years ago after a divorce, so when her dad died the McCords became her family. As it happened, everyone thought Laura and I made a good couple."

"Including you and Laura?" Her breath felt trapped in her chest, Pru thought. Consciously she tried to release the tension that had gripped her.

"Yes," McCord said. "Including Laura and me. She was a beautiful blond angel. Everyone loved her. And she said she loved me."

"Oh." Pru couldn't think of anything to say to that.

"Yes, oh."

"Well?" Pru finally prompted. "What happened?"

McCord looked into his coffee. "I changed my mind about the engagement. I decided I didn't want to marry her. When I told her, she went into a rage. She was almost hysterical. I didn't dare leave her alone that night until she'd calmed down somewhat. I didn't leave her apartment until nearly two in the morning when she finally settled down long enough to throw me out. I left. But almost as soon as I was gone she jumped into a car and went tearing off into the night. The police said she must have been going nearly a hundred miles an hour when she lost control on the freeway."

"Oh, my God," Pru breathed.

McCord's eyes hardened. "She died three hours later at the hospital. My family was gathered around the bedside. It was a very dramatic scene, I assure you. Laura regained consciousness long enough to inform everyone present exactly why she had been roaring along a Los Angeles freeway at close to a hundred miles an hour at two-thirty in the morning."

"She blamed you?" Pru asked, shocked.

McCord nodded. "You might say I was condemned by a dying woman's words. It was a tough act to follow, believe me." He didn't say anything else.

"How awful. What a terrible mess. But didn't your family understand that, while it was a tragedy, it was hardly your fault?"

"No. There were…" He paused, clearly searching for the right word. "Extenuating circumstances, I guess you could say."

"What extenuating circumstances?"

"They don't matter anymore, Pru. It was all over three years ago. The final conclusion was that I really should have married Laura. I had led her on and allowed her to believe she would be my wife. When I cold-bloodedly bowed out of the arrangement, she was distraught. Laura had a very delicate temperament."

McCord had obviously decided he'd said enough on the subject. Pru knew him better than to press for more information at that point. In fact, she was surprised at the amount he'd given her. In the past fifteen minutes she'd learned more about McCord's past and his family than she'd learned in the previous six months. "So the net result was that your father decided your brother was a more worthy son and made him CEO of the company?"

"Something like that. It sounds simple enough now, doesn't it? At the time it seemed damned messy."

"Have you seen much of your parents or your brother and his wife during the past three years?"

"Two years ago I spent Christmas Day with them. It was an awkward occasion for all concerned, to put it mildly. I didn't try to duplicate the experience."

"But now you've decided to introduce me to the family?" Pru asked uneasily.

"It won't be pleasant, but no one's going to attack you, Pru. It's me they blame for the situation. We won't stay long, I promise. I just want to make sure they know who you are and that you're my wife. After all, when the baby comes, they'll have to know about it."

"The baby?" she whispered. "Do we have to tell them about the baby right away? Couldn't we wait?"

"Why do you want to wait?" McCord asked, his eyes narrowing.

Pru groped for reasons she couldn't put into words. "It's too soon. I'm still adjusting to the fact that I'm pregnant. Give me a little time, McCord."

"Nothing's going to change with time," he pointed out gently. "You'll just be more and more pregnant."

"It's not funny," she retorted, seeing the flare of amusement in his eyes.

"I know. I shouldn't tease you. I realize you've been through a lot during the past few weeks. Now I'm asking you to face a pack of in-laws I'm not especially fond of myself. I won't add to the strain by announcing that not only did we get married yesterday, but you're already pregnant."

"Thank you, McCord," she said politely.

"You're embarrassed, aren't you?" he demanded with unexpected masculine insight. "That's the real reason you don't want me to mention that you're pregnant. You don't want everyone thinking you had to get married."

Pru bit her lip. She wasn't sure of her own reasons. She just knew she felt pressured and stressed and all sorts of other emotions that were probably common to mothers-to-be. "I'd just as soon not say anything yet," she murmured stubbornly.

"If you think it's going to be awkward having people think you had to get married because you were pregnant, how the hell did you plan to handle being an unwed mother?"

"That was different."

"How was it different?"

"I can't explain, and I'm sick of trying. Let's just drop the subject. I will announce my pregnancy in my own good time," she flared. It was all wrapped up in knowing she hadn't been married for the right reasons, all bound up with the knowledge that McCord had only married her because he was the kind of man who shouldered his responsibilities. She had been married for all the wrong reasons. She needed time to accept that.

McCord shook his head, half impatient and half sympathetic. "Women," he growled.

"Men," Pru growled back.

CHAPTER SIX

PRU HAD REGAINED a grip on her volatile emotions by the time McCord had the Ferrari packed. She told herself repeatedly she had absolutely no cause for complaint about her situation. She should be downright grateful, in fact, just as Aunt Wilhelmina had advised. Pru knew only too well that many women in similar circumstances would have found themselves on their own. She was lucky enough to be married to the baby's father. She had no grounds for carping about her fate.

But she was feeling perverse.

McCord installed Pru in the passenger seat of the Ferrari and then climbed into the driver's side. He shot Pru a quick, questioning glance as he turned the key in the ignition.

"Are you all right?"

"I'm fine."

"You have an odd look on your face. What are you thinking about?"

Pru deliberately grimaced, making her expression even odder. "I was just giving myself a pep talk."

"About what?" he demanded, guiding the car out of the inn parking lot.

"About not complaining when there is nothing to really complain about," she snapped, feeling goaded.

"You've decided to start feeling grateful instead?"

She didn't like the tone of his voice. "I don't intend to go overboard with it, but, yes, I guess I should be feeling rather grateful."

"I've told you I don't want your gratitude," he said.

"You'd rather have me throwing tantrums and railing against my fate?" she countered.

"As J.P. would say, some folks would complain if they got hung with a new rope."

"That sounds suspiciously like an Aunt Wilhelmina saying. And I am not complaining. I told you, I'm practicing being grateful."

"How about we just drop the subject?"

Pru slanted him a sideways glance and discovered he was making an effort to hang on to his temper. She could always tell when McCord was angry. His jaw became rigid with the force of his restrained emotions. "That might be best," she agreed softly, and turned her attention to the passing scenery.

The sparkling Pacific Ocean stretched to the horizon on the left-hand side of the Ferrari. The morning fog that frequently clouded the coastline in summer had burned off. It would be a warm day.

"Where do your parents live?" Pru asked after thirty minutes of silence.

"They have a place outside of Santa Barbara." McCord's tone was neutral.

"Where's the corporation based?"

"L.A."

"And your brother and his wife? Do they live in Los Angeles?"

"Marina del Rey," McCord said briefly, naming one of the posh oceanfront communities that comprised part of the Los Angeles sprawl.

"Are your parents expecting us?"

"I phoned my mother yesterday and told her we'd be arriving this afternoon. We'll only stay an hour or two, Pru. We should be able to survive that long."

"By then your filial duty will have been done, is that it? You will have introduced your new bride to your family, and that's all that's required under the circumstances?"

"That's all," he confirmed flatly. "I'm not taking you to meet them out of a sense of duty, though."

"Why, then?" She was genuinely curious.

"I'm not sure," he said with surprising honesty. "I think it's got something to do with the fact that I want them to know the family line is continuing through me, whether they approve or not. I want them to be aware of you."

Pru thought for a moment. "Was your mother shocked to hear that you'd married?" she finally asked in a rather tentative voice.

"Very."

Pru groaned silently, wondering what kind of welcome awaited her. "Then I'm definitely glad we've decided to wait to tell them about the baby. I don't want to be responsible for giving your mother too many shocks at once."

THE HOME of McCord's parents was an imposing modern structure set high above the sea and commanding views of both ocean and rolling hills. Pru was a little startled at the size and grandeur of it. For the first time she began to realize just how wealthy the senior McCords were. Pru eyed the sleek, modern, heavily glassed structure as McCord turned the Ferrari into the long, winding drive.

"Were you raised in this house?" she asked, suddenly and intensely curious. "After you left the farm?"

"No. My parents had this place built a few years ago. They used it as a vacation home until my father retired from running McCord Enterprises. They live here full-time now."

"It's quite impressive." Pru couldn't think of anything else to say.

"Do you like it?"

"Nice place to visit, but I wouldn't want to live here," she returned promptly.

He laughed. "Why not?"

"I like our home better."

He flicked her a glance at the words "our home," but he said nothing.

Pru didn't notice the glance. She wasn't paying any attention to him now as he parked the car in the drive. The wide, elegantly proportioned double doors of the house had opened, revealing an attractive woman who must have been nearly sixty but who appeared to be at least ten years younger. Her hair was toned to a rich California blond shade and styled in a short, unswept manner that accented her large, expressive eyes. The beautifully cut khaki slacks and cream-colored blouse that she wore spelled money in a very smooth, understated way.

"Your mother?" Pru asked.

McCord switched off the ignition and stared at the figure on the doorstep. "Her name is Evelyn."

Evelyn McCord came down the steps. As the older woman drew closer, Pru saw the tension and anxiety that couldn't quite be concealed by the bright, welcoming smile. McCord's mother was far more tense about this meeting than Pru was. Nevertheless, Pru held her breath as McCord climbed out of the car and accepted his mother's greeting. It consisted of a very restrained kiss on the cheek. Neither party made any effort to prolong the physical contact.

Pru climbed slowly out of the car as both McCord and his mother turned toward her. It was when Evelyn's hazel gaze met that of her new daughter-in-law that Pru saw there was more than tension in the depths of her eyes. There was a spark of something Pru could have sworn was hope.

The introductions were quickly made. Pru smiled at Evelyn and held out her hand.

"I'm so pleased to meet you," Evelyn said swiftly, rapidly assessing Pru's face. "It was such a surprise to hear from Case yesterday. I had no idea... That is, we didn't dream he was engaged, much less married. Do come inside and meet Hale. Case, why don't you bring in the luggage? You can put it in the west bedroom. It has a lovely view."

"There's no need for me to bring in the luggage, Mother. Pru and I are only going to stay for an hour or so. I just brought her by to meet you and Dad."

Pru winced at the cold, curt refusal. She saw a well-concealed despair replace the flickering hope that had been in Evelyn McCord's eyes.

"Oh, dear," Evelyn said unhappily. "I was so hoping you could stay the night at least. It's been so long. I've invited your brother and his wife for dinner. We're hoping Devin Blanchard can make it, too. They'll be staying overnight and going back to L.A. in the morning."

McCord shot his mother an unreadable glance. "You invited Kyle and Carrie and Devin?"

Evelyn flinched as if he'd made an accusation. Then her mouth firmed. "I thought it only right that they meet your new wife, Case."

Before McCord could respond, a man's voice spoke from the doorway. "The least you could do under the circumstances is stay for dinner. Your mother's gone to a lot of work, Case."

Pru turned to see an older version of Case standing on the threshold of the house. His dark hair was nearly silvered, but the brilliant, dark gaze was as intent and shadowed and proud as that of his son. His face was as fiercely carved, and the underlying masculine arrogance was unmistakable. Hale McCord was still a strong, well-built man although he carried more weight than did his son. Pru would have guessed instantly who he was, even if she hadn't known his name. Now she knew where Case McCord had gotten his pride and his arrogance and his sheer, cussed stubbornness.

"Hello, Dad. I'd like you to meet my wife, Prudence," McCord said coolly. "Pru, in case you haven't guessed, this is my father, Hale McCord." He turned back to face his parent. "I'm sorry about Mother's plans, but I told her yesterday when I called that we wouldn't be here long."

Evelyn looked at him with a pleading expression. "Couldn't you at least stay for dinner, Case? It's been so long." Helplessly she shifted her glance to Pru.

Pru couldn't stand the pain in the woman's eyes. She smiled at

Evelyn and moved forward to take her husband's arm. "There's no reason at all why we can't stay for dinner, is there, McCord? In fact, we can spend the night. We'd love to. We don't have to be back in La Jolla until tomorrow or the next day."

"Pru," McCord began grimly, "there's no need to spend any more than an hour here."

"Nonsense," Pru countered firmly. "This is a beautiful spot, and I would love to spend the night." She felt the tension in McCord's arm and widened her smile. She turned the full force of it on Evelyn McCord. "Thank you very much for the invitation, Mrs. McCord. It's wonderful of you to have us on such short notice."

"Please, call me Evelyn." The rush of maternal gratitude was almost embarrassing.

"Damn it, Pru…" McCord's voice was a low snarl of anger.

Pru released him and started up the steps with a hand extended toward her new father-in-law. "Bring in the luggage, McCord," she ordered casually over her shoulder, silently praying she would get away with the command. "How do you do, Mr. McCord? I would have known you anywhere. I'll bet you were raised on a farm, too. Does wonders for a man's shoulders."

Hale McCord blinked at her as if not knowing quite how to take the outrageous flattery. Then he seemed to decide it was safe to respond to the amusement in Pru's eyes. He accepted her hand in his large paw. "You're right, Prudence. I spent a lot of years picking beans and bailing hay. Who do you think taught Case how to do those things? Call me Hale."

"Call me Pru. Everyone else does." She risked a quick glance back toward the car and gave an inward sigh of relief when she saw that McCord was lifting the luggage out of the Ferrari.

Evelyn's eyes were darting anxiously from the luggage to Pru as if she didn't quite dare to believe her son had agreed to stay the night. When Pru smiled reassuringly at her from the top of the steps, she returned the expression with genuine warmth and came forward quickly. She apparently decided her luck was going to hold. She came up the steps to urge Pru inside the hall.

"Thank you, my dear," she murmured in such a low tone that only Pru heard her. "Thank you very much. I'm in your debt." Then she raised her voice. "Come along and I'll show you your bedroom. Hale, why don't you give Case a hand with the luggage?"

Hale looked toward the Ferrari, as if not quite certain how to handle the simple offer of assistance. Then he nodded abruptly and started down the steps.

"Here, Case. I'll take one of those bags," Hale said brusquely.

"It's all right, Dad, I've got them."

"I said I'll take one, damn it."

Without a word McCord surrendered one of the bags to his father, who turned around and stalked back into the house.

Pru felt the shudder of dismay in the woman beside her and wanted to put her arm around her in sympathy. *My God,* she thought, *what a family. They're all dancing on eggs and juggling dynamite, as Aunt Wilhelmina would say.* At least Aunt Wilhelmina was up front and vocal about her feelings. She didn't try to hide behind the unnerving, barely polite facade.

A young woman appeared in the hall, smiling inquiringly.

"This is Sandra," Evelyn explained. "She helps out around here. She's already got your room made up. Sandra, this is my son's new wife, Prudence."

"How do you do?" Sandra said politely. "Let me know if you need anything."

"Thanks," Pru murmured.

"Here we are, Pru. Hale, you can set the suitcase down over there." Evelyn bustled around the elegant salmon-and-gray bedroom, straightening the already perfectly straight bedspread and flicking an infinitesimally small bit of lint off the sleek lacquer dresser. She glanced anxiously at Pru. "Will this room be all right, Pru?"

Once again Pru felt compelled to summon a brilliantly reassuring smile. "It's fantastic. What a beautiful view. I won't be able to sleep tonight. I'll spend the whole time looking out the window. It's amazing how different the ocean looks from one portion of the coast to another, isn't it? The view from McCord's, I mean *our* home, is completely different."

There was a fraught moment of silence while Evelyn glanced past Pru to her son's set face. "I wouldn't know," she murmured. "I've never visited Case in La Jolla."

McCord said nothing. He set the luggage down and walked over to the window as if he were mildly curious about the view. Hale shifted awkwardly in the doorway. Evelyn bit her lip.

Pru swallowed another silent groan of dismay and prayed she'd be able to keep her foot out of her mouth for the rest of the afternoon and evening. She plowed on with dogged determination. "What time will McCord's brother Kyle and his wife get here? I'm anxious to meet them."

"They should be here by five, don't you think, Hale?" Evelyn jumped to take advantage of the neutral conversational opening.

"Sure. Somewhere around five," Hale muttered.

"Well," Evelyn went on with patently false cheerfulness, "why don't you two freshen up? When you're done, perhaps you'd like to take a walk down on the beach."

"That sounds wonderful," Pru assured her. She almost collapsed in relief when the bedroom door closed behind McCord's parents. She sank down on the bed and watched her husband's broad-shouldered back.

"It's going to be a hell of an evening," McCord said.

"I can see that."

"Just remember," he advised with a sardonic twist of his mouth as he swung around to face her, "that it's all your fault. I was a fool to let you push me into agreeing to stay. I wish you joy of your new in-laws, Pru." He stalked into the adjoining bathroom and slammed the door.

Pru didn't realize just how bad matters were going to get until Kyle and Carrie McCord arrived shortly before five o'clock.

Things might have been tense around McCord's parents, but Pru didn't encounter real hostility until she confronted Carrie McCord.

Kyle and his wife were a handsome couple. Kyle shared his father's dark eyes and thick hair, but he lacked the muscular build of his parent and his brother. Instead, he was slim and dynamic, with a clean-cut, well-dressed, California-executive manner.

Carrie was a lovely blue-eyed redhead. Under normal circumstances, Pru was certain her new sister-in-law would have been slender and well-proportioned. Carrie was, however, quite pregnant. Her designer maternity dress shaped a body that had to be very close to nine months along.

Pru experienced a sudden urge to confide her own pregnant status to Carrie. She found herself abruptly eager to compare notes and ask questions. But the urge disintegrated at once when she saw the anger and resentment in Carrie's blue eyes. The other woman was superficially polite, but there was no welcome for the new member of the family.

She hates me, Pru thought in shock. *I don't even know her and already she hates me.* It was hard to believe that all the anger and tension in this family had been generated by a dying woman's accusation three years ago. There had to be more to the story, and Pru wondered desperately what it might be. It was obvious no one intended to talk about the subject.

"Devin Blanchard decided at the last moment he could come for the evening, Mom," Kyle McCord told his mother as he quietly greeted his brother and prepared to remove luggage from the BMW he drove. "He should be here any minute."

"Wonderful," Evelyn said quickly, casting another anxious glance at her oldest son. "I'm so glad he could make it. You and Devin used to be such good friends, didn't you, Case? I'm sure you'll enjoy seeing him again. Let's go inside. Hale was just about to pour drinks."

Everyone seemed grateful for the small social ritual of the predinner cocktail hour. No one questioned Pru when she seconded Carrie's order of fruit juice. Hale handed out the drinks, and Evelyn and Pru gamely tried to keep the conversation going until the sound of another car was heard in the drive.

"That'll be Dev," Carrie said. She shot McCord an odd look. "You haven't seen him for quite some time, have you, Case? Let's see, the last time would have been three years ago when Laura died."

Pru couldn't believe her sister-in-law had had the gall to introduce the dead woman's name into the conversation. It was so painfully obvious that everyone else was desperately trying to avoid any reference to what had happened three years ago.

McCord merely shrugged and took a swallow of his whiskey. "No. I haven't seen him since then."

"You and Devin worked together on a number of McCord projects," Evelyn said wistfully.

McCord gave her a grim smile. "Things change, don't they?"

Evelyn was saved from having to answer because Hale opened the door at that moment to the newcomer. Pru studied Devin Blanchard curiously.

He was a sandy-haired, green-eyed man who appeared to be about McCord's age. Dressed in an expensive casual linen sport coat and slacks that had a European cut, he was handsome with the kind of sensitive yet rugged look that appealed to women. When he shook hands with Pru, he gave her a warm smile.

"Congratulations on finally trapping him, Pru," Devin said in an easy, bantering tone. "The last time I talked to Case about marriage, he had sworn off it for life."

Pru winced inwardly at the words, but she was so relieved to have someone speak in a normal, friendly tone of voice that she immediately forgave Devin. "It doesn't happen often, because he's a very stubborn man, but believe it or not, McCord does occasionally change his mind," she said lightly.

Devin grinned at her and then at McCord. "Nothing like a pretty woman to help convince a man he might have to reevaluate a decision. How are you doing, Case? It's been a long time."

"Fine, Dev. What about yourself?" McCord was polite, his

voice utterly neutral, although he shook hands with the other man in a reasonably relaxed fashion.

"I'm doing great. Still working for Kyle."

"The board of directors made Dev a vice president three months ago," Kyle informed his brother. "He's become my right-hand man."

"Only because of your recommendation," Devin said, smiling.

Kyle shrugged. "It's about time you got paid for the amount of responsibility you're handling. You've always played a vital role in McCord Enterprises." He turned to Pru. "Devin has been, with the company for several years. He and Case put together some major deals in their time. We're still making money on all of them."

"I see," Pru said politely.

"That was before Kyle took over the reins," Carrie put in with a militant gleam in her eye. "My husband has been running McCord Enterprises for the past three years. The projects Kyle has put together since Case left are considerably larger and more profitable than those earlier deals."

Pru heard the challenge behind the words and wondered at it. Then she remembered that it was Case McCord who had been groomed originally to take over the running of the company. Kyle had got the job more or less by default when McCord and his father had quarreled three years ago.

Pru had a sudden insight into the probable cause of Carrie's overt hostility. It was quite possible Carrie was afraid that, having married at last, her brother-in-law might have decided to reclaim his lost heritage. Pru smiled at the other woman with genuine empathy.

"I understand Kyle is doing an excellent job managing McCord Enterprises," she said easily. "It's strange how things sometimes work out for the best, isn't it? It's quite obvious Kyle has a flair for corporate management and it's just as obvious that it would have been a mistake for McCord to have stayed in that role."

Everyone in the glass-walled living room stared at her. Even

McCord eyed her with an unblinking gaze. But it was Hale who spoke.

"What makes you say that, Pru?"

"I've known McCord for several months now," Pru said gently, "and I can say for certain that he would have been very discontented sitting behind an executive's desk at McCord Enterprises. My husband's true talent is in coaxing the land to produce as much as it's capable of producing. That talent happens to be a very valuable one in certain places around the world where people are systematically starving to death. McCord belongs in the Arlington Foundation's experimental crop fields or in an open-air classroom teaching farmers new techniques. The only kind of office work he enjoys is putting together a research paper on soils or designing a plan to increase plant productivity. He'd be bored and restless playing corporate officer in a high-rise office building. J.P. says he's got the magic touch when it comes to figuring out how to turn a desert into an Eden."

Everyone was still staring at her. Carrie was watching Pru with a distinctly suspicious glare. Devin Blanchard seemed politely interested. Kyle was looking quizzical. McCord's parents appeared startled by Pru's words, and McCord himself had a familiar, amused expression on his face. It was Hale who responded first.

"Who's J.P.?" he asked.

"J. P. Arlington. He's the founder of the Arlington Foundation."

Evelyn nodded slowly. "Case did say something once on the phone about going to work for a foundation of some sort."

Good Lord, Pru thought, *these people barely even know where McCord lives, let alone what he's doing for a living.* Whatever rift had occurred in this family three years ago, it must have been the size of the Grand Canyon. Still, she had a conversational gambit now, and Pru wasn't about to let go. She hadn't been J.P.'s executive hostess for the past six months for nothing. She could handle a roomful of difficult, uneasy, occasionally hostile people.

Pru launched into a glowing report on the Arlington Foundation for Agricultural Research and Development. She hadn't just been J.P.'s hostess, she had also been the editor of the foundation's journal. When called upon, Pru could give an excellent summary of the status of agriculture around the world and who was doing what about it.

To her amazement, she discovered that her audience seemed quite fascinated. They lacked the courage or the nerve to ask McCord what he had been doing for the past three years, but they seized on the opportunity of learning about him through his new wife.

McCord sat back in silence, his glass cradled in his hands, and watched Pru answer questions. Bringing her here had been akin to throwing some poor, unsuspecting nonswimmer into a pool and letting her figure out how to stay afloat. But Pru was learning fast, he thought with admiration. His family and Blanchard were responding the way people always did to her. Her talent for putting people at ease was extraordinary.

She had them all listening and talking now. Some of the tension had seeped out of the room. Even his father was asking genuinely interested questions about the foundation's work. His mother's relief at the nonhostile turn of events was embarrassingly evident.

In general, the reactions of his family were almost amusing. It was Devin Blanchard's intent attention to Pru's conversation that ruffled the latent possessive streak in McCord.

"Of course, Hale," Pru announced glibly, "I'm not saying that his agricultural background is all McCord draws upon in his work. The kind of things you must have taught him about running a large organization come in extremely handy. J.P. relies on McCord to deal with a lot of the management aspects of the foundation's work. There's a fair amount of travel involved, too. McCord has been all over the world in his work for the foundation."

"Case has a natural talent for leadership," Hale said with a reflective look at his son. "He always had a knack for being able to put together a team and get every member working toward a common goal."

"Well, I assure you, it's being put to good use at the foundation. You can't imagine how difficult it is to convince a bunch of poor, desperate farmers on the other side of the world to try a new agricultural technique. They're afraid to try anything new for fear of losing what little they've already got. And then, naturally, there's the business of dealing with various and assorted bureaucratic and academic types. McCord's got a way with those people, too. You're right. He can pull things together."

Carrie's gaze went to her brother-in-law. "You seem to have married a one-woman cheerleading squad, Case."

Pru flushed at the sarcasm, but McCord merely smiled enigmatically. "I'm lucky to have a wife who believes in me so completely," he said blandly. "Every man needs a woman who believes in him, doesn't he? Sometimes there's no one else in the world who does."

There was an appalled silence as everyone in the room appeared to take the remark personally.

"Quite a little treasure," Carrie muttered with a narrow glance at Pru.

Even her husband was somewhat embarrassed by Carrie's comment. He cleared his throat, as though trying to find a new topic of conversation.

McCord ignored his brother's efforts. Instead, he raised his glass in a small, intimate salute to Pru. "She is, indeed, a treasure. I hate to think of how close I was to letting her slip through my fingers."

Pru's embarrassed flush turned to a glowing warmth. She stared at her husband, who was silhouetted against a flaming sunset. His gaze was dark and deep and brilliant. In that moment it was quite easy to believe he meant what he had said.

PRU MANAGED TO AVOID Carrie until after dinner when she found herself alone with her sister-in-law for a few minutes shortly before everyone retired to bed. It had been a mistake to come out alone onto the deck for a breath of sea air. That much was obvious the moment Pru heard the other woman behind her. She didn't turn around. She had a hunch what was coming.

"Well, well, well," Carrie said coldly. "Getting a little tired from playing the role of Great Peacemaker for the McCord family?"

Pru leaned on the railing and gazed out over the night-shrouded sea. "This family could use some peace," she said quietly.

"This family was doing just fine until you entered the picture. How in the world did you trap McCord into marrying you? You don't look like his type."

"What is his type, Carrie?"

"Laura Reynolds was. Tall, blond, classically beautiful, stylish."

"And dead."

"Yes. And dead." Carrie came closer to the railing, her bulky figure moving a little awkwardly. "Has Case told you about her?"

"Yes."

"All of it?"

"Enough," Pru assured her quietly.

"Including the fact that he killed her?"

Pru spun around, incensed. "He did not kill her. That's a horrible thing to say. The woman killed herself in a hundred-mile-an-hour crash on a freeway. There is no one else to be blamed."

Carrie's eyes glittered. "That depends on how you look at it. You weren't around three years ago, Pru. The rest of us were. We know exactly what happened and who was to blame."

"That, as my Aunt Wilhelmina would say, is so much refried chicken manure. If you haven't figured that out by now, then you aren't noticeably brighter than the chickens that make the manure." Pru turned back to the railing.

"You don't fool me for one minute, Pru." Carrie's voice was a tight, angry hiss. "I know exactly why you're here. Case McCord would never have returned if you hadn't found some way of convincing him it might be possible to—" She broke off hastily.

"Possible to do what, Carrie?" But Pru was fairly certain she already knew.

"You think you can patch things up in this family and get Case back into Hale's good graces, don't you? You've found out just how much money and power this family has and you figure you deserve a slice of it because you married the eldest son. It must have come as a shock when you discovered you'd married the wrong son, hmm? You'd picked the black sheep in the family. The one who was kicked out without a penny. I'll bet he didn't mention that small fact before the marriage, did he? Now you're desperately trying to find a way to fix that little problem, aren't you? It must be terrible standing on the outside in the cold, looking in on all this money. But you're smart. You must know Evelyn would give her soul to bring Case back into the fold. So you're going to try to do just that."

"Carrie, you've got this all wrong."

"The hell I have. But I'll tell you one thing, Pru, you'd better live up to your name and exercise a little caution. Because I see right through you. I know what you're up to and I'm not going to let you do it. I won't let you find a way to get your husband put back in charge of McCord Enterprises. Kyle's been running things for three years. He's been brilliant at it. The corporation is richer now than it's ever been. He deserves to go on running the operation. I won't let you wreck everything he's built up during the past few years!"

Stunned, Pru stared after her distraught sister-in-law as Carrie hurried back into the glass-walled living room.

CHAPTER SEVEN

MCCORD LOUNGED in the gray leather chair near the bedroom window, waiting for Pru to emerge from the bathroom. He sat in shadow, naked except for his jeans, which he'd left unsnapped. The only light in the gray-and-salmon room was the crack of yellow that seeped out from under the bathroom door.

The house was quiet now, but it seemed to him that underlying tension still thickened the air. It was as if the place had absorbed the emotions of its occupants while they were awake and was now releasing the essence of their uncertainties, hostility and stubborn pride back into the atmosphere around them.

There should be something more mixed in with the other volatile, aggressive emotions, McCord thought. He should be able to detect some remnant of Pru's glowing pride in him. She had certainly made it plain enough to his relatives and Devin Blanchard. Perhaps, if he concentrated, he could also detect a trace of her fierce refusal to believe he had done anything all that terrible three years ago.

Of course, he reminded himself, *she didn't know the whole story of what had happened three years ago.* McCord stared musingly out over the darkened sea and wondered if her staunch defense of him would survive if she knew all the facts.

The door behind him opened at that moment, and McCord felt another kind of tension in the atmosphere. He didn't turn his head, but he could almost read her mind. She was nervous again tonight about the prospect of sleeping with him.

The knowledge angered him because he wasn't quite sure how to counter her high-strung emotions.

"I warned you it wouldn't be a pleasant visit. If you hadn't decided to ignore my plans to stay for only an hour or two, we could have been long gone by now.'' He felt compelled to point that out and then instantly wished he hadn't sounded so aggressive. He could feel her stop halfway across the room.

"Your mother would have been crushed."

"She would have survived. She's survived the past three years, hasn't she? Besides, she set us up, tried to force us to stay by telling us about her plans for the evening."

"She was desperate," Pru said gently.

"You know how I feel about being manipulated."

"I know." There was a pause and then Pru went on in a cool, polite tone, "Thank you for not making a scene and insisting we leave when I told her we'd stay. I appreciate the fact that you didn't override my decision."

He got up out of the chair in a swift, tense movement, his anger growing. When he swung around to confront her, he found her standing several feet away. Her pale yellow nightgown flowed around her, making her look like a ghost in the shadows. She watched him with wary eyes.

"I decided you might as well learn your lesson the hard way," McCord said roughly. "Maybe after tonight you won't be so eager to restore the bonds of family harmony. What did Carrie say to you out there on the deck?"

She lifted one hand and let it drop back to her side. Slowly she trailed over to the window. "She's afraid."

"Afraid Kyle will lose his position as head of McCord Enterprises if my parents and I resolve our little disagreement?" he scoffed.

"Something like that."

He felt a flash of amusement. "Even though you'd spent most of the evening assuring everyone I was a farmer at heart and wouldn't be happy running the corporation?"

"She doesn't believe me."

McCord shrugged. "Who would? If I were in charge of McCord Enterprises, I'd easily triple my income, not to mention getting my hands on a lot of fringe benefits and a big chunk of real Southern California power.''

"You make plenty of money working for J.P.,'' she tossed back tightly. ''And your power is the ability to make a desert bloom, not force a million-dollar real estate deal to go through.''

"Haven't you learned that when it comes to money and power one never has enough?''

"That's nonsense.''

"You think so? Go ask Carrie. Or my brother, or Devin Blanchard, or my parents.'' He was goading her and he knew it, but he couldn't seem to help himself. It was as if he suddenly had to test her, even though he knew she wouldn't falter. Maybe it wasn't so much a matter of testing her as it was a question of reassuring himself.

"I don't care what the others think. I know you and I know you've got everything you need in your job with the Arlington Foundation.''

He listened to the certainty in her voice and almost smiled. ''Is that right?''

"Yes, it is, and you know it. Why are you behaving like this?'' She glanced back over her shoulder, frowning at him.

He exhaled slowly. ''Maybe because I've just had a lousy evening.''

"It wasn't altogether lousy,'' she protested. ''You and your father managed to talk politely at dinner.''

"Only because you provided a neutral topic.''

"The pros and cons of canal irrigation in sandy soil?'' Pru's mouth tilted slightly. ''Your father really got into that topic, didn't he? I think there is a lot of the farmer left in him, too, even if he did eventually found a corporation and make a fortune in business. Maybe it's a case of being able to take the man away from the farm, but not being able to take the farmer out of the man.''

"My mother would shudder to hear you say that. She hated living on the farm. My brother didn't like it, either.''

"But you were at home there." Pru nodded. "That's what I was trying to explain to everyone all evening."

"They didn't understand," McCord told her grimly, wondering if he did himself.

"They will. Someday." She turned back to stare out the window.

"Maybe. Maybe not." He came up close behind her and found her shoulders with his hands. Leaning down to nuzzle the curve of her throat, he felt the immediate tension that rippled through her. Instinctively his fingers tightened, and she tensed even more.

"McCord, I've been thinking." Her voice was husky and very faint.

"I know. You've been doing far too much thinking the past few weeks. I've got a better idea tonight." He urged her back against him until her soft, rounded derriere came into contact with the taut hardness of him. She could arouse him so easily, he thought in wonder. He doubted that she even realized the extent of her sensual power over him. Pru was sweetly naive about things like power.

"I'm serious, McCord." The words were a little breathless, but very intent. "I know we're married now—"

"Damn right, we're married." he slid his hands down to her hips, holding her tightly. Deliberately he moved his thighs against her in a slow, provocative motion. She shivered.

"But marriage wasn't something you really wanted, McCord. I know that. I realize you went through with it because of the baby and…and I appreciate it, but—"

"Show me," he growled.

"Show you what?" She sounded bewildered.

"How much you appreciate it."

She swallowed. "That's just it, McCord. I'm not sure that's a good enough reason to go to bed with you."

He froze, his fingers digging deeply into the soft curve of her thighs. "What are you trying to say, Pru?" He heard the ice in his own voice, but it was nothing compared to the chill in his gut.

"I'm just suggesting that until we work out the basics of this relationship of ours, perhaps it would be better if we didn't sleep together." She stood very still under his hands. "I know you don't love me and I—"

"They got to you, didn't they?" McCord interrupted savagely. "Who?"

"Carrie and my parents and even Devin Blanchard. They managed to put a few doubts in your head, after all. Oh, you tried to play the loyal, supportive wife, and you did a hell of a job, but deep down you started asking yourself some questions, didn't you? It's occurred to you that a man wouldn't have become estranged from all of these nice, intelligent people if there weren't a fairly good reason. You're starting to wonder what really did happen three years ago."

She whipped around in his arms, her eyes huge in the shadows. "McCord, stop it! You know that's not true."

"Do I?"

"Yes, damn it, you do." She threw her arms around his neck and hugged him violently. "That's not the reason I was having second thoughts about…about our sleeping together."

"Are you sure?"

She looked up at him with pleading eyes. "I'm absolutely positive. You must believe me."

"You've never, ever refused to go to bed with me since you moved in with me," he pointed out coolly. "Nothing's changed in our relationship except that you've got a ring on your hand. Why should you refuse me now unless it's because you've had some second thoughts after meeting my family?"

She blinked and then her eyes narrowed unexpectedly. "Damn you, McCord, you're doing this deliberately, aren't you?"

"Doing what?"

"You're deliberately goading me into feeling I have to sleep with you in order to prove I believe in you."

"It's possible," he said carefully, "that I just need some reassurance."

The last of her shaky barriers collapsed completely under the admission, just as McCord had suspected they would. Pru muttered something slightly incoherent and leaned into him, her arms tightening around his neck.

"Talk about manipulation," she grumbled against his chest.

"Let's not talk about it," McCord whispered thickly as he slid his fingers under her hair and found the nape of her neck. "Let's just go to bed where we belong." He tipped her head up and brushed his mouth lingeringly over hers. When he felt her instant response, the last of his inner tension faded to be replaced by the full force of his need.

He untied the laces at the top of her nightgown and slipped the garment off over her head. The fabric fluttered unheeded to the floor as McCord examined his wife in the moonlight. He knew she didn't think of herself as small for a woman. After all, she was five and a half feet tall. But to him she seemed delicate and fragile and soft. He worried about her carrying the burden of his baby.

She smiled up at him as if she sensed what he was thinking. Then she reached out to take hold of his hand. Her eyes never left his face as she conveyed his palm to her breast and held it there.

"Sweetheart," he muttered, feeling his body react powerfully as he felt the response of her nipple under his palm. "You don't know what you do to me."

"Show me," she challenged softly.

He didn't care that she was taunting him gently with his own words. All he could concentrate on in that moment was the need to have her touch him. He caught hold of her hand, just as she had taken his. Then he placed her fingers at the open V of his unsnapped jeans. McCord knew she felt the shudder that went through him.

"That's it, baby," he breathed urgently. "Touch me. It feels so good when you touch me like that."

She slid her hands inside the waistband of his jeans and pushed them down over his hips, taking his briefs along with the denim.

Pru sank slowly to her knees in front of him as she worked the garments down his thighs to his ankles.

McCord thought he would come apart in a hundred tiny pieces when he felt the soft tendrils of her hair against his thighs. He hastily stepped out of the jeans, but Pru didn't get to her feet immediately. Instead he felt her palms slide around behind his legs as if she would hold him still. When he felt the light, excitingly damp touch of her mouth pressed intimately against him, McCord knew for certain he was going to shatter. His hands tightened fiercely in her hair, and he groaned beneath the sweet, worshipful caress.

"My turn," he whispered in a thick voice as he tugged her to her feet and led her over to the bed.

"McCord?"

"Hush. One good turn deserves another." He pushed her gently onto her back and knelt between her legs.

She cried out softly as he brushed the first kiss against the silk of her inner thigh. McCord was aware of a deep rush of pleasure as he heard and felt her uninhibited reaction. Then he moved closer to the heart of her passion, and very soon Pru was breathless and writhing beneath him.

When he finally moved up along the length of her to claim her body with his own, she reached for him with so much feminine urgency and need that McCord almost laughed aloud.

But the sound was trapped in his throat because his body was too taut with passion to allow the joyous, triumphant laugh to emerge. He held Pru instead, burying himself within her. She gasped and dug her nails into his back.

McCord waited for a moment, luxuriating in the warm, velvet dampness that gripped him so sweetly. When he could stand it no longer, he began to move, slowly easing himself almost completely out of her body.

Pru gave a tiny whimper of protest and lifted her hips to tempt him back into the depths.

"I'm not going anywhere, honey," McCord promised. He

gently caught a nipple between his teeth and tugged. Then he drove slowly back into her, filling her thoroughly.

"McCord, you know how to drive me crazy."

"You're beautiful when you're crazy. I like making you go crazy. I like it very, very much."

He repeated the long, slow thrusts until he felt Pru tightening beneath him. The feminine strength in her at times like this always astonished and excited him. She clung to him as though she would never let go.

"Now, McCord. *Now.*"

He whispered something dark and hungry, and surged into her one last time, feeling the tiny, shimmering waves of release grasp him and hold him. His own deep convulsion poured through him and into her. Together they rode the storm-tossed waves into the quiet pools that waited on the other side.

When it was all over, McCord rolled onto his back and wrapped an arm around Pru, cuddling her comfortably against his damp body. With his free hand he gently eased a heavy, twisting, tangle of hair out of her eyes.

"Sleepy?" he asked.

"Umm." Her eyes were closed.

He touched one rosy nipple. "Are your breasts going to start getting bigger?"

"I don't know. I'm a little vague on some of this yet. I've only had one visit with the clinic doctor, and I spent most of my time trying to absorb the shock of learning I was pregnant. There are a lot of questions I haven't asked." She yawned hugely.

"I'll go with you on the next visit," McCord decided. "We'll ask the questions together. I'm new at this, too."

"So I gathered." There was a smile in her voice.

"Pru?"

"Yes, McCord?"

"Was it a rough shock? Learning you were pregnant, I mean?"

"Let's just say I felt very disoriented," she said dryly.

"You should have told me at once."

Pru said nothing for a moment. "Good night, McCord."

"You're still feeling a little disoriented, aren't you?" For the life of him, he couldn't quite bring himself to let her drift off to sleep. "That's why you don't want to announce the pregnancy yet."

"I guess so."

"Or maybe it's because you're still in shock," he went on meditatively.

"Maybe." She didn't sound very interested. In fact, she sounded almost asleep.

McCord looked down at her. Pru's eyes were still closed, and her breathing was taking on the gentle pattern of sleep. He should let her get plenty of rest, he told himself. She was going to need strength during the next few months. He'd see to it that she took it easy and obeyed the doctor's orders. And he'd take the prenatal classes with her, too.

This was his wife and his baby. They were both an integral part of his life, and he wanted to make certain he was an integral part of theirs.

As he slipped into sleep, he could feel the satisfaction and possessiveness that flowed through him. It seemed to McCord that a lot of the tension that had been seeping out of the walls of the house and into the atmosphere had been dissipated by the act of making love to Pru.

MCCORD AND PRU WERE READY to leave right after breakfast the next morning. Pru was somewhat embarrassed by her husband's blatant desire to be gone from the home of his parents, but she knew she'd pressed her luck far enough. She didn't dare insist they stay any longer.

They did stay for breakfast, however. The entire family and Devin Blanchard sat around a broad glass table in the all-glass dining room and ate fresh strawberries and cheese omelets and coffee prepared by Sandra. Pru, who had suffered another irritating bout of morning sickness, didn't recover her appetite as quickly as she had the previous day.

Everyone except Carrie seemed willing to try to find innocuous topics of conversation. Carrie simply didn't say a word. Evelyn kept sneaking covert glances at her son until Pru wanted to reach out and assure her it wouldn't be another three years until she saw him.

Devin Blanchard was the most at ease in the group, and Pru found herself talking freely with him as the others strained for neutral, polite ground.

He took her aside shortly before she and McCord were due to leave. It was the first time Pru had been alone with Blanchard, and when she looked at him she thought she saw sympathy and understanding in his eyes.

"It looks like you may be able to do something for this family they haven't been able to do for themselves, in spite of all their money and clout," he said quietly.

"I don't know," she answered wistfully. "They're a very stubborn lot."

"Not surprising when you realize just how bad things were three years ago. You've heard about Laura Reynolds?"

"Yes."

"She was like a daughter to Hale and Evelyn. The daughter they never had. They loved her."

"I see."

"She was very beautiful, very loving."

"From the sound of things she must have been somewhat headstrong and perhaps unstable."

Devin frowned. "You're referring to the fact that she killed herself in that crash?"

"Anyone who does a hundred miles an hour on an L.A. freeway must know the risks she's taking."

"She was distraught that night."

"So I hear. A broken engagement isn't a good enough excuse for that kind of idiocy," Pru said hardily.

"Is that what McCord told you? That she was upset because he broke off the engagement?" Devin shook his head sadly. "I'm afraid there was a lot more to it than that. Maybe you should know the whole truth before you make any judgments, Pru."

Pru lifted her chin and said proudly, "If there's any more I need to know, McCord will tell me in his own good time."

Devin's mouth kicked upward in reluctant admiration. "I can see why he thinks he's found a treasure in you. Not many women would trust him so completely. Not after what happened between him and Laura Reynolds."

At that moment Pru spotted Evelyn in the hall and seized on the opportunity of getting away from Devin Blanchard. She didn't want to hear any family secrets from him, she decided.

"There you are, Evelyn," Pru called cheerfully, just as McCord passed his mother in the hall with the luggage. "I almost forgot. I wanted to be sure you and Hale and Kyle and Carrie and Devin had an invitation to J.P.'s first annual ball."

Evelyn's expression was one of astonishment. McCord, over-hearing the comment, slammed a short, narrowed look at Pru.

Pru didn't wait for either of them to say anything. Blithely she explained. "J.P. calls it a shindig, not a ball, naturally. He can't see himself throwing anything as fancy as a gala charity dance. At any rate, I'm stuck with having to organize the whole thing, and McCord and I will be forced to attend. It should be interesting, if nothing else. Why don't you think about coming down to La Jolla for it? We've got extra bedrooms, two of them, so there's plenty of room to stay with us."

"When is it?" Evelyn asked, casting an anxious look at Hale who was staring stonily at his new daughter-in-law.

"Saturday after next." She gave Evelyn the date. "You'll get a kick out of J.P. He's quite a character."

"Pru, it's getting late," McCord said from the doorway.

"I'm coming." She impulsively kissed Evelyn on the cheek, waved to Hale and smiled at Kyle and Carrie. "See you soon," she promised them all. As she turned to follow McCord out the door, her gaze collided with that of Devin Blanchard. "Do try to come, Devin," she said as warmly as possible. "I can get all the tickets I want. After all, I'm the coordinator for the thing. I'm not sure there's room at the house, but—"

"That's all right," he said quietly. "If I can make it down to La Jolla, I'll stay in a hotel."

"Well," Pru said brightly, "that takes care of everything, doesn't it? I'd better get into the car before McCord leaves without me."

She hurried down the steps, slipped into the Ferrari and turned to wave at the cluster of people in the doorway. "I think your mother's crying," she said to McCord as he put the car in gear.

"Does that surprise you?"

"No, I guess not." The beautiful home receded into the distance, and Pru sat back in her seat.

"Don't get your hopes up, Pru," McCord remarked. "I doubt if they'll show up."

"Want to bet?" Pru smiled to herself, feeling smugly hopeful.

FOUR DAYS LATER Pru looked up from her desk in the tiny editorial office of the Arlington Foundation headquarters and decided there was one overriding reason why she shouldn't have run away from Case McCord.

She was swamped with work trying to catch up. Nobody had bothered to take care of her job in her absence. Apparently everyone had been under the impression she was only temporarily gone.

"I told everyone you'd be back right quick," J.P. had explained cheerfully when she'd walked into the office the day after returning to La Jolla. "That McCord may be bullheaded at times, but he ain't completely stupid." Sitting behind his inlaid desk, which was decorated with silver fittings and a set of gilded bullhorns in front, J.P. had appeared quite satisfied with himself. He'd had his dark green lizard-skin boots propped on the desk, and his mint-green Stetson hung on one of the horns in front.

McCord, who was in the hallway behind Pru, overheard the

remark and came to stand in the doorway. "Thanks for your faith in my mental abilities, J.P. What the hell has everyone been up to while I've been gone? The report on the Maraku irrigation project still isn't out of typing, and Harve says you didn't call the meeting to discuss the soil conservation program."

"Well, son, to tell you the truth, we all just sort of sat around and played with our toes while worrying ourselves sick wondering how long it would take you to grovel your way back into Miss Pru's affections. But I guess we can all relax now that you've put a ring on her finger, huh? 'Bout time."

Pru stepped between the two men before McCord could make his retort. "How are the plans for the ball going? Did Mary Ann talk to the caterers?"

"Yeah, but I think there was some problem about the menu. Seems like the caterer didn't want to use my recipe for chili, and he became downright belligerent when she told him I wanted jalapeño-flavored corn bread."

"No kidding? Perhaps that's because your chili recipe is hot enough to set fire to any drapery and furnishings that happen to be nearby. And whoever heard of jalapeño-flavored corn bread?"

"I'll bet you've heard of it," J.P. said slyly.

"Only because I had the poor taste to be born in Spot, Texas." Pru stifled a groan. "I guess I'd better talk to Mary Ann first thing."

After that, she'd been immersed in work. But it was good to be back, she decided as she got her head above the stack of papers on her desk four days later. Her welcome from Martha and Steve had certainly been genuine and heartfelt. She'd had to hide a smile while she'd listened to Martha's complaints about McCord's foul temper during the week he'd spent trying to track her down. Steve's relief upon Pru's arrival was so visible she could only assume his life had been fairly miserable after the big departure scene, too.

There had been no word yet from Evelyn or any of the other McCords, so Pru was still keeping her fingers crossed that they would show up for the ball a week from Saturday. Every little step toward one another would help, she assured herself as she finished editing an article on insect problems in a tiny South American country. The man who had done the initial research was brilliant when it came to insects. Unfortunately he had never learned to spell.

The knock on her office door brought Pru's head up in frowning surprise. When she had her door closed, it was understood she was in the midst of editing and didn't want to be disturbed. Even J.P. respected the closed door.

"Come in," she said formally.

She was startled to see Carrie McCord walk into the small office. Her sister-in-law moved more awkwardly than ever beneath the weight of her advanced pregnancy, and there was no warmth in her eyes as she came to stand in front of Pru's desk.

"Hello," Carrie said evenly. "I've come to talk business with you, Mrs. Prudence McCord." The sarcasm on the Mrs. made Pru wince.

"What kind of business?" Pru asked warily. Her sister-in-law put a hand behind her back to rub her spine. It was obvious she was physically uncomfortable today. "Why don't you sit down?"

"I think," Carrie said deliberately, "that we should go someplace private."

"Why, Carrie?"

"Because I want to find out how much this is going to cost us, and I hate to discuss money in public, don't you?"

Pru held her breath. "How much what is going to cost you?"

"Buying you off, naturally. What did you think I meant? Kyle and I are prepared to make it worth your while to file for divorce immediately."

CHAPTER EIGHT

"WHERE ARE WE GOING?" Carrie demanded as Pru bustled her out to the foundation parking lot and into her small compact. "I want to talk to you alone."

"Don't worry, we'll be alone at the house at this time of day. The housekeeper will have left for the day by now, and the gardener has probably gone surfing," Pru said grimly. She climbed into the driver's seat and turned the key in the ignition.

"What about Case?"

"What about him? Don't you want him to hear this fabulous offer you're going to make to me?" Pru swung the little car out onto the palm-lined street. She was aware of her sister-in-law twisting uncomfortably in the seat beside her. In spite of the anger pulsing through her, Pru felt obliged to ask, "Are you all right, Carrie?"

"I'm fine," Carrie muttered. She stopped massaging her lower back and reclined wearily. "I didn't come here to see Case. I came to see you."

Pru sighed. "Don't worry. We're not likely to run into him at the house. He's got a series of research staff meetings today that will probably last until five or six o'clock."

There was silence in the small car until Pru pulled into the McCord drive. In spite of her tense, bitter mood, Carrie couldn't quite hide her surprise when she saw the lovely home.

"I didn't realize Case had done this well for himself," Carrie said hesitantly as she got out of the car and followed Pru into the house. "He left just about everything behind when he and his father quarreled. And I know Hale has never given him a dime."

"What did you think McCord had been doing for the past three years? Working in a fast-food restaurant to make ends meet? He's a very intelligent man, and what's more, he's a survivor. He's the kind who always lands on his feet. As my Aunt Wilhelmina would probably say, 'put him down in the middle of a cow pasture and he'd make a fortune selling manure.' Come on, Carrie, we'll go out into the garden. It's cool out there. I'd offer you some lemonade, but under the circumstances I'm not feeling terribly sociable.''

Carrie followed Pru through the wide, airy hall and out into the lush gardens at the back of the house. Pru noted that her sister-in-law was still having trouble assimilating the fact that McCord hadn't exactly been living in poverty since he'd been estranged from his family. She also noticed, in spite of herself, that Carrie still seemed to be in some physical discomfort.

Pru thought about her own pregnancy. She wanted to ask Carrie what it really felt like to be almost nine months along, but she didn't bother. They were hardly sisters.

''I think I should warn you,'' Pru said almost gently as she and Carrie sat down in white wicker chairs, ''that if you make me an offer, you'll only make a fool of yourself. It would be better for future family relations if you just decided to turn this little session into an impromptu visit.''

Carrie's chin came up aggressively. ''You think you've done very well for yourself, don't you? You've come a long way from that dull little town in Texas, haven't you? You've even lost your accent. Good manners and enough money for good clothes can really camouflage a lot, can't they?''

Pru was jolted by the unexpected nature of the attack. ''What did you do, Carrie? Hire a private detective to check out my background?''

Carrie tried to look casual about the matter, but there was a dark red flush on her cheeks. ''It didn't take him long. Just a couple of days to verify that you were born to some cheap little truck-stop waitress who slept with just about every trucker who came along. None of them stayed around long enough to marry her, though, did they? You don't even know who your father was.''

Pru came out of the chair, shaking with a rage that was unlike anything she had ever known before. ''Shut up, Carrie! Do you hear me? Just shut up before I lose what's left of my temper. *And leave my mother out of this.* You can insult me all you like, but if you open your mouth about her one more time, I won't be responsible for my actions. The only reason I'm keeping my hands off you right now is because you're nine months' pregnant.''

Carrie flinched, but she didn't back away from the firefight that had erupted. ''You must have thought you'd landed on easy street when you became Case McCord's mistress. He must have looked pretty good to you after what you'd seen in Spot, Texas. You should have been content with that. How did you ever talk him into marriage? After all, you lived openly as his mistress for three months, I'm told. If he was getting what he wanted from you, why should he bother with marriage? Case isn't the noble type, believe me. Laura Reynolds found that out the hard way. You must be something else in bed. But once you realized just how big the prize really was, I'll bet you didn't rest until you'd somehow talked Case into putting a ring on your finger. What did you do? Get him drunk one night and drag him over the border into Mexico for a quickie wedding?''

''Carrie, I'm warning you, don't say anything more. You don't know what you're doing.''

''Oh, yes, I do. You'd better remember that it's almost as easy to get a divorce these days as it is to get married in the first place. When McCord gets tired of playing house with you, you'll find yourself out on the street.''

''That's my problem.'' Pru was trembling with the force of her fury. ''If you're so sure that's what's going to happen, why are you here this afternoon?''

''Because I don't want to see Evelyn and Hale dragged through an emotional wringer because of a mercenary little bitch who thinks she can make life even easier for herself by patching up things between Case and his family.''

"I don't think you give a damn about Evelyn and Hale," Pru said bluntly. "The only thing you care about is protecting your husband's position in McCord Enterprises."

"Kyle's worked long and hard at building the corporation into something more than even Hale imagined it could be," Carrie snapped. "I won't stand aside and see everything my husband's done go down the drain. McCord Enterprises is my child's future. You're not going to steal it."

"I've told you and everyone else that McCord would never be happy running McCord Enterprises!"

"But will you be happy until he reclaims what he probably feels is his heritage? I doubt it. Anyone who's come as far as you have from Texas dirt isn't going to stop now. Not unless she gets a better offer."

"Which you're prepared to make, I suppose?" Pru demanded sarcastically.

"Yes." Carrie challenged her with painfully bright eyes.

"How can you possibly offer me enough to make me walk away from all the McCord family money?" Pru taunted furiously.

Carrie drew herself up stiffly and then winced. Her hand went to her stomach. She caught her breath and continued. "I'm prepared to offer you a large lump sum to leave Case McCord. It won't be anything close to what you think you might be able to drain out of the McCords over the next few years, but it is a great deal of money. And it's *guaranteed* money. You could easily wind up with nothing if you try to play games with the McCords."

"Why should I accept?"

"Because," Carrie said, putting down her ace with grim relish, "if you don't, I will see to it that Case and his parents all see the report I got back from the private investigator."

Pru closed her eyes briefly and shook her head in pity. She turned away and took a few steps toward the flower bed. When she opened her eyes, she was staring at the picture-perfect roses

Steve had been nursing under McCord's guidance all spring. "Oh, Carrie, you're way off base. You don't know what you're doing."

"Don't try to bluff me, Pru. You can't possibly want your husband to know about your past. And even if you thought he could accept it, do you think Hale and Evelyn will? How do you think they'll react to the news that their new daughter-in-law is the illegitimate daughter of a Texas truck-stop waitress?"

"McCord already knows all there is to know about me," Pru said simply. "And I really don't care if Hale and Evelyn find out. I'm sorry to pull the teeth out of your little blackmail scheme, but the truth is, you can't threaten me that way."

"I don't believe you!" Carrie put her hands on the arms of the chair and heaved herself out of it. She was almost shouting now.

"It's the truth." Pru turned back with a slight smile. "If you want to verify it, stay for dinner this evening and bring the subject up with McCord. I'd advise you to do it tactfully, however. My husband is very protective of me. He won't take kindly to any insults."

Carrie stared at her with widening eyes. "I can't believe he married you. I can't believe it. He turned his back on Laura who loved him so much. Laura, who came from a good family and who was so beautiful. She was like a daughter to Evelyn, and McCord knew it. Everyone loved her."

"Except McCord, apparently. Carrie, you can't force love. There must have been good reasons why McCord broke off the engagement. He probably knew he and Laura wouldn't be happy together and saw no reason to put them both through a farce of a marriage. He was not responsible for her wild behavior after that."

Carrie took a step forward and stumbled slightly. Her lovely face grew momentarily taut with pain. "You don't know, do you? You really don't know what happened three years ago."

Pru saw the way Carrie was clutching at her lower back. "Carrie? Are you all right?"

"I told you, I'm fine," Carrie snapped. Then she gave a soft, muffled cry and grabbed at the arm of the chair. "Oh, my God," she whispered.

Pru leaped for her, catching Carrie before she fell and easing her down into the chair. "It's the baby, isn't it?"

"It can't be. I'm not due for another couple of weeks." She gasped again, and a flash of anxiety went through her eyes as she looked helplessly up at Pru. All Carrie's anger and dislike vanished to be replaced by the unsettling fears of incipient motherhood. "They say the first one is always late. This can't be happening. Not here. Not now. What am I going to do?"

"As it happens," Pru announced with determined cheerfulness, "I've been reading some books on the subject lately. Luckily for you, I'm a fast reader. Can you make it to the car?"

"Yes, I think so. I've still got some time. At least, I think I do. Oh, Lord, I didn't know it would happen like this. I wanted Kyle with me. I don't want to be all alone."

"I'll call him as soon as we get you to the hospital." Pru was gently guiding Carrie out of the garden.

"It'll take him hours to get here, even if you locate him right away. I'm going to be all alone." There were tears in Carrie's eyes.

"No, you are not going to be all alone," Pru said stoutly as she eased Carrie into the back seat of the compact. "You've got me. Like it or not, we're sisters-in-law, remember? I'm family and I'm here. You won't be alone."

Whatever Carrie intended to say to that was lost beneath another wave of pain. By the time she recovered, Pru already had the car out of the drive.

Carrie's contractions were coming more frequently by the time Pru reached the hospital. The Emergency Room staff wasted no time. Pru stayed close to the bed as Carrie was whisked down the hall and into an elevator. When she offered her hand to Carrie, Pru was amazed by the desperate strength with which her sister-in-law grabbed it.

"Aren't we supposed to be counting or something?" Pru asked gently.

Carrie groaned. Her nails dug into Pru's palm. "I'm scared," she whispered.

A labor-room nurse leaned over Carrie to undress her. "No need to be scared. It's going to be mighty uncomfortable for a while and a whole lot of hard work, but there's nothing to be afraid of. You're going to be just fine." She flashed a quick glance at Pru. "You're a member of the family?"

"Yes," Pru said calmly.

Carrie opened her eyes for a moment and essayed a weak smile. "She's my sister-in-law."

"Good," said the nurse. "She can stay with you until your husband gets here."

Pru smiled down at Carrie. "If you'll let go of my hand for five minutes, I'll go call him."

Carrie winced and reluctantly released Pru's fingers. "I'm sorry," she said.

"No problem. I'll be right back."

Carrie's head moved in a restless negative motion on the pillow. "No, Pru. I meant I'm sorry about…about everything. I behaved like a fool. I want you to know that Kyle doesn't even know I'm here. This fiasco was all my idea."

"Forget it," Pru advised. She patted Carrie's hand reassuringly.

"Kyle won't be able to get here in time," Carrie fretted.

"I keep telling you, you won't be alone." Pru went to find a phone.

KYLE MCCORD ARRIVED shortly after his brand-new baby son. He found his wife asleep and his new sister-in-law sitting beside the bed, reading a magazine. When he came through the door, his gaze went first to the exhausted face of his wife and then to Pru, who smiled at all the anxious questions she saw in his eyes.

"Everything's fine, Kyle. Congratulations. You've got a beautiful baby son."

"Carrie's okay?"

"Just tired," Pru assured him, getting up out of the chair. "Here, why don't you sit down? I'm sure she'll be happy to see you when she wakes up."

"You're the one who took care of her? Got her to the hospital?" Kyle gave Pru a measuring glance that she decided must be a typical McCord family trait.

"I was the only one around at the time," Pru said dryly.

"You didn't have to stay with her."

"She's family," Pru murmured.

Kyle's gaze narrowed slightly and then he glanced again at his sleeping wife. "She must have come down here to see you."

"Yes."

"She was very upset about my brother's marriage." Kyle sounded as though he were feeling his way through a minefield.

"I know."

Kyle drew a breath and said bluntly, "I'm sorry if she said or did anything to insult you. She's been very emotional during these last few weeks."

"Perfectly understandable," Pru replied lightly. "Stop worrying about it, Kyle. Everything is just fine."

"Are you sure?"

"I'm sure."

He paused. "Does Case know?"

"I called him shortly after the baby arrived. He should be here soon."

Even as she spoke, the door opened to reveal McCord. "He's here now," he said softly. "Congratulations, brother, I understand you have a son."

Kyle nodded, the pride of fatherhood lighting his eyes. "That's what they tell me. I was supposed to be around for the big event, but Pru and Carrie had to handle everything all by themselves."

McCord grinned faintly. "Definitely women's work."

Kyle seemed surprised by his brother's easy smile. Slowly he responded, relaxing at last. "I agree. If you want to know the truth, I'm kind of glad I missed the delivery-room drama. You know how squeamish I am.''

"Both of you had better hush up,'' Pru advised in a low, scolding tone. "You'll wake Carrie.''

Carrie stirred beneath the sheet and sleepily opened her eyes. "I'm awake. Is that you, Kyle? It's about time you got here.''

Kyle went over to the bed and took his wife's hand. "If you'd been at home where you're supposed to be, I would have been around to do my part of this. Just think, I went to all those classes and read all those books for nothing. What the hell did you think you were doing driving down here all by yourself?''

"I thought I had another couple of weeks before I had to worry.'' Her eyes met Pru's. "I just wanted to talk to Pru.''

It was McCord who asked the next question. His voice was a little too quiet. "What did you want to talk to her about, Carrie?''

Carrie bit her lip. "Please,'' she whispered, "I'm very tired.''

"She certainly is,'' Pru announced. "Let's go get a cup of coffee, McCord. We can come back later.'' She took a firm hold on his wrist and led him from the room.

"All right, Pru,'' McCord said bluntly as they walked into the cafeteria. "Tell me what this was all about. Why was Carrie here today?''

Pru set her coffee cup on the tray beside his. "She came to see me.''

"What about?''

"Don't look so suspicious, McCord. She just wanted to get to know me better, that's all. A sisterly visit.''

"Sure. And if I buy that one, you've got a nice bridge you can sell me, right? Come off it, Pru. Tell me what happened.''

Pru sat down across from him and folded her arms on the table. She smiled enigmatically. "Carrie achieved her purpose, that's all.''

"In what way?''

"She got to know me a little better.''

McCord eyed her with a hooded gaze. He said nothing for a

moment while his agile brain turned over the various possibilities. "She tried to buy you off, didn't she?"

Pru blinked in astonishment at his accurate guess. Her reaction gave away the truth. "Now, McCord."

He slouched back in the booth, his mouth twisting wryly. "What a little idiot."

"Me or Carrie?"

"Carrie. She should have known it would be a wasted trip."

Pru was warmed by the implicit faith McCord was showing in her. "She didn't know me very well. She knows me better now."

"Told her to go to hell, huh?"

"I told her she'd made a mistake."

McCord grinned and reached for his coffee. "A big one. There are only a small number of reasons you'd walk out on a man, Pru. Money isn't one of them."

"You sound very sure of yourself."

"I am," he said simply. "Unlike my sister-in-law, I've had several months in which to get to know you."

WHEN PRU AND MCCORD walked back into Carrie's room sometime later, they found the new parents inspecting the son they had produced. The baby had been brought into the room to nurse and was now sleeping contentedly in Carrie's arms. Pru joined in the general admiration, privately wondering if her baby would have the same wisps of dark hair.

"He's beautiful," she murmured.

"Why do women always say that about babies?" McCord complained good-naturedly as he studied the tiny scrap of humanity.

"Because it's a fact," Pru declared staunchly. "Isn't that right, Carrie?"

Carrie glanced uneasily at McCord before nodding. "When you work this hard to create one, you're bound to think it's beautiful. It's only natural for women to be emotional about babies. Men don't always understand how a woman feels when she's pregnant."

There was an awkward silence in the room that Pru didn't understand. She saw the suddenly shuttered look in her husband's eyes and didn't understand it, either. Kyle rushed to cover the small pause. "We called Mom and Dad a few minutes ago. They're thrilled."

"They should be," McCord said calmly. "The dynasty is now assured."

Kyle looked at him. "What's that supposed to mean?"

McCord shrugged. "Isn't it obvious? Now there's someone in line to step into your shoes when you're ready to hand over the reins of McCord Enterprises."

Kyle wrapped one hand around the railing of his wife's bed. His expression was cool, but that didn't hide the intensity in his eyes. "Meaning you're really not interested in taking back your old job?"

"I wouldn't be interested in a million years, Kyle. Weren't you listening at all to what Pru said the other night? I'm a farmer at heart."

Carrie stiffened. The baby in her arms whimpered in his sleep, and his mother instantly relaxed her grasp on the infant. "But if things were patched up between you and Hale..."

McCord glanced at Pru, his eyes brilliant. "Even if my wife pulls off that trick, it wouldn't make any difference as far as my future is concerned. I've got everything I want."

"You're telling the truth," Carrie said in mingled surprise and relief. "Aren't you?"

Pru was shocked. "Of course he's telling the truth. McCord always does. He's much too stubborn and proud to lie. You should know that. Come on McCord, let's go home. I'm getting hungry, and Carrie would probably like some rest. We'll stop back to visit tomorrow." She took McCord's hand and started to lead him from the room. At the doorway she had a last-minute thought. "You'll stay with us tonight, won't you, Kyle?"

"To tell you the truth, I hadn't given much thought to where I'm staying. Are you sure you have room?"

Carrie laughed softly. "Don't worry about it, Kyle. I saw your brother's home earlier today. There's plenty of room. Believe me, they're not living in some run-down little studio apartment. I think you're in for a surprise."

Kyle raised his eyebrows. "I doubt it. You forget I've known Case since I was born. My brother would survive very nicely in whatever situation he found himself."

Carrie smiled across the room at Pru. "That's funny," she said. "Pru said very much the same thing, although she phrased it a little less elegantly. Something about being able to drop Case into a cow pasture and watch him make a fortune selling manure."

"Is that right?" McCord gave Pru a shrewd smile. His eyes were gleaming. "I'm not sure where Pru gets all this boundless faith in me."

"Never mind," Pru said, vaguely flustered. "It's time to go." She urged him through the door, aware that Kyle was smiling behind her.

"A fortune in manure?" McCord repeated with grave interest as he walked down the hospital corridor beside his wife.

"It's an old Aunt Wilhelmina saying."

"Ah. Have you ever noticed how your Aunt Wilhelmina's sayings bear a striking similarity to some of J.P.'s?"

"It's crossed my mind from time to time," Pru admitted.

"Someday," McCord said thoughtfully, "we'll have to introduce them to each other."

Pru grinned. "That's a thought."

KYLE SHOWED UP on his brother's doorstep around eight-thirty that evening. He looked weary but happy.

"Mom and Dad are sure going to get a kick out of the kid," he told McCord and Pru as they sat talking in the living room. "They've been wanting a grandchild ever since you and Laura—" Kyle broke off abruptly, turning red in the face. "Sorry," he muttered. "That was stupid of me."

"I won't argue with that." McCord got to his feet and reached for the brandy bottle. "Here, have another drop of the good stuff. You've had a big day."

Kyle massaged his temples, leaning back in his chair. "That's for sure. I nearly went out of my mind when Pru phoned to tell me Carrie had gone into labor and that she was down here instead of at home. You want to watch out for pregnant ladies, Case. They do crazy things."

"I'll keep it in mind," McCord said neutrally.

Kyle looked at Pru. "I think the folks are going to come down here for that Arlington Foundation ball you mentioned."

"Really?" Pru was pleased.

"Mom's been working on Dad steadily since you left. Don't be surprised if they show up."

"We'll be ready."

"I guess Carrie and I will have to give it a miss now. Looks like we'll be learning how to baby-sit. Sorry. We would have liked to have come."

"Next year," Pru said reassuringly.

Kyle looked at his brother. "I get the feeling your new wife is going to single-handedly change a lot of things in the McCord family, big brother."

"If anyone can do it, she can," McCord replied easily.

Pru stirred on the couch. "I can't believe a bunch of intelligent people have acted this dumb this long. As my Aunt Wilhelmina would say, 'Stupidity is its own reward.'"

Kyle slanted her an odd look. "Your aunt may have had a valid point. In any event, I appreciate what you did for Carrie today, Pru. I can guess what she was doing down here in La Jolla. The very fact that she'd take off like that without letting me know where she was going is all the evidence I need."

"It doesn't matter anymore, Kyle," Pru said gently. When McCord sat back down beside her, she slipped her fingers through his. He gripped them tightly. "She was upset. I understood."

Kyle nodded. "Thanks. You're a very generous woman." He got to his feet and stretched. "Would you two mind if I hit the sack? I know it was Carrie who did all the work today, but I seem to be exhausted.''

"Good night, Kyle.'' McCord nodded at his brother.

Kyle nodded once in return and left the room.

Pru turned to McCord, her eyes gleaming. "I told you they'd show up at J.P.'s ball.''

"My parents?'' McCord smiled. "So you did.'' He ruffled her hair with an affectionate gesture. "You're quite proud of yourself, aren't you?''

"I think it's downright silly for this family to have been at war for nearly three years for no real reason.''

"My family is convinced it has a reason, Pru,'' McCord warned softly.

"Well, they don't. One of these days they'll admit it.''

McCord sighed and poured himself another shot of brandy. "What did Carrie use to blackmail you with this afternoon?''

Pru cleared her throat, not deceived by the seeming casualness of the question. "McCord, it's over. I'd rather not talk about it. Carrie was upset and scared. She said some wild things that she now regrets. Let's let it drop.''

"We will as soon as I know what lever she was using.''

"McCord, there's no need to go into detail.''

"That bad?'' He cocked one brow in polite inquiry.

"Don't be an idiot,'' Pru snapped, incensed. "She just threatened to tell you and your parents about my past. She'd found out about Spot, Texas, and my mother and about my lack of a father and about how far I've come from Texas. Poor Carrie had some silly notion it would matter to you. I told you she wasn't thinking clearly.'' Then Pru groaned. "Now see what you've done? I wasn't going to tell you. How do you do it so easily, McCord?''

He grinned. "It's not me, it's you. You're lousy at keeping secrets. The only one you've ever managed to keep for any length of time was the one about being pregnant. Even there you got tripped up by outside forces.''

"The letter from the clinic?" Pru shook her head. "It's strange to think my whole life was changed because of that bill."

"It didn't change your whole life. It just speeded things up a bit," McCord said. His eyes were suddenly very intent.

"What do you mean?"

"I would have come after you even if I'd never seen that bill, Pru."

She looked away from his glittering gaze. Her fingers twisted in her lap. "You would have?"

"Yes."

She smiled tremulously as she remembered what she had said earlier to Carrie. Case McCord was too proud and too stubborn to bother with lies. "I'm glad."

"Don't kid yourself," McCord growled as he pulled her into his arms. "I didn't have a choice. I wanted you back, Pru."

"I wanted you, too, McCord." She lifted her face for his kiss.

It wasn't until much later that night when Pru lay sleeping beside him that McCord realized she still hadn't admitted she loved him.

Her quiet stubbornness on the subject was beginning to bother him.

CHAPTER NINE

"YOU'RE IN LOVE with my son, aren't you?" Hale McCord asked without any warning as Pru paused midway through the vegetable garden to show off the peas.

Pru was so astonished by the unexpectedly personal question that she almost stumbled over a row of carrots. Then she wondered why she was hesitating to admit the truth aloud. Everyone seemed to know, including her husband. "Yes," she said calmly, as if it were the most natural thing in the world. "I am. Do you want to give me a hand with the carrots and the peas, Hale? Martha sent me out for spinach, but I think it's a little early for it yet."

"I haven't picked fresh vegetables in a while, but I haven't quite forgotten how." Hale smiled and leaned over to pull carrots from the ground with an easy, practiced movement.

Evelyn and Hale McCord had arrived an hour ago. Pru had been delighted to see them. They had been accompanied by Devin Blanchard, who was staying at a nearby hotel. Blanchard had politely declined the offer of a bedroom.

On the surface, McCord had been indulgent about the event, as if it really didn't matter to him one way or another what his parents did, but Pru was certain she'd seen initial surprise and then wary acceptance of the situation in his shuttered gaze.

Evelyn had clearly been slightly taken aback and then delighted by the obvious evidence of the level of success her son had reached in three short years. Hale had appeared curiously satisfied. He had said nothing about the fine home and the superb view, however, apparently content to let his wife exclaim over it.

When Evelyn had declared her intention to take a nap in order to get some rest before facing the big evening ahead, Pru had invited Hale out into the garden. McCord had disappeared into his study. Pru had been explaining the challenge of organic gardening to Hale when her father-in-law had interrupted to ask his blunt question.

There was silence for a moment after the interchange between Pru and Hale. They picked carrots and peas quietly together until Hale spoke again.

"Case seems to have done all right for himself."

Pru smiled slightly. "He's your son. Did you seriously imagine he hadn't been doing all right?"

"No. I hadn't lost complete track of him. I knew he was doing a fair amount of traveling and that he seemed to be establishing himself without any help from me or McCord Enterprises." Hale looked down at the small bundle of golden carrots he was holding. "But I certainly had no idea of just how high he'd climbed in the Arlington Foundation organization."

"J.P. depends on him. McCord plays a key role at the foundation."

"And I get the feeling you play a key role in Case's life." Hale gave her a shrewd glance. "After what he went through three years ago with his family, my son undoubtedly values unquestioning loyalty from those who claim to love him."

Pru's chin came up proudly. "I'm not a blind fool about loyalty, Hale. If there was a reason to question my husband's actions, I'd confront him and demand explanations. But so far I've had absolutely no reason to question him. I trust him completely. I can't believe he was any less trustworthy three years ago."

Hale stripped pea pods from a vine. "Perhaps he was a different man three years ago. Perhaps he's changed."

"Everyone changes, but I don't believe he had a drastically different sense of honor three years ago. His private code of ethics is too thoroughly ingrained in him. He was thirty-three years old then. An adult male and fully responsible for his own actions. I'm certain that, whatever happened, he was functioning within his own personal code. If he were to confront today the same situation he confronted three years ago, I have a hunch he'd handle it in very much the same way. Be honest, Hale. I'll bet your son grew up early, didn't he? He hasn't been a child for a long, long time.''

"The thought doesn't appear to worry you. What would have happened if you had found yourself in the same position Laura Reynolds found herself in?''

Pru smiled. "I've always known where I stood with McCord. He's nothing if not honest. If Laura Reynolds was truly shocked by something McCord did or the way he acted three years ago, then frankly, she had only herself to blame. He wouldn't have pulled any rugs out from under her.''

Hale shook his head in wry admiration of her staunch defense. "My son is a very lucky man. I hope he knows it.''

Pru grinned. "Don't worry. I plan to remind him frequently.''

Hale laughed aloud at that, the robust sound carrying easily through the open windows of the study. McCord, who had been standing at the window watching his wife and his father, found himself smiling slightly in response. He wondered what the joke was. It had been a long time since he'd heard his father's laugh.

Trust Pru to find a way to uncover it.

McCord's gaze went hungrily over the figure of his wife. She was wearing jeans, but she had a slouchy cotton knit top over them. He knew it was because she had reached the point where it was getting uncomfortable to fasten the top button of the denims. Last night in bed he had told her he was beginning to discover a new, added hint of roundness in her soft frame. Pru had told him it was his imagination, but McCord knew better. The changes taking place in her were both sexy and fascinating. They brought out all his protective instincts.

He had made love to her slowly and deliberately, drawing out the process until she was shivering and clinging to him. He had held off the final culmination, waiting expectantly for the words of love he'd been anticipating since the day of the wedding. But Pru hadn't spoken them.

McCord couldn't understand why she didn't admit what he

could read so easily in her eyes. He knew she was in love with him. On the couple of occasions when he'd confronted her with the fact, she hadn't denied it. But although she was excitingly generous with her passion in bed, she had never yet whispered her love to him during their most intimate moments together.

McCord felt the instant changes that started taking place in his own body as thoughts of the previous night's lovemaking drifted through his head. With a small, muttered oath he turned away from the window. He had a long evening ahead of him before he could climb back into bed with Pru.

J. P. ARLINGTON had outdone himself for the occasion of the first annual foundation shindig. He was wearing white. White hat, white shirt, white tie, white western-style jacket, white flared trousers and white leather boots. The outfit was accented with judiciously applied rhinestones and silver. The glittery touches circled the crown of the hat, sprinkled across the yoked shoulders of the jacket and formed long strips down the outside seams of the trousers. There was an additional wedge of silver on the pointed toes of the boots.

All in all, Pru decided in amusement, J.P. was quite a sight. Fortunately the guests loved the outrageous look of their host as well as some of the outrageous Southwestern food that sat side by side with elegant pâtés and choice canapés on the buffet table. J.P. was moving through the well-dressed crowd with ease, enjoying himself enormously.

The hotel ballroom the foundation had rented for the evening was lavishly decorated for the event. The white-and-gilt walls and ceiling sparkled beneath the light of two magnificent chandeliers. The dance floor was filled with couples enjoying the music of the excellent band playing at the far end of the huge room. The opposite end of the room featured the large buffet where the chili and the jalapeño-flavored corn bread were moving quite well. When people commented on the unusual food choices, J.P. explained he liked to get back to his roots occasionally.

It was always interesting, Pru thought, how much easier it was to get large sums of money from people when they were surrounded by lavish hospitality. She had commented on that fact to McCord earlier in the evening when they had been dressing for the event.

"It seems wrong to have to put on such a lavish affair just to convince people to contribute to a foundation that's trying to do something about starvation," Pru had remarked.

"Honey, it's a cold, hard fact of life that it takes money to make money. Right or wrong, that's the way the world works," McCord had told her.

Pru had chosen a free-flowing yellow-and-green silk gown that fell lightly around her figure. She hadn't been able to get into the snug-fitting red gown she had originally planned to wear. While they were dressing, McCord had teased her gently about the small changes that were taking place in her figure, and she had made a face in the mirror.

To her surprise his expression had turned serious. He had come up behind her to help fasten a thin golden chain around her neck. "Are you going to hate being pregnant?" he'd asked.

"It's a little late to worry about that," she'd replied easily, reaching for her earrings.

He'd looked as though he'd wanted to say something else but hadn't been able to formulate the question. Instead he'd leaned down to kiss the nape of her neck, which had been left bare by her upswept hairstyle.

"You won't be alone when your time comes," he'd promised. "I swear I'll be there with you."

He'd been thinking about his sister-in-law's experience, Pru had realized. "Don't make any rash promises. J.P. is always sending you off to some exotic corner of the world. Heck, next week you get to go all the way to mysterious Nebraska to check out that corn experiment."

"What a thrill." He'd touched her cheek, meeting her eyes in the mirror. "I'm going to cut way back on the traveling, Pru.

There are others who can handle that end of things. I'd rather spend my time in the experimental fields and the classroom. And with you and the baby.''

"I'll hold you to that,'' Pru had said lightly.

Remembering the small scene in the bedroom, Pru took her eyes off J.P.'s vivid figure and scanned the room, looking for her husband. She finally spotted him introducing Devin Blanchard to an attractive young woman named Julia from the editorial staff. The social task over, McCord left Devin with his new acquaintance and moved off to join the group of men around J.P. Pru was thinking of how compelling her husband looked in his evening clothes when she heard her mother-in-law's voice at her elbow.

"This sort of thing is more work than fun for you and Case, isn't it?'' Evelyn McCord asked as she and Hale moved up to stand beside Pru.

Pru laughed. "I'm afraid so. J.P.'s fortune forms the financial basis of the foundation, but outside contributions are vitally important. You'd be surprised how much money J.P. will pull out of the woodwork tonight. He'll ply everyone with his jalapeño martinis, and the first thing you know, money will be flowing in right and left. I've seen him at work before.''

"What's Case's role in the money-raising efforts?'' Hale asked with interest.

"Once J.P. gets going, he's pretty good at social chitchat, but he relies on McCord to answer the technical questions a lot of potential contributors will ask.''

"Unfortunately the net result is to leave you to fend for yourself most of the evening,'' Evelyn murmured.

"Oh, I don't mind. This is business, and I've got plenty to do. I'm the one who has to make sure we don't run out of food and that no one gets embarrassingly drunk or left forlorn in a corner. You know, the odd jobs.''

Devin Blanchard's voice interrupted Pru before she could continue. He walked up to join the small group. "Does that mean you might be available to entertain one of your guests on the dance floor?''

Pru turned to smile at him. He had approached from the far side of the room. She wondered what had become of Julia. ''I think I can sneak in a quick dance.''

''Great.'' He nodded at Hale and Evelyn. ''If you'll excuse us?''

''Of course,'' Evelyn said. ''In fact, if I can talk Hale into it, we might join you on the floor. Haven't danced in ages, have we, Hale?''

''I doubt if I've improved since the last time,'' Hale warned good-naturedly.

The two couples slipped onto the crowded floor, and Pru soon lost track of her in-laws as Devin took her in his arms. She was surprised at the forcefulness of his hold. Automatically she tried to put a little distance between them.

''Sorry,'' Devin apologized at once. ''Didn't mean to crush you. I just didn't want you bumping into that couple behind you.'' He smiled engagingly.

''That's all right,'' Pru assured him. ''I'm so glad you could accompany Hale and Evelyn this evening.''

''I think they wanted a little moral support. After three years of estrangement, they don't quite know how to deal with Case. Originally Carrie and Kyle were going to come with them, but those plans fell apart when their son arrived a couple of weeks early.''

''I gather you're practically a member of the family in many ways.''

''Practically,'' Devin emphasized quietly. ''Not completely. There's a big difference, Pru, believe me.''

Pru wondered at the faint trace of bitterness in his voice. ''Does that bother you?''

He looked down into her questioning eyes. ''I accept it. I'm paid very well and I can hardly complain.''

"Then why does it bother you that you're not a McCord?" Pru asked before she could stop to think.

"Let's just say that not being a McCord puts some real limitations on an employee of McCord Enterprises."

"Such as?"

"It's basically a family business," Devin explained. "No matter how good I am or how much I'm trusted, I can only go so far in the organization. A McCord makes all the final decisions and the McCords split all the really big profits."

"Maybe that will change someday," Pru suggested.

"Not a chance. Not as long as there's a McCord male around."

Pru considered the situation. "If you feel that way about the matter, maybe you should go to work for another organization."

Devin favored her with a quick, rueful grin. "Are you kidding? Not many other corporations would match my present salary, and it would take years to work my way up to the kind of status I have now. The McCords listen to me and they trust me. It's the next best thing to actually being in charge. One of these days I may leave for greener pastures, but it would take a pretty good offer to lure me away."

He might resent the fact that he could never be president of the company, but he wasn't about to sacrifice his cushy position by going elsewhere, Pru realized. Devin Blanchard was an eminently practical man.

"It's obvious both Hale and Kyle value your abilities enormously," Pru said, striving for a diplomatic ending to the unexpected conversation.

Devin slanted her an amused glance. "Case valued them at one time, too. You'd never know it, but there was a time when Case and I were like brothers."

"Times change," Pru said cautiously.

"People change."

Pru remembered the conversation with her father-in-law in the garden. "Sometimes. I don't think McCord has changed all that much in the past three years, however. There's something very rock-solid about him. I'd be willing to bet he was always that way."

"You're really in love with him, aren't you?"

"It must be painfully obvious. You're the second person today to comment on it."

Devin looked down at her, concern in his eyes. "I recognize the signs because I saw them in Laura Reynolds."

"I'd rather not talk about her, Devin."

"Sure, I understand." He stopped dancing as the music came to a halt. He glanced over Pru's shoulder. "There go Hale and Evelyn out onto the terrace. Shall we join them? Your husband still seems to be occupied."

Pru glanced around. Everything appeared to be functioning smoothly. No one looked bored or uncomfortable, and the food supply was holding out well. There was no reason not to join the McCords on the terrace for a while. "Sounds good. It's hard to talk above the music, isn't it?"

"That's for sure." Devin led her through the open doors of the ballroom and out onto the lushly landscaped terrace.

"I don't see the McCords," Pru remarked.

"I thought I saw them come this way. Maybe they're over by the fountain." Devin started strolling casually toward the large stone fountain that dominated the hotel gardens. Pru fell into step beside him.

Back in the ballroom, McCord sensed a subtle change in the atmosphere. It was nothing he could name, but it was enough to make him turn his head and search for Pru. He caught sight of her just as Blanchard led her outside onto the terrace. McCord felt his gut tighten.

"Excuse me," he said to the middle-aged scientist with whom he had been discussing soil erosion, "I think I'd better check up on my wife."

The man nodded understandingly. "I'll catch you later. I want to hear about that trip you made to Africa. I've been very curious about what you actually saw."

"Later," McCord promised, and then he was striding through the crowded room.

He encountered his parents near a pair of open French doors. Hale and Evelyn were chatting with J.P. and apparently enjoying themselves.

"There you are, McCord," J.P. said loudly. "I was just explaining the secret of making a perfect jalapeño martini to your dad."

"Don't believe him," Hale said with a lazy grin. "J.P. was leaning on me pretty heavily for a contribution to the foundation. I recognize a pitch when I hear one."

J.P. chuckled, not bothering to deny it. "Your dad's tighter than bark on a tree."

"He just needs to be convinced," McCord said, looking at Hale. "My father likes hard evidence. He isn't easily swayed by sentiment."

Evelyn, at least, appeared to realize the underlying comment extended to more than just J.P.'s efforts to get a contribution from her husband. She stepped into the conversation before it could go any further in what she obviously had concluded was a dangerous direction. "Looking for Pru?"

McCord nodded abruptly. "I saw her go out onto the terrace."

"Hale and I could use some fresh air," Evelyn said quickly, "isn't that right, Hale? Why don't we go with Case?"

"I don't know about fresh air, but it might be a good idea to take a break from J.P. before he finds a way to part me from my money."

J.P. grinned broadly. "I'll be here when you get back."

McCord shrugged, not hesitating any longer. He didn't really care if his parents followed him. He just wanted to locate Pru and bring her back inside.

"This is certainly a lovely event," Evelyn remarked as she hurried to keep up with her son. "I must say the foundation does a first-class job when it comes to entertainment."

"It's a business expense. It'll pay for itself several times over in terms of contributions to the foundation.'' McCord quickened his pace when he realized he couldn't see Pru anywhere in the garden. There was a curious tension flowing in him now. He felt as if he were on the verge of combat. Telling himself that he was being ridiculous didn't do any good. Some primitive instinct had been aroused by the sight of Pru walking away with Devin Blanchard.

Then he heard her voice and started toward the fountain that was located on the other side of a tall hedge. Hale and Evelyn followed.

PRU CAME TO A FIRM HALT beside the fountain. "I don't see them, Devin. They must have gone in another direction. I'd better get back to the party before J.P. wonders what he's paying me for."

Devin shrugged. "I could have sworn I saw them come this way. Oh, well, no harm done. It feels good to get away from the crush for a while."

"If you'll excuse me," Pru began politely, only to stop when she felt Devin's hand clasp her wrist. She looked up at him with point-blank inquiry, and her voice hardened slightly. "What's the matter, Devin?"

"I brought you out here to talk to you, Pru."

"About what?"

"About your husband."

"I don't want to discuss him with you." She tried to pull her wrist free and was irritated when his hold tightened. "Please let me go."

"In a moment, I swear. Pru, this is for your own good."

"I doubt that."

"You have a right to know what really happened three years ago, and it's becoming damn obvious the McCords aren't going to tell you."

"You're wrong. My husband has already told me exactly what happened. I don't need to hear anyone else's version of the truth. Let me go, Devin. You're becoming annoying."

"Listen to me, Pru. I was there. I know the truth. And I know McCord hasn't told you what really went on. If he had, you wouldn't still be with him, believe me. You wouldn't trust him so completely."

She realized he was almost desperate to make his statement, and she wondered what drove him. "What makes you think my husband lied to me?" she demanded angrily. "McCord has never lied to me."

"I'm not saying he lied, only that he can't have told you the full truth. If he had, you wouldn't defend him so fiercely. In fact, if he'd told you what he did to Laura three years ago, you probably would never have married him!"

"That's the most asinine thing I've ever heard. One last time, Devin, let go of my wrist."

"Don't you understand?" Devin flared. "It wasn't just a broken engagement that tore Laura up so much that she killed herself on that freeway. There was a baby. Laura was two months' pregnant, and Case refused to marry her. Hale and Evelyn's first grandchild died along with the woman who was like a daughter to them. All because Case McCord wouldn't marry the woman he'd got pregnant. He told her to get rid of the baby if she wanted to continue the engagement. Laura nearly went crazy."

A woman's anguished gasp of dismay made Pru swing around in astonishment. She found herself confronted by McCord and his parents. Hale looked proud and grim. Evelyn was staring at Pru with such pain in her eyes that Pru almost cried, too.

Case McCord simply looked at his wife as if he were prepared for whatever verdict she chose to render. No one spoke.

Pru met her in-laws' unhappy expressions with a sense of utter amazement. "Is this the reason behind three years of stubbornness? You really believe McCord got Laura Reynolds pregnant and then threatened to break off the engagement if she didn't have an abortion?"

"Oh, Pru," Evelyn said miserably. "There was no need for you to know the whole truth. It's all in the past. I was so hoping it could stay there. It's caused so much pain and turmoil, and there's absolutely nothing anyone can do now to change it. We must all put it behind us and forget it. Three years is a long time. Everyone makes mistakes…'' She turned a pitying gaze on her son. ''But life goes on.''

''For heaven's sake,'' Pru exploded. ''I can't believe this.''

''You have to believe it, Pru,'' Devin said flatly. ''We do.''

''I can't imagine why,'' she retorted.

Hale took a step forward as if to put a consoling hand on her shoulder. But he stopped when she glared at him. ''I told you this afternoon that people change,'' he reminded her.

''And I told you that your son hasn't changed all that much in the past three years. He might be a little older and a little smarter in some ways, but fundamentally he's the same man as he was then. I don't believe he would have acted any differently three years ago than he would act today if he were faced with a similar set of circumstances. If he refused to marry Laura, there was a damn good reason.''

''He didn't want the baby,'' Evelyn whispered. ''He told Laura he didn't want the baby.''

''I suppose those were Laura's famous deathbed words?''

Hale and Evelyn looked at each other. ''Well, yes,'' Evelyn admitted.

''Where is it written,'' Pru muttered, ''that an angry woman is going to be inclined to tell the truth on her deathbed?''

''You don't understand, Pru. She *was* pregnant. The doctor confirmed it.'' Devin came up behind her and touched Pru's shoulder.

She stepped out from under his fingers. Her eyes swung to McCord, who was standing very still and utterly remote in the shadows. ''What is this, McCord? You couldn't be bothered to defend yourself from Laura's accusations?''

McCord shrugged. ''No one doubted Laura's side of things. She was an excellent actress. On her deathbed she gave a very heart-rending performance, believe me.''

Pru threw up her hands. ''I can't believe I'm hearing this nonsense. Three years? Three whole years this family has been at odds because of Laura Reynolds's accusations?''

"They weren't false accusations," Devin said through gritted teeth. "Laura was pregnant, and he refused to marry her. He threw her out of his life when she refused to get rid of the baby. Ask Case, if you don't believe me.''

"I don't have to ask him," Pru said, her voice tight with fury. "If Laura was pregnant and if McCord refused to fulfill his responsibilities, then there is only one explanation on God's green earth why he acted as he did.''

"Why?" Evelyn McCord's single query was almost hushed.

"Because the baby wasn't his and McCord knew it!"

There was absolute silence from the small circle around Pru as they stared at her and tried to absorb the impact of her words.

"Furthermore," Pru continued aggressively, "the one thing McCord won't allow himself to be is manipulated. Any woman who tried to trick him into believing he was the father of her child so that she could force him to marry her was asking for trouble and should have known it. What's the matter with you people?'' She turned on Hale and Evelyn. "McCord is your son. You should have known him better than anyone. You should have been able to figure out for yourselves that there had to be more than Laura's side to the story.''

"Is this what Case has told you?" Hale finally asked tightly. His intent gaze went to his son.

"No, he didn't tell me the baby wasn't his. We never discussed the matter. But there is no other explanation.''

"How do you know that?" Devin snapped.

Pru put her hands on her hips. "Because I am the world's leading authority on what Case McCord would do if he got a woman pregnant. Why on earth do you think he married me? We'd been living together openly for nearly three months. He'd made it very clear he had no interest in marriage. But when I accidentally got pregnant and ran off, he came after me and demanded I marry him. No ifs, ands or buts. No demands that I have an abortion.

No accusations of carelessness. When the chips were down, McCord insisted on fulfilling his responsibilities. He would have done the same three years ago—if the baby had been his. Laura obviously had a lover and, as my Aunt Wilhelmina would say, McCord clearly had no intention of picking up the tab for some other man's stud services.''

Pru didn't wait to see the reaction to her statement. She whirled on her high heels and stalked over to McCord. When she put a demanding hand on his arm and looked up at him, she found his eyes gleaming with dark fire.

''Take me back to the ballroom, McCord. You know it isn't safe to leave J.P. alone in a roomful of potential foundation contributors. He'll go crazy with the jalapeño martinis.''

McCord took her arm in a grip of warm steel. ''Right this way, honey.''

They left the others standing by the fountain and walked silently back toward the brightly lit ballroom.

CHAPTER TEN

McCORD HAD KNOWN the inquisition would come as soon as everyone walked into the house after the conclusion of J.P.'s fancy shindig. He had been expecting it ever since Pru had dropped her little bombshell. It was a rather touching tribute to her sweet streak of naiveté that Pru herself was startled by Hale McCord's demand for further explanations. There had been no opportunity earlier for his parents to corner McCord, probably because he hadn't felt like being cornered and had seen to it Hale and Evelyn were kept busy from the moment they reentered the ballroom. Devin Blanchard had disappeared. Apparently Pru had thought the matter settled.

McCord could have told her things weren't going to be that easy.

"I think," Hale said as he escorted his wife into the living room of his son's home, "that we deserve some further explanations."

McCord said nothing. Instead he headed for the brandy tray Martha had thoughtfully put out earlier. It was Pru who responded. She swung around to confront her in-laws.

"Further explanations about what?"

"You must realize what a shock this has been to us, dear," Evelyn said soothingly. "We had no idea about...about Laura having had a lover."

"Oh, that," Pru said, as if she really had put it all behind her. She frowned at McCord. "You did tell everyone at the time that the baby wasn't yours, didn't you, McCord?"

"I believe I did mention it." McCord poured his brandy, debated about pouring two more for his parents and finally decided it would be churlish not to offer them a drink. He tipped the bottle over two more glasses. "I also remember that no one was particularly interested in listening."

When he turned around to hand the brandy to his parents, he caught the full impact of their shocked gazes. Wordlessly they accepted the glasses. Hale downed half of his almost at once.

"Laura was dying," Evelyn whispered in a heartbroken voice. "She said she hadn't wanted to live after you rejected her and the baby."

"I know what she said." McCord went to stand near Pru, who was glowering at all of them. "I was at her bedside along with everyone else. There's nothing quite like the impact of a deathbed statement, is there?"

"We were all in shock," Evelyn said. Wearily she sat down, her eyes going to her husband's grim face. "She was so dear to us. We loved her like a daughter. And we were certain the two of you were in love."

"Laura was in love with the idea of marrying into the McCord clan," McCord stated flatly. "She was not in love with me."

"She probably needed a sense of security after her father died," Evelyn suggested. "She felt alone in the world. We were the only family she had."

"Umm." McCord made no further comment. It had, after all, happened three years ago. There was no point resurrecting more than necessary.

"But if she was so determined to marry you," Hale pointed out with unerring logic, "why would she have taken another lover?"

"She didn't take *another* lover," McCord said. "She took a lover. It wasn't me. It was never me."

Pru's head snapped up as she realized the significance of his words. "You never touched her?" she asked in amazement.

"No." He was aware of what she was thinking. She knew his sensual appetites. From the moment he'd met Pru, he'd wanted to take her to bed. He'd made no secret of it. It was probably hard for her to imagine him involved in a chaste, platonic engagement.

"She wouldn't let me put a hand on her, not even after we were engaged." McCord smiled wryly down at her. "I told you she was an excellent actress. She wanted all the McCords to believe she was the perfect, untouched angel who wouldn't think of soiling her wings by going to bed with a man without a ring on her finger."

Pru's cheeks turned a sudden, vivid pink, and her eyes slid away from his. McCord was instantly furious with himself as he realized she had misunderstood his meaning. The last thing he had wanted to imply was that he valued the kind of role Laura had played. He wanted to grab Pru and hold her until he'd explained he wanted nothing to do with a cold-hearted woman who used her body like a tool, withholding herself from a man until he had agreed to meet her terms.

But the damage was done, and McCord knew he couldn't correct it in front of his parents. He would only succeed in embarrassing Pru further.

"You never went to bed with Laura." Hale eyed his son speculatively. "And that's why you're so certain the baby wasn't yours. What happened the night she died, Case?"

McCord was irritated at the question. Right now he wanted to talk privately to Pru and instead he was having to rehash old history. With a muttered oath, he turned to face his parents.

"After a few months of playing the chaste ice maiden, Laura was suddenly very insistent on going to bed with me. Unfortunately for her, I had already decided I wanted out of the engagement. Her timing was bad, I'm afraid. When she failed in her seduction efforts, she panicked. She called me that night in tears and told me she had to see me. When I got to her apartment, she threw herself into my arms and told me she wanted to get married right away. The wedding date was still three months off, and I was naturally a little curious about the sudden rush. I was also a little suspicious. I had been for a while, if you want to know the truth. I told her I was seriously considering ending the engagement. That I wasn't sure we were right for each other and that I thought it would be best if we put everything on hold for a while.''

''That's when she told you she couldn't wait? That she was pregnant?'' Evelyn asked.

McCord nodded. ''She gave me an ultimatum. Told me that I had to agree to marry her as soon as possible or she would tell the whole family she was pregnant with my child.''

Out of the corner of his eyes, he saw Pru chewing on her lower lip. Now she knew where he got his dislike of ultimatums, McCord thought.

''You called her bluff?'' Hale asked sharply.

McCord sighed and drained the last of the brandy. ''I told her I had no intention of, uh, picking up the tab for someone else's stud services.''

Pru winced and looked down at her folded hands.

''We argued some more, and eventually I left. The next time I saw her was in the hospital.''

''Where she took what revenge she could get on her deathbed,'' Hale concluded. ''You stated once that the baby wasn't yours and we all jumped down your throat. You never said another word on the subject.''

There was silence in the room for a long moment. Then McCord spoke, feeling obliged to point out the obvious. ''Nothing's changed. The situation is exactly the same as it was three years ago. You've still got my word against Laura's deathbed declaration. Why the big scene tonight?''

Hale looked at Pru. ''Three years ago we saw you the way Laura wanted us to see you—a man with feet of clay. She was our dying daughter, and we were heartsick. But lately your wife has reminded us that we should know you well enough to realize you're not the kind of man who would shirk his responsibilities. We should have known that all along. Instead of seeing you through Laura's eyes, we're suddenly seeing you the way Pru does. The way we'd always seen you until that night three years ago.''

"I think," Evelyn said quietly, "that once the shock had worn off, we wanted to believe you, but by then so much damage had been done. Everyone was so proud and stubborn. Neither side would give an inch. I can't believe we let these three years go by without trying to repair the breach. It took Pru to bring us to our senses."

"You believe me now because Pru believes me?" McCord asked. His mouth twisted sardonically.

Evelyn's expression was thoughtful, her eyes warm as they rested on her new daughter-in-law. "Let's just say that Pru has restored our perspective on the situation. She's reminded us of the kind of man you are. Seeing you again through her eyes has cleared away the fog of doubt and pain that Laura created. Poor Laura. If only we had realized what a troubled young woman she was."

Pru spoke up for the first time in several minutes. "You can't help someone who doesn't want to be helped. Laura made her own decisions, and no one is to blame for what happened three years ago."

Evelyn smiled. "Did my son really marry you because you're pregnant?"

Pru wrinkled her nose. "I'm afraid so. He was very insistent on marriage once he found out he was going to be a father. I hope you don't mind the prospect of being a grandmother for a second time?"

"I am absolutely delighted by the idea." Evelyn's face was alight with pleasure. She came across the room and hugged Pru. "I can't tell you how happy I am tonight, my dear. Thank you for everything."

Hale looked at his son. "You're a lucky man, Case."

"I know," McCord said. He put his arm firmly around Pru's waist. "If you'll excuse us, we're going to bed. It's nearly two in the morning, and Pru needs her rest these days." He steered her toward the hall while everyone murmured good-night.

Pru walked beside him without saying a word. McCord could

feel the tension in her. It made him tense in reaction. When the door of the bedroom closed behind them, he turned her around to face him.

"I didn't want an untouchable angel who claimed she loved me and then had absolutely no problem resisting my lovemaking. I didn't want a woman who withheld herself from me as a means of manipulating me. I wanted a warm, generous, honest woman who, when she fell in love with me, couldn't resist me no matter how hard she tried. A woman who wanted me as much as I wanted her. A woman who believed in me completely. A woman I knew would always be loyal. A woman I could trust. I wanted you, Pru. Just the way you are."

"But you didn't want to have to marry me."

His hands tightened on her shoulders. "Sooner or later we would have been married, honey, believe me. It was inevitable. I've been getting too damn possessive where you're concerned. But when you gave me that ultimatum…"

"All you could think about was the last time a woman had given you an ultimatum," Pru concluded sadly. "I reminded you of Laura."

Irritated by her silly logic, McCord gave her a gentle shake. "No, you did not in any way remind me of Laura. But I'll admit I didn't like being threatened. I thought I could call your bluff and teach you a lesson in the process. I was certain you wouldn't have the nerve to actually leave me. But as my brother Kyle said, women sometimes do crazy things when they're pregnant."

"I suppose you and Kyle think you're authorities on the subject now?"

"We're fast learners." McCord pulled her close and kissed her firmly on the mouth. He could feel her standing stiff and tense in his hold. Deliberately he deepened the kiss, easing apart her lips until he could taste the warmth inside her mouth. When she whimpered softly and began to relax against him, he felt a surge of satisfaction and relief.

"How did you happen to find me with Devin at the fountain?"

she murmured against his lips as she slipped her arms around his neck.

"I saw you leave the room with him." McCord nibbled her ear. "I went after you to bring you back. My parents just came along for the walk. We found you at the fountain just as you launched into your magnificent defense of my conduct three years ago. How the hell did you know Laura had been sleeping with someone else?"

"It was the only logical explanation. If you'd thought the baby was yours, you'd have done your duty."

"Thanks. I think." He nuzzled the nape of her neck, inhaling the sweet warm scent of her skin. "You're still convinced that's the only reason I married you, aren't you? Out of a sense of duty."

"You weren't rushing to marry me before you found out about the baby," she pointed out tartly.

Her obstinateness on the subject was really beginning to annoy him. McCord slid his hands down her back, easing the zipper of her gown. "You know there's a hell of a lot more than obligation involved. You know how much I want you, how much I like having you in my arms. *And you also know how much you like being in my bed.* Admit it, honey."

She shuddered delicately as the gown pooled at her feet. McCord reached out and turned off the light. In the shadows he could see Pru's eyes glowing with the soft light of her love. She smiled tremulously.

"I like being in your bed," she responded with amused obedience. "But, then, you already knew that."

He unfastened her lacy little bra and let the wispy garment flutter to the floor. "I know it, but I like hearing it."

"You're a greedy man."

"Very." He touched her breasts, using his palms to tease her nipples until they blossomed, firm and erect and excitingly hard. McCord lowered his head to kiss the rosy crests. "I'll never be able to get enough of you. If you really believe I could have let you walk away for good, you're out of your mind. Either that or you still don't know the extent of your power over me."

She laced her fingers through his hair, sighing softly as he slid her panty hose down her legs. "Do I have power over you, McCord?"

"An infinite amount." He straightened and smiled down at her. "Come here and I'll show you."

Pru stepped closer, her fingers on the buttons of his shirt, her mouth curved with feminine invitation. "No," she said, "I'll show you."

He grinned in wicked delight and anticipation as she deliberately began to take the initiative. It was only lately that she had become sure enough of her sensuality to do so, and it was still an infrequent occurrence, but McCord took great pleasure in having the tables turned occasionally. He got a kick out of having Pru turn into a sexy, assertive little bundle of demanding femininity.

Her fingers trailed tantalizingly over his bare chest as she undressed him. He could feel the faint trembling in her, and the knowledge that she was as aroused as he was nearly caused him to take back the lead. But he held himself in check, forcing himself to enjoy the unique pleasures to be found in the present situation.

There was a faint metallic clink as the buckle of his belt was undone and then the even softer rasp of his zipper. Pru's hand glided across the opening of the trousers and encountered the evidence of his arousal.

"Ah, McCord," she said with satisfaction, "you are a noble beast."

"You mean I'm in an advanced state of rut."

"Men are so literal."

"That's because we aren't built to be subtle." He caught her fingers when she would have moved her hand. He pressed her palm against himself, glorying in the intimate touch.

"You're right," Pru agreed. "Nothing subtle about you at all, is there?"

"You, I suppose, are much more discreet?"

"Naturally."

He laughed softly and slipped his fingers through the nest of curling hair between her thighs. When he found the spicy dampness, he drew his thumb through it and then over the tiny feminine bud.

Pru moaned and clutched at him, pressing her face into his shoulder.

"Tell me again about female subtlety. You couldn't hide your reaction from me if you tried, could you, sweetheart?" He stroked her softly.

"Probably not," she admitted. "You seem to have the magic touch where I'm concerned."

"I'm glad."

She smiled and took hold of his wrist to lead him across the carpet to the bed. There she pulled back the covers, slid between the sheets and reached up for him.

McCord groaned, going into her arms with a surge of desire that nearly overwhelmed him. She wrapped herself around him, pulling him close, welcoming him until he thought he would explode.

"You're so hot and sweet and sexy," he muttered against her breast as he drove himself into her and felt her legs curl around his hips. "So perfect for me. And you're all mine. What did I ever do without you?"

The question went unanswered as passion claimed them both. The world narrowed its focus to include only the depths of the bed, and McCord lost himself in the woman he had married.

It wasn't until a long while later when they both lay spent and damp with only a sheet pulled over their bodies that Pru reopened the subject of Laura Reynolds.

"Why didn't you fight harder, McCord? Your parents said you made one statement to the effect that Laura had lied and that the baby wasn't yours. You must have known they were in shock. Why didn't you yell until someone listened? You usually don't have that much trouble getting your point across."

He knew what she meant. He could have made a bigger scene three years ago. He could have shouted the truth until someone finally paid attention. "Pru, you have to understand. Laura really was pregnant."

"So?" She propped herself up on her elbow and looked down at him. "We know that much."

He studied her intent frown. She looked cute when she glared at him, he decided. "I knew I wasn't the father."

Pru nodded impatiently. "So?" she prodded again.

"That left open the question of who was."

Pru's eyes widened as the implications set in. "Oh, Lord. Didn't Laura ever tell you who had got her pregnant?"

McCord hesitated and then shrugged. "In the heat of her anger that night, she did give me a name."

"Whose?"

"My brother's," McCord said.

Pru sucked in her breath. "Kyle? She told you she'd been sleeping with Kyle?"

McCord nodded. "I had no reason to doubt her. She and Kyle had always been close, and I knew that Kyle found her attractive. But it had always been understood that Laura would probably marry me. She had no real interest in Kyle, I guess, because she knew I was the one who would inherit the reins of McCord Enterprises. Shortly before Laura died, Kyle and Carrie had begun dating. I knew my brother had fallen head over heels in love and was planning to marry."

"So you made one token protest and then shut up, is that it? You didn't want to ruin your brother's relationship with Carrie."

"I figured it would all work out eventually when the shock of Laura's death was behind us."

"But things didn't work out. You and your father quarreled. You got disinherited. A bad case of McCord stubbornness set in on both sides, and voilà! Total disaster."

McCord looked up at her steadily. "If I hadn't got myself

kicked out of the bosom of the family, I would never have met you. I, for one, do not consider the whole mess a total disaster.''

"Oh.'' She blinked in surprise. Then she smiled. "Thank you, McCord.''

"You're welcome.'' He waited expectantly to hear her say she loved him and was curiously irked when she went on to another topic of conversation.

"Do you think Kyle was the father of Laura's baby? Somehow that doesn't quite fit. I like Kyle. I can't see him having kept quiet about it for three years while the whole family turned against you.''

"I don't know for certain who the father was,'' McCord said patiently. "Laura claimed it was Kyle, figuring I'd feel obliged to marry her to protect the family reputation. She also knew I would have done a hell of a lot for my brother.''

"She really went the whole nine yards when she tried to manipulate you that night, didn't she? No wonder you came down on me like a landslide the day I tried to give you my puny little ultimatum.''

"It wasn't exactly puny,'' McCord growled. "It was a major threat. I should have known that underneath that soft exterior, you've got nerves of steel.''

"I was raised in Texas,'' Pru explained proudly.

"Uh-huh. By an aunt who doesn't make any allowances for weakness, I gather.''

"Aunt Wilhelmina is a good person, but she does have a very forceful personality and an opinion on just about everything.''

"I'm lucky she approves of me. Think she still will after she finds out I got you pregnant before I married you?'' McCord grinned lazily, enjoying the flush on Pru's cheeks. In the shadows he couldn't quite see the fluctuating color, but with his fingertips he could definitely feel the warmth.

"Never mind my aunt,'' Pru said. "What about Kyle?''

"What about him?''

"Well, if we've decided he wasn't the father of Laura's baby, we've still got a problem."

McCord remembered the fury in Devin Blanchard's face as he'd tried to convince Pru that her husband had reneged on his responsibilities to Laura Reynolds. "No, we don't have a problem."

"But, McCord—"

"It all happened three years ago and the woman is dead, Pru. I agree with you. I don't think Kyle was the father. I said I had no reason to doubt Laura's statement that night, but that's not true. I should have doubted it on general principle. We'll probably never know who her lover was, and maybe it's for the best."

"I'm not so sure, McCord…"

He came up onto his elbow, pushing Pru back against the pillows. "I am sure," he said bluntly. "We're going to let the subject drop."

"Are we?" There was a hint of defiance in her voice.

McCord smiled faintly. "Yes," he repeated. "We are." He kissed her lips lingeringly, draining off some of her resentment. "Now go to sleep. You're a pregnant lady and you're supposed to take care of yourself."

"Hmm." A yawn spoiled the muted protest.

McCord lay back and gathered her against him. "There's just one more thing, Pru."

"What?" She was definitely sounding sleepy now.

"No more walks in the garden with Devin Blanchard. Not unless I'm along."

She stirred at his side, rubbing the sole of her foot down the inside of his leg. "Were you jealous?"

"Don't sound so pleased with yourself. Yes, I was jealous."

"Good." She was almost purring.

"Is that why you went out in the garden with him?" McCord asked curiously. "Because you wanted to make me jealous?"

Instantly she was contrite, just as he had known she would be. "No, of course not. We went looking for Hale and Evelyn. Devin thought he'd seen them wander out ahead of us. We decided we'd go out and chat with them while we all got some fresh air.''

"Stay away from him, Pru." McCord heard the steel in his own voice and wondered if Pru heard it, too.

She yawned again and snuggled closer. "You *are* jealous."

"I'm a cautious man."

"Hah."

He tightened his hold on her. "Stop trying to provoke me. Go to sleep."

"All right. McCord?"

"Hmm?"

"Three years ago you knew for certain there was no way Laura's baby was yours. Did you ever wonder about the baby I'm carrying?"

"Not for a split second." The words were blunt and immediate, leaving absolutely no room for doubt. "You and the baby both belong to me."

"Yes, I know, but did you ever wonder?" she persisted.

"You are in a provoking mood tonight, aren't you?" He smiled in the darkness, vaguely aware of the smug certainty he had always felt around Pru. "It would be impossible for you to ever be unfaithful to me, and we both know it. It's not in you."

"I told Annie I trusted you completely," Pru murmured. "I'm glad we both trust each other so much."

"We know each other well enough to be sure of each other, I guess," McCord said matter-of-factly. It was only after the words were out of his mouth that he realized the implications of his statement. He'd never in his life fully trusted a woman the way he trusted Pru.

She was asleep in his arms within a few minutes. McCord cradled her protectively while he gazed thoughtfully at the ceiling. He decided that when he got back from Nebraska he would have a long talk with Devin Blanchard.

That decision made, he gazed at the ceiling a while longer and wondered when his wife would voluntarily confess her love. She did love him, McCord assured himself. She hadn't married him just because of the baby.

He knew it and she knew it. All he had to do was figure out a way to get her to admit it. More and more these days he wanted to hear the words.

SUNDAY EVENING Pru had the house to herself by six o'clock. Hale and Evelyn had left for home, and McCord had reluctantly driven himself to the airport to leave for exotic Nebraska. The house, as usual, seemed quite empty without McCord in it. Pru spent the long summer evening in the garden. Then, mindful of her husband's injunction, she went to bed early.

The next day she went into the office and spent most of the time participating in the general mood of self-congratulation that permeated the atmosphere. J.P. was delighted with the success of the foundation's first big fund-raising event and couldn't stop talking about it.

"With the money that came rolling in Saturday night, we'll be able to add those second farm demonstration programs in a couple of those African countries," he informed everyone. "It will double our presence there. We'll reach twice as many people. Pru, I want you to know I had a phone call from your father-in-law this morning. I take back everything I said about him being tighter than the bark on a tree. He's writing out a real healthy check. Says anything his son is involved in is bound to be successful. Claims his boy always seems to land on his feet."

"I'm glad," Pru said, pleased by Hale's generosity. She knew the check represented much more than a charitable deduction for Hale McCord. It represented restored faith in his son.

"Couldn't have done it without you, Pru," J.P. said expansively. "You put the whole shootin' match together and made it work." Then he winked broadly. "By the way, McCord informed me he wants Bronson and Culpepper to start taking over more of the traveling."

"Really?"

"Yup. Says he's going to be a father and he wants to have plenty of time with his family." J.P. grinned. "I told him the news about being a father came kinda quick, seeing as how you two just got hitched a couple of weeks ago."

Pru coughed discreetly. "Yes, well, these things happen, J.P."

"Don't they just," he agreed blandly. "Good thing, too. Might have taken McCord a year or two to come around to the idea of marriage if he hadn't had a little pressure put on him. That man was happy as a pig in a mud waller in summer while he was living with you. Thought he had everything he needed, and I reckon he did. I knew it was going to take a jolt to make him wake up and do the right thing by you."

"It was a jolt, all right," Pru agreed dryly.

On the way home from work that afternoon, Pru decided to give in to the irresistible craving for pizza that had been consuming her for hours. She stopped by a take-out shop and ordered a pizza with everything to go. Then, with the aroma filling the car, she hurried home to gorge herself. This business of being pregnant could be fun once in a while. It had been years since she'd felt the urge to stuff herself with a pizza.

The thrill of illicit pizza faded rapidly when she spotted a strange car in the drive.

When she saw Devin Blanchard waiting on the front steps, Pru forgot about her dinner plans altogether. Vaguely she recalled McCord's soft warning the night of the ball. She had been almost asleep, but the steel in his words had made itself felt.

Stay away from Devin Blanchard.

CHAPTER ELEVEN

"I CAME TO APOLOGIZE." Devin Blanchard trotted down the steps to take the fragrant box of pizza from Pru's arms.

Pru was still struggling with the idea of having him show up so unexpectedly. His apology jolted her further. "For what?"

His handsome mouth twisted ruefully. "For interfering in the McCord family business the other night. I had no right to get involved as I'm sure some McCord will remind me when I show up at my office."

"You haven't been in to work since the ball?" Then she realized this was only Monday. Automatically Pru put her key into the front-door lock.

"I called my secretary this morning and told her I was taking the day off. I wanted to do some thinking. And I wanted to talk to you."

Pru glanced at him quickly as she stepped into the hall. Short of grabbing her pizza out of his hands and slamming the door in his face, she didn't see any civilized way of keeping him out of the house. "What did you want to talk to me about?"

"First, as I said, to apologize." The door closed behind him, and he was alone with her in the house. Blanchard smiled. "I'm usually a lot more discreet than I was the other night, believe me."

"I believe you."

"Where do you want this?" He indicated the pizza.

"In the kitchen." She turned and led the way down the hall.

"As I was saying, I'm usually very careful when it comes to McCord family business. My only excuse is that I felt sorry for you."

"*Sorry* for me?"

He shrugged as he set the pizza carton down onto the tiled counter. "You're one of those women who brings out a man's protective instincts, I guess." He paused. "Laura was like that."

"Thank you," Pru said tartly, "but I assure you I can take care of myself."

"That's what Laura thought, too."

"I'd rather not discuss her. Look, Devin, I think this has gone far enough. We really don't have much to say to each other. I accept your apology, but now I think you'd better leave."

He held up his hands as if to ward off her anger. "I'm sorry," he said again, shaking his head with a boyish smile. "I seem to keep putting my foot in my mouth. There was something else I wanted to tell you and then I'll leave."

"I don't want to hear it, Devin."

"This has got nothing to do with McCord family business, I swear. It's about something you said the other night at the ball."

"What was that?" she asked suspiciously. She didn't like being confined in the kitchen with him, she realized. Almost unconsciously she opened the back door and stepped out into the late afternoon warmth of the garden. Devin followed.

"You said that if I was unhappy working for the McCords, perhaps I should quit and start over somewhere else."

"I remember." She was a little more comfortable outside with him, Pru decided. Not quite so confined. But she still felt nervous. She began ambling along the vegetable plot. Devin fell into step beside her, his hands jammed into his pockets.

"At the time I told you I didn't want to walk away from such a sweet setup. I'm making good money, lots of perks and—"

"And you're near the seat of power," she finished for him. "You said you liked that."

"I thought it was the next best thing to being the man in charge."

"But not quite the same thing as being the man in charge."

"No," he agreed. "Not quite. I thought a lot about what you said after I got home yesterday, however. It made sense. I don't know why I hadn't figured it out for myself. I've decided you were right. I really shouldn't be working for a McCord. Any McCord. Especially not after what happened three years ago.''

"Why were you so upset about what happened three years ago, Devin?'' Pru asked quietly. "I mean, I know it was a terrible tragedy, but why did you take it so personally?''

He hesitated. "Probably because I admired Case so much. Maybe I'd put him on a pedestal. I couldn't believe he would treat Laura the way he did. She was such a beautiful, loving woman.''

"He didn't do anything to Laura,'' Pru snapped. "She had been cheating on him, and he didn't intend to be manipulated. When he told her that, she lost her temper and climbed into a car. What happened next was strictly her own fault.''

"Do you really believe that?'' He gave her a pitying look.

"Yes, I really believe it!''

"All right, all right. Calm down. It all happened a long time ago, and maybe it's time to put it behind us. In any event, I didn't come here to argue, I promise. I just wanted you to know that I think you were right. I shouldn't be working for McCord Enterprises. I'm going to hand in my notice tomorrow morning. I thought you'd like to know how much influence you've had on me. You seem to have had a lot of influence on the McCords, too. I never thought the family would ever accept Case back into the fold.''

Something clicked in Pru's mind. "You mean you hoped they never would accept him back,'' she said with quiet insight. "You wanted them to punish one another indefinitely, didn't you?''

The boyish expression vanished from Devin's eyes as if it had never existed. It was replaced by a vicious bitterness that made Pru gasp.

"They deserved to be punished,'' Devin snarled. "They were all responsible for what happened. There was no way to hurt the McCords financially, but I knew the family rift was eating all of them alive. That was some satisfaction.''

Pru drew a deep breath and came to a halt near a tree. Steve had left a rake propped against the trunk, she noticed. McCord would be irritated, as usual. She stood looking out toward the ocean, her fingers trembling slightly as she put together the rest of the facts. "It was your baby Laura was carrying, wasn't it, Devin?"

"Yes, it was mine," Blanchard bit out through clenched teeth. "Laura gave herself to me. *Me,* not Case McCord. She never allowed Case to touch her. She used to laugh about that, you know. We both did. McCord thought he was going to be marrying a picture-perfect angel. It gave me great pleasure to know that every time I took Laura to bed I was screwing Case McCord's fiancée."

"You used her. You didn't love her. For you, she was just a means of getting even with the McCords."

"Don't waste any of your sympathy on Laura. She knew exactly what she was doing. She got a kick out of sleeping with me behind her fiancé's back. It was a real thrill for her. Laura didn't like being bored, and waiting around to marry into the McCord clan had grown extremely boring for her. What's more, she was beginning to fear that she was going to be bored after she married, too. The McCords are wealthy and powerful, but they live a quiet life. They're not socialites or jet-setters. After all, they're only one generation away from picking beans, as Laura used to say. She decided to have a little fun on the side. If you want to know the truth, I think she fully intended to continue the affair with me after she got married."

"But she would never have married you, right? And that's what you really wanted. Because she was going to inherit a major portion of McCord Enterprises. Marrying Laura would have given you the position in McCord Enterprises you always wanted to have."

Devin's eyes hardened. The breeze off the sea ruffled his hair slightly as he stood staring down at Pru's profile. "Yes, I wanted to marry her. They accepted her as a daughter, and ultimately she stood to inherit her father's share of the company. If I was Laura's husband, I would have gained a sizable chunk of control in McCord Enterprises. But Laura wasn't interested. She didn't want half the pie when by marrying a McCord she could have all of it. The little bitch. She used me as much as I tried to use her. But she wasn't about to give up her chance of being a McCord. She knew what she wanted. What's more, she always got it.''

"Until the night McCord told her he was breaking off the engagement.''

"She must have been out of her head with rage that night,'' Devin said softly. "Laura had a violent temper, although she was careful to conceal it most of the time. Didn't fit the angel image she always presented to the McCords. When she first learned she was pregnant, she planned to have an abortion. Then she decided that she might be able to use the baby to prod Case into marrying her. I think she knew he was slipping through her greedy little fingers. There had been plenty of signs. She panicked. She had tried to get him to make love to her so that she could claim the baby was his, but I guess he was already suspicious. Or maybe he was just tired of her little sex games. She'd kept him dangling so long he probably just lost interest. Laura thought she had all the McCords on the end of her puppet strings. She used to laugh about how easy it was to get them to do what she wanted. But things went wrong when she started pushing Case.''

"So she lost her temper and tried a rash, stupid tactic. She burst into tears and threw herself into McCord's arms, claiming Kyle had seduced her. She thought McCord would feel obliged to make up for his brother's actions.'' Pru shook her head in silent disgust.

"It was a reasonable assumption. She knew Case would do a lot for Kyle. She'd always been very good at manipulating the McCords and she assumed she could predict their responses.''

"But her luck ran out the night she tried to nail McCord with another man's baby. After that, she knew she was in trouble. She'd burned her bridges.''

"She phoned me after McCord left her apartment that night. Said she had to see me. Claimed I had to help her.''

Pru closed her eyes. "Then she climbed into a car and headed for your home at nearly a hundred miles an hour. What a sad story."

Devin's face was grim with remembered satisfaction. "She managed to extract some revenge against the McCords at the end, though. I was at the hospital that night. I heard her, and I saw the looks on the faces of Hale and Evelyn when she told them McCord had seduced and abandoned her, leaving her pregnant and desperate."

"Yes, she certainly got her revenge, didn't she? Three years' worth." Pru felt a rush of pity for all concerned.

"It's not enough, Pru. Not nearly enough."

She froze at the dangerous bitterness underlying the words. Her fingers dug into the bark of the tree, and she turned her head to stare at Devin. "What are you talking about? It's over. Let it go, Devin."

"Not yet. Not until I've proven to Case McCord that you're no better than Laura was. He thinks he's so damn smart to have finally found a woman who believes in him completely, no questions asked. A woman who gives him all her silly, blind loyalty. He thinks you're at opposite ends of the spectrum from Laura. But he's wrong."

"Get out of here, Devin." Frightened now, Pru tried to put every ounce of command she possessed into her voice.

"Case always lands on his feet. When he lost his whole inheritance, he seemed to take it in stride. He just walked away and didn't look back. It didn't even matter to him."

"You're wrong, Devin. Losing contact with his family mattered to him."

Blanchard waved that aside. "The real loss was the power and prestige he had as the heir to McCord Enterprises. You'd have thought the corporation was so much confetti, the way he reacted when his father kicked him out. McCord created a new career for himself, found a new woman and now he doesn't even want any part of McCord Enterprises. He's always been lucky. Always got what he wanted. He even escaped having to marry Laura after she made a fool of him behind his back. But I'm going to make sure he knows he wasn't so fortunate when he married you. Case McCord is going to learn his luck isn't infallible. You had fun making your grand announcement the other night at the fountain, didn't you? Well, let's see how long McCord goes on believing the baby is his after he knows some other man has had you.''

Pru jumped back instinctively when Devin reached for her. Unfortunately she came up against the tree trunk and couldn't move aside quickly enough to avoid Devin's grasping hands. His fingers closed around her shoulders. When she looked up into his face, she saw nothing but hard, bitter anger. Years of it.

"Let me go, Devin," she snapped. "This isn't going to give you the revenge you want."

"I'm willing to give it a try. You must be pretty damn good in bed for McCord to marry you after he'd been living with you for three months. Laura would be furious if she knew you'd manipulated him into marrying you by using the baby. She thought she was a brilliant manipulator."

"There is one major difference between Laura's situation and mine," Pru gasped, struggling to free herself. "The baby I'm carrying is McCord's, and he knows it."

"How can he be sure?"

Pru was shocked. "He trusts me. He knows I would never cheat on him."

"He won't be so sure of that after today, will he? I'll make certain he knows I've had you, Pru. I'll give him a blow-by-blow account."

"He'll kill you."

"He won't be able to touch me. Besides, it's far more likely he'll take out his anger on you. You're the one who betrayed him. *Just as Laura did.* He'll never forgive you for making a fool of him, Pru."

He was forcing her to the ground beneath the tree. Pru opened her mouth to scream, and instantly Devin clamped a hand over her lips. She twisted furiously in his grasp, using her nails to claw at him.

"Stop it, you little bitch. It won't do any good. You'll only hurt yourself."

He sprawled on top of her, pinning her struggling body with his heavy legs. He kept one hand across her mouth as his other hand went to the front of her dress.

Pru panicked. She was rapidly slipping beyond coherent thought. She only knew she had to get free regardless of the cost. Dimly she remembered the rake that had been propped against the tree trunk. Her hand groped for it as she prayed she wasn't too far away to reach it.

Her fingers encountered the metal prongs just as Devin began tugging at the material of her dress. The fabric was tougher than Pru would have expected. Her assailant was having to work at the task of trying to tear it.

Pru clutched at the rake, seeking a useful grip. She managed to bring the long wooden handle sharply down on Devin's back. It didn't do much damage, but it startled him.

"What the hell...? Damn you!"

His hand came free of her mouth as he reached around to wrest the rake from her fingers. Pru screamed.

"Shut up!"

He tried to cover her mouth again, and as soon as he released the grip on her hand, she grabbed the metal prongs of the rake. This time, she vowed silently, she would do more damage.

Devin yelled and jerked away from his victim as he suddenly became aware of what Pru intended to do. The steel prongs were only an inch away from his back as he rolled free and jumped to his feet.

Pru scrambled to her feet, clutching the rake. She held the implement out in front of her as she backed quickly toward the safety of the house. If she could get inside and slam the door, she would be all right. She could call the police. Devin was coming toward her, his eyes burning with fury. He was waiting for an opening, and Pru knew it. One false step and her makeshift weapon would be wrenched from her hands.

"Stay away from me," she warned.

She had almost reached the kitchen door when it swung open behind her. Pru jumped, swinging around in relief to greet whoever it was who had unwittingly come to her rescue. Expecting Steve or Martha, it came as a shock to see McCord filling the doorway.

"McCord!" she breathed in overwhelming relief. Throwing down the rake, she raced for the safety of his arms.

He caught her as she flew to him, but he didn't hold her. "Get inside." He was shoving her behind him into the kitchen before she could speak. Then he turned to confront Devin Blanchard.

"McCord, no," Pru said urgently as she realized his intention. "I'll call the police."

"Go ahead and call them," he said easily as he started forward. "I've got time to finish this before they get here."

Pru's fingers tightened around the doorknob. She wanted to stop what was going to happen next, but she knew there was nothing she could do. She could only hope McCord wouldn't get hurt.

She should have known better.

McCord always landed on his feet.

IT WAS A LONG TIME before Pru got to her pizza. The police had come and gone, taking a sullen Devin Blanchard with them. Pru and McCord had both made statements and assured the officers they would press charges. All told, some two hours passed before Pru pulled her pizza back out of the refrigerator where she had stored it while McCord dealt with the police. She was starving, she realized.

She turned on the oven and shoved the pizza inside just as McCord stalked into the kitchen. He looked none the worse for wear after the short, violent confrontation with Devin Blanchard. The same couldn't be said about Blanchard. But Pru didn't particularly care about Blanchard's condition. The cops hadn't seemed unduly alarmed, either.

"Do you want some pizza?" Pru asked cheerfully as McCord halted behind her.

"What I want," McCord said grimly, "is an explanation of why you let Blanchard into the house. I told you to stay away from him, Pru."

"Is this going to be an inquisition?"

"Yes."

She smiled, folded her arms and leaned back against the counter to face him. "Then we can start with the question of what you're doing home a day early."

He glowered at her, running his fingers through his hair in annoyance. "I got through with the Nebraska assignment sooner than I expected. There's no great mystery involved. I came rushing back to hearth and home only to discover my wife fighting off an attacker who should never have been allowed into the house in the first place. Hell, Pru, have you any idea of what I felt when I opened the kitchen door and saw what was happening?"

"I know," she said, her voice gentling as she saw the raw emotion in his eyes. "I'm sorry."

He was not in a mood to be placated. "You should be. Are you sure you're all right?"

"I'm sure. I feel fine. He didn't have a chance to hurt me, McCord."

His mouth crooked faintly. "You looked like you were doing a fairly good job of defending yourself."

"Thank you," she murmured. "I come from Spot, Texas, remember. You learn things in Spot, Texas."

"Why was he here, Pru?"

She sighed. "He said he came to apologize for the scene at the fountain the other night. He claimed I'd made him realize he really shouldn't be working for McCord Enterprises. Said I'd made him see the light."

"And you bought that, hook, line and sinker?"

"Well, I certainly didn't expect him to attack me," she flared. "I thought he just wanted to talk."

"I told you to stay away from him."

"But you didn't tell me why, McCord. You didn't tell me that Blanchard was the father of Laura's baby."

He sucked in his breath. "He admitted it?"

"Oh, yes. He admitted it." Pru frowned. "Didn't you know?"

McCord stopped his restless pacing and sprawled into a chair at the kitchen table. "The other night after the ball I began to wonder if he might have been Laura's lover. He was too intent on warning you away from me. I saw his face that night at the fountain. He was too—" McCord lifted one shoulder, searching for the words "—emotionally involved, I guess you could say."

"He was that, all right. He hated you and your family."

McCord stared at her. "I intended to have it out with him when I got back from this trip." He shook his head. "Damn it, Pru, he worked for us for years. We trusted him completely."

"It wasn't enough. He always felt like an outsider. He didn't just want to be a friend of the family, he wanted to be a member of the family, and there was no way that could happen. He resented everything you had, and at the same time he couldn't bring himself to walk away from the cushy position he had. He thought for a while that marrying Laura was the answer. The McCords treated her like a daughter, and she was due to inherit a chunk of McCord Enterprises. But Laura wasn't about to marry an outsider. She was intent on being a McCord."

"She wasn't in love with me," McCord said thoughtfully.

"I'm afraid love had nothing to do with it."

"She played her charming little ingenue games for me and my family while she amused herself with Blanchard on the side." McCord grimaced. "I'd known from the beginning that she wasn't exactly in love with me. But I thought we had a lot in common, and I assumed a marriage between us would work. I cared for her, just as everyone else in the family did. It wasn't until after the engagement when I started seriously thinking about what it would mean to live with her that I began wondering if it was wise for us to marry. She didn't want to talk about any doubts on the subject, though. Probably because she herself wasn't having any. After all, she'd already made up her mind about what she wanted."

"She wanted to secure her place in the family."

"She should have been more careful," McCord pointed out.

"About getting pregnant? I gather that was an accident. One she intended to remedy until she decided she might be able to use it to prod you into marriage. Apparently she had begun to worry about losing you. Unfortunately for her, you weren't easy to prod. You don't take kindly to being manipulated."

McCord swore softly under his breath. "Let's not get started on that subject."

"Suits me." Pru smiled as she bent down to open the oven and remove her pizza. She sniffed appreciatively. "Almost as good as new."

McCord eyed the pizza dubiously. "What have you got on there?"

"Jalapeño peppers, anchovies, olives, onions and hot sauce. I call it a J. P. Arlington Foundation Special. Want some?" She carried it over to the table and set it down.

"You're trying to distract me. In fact, I think you already have distracted me. I'm supposed to be lecturing you on the foolishness of disobeying my clear-cut instructions."

"Darn right. You think I want to sit here eating this fabulous pizza while listening to you rant and rave about how I shouldn't have let Devin Blanchard through the front door?" She sat down and shoveled two fat slices onto the plates she had set out earlier. "You shouldn't yell at a pregnant lady, anyway. Speaking of yelling..."

"What about it?"

"I want you to promise not to yell at Steve about leaving the garden tools lying around for at least a month."

"I never yell," he reminded her.

"Well, I don't want you lecturing him about the matter, then. In fact, I want you to remember to thank him for leaving that rake propped against the tree."

McCord groaned. "I guess I do owe him something for that piece of carelessness, don't I?"

"Yes, you do." She handed him his pizza.

McCord's mouth twitched as he accepted his plate. He glanced down at the pizza and then back at his wife's face. She looked at him, her eyes sparkling as she closed her small teeth around a huge bite of pizza and began to chew. "You never gave me my standard welcome-home kiss," McCord complained suddenly.

Pru stopped chewing, her mouth still full. "Is that right?" Her voice was muffled. "I seem to remember flying to you on winged feet not more than two hours ago."

"Throwing yourself into my arms as you flee an attacker doesn't count."

"Oh." She swallowed the bite of pizza, got up and came around the table to sit in his lap. "I hope you like jalapeños, anchovies, olives and onions." She kissed him soundly.

His arm came around her waist. "I love jalapeños, anchovies, olives and onions. And I love you."

She went very still for a moment, her eyes shining. "Do you, McCord?"

"I've loved you from the beginning," he said quietly. "I don't know why it took me so damn long to say the words."

"You'd been severely traumatized by your experience with Laura," Pru explained generously. "You weren't about to let yourself get manipulated by a woman. I think in your subconscious mind you equated love with the kind of weakness that might leave you open to being manipulated."

"Is that right?" He looked at her admiringly. "Did you figure that out all on your own, or did you take a correspondence course in psychology?"

"I figured it out all on my own."

"You must have spent a lot of time analyzing me."

"Oh, I did," she assured him. "Endless hours."

"Why?"

She smiled and hugged him. "Because I love you, naturally."

He held her close, his mouth in her hair. "I was wondering when you were going to admit it freely."

"You must have known since the beginning."

"I did, or at least I hoped I did. But it's always nice to hear the words."

She shook her head ruefully. "You were always so sure of me."

"You're not very good at hiding your emotions, sweetheart. Every time you look at me I can feel you loving me. I've never known anything like it in my life. Whenever I was away on a trip, all I could think about was getting home so I could have you back in my arms. I'd sit there on the plane coming home from wherever I'd just been and I'd think about how soon I'd be able to tell you all about the trip and what I'd seen and what plans I'd made for foundation activities in that particular region. And then I'd think about sharing a drink with you and a good meal while I unwound and listened to you tell me about what had been happening back here while I was gone. Finally we'd go to bed together, and after we made love you'd curl up beside me and we'd go to sleep. Very simple, very comfortable."

"It all sounds very married."

"But it wasn't. Not quite. And that's where I went wrong, Pru. I should have married you the first day I saw you."

"Yes," Pru agreed, "you should have. It's just like Aunt Wilhelmina always said, 'Give a man free whiskey long enough and he'll get used to the notion of not having to pay for it. It's tough to collect after he's drunk his fill.'"

McCord groaned. "Are you going to throw your aunt's words in my face for the rest of our lives?"

Pru shook her head, grinning. "No, because as it happens I'm glad we did things the way we did."

"Glad!" He gave her an astounded look.

"Uh-uh. This way I got to experience the thrill of an illicit affair. I shall have such wonderfully racy tales to tell my grand-children.''

''Living with a man these days hardly qualifies as an illicit affair,'' McCord pointed out. ''More like a normal event for two people who are as attracted to each other as we are.''

''You can say that because you're from California. Those of us who come from Spot, Texas, view these things differently. Three months of being your live-in lover was just about the most excit-ing thing that's ever happened to me, McCord.''

''I can only hope you're not going to be bored now that the illicit thrill is gone.'' His eyes were gleaming.

''The wonderful thing about being married to you, McCord, is that it's even better than being your live-in lover.''

''I'm glad you feel that way, because there's no going back to the old days.'' There was fascinating determination in McCord's dark eyes. ''You're my wife now. I'll never let you go.''

Pru smiled, all her love shining in her gaze. ''That's just what I wanted to hear.'' She got up off his lap and went around to sit down on her side of the table. ''Have some more pizza before it gets cold.''

He grinned. ''Does it strike you that we're both being rather casual about declaring our love to each other?''

''I expect it's because we've been living together long enough to know we both mean what we're saying,'' Pru said compla-cently.

''No excitement?''

She shook her head. ''No fears or uncertainties,'' she corrected gently.

''You're right.'' McCord smiled. ''It's nice to be sure of each other. Besides, the exciting part comes later. In bed.''

Much later that evening when Pru came out of the bathroom in her nightgown she found McCord lying naked, propped against the pillows with his arms folded behind his head.

He watched her come through the doorway with his usual gleaming, quietly possessive expression. Pru smiled, thinking that some things never change. He had got in the habit of looking at her like this after the first time they had made love. She had a feeling he would still have that look in his eyes the night they celebrated their fiftieth wedding anniversary. It was a pleasant thought.

Pru stopped at the foot of the bed, gazing down at him. The sheet was at his waist, revealing the strong lines of his chest and hinting at the hardness of his lower body.

"What are you thinking, Pru?"

"I'm thinking about what a sexy man I married."

He grinned, thoroughly pleased. His eyes flicked briefly to where the sheet barely covered his arousal. "You've always had this effect on me."

"I'm glad," she said happily. She came around to her side of the bed and climbed in beside him. "It's only fair, considering what you do to me with just a glance or a touch. I love you so much, McCord."

The laughter went out of his eyes to be replaced by the familiar hunger. He reached for her, drawing her into his arms and tangling his legs with hers until they were wound together in a deeply sensual embrace.

"My sweet, beautiful, Pru." He kissed her throat, letting his hand slide over her breast to her hip.

"You make me feel beautiful, McCord," she whispered as she touched her lips to his chest. "When you hold me I feel exotic and gorgeous and sexy."

He laughed huskily. "That's because you are all of those things. You turn to liquid fire in my arms. But it's nothing compared to the way you make me feel."

"How's that?"

"As if I'll explode."

"I'm glad." Boldly she trailed her fingertips down to his thigh and then cupped him intimately. In her palm he was heavy and hard as steel. But the steel was sheathed in velvet, and she was already aching to know the feel of him inside her. She felt his fingers twisting gently in the softness at the juncture of her thighs, and she shivered.

McCord muttered something hot and dark and sensual against her breast and probed her with an excruciatingly slow, teasing movement of his hand. When she cried out and clung to him, he gasped and moved on top of her. The weight of him was deliciously exciting. Pru's senses whirled with the glittering sensations that were pouring through her.

"How could you have believed for even one moment that I wouldn't come after you if you left me?" McCord's voice was raw with emotion as he lifted his head to stare down into her eyes. "I would have followed you to the ends of the world. You belong to me, Pru. Swear you'll never leave me again."

"Never," she vowed. Her arms laced around his neck, holding him close. "In my heart, I never did leave you."

His smile was wicked with latent male satisfaction. "That's what I told myself that day I found you beside your sister's pool. I took one look at the hope and relief I saw in your eyes and I knew you were still mine, that you'd always be mine. All I had to do was make sure you knew that. I figured putting a ring on your finger was as good a way to do that as any."

"Does that mean you are now taking credit for having manipulated me into marriage, not vice versa?"

"Like J.P. says, once you had my attention, there was no stopping me from seeing the light of sweet logic and reason." He covered her mouth with his own and surged into her, filling her with his hard, throbbing steel sheathed in velvet.

Pru sucked in her breath under the sensual impact and then she wrapped her husband in her arms and gave herself up to the wonders of married life.

SEVERAL MONTHS LATER Pru lay back against the pillows of her hospital room bed and handed tiny James Hale McCord to his father. McCord took his sleeping son from his wife and laid the baby carefully in the cradle near the bed. For a long moment he stood gazing down at the infant, examining once more the miniature perfection of the little fingers and toes.

"He's something else, isn't he?" McCord said, not for the first time. He had been saying similar words ever since he'd held his wife's hand in the delivery room and agonized with her as James Hale had made his appearance in the world.

"He's going to look just like you."

"Yeah." McCord was clearly pleased by the idea. He stood looking down at his son for a moment longer and then he came across to the bed. "I love you, Mrs. McCord."

Pru smiled and touched his cheek. "I love you, too."

"I'm going to take very good care of you and our son."

"I never doubted it for a moment," she assured him softly.

McCord's fingers laced through hers, and he kissed the palm of her hand. At that moment the door swung open so abruptly that Pru jumped. McCord glanced up in mild annoyance as he saw who stood in the doorway.

"Do you always have to make an entrance, J.P.?"

J.P., resplendent in lemon yellow from head to toe, grinned broadly. "Only when I have a surprise. Look who I've got with me, Pru." He stood aside, bowing with a grand flourish as a magnificently built woman in her mid-fifties swept into the room. Tall, handsome, with flashing blue eyes and a severely neat bun of graying chestnut hair, the lady was as much a sight to behold as J.P.

Pru stared in amazement and then she laughed. "Aunt Wilhelmina! What are you doing here?"

"Why, I've come to see the baby, of course. This charming Texas gentleman was kind enough to invite me. And thank the good Lord he did. At the rate things were going, the hog wallers would have frozen over before I got an invitation from you, girl." Wilhelmina's handsome eyes were much softer than her accusation.

"Not fair, Aunt Willy. I told you the last time I called you that we'd want you to come see the baby as soon as possible."

J.P. chuckled. "When you work for J. P. Arlington, the possible happens real quick. It's just the impossible that takes a while. How do you like my little surprise, Pru?"

"I'm surprised," she agreed with a grin. "Aunt Willy, this is McCord."

"Hello, Aunt Willy," McCord said easily. His eyes were alight with humor.

Wilhelmina examined McCord with slow deliberation. "I knew it," she finally announced. "Slicker than a greased hog on ice. Congratulations, Pru. You did all right for yourself. You're a lucky gal, and I hope you know it."

"Yes, Aunt Willy. I'm aware of it."

"Good. Now let's see this baby." She advanced across the room to stand beside the crib. "Hmm. Big, isn't he? Not much chance of passing this little guy off as a couple of months premature."

Pru swallowed her amusement. "We weren't even going to try, Aunt Willy."

"Just as well. One small lie always leads to another, and first thing you know you're in more trouble than a dog who's cornered a skunk. Besides," Wilhelmina declared, "it doesn't much matter if you anticipated things a bit, Pru. Your man did right by you in the end, and that's all that counts."

"I'm glad you approve, Aunt Willy. Are you going up to Pasadena to see Annie and Tony while you're on the coast?"

"Of course," Wilhelmina said, "but there's no rush."

Pru coughed a little, wondering how McCord was going to tolerate having Wilhelmina in the house for a few days. "Uh, we're going to be quite busy for a while, Aunt Willy. I'm afraid McCord and I won't have a lot of spare time to show you around La Jolla and San Diego."

"No need to worry about that," J.P. announced. "I hereby claim the privilege of showing Miss Wilhelmina the magnificent California coast. Thought we'd look around San Diego for a few days and then take a leisurely drive up toward Pasadena. Wilhelmina tells me she's never seen Disneyland.''

Pru's eyes widened in amazement. ''Is that right, Aunt Willy?''

''I told you he was a most charming Texas gentleman.'' Wilhelmina gave J.P. a fond glance. It was returned in kind. ''I can't wait to start the sight-seeing.''

''We've got reservations for dinner in an hour,'' J.P. said happily. ''We'd probably best be on our way. Mustn't tire the new mother.''

''Right you are.'' Wilhelmina went over to the bed and dropped one of her brusquely affectionate kisses of greeting on Pru's forehead. ''Fine young son you have, Pru. And a fine husband. You take care of both of them now, you hear?''

''I hear.''

''Good. See you in the morning, dear. Get plenty of rest.'' Wilhelmina patted Pru's hand and started toward the door.

''Aunt Willy?'' Pru wasn't sure what to say next. She needn't have worried. Wilhelmina paused in the doorway as J.P. took her arm.

''Don't you worry about a thing, dear,'' Wilhelmina said airily. ''There aren't a great number of advantages to being my age, but there are one or two. Chief among them is that I'm not likely to get pregnant by accident.''

She swept through the door and disappeared down the hall on J.P.'s arm before Pru could think of a response. As the door closed behind her aunt, Pru shut her mouth and turned to meet her husband's laughing eyes.

''I think J.P. has met his match,'' McCord said. ''It's only fair. After all, I've met mine.''

He leaned down and kissed his wife with a love and a passion that proved his point beyond a shadow of a doubt.

CHANCES ARE
Barbara Delinsky

He wasn't at all what she'd expected of a prominent business-man. For one thing he was holding court in a converted mill, rather than a sleek skyscraper. For another, he wore a crew-neck sweater, soft jeans and sneakers, rather than the traditional three-piece suit. For a third, his hair was longer than the current Park Avenue style, generously brushing his forehead and the collar of his plaid shirt, which edged above his sweater. It was his voice, though, not deep and authoritative but quiet and gentle, that stunned her most—stunned her and mesmerized her as it flowed over the group of foreign businessmen who had come to hear the guru speak.

Lingering near the entrance of the barnlike room where the nation's latest craze—a game called Chimera—was produced, Elizabeth Jerome focused in on the discussion.

"Throughout history people have been drawn to games," Donovan Grant was saying. "They're a form of relaxation, a challenge on a plane less threatening than, say, a job or even a marriage. Board games such as backgammon and chess have been around for centuries. Even more modern ones like Scrabble and Monopoly have become mainstays in modern homes."

One of the visitors spoke up in heavily accented English. "But the market is glutted with games today. What makes yours different?"

"Mine requires nothing more than a pair of dice, a few simple guidelines, and the imagination of the players. It involves fantasy yet appeals to the intellect, where so many recent ones have failed. It challenges the independent mind, the mind that thrives on stimulation and adventure rather than sheer luck. Chimera lets the players determine the nature and scope of the game. This gives them a sense of self-determination, a sense of control that may be lacking in their everyday lives.''

Another of the foreigners interrupted, seeming mildly disgruntled to have found himself in an old mill listening to a laid-back genius discuss his latest baby. ''But this has little to do with big business and the American corporation today.''

Donovan turned to him with a smile Liz found to be disarming. ''That's where you're wrong. The theory behind the success of Chimera applies to big business, as well.''

''We have all read your book, Mr. Grant,'' a third guest injected. ''We have come to hear your theories of economic strategy.''

''Precisely,'' Donovan said smoothly, shifting more comfortably against the long table on which several cartons of Chimera kits lay. ''There's the old economy, the traditional one, involving mass production aimed at mass consumption. And there's the new economy, in which the amount of energy used is honed down, markets are streamlined, jobs are accomplished much more efficiently. Chimera emulates the new economy, forcing players to accomplish a goal by the most efficient means. In a sense it's a learning experience. A player is forced to be more ingenious than his opponents in order to win. That, very simply, is the secret to success in business today.''

The men listened, growing progressively enrapt as he continued to speak softly, elaborating on his economic theory. Several times he gave specific examples, timely examples that dated even his own book. Liz was as fascinated as the others by the time the session ended and the businessmen moved forward to shake the hand of the man responsible for shaping any number of successful business ventures in the past decade. She stayed where she was, though, until the last of the group had filed past and the wizard himself approached.

''You must be Elizabeth Jerome,'' he said in that same fluid tone he'd used to charm his visitors.

Once again she marveled at his manner, so unlike that of corporate heads she'd dealt with in the past. She wondered if it was all an act, but when he offered his hand and a smile as relaxed as he seemed, she abandoned that idea and swallowed hard.

"That's right," she managed, returning his warm handshake with one that was as firm, if more practiced. She tossed her head toward the door. "Very impressive. You took adversity and turned it around. I'm glad to have witnessed it."

His smile grew crooked. "I really didn't plan it that way. I wasn't expecting you until noon."

"I managed to catch an earlier flight to Albany," she explained, gently extricating her hand from his. He was staring at her, in his first show of something other than nonchalance, and she wasn't sure why. Uncomfortable, she averted her gaze to make a cursory study of the massive room. "Your driver was early, too. Thank you for sending him. Why did you pick Troy for this plant, when the rest of your interests are in Manhattan?"

"Manhattan grates after a while. I need the breather. I guess I'm a small-town boy at heart."

She looked back in time to see him grin, and she felt suddenly and strangely vulnerable. He had dimples in his cheeks; their flash seemed to ricochet through her insides. "A small-town boy?" she asked, masking unsureness with skepticism. "But business is your forte. You've made a mark on many large corporations besides your own."

"I don't know about that," he murmured, then took her elbow and lowered his voice to a playful drawl. "Come to my office, my dear. Let me show you my etchings."

She knew he was kidding but she was more ill at ease than ever. He must have felt the tension in her body, for he dropped his hand and stepped before her to lead the way.

His office was little more than a miniature version of the room they'd just left. Its walls were of aged bare brick, bruised at spots. A single file cabinet stood against one, a desk—actually an ancient pine door on sawhorses—against another. The only concession to modernity was a computer, which occupied its own suitably sturdy stand against the third.

Gesturing to one chair, Donovan slid into the only other in the room, a desk model that stood on wheels and swiveled across the oak planks of the floor as he moved closer to her. He leaned forward, propping his forearms on his outspread knees.

"Have you been with Karen long?" he asked.

Liz sat with her legs crossed and her hands anchored neatly in her lap. She prayed that she looked professional. The pose, complemented by the gray suit she wore, had always worked before. But something about the way Donovan Grant's eyes penetrated hers made her feel awkward, as though her legs were too tightly crossed and her hands positively stiff in repose. "Six years," she answered quietly. "I came to her right from graduate school."

"You have a degree in public relations?"

"Yes." She took a quick breath, fearing he had doubts of her ability. "I assure you I'm well qualified to handle your problem. I've handled other sticky ones—"

"I know," he interrupted succinctly, then smiled and leaned back in his chair. "Karen gave me a rundown on the clients you've represented when she recommended you." He paused, staring again. "Relax. I won't bite, y'know."

She looked away, then back. "I know. It's just that...well, you're very...different."

He cocked his head. "In what way?"

"Your clothes. Your manner. I'd expected much more formality."

"Karen didn't tell you about me?" he asked with such tongue-in-cheek caution that Liz couldn't help but be curious. Only later did it occur to her that he might have intended just that.

"She told me about the DIG Group and about the problem you've got. I'd already read about it in the papers."

"She didn't tell you that we knew each other?"

"She mentioned that you were old friends, but she didn't go into detail." When his eyes began to twinkle, Liz prodded. "Where *did* you meet?"

"In college. In the sixties. We were both revolutionaries of sorts."

"Karen...a revolutionary?" Liz conjured an image of her boss and friend, but it was one of sophistication and conventionality. "I don't believe it."

The grin he bestowed upon her was boyish, almost naughty. "She was right there beside me during more than one peace demonstration, waving her sign, holding her ground as staunchly as the rest of us." He shook his head. "She was a vision. Long black hair hanging straight down her back, torn jeans, bare feet, loose peasant shirt with no bra underneath..." He gave a low growl that spoke of his remembered attraction as no words could better do.

Before she knew what she was saying, Liz heard herself ask, "Were you two together? Oh, Lord, I'm sorry. That's none of my business."

"It's okay," he countered easily. "I invited it. We were together for a while, but I haven't seen her in years." His voice took on that same boyish quality that his grin had conveyed moments before. It was a perfectly natural intonation, enthusiastic and innocent. "What does she look like now?"

It was Liz's turn to smile. "Her hair is still black, but it's short and sleek. She wears silk dresses, imported leather heels and I believe she's taken to wearing a...bra. But, if you haven't seen her in so long, what possessed you to call her yesterday?"

"It's part of my philosophy, much as I was trying to tell that group a little while ago. To be successful today you've got to be smart, which means identifying weaknesses and then moving to strengthen them in the most efficient way possible. Karen Reynolds's firm is the best. I may not have been in personal touch with Karen over the years, but I'm well aware of her reputation. I like it better when you smile."

"Excuse me?"

"You smiled a minute ago. It was pretty. But now you're frowning. Did I say something wrong?"

Liz ignored his compliment without a second thought. "I'm wondering if you're disappointed that Karen sent me."

"Why on earth would I be disappointed?" he asked with genuine puzzlement.

"I'm not Karen."

Donovan could see that she wasn't Karen, yet there was definitely something familiar about her. He decided that it had to be her hair, which was a warm shade of brown, worn parted in the center and flowing down her back. There was a simplicity about it, an unadorned attractiveness reminiscent of days gone by, so unusual to the modern career woman. Her eyes captivated him even more. They were hazel and, as true windows of the soul, bore an intelligence that appealed to him, a hint of defiance that intrigued him.

"You've been trained by her and she thought you'd do the best job for me. I never expected that she'd personally handle this. In fact, if she'd suggested it, I'd have been skeptical."

"Why?"

"Because I want your full attention. I'll *need* it if this job's going to be done right. Karen is an administrator. She's got to keep tabs on many things at once if she's going to keep her organization operating smoothly. You don't have those administrative duties to dilute the time you give to me."

Something in his words made Liz uneasy. Or maybe it wasn't his words as much as his eyes. They were penetrating again, demanding in a way that neither his voice nor his casual pose suggested. If she'd been another woman, she might have been tempted to add deeper meaning to his words. But she wasn't another woman. She was Elizabeth Jerome. Plain, professional Elizabeth Jerome.

At the personal reminder, she sat straighter. "Let's talk about what you need done."

"Right." But he was out of his chair and grabbing her hand to draw her with him toward the door. "Over lunch. I'm starved."

She had no choice but to follow him, half trotting to keep up with his strides. When she was tucked safely in the passenger seat of his sporty Audi, he slid behind the wheel.

"Nice car...for an ex-revolutionary," she commented with a grin. She couldn't picture him in the role of the corporate giant, and she was content, under the guise of professional research, to explore the man himself. Knowing what made him tick would be invaluable if she was to be his champion in the weeks to come.

"Revolutionaries grow up," he said good-naturedly as he started the car and headed from the parking lot. "We also develop tastes for the good life. Oh, our personalities don't change; we still like to be different. But we learn to temper our urges, to channel them appropriately."

"Then you've sworn off demonstrations?"

"Not completely. If I believed very strongly in a cause and felt that a public demonstration was the most effective statement, I'd be out there marching. But I have alternatives now. I have more influence, power, if you will, to affect things. It's a matter of working from the inside to change what I believe is wrong."

"Is that what your consulting is about?"

He shot her a glance. "You know about that? You've done your homework."

"Only in the broadest sense, with the resources that were at my disposal at the last minute. I know, obviously, that you're involved with health foods, and that you've got a thriving courier service and a commuter airline. But from what I've read, it's the consulting you're really known for. A cult following?"

His mouth slanted on the mild side of a grimace. "I wouldn't call it that exactly. It's just that people are always looking to grab on to something—or someone—who can give them hope. I get calls all the time from would-be entrepreneurs wondering if one scheme or another of theirs is worth pursuing. More often than not I tell them to forget it, but even that impresses them."

"You're being too modest," Liz chided. "Much of the consulting you do is on a larger scale. You've been called in by some of the largest corporations in the country to make suggestions on how they can better manage their interests."

"Their interests are monstrosities, which is the major source of the problem. Unchecked growth gets quickly out of hand. The right doesn't know what the left is doing. It doesn't take genius to see that or to tell them to streamline. Where are you from, Elizabeth Jerome?"

The abrupt shift in conversation, accompanied as it was by no shift in tone, took her off guard for a minute. She blinked once, then steadied herself. "Baltimore, originally. Tell me about your interest in health foods."

He cast her a quick glance, but acquiesced. His hands were relaxed on the wheel; the car seemed little more than a smoothly operating extension of the man himself. "Health foods and I go way back. In my early, uh, nonconformist days, I was often in the midst of discussions about chemical additives in foods. When I finally realized I was going to have to do something to earn a living, it seemed only natural that I should turn to the manufacture and marketing of organically grown products. Actually, luck had more than a little to do with my success. Luck, and timing, and patience. I got into the field just early enough to find my sources and set up an efficient operation before the American public tuned in to health foods. I was there and ready when the market mushroomed."

"Was it luck or foresight?"

He shrugged. "I wish I could say it was foresight, but at the time I wasn't exactly into making money. I was still pretty much of a hippie."

"But you knew enough to do things right."

"I suppose that was instinct, though I only recognized it later. I started with a single small outlet in Los Angeles and would have been satisfied at the time if it had simply given me enough to live on. When it did better than that, the challenge grew. I contracted more growers and opened a second outlet, then a third and so on. It was like a game, and I was calling the shots. Before I'd realized it, I'd become a full-fledged entrepreneur."

"And today? How large is the business?"

"I've got processing plants in six states, better than ninety thousand acres of land being planted, nearly a thousand employees and a source network that extends to a dozen foreign countries. It's pretty large, I guess."

"Large enough to inspire sabotage," Liz commented thoughtfully. Donovan held up a hand in a gesture that might have been harsh had it not been delivered simultaneously with a smile. "Not yet. I can't discuss that on an empty stomach. When did you leave Baltimore, Elizabeth?"

She wanted to say that everyone called her Liz, but she didn't. There was something about the way her full name flowed from his tongue that made it sound pretty to her as it never had. There was also something warm and comforting about him that quelled any objection she might have had to this detour from business. "When I went off to college."

"Where did you go?"

"Emery."

"In Atlanta? That's a great place!"

"I got a good education there."

"And the graduate degree?"

"Boston University."

"Had you always wanted to work in Manhattan?"

"Only once I realized that the best jobs were there." She glanced out the window of the car to find that they'd long since left the urban confines of Troy and were traveling along a road bordered by open fields and trees. "Where are we going?"

"My place. I make the best cheeseburgers around."

Liz tensed, only realizing by contrast how slyly Donovan Grant had put her at ease. "I, uh, we could have grabbed something in town." She didn't look at him. She didn't dare. But she heard the smile in his words and knew he was laughing at her.

"I felt this would be better. We need privacy for what we have to discuss."

"We could have stayed in your office."

"Nah. Too impersonal."

"This is an impersonal issue."

"I certainly hope not!"

When Liz's gaze flew to his in alarm, she met a pair of dancing brown eyes. But the dancing abruptly ceased when Donovan sensed her fright.

"It's okay," he soothed, though he was clearly puzzled. "I was only talking about work. It is a personal issue—for me at least."

He paused, darting intermittent glances at Liz as she gnawed on her lower lip. ''You're edgy. Do men come on to you often?''

''No!'' She'd never had to worry about come-ons...or double entendres...or embarrassment, which was what she felt most noticeably now. A man like Donovan Grant—successful, charming and good-looking to boot—wouldn't be interested in her. Why she'd even jumped to the conclusion she had she couldn't fathom. ''I just like to stick to business.''

''You don't ever mix work with fun?''

''No.'' She sat straight-faced, staring out the windshield.

''Not even a little?'' His voice was higher, teasing.

Liz realized she was making too much out of nothing, and she forced herself to relax. ''No,'' she said more quietly. It was just as well he knew at the start where she stood. She didn't think she could bear being humiliated by someone as bright, as confident, as handsome as the man at the wheel.

''That's a shame,'' he said very softly, almost to himself, then raised his voice. ''What *do* you do for fun?''

She shrugged the edge off her unease. ''The same things other people do.''

''Like...?''

''Read. Eat out. Go to the theater.''

''Alone?''

''Sometimes. Sometimes not. Tell me more about the DIG Group. Anything else beside the courier service, the airline and health foods?''

''Chimera. Have you ever played?''

''No. I went to buy it once but the store was sold out.'' She looked over at him. ''There's been a shortage. Was that intentional?''

''Not really, though it did serve to whet the public's appetite. We really hadn't anticipated the demand, or rather, we'd planned conservatively at the start. Production's been stepped up, though, so the problem should be solved. I'll give you a kit and some booklets with potential scenarios before you leave.''

''That's not necessary. I can buy—''

"I'd like to *give* them to you. Consider it an advance on payment for your services."

Again Liz felt a tremor of discomfort. Something about the way he'd spoken of services conjured other images. She told herself that she was being neurotic and wondered why she couldn't simply take this man at face value. Perhaps it was because his tone of voice was somehow intimate, or because his gaze penetrated her each time it left the road. Then again, perhaps it was her own very foolish imagination.

"Where are we now?" she asked, needing to steer the talk along less threatening lines.

Again Donovan yielded, though not before he'd thrown her a knowing glance. "We're heading northwest. If we were to continue in this direction we'd hit the Adirondacks. Ever explore them?"

"No. I hear they're beautiful."

"The park itself is the largest of its kind in the country. Six million acres in northern New York. It's also considered to be one of the most beautiful. The northern areas are less traveled and almost completely unspoiled. As inhospitable as they can be in bad weather, they're breathtaking when tackled properly."

Liz swiveled in her seat to study him more easily. "You've tackled them?"

"Only parts. I'll cover them all if I live long enough. There's something about hiking through dense woods, around and over mountains. I mean, we may not be talking the Rockies, but the wilderness here is every bit as inspiring. When you're out there alone surrounded by nothing but the sights and sounds of nature…" His voice trailed off and he breathed a soft growl not unlike the one he'd made when recalling Karen Reynolds's braless past.

Liz had to smile. "So it's not just women who turn you on?"

The corner of his lips twitched. "Not by a long shot. Nature turns me on. So does business. In different ways than a good woman would, of course."

"Of course."

"Where was I?"

"A geography lesson."

"Ah, a geography lesson. The male physique—"

"Of the Adirondacks."

"Mmm. Actually, the other's just as interesting."

"It's irrelevant."

"Now just a minute. I wouldn't say that my body's irrelevant." He dropped a fast glance to the subject in question. "The male geography can be—"

"The Adirondacks?" Liz interrupted in gently pointed reminder. But she'd begun to relax again and took no offense in the sexual banter. "If you refuse to discuss business, the least you can do is to educate me a little."

"That's what I was trying to do," he countered innocently.

"The Adirondacks...?"

He set his lips in mock show of discipline. "Right." He took a breath. "The Adirondacks cover six million acres—"

"You've told me that."

"I have? Oh. Okay, where did I leave off when I was so rudely interrupted?"

"You weren't rudely interrupted."

"I was, too. *You* were the one who raised the subject of turnons."

"Only when you started to pant at mention of the wilderness."

"The wilderness. Okay, let's take it from there. Did you know that the human body is a wilderness—self-generating, sustained directly or indirectly by the sun, filled with nooks and crannies waiting to be explored?"

Liz dropped her head to her hands and shook it slowly. For a split second Donovan was mesmerized by the shimmer of her hair, so clean and soft and natural, striking that familiar chord in him. Then he heeded her gesture. He spoke quickly, though, as if he desperately wanted to be done with this particular geography lesson.

"The southern areas of the Adirondacks were heavily logged in the 1800s. Fortunately much of the forest has grown back, though old logging roads still wind through it. Small pockets of privately owned land intermingle with what the government now owns, but even the private landowners are protective.''

"Do you live in one of those pockets?''

"Couldn't get one. Private landowners are not only protective but possessive. Here, this is my road.'' He'd slowed the car and was turning off onto a narrow strip of rutted pavement. Had Liz been alone she might have completely missed the road, hidden as it was by thickly canopied growth. Pines and hemlocks were interspersed with deciduous trees whose leaves had just begun their autumnal change.

"This is country!'' Liz remarked appreciatively. "It's hard to believe we're less than an hour's flying time from Manhattan.''

"That's what's so fantastic about living here.''

"Do you commute daily?''

"To and from the city? No. I have a place there, but this is my haven.''

"Some haven,'' she crooned in envy. They were cruising slowly down the road, which showed no sign of ending. "Where is the house?''

"Another three-quarters of a mile.''

"My Lord, how do you manage when it snows?''

"I'm plowed out. And this car's got four-wheel drive. Not that there haven't been a couple of hairy times...''

"I can imagine. You're really isolated out here, aren't you?''

"Yup. And I live alone.'' He looked at her. "No wife. No girlfriend. No housekeeper.''

"Are you trying to scare me?''

"Nope. Just want you to know I'm available.''

"But I'm not.''

"You're not married.''

She flexed the bare fingers of her left hand and lowered her eyes to study them. "No. But we have a business relationship. It can't be anything more.''

"Why not?''

The innocent way he'd asked brought her gaze back up, but he was concentrating on negotiating the increasingly winding, occasionally hilly road. She felt an inkling of annoyance that he should tease her so.

"Because."

"Because why?"

Because I'm plain and you're gorgeous. Because I'm inexperienced and you've been around. Because I'm spinster material and you'll be snatched up before long. "Just…because."

"Not good enough."

"Where *is* this place of yours, anyway?"

"Right…there."

Sure enough, a house suddenly materialized from amid the forest. It was built of stone and looked like a relic of bygone days, except it was dated by huge expanses of windows and a skylight or two.

Enchanted, Liz promptly forgot all annoyance. "It's charming," she breathed.

"Thank you. I like it." Bringing the car to a full stop, he swung from behind the wheel and trotted around to help her out. The hand that took her elbow slid down to firmly grasp her hand. She didn't resist as he buoyantly led her up the walk.

The inside of the house was delightful, if slightly disorderly. Even Donovan seemed taken aback by the newspapers and magazines that graced the upholstered sofa and the sweat suit that was flung over the arm of one chair.

"Uh, sorry about this." He gathered the papers together in one large sweep and anchored them under his arm. "I hadn't anticipated having guests."

Liz wanted to ask him what he *had* anticipated. He'd known she was coming. If he'd originally planned on a lunch meeting in Troy, why was she here? But he had scooped the sweat suit from the chair and was off before she could say a thing.

"Make yourself comfortable," he called over his shoulder. "I'll go put the meat in the microwave to defrost. It'll only take a minute."

Wary of making herself too comfortable, Liz simply stood

where she was, hands clenched around the top of her oversized purse as she looked around the room. It was large, decorated sparsely but with warm things—the upholstered furniture was beige-and-navy plaid and cushiony, the pictures on the walls were of local origin and decidedly homey, the high bookshelves were crammed with volumes arranged in haphazard fashion. A low glass table stood atop a rag rug that lay atop the highly polished wood floor. A large fireplace, its grate covered with ashes, broke up one wall. Beside it was a basket of logs.

In an open loft high above was another sofa, a television and a stereo. Books and magazines littered this area, as well, but they merely enhanced the lived-in look that gave the house such charm.

The sounds of activity in the kitchen brought Liz's attention back to the ground floor. She was tempted to follow the noise, then thought better of it and slowly edged toward one of the armchairs and settled cautiously into it. She folded her hands in her lap. She looked around. Her eye fell on the bookshelf again and she left her chair to peruse the books it held. Some of the volumes related to business, but the bulk covered other diverse topics. There were books on travel, books on art, books on mountain climbing, books on self-improvement. And there were novels— many of which she'd read herself—both recent and not.

"Ah," came a voice from close behind her, and she jumped. "You're studying my collection. Even better than etchings. You can learn a whole lot about a man by what he reads."

"So I was thinking," she murmured, then firmed up her voice. "Every little bit helps if I'm to represent you well."

Donovan's arm brushed her shoulder when he reached behind her to finger the binding of one particular book. "You're not going to announce to the world that I read escapist literature, are you?"

She stepped aside and looked back at the shelf. "There's nothing wrong with it, though I really liked the book L'Amour wrote before that one better."

"You read him, too?" Donovan asked in surprise.

"Doesn't everyone?"

"But I thought men mainly liked westerns."

"Now that," she said with a grin, "is a sexist comment if I've ever heard one. And coming from a former hippie, it's shocking."

The book forgotten, he was concentrating on her face. Her eyes were gentle, almost shy despite the surface boldness of her grin. She seemed a rarity amid the ultrasophistication of New York. "I like to shock. It's part of the game."

Liz grew uneasy then. He was standing far too close, studying her far too intently. She wanted to run, to escape, to hide, but her purpose in being there held her rooted to the spot. "What game?" she asked nervously.

"Life. Love."

When the last word slid from his mobile lips, she did bolt. Quickly crossing the room, she leaned against the back of the chair in which she'd rested moments before. She didn't like games, particularly ones dealing with love. Or lust. Or physical need. Or whatever the head player chose to call it.

Donovan followed her flight, unrelenting in his scrutiny. She darted him a glance, then looked away and was about to remind him of the purpose of their meeting when he spoke softly.

"I didn't mean to frighten you. I seem to do that a lot, though, don't I?"

"I'm not frightened."

"Then threatened. Why?"

"I'm not threatened," she lied.

"Call it what you will, but the fact remains that I make you nervous. I don't understand, Elizabeth. You're an attractive woman. Surely you're used to men who tease."

You're an attractive woman. You're an attractive woman. "I don't like teasing. Look, maybe you should be working with someone else from the office. I could go back and speak to Karen—"

"I don't want to work with someone else. I want to work with you."

"But we've obviously hit an impasse—"

"You're the one who's hit an impasse. I don't see any problem. I'm not going to jump you and ravish you on the floor. And I really didn't have anything sinister in mind when I brought you here, unless you call getting to know someone better sinister. Maybe if you try to relax, to take my teasing with a grain of salt, you'll find that I'm a nice guy after all.''

She met his gaze with some hesitancy. ''You are a nice guy. It's just that…well, I guess I'm not used to teasing. It makes me uncomfortable.''

He thought for a minute. ''I can handle that.'' He took a step toward her, then stopped. ''Can you cook?''

She frowned for just an instant before realizing that, in the way that appeared to be characteristic of him, Donovan was changing the subject. ''Not in the gourmet sense.''

''Good.'' He resumed walking, but back toward the kitchen. ''Then I don't have to worry that you'll cringe when you see what I mix with the hamburg.'' He was about to gesture for her to follow when he glanced back, paused, then backtracked to gently pry her fingers from her bag and set the latter on the chair. ''Come,'' was all he said before he left her alone.

Liz half wished he'd taken her hand, as he'd done several times that day, and led her. Then she wouldn't have had a choice. As things stood now, she had to decide whether to be a coward and remain in the living room or to trust Donovan. With a deep breath she pulled herself up straight. She was twenty-nine, independent and professional. If it was instinct that advised trust, it was that sense of professionalism that gave her the courage to move.

Donovan's back was to her when she appeared at the door of the kitchen. He was rummaging in a cabinet, extracting one bottle, then another and several spice tins. His momentary distraction gave her time to examine her surroundings, which she did with growing pleasure.

This was no backwoods stove-and-icebox kitchen, but rather a thoroughly modern, well-equipped room containing a double oven, a separately mounted microwave, abundant cabinet space and spacious countertops. The far end of the room opened into a dining area made bright by hip-to-ceiling windows. Just as in the living room, there were no drapes to shield the sunlight, which streamed freely over the lacquered table and across the ceramic-tiled floor.

"Okay?" Donovan asked. His expression held a hint of unsureness.

"It's great!" Liz responded readily. Though his question and its attendant gaze lent deeper meaning to his inquiry, she concentrated on the room. "You must have done a lot of work when you bought this place. I didn't expect anything as modern."

He ran his hand along the shiny countertop. "I figured that if it was food that earned me the down payment on this place, I'd better show respect in the kitchen."

"Since when do cheeseburgers qualify as health food?"

His lean cheeks grew flushed, but only for an instant. "I'm not the fanatic I used to be. Besides, lean meat and cheese provide protein for a balanced diet. I mean, I buy the best, stuff that's not piled with preservatives, and I won't be offering you marshmallow fluff on the side. We can have fresh fruit for dessert. In fact, I may slice some fresh carrots to go with the burgers. I love raw carrots. They're great munchies. Don't look at me that way. They *are* good."

"For rabbits."

"Don't knock 'em. Rabbits are healthy little creatures. They're sure as hell good at reproducing ...don't *look* at me that way." He gave a low growl, this time in frustration. "I'm beyond redemption. Face it. I've got a one-track mind."

"Mmm. But you can switch tracks. I've seen you do it. Maybe if we talk about the maniac who poisoned your fields—"

Donovan held up a hand. "Uh! Not yet. First, we eat."

Liz raised a brow and eyed the raw hamburg he'd just removed from the microwave. "First, you'd better cook, don't you think?"

"Cook. Right." He slid the miscellaneous whatevers he'd taken from the cabinet across the counter to the hamburg, reached into another cabinet for a mixing bowl and began to work. "Have a seat and tell me about your life."

She walked to the table, slid into a chair and held herself straight. "I already have."

"Where do you live? Co-op? Apartment? House? In the city or out of it?"

"If I lived in a suburb, I wouldn't be as green with envy over this place. No, I've got an apartment in the city."

"Do you walk to work?" His back was to her and he was dumping things into the mixing bowl with such abandon that Liz wondered if she *should* supervise. Unfortunately that would have meant being near him, and she valued the distance.

"In good weather, yes. Otherwise I take a bus."

"What are your work hours like?"

Had he been looking at her in that intense way of his, she might have evaded the directness of his questioning. But his attention was on his work and his curiosity seemed so totally innocent that she didn't have the heart to rebuff him. "Pretty sporadic. I'm a morning person, so I try to get in early every day. Dinners with clients—or with people to be courted on behalf of clients—keep me working late. When I travel I lose track of *all* time."

His arms were working at blending the mess he'd concocted. "You like traveling?"

"I love it. Seeing different parts of the country, meeting new people—it's exciting."

"Did you travel with your family when you were growing up?"

She paused for an instant and chose her words with care. "Yes, but never with the kind of freedom I have now."

"There can't be much freedom when you're working on a case." He began to form his mixture into patties with the verve of a child making snowballs. Liz wondered at the energy he poured into it and found herself suddenly eager to taste these cheeseburgers.

"Some cases, some trips, are more demanding than others. I can usually find time to do a little sightseeing, a little shopping."

"You like to shop?"

"For other people." She smiled. "There's always someone who's got a birthday or an anniversary or some other kind of milestone coming up. If I can pick up something to mark an occasion, I feel good."

"February 25. October 3. June 4."

"Excuse me?"

He slapped one of the meatballs onto the counter, then peeled it off and popped it directly onto the built-in grill. "February 25. My birthday. October 3. The anniversary of the Group's incorporation." A second patty hit the counter and went the way of the first. "June 4. My graduation from college. Now *that* was a milestone. It was a miracle I made it, a miracle the university swallowed its pride and presented me my diploma. Not that I saw the graduation exercises myself. I was in the parking lot slipping propaganda leaflets under windshield wipers." Having set two more patties onto the grill, he turned with his fist on his hip and his eyes skyward. "What was it that time? Fraternity discrimination? Fluoridation of the water?" He threw a hand in the air, then held up a finger. "Ah. One more. November 23."

When he offered no significance for the date, Liz eyed him strangely. "The day Kennedy was shot?"

Donovan grew serious, but in a soft and vulnerable way. "The day my son was born."

"Your son? But I thought…"

"We never married, Ginny and I. David was a love child. Unfortunately, Ginny and I outgrew our love—and each other—pretty soon after we graduated. It was one of those really quick things. We met, we loved, we parted. She met someone else within a year and got married."

"And…David?"

"David got a stepfather who loved him, thank God. Ron adopted him legally, as a matter of fact, and gave him his name. He and Ginny have three other children now, and David's been happy."

"Do you ever see him?"

"More, now that he's older." Wiping his hands on a dish towel, Donovan pulled his wallet from his back pocket and dug out a picture, which he handed to Liz. "It was taken a year ago."

Liz studied the picture for a long time. She could see Donovan's healthy coloring in David's face, as well as the same deep-brown eyes and firm jaw. "He's a handsome boy."

"Almost a man. He'll be seventeen next month."

She looked at the picture for a minute longer before handing it back. "You must be proud of him."

"I am, though I don't really have a right to be. I contributed to his gene composition. That's about it."

"You're his father."

"But I've had little to do with his upbringing."

"Did you want it differently?"

Having returned the picture to its place, Donovan tucked the wallet into his pocket. He drew a spatula from a nearby drawer and tended to the quickly broiling patties. She wondered why he kept his back to her, then understood when he spoke slowly and with an unmistakable note of shame. "At the time, no. I was into doing my own thing—the 'me-generation' personified. But I outgrew that particular self-indulgence, too. And now I'm sorry for all I missed of David's life. He's a super guy. I guess I should be grateful that Ginny and Ron made him that way." He flipped the burgers before turning around. "I don't know why I'm telling you all this."

Liz wasn't at all puzzled. "I'm a good listener."

"I haven't told many people about David. It's …difficult to admit that I was so irresponsible when I was young."

"You were young. That says it all."

"Ginny was young, too, but she was a wonderful mother."

"She had nine months of practice even before David was born. Besides, if she married soon after graduation and had three more children, she must have wanted that kind of life. She must have been ready for it. You just…took a little longer."

He tipped his head. "Why are you so understanding?"

His perplexity brought a gentle smile to Liz's lips. "Because it all makes sense. If you'd forced yourself to settle down then, you'd probably have been miserable. And you might never have been able to achieve what you have since. Besides, I'm looking from the outside in. It's easier to put things in perspective when you're not personally involved."

"Did you ever want kids?"

"I love kids."

"But did you ever want to have your own?"

Did she ever! But it was a dream, nothing more. Seeking a diversion, she focused on the thin tendrils of smoke rising from the Jenn-Air. "I think our lunch is burning."

Whirling around, Donovan rescued the burgers. Within minutes he'd heated buns, melted cheese atop the patties and presented Liz with what truly were the most delicious cheeseburgers she'd ever tasted.

By the next morning, though, she had a case of heartburn that had nothing to do with what she'd eaten.

"I think Veronica should be handling the DIG Group," Liz informed her boss soon after the latter had arrived at the office.

Karen Reynolds set down the coffee she'd been sipping and eyed Liz over the rims of her tortoiseshell spectacles. "Why Veronica?"

"She's been with you longer than I have. She's more experienced."

"You're brighter."

"Then...maybe Julie. She's *brilliant*."

"Julie has her hands filled with the book tour for Jonathan Douglass."

"I've got my hands filled, too. There's publicity to be arranged for Eastern Leather and the quarterly report to be done for Humbart, and I've got to set up meetings with the media to stir up interest in the *Women's Journal*...."

Karen's brows met as she studied Liz's agitated state. "What's wrong, Liz? What happened yesterday?"

Liz began to pace across the plush mauve carpet. "I met with him. We talked. I just think that I'm the wrong person to be working on this case."

"You're my troubleshooter. You're the *best* one for this case."

Liz stopped in front of the desk, her worried eyes suddenly brightening. "How about Donna? She's as much of a troubleshooter as I am."

"Donna's got a husband and two kids and her hours are more limited. Besides, I want *you*. Damn it, Liz. Don't start pacing on me again. Sit down and tell me what the problem is."

Liz sent her a frustrated glance from midway across the room. "The problem is Donovan Grant."

"Donovan a *problem*? I don't believe it. He was always the most easygoing, nicest guy."

"I don't think I can work with him."

Karen settled back in her chair, clearly perplexed. "I thought you two would hit it off well." Indeed that was what she'd intended, for more than business reasons. She wasn't usually a matchmaker, but somehow the image of Donovan and Liz together had struck an instant chord in her. "What happened?"

"He's a tease."

"*Donovan Grant?* Are you sure we're talking about the same man? The Donovan I knew was soft-spoken and earnest. A tease? No. Charming maybe." She grinned. "And gorgeous without a doubt." She shook her head, then paused with a hint of that same innocent curiosity Donovan had shown when he and Liz had discussed Karen. "What does he look like now?"

For the first time that day, Liz smiled. "He wondered about you, too."

"It's been better than seventeen years since I've seen him—other than grainy photos in magazines. Has he aged well?"

Liz's lips thinned. "I don't think he's aged."

"Come on. Time passes. What does he look like?" When Liz turned to stalk to the far side of the office, Karen rolled her eyes. "Liz, *sit down*." Only after Liz had begrudgingly settled into the nearest chair did she prod. "Well?"

Liz reluctantly met her gaze. "I didn't know him before, but he looks…good."

"He always looked good. Come on, Liz. Give."

Liz forced herself to paint with words the picture that had been so vividly in her mind's eye for the past hours. "He's tall and lean but solid. Clear brown eyes. A full head of brown hair with lighter streaks near the temples."

"Grey?" Karen asked with a wide grin. She was thinking of her monthly trips to the colorist and was delighted to know that she wasn't the only one showing telltale signs of middle age. Liz, God bless her, didn't have that problem, and she'd never have tried to cover it up if she did, Karen knew.

"Gray? Uh...I'm not sure. Maybe, but he seemed so boyish."

"The man has to be thirty-nine, if not forty. It *has* to be gray."

"Whatever it is, it becomes him. Like the crow's-feet at the corners of his eyes. And the tiny lines on his forehead. And his dimples—"

"His dimples! God, how could I forget those. They always did the weirdest things to my insides."

"Exactly." Liz also recalled the fine sprinkling of dark hair on the back of his hands, the way his Adam's apple bobbed gently when he swallowed, the litheness of his walk that suggested long, firmly corded legs hidden beneath the oh-so-soft denim of his jeans. But she didn't want to tell Karen about those things. She didn't want to think about those things, yet they persisted in haunting her. Even the memory of his voice, warm and soothing, was a balm that grated.

"So, what's the problem?" Karen broke into her thoughts, then grew smug with suspicion when Liz's glazed look registered. "You did discuss the contamination of his fields, didn't you?"

The glazed look vanished, replaced by the professional one Karen was so much more familiar with. "Oh yes. Some of what he said I already knew from the newspapers—that the fields in question are in Southern California and produce lettuce. *Organically grown* lettuce."

"Which means?"

"Lettuce grown on composted soil without manufactured fertilizers, pesticides or herbicides. According to Donovan, the only sprays used on organically grown products are those derived directly from plants such as garlic and nettle. Someone obviously went out of his way to spray something else."

"Does he have any idea who?"

Liz shook her head. "He's as much in the dark about who might have done it as the authorities are. He's been in touch with the families of the two women who died, and he makes daily calls to the hospital in Sacramento where other patients are being watched. It's impossible to know exactly how many people were affected in all; some suffered nothing more than intense cases of indigestion, which worked themselves out in a day. We agreed that the best thing would be for him to go public, discussing the problem and the security measures he's taken to make sure nothing like this happens again.''

"Security measures?"

"He's hired guards and is in the process of buying a radar-type detector that can scan his fields and make sure nothing hits them from the air. That's how it was done before—a fine-grain poison dusted over one of the fields at night. No one really noticed a plane buzzing low, and it was foggy besides.''

"It was a miracle the plane didn't crash in the fog,'' Karen mused dryly.

"Whoever did it had guts, that's for sure.''

"And there are no leads at all as to who it was?"

Liz shook her head. "Investigators have gone through logs at every airport in the area. It was probably a private plane taking off from a private airstrip. The authorities are hoping for a tip from someone somewhere. Otherwise...''

"Otherwise they'll never know.''

"Right. From a selfish point of view, it would make matters that much better if the case were solved. Then we could attribute the whole thing to one particular crackpot.''

"Is that what Donovan thinks? That it was a crackpot?''

"You mean, rather than someone who specifically had something against him?" Liz countered. "I asked him that, but he says he doesn't have any enemies." She clearly remembered the innocent way he'd said it, and her subsequent chiding. "I suggested that it might have been someone jealous of his success, but he brushed that possibility aside. Anyway, if whoever it was is caught, the situation will be better for all of us.''

Karen retrieved her coffee and took a thoughtful sip. "Okay. So you'll go public. I agree that that's the best tack." Realizing that for the moment Liz had forgotten her request to be removed from the case, she eyed her with studied nonchalance. "What, specifically, did you have in mind?"

Liz didn't even see herself as stepping into a trap, because professionalism had taken over and she was drawn into the excitement of plotting a new and challenging case. "There should be letters to stockholders and associates of the DIG Group, of course, and to the distributors and retailers. But the most effective thing would be a barrage of television and radio talk shows and news spots—Donovan would be perfect for that—and large ads in prominent newspapers. At this point the general public is the problem. If fear leads to a boycott of his entire line of health foods—even though all of the contaminated items have already been removed from the shelves—it could cause irreparable damage to the future of the division. It's too early to get concrete figures, but the communication Donovan's had with distributors tells him that sales are definitely off. That's why we have to hit soon and hard."

Karen sat forward. "Go to it then. I assume you can get the background information you need from someone at DIG headquarters. It's not far from here. Did you arrange something with Donovan?"

Did I arrange something with Donovan? The question brought Liz from the professional to the personal with a jolt. Bounding from her seat, she made it to the window before she turned back. "He said he'd be by later to take me over. I thought that you and I could agree on a replacement by then."

"A replacement? But you've barely started. And you've got such good ideas. This case is tailor-made for you."

"I'm going to have trouble, Karen," Liz countered beseechingly.

Karen studied her friend's face, then spoke softly. "Donovan scares you, and it's got nothing to do with business."

Liz dropped her gaze. "I feel uncomfortable with him."

"It's natural to feel a little uncomfortable with a new client."

"Not a little uncomfortable. A *lot* uncomfortable."

"You'll get over it once you start working."

But Liz was shaking her head. "I don't think so."

"Why not?"

"Because…because he's so…so…"

"Good-looking? You've worked with good-looking men before."

"It's not that. He's so…so…"

"Charming? That'll only make it all the more pleasant."

Again Liz was shaking her head, but she was no closer to finding the word that explained her problem. Sure, she'd worked with good-looking men before, many of whom had been charming, as well. But she'd never felt so threatened. Something in her gut stirred when she thought of Donovan Grant, and it set her on edge.

"I just can't relax with him," she ventured at last, launching an appeal to Karen's business sense. "And if I can't do that, I doubt I'll be able to do the kind of job this firm prides itself on."

Karen wasn't fooled for an instant, but then, just as she was an expert at constructing credible facades, so she could easily see through ones that weren't quite so credible. She knew that Liz had the same aptitude and therefore she had no qualms about calling her bluff. Perhaps bluntness was what was needed. "Tell me something, Liz," she commanded gently. "Do you *like* Donovan? Is that what's worrying you?"

Liz scowled. "Of course not."

"Of course not…what? You don't like him, or that's not what's bothering you?"

Liz sensed she was getting in over her head. "I don't think in terms of *liking* my clients. You know that."

"It wouldn't be so bad…with someone like Donovan."

"That doesn't make good business sense."

"I'm not talking business."

Liz sent her an imploring look. "How can you do this to me?"

Pushing herself from her chair, Karen came around the desk to put an arm across Liz's shoulders. "I can do it because I'm your friend. Because I *care* about you. Because I think that at first sight Donovan Grant got under your skin. And because I know what that feeling's like."

"Maybe *you* should be working with him."

Karen laughed, then proceeded to echo Donovan's own thoughts. "I can't give him the attention his case deserves. If there's one thing I've learned in twelve years of building this business, it's to delegate work. Besides, I've had my day with Donovan. We enjoyed each other, then moved on. Donovan's not right for me. He's too...too soft. I was always more aggressive than he was, more ambitious.''

"How can you say that, looking at the corporation he's built for himself? He has to be aggressive *and* ambitious."

"I know Donovan better than that. He may look a little different now. He may be more sophisticated, more experienced. But he's still sensitive and, from what I've read, he's a pragmatist. I'd dare say that if the DIG Group fell apart tomorrow and there was no possible way it could be retrieved, he'd very calmly turn his sights to something else."

"If that's true, why is he so worried about the damage this poison business will do?"

"Because he's bright. And this is a new challenge to face. Donovan always thrived on new things—new people, new ventures. Why do you think he keeps inventing new divisions for the Group? This year it's Chimera. Next year it'll be something else."

She grew more pensive before speaking again. "It's not that he loses interest in the old things, because I doubt he does and his record doesn't suggest it. He was always dedicated to whatever cause he chose to espouse. Mind you, when we were in school together, he was as carefree as the rest of us. But I always had a feeling about him, about what was lurking behind that carefree front. He's become a very responsible individual." She gave Liz's shoulder a squeeze. "I'd guess it's loyalty to his health-foods business that makes him want to fight to keep it alive."

Liz was thinking about responsibility and what Donovan had said about his son, and wondered if Karen was right in guessing that he'd finally found himself. If so, she admired him for it, though that didn't do anything to ease her own predicament.

"I'd really feel better if you put someone else on his case," she pleaded softly.

"And I think I'd never forgive myself if I did," Karen countered, walking Liz to the door while she was ahead in the game.

She knew how her mother must have felt sending her only daughter, crying and pleading, off to overnight camp; once she'd overcome her homesickness, Karen had loved it. As her mother must
have done then, so Karen now prayed that she was doing the right
thing by sticking to her guns. "Look, just give it a little longer.
Get going on the work. If things continue to bother you, we can
talk about it again. Just remember that Donovan's a special friend
of mine and I *know* that you're the best one for this job."

Liz sent her a look that said she saw right through the flattery,
but she also knew that, for the time being at least, the issue was
dead. Karen was her boss and, despite their friendship, Liz wasn't
about to push her too far. Contrariness wasn't one of Liz's natural
traits. Nor was recklessness. Her position at Reynolds Associates
meant far too much to her to jeopardize because of one client.

Come lunchtime, though, Liz had second thoughts about that.
With a surprisingly productive morning behind her, she was just
beginning to feel confident when Donovan appeared at the door
of her office and threw her off balance again.

"Hi," he said in that soft, flowing way of his as he stepped
into the room. This time it wasn't his balmy voice that disturbed
her, or even his smile, which was as brilliant as ever. Rather it
was the way he looked. "Uh, is everything all right?" he asked,
hesitating at her stricken expression.

For a moment she couldn't reply. He glanced down at himself,
then sheepishly met her wide-eyed gaze. "I wanted you to be
more comfortable today. This was—is more what you expect, isn't
it?"

He wore a three-piece suit of the finest beige wool and looked
positively gorgeous. "What I expect?" she echoed dumbly.

"Formality and all?" He ran a finger inside the collar of his
shirt, as though he was ill at ease, when in fact Liz could only
marvel at the positively masterful way he wore the suit.

"You look fine," she finally managed, at which point he
grinned again and, in sheer self-defence, she dropped her gaze to
the desk. "What're you doing?" he asked, walking quietly toward
her.

"Hmm?"

He cocked his head toward the papers at her fingertips. "Anything good?"

"Uh, a quarterly report for one of our clients."

"Would you rather I come back later?"

"No, no." She quickly gathered the papers into a pile and pushed them aside, then stood. "You're a client, too, and we did have an appointment." She was determined to remember that, despite what Karen had said, he was *only* a client. "Would you like to stop in and say hi to the boss?"

"I already have. It was wonderful seeing her again."

Liz nodded, unsure as to what to say next. Donovan took that responsibility out of her hands in a way that forced her to respond, and quickly.

"You look lovely today." He marveled again at the natural look to her, the faint flush on her cheeks, the guileless lowering of her lids. Then he gave an approving once-over to her plum-hued suit and the matching necktie that bisected the front of her white blouse.

"Shall we go? We've got a lot of ground to cover." She kept her eyes averted, focusing first on the pads of paper and pens she was stuffing into her bag, then on the coat she crossed the room to retrieve from behind the door.

"I thought we'd stop for lunch before we hit the office."

"That's not necessary. I'm sure you've got plenty else to do."

"I've got time for lunch. I'm hungry. Aren't you?"

She ventured a skeptical glance at him. "You're always hungry."

"At mealtimes, yes." He grinned. "See, I'm trying."

"Trying?"

"To watch myself. That comment about hunger could have easily drawn a less innocent response."

Her lips thinned, but there was no anger in her eyes. How could there be when her gaze was filled with Donovan's boyish innocence? "But you've made your point anyway, haven't you?"

"I just want you to know that I'm trying, that I'll *continue* to try not to be offensive."

"You're not offensive."

"But I say things that upset you."

She took a deep breath, then let it out. "I'm just supersensitive, but it's my problem, not yours. You've got a job that needs to be done. I have no problems on that score."

"Then you're saying that if I keep things on a business level we'll be okay?"

"Yes. That's what I was trying to say yesterday."

He paused for an instant, regarding her thoughtfully. Then his expression took on a note of pleading that would have been humorous had she not been particularly susceptible to everything else about him. "Can't we be...friends?"

She'd barely begun to search for an answer when her phone rang and, grateful for the diversion, she excused herself softly and turned to answer it.

"Elizabeth Jerome here."

"Liz? It's Cheryl. I think we've got a problem."

Cheryl Obermeyer was the executive vice-president and chief executive officer of her own family's corporation. Encompassing a nationwide chain of discount department stores, it was presently having its share of financial worries. Liz, who'd spearheaded the chain's public-relations efforts for the past five years, was intimately aware of them.

"Uh-oh. Not something with the designer contract?" In an attempt to bolster its image, the chain had recently paid dearly for the right to carry, at a discount, the clothing of an internationally known designer. The bulk of Liz's recent efforts had gone into notifying stockholders, investors and the media of this upgrading of the store's inventory.

"No, thank heavens. This time it's Ray."

"Ray?" Ray Obermeyer was Cheryl's younger brother and a lesser vice-president of the company.

"He's threatening to leave if he's not given more responsibility, and he's making a lot of noise about it."

"Why all of a sudden?"

"He says it's not so sudden, that he's been trying to get more to do for a year. I'm sure it's coming from that bitch of a wife of his—excuse me for saying that, but my sister-in-law has always been a climber. She's probably nagging him about where he'll be in five or ten years and he's getting nervous."

Aware of Donovan standing close behind her, Liz spoke quietly into the phone. "Isn't this something for your father to handle?"

"He's tried, but he's getting nowhere and I'm worried because he doesn't need the strain. He's already had one heart attack. It's bad enough that Ray seems to bungle whatever he's given, but now that he's asking—no, demanding—more, he's really putting Dad on the spot. Me, too, for that matter. I'm the one who's supposed to be running the show."

"Ray knows that and it probably eats at him."

"But what am I supposed to do about it, Liz?" Cheryl asked imploringly. "I can't give him more responsibility if he can't handle what he's already got, and if I don't and he walks out on us, he'll take the image of the family operation right along with him."

Liz fully understood the problem. She'd been behind the image of the family operation from the start. She also empathized with Cheryl and her father, both of whom she'd grown very close to in the past years.

"Maybe it's time to start rethinking the family approach," she suggested softly, but Cheryl's resistance was immediate.

"Not yet. Not until we've tried to work all this out. There's got to be some way of calming Ray down. That's why I'm calling."

Liz waited for the other shoe to fall. She cast an apologetic glance over her shoulder at Donovan, but when he seemed engrossed in a survey of her office, she returned her attention to the phone. "Yes?"

"If you could speak to Ray—"

"Me? But it's a family matter, Cheryl."

"But you've been so close to all of us, and you're so diplomatic. I'm sure Ray would listen to you."

Liz wasn't so sure. From the start she'd sensed something brewing beneath Ray Obermeyer's relatively amiable exterior, and though she knew that he liked her, she was wary. "I could do more harm than good. If he feels that I'm sticking my nose in where it doesn't belong, it could demolish the rapport we've had."

"If he walks out, that rapport would be gone anyway," was Cheryl's pointed response.

"But I'm in no position—"

"You're familiar with the company and with all of us. And you're good, Liz. You're soft-spoken and tactful and intelligent. If you were to suggest to Ray that he'd do well to shine with what he's already got, he'd listen. He respects you. You could tell him that he'll be getting more as time goes on, but that for now the responsibility he's got is plenty. Appeal to his ego. Tell him that he's needed right where he is, that there's no one else who can fill his shoes right now."

"*You're* the one with all the arguments. Why can't *you* make them?"

"Because I'm his sister and coincidentally the CEO of this company. I could say the words and they'd sound either condescending or patronizing. From you, they'd sound like common sense."

Liz closed her eyes for a minute. When she opened them, she caught sight of movement reflected in the brass pen set on her desk. "Listen, Cheryl, can we talk more about this later?"

"I'm leaving for L.A. this afternoon. I won't be back till the beginning of next week. Please, Liz? Will you do it? You'll have the perfect opportunity to talk with him while I'm out of the picture."

"I don't know, Cheryl. It's really not my place."

"As a friend, Liz? That's how I see you and that's why I've called. Will you do me this one favor?"

This last argument was more potent than any that had come before, because Liz was a sucker for friendship and she knew it. "Dirty play, Cheryl."

"I know. But will you?"

Liz sighed. "All right. I'll give it a shot. But I can't promise results. This isn't my usual line of work."

"That's baloney. It's what you do best—dealing with people, making them see varied aspects of a picture. He'll listen to you. I know he will. I'll give you a call when I get back. Maybe we can meet for lunch. Okay?"

That sounds good," Liz said with a smile. She did enjoy Cheryl and the occasional lunches they shared. As for her brother, well, she'd simply have to try her best.

Replacing the receiver in its cradle, she turned back to Donovan. "Sorry about that. She's going out of town and I couldn't get her off the phone."

Donovan didn't seem any the worse for his wait. "Everything okay?"

"I hope so."

"A client?"

"And friend." She rolled her eyes. "There's the catch." Then she abruptly narrowed her gaze on Donovan. "See? That's what I've been trying to tell you. It's a mistake to mix business with pleasure."

"Is it a mistake to have friends?"

"Of course not. But—"

"And if those friends just happen to be people you meet through your work?"

"In theory, it's fine. But—"

"That woman—Cheryl? Do you value her friendship?"

"Of course, but—"

"And if you hadn't happened to work for her, you'd never have met her." He grinned and reached to take her coat from her. "So there's hope for us after all."

Struggling to find further words of protest, Liz turned her back and slid her arms into the sleeves that were deftly offered. But before she could turn back, Donovan's hands settled on her shoulders. His long body was suddenly close, his breath fanning the dark hair by her ear.

"Friends?" was all he said, but it was the way he said it, softly and gently, that would have been her undoing if his nearness hadn't already set her insides to quivering.

Dumbly she nodded, unable to muster a sound as he confidently took her elbow and escorted her from her office. By the time they'd reached the street and the cool October air had revived her somewhat, she'd realized that she couldn't very well turn down his offer. In the first place, it would have been rude to do so; he was a new client, a good friend of Karen's and not to be offended. In the second place, she *did* value friendship. And if that was indeed all he wanted, she stood to benefit from the arrangement. Donovan Grant was interesting and companionable. As for his ability to pierce her soul with a glance, to make her insides stir by dint of his mere presence, well, that was something she was simply going to have to learn to control.

Sliding his palm down her arm, Donovan took her hand and began to walk. "You don't mind, do you? Walking, that is? It's not far to my office and there's a super restaurant along the way."

"I don't mind walking," she said quietly. She made no effort to remove her hand from his. His touch imbued her with a sense of protection, one she'd never missed in the past but which was as pleasant a momentary indulgence as any. "It's a beautiful day. I'm used to walking."

He looked down at her, catching her gaze when it flicked toward his. "That's right. You walk to and from work. Don't you ever get worried in the dark? New York's not the safest city in the world."

"No one notices me. I'm perfectly safe."

"You're a pretty woman in a concrete jungle. I'd say you stand out." When he tipped his head to study her, she tore her gaze away and looked straight ahead. "Of course, you don't wear flashy jewelry. No diamonds or gold chains just begging to be grabbed. Why the scowl?"

"What scowl?"

"The one you're wearing. Listen, it's okay. I'm not big on jewelry myself, either."

Her scowl had nothing to do with jewelry, but she didn't care to enlighten him on that score. Rather, she lifted his hand, their fingers still entwined, and glanced curiously at what little bit of cuff peered from the end of his jacket. Her hunch confirmed, she sent him a pointed look before returning her eyes to the street.

"Okay, okay, so my cuff links are gold. But they were a present from my mother on my sixteenth birthday and I needed *something* to keep these damned cuffs together."

Liz grinned in spite of herself. "Your sixteenth birthday? We're talking history here. Your mother must have been a seer."

"More like a dreamer, at least for a time. She'd just about given up hope on me ever making anything of my life."

"But now you have, and she must be in seventh heaven."

"Not seventh. Just heaven."

Liz caught her breath at her own stupidity. "Hey, Donovan, I'm sorry."

"So am I," he said with a rueful smile. "She deserved some kind of reward after the hell I put her through when I was younger. I wish I could have done something to make it all up to her—not that she needed money. My dad did well. He still does. He's an orthopedic surgeon."

"Really? Where?"

"St. Louis."

"That's where you grew up?"

"Yup." He smoothly steered her around a threesome walking at a snail's pace ahead of them.

"Do you have brothers or sisters?"

"One of each. They're both super achievers, always were. Rather than compete with them, I decided to be different." He chuckled as he guided her around a corner. "Looks like I blew it."

"Does that bother you? I mean, it can't be a matter of competition at this point." She slipped past the door Donovan held and entered the restaurant. He was quickly by her side again.

"It's not, and, no, it doesn't bother me. We're in different fields—my sister's a doctor like Dad and my brother's in real estate. They kinda get a kick out of my showing up for family events wearing peasant pants and a dashiki.''

''You don't,'' Liz chided in response to his mischievous grin.

''Well, maybe only once in a while. Just to remind them I'm me.''

''I can't picture *anyone* not knowing you're you.''

''If that's a compliment, I thank you.'' The smile he bestowed upon her was heart-stopping, and for an instant Liz couldn't look away. ''Would you like me to check your coat?''

''My coat?'' Abruptly she looked down at the simple topcoat, then, with a blush, corralled her senses to obedience. ''Uh, no, it's okay. I'll keep it with me.''

''For protection?'' he teased.

''For warmth,'' she replied. ''I've been here before. The management spares nothing when it comes to air conditioning, even in October.''

Donovan's eyes clouded and, three-piece suit and all, he seemed suddenly uncertain. ''Would you rather go elsewhere?'' he asked quickly.

As had happened before, Liz found his unsureness endearing. It was only second nature for her to reassure him with a gentle smile. ''This is fine. And the food's great here.''

''Ah.'' Buoyant once more, he held two fingers up to the hostess and put his hand lightly to Liz's back to guide her through the crowd when they were gestured onward. He stayed close by her side as they walked to the small corner table, drew her chair out and seated her before dropping into his own chair and pulling it close to the table. Then he leaned forward with his forearms straddling his plate and simply grinned.

Discomfited by his obviously undivided attention, Liz dragged her gaze from his and scanned the room. ''They always get a good lunch crowd here.''

''You come often?''

''Not really. But the few times I have it's been packed. I'm actually surprised we were seated so quickly. Those others waiting must have needed bigger tables.''

"I paid the hostess off."

"You what? I didn't see—"

"I stopped in on my way to your office and, uh, reserved a table."

"But they don't take reservations—"

"Anyone takes reservations with the proper incentive. I didn't care to stand around in a crowd. I wanted you all to myself."

"Donovan, you promised..." But he was still grinning and she sensed that it was futile to try to argue. Besides, his grin was contagious. "You look like a Cheshire cat. Are you always this way?"

"Nope."

"Then something must be up. Tell me the police have a lead on the mad poison duster."

"If only."

"Oh. By the way, Karen agreed with everything we discussed yesterday."

"I know. Not that it would have mattered. You're the one who's handling my case, and if you and I agree on a course of action, that's all that counts."

"Still, it's nice to have the reassurance."

"I don't need it. I trust you. Do you trust me?"

She looked him in the eye. "No."

"Mmm. That's what I thought." He sighed and sat straighter, but his grin persisted. "Well, that's something I'll have to work on."

When he continued to look at her, Liz made a ceremony of studying her menu. "Do you know what you want?"

He didn't even glance at the selection printed. "Uh-huh."

She looked up sharply, sure she'd caught a hint of suggestiveness in his drawl, but when she would have glared at him in punishment, he spoke quickly.

"The croissant club."

Her hackles settled down. "So you've eaten here before, too?"

"Yup. But I'm sure you weren't here. I would have noticed."

"Donovan..." she warned.

"What are you having?"

She stared at him a minute longer, then looked down at her menu. "I thought I'd have the quiche of the day."

"Without knowing what it is?"

"I like surprises."

"What if it's got spinach in it?"

"I like spinach."

"What about capers?"

She pondered that thought. "I've never had a quiche with capers in it. It'd be interesting."

"Then you are adventurous?"

"I ate your cheeseburgers, didn't I?"

"I like your eyes. Especially when they twinkle like that...oops, there it goes. Hey, don't glare. I didn't mean any harm. I *do* like your eyes."

What Liz was thinking was that she liked Donovan's eyes, too—so clear and chocolaty—and she wished she didn't. His eyes could see so much. Certainly they could see the beautiful blonde at the next table or the stunning brunette at the table beyond that. And here she sat, with straight brown hair, nondescript features and a figure as plain as the rest of her. Donovan's attentiveness had to be a sham. Not for the first time she felt she was being played with. And Donovan seemed so sincere about it that if she didn't watch herself, she'd begin to believe that he *did* like her eyes.

Just then the waitress arrived and Donovan quietly ordered for them both. When they were alone once again, he relaxed back in his chair, though his gaze remained every bit as direct. "So, where do we start this afternoon?"

Liz, too, relaxed. "I'd like to learn as much as possible about the DIG Group. Any written material you can give me would be a help, as would talking with your ad people."

"Are you surprised that I've gone over their heads to hire you to handle this problem?"

"No. It happens all the time. Advertising and public relations may not be mutually exclusive, but they are separate fields. For one thing, my contacts are different from those of your ad department. For another, I don't approach a member of the financial press and try to buy space in his column; that would defeat our purpose and lessen the legitimacy of our case. Oh, and I'd like to meet with your sales and marketing people."

"I can arrange that. Then what?"

"Then I digest it all and come up with a specific plan of attack. It would be great if I could take a look at the media coverage you've had in the past—newspaper and magazine kind of thing."

"Sure. It's all been pretty straightforward, though. We never went looking for publicity because our products and services have sold themselves, which is one of the reasons our ad department is small. This is the first time we've had to specifically think about PR. When I first spoke with Karen on the phone the other day, she mentioned several of the other crisis cases you've handled. Do you thrive in crises?"

"Thrive? I wouldn't necessarily say that. There is an added excitement in crisis cases, as you call them, purely because of the immediacy of the situation. Do you remember the accident in one of the Driscoll hotels several years back, where fourteen people were killed when the roof of the restaurant caved in?"

When he nodded, she went on. "Immediately after the accident there was a deluge of cancellations that threatened to cripple the entire hotel chain. The Driscoll people hired us, and it was nonstop work for a month. We sent letters of reassurance to anyone and everyone involved or planning to be involved with the hotels. We hit the media—much as we'll do with you—and focused directly on the cause of the accident and the subsequent safety checks that had been made on all of the hotels in the chain. Basically, we were able to stem, then turn around the kind of mindless panic that the accident caused."

"The campaign was a success."

"Very much so. We saw results almost instantly, which was rewarding and therefore exciting. Actually, though, noncrisis cases are probably harder to handle."

"In what sense?"

"You've often got to make something out of nothing. In your case, for example, we're starting with a newsworthy event, so that when I approach the media they'll jump at the opportunity to interview you. In the case of, say, an educational-publishing house that may want to push one or another of its publications, you have to really *work* to drum up public interest. Then again there are corporate quarterly reports such as the one I was working on this morning. It's sometimes nearly impossible to come up with the slightly unusual that will catch the eye of the thousands of stock-holders who would otherwise throw the thing into the trash. We can spend weeks brainstorming in-house before we finally hit on the tack we want."

"Is Karen's organization a tight-knit one?"

"You mean, do we work together? Yes. That's the beauty of it. Some PR firms in New York have upward of two hundred employees, each assigned to a particular division, whereas there are only twenty of us at Reynolds Associates. We meet as a firm once a week, in smaller groups more often. We get to interact on different accounts and therefore get exposure to many different kinds of cases."

"And you're all women."

Liz grinned. "Each and every one of us."

"Was that a drawing card for you?"

She paused for a minute, wondering whether Donovan implied criticism in his question. As though sensing her wariness, he ventured a smile. "Hey, it's okay. The makeup of Karen's firm certainly didn't deter me. To the contrary. I respect women. They've got creative minds and they're often far more organized than men are. I was just curious about your own feelings."

The problem, Liz realized, was that she *had* been attracted to Reynolds Associates because it was an all-female firm. From the very start of her interviewing process she'd felt more comfortable there than she had at some of the other places at which she'd applied. Unfortunately, she didn't want to have to explain the reason for it to Donovan.

"Karen and I hit it off from the first. I admire her for what she's built, and I share her views on public relations. What with the client list she had even then, I couldn't have refused her offer.''

"You haven't answered my question." This time it was Donovan's eyes that twinkled.

But Liz wasn't about to answer his question. "We've had some pretty funny experiences with men, actually. There was one fellow who went from office to office looking for the 'associates.' All he could see were 'secretaries.' Then there was the time we were hired to do a publicity campaign for an underwear manufacturing company and four of us showed up in its boardroom to hear a team of men stammer and sputter about one style of jockey short or another. You see, we don't advertise the fact that there aren't any men in the firm. It's really flattering when men hire us without realizing what they've done.''

"But you do the job."

"You bet. How did *you* know we were all women?"

"I had a hunch, knowing Karen. She was a libber even way back then. I think that was one of the reasons we didn't work out as a twosome.''

"You don't believe in women's lib?"

"Oh, I believe in it. I just think it goes too far. Too many women seem to have sacrificed the softer side of themselves for the sake of professional advancement.''

"Ah. In your old age you'd kind of like to have a woman at home waiting for you, all dolled up and counting the minutes until you step through the door?'' she teased.

But Donovan was very serious. "Not at all. I wouldn't respect a woman who did nothing with her time but wait for me, and very honestly, I wouldn't want that kind of responsibility.''

"Then what would you want?"

"A woman who had a career but who realized that it wasn't the be-all and end-all of life. A woman who prized her quiet times with me as much as her hectic ones at the office. A woman who was willing to share the responsibilities of a home and family and thereby enable both of us to do more and have more than either of us could do or have alone.''

Liz felt her throat grow tight for an instant. What he suggested sounded forbidden yet marvelous. She wondered at the pang of yearning that had momentarily stolen through her iron guard and quickly strove to squelch it. ''You're an idealist, Donovan. What you say sounds fine in theory, but statistics have shown that it's the woman who usually ends up shouldering the larger share.''

''I cook. I do laundry. Okay, so I hire someone to do the cleaning. But I've lived alone long enough to know that I want more from life than a dark and empty house. Maybe I am a dreamer.'' He sighed. ''God knows I haven't been able to find a woman who fits my qualifications.'' His expression grew suddenly softer, more vulnerable, and his gaze fell to her lips. ''Would you, Elizabeth?''

''Would I what?''

''Be willing to share my dark and empty house?''

For a minute Liz could scarcely breathe because her imagination was running away with her. She could have sworn she was being kissed; Donovan's eyes silently but thoroughly savored her lips. She could have sworn he was making a proposal.

But she knew better. She knew that she couldn't begin to compare in either looks or experience with most of the women in the restaurant, certainly not with the women who had to have previously passed through Donovan's life. She knew that Donovan liked to tease, and that he knew she was susceptible to it. Moreover, she knew she wouldn't ever have what he, albeit hypothetically, dangled before her eyes.

Corralling her senses, she wrinkled up her nose and played along. "I hate dark and empty houses."

His gaze slid from her lips to her eyes and was every bit as embracing. "It wouldn't be dark and empty if we were sharing it."

"But I already have a place to live," she countered with respectable serenity.

"You could move."

"I've got a two-year lease."

"I could get you out of it."

"I don't want to get out of it."

"Then...you're not the kind of woman I'm looking for?"

She rolled her eyes and sighed, feeling in touch with reality once more. "Ah. I'm finally getting through."

His brows met for an instant. "Why did I think you might be?"

"Don't ask me. I've never understood the male mind."

"Never? Wasn't there ever a special man in your life?"

"No."

"Why not?"

"Because I've been busy building a career."

"So you *are* one of them?" A hint of teasing had returned to his voice and Liz was relieved. She was also proud of herself. She'd dealt with Donovan in a calm, sensible manner. This time, for once, she hadn't let his teasing get to her.

"I suppose you could say so," she responded, then smiled graciously as the waitress set her quiche before her.

As though a prime hurdle had been cleared, the rest of their lunchtime passed without a hitch. Donovan made easy conversation, talking of other restaurants he liked, about a show he'd seen the week before that coincidentally she'd seen, too, about skiing prospects for the upcoming winter season. Though Liz didn't ski, she smiled and nodded when he suggested he'd teach her how. Perhaps he'd been right, she mused, when he'd suggested that if she learned to take his teasing in stride she'd discover what a nice guy he was. She *did* like him. Moreover, she felt good being with him. In her eyes he was the best-looking man in the entire restaurant. He didn't glance around to take stock of the other diners. He didn't yawn or look bored when she talked. He was attentive and interested. She couldn't have asked for a more pleasant client.

When they finished lunch he walked her to his office. He didn't hold her hand this time and although one tiny part of her missed the warmth of his strong fingers, the larger part felt she'd scored a victory for detachment.

Negotiating the afternoon foot traffic with ease, he maintained a running commentary on the history of the DIG Group and its installation in the Park Avenue office toward which he guided her. After the elevator had carried them to a floor high above the city street and deposited them in an attractive reception area, he led her from office to office, introducing her to his employees.

Donovan was well liked by his staff. Liz could see it in the smiles that lit faces when he appeared, in the respect, clearly neither obligatory nor reluctant, which greeted his introduction of her. He paved the way and she was welcomed warmly. She felt mildly bereft when he deposited her with the head of his sales department and took his leave, but she was soon engrossed in discussion and busily taking notes.

From sales she was shuttled to marketing, then to advertising. Somewhere along the way a conference room was put at her disposal, and when her meetings were done she found there, as promised, a stack of printed matter for her study.

In the course of the afternoon she learned that, in addition to those endeavors she already knew about, the DIG Group had divisions that sold running and outdoor gear as well as spa equipment. As if that weren't enough to keep one Donovan Grant occupied, she learned that even beyond the consulting he did, he regularly ran management-training sessions for upper-echelon employees of companies from coast to coast.

As he'd suggested, the publicity the Group had hitherto received had been straightforward. Indeed it was positive overall, even glowing on occasion, but in no instance did it appear that Donovan had personally capitalized on the attention.

His modesty suited Liz's purposes beautifully. The fact that he'd kept a low profile in the past would be an asset when she approached the media. His would be a fresh face, a new voice. And he'd go over famously.

"You're looking very pleased with yourself," came that "new" voice, which wasn't new at all but by now hauntingly familiar to Liz.

Her eyes shot toward the doorway in which Donovan leaned, and her pulse quickened. "I didn't realize you were there."

"You seemed totally involved with whatever it is you're smiling about. I take it you like what you've read?"

"I'm impressed." She dropped her gaze to the report she was holding to buy a moment's time in which to compose herself. She desperately wished that her insides would behave, that they wouldn't start jumping each time Donovan was near. "Your organization's well run. Your reputation's well earned."

With a smile, he lazily pushed off from the doorjamb and approached her. "It'd be awful if I didn't practice what I preach."

"I think it's the other way around. You preach what you practice. I hadn't realized you were into sporting gear, as well."

"The motivation for that was selfish. I like sports." He perched on the edge of the table near her. Defensively she sat farther back in her seat.

"Do you run?" she asked.

"Several times a week."

"And I know that you ski."

"I also scuba dive when I can. And go rafting. And sky-dive."

"Ah-hah. You like to tempt the fates." She sounded more cocky than she felt. It was hard, with him so close, with those eyes of his spearing her in such a gentle, if deceptive, way.

"That I do. How about dinner?"

"Dinner?" She glanced at her watch and gasped. "Oh, Lord, I hadn't realized it was so late." She quickly stood and began to gather together the reports she'd been reading.

"It's not late. It's a perfect time for dinner."

"I have to run."

"You run, too?"

"When I'm late," she snapped. "Yes."

He seemed undaunted by her tone, his own softer than ever. "But you haven't given me an answer."

Unable to meet his gaze, she reached for her purse and thrust her notebook inside. "I thought I had. I've got to be going."

"You have plans for the evening?"

"Yes."

"A date?"

"No." She was about to lift the stack of reports when Donovan's hand caught her wrist.

"You don't have to work at night," he said soberly. "Not for me, at least."

Her gaze settled on his fingers and she swallowed. "I wasn't planning to work."

"Then what?" He raised his other hand to her arm and began to lightly, lightly stroke it from elbow to shoulder.

Liz wanted to step away, but she couldn't. As gently as he held her, she felt totally immobilized. "Don't," she whispered. Something had slipped beyond her control and she was frightened.

"What do you have to do tonight?"

She focused on his shirtfront, which didn't help her much because it looked so soft and she could all but see the warm flesh beneath.

"I've got to baby-sit."

"Baby-sit? You're moonlighting?"

"It's for a friend."

He tipped her chin up with his forefinger and she was forced to meet his gaze. "For a friend."

"Yes," she whispered. Further sound seemed beyond her. She shrank into herself but couldn't go far because Donovan's free arm was around her waist, drawing her forward almost imperceptibly.

His eyes skimmed each of her features, soothing her, ruffling her. She tried to steady her breathing, which had suddenly grown shallow and quick, and she was sure he saw the agitated rise and fall of her chest though his eyes didn't venture that low.

"And you don't have time for a quick bite on the way?" His voice was a whisper now, too, though rather than being fearful as hers had been it was tinged with hoarseness and infinitely seductive.

She shook her head, then swallowed convulsively when he dipped his head and feather-touched her cheek with his mouth. "Don't," she whispered again, but she couldn't turn her head, couldn't free herself from his grasp, couldn't run. His lips moved higher and she shut her eyes. The warmth of his body incited her, his clean male smell entranced her. She was helpless to resist the ghostlike kisses he rained slowly over her face. They were soft and beckoning, tempting her with something she'd never in her life known before.

A tiny whimper slipped from her throat and she swayed, only to find herself supported in the cradle of his thighs, with his hands splayed across her back. When he raised his head, she opened her eyes and looked up at him.

He said nothing at first, simply continued to explore her features with a slumberous gaze. While his thighs held her, he brought his hands to her shoulders, caressing them, then her collarbone. His palms slid over the silk of her blouse, making a slithering sound that reverberated through her body.

"You're very soft," he murmured.

She shook her head, but slowly this time. The heels of his hands were perilously close to her breasts, which to her dismay tingled and swelled. She felt awakened, and scared.

"I knew it would be this way."

"What way?"

"My burning, your melting."

"It's not."

"But you're trembling."

"You're frightening me."

"No. You're frightening yourself, and needlessly."

"I'm...not."

His hands continued their slow torment and she brought her own up to press them still. It didn't occur to her that she was holding him closer, but he wasn't as naive as she was.

"It's inevitable, Elizabeth," he whispered. "Why do you fight it?"

"Nothing's inevitable," she answered painfully.

"This is. We affect each other. My heart's beating as fast as yours is." As though her hand weighed no more than thistledown, he moved his own beneath it to cover her breast. She sucked in a breath and bit her lip, afraid that she'd make a sound to belie what she knew she had to say.

"I told you. You're scaring me. I don't like your kind of play."

"Is that why your breasts are fuller? You're responding to me."

"No..."

"There's nothing wrong with it, love. It's beautiful. Even when I touch you here..." His thumb grazed her nipple and a flare of electricity shot through her. The newness of it, its mind-blowing force gave her the strength to push back from him, but his thighs only tightened to keep her close. "I'd never hurt you. Is that what's got you scared?"

She was breathing heavily, her chin tucked to her chest. Even with his hands safely removed to her waist, she felt threatened. "I don't want this."

"You want to baby-sit."

She nodded.

"Then kiss me and I'll let you go."

"No."

"Aren't you curious? I haven't kissed you yet."

"Yes, you did. Before."

"Not on your lips. Not with you responding that way."

She shook her head in denial of his request, but again he forced her head up. "I'm not letting you go until you do."

"Please don't do this to me," she begged. "Play your games with someone who can handle them."

"I think you can handle them just fine. That's why I'm challenging you."

"But I don't *want* to play."

"One kiss."

She pressed her lips together.

"You're chicken."

She nodded.

"Come on, Elizabeth."

"It's *Liz*," she cried, having had just about enough of his seductive tone. "Everybody calls me *Liz*."

"I'm not everybody. I'll call you Elizabeth."

She closed her eyes and moaned, but the sound was barely half out when it was swallowed by Donovan's mouth. With a muted groan of protest, she tried to push him away, but his fingers were suddenly tangled in her hair, holding her head so that she couldn't escape his lips.

Later, Liz was to analyze that kiss, from its first unrelenting claim, through its gradual softening, to its final devastating persuasiveness. She'd remember the way his mouth had slanted over hers, firmly and possessively, then with finesse and a tempered hunger. She'd remember the way his tongue had stroked hers, challenging it, calling it from hiding, tempting it, finally mating so fully with it. She'd remember the way his teeth had nibbled on her lips, the way his breath had mingled with hers. And she'd be shocked that she'd allowed herself this cruel glimpse of paradise.

For now, though, she could only go with the flow, too weakened to fight, too inflamed to resist. When he finally set her back, her cheeks were hot and her entire body throbbed.

"There," he said with a satisfied grin, "*now* we can go."

Ignoring the "we" and the way her limbs quaked, she reached for the reports, but he lifted them first and balanced them in one arm. With the other he took her coat from the chair and held it while she put it on. When she'd thrust her pocketbook strap over her shoulder, she held her arms out for the reports.

"I'll carry them down and get you a cab."

"That won't be necessary."

"Still, I'll do it."

Determined only on escaping this room, this building, this man, Liz stormed ahead. She didn't look at him once during the wait for the elevator or the purring ride down, and she hailed her own cab, though in other circumstances she would have walked. Only after she'd somewhat ungraciously flounced into the cab did she hold out her arms for the reports. Not relinquishing them yet, Donovan bent low.

"I'm off to New Orleans tomorrow morning but I'll be back the next day. I'll call you then. Okay?"

"Fine," she gritted. "I'll pass these reports and my notes on to whomever will be taking over your case."

"You'll be handling it."

"No way."

"It's either you or no one."

She stared at him angrily. "You mean that you'd actually go to another firm if you don't get your way?"

"Yes."

"That's childish."

"See? We're alike that way, too."

Before Liz could think of a suitably cutting remark, he'd deposited the reports in her lap, closed the door and given it two taps in indication that the cabbie should move. Which he did.

"I'm sorry, Karen, but I've tried and it won't work. You're going to *have* to put someone else on Donovan Grant's case."

Karen had been waiting for Liz's visit, well prepared for agitation this time. "Donovan told me you wanted out."

"He *told* you?"

"He called me last night. We had quite a talk."

"Did he tell you that he attacked me?"

"That…wasn't exactly the word he used."

Liz felt mortification begin to mix with her annoyance, because she half suspected that Donovan had told Karen exactly what he'd done. "What did he say?" she asked more timidly. She had to know exactly how far the man would go.

Karen shrugged. "He said that he'd kissed you and that you hadn't liked it."

"That was very perceptive of him."

"He said you were frightened."

"You bet I was. Social rape isn't any more pleasant than the other kind."

"Do you know about…the other kind?"

Liz looked at her sharply, then relaxed slightly when she saw that Karen was both curious and genuinely concerned. "No. I've never been raped."

"I was wondering."

"You mean, because I seem so resistant to Donovan?"

"Actually, I was thinking about men in general," Karen went on gently. "In the six years I've known you, you haven't dated any man more than once or twice, and even then the dates have been few and far between. When I've tried to fix you up, you've refused. I…it's only natural that I'd wonder…"

"Well, you don't have to," Liz murmured grudgingly. "Men don't enthrall me. That's all. I don't see that my life is missing anything without them."

"What you don't know, you can't miss."

"That works both ways. And why should I ask for trouble?"

"There doesn't have to be trouble."

Liz eased into a chair and folded her hands in her lap. "Okay, Karen. Why haven't *you* settled down?"

"I have settled down. With this business. I don't need the burden of a husband or children. But I wasn't talking about settling down. I was talking about dating. I do plenty of that. And I enjoy it. There are some things men are good for."

The tiny tilt in Karen's lips spoke volumes. Liz eyed her skeptically. "You don't sleep around, Karen. I know you haven't been seeing anyone but David Brewer for the past six months."

Karen gave a small toss of her head, both acknowledging Liz's statement and shrugging it off at the same time. "David happens to do it very well. And he's not demanding or bothersome. He knows that if he talks marriage I'll be gone. But...I'm not the issue here. You are."

Liz sighed wearily. Karen couldn't know that she'd spent her night pacing the floor, but she certainly felt it herself. Her muscles were tense, she'd already taken three aspirin for her headache, and the abundant caffeine she'd consumed this morning had done nothing for her edginess. "I just want off this case. Karen, I've never asked anything like this before, and I know that I may be jeopardizing our relationship. Donovan was—is—a good friend of yours. And I apologize. But I just can't work with him."

"He said he wanted you."

"Or no one? Umm. That's what he told me."

"He said he'd take his case to another firm," Karen stated calmly.

"He's bluffing. He loves games, and this is game playing to the hilt."

"You sound sure that he won't do it."

"I am. The first time I met him he told me that he chose our firm because he felt it was the best. Going to the best is part of his economic philosophy. Listen, Donovan's out of town now for at least a day. If you were to reassign the case, whoever takes over will have time to talk with me, to study my notes, to read the papers and reports I got at his office yesterday. The transfer can be a fait accompli by the time Donovan returns, and once he gets a look at either Veronica or Julie or…or Brenda or Sheila, he'll forget me in an instant."

"I doubt that," Karen began, only to be interrupted when her secretary rushed in with a pained look on her face.

"I told him he'd have to wait, but he insisted." She darted nervous glances from Liz to Karen and back, and Liz's eyes widened, expecting Donovan's momentary entrance. But another man stepped into view. He was younger, tall and rather gangly, with shaggy brown hair that accentuated his pallor.

Liz was on her feet in an instant. "Jamie! What are *you* doing here?"

"I had to see you, Liz." He looked briefly at Karen, but seemed more annoyed than penitent. "We have to talk."

It had been over six months since Liz had seen Jamie, and she was taken totally off guard by his sudden appearance, particularly since he lived better than twenty-five hundred miles away. "Uh, sure. Jamie…uh, Karen, this is my kid brother. Jamie, Karen Reynolds, my boss."

If she'd put the "kid" on as a way of telling Karen that Jamie was to be excused for his behavior, it seemed to have worked, because Karen nodded and smiled warmly. Conversely, if Liz had added "my boss" as a means of conveying a message to Jamie Jerome, it fell flat. Jamie nodded once in Karen's direction, but his attention was quickly back on Liz.

"Can we go somewhere?" he asked tersely.

"Uh, sure." Clutching her hands together, she looked at Karen. "We'll finish this discussion later?" she asked softly.

Karen gave a quick nod of understanding and waved her hand, gesturing the two Jeromes out the door. Liz waited until they were in the hall and walking at a fast clip toward her office before she looked up at her brother and spoke.

"What's wrong?"

"What isn't?"

"Has something happened?"

"You could say that. Where's your office?"

"Right up ahead." Without trying to draw anything further from him, she led him past the few remaining doors to her own, then closed it quietly when he'd entered and thrown himself into the nearest chair. "Okay, Jamie," she said gently. "Nice and slow. What's brought you to New York?"

"I'm in trouble."

It was nothing new, though Liz had hoped that with maturity and the professional help he was receiving Jamie would have begun to gain greater control over his impulses. "What is it?" She might have added "this time," had it not been for the personal responsibility she felt.

"I've been going with this girl—"

"Anne?"

"No. Another one. Her name's Susan. We got into a fight and, well, I guess I hit her."

Liz closed her eyes for a pain-filled minute, then opened them and slowly stepped over Jamie's sprawled legs and made her way to the other chair. She needed to sit down. This day had been rotten from the start and was promising to get no better.

She eased herself down and took a shaky breath. "You hit her. Is that it?"

"Well, I guess I did it a couple of times."

"How badly was she hurt?"

"Not terribly."

"Did she have to go to the hospital?"

"Yes."

With a soft moan Liz let her head fall back. "Oh, Jamie," she whispered. "Why?"

"I broke her nose."

"Why did you *hit* her?"

"Because she was taunting me. She was making me feel like a jerk, and I don't have to take that from anyone."

"But to *hit* her…that doesn't accomplish anything."

He gave a grunt. "Now you tell me. She's pressing charges."

Liz bolted forward. "She went to the police?"

"Yes."

"Were you...booked?"

"I was on a plane before they could reach me. Susan, dummy that she is, called to tell me they were on their way."

Liz pressed her fingers to her temple, which had begun to throb worse than ever. She knew she had a migraine coming on. She just knew it. "Have you spoken with Dr. Branowitz?"

"No."

"When did you see him last?"

"Last Friday. I was due to see him again tomorrow."

"I think we should call him."

"What good would that do? He's only a shrink, for God's sake, not a miracle worker."

"But he'll know of a lawyer in San Francisco." She leaned toward him. "Jamie, you've got to go back. There's a good chance that you'll get away with probation, especially since you're already under a doctor's care. And you haven't got a record." Which was truly the miracle. Mercifully, the system of justice took no interest in how many different schools a person dropped out of or how many jobs he'd gained and lost.

Jamie simply shrugged. "I don't know. It was getting time to leave anyway. I've been in San Francisco for four years. I think I'd like something new."

"That's just fine, once you settle this thing with Susan."

"She doesn't have to know where I've gone."

"And the warrant that must be out for your arrest? Are you going to let that just...hang?"

He shrugged again, but said nothing.

"Jamie," Liz began, trying to be understanding and gentle even as she felt exasperated, "you've got to be realistic. You have a decent job—"

"It's lousy."

"I thought you liked this one. You're with one of the better architectural firms in San Francisco."

"And I'm at the very bottom rung of the ladder. Do you have any idea how distant that top rung looks?"

"Don't worry about the top rung. Worry about the one directly above yours. Rome wasn't built in—"

"Oh, God, spare me!"

"Then *listen* to me, Jamie. You're at the bottom rung of the ladder because you haven't given yourself time enough in any one firm to climb higher. This is the third job you've had in as many years. Okay, so this firm's bigger and more bureaucratic. It might be harder to climb to the top, but at least there should be a handful of people you can get along with."

"They're all snobs."

"They can't be. They hired you."

He'd turned to her, about to argue, when he caught her soft smile. His belligerence faded, and he gave her a begrudging grin. "Yeah. I guess they did."

"Okay. So that's one good thing going for you. Even in spite of the problems you'd had at the other firms, this one saw potential in your work. You've got to give it a chance, Jamie. And San Francisco's a terrific place to be. You've got a good apartment, and then there's Dr. Branowitz."

"For all the good he's doing. Look what happened."

"So you lost control," Liz countered, sounding less concerned than she felt. Losing control to the point of striking out physically was precisely what she'd feared most in Jamie. She didn't want history repeating itself. "But this is the first time...isn't it?" For a minute, when Jamie looked hesitant, Liz felt a sudden chill. "Well, isn't it?"

"Yes."

"Okay. So this is something you can work out with Dr. Branowitz."

"What if I do it again? I didn't mean to hit Susan. I didn't plan it beforehand. It just happened. Maybe I'm just like *him*."

"You're not," Liz snapped, then quickly slipped from her chair to kneel beside her brother. She clasped the hand that lay outspread on his knee. "You're not one bit like Dad," she vowed. "For one thing, you're sensitive and aware and you've got a future ahead of you. For another, you know what it's like to be at the wrong end of a strap and that's pretty awful. For a third, you've got Dr. Branowitz. He's been a help, hasn't he? And you're twenty-five years old. Dad was past forty when he turned on us, and by then he'd just about soured on everything.''

''Still, maybe it's in the genes.''

''That's a cop-out and you know it, Jamie.'' She stood, using his knee for leverage, then stared down at him with her jaw hard. ''I'm sorry, but I refuse to believe that you're a malicious person. You can go ahead and take the easy way out and blame everything on genes, or a poor role model, or whatever, but it's bull.''

''Bull…what?'' he teased, evidently bolstered by her pep talk. ''Come on, Lizzie. Say it.''

''You know what I mean,'' she snapped crossly.

The roles were suddenly turned and Jamie was the one to be gentle and coaxing, if with a mocking twist. ''But it's good to express yourself. Got to get it all out. If you're angry, you need an outlet.''

She glared at him, but the corners of her lips were beginning to twitch. ''Maybe you've seen *too* much of your doctor friend. Besides, I have an outlet. A headache.''

He was serious again. ''Hey, I'm sorry. I didn't mean to dump all this on you—''

''You did so. But it's okay. What are big sisters for anyway? And I had the headache before you showed up.''

''Bad day.''

''You could say that.''

''But work's going well…''

''Yes, Jamie. Work is going well. I will be able to keep sending you checks. You're paying the doctor on time, aren't you?''

''Sure.''

''And the rent? You don't need another eviction notice.''

''Naw. I'm all paid up.''

She inhaled deeply, then let her breath out slowly. ''So. It's only the…present problem we have to deal with. How did you get away from the office today? And when *did* you fly in, anyway?''

"I took the red eye last night. And I've got sick time coming. I called one of the other guys before I left and said you were sick."

"*Me?*"

"Yeah. I have to make sure you're okay. After all, you're the only sister I've got."

"How could I forget. Do you think the police will look for you at work?"

Whether or not the thought had occurred to Jamie before, he looked sufficiently disturbed. "Jeez, I hope not."

Liz reached for the phone. "What's Branowitz's number?"

Jamie yawned. "Listen, I'm really exhausted. Jet lag and all. Couldn't we call him later?"

"We'll call him now. At least he can start the ball rolling. It's still early enough there that he might be able to contact the police before they show up at your office…if they haven't already. When was it you heard from Susan?"

"When I got home from work yesterday. I might be safe."

Liz sent him a dubious look. "Branowitz's number?" She jotted it down as Jamie recited it, then promptly dialed. Had she been more familiar with psychiatrists, she would have known she'd only reach an answering service. But she wasn't familiar with them, or rather she'd never felt such urgency. Frustrated, she left her number with a message for the doctor to call back. Replacing the receiver, she eyed Jamie again.

"How long does he take?"

He shrugged. "Fifteen minutes. An hour. Six. Who knows? You made it sound like a matter of life and death, so my guess is it'll be sooner rather than later."

"It *is* a matter of life and death—well, figuratively speaking. Jamie, there's an *assault* charge against you. I mean, if you want to look at the worst of the possibilities, you could go to prison. You'd have a criminal record. And I doubt your firm would take kindly to that."

"The worst won't happen. I knew you'd be able to help. That's why I'm here."

Liz hadn't stopped to wonder why he'd come. She hadn't had to. It wasn't the first time that Jamie had run to her in moments of trial. He'd done it each time he'd dropped out of school, then again when his graduation was threatened at the last minute because of an argument he'd had with one of his professors, then again when he was given his walking papers from the first job he'd had. Though he counted on the money she sent him, she knew that he needed emotional support, as well. She also knew that she'd always be there for him.

"Well," she sighed, walking to her desk. "I guess we just wait for that call."

"I could really use some sleep."

So could I. "Put your head back and rest here. Once we've spoken to Dr. Branowitz you can go over to my place."

It was nearly an hour before the call came through, and during that time, though Liz tried to focus on the quarterly report she'd been working on the morning before, she couldn't involve herself in it. Rather, her mind was on Jamie and his problems. She thought ahead to the possibility of his being incarcerated, and her headache worsened. She knew she'd simply *die* if *she* herself was ever imprisoned. The thought of others having total control of her, of hostile forces being able to make her do whatever they chose, sent terror-filled tremors through her being. And she knew that despite the bravado Jamie showed at times, he'd be terrified, too.

Dr. Branowitz was grateful for her call and thoroughly understanding of the situation. He wondered if a warrant had actually been issued, but agreed to contact the police, as well as a skilled attorney who would represent Jamie. For her part Liz promised to have Jamie on an evening flight back to San Francisco. After giving the doctor her home phone number and extracting a promise that he'd call to report on the progress at his end later in the day, she hung up the phone and dug through her bag for the keys to her apartment. On second thought, she dropped the keys back in her bag and reached for her coat. Much as she loved him, she wasn't sure if she trusted Jamie. If he got to thinking about the things that had shaken *her* in the past hour, he was apt to disappear rather than make that flight to the coast. Far better, she decided, to stay with him until he had safely boarded his plane. She owed it to him. Besides, what was a day off from work? She doubted she'd get much done anyway, given the emotional state she was in. And the throbbing behind her eyes was sheer agony.

Liz left word with her secretary as to where she'd be, then she and Jamie walked home. Though she gently questioned him on what was new in his life, aside from Susan, conversation between them was sparse. As always, Jamie asked few questions himself. Liz had long ago decided that rather than being disinterested, he was simply expressing a kind of confidence that she was fully in command of her life. She was satisfied with that if it made him feel better.

While Jamie slept in her bed, she rested on the sofa. She'd taken more aspirin and had pressed a warm cloth to her eyes. By the time the doctor called back, she felt slightly better, and his news was encouraging. The lawyer, who had agreed to meet with Jamie early the next morning, had already been in touch with the police. It seemed that before a formal complaint could be filed, there would be a preliminary hearing to determine if there was cause for such action. The hearing was set for several days hence, and the lawyer felt confident he could help Jamie.

Liz thanked the doctor profusely, then sagged back into the sofa feeling drained. She tried to sleep, but her mind wouldn't rest. Images of the past rose to haunt her, and she knew she'd get no peace until Jamie was back in San Francisco. Selfish though it might be, she could never live in the same city as her brother. His presence was a reminder of the past and of the responsibility she felt. Oh, she'd always take care of him, send him money, bolster him when he ran to her. But she'd always be relieved when he left. And that compounded her guilt.

Giving up on the idea of sleep, she phoned the airport for Jamie's reservation, then put a beef stew on to cook. Since they hadn't had lunch, she mused, they'd have an early dinner, and there'd be plenty of time to get to the airport afterward.

She was about to wake Jamie when she heard sounds from the

shower. A bit later, clean and fresh-shaven, he joined her in the kitchen.

"You need new blades," was the first thing he said. "I used the last one and it was pretty dull."

"And good morning to you."

He was prowling around the small room, seeming unsettled despite his rest. "It's not morning."

"How about some juice?" She started toward the refrigerator, but he waved her away. "Dinner will be ready soon, then," she offered. She waited for him to ask if Dr. Branowitz had called back, but he didn't, so she broached the subject herself. When Jamie took her news with a minimum of enthusiasm, she looked at him in dismay. "I thought you'd be pleased. At least you're not on the verge of arrest."

"You committed me to flying back tonight."

"You have to. You know that."

"I was kind of thinking I'd spend the weekend here. Monday's soon enough to face what's out there."

"Monday's too late. Even Friday's bad enough. You should have been meeting with the lawyer *today*—"

"You don't want me here," he interrupted. There was a sullenness to him that Liz resented, but she'd seen it before and was sure she'd see it again.

"That's not true, Jamie. You know I love you."

"Maybe I cramp your style."

"You do no such thing."

"Maybe you've got a hot date for the weekend."

"Wrong again. I don't go in for 'hot dates.'"

"Ah, I forgot. My sister, the Madonna."

"Why are you doing this to me?" Liz asked, feeling more hurt than anything.

"Doing what?"

"Cutting me down. I don't do it to you."

"And by rights you'd be justified? Is that it?"

"I didn't say that. We're brother and sister, and it looks like we're all we've got. Don't you think it would be better to share a little respect?''

"Do you respect me?''

"Of course I do.''

"Even in spite of what you've had to put up with?''

"Even in spite of that. I know what you can do and be if you put your mind to it. All along I've been telling you that.''

"I know. It's just that sometimes I don't believe it myself.''

"Then that's another thing you'll have to work out with Dr. Branowitz.''

"Dr. Branowitz, Dr. Branowitz…it always comes down to him, doesn't it?''

"I have faith in him.''

"More than you do in me.''

With a sad sigh, Liz put her arm around her brother's waist and gave him a tight squeeze. "*I* have faith in you, but it looks like it's the good doctor who's going to have to help you build that faith in yourself.''

All told, it was a trying afternoon and evening. When Jamie finally agreed to return to San Francisco, he announced that he didn't have money for the ticket. His bank balance was next to nothing, he claimed, and Liz didn't dare ask him where his salary went. So she left him to watch the stew while she dashed to the bank before it closed. By the time she returned, he was having second thoughts again, so she launched into argument once more.

It was nearly nine-thirty before she was finally back home after taking Jamie to the airport and seeing him off. Her headache had escalated to migraine proportions, with the accompanying nausea and sensitivity to light that she'd come to recognize. Her only desire was for her dark room and bed, and utter silence.

When the phone rang shortly after ten, she moaned. Half expecting to hear Jamie on the other end of the line with a song and dance about the plane being delayed, his disembarking and wandering around the terminal, then missing the takeoff, she steeled herself.

It was Donovan.

"Donovan?" She breathed a sigh of sheer relief. "But…I thought…"

"I just wanted to say hi."

"Where…where are you?" She was having trouble getting her own bearings, and couldn't seem to lift her head from the pillow.

"In New Orleans. Uh-oh. I woke you up. Hey, I'm sorry. I didn't dream you'd be in bed at nine."

She put her hand to her head. "I think it's ten here."

There was a pause, then a soft curse. "Hell. I blew it. I was in such a rush to call that I didn't stop to think. Man, I haven't done that in ages and it was only this morning when I turned my watch back.'' He paused again, but heard no response. ''Liz, are you all right?''

The genuine worry in his voice prevented her from lying. ''I'm not feeling well, that's all.''

''What's wrong?''

''I have an awful headache.''

''Did you take something for it?''

''Aspirin. There's not much else I can do.''

''Maybe you should call a doctor.''

''For a headache? Don't be silly.''

''Do you have a temperature?''

''I don't think so.''

''Maybe you should find out.''

''I don't have a thermometer...and besides, it can't be much if it's up, and the aspirin will take care of it, too...if I could only get some sleep.''

''I can take a hint.''

''No, no, Donovan,'' she returned quickly, and in earnest. ''I didn't mean it that way.'' And she didn't. The sound of Donovan's voice was strangely reassuring, particularly after the to-do with Jamie. ''It's just that I didn't sleep well last night, and I lie here with my eyes closed and feel so tired but I *still* can't sleep.''

''Try a little warm milk.''

She groaned. ''I don't think I could get it down.''

''How about a warm bath?''

''I *know* I couldn't drink that.''

Only when Donovan chuckled did Liz realize what she'd said. In the darkness she smiled. She didn't understand why talking with him should make her feel better, but it did.

''That's better,'' he said, as though he'd seen her smile. ''I'm going to hang up now so you can rest. Can I take you to dinner tomorrow night?''

''That's a sly move.''

''What is?''

''Trying to take advantage of me when my brain is all muzzied, but it won't work.''

"You won't have dinner with me?"

"No. I'm going to a baby shower for a friend."

"How about Saturday night?"

"I can't."

"Tell me you're tending bar at your cousin's dinner party."

"I don't have a cousin and I can't mix drinks."

"Then you've got a date?"

"Mmm. With this bed. I'm planning to sleep off every bit of the aggravation you've caused me this week." Her annoyance was very much put on. She knew it because at the moment she couldn't seem to remember much of the aggravation he'd caused. He knew it because there was an unmistakable note of humor in her voice.

"Come on, Liz. We could have an early dinner and *then* you could sleep."

"No. Thanks, Donovan, but no."

"Is that firm?"

"Yes."

"No dinner?"

"No."

His exaggerated sigh traveled easily across the miles. "Shot down again. You're terrible for my ego."

"Sorry about that."

"No, you're not. If you were really sorry, you'd reconsider."

"I feel so lousy, Donovan. Please, not now?"

"Okay. Listen, love, you take care. If you don't feel right in the morning, stay home."

"Yes, Donovan."

"And call a doctor."

"Yes, Donovan."

"And when I get back I'll come over and play nurse."

"No, Donovan."

"Good night, love."

"'Night, Donovan." *And thank you for calling.*

By morning her migraine was nothing but a dull ache that responded, at last, to aspirin. She went into the office, determined to bury her worries in work, and she did just that. In addition to

making up for all she hadn't done the day before, she met Ray
Obermeyer for lunch and put in a most delicately framed plea,
then returned and made significant progress on the quarterly report
she'd been struggling over.

When one of her fellow workers, newly married and having
differences with her husband, rushed into her office in tears, she
spent a while calming her. When another dashed in, in a frenzy
because the bakery had misplaced the order for the baby-shower
cake, Liz calmly called the baker, then another that was willing
to create something on such short notice.

Somewhere along the way, she decided against giving up on
Donovan Grant.

She wasn't sure when it happened and didn't care to analyze
the why of it lest she change her mind. But she drew up preliminary drafts of letters to go to various organizations and individ-
uals associated with the DIG Group, and when Karen came in to
see her late that afternoon, Donovan's name didn't come up.

"If there's anything I can do to help with Jamie, just yell,"
Karen offered, after Liz had briefly explained the immediate problem.

"I will, and thanks, but I think things are going to be okay. I
got a call from his lawyer a little while ago—" Jamie himself
hadn't bothered to call, but the lawyer evidently knew who was
buttering his bread "—and he thinks he can get the girl to drop
her complaint. At worst, if she refuses and the case goes forward,
Jamie will get a suspended sentence. But he's already back at
work, and that's what's important."

"Right. But remember, the offer's open. I've got resources in
the Bay Area that I wouldn't hesitate to tap if it would help."

Liz smiled gratefully. "Thanks, Karen. I'll remember."

The baby shower, last-minute cake and all, was a grand success.
Liz didn't get home until late, so she slept late on Saturday morning, awakening only in time to do a cursory cleaning of the apartment, then shower and dress and meet several friends for the mat-
inee they'd had tickets for for weeks. The show was as good as
they'd hoped it would be, as was the dinner they shared afterward.

By the time Liz was back in her apartment, she felt relaxed enough to read long into the night. Hence, when her front buzzer rang early Sunday morning, she had to practically pry her eyes open and drag herself from bed.

The sight she met in her peephole brought her fully awake. So much for security precautions, with neighbors who defied them by holding the front door open for strangers. "Go away, Donovan! I'm sleeping!"

His voice was muffled through the door, though distinct nonetheless. "You had all last night to sleep. And I've got breakfast. Come on, open up. The damn coffee's spilled all over the bag and it's burning my hands!"

She pressed her forehead to the door, knowing that if she ignored him long enough he'd leave. But she couldn't ignore him. She'd *never* been able to ignore him. Straightening, she slowly released the chain, slid back the bolt and opened the door.

Without so much as a hello, Donovan dashed past her and headed for the kitchen, which wasn't hard to find since Liz's apartment consisted of a living room, a single bedroom and bath, both of which were off a short hall, and the kitchen, which lay just beyond an archway at the far end of the living room.

"God, what a mess," she heard him say as she slowly approached. Having set the bag on the counter, he was flinging the moisture from his hands into the sink. Then he began to search for a cloth.

"In the cabinet under the sink," she prompted quietly.

He opened it, tore off a lengthy strip of paper towel, mopped his hands, then wadded the towels beneath the sodden bag and went to work unloading what he'd brought.

"Bagels and cream cheese and lox," he announced, placing each package on the counter. "And orange juice." He set the half-pint cartons beside the rest. "And coffee that didn't quite make it."

"I could have made coffee. It's easy enough."

"I know," he said, only then turning to face her. "But I wasn't sure—'' his gaze fell and his voice slowed ''—if I'd...be, uh, welcome...''

Only then realizing—and with instant dismay—that she wore nothing but her nightgown, Liz turned and fled to the bedroom, returning only after she'd belted a long terry robe around her and put on slippers.

Donovan had already taken plates from the cupboard and was in the process of setting things on the table. ''You looked fine the other way.''

''It was my nightgown, for God's sake.''

''I know, I know,'' he muttered beneath his breath, then raised his voice. ''But it covered everything. You needn't have worried. Here, have a seat. Uh, on second thought, you'd better not.'' He gave her a sheepish grin. ''I couldn't figure out how to work your coffeemaker.''

She gave him a well-what-did-you-expect-since-believe-it-or-not-this-isn't-your-home-after-all look, then went by without a word and set up the coffee. She turned to find that he'd already poured her juice into a glass and spread cream cheese on a bagel half, then topped it with lox.

''What would you have done if I didn't like lox?''

''You said you were adventurous when it came to food.'' He patted the chair next to him. ''Have a seat like a good girl. I can't eat until my hostess begins.''

''Seems to me you're very much the host.'' She put one hand on the back of her chair and the other on her hip. ''What are you doing here, Donovan?''

''Having breakfast with you—at least I will be once you sit down.''

''I told you I didn't want to go out with you.''

He held up a hand. ''Unnh. We're not 'out.' And you said no to dinner. You didn't say anything against breakfast.''

''I thought it was understood,'' she said, but she sat in the chair anyway and watched Donovan take a mammoth bite of his bagel.

''Mmm.'' He closed his eyes for the time it took him to chew his mouthful slowly, then swallow. ''This...is...good. There's something about the way the foods blend—bagel and cream cheese and lox—that does it. No one of them is as good by itself, and when you've got all three, that's paradise.''

"Donovan, you're changing the subject. I wanted the weekend to myself. I need *some* break from work.''

"This isn't work. This is fun.''

"But I told you I didn't want that.''

"I thought we were friends.''

"We are, but—''

"I'm a friend taking care of you at the moment, and I'm telling you to eat.''

"I don't need taking care of.''

For the first time in the repartee, his confidence faltered and his expression grew serious. "You sounded pretty lousy the other night. Are you feeling better now?''

She stared at him for a final moment, wishing she could fight him but unable to when he grew concerned and gentle, as he was now. "Yes,'' she answered more softly, "I'm feeling better.''

"I'm glad. Eat up. I want to hear what you've been doing since I've been gone.''

She bit into the bagel, aware that he was eagerly awaiting her verdict. "You're right,'' she said at last. "This *is* good.''

He smiled and sat back to take a long drink of juice.

"Did everything go well in New Orleans?'' she asked.

"Very well. There's a company down there looking for a buyer, a so-called white knight.''

"The company's facing a hostile takeover?''

"So you *are* familiar with business antics.''

"I have to be in my line of work. Are you looking to buy?''

"Possibly. Not that the company's sure if there *is* a hostile takeover in the offing, but company stocks are being bought by some questionable groups and the directors want to be covered. The company is a major book distributor in the south. It'd be something new for us.''

"Is it a sound investment?''

"That's what I've got to find out…and fast. The management

setup isn't bad, from what I saw in New Orleans. And the scope of the business is huge. But my accountants have to go over the books before we really know much else."

"If the merger went through, it'd be another division of the DIG Group?"

"Right. A diversifying one. I think it could be a good move."

Liz bit into her bagel but her teeth failed to break through the lox, which slithered across the cream cheese and threatened to trail down her chin. In response to her muffled cry, Donovan reached over and secured the stubborn piece so that she could more easily bite it. When she'd finally swallowed what was in her mouth, she was blushing. "Thanks. That was tricky."

He licked the cream cheese on his finger and grinned. "My pleasure. But it's your turn. Tell me about your baby shower."

"There's nothing tricky about a baby shower. On the other hand, I take that back." Smiling, she told him about the cake that nearly wasn't. "In the end it was a great shower, though. Jill—the one who's having the baby—looked fantastic. She worked as Karen's secretary up until two months ago. She's due in another few weeks."

"I bet you'd like to have a baby."

"What makes you say that?"

"The way you lit up when you talked of Jill."

"I'm happy for her. That doesn't mean I want to be in her shoes." At his chiding look, she backed down. "Well, maybe a little. But she didn't have a major investment in a career, so it was an easier decision to make."

"But you admit that you'd like to have a baby—okay, that some teeny-weeny part of you would like it?"

Liz left the table to pour their coffee. She spoke softly, with her back to Donovan. Not for the first time was she stunned by the direction in which he forced her thoughts. Forever and ever, it seemed, she'd managed to avoid thinking of things like a home and family. But he brought it all back, and she grew defensive. "Of course I would. But I doubt it'll happen."

"Why not?"

"Because…I'm busy with other things."

"That's a matter of choice, isn't it? If you wanted to be less busy, you could."

"But I choose not to be. I like my work. I like my life as it is. Milk, no sugar?"

"You remembered."

"How could I forget? You made quite a thing over my adding two sugars to mine that day at lunch."

"I was only kidding."

She turned then and smiled as she set his coffee before him. "I know. I'm learning."

"I'm glad," he said with such quiet intensity that for a minute Liz couldn't think of a thing to say. Concentrating on her own coffee cup, she sat down dumbly. "What else have you done," Donovan went on quietly, "besides go to a baby shower?"

"I worked. I drew up some preliminary letters for you to see. Unfortunately they're at the office. I didn't expect to…see you sooner."

"That's okay. You were right. The weekend isn't for working. It'll be soon enough for me to see them tomorrow."

"I think we should get something out this week. Each day that passes is a day lost. I also made a few calls to some press contacts, and I've got a list of others to phone this week. As soon as the letters are out, we ought to start in with the newspapers and electronic media."

"Sounds good."

She studied him for a minute. "You're very laid-back about it all."

"Shouldn't I be?"

"Well, it *is* a crisis situation. One of your divisions—your very first—is in danger of dying a slow and costly death. I'd have thought you'd be champing at the bit to get a campaign rolling to prevent it."

He shrugged. "There's no point in doing it if it's not done right and to do it right takes sane planning. Besides," he said grinning brightly, "I've hired *you* to do the champing. I know you'll save my baby."

She smirked. "You do, do you."

"Yup. So, what else have you been up to since I went away?"

"What *else*? There are only so many hours in a day, and you were only gone for one day."

"But I didn't see you for two others. You couldn't have been working or giving baby showers all that time."

"You're right. I cleaned house. And saw some friends yesterday afternoon."

"And you slept."

"Yes."

"What brought on the headache the other night? I hope it wasn't me."

If only he hadn't sounded so truly concerned she might have had a chance. But he had, and she didn't, so quite helplessly she found herself talking of Jamie. Donovan listened, asking thoughtful questions from time to time, expressing sympathy, giving support. As she'd done with Karen, so Liz told only of the most recent crisis. She wasn't *that* taken with the man's interest that she'd go into a family history. Unfortunately, that was just what Donovan wanted.

"You haven't talked of your family at all. This is the first time you've mentioned a word. Are your parents still alive?"

She hesitated for an instant, tracing the curved handle of her coffee mug. "My father, yes. My mother died years ago."

"Is he still in Baltimore?" When she looked up sharply, he explained. "You mentioned the first time we met that you were from Baltimore."

"I forgot. Yes, he's still in Baltimore."

"What does he do?"

"Sells insurance."

"Baltimore's not that far. It must be nice to be able to see him often."

"I don't. We're not very close."

"How come?"

"Oh," she waffled, and scrunched up her nose, "you know how it can be. We have different ideas about lots of things."

"You're right; I do know how that can be. But still, often the differences fade as we get older."

"They haven't," she responded quietly.

"How about Jamie? Barring emergencies like the one this week, do you see him much?"

"He's far away. It's pretty expensive…flying across the country."

"You can afford it."

"Well," she sighed, unable to refute his claim, "it's still hard. I do call him once a week."

"But you three must get together for holidays."

"Actually, no."

"Then what *do* you do…for Thanksgiving and Christmas and all?"

She looked up then and forced a smile. "I'm usually with friends. Why does this feel like an inquisition?"

"I'm just curious. It's strange." He did look puzzled, and that took the edge off his comments. "I'd have pictured you surrounded by family as well as friends. You're so giving and easy to talk to."

"Coming from you that's a compliment, since you've certainly seen my acid side."

"Nah. Never acid. Maybe nervous or defensive. But you're getting over it. You're more comfortable with me now than you were. I can tell."

"Oh?"

"Sure. Just look at you. You're fresh from bed, sitting here in your nightgown and robe having Sunday-morning breakfast with me."

"I'm only doing this so you'll see reason," she retorted defiantly. "I'm perfectly ugly in the morning. My hair's a mess and my skin is as sallow—"

"Are you kidding? Whoever told you that?"

"I've got eyes. I see me this way every morning."

Donovan's voice grew very quiet. "You're not looking through *my* eyes, and I see something very different."

"Donovan, don't—"

"I see a warm and gentle woman, who looks that much softer and more desirable coming straight from bed."

Liz jumped from her chair, but he caught her wrist and, tipping her off balance, brought her down on his lap.

"You don't believe me, do you?" he asked.

"Not for a minute. Now let me up." She was holding her body rigid, but Donovan seemed unperturbed.

"Not until I show you how you affect me first thing in the morning."

She tried to rise, but his arm tightened about her waist. When he put his lips to her neck, she began to squirm.

"Hold still," he commanded, his breath warm against her skin. "You smell so good."

"It's...it's the fabric softener—" she pushed against his arms, but to no avail "—that I put in...the wash...Donovan, let go!"

He didn't bother to answer, but began to lightly kiss the underside of her jaw. She closed her eyes and tried to rein in her senses, but the war she was waging was hopeless because she could smell the clean, lemon-tinged scent of his hair, could feel the liquid heat of his mouth, could fully appreciate the strength of the body that imprisoned her so effortlessly. He was male from head to toe, and, God help her, he made her feel female.

A final moan of protest slipped from her throat and then he was kissing her, warming her from the inside out, showing her the unbelievable pleasure to be gotten from the meeting and meshing of lips and teeth and tongues. Before she knew it she was clutching his shoulders, bunching the wool of his sweater in her fists as though she were drowning and needed a lifeline.

He kissed her again and again, taking but the briefest of breaths between forays. She couldn't pull away because he suddenly seemed her sustenance, more so even than air or light or the blood that pumped so rapidly through her veins.

Her lips were against his hair then, and she was cupping his head while his mouth moved lower, lower. His hands, which had been stroking her from shoulder to hip, moved frontward, gently raising her breasts without quite touching them, until his face was buried between their gentle swells.

Sustenance or sustainer...for a minute she wondered whether she was the receiver or the giver. Donovan seemed to be feeding off her nearness, as though she offered him something he couldn't live without. She knew it wasn't so, but for the moment she was willing to believe that she was different and special and, yes, desirable. He muddled her mind, but she loved it. It was fantasy-playing at its most glorious.

His fingers skimmed her breasts en route to the tiny buttons at her throat, then he was releasing them one by one, covering each inch of revealed flesh with his mouth. He'd just about reached her breasts when she realized what was happening.

"No..." she whispered, but he was spreading the vee of her robe farther apart to reach those buttons it had hidden. "Don't...oh, no..." Torn apart inside, she begged, "No...please, no..." She was whimpering and close to tears as utter terror filled her. It was only the latter that gave her the strength to dig her fingers into his neck and tug him away. When he looked up in surprise, she clutched the lapels of the robe close together.

"I...I don't understand," he began hoarsely.

"You can't do that," she whispered with her head tucked low.

He took a ragged breath. "But...you were...it felt..."

She was shaking her head, trying to free herself of the thoughts that tormented her, but she couldn't.

"Elizabeth?"

In response she moved awkwardly to her own chair. Fleeing the room would have been too much to ask of her trembling legs, so she simply sat with her knuckles white at the neck of her robe, her head bent.

Donovan raised a hand and stroked her hair once, lightly, then sat back in his chair and closed his eyes for a minute. When he'd opened them, he was in control.

"Why don't you get dressed," he suggested quietly, gently.

"We can take a ride up to my place and go for a walk in the woods."

Liz didn't answer for a while, and when she did it was still without raising her eyes. "I don't think...I should."

"Why not? That was the main thing I had in mind when I came over here so early."

His place. She finally looked up, but timidly. "That's right. It's your hideway. Why aren't you there now?"

"Because I'm here."

She frowned. "How *did* you get here?"

He gave her a gentle smile. "I drove."

"No, I mean, how did you know where I live?"

"The same way I was able to call you the other night. The phone book. 'E. Jerome.' The initial is a sure sign of a woman, and since there were no other E. Jeromes, only Edwards and Edgars and Eugenes and Evans—"

"Where does Innis come from?"

"Innis?"

"Your middle name. I thought it was so clever to call your group the DIG Group, since you started out growing foods and all, until I realized that those were your initials. I read the Innis part on your biographical sketch."

"It's my mother's maiden name. She hated to see it die, particularly since her only brother has four daughters."

Liz nodded, then, uncomfortable, looked away again.

"How about it?" he asked softly. "I've got to come back to the city tonight, anyway. We could take a ride up and just relax. It's a beautiful day. There might not be too many more like it."

"I know. But I...I'm not sure..."

"I wouldn't try anything Liz. I swear it. I just want to spend some time with you. Totally innocent. Brother and sister, if you'd like." Inwardly he cringed at his own offer, but he knew he'd settle for that if it was all she could give him at the moment. She charmed him with her innocence, her lack of demand. He simply needed to be with her.

It wasn't so much what he'd said as the undercurrent of urgency in his voice that swayed Liz. She remembered when he'd been kissing her, when she'd felt, albeit dreamily, that he needed her desperately. The urgency she'd sensed then was similar in its way to that she heard now. And she couldn't resist. Perhaps it was what she needed in life—to be needed. She thrived on having friends come to her with problems, thrived on doing favors for other people. And Donovan was her...friend, wasn't he?

"Brother and sister?" she echoed, eyeing him shyly.

"Brother and sister. I promise."

She stood slowly, dropping her hands to fidget nervously with her belt. "I really shouldn't be doing this."

Donovan stood, physically turned her and gave her a light shove. "Get dressed. I'll clean this stuff up. If we don't leave soon we'll miss the best part of the day."

They arrived at the house shortly before noon. As Donovan had said, it was a beautiful day, all the more beautiful with the woodlands at their autumnal best.

"You miss this in the city," Liz mused, standing by the side of the car and taking the scenery in. "I think the color's at its height. It's lovely."

Her smile of delight was what Donovan found most lovely, but he didn't say it. Though he didn't understand why, she didn't take to his compliments. And he had promised...

"Why don't you wander out back. I'll open up the house and then we'll go exploring."

She nodded and headed around the house, walking on a mat of pine needles, occasionally overstepping gnarled fingers of tree roots that had found their way to the earth's surface. The sound of gurgling water lured her on, and she soon found herself by a brook that wound through Donovan's property and into the woods. It was charming and peaceful. She felt decidedly cheerful.

Kneeling, she ran a finger through the clear water, then tipped her head back and basked in the sun's warmth.

It was in that position that Donovan found her moments later. "Nice?"

"Mmm. Wonderful. Such a marvelous retreat."

"The brook doesn't freeze till dead of winter, and then it's beautiful in a different way." He sank to the ground on a cushion of moss several feet from her. "Early some mornings you can see deer here."

"I thought I saw a chipmunk as I was walking back."

"You probably did. They're all over the place. And rabbits, and woodchucks, even a fox once in a while."

"A fox?"

"Oh, the fox is harmless enough. He runs in the opposite direction well before you do." He was trying not to smile. "No, it's the skunks you have to worry about. Lazy buggers, skunks are. You walk out in your own backyard to admire the moon, and a pudgy black-and-white thing waddles across your path. You don't know whether to freeze or run, and the damned animal continues to saunter, just as cocky as you please, while you're racking your brain trying to remember what it is that will get out the stench if you're sprayed."

"Have you ever been?" she asked, wide-eyed.

"Once."

"What *does* get the smell out?"

"A quick trip to the nearest dump with your clothes...or a bonfire in the backyard. And cologne, gobs of it, for days."

She laughed at his drawling tone and readily let him draw her to her feet and toward a path that led into the woods. The growth on either side was lush and had the poignant fragrance of autumn. The crackle of twigs underfoot blended with the sounds of the breeze and the scurry of wildlife that eluded Liz's untrained eye. Donovan's eye wasn't as untrained. In a voice as soft and airy as a whisper of the leaves overhead, he pointed out various animal habitats and identified the calls of the migrating birds.

In time they came to an open meadow whose swaying grasses were gilded by the sun. Shrugging out of their sweaters in deference to the warmth of the early-afternoon air, they walked to an old tree stump and sat, side by side, enjoying the serenity in silence. At length Donovan broke it with an indrawn breath, as though he'd been millions of miles away and had suddenly returned.

"When I was a kid, my parents used to take us off to fancy resorts in the mountains. At first I thought it was boring; I wanted to be *doing* things. By the time I was fifteen I was arguing that it was a grand waste of money to pay so much for a luxury resort, when we could just walk into the nearest park if we wanted fresh air." He chuckled. "I think I was missing the point."

"Which was?"

"To get us all together. To break the routine of our everyday lives. To remind us that we were a family and that, even in the woods, miles from civilization, we had each other. I wish I'd understood it sooner."

"Maybe you did."

"What do you mean?"

"Maybe that's what you were rebelling against, the idea that you were dependent on others. You were trying to form an identity of your own, and the reminder that you were irrevocably part of a larger group, in this case your family, was hard for you to accept."

"Well, I wish I had accepted it. I missed out on a lot of warmth because I was too stubborn to try to see things as my parents did."

"Most kids are that way."

"Were you?"

"I suppose. Then again, my situation was different."

"How so?"

"With my mother dead and all, we didn't have much of a family life."

"Didn't your dad do things with you?"

"Not often. He was busy with work, doubly busy, he said, since he couldn't travel because of us."

"How old were you?"

"When my mother died? I was ten. Jamie was six."

Donovan winced. "It must have been tough for *all* of you."

"It was. But she'd been sick for a long time. Her death was a blessing."

"Awful to think of death as a blessing." He looked off into the distance. "It's what frightens me most sometimes, because there's still so much I haven't done."

"But you're so successful."

"Professionally, yes. Personally, well, that's up for grabs." He seemed about to say more, then changed his mind. "How did your father manage after your mother died?"

"Not well."

"What do you mean?"

"He'd always been something of a cynic. Her death made things worse."

"Who took care of Jamie and you?"

"Oh, we had a housekeeper. We'd always had help because my mother wasn't able to do much, but in the later years of her illness Dad got harder to live with, so there was a pretty fair turnover."

"Not great when two kids need stability and love."

She lowered her voice and looked down. "No."

"Did you *ever* do things as a family? You mentioned once that you traveled."

"Oh, yes. My father had certain priorities, one of which was traveling. Actually, it was a matter of taking us with him on business trips when they coincided with school vacations."

"Not much fun, then?"

"Not much. Well, maybe I shouldn't say that. We did our share of sightseeing."

Donovan's voice was tight. "With a paid guide, while your father worked?"

She looked at him in surprise, then quickly recovered. "It wasn't bad. Actually, some of the guides were more fun than Dad would have been. They were certainly knowledgeable."

"But they weren't your father. That must have hurt."

"Lots of things hurt. You just learn to concentrate on those things that don't."

They'd come full circle. "And that's where you differ from your father."

"It's...one of the ways. He also happens to be a chauvinist. He can't understand the work I do, other than to feel that I'm taking a job away from a man who needs it to support his family."

Donovan was grinning. "What do you say to that?"

"Not a thing. I can't change the way he thinks. It'd be a waste of my time and effort to try, and there are too many things I'd rather be doing."

"Does *he* seek out any contact with you?"

"No."

"He must be a lonely man."

"I wouldn't know," Liz stated simply.

Donovan couldn't help but think it was odd that she was so open and willing to discuss others' feelings and motivations, yet totally turned off to her own father.

"Is there other family—aunts and uncles and cousins?"

"Nothing on Dad's side—well, he did have a sister but he never saw her. There were some relatives on my mother's side, but we lost contact with them soon after she died." She shot him a sad glance. "Loving family I've got, isn't it?"

But he was feeling a sadness of his own. "I could have had all you didn't, and I threw it away. It's pathetic, when you stop to think of it."

"Not pathetic. And you didn't throw it away. You simply...deferred it."

"Yeah. But I lost a whole lot in the process."

"You'll gain it back, and it'll be that much more meaningful for the value you put on it now."

"Some things you can't gain back. My mother's gone. My father's getting older. My sister and brother have their own families and lives. And David...well, those early years are gone."

Liz put her hand on Donovan's arm and shook it gently. "Where's that old optimism, Donovan? It's not like you to bemoan the fates."

"I know," he said, his eyes meeting hers. "But you bring some things out, make me think about others. You're good to talk to. You listen and respond. I know I've said as much before, but I mean it. You seem to be everyone's confidante. Who's yours?''

She laughed, but there was a melancholy sound to it. "I'm the lady of steel. I don't need a confidante. And anyway, I think I've told you more today…'' Her voice trailed off and she looked away, realizing how much she *had* said, perplexed that she should have told Donovan so much about herself. It was frightening to think of how easy it had been, to envision becoming dependent on his ear, only to have it withdrawn.

"You're cold. You've got goose bumps." He reached for her sweater. "Better put this on."

She did, and frightened of pushing her, Donovan began to talk of other things. They left their tree stump and walked farther before finally retracing their route to the house. By the time he'd built a fire—she argued that it was too early in the season, but he insisted that a fire in the hearth was good for the soul—she felt relaxed and surprisingly happy.

True to his word, Donovan was perfectly brotherly, though so much more thoughtful than Jamie had ever been that Liz had to redefine the term. Jamie leaned on her. Jamie took from her. Jamie used her. And she let him. It was the least she could do to make up for all she hadn't been able to do when they'd been younger.

She and Donovan made dinner together and ate before the fire, talking all the while of inconsequential things that somehow seemed less inconsequential what with the insights the other lent them. Liz was stunned that she and Donovan shared so many views. And while they also had their differences, they were able to discuss and accept them.

All too soon, the day ended. While Donovan drove back to the city, Liz sat contented in the passenger's seat, dozing at the last. She was groggy when he walked her to her apartment, and she only half heard herself ask him in for coffee before she dozed off again on the sofa.

When she awoke the brother was gone, replaced by the man who'd been tethered all day.

Liz opened her eyes to find herself cradled in Donovan's arms. His head was buried against her neck, where his lips moved lightly, moistly. She sighed softly and indulged herself the momentary luxury, pretending she was dreaming and that this was her dashing knight, the man set upon the earth for no other reason than to protect her, to care for her, to give her what she'd never dared wish for.

Her lashes lowered as she dreamed, and her fingers combed through the hair at his nape. It was thick and soft and yielded vibrantly, beckoning her touch.

She felt Donovan shift slightly and tipped her head to ease his access, only to have her chin brought back by his gentle hand when his lips sought hers. What had been totally new once was now familiar and irresistible. She responded to the lead of his mouth, opening her own and welcoming him with a verve that was instinctive. She didn't have to clutch his shoulders this time because the drowning sensation she'd known that morning seemed now more exciting than overwhelming. Instead her hands found their way to his back, moving slowly, charting by inches the sturdy cording of muscles they found.

A tiny part of her tried to temper the fantasy, but failed. With each tilt of his lips, with each sweep of his tongue she was more deeply enveloped in it and in the glorious sense of awakening that it spawned. Her body thrummed with pleasure. Warm bursts of delight spread through her.

Drugged by his sensual assault, she made no protest when he shifted her to lie on the cushions, freeing his hands to span her waist, then her ribs. But she wanted more; her breasts swelled in anticipation. A small purr of satisfaction slipped from her throat when he gently covered them and began to move his palms in devastatingly light circles over their fullness.

Even had his mouth not continued to monopolize hers, she couldn't have uttered a word, for she was momentarily beyond rational thought, totally swept away in a world of sensation. She arched her back, strained closer to those heavenly hands, and was rewarded when he increased the pressure.

She was gasping when he released her lips and slid his mouth across her cheek to her ear, but she could hear his own ragged breathing and it perfectly justified her state. She became so wrapped up with what he was doing to her ear that she didn't notice he'd slipped his hand under her shirt and sweater until she felt an encompassing warmth on her breasts, distinctly different from the simple nylon of her bra. Her flesh felt seared, yet it ached for more, and her body conveyed the message quite eloquently.

The tiny part of her that had tried to break through did so again, but she fought its warning. For so many long years she hadn't known what she'd been missing, but she knew it now, and it felt right. The quivering tendrils that shot to the pit of her stomach when his fingers homed in on her budded nipples had her arching her hips. Everything in her body responded so naturally to Donovan that surely it was meant to be, she reasoned from amid her dream.

Then he was kissing her again, sliding his body over hers, abandoning her breasts to shape her hip, the inside of her thigh, the warm apex that had never been so shaped, so caressed. Donovan's deep groan sparked another warning in the back of her mind, but she had to know what came next, where the anticipation that coiled in her belly would lead.

Somehow he was between her thighs then, rubbing against her, undulating his hips in a way that taunted rather than eased. But when he raised his body to allow his fingers a hasty release of the snap of her jeans, the sound reverberated in her brain and her bubble popped.

"Oh, God!" She gulped and grabbed his wrists to halt the work of his hands. "No, Donovan...oh, my God...stop!"

His breath was rough and panting as he held himself over her and stared down incredulously.

Her eyes were wide and pleading. "Please," she whispered, and swallowed convulsively, "please...I can't..."

"Sure, you can," he murmured, lowering his head to kiss her, but she turned her face aside and squeezed her eyes shut. Her body, so hot and pliant moments before, was suddenly rigid. He raised his head and stared at her, dropped his gaze to study the stiff way she lay, then slowly pushed himself up until he sat an arm's length away. "All right, Liz," he said with remarkable calm, "you're going to tell me why. You're going to tell me why a woman in this day and age can't make love with a man who turns her on."

Drawing her knees sideways, Liz rolled up, then huddled into the opposite corner of the sofa. Her arms were crossed over her waist, covering the condemning snap of her jeans. She stared at the floor, wincing when Donovan spoke with greater force.

"Tell me, Elizabeth. You owe me an explanation. It's not right to lead a man on. Didn't anyone ever teach you that?"

Mutely, she shook her head. She didn't see Donovan thrust an agitated hand through his hair, but she heard his growl of frustration and felt worse.

"Why did you ask me to stop?"

"Because...I don't want to...make love."

"Sure as hell could've fooled me, what with the way you were responding." When she grimaced and tightened her arms around herself, he modulated his tone. "Okay. We agree that it's not a matter of physical revulsion. And you've said that there isn't another man in your life. Was there one in the past who hurt you? A minute ago I saw terror in your eyes. That had to be it. You've been abused."

She quickly shook her head, unable to speak, much less look at him. He was too close to the truth, but it wasn't the way he thought and she just couldn't go into it.

"*Was* there someone?" Again she shook her head. "Never?" She shook her head a third time. Donovan seemed to hold his breath, then let it out slowly. His voice was quiet. "You're a virgin." When she didn't respond but squeezed her eyes shut, he coaxed her more gently. "Elizabeth? Tell me. Please. I have to know. Is it something about me? Or you? Or the situation?"

"It's me," she whispered at last.

"You are a virgin."

Very slowly, she nodded.

He was closing the distance between them then, taking her in his arms, holding her tenderly. "God, Liz. I wish I'd realized it sooner. It's just that I didn't expect...I mean, you're nearly thirty...I just assumed..." He pressed her head to his chest and stroked her hair until he felt her first sign of relaxation. "Do you know how wonderful that is, what a gift? Do you have any idea how good it makes me feel to know that I'll be the first?"

Any momentary relaxation he'd felt in her vanished, and she levered herself away. "You won't be," she stated sharply. With the dissolution of her passion-induced dream, she saw the light. Donovan's words had helped. She was a virgin, to him little more than a new and rather pathetic challenge. And he was the master game player.

"That doesn't make sense."

"To me it does."

"You're a passionate woman, Liz."

"What does *that* have to do with anything?" Her eyes sparked with anger, and Donovan stared, disbelieving.

"I don't understnd," he finally managed. "We go well together both intellectually and physically—"

"No, we don't. *You* go well with just about anybody. Not me."

"What's that supposed to mean?"

Returning his gaze, she found her anger dissipating. In its stead was a soul-rending sadness. "It means that I'm not good for you. You can have any woman you want. You can take your pick of the most beautiful of the beautiful, the most brilliant of the brilliant. You don't need me. I'm just a...a plaything."

"Like hell you are," he growled, but Liz was jumping from the sofa and pacing across the room.

"You can do better, Donovan," she said with her back to him. "You can do much better than me."

"Is that what you think? Man, you're crazy! Do you have any idea how long I've looked for the right woman?"

"And you haven't been able to find her, so you're temporarily amusing yourself with me."

"Damn it, that's *not* what I meant. You're jumping to conclusions, and every one of them is wrong. I'm not 'amusing' myself with you. And there's nothing temporary about what I want."

She gave a bitter laugh. "Which would make hell that much hotter for me."

Donovan was off the sofa then and turning her around. Though his hand was insistent, his gaze was beseechful. "You don't believe that I'm serious, when I say I am. Why is it you find it so hard to believe that I want you?"

She spared him a pained glance before looking away. "I believe that you want me. I'm not that dumb that I don't know when a man's aroused."

"Forget sex. I'm talking in the broader sense."

"I can't forget sex. It…tinges everything else."

"It doesn't have to," he countered softly, "not that I see it as being a problem. We'd be great together, Liz. I've held you and kissed you. I've felt you respond. You body is perfect for mine. If you'd let me, I'd show you. We could go into your bedroom and undress and—"

"No!" she cried in fright, pressing her hands to her ears so that she wouldn't have to hear more. When she saw that he'd stopped speaking and was staring at her in amazement, she lowered her hands and pleaded. "Look at me, Donovan. I'm nothing. I'm plain and unattractive and—"

"You've hinted at that before, but you're wrong. There's nothing plain and unattractive about you. You're a beautiful woman from the inside out."

"Now that," she stated baldly, "is an outright lie."

"I don't lie, Liz. You just refuse to see what I'm saying." He put his hands on her shoulders to hold her when she looked about to bolt again. "Okay, so you're not Miss America. I'm not Mr. America, for that matter. But there are things inside you—warmth and sensitivity and generosity—that make you shine."

"My hair is yuk brown. My eyes are sunken. My nose sits in the middle of my face like a bump on a log. My lips are bottom-heavy. And my body...God, I wouldn't know *where* to begin on that."

"I would know, because I've felt it beneath mine. It curves where it should and pulses when it should and it turns me on in a way no other body has ever done." He shook her shoulders lightly. "Beauty isn't skin-deep, Liz. It comes from within. At least true beauty does. And that's what I see in you."

Liz sighed and dropped her chin. "I don't need flattering, Donovan. I'm a realist." She paused. "I think you'd better leave now. It's been a nice day, but I'm really exhausted, and I have to be in the office early tomorrow."

"You'd just forget this whole thing as if it never happened?"

She tipped up her chin and held it firm. "I already have."

He eyed her intently for a minute, then dropped his hands from her shoulders and stepped back. "Okay. I've got a little pride left. Have it your way for now. If it's work you want, work you'll get. I'll stop in tomorrow afternoon to look over the letters."

"I have an appointment at one. You'll have to make it after two-thirty."

"I'll see you at three then." One corner of his mouth curved into a wry half smile. "Sweet dreams, Liz."

She simply stared at him until he turned and left. Then she crumpled onto the sofa and cried.

By three o'clock the following afternoon Liz was all business. She had separate letters drawn up, one for stockholders and in-vestors, one for employees, one for distributors, each with its own appropriate slant. Donovan read then carefully, made several mi-nor suggestions, then approved them. He ran through the list of media outlets she'd prepared and asked questions about one or two, but could find no fault with her overall plan.

If he was more somber than usual, Liz told herself to be grateful. She'd let things go too far, and it was her own fault. She should never have agreed to spend Sunday with him...nor let him get so close to her that she'd lost control. She didn't know why she'd done it. She'd never harbored illusions of loving and being loved by a man before, yet Donovan did strange, strange things to her.

On one level she missed the twinkle in his eye, the verbal sparring that had almost always had sexual overtones, his teasing. On another, a more rational level, she knew that this way was better. It was more businesslike. It was more conducive to productivity. It was how things should be with a client, and that was all Donovan Grant could ever be.

The week passed quickly. Liz completed the quarterly report she'd been working on. She made headway with arrangements for publicity for the *Women's Journal*. She spoke with Cheryl Obermeyer and learned that Ray had indeed calmed down and seemed content, for the moment, to stick with his current responsibilities.

The DIG Group letters went out, and Donovan's media blitz took shape. Liz met on five different occasions with various media representatives. She spent time on the phone with others. By the end of the week she was able to present Donovan with a list of a dozen appearances and interviews she'd set up for the next two weeks, with additional ones in different parts of the country still to be confirmed and scheduled.

For his part, Donovan was thoroughly accessible. When she called, he came. When she spoke, he listened. She prepped him on ways to most effectively handle the press, posing questions interviewers might ask, then helping him to analyze and strengthen his answers.

At each of their meetings, and there were three that week, his behavior was without fault. He was the perfect gentleman, the quick-minded and attentive businessman. She couldn't even begrudge him showing up one day in a sweater and jeans, because her hungry eye savored it and she indulged herself the passing fancy. Indeed, his outward manner was justification that she'd been right in what she'd said and done. He'd obviously and, without great effort, given up on her as a playmate. His attraction to her wasn't that strong after all.

Of course she knew nothing about the meeting he had with her boss.

"I need your help, Karen," he said soon after he'd entered her office. It was shortly after his third session with Liz. "Something's odd, and for the life of me, I can't figure it out."

"That's not like you, Donovan. You're not often…perplexed."

"I'm dead serious, so you can wipe that grin off your face, friend. I've got a problem, and it's all your fault."

"Mine?"

"You were the one who introduced me to Elizabeth Jerome."

Teasing suddenly forgotten, Karen frowned. "What's wrong? You're not displeased with what she's doing, are you?"

"Of course not. She's wonderful. Insightful, efficient and a hard worker."

"Then…"

"It's her. Personally. I can't seem to get through to her."

Now that she knew the problem had nothing to do with work, Karen eased back and smiled. "That's *really* not like you. I never thought you'd have trouble on that score."

"*No* score. And it doesn't make sense. We get along perfectly when it comes to work, and even when it comes to doing simple things for fun. I brought her up to my place last Sunday and we had a terrific time."

"But you can't get her into bed," Karen prompted dryly.

"It's not that that's all I want, but there does seem to be a major stumbling block in that area."

"I don't know, Donovan. You must be losing your touch with age."

"I am *not* losing my touch, and stop laughing at me, Karen. You seem to think this is pretty funny, but I don't."

"It's okay," she cooed, her eyes still dancing, "I'm told it's a common problem. Maybe part of a midlife crisis—okay, okay, I'll be serious. You are, aren't you?"

"Serious? Very. I'm taken with Liz. But then, you knew I would be. That's why you threw us together."

"I didn't 'throw' you together. I simply assigned her to your case."

"Well, she's on it, and now I'm on hers. How well do you know her, Karen?"

"As well as anybody, I guess, which isn't saying all that much. She's a private person when it comes to her inner thoughts and feelings."

"She says that there haven't been any men in her life."

"Believe it. I've tried before, but nothing's worked."

"Any ideas why not?"

"She claims not to be interested. She says she's perfectly happy with her life as it is now and doesn't need anything else. I could almost believe her. She loves her work and she's got loads of friends. People take to her because—"

"She's such a great listener. I know. She's a born counselor. Her instincts about people's emotions are solid, and she has all the patience in the world when it comes to hand holding." His voice dropped. "But she doesn't have relationships with men."

"Not sexual ones."

"Then she does have male *friends*?"

"I'm not sure about even that. She gets along well with male clients, but whether any of them have become friends or whether she has any other long-standing male friends, I just don't know." Karen looked at him, hesitated, then spoke. "I do know that you threaten her somehow. After she met you the first time, she asked me to take her off the case."

"She really did?"

"Mmm. But she couldn't give me a reason, at least not one I thought to be legitimate. She did a lot of beating around the bush, but I think she was really scared."

"But why...and of me, of all people?"

"Come on, Donovan," Karen drawled. "You know the answer to that as well as me. You affect her in ways that no one else ever has."

"That's no cause for her to be terrified, yet she is. I see it in her eyes sometimes. Sheer terror."

"I asked her once..." Karen began, only to bite her lip.

"You asked her what?"

"I really shouldn't betray her confidence this way."

"Karen, I'm on my way to falling in *love* with the woman. I'm asking you to help me understand her. Something's got to be hanging her up so she can't let herself go. And I'm not talking only of sex."

Hearing the desperation in his voice, Karen resolved her dilemma in his favor. "I asked her if she'd been raped."

He hadn't had the guts to ask it as bluntly himself. "And?"

"She said no."

"Do you think she was telling the truth? Women often feel guilt after something like that. They come to believe that they somehow invited it."

"No," Karen mused thoughtfully, "I think she was being honest. But I agree with you. Something *is* hanging her up."

"Any theories?"

Karen shrugged with her brows. "I could speculate...but I'm not sure it'd be fair to her."

"It'd be only fair to *me*. Go on. Speculate. I'm listening."

"There's got to be something in her background that's deeply affected her. Do you know anything about her brother?"

"Jamie? She told me about him last week."

"He's been a worry to her for years. She feels responsible for him. He's constantly getting into trouble, and I have to ask myself why. When you see a kid like that who can't seem to settle down, there's usually a reason."

Donovan pondered that for a minute. "I know she didn't have a happy home life when she was growing up. Her father sounds like a bastard."

"You know more than I do then. She's never said much of anything about the man to me, other than a passing reference here or there."

"She didn't say all that much to me, either, and it wasn't that she was blatantly critical. She seemed almost...detached when she spoke of him, like he's part of her past that she can factually accept but that she'd just as soon never tangle with again. I can't believe she's sexually hung up on him. Maybe angry deep down inside at the way he let Jamie and her down. But sexually hung up? Nah.''

"Did she say anything about her parents' personal relationship?''

"No. Her mother died early on and was sick for a long time before that. I doubt there was much of a sexual thing there, if you're thinking that maybe Liz was traumatized by something she'd seen. As for Jamie's problems, they could well have been from lack of interest on the father's part.''

Karen made a face. "We sound like a pair of amateur psychiatrists. I don't know, Donovan. I just don't know. But listen,'' she leaned forward, "don't give up on Liz. I think she's a fantastic girl.''

"You don't have to tell *me* that. And believe me, I have no *intention* of giving up on her, not while there's still a chance.''

"I believe you,'' she said with a smile. "That's the Donovan I *do* know.''

The following week the media campaign Liz had engineered for Donovan began. She was present during most of the interviews, some of which were held at his office, others at restaurants over breakfast or lunch, still others at television or radio studios.

The week after that they made day trips to hit the media in Boston, Philadelphia and Washington, and by the end of that second week, Liz was confident that the campaign would be a success. Wherever he went, Donovan was received well. He was personable, articulate and effective. He handled even sticky questions with ease and managed to charm the most wary of interviewers. Though it would be a while longer before they knew whether the public was buying their case, Liz was personally pleased with the articles that appeared in print. She studied videotapes over and over again with the same satisfaction that was expressed by other members of her firm and Donovan's.

During the two-week period Liz found herself enjoying Donovan again. He made no mention of what had happened the night at her apartment. Nor did he try anything further, other than to issue an occasional invitation to dinner that she refused in the same teasing tone in which it was offered. But she always felt an inkling of excitement waking up on a morning when she knew she'd be seeing him, and he never failed to make her laugh at least once on those days. If there was method to his madness in giving her space, she was unaware of it. She only knew that she enjoyed talking business with him—which they did regularly— and that on practically any other subject he was good for conversation.

Then it came time for him to travel, to meet the press in Chicago and Detroit and Dallas and the West. When he launched his own campaign to entice her along, she politely but firmly refused, insisting that he'd been fully trained, that he handled himself like a pro, that she simply couldn't be spared that long from the office. In fact, she was fearful of what might happen given a hotel room in a distant place. She wanted no opportunity for mischief. She didn't think she could cope with that. It was going to be difficult enough for her when her job was done and she no longer saw him from day to day. A small part of her had grown dependent on his friendship, and she wasn't sure how, without the convenience of working together, they'd be able to maintain it.

As it happened, while he was on the road he called her at least once a day in the office and then again at her apartment at night. He seemed to need to know she was there, to discuss his day with her, to hear about what she'd done herself. And again they lapsed into the sexual bantering she'd thought they'd left behind. She told herself that it was the distance between them that inspired it, told herself that Donovan needed this warm touch, told herself that it was really harmless. But she spent more and more time thinking about it, thinking about *him*, thinking about what she felt and what she believed, and fearing that, eventually, there would be trouble.

It began the following week, on the very day that Donovan

returned from Seattle, the last stop on his tour. She'd just arrived in the office when her phone rang.

"I'm back!"

Her heart flip-flopped and she broke into a smile. "So you are. How did it go?"

"Not bad. Would have been better if you'd been along."

"Flattery will get you nowhere. Did you make it to all the interviews?" There had been some question, even as late as the morning before, as to whether several of those scheduled would pan out.

"All except the one at the cable station. But the others went well. And I'm glad to be back. Listen, I'm going home to get some sleep. How about dinner tonight?"

"I can't, Donovan. I'm meeting with another client."

"Oh. How about breakfast tomorrow then?"

"Why don't you just come by here in the morning? I have a nine-o'clock appointment, but I should be free by ten."

"We could have breakfast at eight. Come on, Liz. I want to see you."

"Ten o'clock?"

There was a long pause before he answered. "Right. See you then."

But the following morning he called her at seven to say that he had to make an emergency trip to New Orleans that day.

"It looks really good for the merger, but there are a couple of things I've still got to iron out. I should be back by tomorrow night. Meet me then?"

"I can't, Donovan. I'll be with a client all afternoon and it's sure to run through dinner."

"Damn it, Liz. There's always something."

"I...I can't help it. I told you at the start that my hours were sporadic."

"Yeah, but every time I want to see you you've got something else planned. You're avoiding me, aren't you?"

"We could meet here in the office the morning after you get back."

"How about at the Park Lane for breakfast?"

"Nine-thirty...here?"

"See? You won't do it. Hell, there's nothing I can do in a public restaurant, Liz."

She clicked her tongue. "You're in a temper this morning."

"Damn right, I am. I wanted to be seeing you, not running to New Orleans. Come on, Liz. Make my day. Promise to meet me for breakfast Friday morning. You meet your other clients for meals. Well, I need to consult with you, too, and I'm a busy man. What with the circles you've had me running in for the past few weeks, I've gotten zilch done at the office. It'd save both of us time if we could kill two birds with one stone. Breakfast?"

Feeling unbelievably helpless, Liz nodded. "What time?"

His tone picked up instantly, the words coming faster. "Eight-thirty. Hey, thanks, Liz. I'll look forward to it. See you then."

"Donovan? Have a good trip."

"Thanks, love. So long."

Donovan was looking bright and chipper when Liz arrived at the Park Lane dining room on Friday morning. They were seated at a round table by the window overlooking Central Park, and their coffee was poured in an instant.

"It's good to see you, Liz."

It was good to see him, too—just how much she tried to ignore. "How did it go in New Orleans?"

"Great. We're on our way."

"Then the deal will go through."

"Looks that way. How've *you* been?"

"Fine. I've got a terrific bunch of articles from the interviews you did on the road," she offered enthusiastically. "Any word yet on the latest sales figures?"

"Not yet. I'm hoping to get a look at them today."

They ordered breakfast, and Liz looked up to find him staring at her. "Don't look at me that way, Donovan."

"What way?"

"*That* way."

"I enjoy looking at you. I feel like I'm finally home."

She rolled her eyes. "Must be all the flying you've been doing. You're still in the clouds."

He grinned. "You bet. Hey, what's the word on Jamie? Is everything okay?"

"For the time being, yes. The girl decided to drop her complaint. Not that she didn't have a case. But Jamie's lawyer was able to convince her that it would cost *both* of them if they were to end up in court. Jamie's agreed to stay away from her, and he knows that if he dares lift a finger again he'll be in real trouble."

"Will the scare work?"

"God, I hope so," Liz said with a sigh. "The lawyer told me he was fully apologetic when he saw Susan."

"Did he sound it to you?"

"Jamie? I don't know. I haven't spoken with him since he left here." She realized how odd that sounded and rushed on. "I didn't want to push things. I'm sure he feels ashamed, and it must be worse when he has to face me."

"But he ran to you when it first happened?"

"He didn't know what to do. He's always run to me like that. I'll talk to him next week, when things have died down."

"Next week's Thanksgiving. Have you made plans?"

She brightened. "I'm going for dinner on Long Island with some friends from the office. One of them has family there and we were all invited. How about you?"

"If you'd been free, I would have stayed here. But since you're deserting me, I guess I'll have to put in an appearance in St. Louis."

Teasing him right back, she eyed him boldly. "Don't give me that 'since you're deserting me' line. I know as well as anyone that you've had to have reservations for months to get on a plane going anywhere for Thanksgiving. It's the busiest time of year at airports."

"Well, I did make reservations early, but I could wangle another if you'd come with me. How about it? You'd like my family."

"I'm sure I would, but I can't go. I told you. I've already got plans."

"With friends. This is something else."

"Oh...?" Liz was steeling herself for a protest when another thought intruded. "Do you see David for the holidays?"

Donovan, too, seemed distracted by the question. "Uh, no. He stays with Ginny and Ron. They mean so much to him. I couldn't ask him to leave."

"Does he know your family?"

"I've taken him to St. Louis a couple of times. It was nice. Well, maybe a little awkward. I mean, the two of us are finally comfortable with one another, but introducing my whole family into the picture is a little overwhelming." He thought for a minute, then shrugged. "Maybe I'm selfish and want him all to myself. Then again, maybe I'm afraid my family will say I'm doing something wrong. I guess I'm not too sure of myself in the role of a father."

"The fact that you recognize it probably makes you a that much better one," she reasoned gently. "It's the parents who take their children for granted who present the real problem. Being born is something none of us asks for."

Donovan studied her intently, then chose his words with care. "Do you think your father regretted having children?"

It took her a long time to answer, and when she did it was a simple, "I don't know." Then she turned the conversation back to him. "Will you be seeing David at all?"

"He's coming east to spend time with me for Christmas. I'm looking forward to it."

"That should be nice."

"I'd like you to meet him."

"You don't need *me* complicating the picture," she said, alluding to his earlier comment.

"You're different. I'd like it. I'll even bring him to the office," he teased in a drawl, "if that'll make you feel better."

Strangely, Liz did want to meet David. "That might be okay."

Their breakfast arrived then, and they set to work eating. It was only as they prepared to leave that Donovan reached into his pocket and withdrew a small box. "Here. This is for you."

Liz stared at the box, then Donovan, then the box again. She was about to protest when he took the wind from her sails.

"It's a pair of earrings I bought in San Francisco. I remembered your saying that you loved buyings things for people, so I decided to give it a try. You were right. I had a ball shopping. Go on. Open the box. I want to know what you think."

For a minute Liz couldn't speak because her throat was tight. She couldn't remember the last time someone had bought her something just for the fun of it. Hands trembling slightly, she slid the ribbon from the box and lifted its lid. Inside, nestled in a bed of cotton, was a pair of solid-gold hoops. They were small but wide, actually three bands joined together, and positively beautiful in their simplicity.

"They're stunning," she breathed.

His face glowed. "You like them?"

"Oh, yes. But you shouldn't have…and…there's one problem."

"They're for pierced ears. I know. That was what I debated about for the longest time. But your lobes are tiny and just right for piercing, and if you decide not to do it I can have them converted." Actually, what he'd spent the longest time thinking about were the *other* earrings be'd buy her in time. He wanted her to have pearl ones and onyx, and of course, diamonds. Nothing elaborate in design, because that wasn't her style, but simple, and classy, and…only from him.

Gazing at the earrings, Liz knew Donovan was right. Her lobe was small, a perfect size for the hoops to curve snugly around. They would be nothing more than a fine gold extension, in no way showy or burdensome.

"I've never thought of having my ears pierced."

"There's nothing to it. I've got a doctor friend who'd do it in a minute."

"I don't know, Donovan." She spoke very softly, her gaze focused on the earrings. "They're so beautiful…"

He took her hand then and squeezed it. "Think about it for a while. I'll take you if you want to have your ears pierced. If not, I'll have a jeweler put on a conventional back."

She still didn't look up. "I'm...I'm stunned. You didn't have to buy me anything."

"I know. That's what made it so much fun. Will you...think about it?" One part of him had been worried that she'd refuse to accept his gift, and he was jubilant that she hadn't.

"Yes." She looked up then, her eyes suspiciously moist. "Thank you. I can't remember when I've ever received anything quite as lovely."

He simply smiled at her, and his own throat was tight. He cleared it after a minute and, putting the lid back on the box, reached down and thrust it into her bag. Then, taking her hand, he led her from the dining room. Neither of them spoke during the short ride to her office, and Donovan continued on in the cab to his own. He was pleased with the breakfast that had just been and sensed that to push Liz to see him the next day, or the day after that, would only be to jeopardize what he felt was building. It was a matter of strategy in a game that meant the world to him. He had to give her time without pressure, time to adapt to their relationship, to realize that it was more than simply a business one. He had to give her time to understand that she could love him, if she wanted, and that he'd never hurt her.

Liz didn't hear from Donovan that weekend. She spent time thinking about the Sunday they'd spent at his house north of Troy, spent time thinking about the closeness she felt toward him, spent time looking at the earrings he'd given her and knowing that she'd cherish them for life.

He dropped by the office on Monday to give her the good news. Preliminary figures showed that the health-food sales, which two weeks before had been in a serious slump, were beginning to pick up. Whether it was Donovan's television appeal or the full-page ads she'd had placed in prominent newspapers that had done it, they weren't sure, but things were looking up, and they were both ecstatic.

On Tuesday there was more good news. An anonymous tip had led federal authorities to a man suspected of poison-dusting Donovan's fields. He was being booked for the two murders. It turned out that Donovan did know the culprit—or had known him once. He was a fellow revolutionary, a psychedelic tripper, an aging hippie who had lashed out at what he perceived to be Donovan's defection to big-time establishment. Though Donovan was deeply dismayed at the thought that people had died because of him, he was nonetheless relieved that the mystery had been solved.

"Today is worth marking," he announced on the phone. "I'll pick you up at the office tonight and we can—"

"I can't, Donovan," Liz broke in before he got carried away. Of the thinking she'd done since the Friday before, a good deal had centered on the ramifications of her accepting his gift. At the time she'd been taken off guard, too pleased to question his motives. Though she still wasn't sure what those were, she knew that, though she'd cherish the earrings always, she had to keep her relationship with him in perspective. "I'm taking the train to Philadelphia for a meeting this afternoon. I'll be back tonight but I don't know when."

"That's okay. You can give me a call before you leave Phillie and I'll meet the train—"

"It'll be late and I'll be exhausted."

He breathed an undisguised sigh of frustration. "And I'm leaving for St. Louis at noontime tomorrow, with a million appointments crammed into the morning. I won't see you before Thanksgiving."

"No," she acknowledged quietly, then waited out a long pause until at last Donovan spoke again.

"I'm sorry about that. I was really hoping…ah, hell, I sometimes wonder…" He seemed to be rolling his dice the wrong way.

There was another pause. This time Liz bit her lip. She didn't want to know what he was hoping, what he sometimes wondered. She sensed she wouldn't like what she learned.

"Okay, Liz. Well, have a nice Thanksgiving."

"You, too, Donovan," she said softly.

"Sure. Talk with you later."

When he hung up the phone, Liz slowly did the same. She knew she'd hurt him, knew that he was annoyed with her, but she couldn't help it. He was going to have to accept the lines she'd drawn. She had her own life, one she'd put together and built through sheer grit. The disappointment she felt right now would be nothing, she knew, compared with the anguish she'd suffer later if she let Donovan have his way.

Yet there was guilt. Always guilt. She liked Donovan so much, and it hurt her to hurt him. She thought about him during the train ride to Philadelphia and back, then long into the night, and was still thinking about him when she was at her desk, supposedly working, on Wednesday morning.

That afternoon she had her ears pierced.

"Elizabeth?"

"Donovan! Perfect timing. I just walked in." She was taking her coat off even as she talked, and she was grinning broadly.

"Happy Thanksgiving."

"Same to you."

"Did you have a nice dinner?"

"It was great. There were eighteen of us, including Sheila's parents and family. They're wonderful people. How about you? Good dinner?"

"My sister cooked…or tried. The turkey was dry, the peas were all wrinkled and the lemon soufflé collapsed."

"Poor baby."

"I have to admit it was fun, though. It's nice seeing everyone."

"The nieces and nephews are all well?" Liz knew that though Donovan's sister hadn't married, his brother had. He and his wife had five young children.

"Oh, yeah. Noisy as hell, but terrific. I wish you were here, though. It would be icing on the cake."

"On the sunken soufflé, you mean," she teased.

"No, that's not what I mean. I was thinking of the magnificent pecan pie that *I* brought to the feast. Funny thing about pecan pies. They're not as elaborate to look at as some fancy desserts, but, man, do they ever taste good."

Liz was too high-spirited to give thought to any message there might have been in his words. "They're very fattening. You'd better watch it, Donovan. Wouldn't want to put on weight."

"I ran five miles this morning. You sound happy."

"I am."

"Tell me one of the eighteen people at your friend's house was a gorgeous guy who bowled you over."

"Not quite."

"Then a homely guy who bowled you over."

She grinned. "Nope. I just feel good. That's all." She wasn't about to say that her spirits had soared with his call, much less admit it to herself.

"Then I'm glad. What are your plans for tomorrow?"

"I'll be working."

"Come on, Liz. Everyone takes the day after Thanksgiving off."

"Which is why I'm going in. Half of the office is out of town, and we've got to have some kind of skeletal staff there to cover."

"So you volunteered. I bet it'll be dead as anything."

"Probably, in which case I'll be able to catch up on my own work."

"You're a glutton for punishment."

"Not punishment. It'll be fun. Very relaxed. And quiet. I like days like those."

"You would," he muttered, but she knew his grudging tone was put on, for it vanished with his next breath. "I'll let you go, then. I'm glad you had a nice day."

"Same here. Thanks for calling, Donovan."

"My pleasure."

He called her the office the following afternoon, just to give her something to do, he explained, then again at home that night, when she was in her nightgown getting ready for bed.

"I'm flying back tomorrow," he began quickly.

"Oh? Is something wrong?"

"Yeah. I want to see you."

"Donovan—"

"A date. Tomorrow night."

"But we—"

"Have a business relationship? We've *had* that. But you've done what I hired you to do, so now it's time to move on. Or haven't you thought about that?"

"I've thought about it," she said softly.

"Good. Because from here on in, we're something else." He'd decided, among other things, that it was time to shift tactics. Her game had been to stall, and as game master, he wanted to move on.

"We're friends."

"That, too. But I want more."

Liz closed her eyes. She'd known it was coming. Donovan just didn't give up. She'd sensed he was biding his time, and she could hear from the impatience in his tone that the biding had taken its toll.

"There's no point," she whispered.

"This connection stinks. I can't hear you."

"I said," she raised her voice, "that there's no point. I've already told you that I don't play your way."

"I'm not talking play. I'm dead serious."

"So am I. If we can't be friends and leave it at that, I guess we'll have to go our separate ways."

"Is that what you want—to go separate ways?"

"No, it's not what I want," she cried. "I want to be friends. But I can't give you anything more."

There was a momentary silence from the other end of the line, then a more gentle, "What're you afraid of, Liz? I won't hurt you. I've told you that before. I've tried to prove it to you by taking things slow. I haven't pushed you lately, have I?"

"No. But you're pushing me now."

"That's because I've been sitting here for two full days thinking of nothing but how much nicer it would be if you were here, if we were together. I want you, Liz. Don't you know that?"

"You don't want me. Not really. You've just built something up in your mind, a challenge you're convinced you've got to meet. But I'm not a challenge. I don't have anything to offer—"

"Christ, we're going in circles. Look, I guess it was a mistake trying to talk this out over the phone. If I was there with you, I'd *show* you what you have to offer. I'm flying in tomorrow and I'll be at your place by seven."

"I won't be here."

"Where *will* you be?"

"That's none of your business." When she heard him grunt she relented. "I'm going to a party." It was a cocktail party at Cheryl Obermeyer's home. Actually she'd been on the fence about going, but it seemed the perfect out now.

"When will you be back?"

"Late. Please, Donovan, leave well enough alone."

"What we've got *isn't* well enough.

"For me it is. Good night, Donovan."

"Damn it, Liz. I want—"

She hung up on him before he could say what he wanted. She knew what it was, and she wouldn't—she just couldn't—give it to him.

And so Saturday night found her at the cocktail party she'd rather have skipped. It wasn't that she disliked parties. She enjoyed being with friends and the Obermeyers always welcomed her with open arms. Unfortunately, though, their parties were gathering places for one beautiful couple after another. By contrast, Liz felt conspicuously single and distinctly outclassed.

"I want to talk to you," Cheryl drawled leading her away from the group on whose fringes she'd been standing for what had seemed hours. "You look subdued."

"I'm not. Actually, I'm feeling rather good."

"That's because you've had...how many drinks?"

"Just two."

"Which is more than you usually have. And since the first goes right to your head, you probably *are* tipsy, which makes your somber expression that much more mystifying. Something's bothering you."

"Nah. Everything's fine." She lifted her glass to her lips and would have taken a healthy swallow of whatever it was the bartender had handed her. But Cheryl removed the glass from her fingers and set it on a passing tray.

"Talk to me, Liz. You've helped me out when I've needed you.

Now it's my turn. And don't tell me nothing's wrong. I know you too well. Your mind has been on anything but this party tonight."

"I'm sorry, Cheryl. I didn't mean—"

"I'm not offended. Just worried. Friends have a right to be that way once in a while, y'know?"

"I know. And I appreciate it, really I do, but—"

"Who is he?"

"He?"

"Whatever man it is you're thinking about. That's the only conclusion I can come to. I'm only annoyed that you didn't bring him here."

"Uh...it's not like that."

"What is it like?"

Later Liz would blame her loose tongue on liquor. But for the moment she was beyond anything but sharing her woes with Cheryl, who was so very willing to listen and give advice. "He's a client. His name's Donovan Grant."

Cheryl gave a low whistle. "Donovan Grant. The DIG Group. Didn't I see him on television recently?"

"That was part of the work I did for him. We're trying to counter the adverse effect on sales—"

"Of health foods. I know the case. All the time I was reading about it, I kept wondering what *we'd* do if our customers suddenly developed a rash from a lethal something that was used in the manufacture of our clothes. They've caught the guy who did it, though, thank God. Donovan Grant. Now there's a super catch. Gorgeous, and from what I've read, he mans four very profitable divisions—"

"Six, actually. And he's about to take over the Ullman conglomerate in New Orleans."

Cheryl's eyes widened, then darted from Liz and narrowed on her brother, who had sidled up sometime during the conversation. "We're having a private discussion, Raymond. You can talk with Liz later." Tightening her grip on Liz's elbow, she inched her farther away from the other guests. "Donovan Grant is one very shrewd businessman. And available. So he's the one who's got you in a dither?''

Liz nodded, her expression pained.

"Have you two been dating?''

"Not...really. Well, maybe you could call it dating, but he wants more and I'm not sure I do, and it bothers me. I don't want to hurt him. He's really a wonderful guy.''

"Why ever wouldn't you want to date him?''

Given her light head, Liz had to struggle all the more to express herself. "He's too good and too successful and too handsome. He's everything I'm not. We're poorly matched.''

"I wouldn't think so, and neither must he, if he's the one who's doing the chasing.''

"That's just it. It's a game. He's big with things like that. But I'm not. I take life more seriously.''

"Maybe you shouldn't. I mean, maybe you should let him chase you and see where it leads.''

"I'll only be hurt in the process. What do I need it for, Cheryl? I've got a good life, a good career.''

"So do I, but I'd give my right arm for a good man. Don't you ever sit back and picture yourself ten or twenty years down the road? I do and I'm not sure I like what I see. I'll have poured blood and sweat into the business, and to what end?''

"You'll be well respected and wealthy.''

"Sure, I'll be wealthy, but if I've got no one to share it with, what good is it? Okay, maybe wealth isn't your thing. What will *you* have?''

Liz forced a grin. "This is getting too serious for me. I can't think straight.''

"You're just avoiding the issue.''

"No, really...''

"Okay, I'll let you off the hook for now. But think about it later. Think about what I've said. If you decide then that you still don't want Donovan Grant,'' she said grinning slyly, "give him my number.'' With that, Cheryl eased Liz back into the mainstream of the party.

It was, ironically, those last words and their accompanying grin that stuck most in Liz's mind. Though she'd never have imagined herself capable of it, she felt distinct jealousy when she pictured Cheryl with Donovan. That jealousy shocked and disappointed her so much that when Donovan showed up unannounced at her front door on Sunday, she was spoiling for a fight.

"Back to your old tricks?" she said, standing aside to let him in. She was dressed this time in slacks and a sweater, and hadn't even bothered to tell him to go away.

Donovan shrugged. "There's always someone going in or out of this building. If the downstairs door's wide open, what can I do?"

"You could have buzzed up anyway."

"And you would have told me to get lost."

"Not this time. This time we've got to talk."

But he was staring at her, then a slow smile spread over his face. His voice was suddenly as gentle as his expression. "You had yours ears pierced."

Liz found herself melting. It happened whenever he looked at her that way. Almost shyly, she fingered one earlobe. "I...I decided the earrings were too beautiful to sit in a drawer."

"When did you do it?"

"Wednesday."

"You should have waited for me. I would have taken you."

"I would have been embarrassed. I'm not terribly good when it comes to pain."

He was touching her ear ever so lightly, his fingers brushing, lingering against hers. "Tell me they had to strap you down."

"No. But I practically passed out."

"You didn't."

"I did. The nurse made me stay at the office for a whole hour afterward before she'd let me go."

"It doesn't hurt now, does it?"

She shook her head, unable to speak with Donovan so close, so dear, his body so vibrantly stirring her own.

"They look great," he murmured, pushing aside her hair and touching the upper curve of her ear with his lips.

She wanted to tell him not to do it, but the words wouldn't come because his breath was warm, sending shivers of heat through her, and his hands whispered over her back, and she felt good, so good, and cherished. So she told herself she'd enjoy this last bit of heaven before she put it behind her.

She didn't object when he murmured soft words of encouragement against her cheek or when his hands left her back to skim her thighs, her ribs, her breasts, or even when he framed her face and tipped it up. His lips opened, dusting her eyes, her nose, her chin, and she was waiting when they finally teased her own with the same airy ghost of a kiss. Needing firmer contact, she tried to catch him, but his mouth eluded hers and continued its tantalizing butterfly play.

"Donovan," she moaned, clutching his wrists, "you're torturing me."

He hummed a smile against her cheek, then ended the torment and seized her lips with a force that stole what little breath she had. His mouth slanted and sucked. He thrust his tongue deeply and she willingly received it. She was ravaged and devoured, but felt more whole than ever before.

When at last he tore his lips from hers, his body was a mass of coiled sexuality. "This is what I've needed, what I've missed," he growled, holding her face and looking into her eyes. "Tell me it's not the same for you."

If only he hadn't spoken...thank God he'd spoken! Liz blinked once before she registered his words and the look of intent on his face. She opened her mouth to speak but her throat was knotted. He wanted to make love to her. Unmistakably. Urgently. She began to shake, but not in passion.

He gripped her shoulders as she tried to ease back. "Oh, no. Don't back out on me now, Liz!"

"I have to," she whispered.

"Damn it, you don't!"

"I never promised you this, Donovan. All along I've been telling you I didn't want it."

"Your body tells me differently. And so does mine, damn it!" But he saw the fear in her eyes, and it quickly dulled his physical drive. He held up both hands and stepped back. "Okay. You said you wanted to talk. Let's talk." Turning, he walked to the sofa and settled into it with his arm along its back and one knee crossed over the other. Though his pose was casual, his expression was anything but.

Liz stood clutching her hands in front of her for a minute, then slowly walked to the window. She stood staring out with her back to him and began to speak quietly.

"I've led a very different life from you, Donovan. I never rebelled. I never sowed any wild oats. And I never wanted to. What I wanted was a secure life, a life where I was the one in control. I wanted freedom, but a freedom to do what *I* wanted, *when* I wanted it, even if that all fell along very conventional lines." She took a deep breath. "I've never included a man in that vision."

"That's what I don't understand," Donovan stated. "If you're as conventional as all that, there's got to be a husband and kids somewhere in the picture. Isn't that the meaning of security?"

She turned slowly and rested back against the sill. "It's one meaning. For some women. But not for me. I define security as self-determination. I *choose* to lead the life I do, and I'm happy that way."

"But you're not a hermit. You do have friends. Friends who depend on you, who ask things of you. You help one by babysitting when she and her husband need time alone. You help another out by talking with her brother when he starts to act up. It's not a question of being selfish."

"I never said it was. But I'm free. I can pick and choose what I want to do. I can pick and choose the context in which I want to do it. If something is too uncomfortable or threatening, I don't have to do it."

"And the thought of a relationship with me makes you uncomfortable. It threatens you."

"Yes."

"But *why*? That's what I don't understand."

"You wouldn't. You've always been on top of the heap." When he opened his mouth to object, she rushed on. "Anything you've done, you've done well. Even when you were a revolutionary, as you call it, you were respected and admired. I never had that, Donovan. Growing up, I was an outcast. I was shy and withdrawn. I didn't have friends to speak of, because I couldn't begin to compete with the other kids. Oh, yes, I could be a follower. I could tag along with the group until they got tired of me and left me by the wayside. But I didn't want that. It hurt too much. So I stayed by myself until I got through college and into graduate school. It was only then that I met more accepting people."

"Hell, you talk as if you've got leprosy or something," he sneered, looking away.

"Not leprosy. But I can't run in the fast lane. I can't keep up. I'm still shy. Okay, I've learned to handle myself professionally; and socially to an extent. But that's because I *do* pick and choose those professional and social situations."

There was a long silence while Donovan gnawed on his lip. He looked up with an abruptness that momentarily shook Liz. "So what's this got to do with me? With us?"

"Don't you see? I can't keep up with you. You're suave and sophisticated. You're good-looking and personable. You can handle yourself in any and every situation that crosses your path. *I* could never have faced those interviewers or those television cameras. It's one thing to understand what's needed for things like that, and I do, which is why I could talk with you beforehand and prepare you. But to be on the firing line myself...I'd wither."

"Not everyone can be on the firing line. And I may have looked like Mr. Cool during those interviews, but my stomach did its share of jumping."

"Still, you *thrive* on new adventures, new challenges. I don't. I want things gentle and manageable."

"You constantly face challenges in your work."

"But it's all within a context I know I can handle. Do you remember when we were talking last Thursday and I said I was looking forward to working on Friday? Well, I was. The office, for me, is a haven. It's something I know, something I can manage. Sure, problems crop up all the time. But there are guidelines to follow, and there are other people, people I can trust, to give me advice."

"I'm sure you give *them* advice as often. Damn it, Liz, why do you keep putting yourself down? You've convinced yourself that you're this little wilting daisy, and it just isn't so."

"Isn't it? I'm nothing to look at. You can do better in a minute."

He groaned and rolled his head to the side. "Here we go again." Then he met her gaze squarely. "I've never had any problem with your looks, Liz. You're the only one who's hung up on it."

"I'm a realist," she returned crossly. "I know what my limits are."

"But what about stretching them? What about growing?" His eyes widened for a fleeting instant. "I mean, maybe I'm missing something here. You do like me, don't you?"

"Yes. I like you. You've been a more agreeable client than some—"

"Forget client. Think person. Better still, think man. Do you like me?"

"As a person, yes."

"And as a man?"

"I...I don't want to think of you that way."

"Because you *do* like me that way and it scares you."

"That's not the point," she countered, eyes flashing. "If I chose not to look at you in sexual terms, it's my right!"

"But you're fighting it," he said more softly. "You *do* see me in sexual terms, and you're fighting it. I want to know why."

"I don't want sex."

"Why?"

"Because...I don't."

"I thought you wanted to talk, Liz, but you're not doing it. You happen to be the most thoughtful, understanding person I know. Why can't you turn that strength toward yourself and express your feelings to me?"

Liz knew they'd reached an impasse and she grew more frustrated than ever. "Because they're *my* feelings and I choose not to express them!"

Donovan stared at her thoughtfully, absently rubbing his upper lip. She held her breath, wondering where he'd go from here. Of all the directions she imagined him taking, she wasn't prepared for the one he did.

"I've given this lots of thought, Liz. Lots of thought. You're open to a relationship, but only to the point of sex. You back off then, and with pure terror. You say that you're a virgin, that there haven't been any men in your life, but you're terrified, and there's got to be cause. It's my guess that your father abused you."

For a minute Liz couldn't answer, but only for a minute. "He did not! He never once raised a hand against me!"

"There are many different kinds of abuse, some of which don't involve physical force."

"You're way out of line, Donovan!" she cried. "And it's because you're too bullheaded to believe that I don't want you in my life. I've been saying it from the first, but you've refused to listen. Because it's all a game to you! All a game!"

"Hold on now," he gritted, rising from his seat and approaching her. "I'm not bullheaded, and if you assume that a game implies I'm just toying with you, you're wrong. I'm dead serious about my interest in you." Liz was backed to the window and he was within arm's reach. "Is that what's got you worried? That I'll love you and leave you?"

She scrunched up her face and squeezed her eyes shut. "I don't *want* you to love me! You're not listening! I don't want any *part* of you!"

"No?" He reached for her, but she twisted to the side and ran to the door, swinging it open with a flourish.

"Get out, Donovan." Her voice shook, though her entire body was stiff. "I don't need you, and I don't want you."

He was beside her in an instant, slamming the door shut again with one hand. "I don't believe you. I think you're just scared. You're nearly thirty years old, Liz. Isn't it about time you grew up?"

"Get out," she repeated, this time through gritted teeth. When he didn't budge, she was livid. "So help me, I'll call the police."

"You wouldn't do that. You like me too much."

"I *don't* like you!" she yelled. "You're an arrogant bastard who thinks he knows everything. Well, you don't, buster. You don't know what I—" she prodded her chest with her forefinger "—think. *I* think that you're thick. *Thick*! Liberal—hah! You're one of the most narrow-minded people I've had the misfortune to meet, because you can't accept the fact that someone else sees differently from you. You play games and they're cruel! You'd stamp all over me if you had the chance, because you're so damned sure that you know what's best! Well, you don't!" Her chest was rising and falling rapidly with the labored working of her lungs. "And who are *you* to tell me what to do with my life? You blew it with your son, because you just couldn't accept the responsibility!" When he recoiled as though he'd been slapped, she gloated. "And you're nearly *forty* and only now thinking of all you've missed."

She took a gasping breath and narrowed her eyes. "So don't tell me what I should or shouldn't be doing. You might be the idol of the business world, but in *my* world, you're nothing! Do you hear me? *Nothing!*"

Donovan's face was pale and for a minute he said nothing. Then he spoke slowly, distinctly. "I hear you. For all else I may be, I'm not deaf." Lowering his hand, he pulled the door open. He turned on the threshold to look at her a final time, but his eyes were hard. "I won't bother you again. Goodbye, Elizabeth."

It was all she could do to hold her head high until she'd shut the door on him. Then she sagged back against it and closed her eyes, taking long, shuddering breaths. A minute later she pushed herself from the door, and, in a flurry, raced to the kitchen for a dust rag.

The apartment, bathroom and all, was gleaming by the time she'd finished, and still she looked around for more to do. On impulse, she dashed into her bedroom and changed into a skirt, then threw on her coat and headed for the nearest museum. There she stared at one painting after another until she had a headache.

In search of fresh air, she went outside and started walking, aimlessly but at a rapid pace. She kept her hands buried deep in her pockets because she'd not thought to bring gloves and the late November chill seemed to penetrate her very being. She bought a bag of roasted chestnuts from a corner vendor, but she seemed to have lost her knack for removing the shells, for they ended up more often than not in her mouth. Finally she tossed the bag in the nearest trash can and ducked, instead, into a coffee shop.

Neither hot coffee nor steaming chowder made a dent in the chill she felt. But she couldn't bear the thought of returning to her apartment, and she couldn't think of anyone she wanted to visit, so she began walking again. When she passed a theater, she doubled back, bought a ticket and went inside. There, with a large buttered popcorn propped in her lap, she sat. And watched. Or tried to watch. Her mind kept wandering, to the point that once, when the background music rose abruptly, she jumped in alarm and spilled the entire bucket of popcorn onto her skirt and the floor. Flustered, she tried to brush it off, but her embarrassment only increased when she found the motion attracting the attention of those around her. Grateful only for the dark of the theater which would surely hide her true identity from any who might wonder, she pulled herself together, ignoring a snicker, and left.

Dusk was beginning to fall, but she walked on. And on. Finally, she found herself on the edge of Central Park. Exhausted by now, she collapsed onto a bench facing Fifth Avenue. Cars passed and taxis and limousines. She watched their progression, wondering who was inside and where they were headed, until she realized that she just didn't care. *They* didn't care. They were strangers, people with their own lives, their own destinations. They wouldn't even notice her, sitting alone on her bench.

It was then that her eyes filled with tears. Slowly they trickled down her cold cheeks and then her nose began to run. Liz dug into her purse for a Kleenex, which she pressed to her lips to muffle the quiet sobs. She couldn't seem to stop. Yes, she was alone. She was alone, and by choice. And for the first time in her life she regretted it. For the first time in her life she felt truly lonely.

"That was a really dumb thing to do," Karen informed her after Liz had poured out her heart the following Thursday morning. "You could have been mugged, or worse, raped, sitting by the park at night that way."

"I think I would have welcomed it at the time. *Anything* for human contact."

"You should have called me...or come over. I was home all day Sunday."

"Alone?" Liz prompted, knowing the answer.

"Well, David was there, but he would have understood if we'd had to talk."

"I couldn't talk then. I couldn't think. I just felt so...so numb.... Not numb because I was freezing, but numb *inside*...do you know what I mean?" She looked down. "I'm even amazed that I've talked now."

"You talked because I dragged you in here and demanded that you explain why you've been a walking zombie all week."

"That bad?" Liz asked timidly.

"That bad. Well, maybe not so obvious to someone who doesn't know you and care, but I'm not the only one who's been concerned. Julie and Veronica approached me individually, and I know that Donna's worried, too." She donned a mischievous grin. "They're convinced you're pregnant."

"They are not."

"So, what are you going to do about it?"

"About not being pregnant?"

"About Donovan. Do you love him?"

"*Love* him! You haven't been listening to me. What I feel has nothing to *do* with love. I just feel...awful for having said such terrible things to him." Her voice dropped. "And I'm sorry to have lost him as a friend."

"Do you want to see him and apologize?"

Liz thought about that for a minute, but she'd thought about it before and had ruled it out for the same reasons she now gave Karen. "It wouldn't do any good, other than to ease my conscience. Some words you can't take back. Apology or no, I'll always hear myself saying them. I'm sure Donovan will, too. And if he doesn't, and I apologize, he's apt to think the game is on again, and I don't want that."

"Are you sure? Isn't there some small part of you that's upset to have lost Donovan...for other reasons?"

"No. Definitely no."

"You say that with such conviction. Almost too much."

"Then blame it on the past week. I'm telling you, Karen, I don't want what he wants. It's as simple as that. Regrettably, I had to say a lot of ugly things to get Donovan to believe it, but now that he does, I'm relieved."

"Could have fooled me," Karen mumbled, then pulled herself up and took a breath. "Okay. The question is where do I go from here. I got a call this morning from a greeting card company in Kansas City that wants us to do some work for them. It'd mean a trip out there...as soon as possible. I think what you need to pick up your spirits is a change of scenery. Does it sound...appealing?"

"Right on the button," Liz responded, brightening for the first time in days. "If I clean up some things this afternoon, I could be on my way tomorrow morning."

"Good. Why don't you plan on it, then. I'll call Kansas City and let them know you're coming. My secretary will type up the specifics of the case and get them to you. You won't work through the weekend, though, will you?"

Liz was on her feet, revived by the thought of a new case, a new city. "Nah. I'll just wander around. I can work tomorrow, then as many days next week as I have to. Since there's nothing pressing here, it'll work out well.''

Karen walked her to the door. ''I hope it does…for you. I, well, I was really hoping things would work out with Donovan, but I've never been one to beat a dead horse. I want you to be happy, Liz. You know that, don't you?''

''I do, Karen. And thanks.'' On impulse Liz gave her a hug, then headed for her office to make arrangements for the trip.

She left for Kansas City the following morning and spent a relatively relaxing five days away from New York, getting to know a new client and its product, letting the wounds of the past days heal. Though she continued to be bothered by the things she'd said to Donovan, she became more and more convinced that the outcome was for the best. If she'd lost one friend, she had others. It was time to pick up where she'd left off on that day she'd flown to Troy.

If she assumed that Reynolds Associates had completed its work for the DIG Group, though, she'd been mistaken. It seemed that Donovan had decided to retain the firm to do future publicity on the merger with Ullman. At his request Liz had been removed from the account.

"Got a minute, Liz?"

Liz looked up quickly from her work to find Brenda Nussbaum at her door. She smiled and sat back. "Sure, Brenda. Come on in."

"Am I interrupting anything urgent?"

"I was just going over some of the figures I brought back with me from Kansas City. I want to get the ball rolling on this thing." It had been over a week since she'd been back, and only during the past few days had she felt she was working up to par.

"Is there a problem?"

"Just piles of figures to wade through. The annual reports this company has put out in the past leave something to be desired."

"That's why they hired you, I'm sure."

"Us. They hired us."

Brenda slipped into a seat, looking decidedly sheepish. "Yeah, well, I'm glad you feel that way, because *I* need your help. And since the DIG Group hired *us*..."

"Uh-oh." Liz's easy smile faded. "What's wrong?"

Brenda threw a hand in the air and shook her head. "It's Donovan Grant. I don't understand him. How a man could come across as being so congenial, so easygoing in the press and turn out to be a man of stone in person mystifies me."

"Man of stone?"

"Exactly. Oh, he always says and does the right things, but he's so...so formal about it."

"Formal?"

"I mean, I think he's the best thing to come along since Robert Redford. All he has to do is to walk into the room and my heart starts pounding." She looked up from pleating her skirt. "I suppose I shouldn't be telling you this...or even feeling it, for that matter...and I know that a professional relationship should be just that, and I'm ready to settle for it if only he'd let me.''

Liz felt her own heart pound. ''He's coming on to you?''

''Just the opposite. He insists on my coming to his office, and when I dare suggest, even innocently, that we might discuss something over lunch or dinner he all but turns me into ice with those eyes of his.'' She was frowning. ''I thought you might be able to give me some hints.''

''Hints...on what?'' There was a sudden chill in Liz's voice, but she was unaware of it. Brenda wasn't.

''Uh-oh. I've offended you. You must think I'm awful. Oh, Liz, I'm sorry.''

''You haven't offended me. I'm just not sure what it is you want.''

''I want a comfortable working relationship with him. I mean, it'd be nice if he'd notice me as a woman, but I can only do so much. I agonize over what I'm going to wear on the days I see him. I make sure I don't eat anything with garlic in it for lunch. I rack my brain trying to come up with novel ways to present the Ullman merger to the public. And he takes it all in, then quickly ushers me to the door.''

Liz was amazed. Brenda was young, redheaded, adorable and available. If Donovan had wanted a playmate, she was his for the asking. But he wasn't asking. And now Brenda had come to her for advice. How do you tell a girl that the game was only fun if the object was unadorable, inexperienced and disinterested, and therein lay the challenge?

''You've worked with him, Liz. Was he that way with you?''

Liz felt a bitter laugh bubbling but squelched it. It was really ludicrous, a first, that a woman as appealing as Brenda should come to one as unappealing as herself and innocently ask how a man had been with her. On the other hand, maybe Brenda needed the reassurance that it wasn't just her, and who better to come to than the ugly duckling of the firm?

"He...had his moments. But I think he's very wrapped up in the Ullman thing and—"

"You can say that again! You'd think his entire future depended on this acquisition. He put me through the second degree yesterday because some idiot is suddenly buying huge chunks of Ullman stock. Just because the guy's family is one of our clients—"

"Whoa. What did you say?"

"I met with Donovan at his office yesterday and he all but accused me of selling inside information to another client."

"Which client?"

"The Obermeyers. Actually, it's the son, Raymond, who's been snatching up stock in Ullman, at least that's what Donovan's sources claim."

For a minute Liz couldn't breathe. "It's a federal crime to pass on inside information like that," she murmured. "Whoever buys stock just prior to a merger stands to make a bundle as soon as the merger is announced."

"That's what Donovan said. I assured him that we don't discuss one client with another, but I'm not sure he believed me. He seems to think I'm pretty raw in this business."

She was, though Liz wouldn't have said so. Brenda, evidently, didn't realize that the Obermeyers were *Liz's* clients. But the more Liz thought about it, the more uncomfortable she grew. It could be a coincidence, Ray's buying Ullman stock. On the other hand, there'd been that cocktail party after Thanksgiving...and Liz had had one too many...and she'd talked with Cheryl. What *had* she said...

"I don't know, Liz. Am I doing something wrong?"

"Uh-uh, Bren," she answered distractedly. "You're doing just fine. Bear with Donovan. He tends to be intense about some things. It must be a trying time for him."

"God, I hope that's all." She talked on a little longer about what she planned to do to publicize the Ullman merger, and Liz nodded from time to time. Then she stood up and shook her head as she started for the door. "Another Redford…just slipping through my fingers…"

Fortunately Brenda didn't look back, because Liz wasn't smiling. Her heart was pounding, and it wasn't even Donovan she was thinking of at that moment. Lifting the phone, she called Cheryl Obermeyer.

"I have to see you, Cheryl. Can we meet somewhere for lunch?"

"You sound uptight. What's wrong?"

"I…I can't talk about it now. Can we meet?"

"Sure, but not until two o'clock."

"That's fine."

Cheryl named a place they'd been to together several times before, and Liz hung up the phone feeling that at least she'd taken the first step. She accomplished nothing between then and two, though, because thought of the steps to follow had her tied up in knots. She waited until she and Cheryl had been seated before broaching the subject.

"Cheryl, do you remember that night at your party when we were talking?"

"Of course." She grinned. "You were a mite tipsy and told me all about Donovan Grant."

"What 'all' did I tell you?"

"Just that he wanted to date you and that you didn't want to."

"Did I say anything about his business interests?"

Cheryl was no longer grinning, because she couldn't help but sense Liz's distress. "I don't remember. Why? What's this all about?"

With a grimace, Liz hung her head. When she looked up again, there was a pleading slant to her eyes. "I…I think I told you something I shouldn't have. Something about a merger."

With the prompting Cheryl remembered. She frowned, struggling to draw back the facts. "Mmm. With the Ullman Distributorship, wasn't it?" Liz nodded. "Well?"

"Someone has been buying Ullman stock in bulk. I believe it's Ray."

"Ray? But how could he...he wouldn't..." Her eyes widened. "Oh dear. He was right behind you when you told me. He must have heard."

It was all the confirmation Liz needed to support her suspicion. "I was hoping I was wrong. I've been trying to dredge up every detail of that conversation since I learned of the problem this morning. I kept thinking Ray's sudden interest in Ullman was a coincidence. But he *did* hear me that night. And we both know he'd be tempted."

"He would, damn his soul. Liz, who knows about this?"

"Donovan does."

"Did he accuse you?"

She shook her head. "We're not working together anymore."

"You're kidding. Why not?"

"I can't go into it, Cheryl. There's too much else we have to worry about. I learned about the stock business by accident, in the course of a discussion with the woman who's now working with Donovan. She said he's livid."

"Has he made the connection between you and Ray?"

"No. Neither did she. I called you as soon as she left my office."

"Thank God you did," Cheryl murmured, frowning down at her plate. "We've got to figure out the best thing to do. Damn it, both you *and* Ray could be in serious legal trouble if something's not done." She put her hand on Liz's. "You weren't really hungry, were you? It'd be best if I got back to the office and spoke with our lawyer."

"And Ray."

"Right...damn him. How could he do this?"

"Maybe he's trying to get back at me for having cajoled him into staying put."

"Maybe, but I doubt it. I doubt he'd put his own neck on the line just to spite you. On the other hand, he may be too dumb to realize what he's done. He's probably only thinking of the profit he'll make and what he'll be able to do with it." She grabbed her purse and stood. "I'll get back to you as soon as I know anything, okay?"

"I'd appreciate it, Cheryl. I'll be a nervous wreck until you do."

Cheryl bent low for a final minute. "You relax. If push comes to shove, I'll testify that you didn't intentionally divulge privileged information. No one will be able to prove intent, and that's what counts in cases like these."

Liz's smile was weak. "I'd like to believe that, but..."

Cheryl patted her arm. "I'll get back to you."

"Thanks."

Liz sat through a long afternoon and an even longer evening at the office waiting for Cheryl's call, but it didn't come. Finally she went home, knowing that Cheryl would call her there if she had anything to report. By morning, though, when there was still no word, Liz knew that she had to do something else. Dressing carefully, she stopped in at the office for only the time it took to postpone two appointments, then she headed for DIG headquarters.

Donovan was in Troy, but was expected back before noon, she was told. She decided to wait, fearing that if she left she'd lose her nerve and never return. And, she reasoned, the longer the receptionist saw her sitting there, the harder it would be to run out, which was what she wanted to do more than anything else in the world at that moment. It would have been difficult enough three weeks before, to confess to Donovan what she'd done. But now, given what had happened, given what she'd said to him the last time they'd seen each other, it was a truly terrifying prospect.

By eleven-thirty, when Donovan walked past her into the reception area, she was pale and tense. The receptionist smiled in greeting, then shifted her gaze to Liz. Only then did he turn. His surprise was momentary and was quickly checked, as was the relief that surged through him.

When he'd seen Liz last, she'd hurt him with her words—until he realized that she'd struck out in self-defense. She'd been running scared from his feelings and, more importantly, from her own. He'd realized then that he had to wait for her to come to him, and he'd reminded himself of that each time he'd lifted the phone to call her.

It was her turn. She had the dice in her hand. All he could do was to patiently wait for her to roll them and make her move.

"Did you want to see me?" he asked evenly.

She prayed for as even a tone, but only managed a slightly timid, "If you've got a minute."

He hesitated, then gave a short nod. She rose and preceded him to his office, where he closed the door and went straight to his desk. "What is it, Liz?" He thumbed through his mail, then tossed it down and leaned back in his seat. It was all he could do not to round the desk and take her in his arms, but he knew that wouldn't help her. He had to wait.

"I've...got a problem."

He shrugged. "Why are you coming to me?"

"Because it concerns you. It's about the Ullman merger." She saw alertness flicker through his otherwise controlled gaze.

"What about it?"

"I've made an awful mistake. I didn't mean to do it, and I didn't realize I'd even done it at the time—"

"Sit down, Liz, and spit it out."

She knew then that he wouldn't make things any easier for her, that she couldn't expect any of the warmth, the gentle understanding that had once seemed such an integral part of his nature. She also knew that she'd accomplish nothing by hedging. She looked at him and swallowed, awkwardly settled on the edge of the chair facing his desk, then summoned every bit of her inner strength and spoke.

"I went to a cocktail party—maybe you remember—the Saturday night after Thanksgiving. It was at Cheryl Obermeyer's. Cheryl and I are close, and on occasion I've been to family affairs with her. This wasn't exactly a family thing, though, and I felt a little out of the place. I had had two drinks before Cheryl dragged me aside and wanted to know what was bothering me. She could see that I was distracted." Liz looked down. "And I was. In the, uh, process of conversation I mentioned you, and Cheryl went on about how successful you are, and very carelessly I mentioned Ullman." She waited for Donovan to say something. When he didn't, she looked up. "I didn't even realize I'd betrayed your confidence because I was a little fuzzy-headed, and anyway, Cheryl would never have done anything with the information."

"Someone did," Donovan stated somberly. Somehow he hadn't expected this.

"Ray did. Cheryl's brother. He'd come up from behind, and I didn't even know he was there until Cheryl told him to get lost. By then it was too late. Honestly, Donovan, I would never have even mentioned your name if I'd known he was listening." She focused on her fingers, which were kneading her purse. "I don't think he was there long, but he obviously heard enough."

A muscle flexed in Donovan's jaw. Yes, he was angry that Liz had been the one to betray him, yet he couldn't sustain his anger long. She'd come to him on her own with the truth. Perhaps it was the move he needed to force her hand. "He's been buying Ullman stock."

"I know."

"Do you know that given the upcoming merger that's a federal offense?" Germs of an idea were taking shape.

"Yes."

"And that you're as guilty as he is?"

"I didn't do it intentionally—"

"But you did it," he said. "You passed on inside information. For all I know you may be getting a cut in Obermeyer's profit." He knew it wasn't true, but he had to push. He had to know exactly where he stood...and he was buying time to plan his strategy.

"I'm not! I told you, I didn't know anything about this until Brenda mentioned it yesterday. She didn't even realize that the Obermeyers were my clients."

She blotted her dry lips together, a nervous gesture. "As soon as Brenda left I called Cheryl, and we met yesterday afternoon. She's as upset as I am. She promised to speak to her lawyer and to Ray, then get back to me. But I haven't heard from her." She threw up a hand. "Maybe she couldn't get either of them. Maybe Ray denied that he'd overheard anything and claimed that he's been buying Ullman stock purely on instinct. I just don't know, but I couldn't sit back and do nothing forever."

Donovan sat staring at her like the man of stone Brenda had accused him of being. "What do you want from me?"

"I don't know. I...just wanted you to know the truth."

"You and I seem to have different perceptions of the truth," he countered, and she knew he was thinking of the things she'd said to him when last they'd seen each other.

She averted her gaze, unable to face him. "I'm sorry," she whispered. "I shouldn't have said those things. I was angry and...and I didn't know what else to do."

"You were terrified. But then, you've been terrified of me ever since we met. The only difference is that now you've got due cause."

That there was terror now, she couldn't deny. It showed in the rigidity of her body, in her face, in her eyes as they shot to his. "You wouldn't...prosecute...would you?"

"It is illegal, what you did."

"But I didn't mean to do it. I didn't do it with ill intent. It was a mistake, and I've said I'm sorry, and if Ray can be convinced to get rid of his stock before the merger is made public and he makes any profit..."

"The fact remains that the SEC may already be on to you both."

She caught her breath. "Is it?"

He gave a negligent shrug. "I don't really know. I got my initial information from the people in New Orleans. To my knowledge, they haven't gone to the authorities...yet."

She sat farther forward. "Stop them, Donovan! You can, if you want. Explain that it was a mistake and that it's going to be corrected before anything comes of it."

"But I don't know that. You said it yourself. You don't know what Obermeyer's response is. And forgetting even that, why should I help you?'' He was pressuring her as he never had before, and while it tore him apart to do so, he sensed he needed to do it for her sake, for *their* sake.

She looked around vainly for an answer. "Because...because we were friends once...and if you knew me at all you'd understand how badly I feel.''

He took his time in responding, pensively rubbing his upper lip before dropping his hand. "How badly *do* you feel?''

"I feel awful! I'd never have come here today if that hadn't been so! After the things I said to you, you've got every right to kick me out. I'm ashamed of *everything*. You do know that, don't you, Donovan?''

He raised one brow, then lowered it. "I know that you don't think terribly highly of me as a person. You made that clear—''

"I was frightened! All right, that's what you want to hear, isn't it? I was frightened and I lashed out.''

"And now you claim you didn't mean a word? Now that you need my help, you're apologizing? You've had a good long time to apologize, Liz. Why only now? Damn it, put that purse down! You'll ruin the leather if you keep strangling it that way.'' He heard his own harshness and knew that it was born of frustration. It killed him to be causing her pain, but he had to!

As though it were a hot potato, she dropped the purse to the floor and clutched her hands in her lap. "I couldn't face you before. I...I was afraid that you'd take my apology as a sign that I...that I...''

"Want me? I know you do, well, on one level at least. But that's where the terror comes in, doesn't it? You'll go to your grave a virgin because you're scared of making love.''

Her voice was a mere breath. "It's not that.''

"Then what is it?''

She simply shrugged and kept her chin low, her eyes downcast.

"But now you want my help.'' He leaned farther back in his chair and laced his fingers together over his middle. "Okay, Liz. I'll help you.'' She looked up at him, only to have the hope in her eyes fade when he went on. "But on one condition.''

"What's...that?"

He hesitated for only an instant. She'd made her move; now he had to counter it. He didn't like what he was about to say, but he had to force a showdown. He had to free her of the shadow that dogged her, even if it meant coming across like a bastard. "That you move in with me. That you become my lover."

The blood rushed from her head and she felt dizzy. She clutched the arms of the chair but found little support. "You can't be serious."

"I am. Very much so. I know that you prize your freedom, that you like to make your own choices. Well, the choices are these. You can come to me of your own free will, or I'll go to the authorities. It's as simple as that." It wasn't really, because he'd never be able to turn her in. He was bluffing as never before. But hadn't he been the one to say that to win one had to operate in the most efficient manner possible?

She was shaking her head very slowly, trying to deny the fleeting images that crossed her mind, but tears began to gather at her lower lids and she sensed she was cornered. "Why are you doing this?" she whispered brokenly.

"Because I want you. I always have. I'd pretty much given up on you after last time, but since you've walked in here and put the tool right in my hands—"

"The weapon, you mean."

Determinedly he held his gaze steady. "Whatever. I still feel the same about you, and I've got you where I want you. You know, you were wrong about my being arrogant and cruel. The problem was that I was too *nice* where you were concerned. I should have been more forceful from the start. Then there wouldn't have been all this prancing around on tiptoes. My strategy was all wrong."

"A game. That's all it is. But I'm a nobody. You could play games with anyone else."

"I'm not looking to play games with anyone else."

"You want to make an example of me."

"No. This is private, between you and me. The rest of the world doesn't have to know a thing."

"You're having fun."

"I hope to. For that matter, I hope you will, too."

"You are cruel."

"Come on," he grumbled wearily. "We don't need more name-calling. That's what got you into trouble before."

"I bruised your ego then. You're taking revenge for what I said."

He didn't refute her charge. To do so would have been to tip his hand, and he felt shaky enough inside as it was.

"Donovan...please? Don't ask this of me."

He forced his mind away from the pain he was inflicting. It was for her own good, he told himself. *It had to work!* "You could refuse my offer, in which case the legal system will take over. You might not like that. I mean, white-collar crime or no, there's still the booking process and bail and a trial. And if you were to be convicted, you might be able to get away with a stiff fine, but I'm not sure you've got that kind of money. Chances are you'd spend a little time in jail. I doubt the judge would be too hard on you, though."

Liz stumbled from her chair and made for the door, but her knees were wobbling so badly that she could only clutch its knob and press her forehead to the wood.

"What's the matter, Liz? Finally putting terror in perspective?"

"My job...my future...it'd all be gone..."

"It's either that or your virginity. Seems to me the choice is pretty clear-cut. Of course, it's your choice. Your free choice. That's what you've always wanted, isn't it?"

"You really hate me, don't you?" she breathed.

She heard movement from her desk and when next he spoke it was from directly behind her. "Hate you? No." He put a light hand on her shoulder, then ran it over her back. Fortunately she couldn't see the agony in his eyes. "I just want to see this trembling put to better use. You'll tremble when I make love to you, Liz. You'll tremble and cry out and wonder what it was you ever fought.'' His voice grew soft in the way she'd known so well, ''Because you'll feel like a million with me inside you, and so will I. Does that sound like hate to you?''

She was breathing hard, trying desperately not to cry. ''I swore this...would never happen to me again. I swore I wouldn't let...anyone do this...''

He leaned into her, but she was beyond appreciating the support or the fact that his tone was more gentle and that he seemed to be talking as much to himself as to her. ''Sometimes choices aren't much fun. Sometimes it's a matter of opting for the lesser of two evils. I wouldn't have had it this way, either, but things didn't quite work out the way I'd hoped.''

She pressed pale fingers to the door. ''How long...'' Her voice was garbled, so she cleared her throat. ''How long would this...arrangement last?''

''At least until the Ullman merger is formalized and made public. I'd want you under my thumb until then. As for the future, well, who's to say. You might find that you'll like what you've got.''

''Please...don't make me...''

''I'm not making you do anything. You've got a choice.''

''But...I can't...''

He straightened to his full height then. ''Today's Thursday. You've got until Sunday noon to make your decision.'' He returned to his desk, and Liz turned her head to see him jotting on a small pad. He tore the top sheet off, then approached her. ''My Manhattan address. I don't think you've ever been to my place here.'' She stared at the piece of paper. ''Take it, Liz.'' When she still didn't move, he ducked away to retrieve her purse from the floor. He opened it, stuck the paper inside, then held it out. ''Noon Sunday. If I haven't heard from you by then, I'll put in a call to a friend who happens to be on the SEC. He'll take it from there.''

Quivering, Liz took the bag and paused only to blot her wet cheeks before passing through the door he'd opened. How she found her way out of the building she didn't know, or for that matter, how she managed to find her way home. She felt ill and more than once paused to lean against the side of a building, praying only that she wouldn't disgrace herself by being sick all over the pavement. She was marginally aware that more than one person stared at her, but she was beyond caring. The only thing that seemed to matter was reaching the familiar confines of her apartment, climbing into bed and pulling the covers over her head.

It was late in the afternoon when the phone rang. She listened to its peal, debating whether to answer it until she realized that Donovan might be calling with a reprieve. Scrambling free of the blankets, she grabbed up the receiver, only to find that it was her secretary, concerned when she hadn't returned. Not only had she missed a meeting, Cheryl Obermeyer had also been trying to reach her.

Liz explained that she wasn't feeling well and asked that any appointments she had scheduled for Friday be canceled. After pressing the button, Liz phoned Cheryl.

"He's a bastard, Liz. What else can I say. I've been working on him, our lawyer's been working on him, but he won't budge from his claim that he never heard a word from you. I mean, the guy may be my brother, but you know as well as I do that he's got no instinct for business, much less the stock market. He expects me to believe that his buying that Ullman stock is a shot in the dark. Who's he kidding? He's a waste! He refuses to believe that he's in legal trouble, and by the time he does it'll be too late."

Liz let out a long breath and fell back to the pillow. Ray's getting rid of the stock had been her only hope, and even then it had been a long shot that Donovan would have dropped things there. "It's okay, Cheryl. He'll be all right."

"How can he be all right? He's breaking the law. You know as well as I do that his buying that stock was no fluke."

"But he won't be prosecuted. I've...taken care of it."

"You've what? But how?"

"I talked with Donovan today. He won't report it. No one will ever know that it was anything but sheer luck that Ray chose this particular time to invest in Ullman."

"Are you sure? But even then, we'll know. I feel tainted simply by being related to Ray. You sound awful, Liz. You're not at the office, are you? I've been trying you there."

"I'm home."

"Are you sick?"

"I...I must have the flu or something. I'll be okay."

"Is there anything I can do? God, you've been wonderful about all this. It's a miracle you haven't washed your hands of us already, what with all we've put you through."

"It was my own fault, Cheryl. I was the one who let it slip."

. "I asked Ray what he intended to do with the money he makes, and he informed me that he has designs on his own company. You know, Liz, I hope to God he does, because if he doesn't come to his senses and divest himself of that stock soon, hell will freeze over before I give him a thing. Dad's got limited time, and then the company will be mine, and there's *no way* I'll let him touch it!"

"Take it easy, Cheryl. He's your brother. He's immature and he's frustrated and—"

"He's stupid!"

"Well, there's no point in our rehashing that. Listen, I really do feel pretty lousy. I'm going to try to sleep. Can I talk with you another time?"

"Sure, Liz. *Is* there anything I can do?"

"No. But thanks anyway, Cheryl. And thanks for trying to talk with Ray. It's not your fault that he is the way he is."

"Mmm. I sometimes wonder about that. But...enough said for now. You take care of yourself. Will you let me know if you need anything?"

"I will. Bye, Cheryl."

Liz had known what her choice had to be even before she'd left Donovan's office, yet through the next two days she agonized. She could barely eat, and what little sleep she got was inevitably interrupted by a nightmare that seemed to continue even after she'd woken.

She pictured herself being charged with the misuse of inside information, with conspiracy, with stock fraud or theft or embezzlement or whatever the official words were. She pictured herself going through the legal processes Donovan had described and remembered so recently having thought about many of the same things with regard to Jamie. The irony of it was too much. Too much.

She considered the possibility that Donovan was bluffing and thought of calling him on it. But the penalties were too harsh. Even aside from the legal ramifications, her job, her reputation in the field, her security would all be gone. And without a job she wouldn't be able to help Jamie. While one part of her said that it would be good for him to have to stand on his own two feet for once, the other, larger part couldn't bear the thought of letting him down this way. She'd let him down many times when they were children. She just couldn't do it again.

So she accustomed herself to the only option that remained. She would go to Donovan's apartment at noon on Sunday and submit to whatever he wished to do. She tried to steel herself against the humiliation, the mental pain she knew she'd have to endure, but she only ended up more and more anguished. She felt so much for Donovan…yet he'd see her and taunt her and, in the end, find that the game wasn't half as much fun as he'd anticipated.

Anticipation. What might be for him the best part was for her the worst. As the hours passed she came to realize this, and it was her sole saving grace. The pain, the torment she was suffering now *had* to be worse than the actuality.

She also realized something else. Perhaps it was by way of rationalization, but a tiny part of her did want to be Donovan's lover. She was stunned by the knowledge, but then, Donovan had been stunning her for weeks, awakening feelings in her she'd thought herself immune to. He aroused her physically. She knew all too well how wonderful she felt in his arms. So what if he'd send her home later? He was the one who was forcing her into it. He was giving her the excuse to taste heaven, if only once in her life. When Donovan was done with her, her job, her future would still be intact. She'd simply have to pick up the pieces of her personal life and put them together again.

Sunday morning found her utterly calm. Numbness did that to a person, she knew, and she was grateful. She cleaned the apartment and put in a wash, then showered and put on a pair of slacks and a sweater. Taking a suit bag with her clothes for work and a small overnight bag for the few personal essentials she'd need, she left her apartment and started the walk to Donovan's.

It wasn't far, but the air was cold, as by rights December should be. And the spiritual warmth of the Christmas decorations in store windows eluded her as she walked on, barely seeing, intent only on reaching her destination.

At 11:55 Liz reached the address Donovan had scrawled on the small piece of paper. It was an elegant high rise in the East Eighties, with large glass doors in shining brass frames. Her hand was steady as she let herself in, her voice quiet when she gave the attendant her name. She watched him press a button on his phone, then announce her arrival, then nod at the response he received.

"Fifteenth floor, Ms. Jerome," he said as he replaced the phone. "Mr. Grant's door is the second on the right."

"Thank you."

Had she been capable of feeling at that moment, she would have been proud of the way she walked toward the waiting elevator and stepped inside. She would have been proud of the way she walked out on the fifteenth floor, turned to the right and approached the second door. She looked composed and sure, and that composure barely faltered when Donovan opened the door.

His expression was shuttered as he raised his hand to look at his watch. "You're right on time. It's just noon." Then he surveyed her and her bags. "Is this all you've brought?"

"Yes," she answered quietly.

"Not very much for a prolonged stay."

"It may not be prolonged. After tonight the game will be done. You'll be glad to see me go."

"That wasn't our arrangement," he gently reminded her as he took the suit bag and overnight case from her hands. "You can pick up the rest tomorrow. Come on in and take off your coat. I've got brunch nearly ready."

Holding herself straight, she stepped inside. She blotted the sound of the closing door from her mind, much as she'd blotted out everything else all morning. "I'm not very hungry."

After setting her things down on a chair by the door, he helped her off with her coat, studying her closely all the while. She might have seen his concern if she'd been looking for it, but she wasn't. "You look like hell, Liz. Are you sick?"

"It's my usual pallor."

"Are you sick?"

"I...I haven't been able to sleep. That's all."

"Or eat. When was the last square meal you had?"

"I don't know."

"Then I'm glad I cooked."

"You were that sure I'd come?"

Without answering her he lifted the suit bag and overnight case again, headed down the hall and disappeared from view. She was still by the door when he returned. "You don't have to stand there, Liz. You can come in and sit down."

"I'm not sure what I'm supposed to be doing."

"For now you're supposed to be making yourself at home here, since this will be home for a while."

"You'll...we'll be staying here then?"

"Until the weekend. Then we'll go up to the house."

She nodded and walked forward, about to descend the two steps into the living room when Donovan stopped her. "Why don't you come into the kitchen with me. I've got to put everything out."

As though she'd only been waiting for his command, she turned and followed him. She watched from the door of the kitchen as he donned mitts and bent to take a large glass pan from the oven.

"What made you decide to come?" He set the pan on the stove top and reached toward the refrigerator, carefully hiding his relief that she'd showed, and his pleasure. He hesitated to soften outwardly, fearing that she might then plead for a reprieve, fearing that he might give in. But he had to go through with what he'd started.

"I didn't have much of a choice."

"You did have a choice." He'd taken out a container of orange juice and a bottle of wine.

"Then it was, as you put it yourself, a matter of choosing between the lesser of two evils."

He turned to lean back against the counter, facing her. "The other was that bad?"

"Yes."

"Did you hear from your friend?"

"Her brother's denying it."

Donovan shook his head in dismay, then shrugged. "You know, even if it all came to a trial, you'd probably get off with probation. You could argue that you were innocent of malicious intent. The judge might believe you."

"Then again, he might not. I can't take that chance." She'd thought it all out before, looking into any and every possibility, but she'd seen no escape. "My career is at stake. It would be damaged by the simple fact of the accusation being made, regardless of the outcome."

"Your career means that much to you?"

"Yes."

"Why?"

"It's just about the only source of self-respect I have. And I need the money to help Jamie out with his therapist."

Donovan considered that for a minute. Then he turned around, took two tall glasses from a cupboard and filled them with a mixture of orange juice and wine. Champagne, actually, Liz realized when he explained what he'd made.

"Mimosas. And a blintz soufflé. And fresh fruit." He sent her a pensive glance. "I think I'll heat muffins, too. You could use some fattening up."

Liz said nothing, but stood with her hands balled in the pockets of her slacks.

"Well, what do you think of my place?"

"I don't know. I haven't looked around."

"Then look. Start with this room. You liked my country kitchen. This is its city cousin."

Dutifully she ran her eye around the room. "Very nice."

His grin was weak. "Such enthusiasm. Close your eyes." When

she looked puzzled, he repeated himself. "Close your eyes." She did. "Now tell me what you saw."

She hesitated for as long as she dared. "I...can't."

"That's what I thought." He sighed. "Well, you'll know later. Liz...open your eyes. Damn it, you're not a machine, y'know. I've got no intention of leading you through life here as though you didn't have a brain in your head."

"I'm sorry. You can always send me home."

"Oh-ho, no. The deal was that we'd be lovers, and that's exactly what we're going to be." He was purposely goading her to get a response, and if it hurt him to do it, he told himself it was necessary. "If you want to stand around here like a mummy, that's fine. But you're not going to weasel out of this by acting like an idiot."

Liz felt an inkling of anger, the first stirring of emotion she'd experienced in hours. "I'm not acting like an idiot. You've put me in a situation that's totally foreign to me. It's awkward, and I feel strange. What would you have me do—waltz in here all smiles when I'd rather be anywhere else?"

"Unnh!" He held up a finger. "The deal was that you'd come to me of your own free will."

"Words. Only words."

"And they'll be only words I pass to my SEC friend if I sense any more antagonism. You had your shot at me that day in your apartment. I've got enough ugliness to remember, without having more. Understood?"

Imprisoned by the determination in his gaze, she nodded once, then swallowed.

"Sit down," he murmured. "I'll just put the muffins in and then we'll eat."

Liz sat down at the small round table and stared at her place setting until the empty plate was removed and replaced by one filled to the brim with the goodies Donovan had prepared.

"I don't think I can eat all this," she said quietly.

"You can try. That's all I ask."

Lifting her fork, she began to pick at the soufflé.

"Why don't you take a drink. It'll loosen you up."

"I don't need loosening."

"You're tight as wire. Drink it, Liz. Then you'll *have* to eat, unless you want the champagne to go to your head, in which case you're apt to do something foolish."

"That's how this all happened. If only I hadn't had that second drink…"

"It's water over the dam. You've got to move on." That play was long since done, though it had been instrumental in setting up the one they were working through now. He took a drink, then a forkful of the soufflé. "Mmm. Not bad. You weren't at work yesterday."

She eyed him. "You checked up on me?"

"No. But I did see Brenda, and your name came up. She said you were sick. Were you that disturbed after our talk Thursday?"

"Yes."

"But you seem cool as a cuke now."

"You gave me two choices. I picked one."

"And you've accepted your fate."

"Only because I have to. That doesn't mean I have to like it." She wasn't being wholly truthful, she knew. But that small part of her that tingled at the thought of Donovan making love to her was being overpowered by nervousness, which in turn was tempered by the numbness she'd set protectively about herself.

"Careful, Liz. I can still make the call… For God's sake, eat!"

Liz ate, thought it might have been cardboard that agonizingly worked its way down her throat and into her stomach. The drink did little to loosen her up. And Donovan remained silent until they were done.

"Coffee?" he asked as he carried their dishes to the sink.

"No, thank you."

"Then I'll clean up here. Why don't you wander around. I'll be done in a minute and we can take a walk."

Liz went into the living room and sat in a chair until Donovan joined her.

"Will you be warm enough?" he asked as he held her coat for her. "You don't have a hat or anything, and it's pretty cold out."

"I'll be fine." She buttoned the coat up to her neck and buried her hands in her pockets, but Donovan insistently retrieved one and closed his fingers around it.

They took the elevator down and left the building, heading toward Fifth Avenue.

"At least you've got comfortable shoes on," he commented, eyeing her soft leather flats. "You'll have to bring boots over, though. We're apt to get snow any day, and there's nothing more fun, especially upstate, than going out for walks in the snow."

"I've got heels in my bag for work tomorrow," was all she said.

By the time they'd walked several blocks Liz was shivering. She freed her hand to turn up the collar of her coat, but Donovan quickly snatched it back and tucked it, along with his own, into the pocket of his heavy jacket.

"If you're too cold, we can turn back." He had so many second thoughts about what he was forcing, but this was the only one he could express.

"I'm fine. The cold feels good."

"Numbing? Is that what you want?"

"It helps."

He tipped up his chin and smiled. "Y'know, tomorrow you'll be laughing at all this. You don't want to be numb, Liz. You want to enjoy yourself."

"I want to be numb."

"Don't have much faith in my ability as a lover?"

"It's not your ability I'm worried about."

"Then yours? Hell, Liz, you'll be terrific. I've never been worried about that. I mean, it'll be new at first, maybe a little painful, but if you trust me and let yourself go, you'll get over that and it'll be great."

Liz felt her cheeks flare beneath their chill, but she simply stared ahead. Donovan looked at her from time to time, but she refused to return his gaze. So they walked, briskly and in silence.

As they approached the Plaza, the sidewalk traffic picked up and she was forced closer to him. Each time their hips brushed she stiffened; each time he ordered her to relax. But relaxation was beyond her. The only thing she could do was concentrate on keeping one foot moving after the other.

Rockefeller Center was seasonally cheerful, with Christmas lights in abundance and a huge tree surveying all. Donovan edged to the front of the gathered crowd so that he and Liz could look down at the skaters on the rink for a time. Then they headed for a coffee shop on Sixth Avenue, where he ordered hot chocolates for them both.

"I'll pick you up from work tomorrow and we can go back to your apartment for more clothes. There's a party on Thursday night we'll be going to, and—"

"You don't need me along. I thought you said that this wasn't going to be a public spectacle."

"It's not going to be a public spectacle. What happens in the privacy of our bedroom is between you and me. As far as anyone else is concerned, Thursday night you're my date. You're right. I don't *need* you along. But I *want* you along, which is why you'll be coming."

"Why would you want me along, other than to make a spectacle of me?"

In a moment's exasperation Donovan scowled at her. Then, regaining control, he softened. "I want you with me because I enjoy your company—"

"Even now? I can't believe it."

He grinned. "Right now, you're a real challenge. You've convinced yourself that you don't feel a thing, like a martyr being led to the stake, and it's rather fun trying to poke holes in that bravado. But don't forget, I've seen you differently. Which is why I say that I enjoy your company. You're intelligent and thoughtful." He tipped his head as he stared at her, into her. "There's something about you, a warmth, a compassion, that appeals to people—at least, it did to me from the first. And besides—" he smiled his thanks at the waitress who delivered their drinks and left "—by Thursday night you'll be feeling very good."

"Thanks to you?"

"Thanks to *you*. Liz, you don't seem to realize that you're your own worst enemy. You've got yourself convinced that you're ugly and unappealing, that there's no credible reason I should be attracted to you. But you're wrong. And you're going to find that out for yourself before long." He paused to sip from the steaming cup before him and motioned for her to do the same.

"It's too hot."

"Then blow on it. At least hold the cup. It'll warm your hands."

She did hold the cup, though it did little to warm her, so she set it down, at which point Donovan took her hands between his and chafed them. "Before, you said that your job was your only source of self-respect. That's what I don't understand. You've got a hell of a lot to be proud of besides your job. You've got character and presence, and I'm sure that legion of friends you've got could say a whole lot more."

She shrugged and put her hands back around her hot chocolate.

"No comment?" he prodded.

"No."

"Why not? You're usually right on the stick telling me off when I give you compliments."

"It's not worth the effort." She lifted the cup and sipped from it, staring straight ahead.

"But you're depriving me of fun if you don't argue."

"That's the point."

"Then you're seething inside, but biting your tongue."

"I'm not seething."

"It'd give me too much satisfaction, right?"

"Something like that." Actually, she realized that she was testing him. She wondered how much he'd take before disillusionment set in.

He laughed. "You are a gem, Liz. And speaking of gems, how

are your ears? I see you're still wearing the earrings. I'd have thought you'd have ripped them out after Thursday.''

Lowering her gaze, she admitted softly, ''I can't.''

''What do you mean, you can't?''

''I'm afraid to take them out. I have a squeamish stomach. I told you I'm not good at dealing with pain.''

''But you've had to do…something with them, haven't you?''

''I put alcohol on them twice a day and twist them. The doctor told me not to take them out for a couple of weeks.''

''And it's been a couple of weeks. Weren't you planning to change them at some point?''

''I…suppose.''

''But—'' he held up a finger ''—you don't have any others. *That's* what we can do one other night this week. We can go shopping for earrings.''

''I'm not spending good money on jewelry.''

''Fine. I will.''

She looked at him sharply. ''You will not. I may be forced to share your bed, but I'm *not* going to be paid for it.''

He grinned and punched the air with his fist. ''Atta girl. Fight with me. Tell me where to get off.''

She glared, then carefully schooled her expression to one of blandness and looked away. Donovan was undaunted.

''Then it's settled. Mmm, I think pearls would be nice. Very simple. Very elegant. And don't worry, love. I'll help you put them in. I've got a strong stomach, so you can pass out or throw up or do whatever your little heart desires, but when you come to, your ears will look super.''

''It was dumb,'' she muttered. ''I never should have had them pierced.''

''Don't be silly. Now that it's done, I can buy you really *expensive* earrings without having to worry about their falling off.''

Realizing she was being goaded to once again speak out against being ''kept,'' Liz ignored him and took another drink. When she set the cup down, Donovan lifted her coat from the back of the chair.

"Shall we go?"

She hesitated for an instant, almost regretting leaving the coffee shop, which was so clearly, if relatively, safe ground. Then she caught herself. She wanted this over. She wanted Donovan to do what he would and then let her go home.

Without a word she slipped her arms into her coat, stood and buttoned it. As he had before, Donovan tucked her hand into his pocket, and they started back the way they'd come. This time, though, Liz had trouble keeping up, so Donovan slowed the pace.

"Got cold feet?" he teased, leaning close to her ear.

"They've been cold for three days."

"I'll have to warm them up for you when we get home."

"They'll be fine."

"Maybe you'd like a hot bath. That'd warm you up."

"I had a hot shower this morning and it didn't help."

"Getting ready for me, were you?"

She gave him a quelling stare but said nothing more.

By the time they reached his building, Liz understood why Donovan had walked her so far. She was exhausted, and she cursed the fact, because she needed every bit of her strength to remain composed through what she was sure lay ahead.

Once inside his condominium, she braced herself as best she could. Donovan removed his coat and took hers, hanging them both in the closet by the door. Then he took her hand and she stumbled after him down the hall, fully expecting to find herself in his bedroom, with the awesome moment at hand. To her amazement he drew her into a room opposite the other door.

"I want to catch the end of the Knicks' game. Okay?"

She nodded dumbly, then found herself being led to a long leather couch. After depositing her in its richly scented folds, he crossed to a television set, turned it on, switched the channel, then returned. The game was in its third quarter, with the Knicks trailing. Donovan grunted when the opposing team scored another basket, then he spoke to Liz without taking his eyes from the screen.

"Do you like basketball?"

"Not particularly."

"That's probably because you've never watched enough of it to get involved in the game. Oooooh!" A Bernard King lay-up whirled around the rim of the basket before falling off, but King made the rebound himself and promptly dunked the ball. "Heeey! Good goin', Bernard!"

"I'm sure he can hear you."

Donovan ignored her dry comment. "The Knicks are a super team this year. Something seems to have jelled. 'Course, the same's true of both the Celtics and the Sixers. Their records are better, though Bernard, God bless him, is the top scorer in the league. Whoa. Did you see that? A three-pointer! Atta way, Knicks!"

Liz looked away from the screen. She focused first on the stereo set, then the nearby bookshelves, then an oil painting that hung on one wall. It was an abstract.

"No, not a time out now, you dummy!" Donovan screamed at the opposite coach, then directed quieter words at Liz. "Do you like it?"

"Like what?"

"The painting."

"It's bizarre," she mumbled.

Donovan grinned in intentional misinterpretation. "I think so, too. It's challenging, somehow. I can sit here for hours staring at it, trying to decide what I see, but what I see always seems to reflect my mood. What do you see?"

"A blinding nightmare."

"I see excitement...discovery. The artist is a friend of mine. From the old days, actually. He's a little bizarre himself, but I love him. There we go. All tied up." He lowered his voice in urging. "Come on, Knicks, come on."

Suddenly feeling the need to move, Liz jumped from the sofa and walked to the bookshelves. She stared at their contents for a minute, then walked to the window. Minutes later she was prowling the room.

"Sit down and relax, Liz."

"I *can't* relax."

"The waiting's finally getting to you, is it?"

He'd hit the nail on the head. "I don't like basketball, and there's nothing else for me to do."

"I could give you some crayons and a piece of paper and you could draw me a picture."

"I'm not a child."

"So you're not," he said, slowly twisting to face her. Having made a complete circle of the room, she was back where she'd begun by the bookshelves. "I'd say you're impatient. Maybe excited?"

Liz had had it. Her outward calm fled, along with the numbness that had protected her earlier. Excited? Oh, yes. But she was also terrified, and that made her perverse. "Don't flatter yourself, Donovan," she gritted. "It's occurring to me, more and more each minute, that I wasn't so wrong in what I said to you that day. You *are* arrogant. *And* bullheaded. *And* narrow-minded. And some day that cockiness of yours is going to get you into a whole load of trouble."

As she railed on, the easy indulgence that had dominated Donovan's expression for much of the afternoon fled. In its place was a certain grimness. "I told you to be careful, Liz," he warned. "You're skating on thin ice."

She threw up her hands. "I don't care! Falling in and drowning would be better than what I'm going through now. You're playing with me, just like you've always played with me. Well, I'm not a toy! And I'm not made of steel!"

He looked at her for a minute, then finally spoke in a tone of deadly calm. "Is that the way you feel?"

"That's *precisely* the way I feel."

"Are you sure?"

"Of course, I'm sure!"

He thought a moment longer, then sat deeper into the sofa and spread his arms to either side atop the back cushions. Though he looked confident and relaxed, inside he was a bundle of nerves. "Okay," he said quietly. "Take off your clothes."

Liz stood perfectly still. She couldn't believe what he'd said. "Ex-excuse me?"

"I said, take off your clothes."

She took a step back, but came up against the bookshelves. "Uh, look, it's okay. I'll just, uh, I'll just watch your game—" But he was shaking his head in a determined manner. "Hey, Donovan, I'm really sorry. It's just that I'm nervous and I'm not really in control—"

"Take them off now," he said softly, "or I'll make that call."

"This isn't like you," she said, gulping. "It's out of character. You were always so understanding."

He didn't want to feel understanding now. He was pushing himself as desperately as he was pushing her. "It's what you've done to me."

She stared at him, but there was no yielding in his face, no compassion in his tone. Very slowly he lowered one hand toward the phone, which sat on the end table.

"Please, Donovan," she whispered, her eyes wide, "don't do this to me." The tiny part of her that had wanted his lovemaking was stunned into neutrality. She hadn't dreamed he'd approach it this way!

"You can start with the sweater."

"I...but it's...broad daylight."

"So much the better. Go on. The sweater."

Her breath was coming in short gasps. "I can't...don't make me..."

"You can and you will. I'll give you ten seconds to start. Ten, nine, eight, seven..."

Hands trembling, Liz reached for the hem of her sweater and drew it up. It was over her head and on the floor before she looked at him again. The pleading in her eyes went unheeded.

"Now the blouse."

"Donovan...I'm begging you..."

His fingers brushed the telephone. "The blouse, Liz."

The threat of that gesture, coupled with that in his gaze, made her swallow hard. Tucking her chin low, she began to release the buttons of her blouse. When she was done, she clutched the center tabs together.

"Off, Liz."

She glanced toward the television. "In front of...of them?"

He made a gutteral sound before bounding from the sofa and turning off the set. "They wouldn't see a thing, but if it makes you feel better..." He resumed the pose of the relaxed spectator, though his insides were in knots. His hand dangled ever closer to the phone. "Six, five..."

She struggled out of the blouse and dropped it, then stood with her shoulders hunched forward and her eyes downcast.

"Go on, Liz. You know what to do."

"No!" she whispered.

"You won't do it?" He lifted the receiver, dropping it only when she reached for the snap of her jeans. He watched her bend over, pushing the jeans down her legs, stepping out of her flats to push the denim from her feet.

She didn't straighten all the way. She couldn't. Even if her stomach hadn't been cramped, the humiliation she felt would have prevented it.

"Take off the tights."

"Please..." she begged.

"Do it!" He was furious at her for making him drag it on this way.

She peeled the navy tights from her hips and legs and had to struggle to keep her balance as she pulled them from her feet. Her legs were shaking, as were her hands. She wrapped her arms around her waist, feeling chilled inside and out.

"You're almost there, Liz. Now the bra."

Frantically she tried to think of some way to escape the hell she was in, but she was trapped. She could refuse outright, but the consequences... It took her a minute to release the back catch because her fingers seemed boneless, but finally she added that piece of nylon to the pile by her feet. Instinctively she shielded herself with her hands, but he wouldn't have it.

"Put your arms down. I want to see you."

Only with a determined effort did she do as he'd ordered. Donovan said nothing for a minute. She felt tears well in her eyes, then trickle down her cheeks, but she kept her head bent, unable to look at him.

"Okay," he said more quietly. "Now take off your panties."

She hunched her shoulders even more, doing the only thing she could to protect herself from his gaze. If only they were in the bedroom and it was dark...but...like this?

"Liz..." he warned.

Crying quietly, she slipped her cold hands inside the elastic band at her waist and pushed the panties off. Then she stood before him totally naked, trembling as she endured one nightmare and relived another.

"He...he made me...do this, too," she sobbed softly, unable to stem the words because embarrassment, humiliation, defeat had robbed her of what little pride she might have had. She was shaking uncontrollably. "He made me...stand...in front of him...and take my clothes...off...just like this...and then—"

"What?" Donovan cut in in a whisper, suddenly before her, his hands on her cold quaking shoulders.

She barely registered his presence. The words just seemed to spill. "My father...he told me how...how ashamed I should be...how disgraceful I was. That I shouldn't...shouldn't ever think that...that someone might want...me..." She broke down completely then, weeping copiously. But Donovan pulled her instantly against him, her face pressed to his chest, his trembling hands roaming her back as though he had to warm, to soothe, to protect every inch of her.

"Oh my God," he murmured brokenly, agonizingly, "oh my God...what have I done."

He hugged her to him and rocked her gently, then, keeping her upper body pressed close, he slipped an arm beneath her knees, lifted her and hurried from the den. She continued to cry, and he ran the last few steps to his bedroom, only releasing her legs to snatch his robe from the closet. As quickly as he could he slipped her arms into the sleeves and belted the lush terry fabric around

her waist. Then, lifting her against him again, he sat down on the
edge of the bed and held her tightly.

"I'm sorry, Elizabeth," he cried against her hair. "So sorry. I
didn't know...I'd never have made you do that...if only you'd
told me sooner...I knew that there had to be something, but you
wouldn't tell me and I got so damned impatient with loving you
and being blocked out."

She cried for a while longer, her body curled into a ball on his
lap. Over and over he whispered soft words of apology and love,
while he hugged her and rocked her. He felt her pain and suffered.
He understood her humiliation and was filled with shame. He held
her tighter, loving her with every ounce of his being. Then, when
her sobs had finally begun to ease, he took her face in his hands
and turned it to his.

"Look at me," he whispered. Her eyes were closed. He brushed
damp tendrils of hair from her brow. "Please, sweetheart, look at
me. I know you've got every right not to, but I need you to see
me and hear me and know what I'm feeling."

She hiccuped softly and squeezed her eyes shut, pushing the
last tears from her lids. He blotted them with his thumbs.

"Elizabeth...?"

She opened her eyes, looked at him, then away.

"Liz...?"

She met his gaze then, but with timidity.

"I don't want you to be frightened of me. I've never wanted
that," he said, speaking very, very softly and gently. "I love you,
Elizabeth. No, don't shake your head. It's the truth. I would have
told you sooner but I was trying to go slow when you seemed
threatened, and I didn't know what it was that was bothering you.
I didn't think you'd believe me, and you don't, but that's okay
because I'm going to spend the rest of my life proving it to you.
Don't shut your eyes again, sweetheart. Please?" Only when she
opened them did he go on.

"How old were you when your father did that to you?"

She bit her lip, but he prodded, still in that doe-soft tone. "How
old were you?"

"Tw-twelve…and thirteen…and on…"

"Just when you were reaching adolescence. Just when you were developing as a woman." With a groan he pressed her head to his chest and held her that way until he'd regained his composure. "No wonder you're convinced that you're ugly and unappealing," he murmured, then held her back so he could look at her again. There was an intensity in his gaze this time. "Your father must be a very, very sick man. I wouldn't begin to try to explain why he did what he did. And it does no good rehashing the past. It's the present and the future I'm thinking about." Again he framed her face with his hands. "Elizabeth, you *are* beautiful. I know you don't believe it, but you *are*. I've seen your body, and there's *nothing wrong* with it. It's just as it should be." He cocked his head. "I mean, it's not like you've got a breast sticking out of your navel."

He was rewarded by a self-conscious laugh, which died as soon as it emerged but was a victory of sorts nonetheless.

"That's better." Smiling, he feather-brushed her lips with his thumbs. "Beauty is as beauty does. Have you ever heard that expression?" Very slowly, she nodded. "It applies to you as I've never known it to apply to anyone else. Especially now that I know what you've lived with all these years. You give so much to people, to friends, business associates. Look at what you do for Jamie."

When another thought intruded he frowned. "Liz, what did your father do to him?" When she simply stared at him unsurely, he coaxed. "Please. I want to know, to understand."

It took Liz a long time before she could answer, and then it was in a whisper. "He beat him."

Donovan closed his eyes for a moment. "Oh, God."

But Liz wasn't done. Her words spilled quickly, slurring together at times. "I used to stand in another room wanting to go to Jamie's defense, but I was too scared that Dad would turn on me instead so all I could do was to comfort Jamie afterward and hurt for him and always feel so guilty."

"Oh, God," Donovan murmured again, then grew suddenly

fierce. "Did he ever touch you?" She shook her head quickly. "He never tried to molest you?"

"No. He only did what I told you...and more often it was just words...ugly words."

Donovan had to know there was nothing else. "I don't want you hiding anything from me. The time for that's over."

"No. That was all."

Donovan took a deep, slightly ragged breath. "That was enough." He propped her more comfortably in the crook of his shoulder. "You've never told anyone about this before, have you?" She shook her head. "And all this time you've gone through life believing that you'd repulse any man who looked at you...God, he should be beaten himself. To do that to his own daughter, when she's such a beautiful, beautiful person." He saw that she hadn't opened her mouth to argue, so he pressed on. "I do love you, Liz. I want you to know that. I do love you."

"But you'd given up on me. You were ready to turn me in to the police."

"I wouldn't have done that. It was an empty threat. I knew I had to bring this all to a head somehow. That seemed the only way. You were right. It was out of character. Donovan Grant, the laid-back, happy-go-lucky genius. Well," he sighed, "he's got feelings like the rest of us, and when he's in love, I'm afraid he's not quite so laid-back and happy-go-lucky. At least, not when he's dying inside because the woman he loves wants him out of her life."

"I never wanted that," she murmured. "I was just...just so afraid of letting it go further."

She felt a tension enter him, saw the vulnerability on his face. "I know this may be too much to ask after all I've done, but I've got to ask. I trust that you'll tell me the truth." He hesitated, never once taking his eyes from hers. "Do you, uh, could you love me, even just a little?"

He was the old Donovan then, baring himself, speaking sincerely and Liz felt her chill begin to fade. It was one thing for him to say that he loved her, another for him to ask—not tell, but ask—if she loved him back. But he'd trusted her to tell him the truth, and much as it hurt her, she couldn't lie.

"I don't know, Donovan," she said very softly. "I've pushed the idea of love from my mind for so long that I'm not sure I'm ready to believe in it. Maybe I do love you. Maybe that's why I was so threatened, because I wanted so badly to please you but knew I'd only disappoint you—"

"You *haven't* disappointed me, love. Nothing you've done has disappointed me, except maybe that day when you lashed out at me, and if that was because the seeds of love were there and you were torn and upset, I honestly can't blame you. Knowing what I do now, I can understand why you were so threatened. Not agree, mind you, because I love the way you look, but I do understand now why you don't believe in yourself." His smile was gentle enough to melt another layer of her chill. "That's what we're going to have to work on, you and me."

"Are you...going to keep me here?"

"By force, no. I only did it before out of desperation. But I won't do it again, Liz. No more threats. No more secrets. We've gone beyond those. When I think of a future without you it's pretty dismal, and if there's any chance that you could grow to love me...well, I can live with that." He grinned. "It's a challenge, really, getting you to love me back."

"What about..." Her eyes shifted briefly to the bed.

"I still want to make love to you. I don't think that'll ever change. But I want you to feel better about yourself first, and better about me." He paused. "I would like you to stay with me. There's so little other time, what with both of our jobs—though I want you to take over the DIG Group work again."

"You don't like Brenda? She's very good, and she's adorable."

"I want *you.* And I want every minute we spend together to be good." He hesitated once more. "Liz, if you stay here I won't push you. I mean, there's only this one bed, but it's plenty big and I'll put pillows between us if you want, but what I'd really like is to be able to hold you in the night. We don't have to make love. Only when you want it. But I've dreamed of waking up with you there, and…and…you have to take *some* pity on me…''

His lips were curving into a boyish grin that she simply couldn't resist. If she wanted to be truthful with herself, she'd never been able to resist it, though she'd tried, how she'd tried.

Her own grin was more tentative. ''I will.''

''You'll stay?''

She nodded, buoyed by his obvious pleasure.

He hugged her so tightly his arms trembled and she feared for a minute her ribs would crack. ''O-kay!'' he said with feeling, then set her back. ''What say you get dressed, then we can go to your place and get more of your things and drop them back here, then go out to dinner somewhere special—I have just the place in mind—then—''

''Donovan?''

''Yes, love?''

''Could we make the dinner another time?''

His face fell. ''This sounds familiar.''

''No, it's not that,'' she was quick to reassure him. ''After we get my things, could we just come back here and eat? I'm…I'm afraid I'll fall asleep if we have to sit out dinner at a fancy restaurant. It's been a…tiring week.''

The relief in his expression was as good as a prize. ''Sure, Liz. And you do look beat. But beautiful.'' He grinned, and on impulse swooped down and sealed her lips with a kiss. Then, nearly as quickly, he pulled back. ''I'm sorry. Would you rather I not do that?''

The smile she gave him was the first honest-to-goodness one she'd manufactured in days. ''I kind of liked it,'' she said shyly.

But rather than repeating the kiss, Donovan put his arms around her and hugged her.

Very slowly she slid her arms up and hugged him back.

Donovan left Liz in the bedroom while he retrieved her clothes, then waited in the living room, giving her the privacy she needed, until she'd dressed and joined him. They took a cab to her apartment, and an hour later, another back to his place with two suitcases in hand. He set some steaks on to broil while she neatly placed her things in the drawers and closets he'd cleared. By the time she'd followed her nose to the kitchen, she was starved.

"It's about time," was his reaction when she told him as much. "You really haven't eaten all week, have you?"

"Not much."

"Well," he declared, setting filled plates on the table, "you can make up for it now." He halted just before sitting to gently stroke her hair. "Feeling better?"

She smiled. "Much."

"I'm glad." He pressed a quick kiss to her head, then sat and began to eat. "I'll pick up a telephone-answering machine tomorrow, and we can set it up at your place after work. No one knows where you are, and if someone tries to reach you there'll be no problem. All you have to do is to leave my number on the recorder...better still, let me call the phone company first. They may be able to automatically forward your calls. That'd spare you having to make explanations."

She finished chewing a mouthful of steak and cut into her baked potato. Though hunger seemed her first priority, she was touched by his concern that she not be put in an awkward position. "And when a man answers 'my' number?"

"You can, uh, say it's your cleaning person."

She grinned. "I don't have a cleaning person."

"Then...the plumber?"

"I could just say that you're my boyfriend."

He grinned back. "I'd like that."

"'Course, most of my friends won't believe me and then I'll *really* have explaining to do. Maybe I'd better stick with the plumber."

Donovan could see she was teasing because her grin lingered. "You can tell anyone who's interested that it's your boyfriend and that anything more is none of their business. A little smugness wouldn't hurt. You haven't had much experience with that, have you?"

"Afraid not."

"Well, it's about time you begin. You've got a brilliant, successful, good-looking-as-hell guy in love with you. You have a right to be smug."

Blushing, Liz directed her gaze to her food.

"Liz?"

"Mmm?"

"What are you feeling? I mean, in many ways it's been an awful day for you, and I know you're exhausted, but I keep wondering whether you're happy...or frightened...or embarrassed...or excited."

She thought for a minute. "A little of each, I guess."

"Explain. Tell me."

Setting her fork down, she eyed him hesitantly. "You do have a beautiful place here, Donovan. I think the country house is still my favorite, but I can be very comfortable here."

"About *me*. Tell me what you're feeling about me."

It was harder to explain her feelings because their expression was all so new to her. But she tried, sensing Donovan's genuine need to know. "I'm feeling happy. You're right. You're brilliant and successful and good-looking as hell. In the minutes I let myself believe that you love me, I feel happy and excited, almost overwhelmingly so."

"But in the other minutes?"

Her eyes clouded. "I feel scared. Scared that it's all a fluke, too good to believe. Scared that you'll tire of me in a few days or a week or a month and that you'll see me for what I am."

"You are *not*—"

"For what I've always *seen* myself as being," she corrected. "I do still see myself that way, Donovan. It's habit, perhaps. Or reality," she said more softly, then raced on before he could argue. "And I also feel a little frightened. I've never lived with a man...well, not in that sense."

"I'll give you all the privacy you need, sweetheart. You've got space until you decide you don't need it as much."

"I know," she said quietly, lifting her fork, then holding it suspended above her steak. Once started, her thoughts flowed. "I'm also worried that my insecurities will haunt me whenever we're out somewhere and there are other women in the room." She pressed her lips together for a minute. "When I was talking with Cheryl at her party that night, she said that if I didn't want you, I should give you her number. I felt it then—jealousy, unsureness. And again when Brenda was talking about everything she was doing to make you see her as a woman."

"Brenda was doing that? I didn't notice a thing because I couldn't stop thinking of you. As for Cheryl, I've never met the woman. But—" he reached over and squeezed her hand "—believe me, I have met lots and lots of others, and not one of them has captivated me the way you have."

She chewed on her lip, then darted him a sidelong glance. "What if I don't please you in bed?"

"You will. I told you, I've never had doubts about that."

"But I don't know what to do."

"I'll show you. And because I'll have been able to do that, it'll be all that much better. If you want to look at it one way, I'll be to blame if things aren't right. After all, I'm supposed to be the experienced one. And I *know* the passion's there in you, Liz. I've had glimpses of it from time to time. Hey, don't get all flustered. That was a compliment. Do you remember when you first told me you were a virgin and I said that it was a gift?" He waited until she'd nodded. "Well, it is. I've been with women who are as experienced as the local madam, and I've spent my time with them wondering who taught them what they know and who'll be the one to teach them more. It's definitely taken something from the relationship, at least from my own feelings toward the relationship." He paused, thinking. "But I think it'd be different even if you weren't a virgin. *You're* different. And special. And when you look at me the way you are now, I feel like I'm the only man on earth. It's a nice feeling, Liz. Believe me, it's a very, very nice feeling." He smiled at her a minute longer, then gave her hand a parting pat. "Eat up. You warned me you might fall asleep, and that'd *really* bruise my ego."

"I said in a restaurant."

"Methinks here, too. You can only prop those lids up so long."

"It's all the wine I've drunk," she teased, making no effort to deny his claim.

He eyed the glasses, which were filled with nothing more potent than water. "Good thing I broke out the best," he said with a chuckle. "Lord only knows *what* would have happened with the cheap stuff."

Liz chuckled, too, then set to finishing every last bit of food on her plate. By then her head was all but wobbling on her neck, so Donovan suggested she go to bed. He walked her to the door of the kitchen, then turned her to him.

"Should I put pillows between us?"

"No."

"Will you be frightened if you wake up in the morning and find me holding you?"

"Maybe a little…at first."

"Just remember that I love you and that I won't do anything but hold you. It might be my own personal need to reassure myself that you're really here. Okay?"

She nodded, and he turned her and sent her off while he stayed in the kitchen. She was nervous taking her nightgown from the drawer and went into the bathroom to undress. But minutes after she'd carefully let herself into the far side of the bed she was asleep.

The next morning when she woke, Donovan was quietly holding her, and she found that she liked it very, very much.

Monday went by in a whirl for Liz, with no less than five of her associates commenting on how wonderful she looked. Well rested, they said, and full of color. She had a smile—yes, a smug one—for each of them.

Tuesday morning when she awoke, she was in Donovan's arms again. This time, she took stock of her surroundings, namely his chest, which was solid and covered by a soft furring of hair and fragrant in an utterly manly way beneath her cheek. She touched him, timidly skirting one nipple, then lifted her lips for his kiss when his quiet gasp told her he was awake.

"I like it when you touch me," he murmured against her mouth.

"It felt good. You're very warm."

"Mmm." He kissed her again, more thoroughly this time, then set her gently back. "We have to get up. You've got a nine-o'clock appointment. Want to take the bathroom first?"

She nodded and rolled to her side of the bed, tugging her nightgown down as she climbed out. She was halfway to the bathroom when Donovan called her back.

"Liz? One more kiss?"

Cheeks rosy, she returned to him, savoring his kiss until, with a light pat to her bottom, he sent her off.

By Wednesday morning her legs were entwined with his when she awoke. She felt comfortable and surprisingly secure, and grew more adventurous with the exploratory hand she ran over his chest and his arms. His tempered strength delighted her.

"Do you always wear pajama bottoms, or have you put them on for my benefit?" she asked after he'd given her a good-morning kiss.

"The latter, I'm afraid. I usually sleep in the buff."

She set her head down on his chest and dropped her gaze to his hips where his pajamas rode low. Then, without thinking of the consequences, she slid her palm down the dark, narrowing trail of hair to that point.

Donovan sucked in a sharp breath. "Oooh, sweetheart, you're playing with fire."

She snatched her hand away and quickly raised her head. "I'm sorry. I didn't think—"

"Shh." He pressed her head back down. "It's okay. It's just that I want you to touch me there, too. Just thinking of it does things to me."

The idea that she could so easily excite him was almost incredible, yet when she looked down his body she saw it was so. Her fingers itched, unsure but tempted. In the end it was curiosity that gave movement to her hand. It inched slowly past his waist, then his navel, then over the band of his pajamas until his tumescence was not mere vision but hard fact.

"That's it," he whispered hoarsely. He covered her hand with his and moved it gently up and down, up and down, until his breath was uneven, his entire body tense. "I, uh, I think that's enough." He swallowed loudly, then cleared his throat. "I'm a little short on control this time of day." He drew her hand up to cover his heart, which beat strong and fast against it.

What Liz hadn't expected was that the feel of his sex would touch off sensual reverberations in her own body, yet it did. A warmth spread from her breasts to her loins, and for the first time she knew true frustration. But Donovan was setting her gently back to her side of the bed.

"Can we meet at lunchtime? I thought we might go shopping."

"Shopping?"

"I'd like to buy you a dress for Thursday night."

"Donovan, you don't have to—"

"I know I don't have to, and I know you've got a perfectly beautiful dress hanging in the closet, and you've already told me your feelings about being 'kept.' But I *want* to buy you something. My motives are purely selfish. Will you deny me the pleasure?"

She rolled her eyes. "Talk about guilt trips. How can I refuse when you put it that way?" In truth, she was tickled pink, even more so when he beamed.

So he picked her up at the office and, hand in hand, they headed for the exclusive department store Donovan had in mind. He stayed with her until she'd selected—actually, he had to help with the selecting because he wanted the best, which she shied away from when she caught sight of the price tag—and tried on a stunning silk dress of a burgundy shade that brought out rather than overpowered her features. After settling the account with the salesperson, he excused himself, claiming he had one or two purchases of his own to make, and arranged to meet Liz by the front door in ten minutes.

When she arrived, he had a box under one arm and was looking vaguely sheepish. "Okay," she grinned. "What did you buy?"

"Oh, something…personal."

Envisioning briefs or an athletic support, or some other bit of intimate male attire, she blushed and asked no more. Grinning, he took the dress box from her arms and ushered her across the street to a jewelry store, where he insisted on buying her a pair of elegant pearl studs.

"Donovan, I can't let you—"

"Of course you can. They'll look smashing with the dress, even more smashing with your complexion. Besides, I haven't had this much fun since…since I shopped for you in San Francisco, and before that, well, I can't even remember."

One side of her lips turned down. "What if I can't put them on?"

"I told you I'd help. We can do it tonight, and you'll have plenty of time to recover before the party."

"I don't know. I'm starting to get really nervous about this party. New dress, new earrings…there's probably going to be royalty there."

"Sure is. *You.* Indulge me, Liz. I'm so proud of you, and it'll make me that much prouder to know that I've contributed something to all this."

She blushed. "I think you've lost your marbles."

He simply wiggled his brows, then pocketed the box with the earrings, took her arm and escorted her to a small sandwich shop near her office before he dropped her off.

That night she discovered precisely what personal somethings he'd bought during those ten minutes he'd been alone in the store. He waited until after they'd had dinner, until she stood in front of the bathroom mirror admiring the pearl earrings that, to her surprise and infinite relief, he'd had no trouble inserting. Then he disappeared and returned carrying the box, which he handed to her.

"This is for you."

"For me? But I thought—"

"I figured as much," he said with a grin. "Go ahead, open it."

She slid the top off and pressed back the layers of tissue, then bit her lip and shyly looked up.

"Not for the party," he instructed, but ever so gently, "or for me. Just for you."

The color rose in Liz's cheeks as she timidly touched the lace-and-silk confection of an ivory-hued bra, panties and matching slip.

"I want you to wear them," he went on in that same gentle tone, "just so you can see how super they look on you, so you can feel really…feminine, on the inside, privately. No one has to know they're there but you."

"I've never worn anything like this," she breathed. She didn't look at him because she felt slightly embarrassed, but she also felt excited and, yes, feminine.

"Then it's long overdue. You'd be amazed at what little noth- ings like these can do for the ego."

"You've had personal experience?" she teased, pleased to see his own cheeks grow red.

"Well, not in exactly the same way, but I do know that what I wear can make a difference in the way I feel. Right about now I'm feeling pretty stuffy because I've had to wear a suit all week. I'm really looking forward to going north. You've got plenty of jeans, don't you? And heavy sweaters—"

She cut him off with a laugh. "Yes, Donovan. I've got plenty for the country. And if I don't, I'm sure you'll shanghai me to the nearest sportswear store to rectify the situation."

"Would that be horrible?" he asked softly. "I really do love buying you things."

"I know," she said as softly, looking at him then, feeling her insides positively melt at the tenderness of his expression. "That's what makes receiving them so nice." She gave the lingerie a lingering caress. "Thank you for these…and for the dress…and the earrings. I do love them all."

He put his arms around her then and ran an adoring gaze over her face. "I'm glad. So glad," he murmured, kissing her gently before leading her back to the den, where they'd both left work they'd brought home from the office.

Donovan was the one in for a surprise when he showed up at her office late Thursday afternoon to take her home. He walked in, then brought himself up short and stared. She'd been concentrating on a report when he arrived and had jerked her head up, then sat still, holding her breath.

He continued to stare, but his eyes widened, mirroring the growing smile on his face. "Your hair looks fantastic!" he breathed at last. "When did you do it?"

She shyly touched the ends, which barely reached her shoulders. "At lunchtime. Are you sure it looks okay? I feel naked. I think it's been hanging down to the middle of my back since I was eight."

"It looks unbelievable! And that's natural wave, isn't it?"

She blushed and nodded. "I didn't know I had it until the guy started cutting and there it was." She scrunched up her nose. "I'm not sure I like the front. I told him I didn't want bangs, but he insisted that I'd really outgrown a center part with everything hanging to one length. They're not really bangs, just kind of—" she gestured with her hand "—wispy things."

Beaming, Donovan walked toward her. "Whatever they are, they look great!" Unable to resist, he gently touched the shining brown tresses, first by her temples, then her crown, then her nape. "You look so soft." He cleared his throat of its frogginess. "I hope you know that this is going to do nothing for my peace of mind."

"It really looks okay?"

"More than okay. It looks beautiful, Elizabeth. I love it. I love *you*," he murmured as he dropped his head to give her a soft kiss. By the time he was done, he had to clear his throat again. "Uh, we'd better be going. Are you almost finished?"

It took Liz a minute to refocus, because his kiss had reawakened those little yearnings in her. She forced her eyes to the desk top, only to close the report she'd been reading. "I can finish in the morning."

So they headed home to change for the party.

Liz had had a hot bath and was finishing applying a touch of blusher and mascara—both new purchases—when Donovan called from the bedroom.

"Are you decent?"

She looked down and automatically crossed an arm over her breasts, then glanced back in the mirrow. Slowly and determinedly she lowered her arm.

"Yes."

The door swung open and Donovan sauntered in wearing his dark dress pants and a fine white shirt, which hung open. At the sight of her, he stopped short. His eyes ran over her breasts, which were delicately encased in the new bra, and her panties, outlined clearly beneath the slip. With a low moan he turned to the wall and put his forehead on the arm he braced there.

"Oh God," Liz breathed, distraught. "You don't like it."

"Just the opposite," was his deep groan. Very slowly he straightened, then as slowly turned to her. "The problem is that we might well not make it to that party at all. I thought you were dressed."

Self-consciously she looked down and frowned. "I guess I wanted you to see me...wearing these...."

"I do," he rasped, taking her in trembling arms and pressing her full length against him. "I've been imagining it all day. Needless to say, I haven't gotten a helluva lot of work done."

Liz relaxed, then grew almost giddy. She did feel feminine at that moment. And sexy. And...almost beautiful.

"I'm glad," she whispered against the warmth of his throat. She felt the tension in him, but it was a good tension, and with her body molded to his as it was, the tension became an internal thing for her, as well.

He held her back and gave her a hungry look, then kissed her deeply and thoroughly. She was beginning to think that it wouldn't be so awful if they did miss the party when he wrenched his mouth away and dug into his trousers pocket.

"Here," he said hoarsely. "These go with the earrings."

Before she could know what he was up to, he had a single strand of pearls around her throat. He turned her to the mirror and stood behind her to fumble with the catch. His fingers were none too steady, and he swore once before he finally smoothed the beads down on her chest. Hands on her shoulders, he looked at her reflection.

Liz was entranced by the pearls. "They're beautiful," she whispered. "Too much...."

"Not enough," he whispered back, lowering his mouth to her neck, where he pressed a series of soft kisses that had her closing her eyes and leaning back against him. "God, Liz, I want you so badly."

She could feel how badly, because his hips were arched against hers, but she could only concentrate on the gentle caress of his lips, then on his hands, which slid to cover her breasts. He lifted them, then kneaded softly, as she sighed at the flush of heat that spread through her.

He turned her in his arms and looked down at her, tracing her features with fingers that were light and shaking, sliding his hands down to her throat, then over the pearls to her breasts again. She felt an instinctive glimmer of apprehension, because he was watching his hands and what they touched, but that apprehension was soon overcome by the rising pleasure she felt. When he slipped his fingers inside the cups of her bra and explored the soft swelling of flesh there, a sound of delight escaped her lips.

"You're so lovely," he whispered, inching his fingers farther until they glanced past her nipples. "So lovely."

Eyes closed, she sighed his name. She wanted to touch him, too, but her hands were anchored on his shoulders if for no other purpose than to keep her upright. She nearly cried out in frustration when his fingers withdrew, but he was spreading his shirt open and lifting her against him.

"We have to leave," he rasped as though to remind himself, but he didn't release her. His hands were roaming her back, finally homing in on the catch of her bra, which he undid so quickly she could only gasp.

"It's okay, love. I just need to feel you against me. Just for a minute." The same hand was forward in an instant, tugging the bra up to her armpits. Her bare breasts touched his chest then, and the electricity of it curled through her. "See? It's wonderful...oh, Liz, I need you. Oh, God..."

She felt the same. Her body was coiled and trembling, and she suddenly wanted him to touch her all over, to kiss her all over, to finally relieve the awful knot of need so low in her belly.

But he was setting her back, replacing her bra and fastening it while she struggled to regain her composure. She was disappointed and frustrated.

"I...I thought you wanted me," she heard herself say. Such a short while ago she would have been appalled to hear the words, but she could only think of what he'd kindled, of what still burned.

Raking an unsteady hand through his hair, he gave her a crooked smile. "I do want you, but I want you to want me as badly."

"I do want you," she whispered.

"Not as badly. Not yet. When that time comes, you'll know. We'll both know." He took her face in his hands and kissed away her perplexed expression. "I love you, Liz. Keep that in mind while they're falling all over you tonight at the party."

They didn't exactly "fall over" her at the party, Liz mused, but the attention she got, the admiring glances didn't fail to stun her.

"It must be the dress...or the pearls," she murmured, when Donovan swept her away for a minute alone.

"It's not the dress or the pearls. It's *you*."

"I think it's *you*. I'm floating on the coattails of your charisma. I've never received compliments like these."

"You probably have, but you've ignored them. I know." He arched a pointed brow. "You ignored most of mine from the start. And don't give me that baloney about my charisma. You heard Donaldson. He said that old man Obermeyer never stops raving about you. I wouldn't be surprised if you get a new client out of this."

She blushed. "That wasn't why I came."

"I know that, but it'd be a nice side effect." He hooked a firm arm around her waist. "Come on. There's someone else I want you to meet...."

When they got home that night, Donovan turned her to him. "Thank you for coming, Liz. You made me very happy. Were you? I mean, was it as bad as you thought it would be?"

She gave a soft laugh and looked down. "I wasn't expecting the worst."

"But you've said how you often feel at parties like that. Did you feel...awkward or outclassed?"

"No. Well, maybe just a little, once in a while."

"And the next time will be even better. It's all a matter of self-confidence, and that's bound to grow. I'm telling you, Liz, you had more going for you than any other woman in that room."

There was a tiny catch in her voice. "I don't know about that. There were some lovely women there—"

"Every one of whom you can compete with on the outside and none of whom can come close to you on the inside. As far as I was concerned, you were the only woman worth talking to in the room."

Liz studied his earnest expression. Indeed, he hadn't given more than a passing glance at another woman, and she'd been purposely looking to see if he would. "You made me feel special, Donovan. Thank you."

"You made my night. Thank *you*." He paused. An inkling of unsureness wrinkled his brow. "Let's go to bed," he said quietly, then added quickly, "Not to make love, just to be together. I want to be with you when you fall asleep tonight. Is that okay?"

She gave him a soft smile, then nodded. Even now the memory of what she'd felt earlier that evening was fresh in her mind, and with Donovan's tall, sturdy body so close to her she felt new waves of desire stirring. "I'd like that." She hesitated for an instant. "You can even…if you like…"

He draped an arm around her shoulders and led her down the hall. "What? And let you think I'm an easy lay? No way! I'd never make love to a woman after living with her for only four days. Nope. Tonight we'll sleep. Besides," he murmured more naughtily, "it'll take most of the night to do what I'd like, and we've both got to work tomorrow…"

Left unsaid was that tomorrow was Friday and they didn't have to work on Saturday.

The drive to the country was slow, what with the weekend automotive exodus from the city and the snow that was lightly falling. By the time Donovan and Liz left the highway, the snow wasn't falling so lightly anymore and he was growing concerned.

"I'd like to go straight to the house, but if we don't make a stop at the supermarket, we may have to subsist on canned goods all weekend."

"We could make do. I'm sure you've got soup, and there must be things in the freezer."

"Yeah, but I really like fresh orange juice, and cereal's no good without milk."

He sounded like such a little boy at that minute that Liz couldn't help but laugh. So they did stop at the market, and by the time they reached the road leading to the house, Donovan was singing the praises of four-wheel drive. Four inches of snow had fallen, which wouldn't have been so terrible had the temperature not fallen even more quickly, turning the ground beneath the snow to a sheet of ice. He negotiated the twisting road with great care, and they both breathed a sigh of relief when at last they arrived at the house.

After they'd turned on the heat, built a fire and made dinner, they sat together in the loft watching a movie. Curled comfortably against Donovan, with an afghan spread liberally over them both, Liz tried to concentrate on the movie, but she couldn't. She felt happy and content, but restless, as well, for neither her mind nor her body could ignore the man who breathed so evenly nearby.

He'd been wonderful all week. He'd anticipated her needs, catered to them, respected them. He'd done everything in his power to let her know that he did truly find her attractive, that he did truly love her.

She wanted him. She wanted to touch him, to kiss him. She wanted him to do the same, and when she thought of that, she grew all the more restless. She marveled at the way he could lie there so unaffected, and she wondered if she was wrong, if he didn't really want her.

Tipping her head back so that she could study his face, she found her answer. A helpless smile spread across her features, and she felt a world of tenderness well up in her.

His dark lashes rested atop his cheekbones. His hair fell rakishly across his brow. His cheeks bore a slight flush. He was fast asleep.

"Donovan?" she whispered. "Donovan? Wake up." She gently shook his arm, rewarded when his eyes fluttered open. "You're exhausted. Why don't we go to bed?"

It took him a minute to realize where he was, and Liz grinned at the lost way he looked around.

"What happened?" he murmured groggily.

"You fell asleep is what happened." She threw back the afghan and pushed herself up, then reached for his hand. "Come on. To bed with you." She felt a little like a mother as she led him to the bedroom, but she kind of liked it. He'd taken such good care of her all week that she welcomed the chance to do something in return.

While Donovan stood by the side of the bed absently fumbling with his shirt buttons, she drew back the quilt and puffed the pillow, then turned to help him undress. Since she hadn't turned on a light for fear of disturbing his sleepy state, the room was in semidarkness, lighted only by the dusky glow of the snow outside.

One part of her was grateful; she'd never undressed Donovan before and she felt vaguely self-conscious. The other part of her wanted to see more but had to settle for the faint outlines of his body. To her astonishment she discovered that these were as inflammatory to her senses as a fully lighted scene, for what the dimness failed to provide her imagination did. By the time he was stripped down to his shorts, she was trembling.

Dutifully she helped him into bed.

"You're coming, too, aren't you?" he mumbled, tugging the quilt to his armpits.

"In a minute," she whispered, then stood watching as his lids closed. He was beautiful lying there, his features in such thorough repose. Between his mussed hair and the shadow of his beard, he had the look of a rogue and the air of a child. It was a point in between that Liz craved.

Sighing, she turned and fished her nightgown from the drawer she'd set it in earlier. She closed the bathroom door behind her before she switched on the light and switched it off before she reemerged a few minutes later.

She padded softly to where Donovan lay and found that he hadn't moved. Gliding quietly around the bed, she pulled back the quilt on her side and settled gently down on the sheets. Rather than lie back, though, she turned her head to look again at the man beside her. He *was* beautiful, all the more so in the pale-blue light that should have been eerie but was somehow romantic.

Rising from the bed, she crept to the window. So cold outside...so warm inside. She thought of Donovan lying beneath the sheets in nothing but his shorts, and she grew even warmer, but in private places, places that had yet to know the fullest meaning of heat. She who hadn't dared once to dream now wanted so much...so much...

"Liz?"

His quiet voice came to her and her heart skipped a beat.

"Is something wrong, sweetheart?"

She turned and met his gaze. "No," she whispered. "I just..."

"Just what?"

She knew he couldn't possibly see the yearning in her eyes because it was so dark and there was still so much space separating them, and even if he did see it, she knew that he wouldn't push her to do what she didn't want to do. But she did—she did want him....

Quelling an unsteadiness born of anticipation, she slowly crossed the room to stand beside him. "Donovan, I...I..."

He was studying the way she twisted her hands together, the way her eyes were wide, almost pleading, the way her breath was coming in hesitant bursts. He knew what *he* wanted, and could only pray that she wanted the same. He raised the corner of the blanket in silent invitation that she join him, then held his breath.

He didn't have to hold it long—either his breath or the blanket—because she was quickly in bed with him and his arms were around her. "Oh, love," he gasped seconds before he captured her lips in a kiss she returned with the same hunger he felt. "Are you sure?" he whispered when at last he drew his head back.

She nodded.

"You do want me?"

She nodded again.

"As badly as I want you?"

She had only to feel the hardness of his body pressing against her and the answering thrill that surged through her to know that she did. "Yes."

A shudder went through him as he hugged her again. Then he rolled her to her back and moved over her, kissing her, pressing himself into her softness. He was gasping when he released her lips. "Slow. We'll...take it slow!" It was almost a command, and clearly directed at himself because he hadn't realized how fiercely his body would react to her simple yes.

He did kiss her more slowly, savoring every corner of her mouth, then the soft insides. Entwining his fingers with hers, he pressed her hands back to the sheets while he explored her face, her neck, her throat. Her hands remained where they were even when he released them to touch her breasts, and she was straining upward when he spoke again.

"Liz? Can I slip your nightgown off? You're so beautiful. I want to touch you."

A frisson of apprehension skipped through her, but she only had to look at his face and see the desire there to realize she wanted him, too. She nodded, then held her breath while he rolled off her and carefully eased the nightgown up over her thighs and her hips, then her waist and breasts, until it was over her head and discarded.

"There," he whispered as he reached up to unball her fists and hold her hands, "that wasn't so bad." Rather than take his time looking at her body, as she'd been afraid he might do, he eased over her again. Eyes closed, he tipped his head back. "Ahh. That feels so good. Oh, Liz, you can't imagine—"

But she could, because the feel of his nearly bare skin against hers was instantly rewarding. Her lips were parted when he caught them again, and he took a long while kissing her, letting her adjust to the feel of his warmth against hers. Only when he heard her soft, purring response did he slip to her side and very gently run a hand from her navel to her collarbone and back.

"I can't believe you're actually here," he murmured. His eyes followed the progress of his hand, but Liz didn't mind because he seemed so pleased and what he was doing felt so good. He continued to look at her and touch her, covering each of her breasts in turn before he bent his head and took one dark areola into his mouth.

Unprepared for the tugging sensation that ignited a fire to her womb, Liz gasped. But he continued to suck, raising his mouth only to touch the tip of his tongue to her nipple, and soon she was holding him closer, arching into his moist grasp, breathing raggedly.

His hands wandered farther then, coasting over her stomach to her thighs, returning over the juncture of her legs. With a quick indrawn breath, she pressed her knees together, but in an instant he was murmuring words of encouragement.

"It's okay, love. Let me touch you there. You're beautiful...every sweet inch." His hand crept lower again and began a slow, sensual stroking. "Relax, love. That's it. Open for me..."

She had no choice, because the fire there was so hot that she needed all the relief he could offer. Soon enough she learned that it was only temporary. Wherever his fingers delved the fire raged hotter, and she was clutching his waist, instinctively urging him toward her.

He paused only to rid himself of his briefs, and then he was back, tormenting her with his lips, his teeth, his tongue, his fingers.

"Donovan!" she breathed, unable to cope with the pleasure-pain a minute longer. Yet she did, for another minute, then two and more. Only when Donovan was satisfied that she was fully ready did he slide between her thighs.

"I love you, Elizabeth," he moaned as, with one magnificent thrust, he surged forward.

Liz cried out softly and arched her back in a reflexive attempt to escape the sharp pain of his entrance, but he held himself deeply embedded in her while he murmured soft, soothing words.

"That's it, love. It's done. The worst is over. Just relax. It'll ease."

She bit her lip against the shallow panting she couldn't control, but he was right. The pain was easing. He held himself still, filling her but demanding nothing. When he felt her thighs slowly fall back, he propped himself on his elbows and framed her face with his hands.

"I love you," he murmured between whispered kisses. "You have no idea how much." He drew his mouth over her eyes and brushed her lips with his thumbs. "Better?"

She gave a jerky nod. "I'm...sorry."

"For what?"

"For being such a ninny. It wasn't so bad...the pain."

"But it was sudden and it had to be, and *I'm* the one who's sorry about that," he crooned. "The wonderful thing is that it'll never be like that again. It only gets better and better. Do you believe me?"

She gave a short laugh. "I think I'd believe most anything you tell me since you've gotten me this far."

"And it is far, love. You're not a virgin anymore. You're mine now. All mine." He sealed the vow with a kiss that grew slowly seductive, then he began to touch her again, teasing her, coaxing her, stimulating her with his caresses until she was the one to move her hips in demand for his active possession.

Carefully he withdrew from her, then eased back inside, repeating the tempered motion until she joined it. From then on the pleasure spiraled for them both. From time to time he whispered endearments, but soon he was too caught up in her flame to do anything but gasp and drive onward.

As for Liz, she was whirling in an eddy of delight, reaching one plateau then surging to another higher and hotter. Stunned by the power of what she felt, she responded with an intuitive sense of rhythm. Her fingers dug into the slick muscles of his back, and she held on for dear life when she felt she would shatter into a million star-flung pieces.

"Donovan...?" she cried, frightened at the end.

"Let it come, love. It's there. Let it come. I'll hold you."

He did, but it was for his own sake, as well, for with the first of her spasms his own body erupted, and he could think of nothing but clinging to this woman, to the pleasure she brought him, to the love he'd never known before and that he cherished nearly above life itself.

It was a long time before their harsh pants eased and either of them could speak. Donovan kissed the moistness from her brow and the tip of her nose, then slowly, relunctantly slid to the side and drew her to nestle against him.

"Oh, Donovan," she breathed, her smile audible even in that whisper. "I can't believe it."

He was smiling, too, then chuckling aloud. "It was good, wasn't it?"

"Good? No. It was fantastic!"

He chuckled again and hugged her tightly.

"Is it always that way?" she asked, rubbing her cheek against the damply curling hair on his chest.

"Not for everyone, especially the first time. For us, though, it'll always be as good, then better, and better, and better…I love you, Liz." When she tipped back her head and opened her mouth, he put a long finger against it. "Shh. Just let me say the words. If you say anything now, I'll always wonder if it was leftover passion or gratitude or simply sheer exhaustion. When you say those words to me, I want it to be at a time when I least expect it. But when you say them, you'd better mean them. Because as soon as I hear them, I'm going to ask you to marry me, and you'd better be prepared to say yes. Understood?"

Liz smiled against his finger, which had lingered to lightly stroke her lips. She knew that she loved him, but she also knew that he was right. When she said the words, she wanted them to carry the full weight they deserved. When she said them, she wanted to be able to say yes.

With a gentle kiss to his fingertip, she nodded, then settled down to enjoy the spanking new happiness of the moment.

They spent the weekend deliciously snowbound, if only in spirit since the plow came through Saturday morning and Donovan shoveled the walks that afternoon. Other than a frivolous romp in the snow on Sunday morning, though, they didn't budge.

The majority of their time was spent in a bed of one sort or another. They made love beneath the covers in the bedroom, on a pallet of cushions before the living-room fire, on the sofa in the loft. Donovan taught Liz the passionate art with the tenderness, the consideration that was so much a part of his nature. Ever aware of her ingrained self-consciousness, he conquered her body by steps until there was nothing she hid from his hands or his lips or his tongue. When she felt comfortable enough to stand nude with him in broad daylight, he was filled with pride and no small sense of victory.

He insisted she take long hot baths, then proceeded to join her and show her the pleasures of fluidity. More than once he took to massaging her aching muscles, only to have the massage end in another passionate bout. When Liz swore she would never walk again, he laughed and strolled out of the room, knowing she'd soon follow on his heels. Inevitably she did.

The woman who returned to Manhattan with him very early Monday morning was a far cry from the one who'd left there the Friday before. Liz glowed. She felt fulfilled in a very feminine way and more self-confident than she'd ever been before. True, that self-confidence always faltered a bit when she and Donovan were apart during the day, but their reunions were always so sweet that she gradually managed to control those daytime insecurities, as well.

Little by little she let slip to her friends that she was staying with Donovan. Where she'd half-suspected they'd be surprised that Donovan should remain interested in her, they weren't. Rather they accepted the news as though she fully deserved both him and the happiness he gave her. They were thrilled for her, and that fact bolstered her all the more.

As the weeks passed, Donovan took her out more and more, introducing her to his friends and business associates. On each instance he made her feel as though she was the best thing to ever come along in his life. His pride was boundless, as was his attentiveness. Never once did he so much as show a passing interest in another woman. It never ceased to amaze Liz that a perfectly beautiful woman could be standing next to him, yet he'd only have eyes for her.

Thus encouraged, she began to take more of the initiative when she was with him. More frequently she took on the cooking of dinner. She invited him to a get-together of several of her associates and their dates. She splurged on clothes and underthings, all of which were far more stylish than anything she'd bought before, and took new interest in her appearance.

In lovemaking, as well, she grew bolder, though in truth it came quite naturally. She was curious about Donovan's body, wanting to explore him, to taste him, to discover what aroused him most. And since that arousal was very definitely two-way, she never once regretted her forwardness. Nor did Donovan. He called her a born seductress, and occasionally, when his body was limp and drained, bemoaned the Pandora's box he'd opened. But his words of love were always soon to follow, and Liz felt on top of the world.

Work-wise, their lives meshed as comfortably. Shortly before Christmas the Ullman merger went public, and though its attendant fanfare demanded much of their time, it was time spent together and therefore pleasurable. Donovan took the news of Ray Obermeyer's windfall in stride and even insisted on taking Liz and Cheryl to lunch one day to let the latter know he held no ill will toward her. Indeed, he laughed, he was almost grateful for what Ray had done, since it had brought Liz and him together. Liz blushed, but couldn't argue.

Where once Liz thought that her career had to take precedence over all else, now she found that she could easily arrange her schedule to accommodate the times she spent with Donovan. Karen Reynolds was a big help on that score, encouraging her to plan appointments for those days when she'd be in the city and to take paperwork with her when Donovan had to be in Troy.

Christmas came and went, and was the happiest one Liz could remember. She and Donovan spent it alone in the country house with a small, gaily decorated tree by the window and an ever-burning fire in the hearth. It was all the more meaningful, this time together, because two days later Donovan's son arrived and Liz temporarily moved back to her apartment.

It had been a mutual decision, given Donovan's growing relationship with his son, that David shouldn't be overwhelmed by the fact that his father was living with a woman. As it happened, though, Liz spent every free minute with the two of them, and at Donovan's insistence. It was almost as if he was more sure of himself when he was with her, and it worked out well all around. Donovan seemed more at ease with David, what with Liz's helping hand. David seemed more at ease with Donovan, what with not having every bit of his father's attention centered on him. Liz and David got along famously, such that by the time he boarded his plane to return home, David was instructing his father that he should marry Liz before losing her.

Donovan thought about that often. He hadn't mentioned marriage again, and Liz still hadn't said the words. But he no longer thought of their relationship in terms of a game with players making alternating moves. He and Liz were together, which had been his primary goal all along.

He knew that she loved him. He could see it in her eyes when she looked at him, feel it in her body when she made love to him. And there weren't any other men in her life—except her father and Jamie. The former was no problem. Though Liz hadn't been in touch with the elder Jerome, Donovan felt confident that Liz could hold her own now where her father and his perversities were concerned.

Jamie was another matter. Religiously Liz phoned him every week, and Donovan sensed that any qualms she might still have about herself related to the responsibility she felt for Jamie. She was always subdued for a few minutes after those calls, and though Donovan talked with her and tried to make her understand that she was doing everything she could for Jamie, certainly enough to cancel out the long-standing guilt she felt, he wasn't sure if he was getting through. It appeared that Liz was going to have to work things out for herself on that score, and all Donovan could do was love her, support her and wait.

The wait wasn't as long as he'd feared it might be. Two weeks into January, on a Wednesday night shortly after he and Liz had arrived home, the phone rang. Donovan reached it first.

"Hello?"

There was a long silence, then a click. He replaced the receiver and headed for the kitchen after Liz, but within seconds the phone pealed again. He grabbed it from the wall just inside the kitchen door.

"Hello?"

Again there was a long silence.

"Hello!" he repeated, puzzled.

At last a man's voice came through, somewhat irritably giving the number he'd dialed and asking if he'd reached it.

"Yes," Donovan answered. "You've dialed correctly."

"But this is supposed to be Elizabeth Jerome's number."

Donovan felt a certain premonition. "It is. Hold on. I'll get her." He put the phone against his chest, then held it out to a questioning Liz.

"Hello?"

"Who was that?" a familiar voice asked.

She let out a sigh, then looked at Donovan. "Jamie. Hi! Is everything okay?" He never lifted his own phone to call her unless there was a problem, and she'd called him just the Sunday before.

"Who *was* that, Liz?"

"That? Uh, that was Donovan Grant."

"Who's he?"

"The man I've been seeing."

Jamie laughed, but it had a sneering twist. "That's a new one. I didn't think you dated."

"I do."

"What's he doing at your apartment?" The tone was definitely one of demand, almost indignation, rather than brotherly concern.

Liz felt her hackles rising, but she couldn't quite come out with the truth. Jamie needed time. "Where are you? You sound very close."

"I am very close. I'm at the airport."

"Here?" She paled, and Donovan put a gently supportive hand on her shoulder. "*Is* something wrong?"

"Nah. Work's just getting to me, so I thought I'd take a while off."

"Oh, no, Jamie. You haven't been let go, have you?"

"I may just quit, but I haven't been fired yet. This is vacation time, which my boss is generous enough to dole out." His sarcasm did nothing for Liz's peace of mind.

"Okay. Vacation is fine. After you've had a break you'll feel better about things."

He didn't address that particular issue, but was obviously more concerned for his immediate well-being. "I thought I'd stay with you for a couple of days. You're not running out of town, are you?"

"Uh, no."

"Good. I'll be over soon."

"Jamie, maybe—Jamie?" She waited, then slowly replaced the phone and looked up at Donovan. "He hung up. He's on his way to my apartment."

Donovan gently kneaded her shoulders, easing them back when they tried to slump forward. "That's okay, love. He can stay there."

"But he'll expect me to be there."

He spoke after a minute's pause. "You could."

"No! I want to be here with you, not there. But I'll have to tell Jamie where I am and why."

"You don't owe him elaborate explanations, Liz," he reminded her quietly, repeating arguments he'd used before. "You're an adult. So is he. You've got every right to live your own life."

She hung her head. "I know."

"Listen, put your coat on and I'll take you over. You can let Jamie in and get him settled. We can even take him to dinner. Then you and I can come back here. Jamie will be fine. He's used to being alone."

"I know, which is one of the reasons I feel so awful. I'm the only family he's got. I'll feel guilty leaving him alone when he's here."

"But you say you don't want to stay there."

"I don't!"

"So we can do second best. We can spend time with him in the evenings. I can get tickets to a show or, if you can bear it, a basketball game."

That drew a tentative if sheepish smile from her. "You were right about that, y'know. It's not such an awful game once you get to know it. And since I've had to sit through—" she eyed the ceiling "—how many televised games? Seven? Eight?"

"Is that a complaint?" he drawled, eyes twinkling.

Liz stood on tiptoe and cinched her arms around his neck. "No. It's not a complaint. I love hearing you cheer for your team!" She kissed his cheek and let herself down. "Okay. Let's go to my place. I might as well get this over with."

Within ten minutes they were at her apartment, turning on the lights and increasing the heat, then waiting until Jamie arrived twenty minutes later. His hair was as unruly as ever, but he was dressed neatly and this time carried a suitcase. Self-consciously Liz introduced Donovan, whom Jamie had been staring at since he'd entered. She knew she saw annoyance in his eyes, perhaps cynicism, but she reminded herself, as she had earlier, that he simply needed time to adjust to the change in her status.

At Donovan's suggestion they went out for dinner, and if Jamie was less than gracious, Donovan made up for it, doing everything he could to coax the sullen expression from the younger man's face. Liz was conscious of Jamie glaring at her from time to time, but she made no mention of the fact that she wouldn't be staying with him until they'd returned to her apartment. Then, it seemed, she had no choice.

"Well, uh, listen, Jamie," she began, knotting her fingers tightly together, "you can have the run of the place for as long as you want. I'll, uh, I'll be staying at Donovan's."

Jamie looked utterly dumbfounded. "You'll what?"

"I'll be staying with Donovan."

"Hey, listen, Lizzie. You don't want to do that. I've never needed the place to myself before. And it wouldn't be much fun for Donovan to be imposed upon that way."

"It's not an imposition," Donovan stated. He'd just about exhausted his supply of graciousness for the night, and he didn't like Jamie's tone of voice.

"What Donovan means," Liz hurried to explain, "is that I've been staying with him for a while now."

Jamie darted a cursory glance around the apartment. "What's the matter? This place low on heat or running water or something?"

"No. It's fine. I've chosen to live with Donovan."

"Why would you do a thing like that?" His gaze narrowed. It wasn't that he was being purposely obtuse, Liz knew, just that he had a very specific view of her. "Are you getting crank calls or something? Is it the protection you need? If that's the case, I'll be here—"

"That's *not* the case," Liz interrupted more firmly. She was aware of Donovan standing close, growing more tense by the minute, and the last thing she wanted was an unpleasant exchange between the two. "You don't understand. Donovan and I are *living* together."

Jamie stared at her, his eyes wide, then he threw back his head and laughed. "That's a good one, Liz. I never thought I'd hear that coming from you."

"Why ever not?" she asked. Strangely, she'd known how Jamie would react, yet now that he'd done so she felt a slow anger burning inside her.

"I mean, look, Liz, you're not exactly a temptress."

"Now, just a minute—" Donovan gritted, only to be restrained by Liz's tight grip on his arm.

"I'll handle this, Donovan. Jamie, go on. Say what you mean."

"Come on, Lizzie. You've never been a looker. You were the perennial wallflower back home, and you've lived the life of a nun since you left. Do you honestly expect me to believe that you've taken a lover—or, more to the point, that he's taken *you*?"

"That's exactly what I expect you to believe," Liz ground out. "I also expect—have a *right* to expect—that you'll be happy for me."

"Right? What right do you have? Damn it, you heard Dad, Liz. You're nothing—"

"That's enough!" Donovan exploded, but again Liz kept him from saying more. Her tone was taut, but quiet.

"Let me handle this, Donovan. There's an awful lot I have to say to Jamie, and it's long overdue." She turned to her brother, one arm stiff by her side, the other connecting to Donovan's arm as though, despite her disclaimer, she needed the lifeline.

"Dad was wrong, Jamie. Dead wrong. I've finally come to see that, thanks to Donovan."

Jamie gave an ugly laugh. "Donovan? What could he ever see in you?"

"I've asked myself the same question a hundred times, and there are times when I still ask it, when I can't quite believe the answer. But Donovan does, and that's what matters. He loves me, Jamie. He loves me despite every little fault I've got!" When Donovan started to argue, she squeezed his arm in a bid for silence. "And what would be so awful, from your point of view, if he loves me? It doesn't change the way I feel toward you. It doesn't change the fact that I'll continue to love you, to help you whenever I can. You don't have to be threatened by Donovan. I was for weeks, until I realized how foolish it was.''

"I'm not *threatened* by him.''

''Then why are you so upset that I'm living with him?''

''I'm not upset. I'm just…shocked. You…living with someone like him…it's incredible.''

"What do you mean, 'someone like him'?'' she spat. It was one thing for Jamie to insult her, quite another for him to attack Donovan. As it happened, in her rush to defend Donovan she'd misinterpreted Jamie, who proceeded to set her straight.

"Oh, there's nothing wrong with him,'' Jamie said impudently. "In fact, I got the impression from what he said over dinner that he's got a hell of a lot going for him. Which is what makes it all so astounding. He's good-looking and successful. He can have any woman he wants. That he should choose you…'' He shook his head for effect.

Donovan couldn't keep still. "Liz, I think we ought to go. You don't need this—''

"No, Donovan. There's more I have to say.'' She turned back to Jamie and her soft voice took on a sheath of steel. "You know, you've been putting me down for years. Oh, maybe more subtly than Dad did, but it's always been there. You've held me responsible for everything you've suffered, and maybe I'm to blame because I let you do it. I've lived with guilt for so long—guilt at thinking that I might have somehow spared you Dad's beatings—''

''Damn it, Liz!'' Jamie cut in, slicing an angry glance at Donovan. "Not in front of him!''

But Liz was livid. "He knows it all, but that's beside the point. The point *is* that there *wasn't* anything I could have done to help you. I took my own beatings, Jamie. Where were *you* when I could have used help?''

"I was just a kid!''

"*So was I!* I suffered then, and I suffered long after, and never once have you given me support or understanding or encouragement. No, you let me go on believing everything Dad said, seeing myself as the ugly little nothing he seemed to think I was. But I'm through now. I've had it. Evidently your Dr. Branowitz hasn't done all that much, if he's never gotten going on your feelings toward me. Or maybe he simply takes your word and honestly believes I'm the dog you think I am. Well, *I'm not!*''

Fury had her shaking all over, but she wasn't about to stop. ''We're all grown up now, Jamie, and I for one need to put the past to rest. I may never be a looker, as you call it, but I'm not ugly and repulsive, and I'm not some kind of freak. I've got friends who like me and business associates who respect me, and Donovan who loves me. And you know something? *I love him!*'' Her expression still cross, she looked at Donovan. ''The answer is yes.''

Then she turned back to Jamie, but her tone gradually softened. ''I love him, and I'm going to marry him, and it would make me very happy to know that you can accept it, that you can come to like both of us. Because I do love you, Jamie. You're my only brother. I'd like you to share some of what Donovan and I have. Our life is going to be wonderful, far different from anything you and I ever knew, and we'd like it if you could be with us sometimes. If you find you can't, then I'll accept that and move on, because nothing, *nothing*, is going to cast a shadow on the rest of my life. I've lived in the dark for too long. And so have you. Think about it, Jamie.''

When Donovan put an arm around her shoulder, she looked up at him and smiled. The pride in his face was as unmistakable as the love, and she felt suddenly light-headed and free.

''He's got you brainwashed,'' Jamie muttered.

''Well,'' Liz mused serenely, hooking her arm through Donovan's and starting for the door, ''If that's so, I love it. Because I've never been happier in my life.''

''Did you mean it?'' Donovan asked, crowding her against the wall just outside her building.

''Every word. Boy, did that feel good!''

''You do love me?''

''I do love you.''

"And you'll marry me?"

"In a minute."

"It'll have to be longer than that. There's a tiny matter of the law to contend with."

Liz's eyes widened. "The law?" She couldn't help but recall the fateful instrument of their union.

Donovan grinned and popped a kiss on her nose. "Not *that* law. The one governing things like blood tests and licenses and marriages in the eyes of the Lord and the state of New York."

She laughed and threw her head back. "*That* law. Well, I'll leave all that to you. You're the one who's got friends in high places. But I'm telling you, buddy, if you lean into me any closer you may have to worry about charges of indecency. I don't think they allow lovemaking on the streets of New York."

"Mmm. I think you're right. Come on. Let's go home."

"Now that's the best idea you've had all night."

Actually, it wasn't, but Liz didn't find out about the other until she got out of her bath and went looking for Donovan. He was walking down the hall toward the bedroom when she emerged.

"Where were you?" she asked softly. "I was beginning to worry."

"I just called Jamie."

"You did?"

"I'm meeting him for lunch at the office tomorrow."

"You don't have to do that, Donovan."

"But I do. You're still angry at him, but by tomorrow you'll be feeling badly. *I* feel badly. All things considered, Jamie must be feeling lost. He's had some mean shakes in life, and he's bound to be thrown by what he sees as your defection. I'm not sure how much of what you said tonight he absorbed, especially the part about his being welcome to spend time with us, but I want to reinforce it. I don't know if it'll do any good, but I don't think I'd forgive myself if I didn't give it a try."

For a minute Liz was speechless. Then she threw her arms around Donovan's neck and hugged him tightly. "Have I ever told you how wonderful you are?"

"That's not what I need to hear. It's those other words…"

"I love you? I love you…love you…love you…"

She was still chanting when he lifted her in his arms and carried her to bed.

PRESUMED GUILTY
Tess Gerritsen

CHAPTER ONE

He called at ten o'clock, the same time he always did.

Even before Miranda answered it, she knew it was him. She also knew that if she ignored it the phone would keep on ringing and ringing, until the sound would drive her crazy. Miranda paced the bedroom, thinking, *I don't have to answer it. I don't have to talk to him. I don't owe him a thing, not a damn thing.*

The ringing stopped. In the sudden silence she held her breath, hoping that this time he would relent, this time he would understand she'd meant what she told him.

The renewed jangling made her start. Every ring was like sandpaper scraping across her raw nerves.

Miranda couldn't stand it any longer. Even as she picked up the receiver she knew it was a mistake. "Hello?"

"I miss you," he said. It was the same whisper, resonant with the undertones of old intimacies shared, enjoyed.

"I don't want you to call me anymore," she said.

"I couldn't help it. All day I've wanted to call you. Miranda, it's been hell without you."

Tears stung her eyes. She took a breath, forcing them back.

"Can't we try again?" he pleaded.

"No, Richard."

"Please. This time it'll be different."

"It'll never be different."

"Yes! It will—"

"It was a mistake. From the very beginning."

"You still love me. I know you do. God, Miranda, all these weeks, seeing you every day. Not being able to touch you. Or even be alone with you—"

"You won't have to deal with that any longer, Richard. You have my letter of resignation. I meant it."

There was a long silence, as though the impact of her words had pummeled him like some physical blow. She felt euphoric and guilty all at once. Guilty for having broken free, for being, at last, her own woman.

Softly he said, "I told her."

Miranda didn't respond.

"Did you hear me?" he asked. "I told her. Everything about us. And I've been to see my lawyer. I've changed the terms of my—"

"Richard," she said slowly. "It doesn't make a difference. Whether you're married or divorced, I don't want to see you."

"Just one more time."

"No."

"I'm coming over. Right now—"

"No."

"You have to see me, Miranda!"

"I don't have to do anything!" she cried.

"I'll be there in fifteen minutes."

Miranda stared in disbelief at the receiver. He'd hung up. Damn him, he'd hung up, and fifteen minutes from now he'd be knocking on her door. She'd managed to carry on so bravely these past three weeks, working side by side with him, keeping her smile polite, her voice neutral. But now he was coming and he'd rip away her mask of control and there they'd be again, spiraling into the same old trap she'd just managed to crawl out of.

She ran to the closet and yanked out a sweatshirt. She had to get away. Somewhere he wouldn't find her, somewhere she could be alone.

She fled out the front door and down the porch steps and began to walk, swiftly, fiercely, down Willow Street. At ten-thirty, the neighborhood was already tucked in for the night. Through the windows she passed she saw the glow of lamplight, the silhouettes of families in various domestic poses, the occasional flicker of a fire in a hearth. She felt that old envy stir inside her again, the longing to be part of the same loving whole, to be stirring the embers of her own hearth. Foolish dreams.

Shivering, she hugged her arms to her chest. There was a chill in the air, not unseasonable for August in Maine. She was angry now, angry about being cold, about being driven from her own home. Angry at *him.* But she didn't stop; she kept walking.

At Bayview Street she turned right, toward the sea.

The mist was rolling in. It blotted out the stars, crept along the road in a sullen vapor. She headed through it, the fog swirling in her wake. From the road she turned onto a footpath, followed it to a series of granite steps, now slick with mist. At the bottom was a wood bench—she thought of it as her bench—set on the beach of stones. There she sat, drew her legs up against her chest and stared out toward the sea. Somewhere, drifting on the bay, a buoy was clanging. She could dimly make out the green channel light, bobbing in the fog.

By now he would be at her house. She wondered how long he'd knock at the door. Whether he'd keep knocking until her neighbor Mr. Lanzo complained. Whether he'd give up and just go home, to his wife, to his son and daughter.

She lowered her face against her knees, trying to blot out the image of the happy little Tremain family. *Happy* was not the picture Richard had painted. *At the breaking point* was the way he'd described his marriage. It was love for Phillip and Cassie, his children, that had kept him from divorcing Evelyn years ago. Now the twins were nineteen, old enough to accept the truth about their parents' marriage. What stopped him from divorce now was his concern for Evelyn, his wife. She needed time to adjust, and if Miranda would just be patient, would just love him enough, the way he loved her, it would all work out....

Oh, yes. Hasn't it worked out just fine?

Miranda gave a little laugh. She raised her head, looked out to sea and laughed again, not a hysterical laugh but one of relief. She felt as if she'd just awakened from a long fever, to find that her mind was sharp again, clear again. The mist felt good against her face, its chill touch sweeping her soul clean. How she needed such a cleansing! The months of guilt had piled up like layers of dirt, until she thought she could scarcely see herself, her real self, beneath the filth.

Now it was over. This time it was really, truly over.

She smiled at the sea. *My soul is mine again,* she thought. A calmness, a serenity she had not felt in months, settled over her. She rose to her feet and started for home.

Two blocks from her house she spotted the blue Peugeot, parked near the intersection of Willow and Spring Streets. So he was still waiting for her. She paused by the car, gazing in at the black leather upholstery, the sheepskin seat covers, all of it too familiar. *The scene of the crime,* she thought. *The first kiss. I've paid for it, in pain. Now it's his turn.*

She left the car and headed purposefully to her house. She climbed the porch steps; the front door was unlocked, as she'd left it. Inside, the lights were still on. He wasn't in the living room.

"Richard?" she said.

No answer.

The smell of coffee brewing drew her to the kitchen. She saw a fresh pot on the burner, a half-filled mug on the countertop. One of the kitchen drawers had been left wide open. She slammed it shut. *Well. You came right in and made yourself at home, didn't you?* She grabbed the mug and tossed the contents into the sink. The coffee splashed her hand; it was barely lukewarm.

She moved along the hall, past the bathroom. The light was on, and water trickled from the faucet. She shut it off. "You have no right to come in here!" she yelled. "It's my house. I could call the police and have you arrested for trespassing."

She turned toward the bedroom. Even before she reached the doorway she knew what to expect, knew what she'd have to contend with. He'd be sprawled on her bed, naked, a grin on his face. That was the way he'd greeted her the last time. This time she'd toss him out, clothes or no clothes. This time he'd be in for a surprise.

The bedroom was dark. She switched on the lights.

He was sprawled on the bed, as she'd predicted. His arms were flung out, his legs tangled in the sheets. And he was naked. But it wasn't a grin she saw on his face. It was a frozen look of terror, the mouth thrown open in a silent scream, the eyes staring at some fearful image of eternity. A corner of the bed sheet, saturated with blood, sagged over the side. Except for the quiet tap, tap of the crimson liquid slowly dripping onto the floor, the room was silent.

Miranda managed to take two steps into the room before nausea assailed her. She dropped to her knees, gasping, retching. Only when she managed to raise her head again did she see the chef's knife lying nearby on the floor. She didn't have to look twice at it. She recognized the handle, the twelve-inch steel blade, and she knew exactly where it had come from: the kitchen drawer.

It was her knife; it would have her fingerprints on it.

And now it was steeped in blood.

Chase Tremain drove straight through the night and into the dawn. The rhythm of the road under his wheels, the glow of the dashboard lights, the radio softly scratching out some Muzak melody all receded to little more than the fuzzy background of a dream—a very bad dream. The only reality was what he kept telling himself as he drove, what he repeated over and over in his head as he pushed onward down that dark highway.

Richard is dead. Richard is dead.

He was startled to hear himself say the words aloud. Briefly it shook him from his trancelike state, the sound of those words uttered in the darkness of his car. He glanced at the clock. It was four in the morning. He had been driving for four hours now. The New Hampshire-Maine border lay ahead. How many hours to go? How many miles? He wondered if it was cold outside, if the air smelled of the sea. The car had become a sensory deprivation box, a self-contained purgatory of glowing green lights and elevator music. He switched off the radio.

Richard is dead.

He heard those words again, mentally replayed them from the hazy memory of that phone call. Evelyn hadn't bothered to soften the blow. He had scarcely registered the fact it was his sister-in-law's voice calling when she hit him with the news. No preambles, no are-you-sitting-down warnings. Just the bare facts, delivered in the familiar Evelyn half whisper. *Richard is dead,* she'd told him. *Murdered. By a woman....*

And then, in the next breath, *I need you, Chase.*

He hadn't expected that part. Chase was the outsider, the Tremain no one ever bothered to call, the one who'd picked up and left the state, left the family, for good. The brother with the embarrassing past. Chase, the outcast. Chase, the black sheep.

Chase, the weary, he thought, shaking off the cobwebs of sleep that threatened to ensnare him. He opened the window, inhaled the rush of cold air, the scent of pines and sea. The smell of Maine. It brought back, like nothing else could, all those boyhood memories. Scrabbling across the beach rocks, ankle deep in seaweed. The freshly gathered mussels clattering together in his bucket. The foghorn, moaning through the mist. All of it came back to him in that one whiff of air, that perfume of childhood, of good times, the early days when he had thought Richard was the boldest, the cleverest, the very best brother anyone could have. The days before he had understood Richard's true nature.

Murdered. By a woman.

That part Chase found entirely unsurprising.

He wondered who she was, what could have ignited an anger so white-hot it had driven her to plunge a knife into his brother's chest. Oh, he could make an educated guess. An affair turned sour. Jealousy over some new mistress. The inevitable abandonment. And then rage, at being used, at being lied to, a rage that would have overwhelmed all sense of logic or self-preservation. Chase could sketch in the whole scenario. He could even picture the woman, a woman like all the others who'd drifted through Richard's life. She'd be attractive, of course. Richard would insist on that much. But there'd be something a little desperate about her. Perhaps her laugh would be too loud or her smile too automatic, or the lines around her eyes would reveal a woman on the downhill slide. Yes, he could see the woman clearly, and the image stirred both pity and repulsion.

And rage. Whatever resentment he still bore Richard, nothing could change the fact they were brothers. They'd shared the same pool of memories, the same lazy afternoons drifting on the lake, the strolls on the breakwater, the quiet snickerings in the darkness. Their last falling-out had been a serious one, but in the back of his mind Chase had always assumed they'd smooth it over. There was always time to make things right again, to be friends again.

That's what he had thought until that phone call from Evelyn.

His anger swelled, washed through him like a full-moon tide. Opportunities lost. No more chances to say, *I care about you.* No more chances to say, *Remember when?* The road blurred before him. He blinked and gripped the steering wheel tighter.

He drove on, into the morning.

By ten o'clock he had reached Bass Harbor. By eleven he was aboard the *Jenny B,* his face to the wind, his hands clutching the ferry rail. In the distance, Shepherd's Island rose in a low green hump in the mist. *Jenny B*'s bow heaved across the swells and Chase felt that familiar nausea roil his stomach, sour his throat. *Always the seasick one,* he thought. In a family of sailors, Chase was the landlubber, the son who preferred solid ground beneath his feet. The racing trophies had all gone to Richard. Catboats, sloops, you name the class, Richard had the trophy. And these were the waters where he'd honed his skills, tacking, jibbing, shouting out orders. Spinnaker up, spinnaker down. To Chase it had all seemed a bunch of frantic nonsense. And then, there'd been that miserable nausea....

Chase inhaled a deep breath of salt air, felt his stomach settle as the *Jenny B* pulled up to the dock. He returned to the car and waited his turn to drive up the ramp. There were eight cars before him, out-of-state license plates on every one. Half of Massachusetts seemed to come north every summer. You could almost hear the state of Maine groan under the the weight of all those damn cars.

The ferryman waved him forward. Chase put the car in gear and drove up the ramp, onto Shepherd's Island.

It amazed him how little the place seemed to change over the years. The same old buildings faced Sea Street: the Island Bakery, the bank, FitzGerald's Café, the five-and-dime, Lappin's General Store. A few new names had sprung up in old places. The Vogue Beauty Shop was now Gorham's Books, and Village Hardware had been replaced by Country Antiques and a realty office. Lord, what changes the tourists wrought.

He drove around the corner, up Limerock Street. On his left, housed in the same brick building, was the *Island Herald*. He wondered if any of it had changed inside. He remembered it well, the decorative tin ceiling, the battered desks, the wall hung with portraits of the publishers, every one a Tremain. He could picture it all, right down to the Remington typewriter on his father's old desk. Of course, the Remingtons would be long gone. There'd be computers now, sleek and impersonal. That's how Richard would run the newspaper, anyway. Out with the old, in with the new.

Bring on the next Tremain.

Chase drove on and turned onto Chestnut Hill. Half a mile up, near the highest point on the island, sat the Tremain mansion. A monstrous yellow wedding cake was what it used to remind him of, with its Victorian turrets and gingerbread trim. The house had since been repainted a distinguished gray and white. It seemed tamer now, subdued, a faded beauty. Chase almost preferred the old wedding-cake yellow.

He parked the car, grabbed his suitcase from the trunk and headed up the walkway. Even before he'd reached the porch steps the door opened and Evelyn was standing there, waiting for him.

"Chase!" she cried. "Oh, Chase, you're here. Thank God you're here."

At once she fell into his arms. Automatically he held her against him, felt the shuddering of her body, the warmth of her breath against his neck. He let her cling to him as long as she needed to.

At last she pulled away and gazed up at him. Those brilliant green eyes were as startling as ever. Her hair, shoulder length and honey blond, had been swept back into a French braid. Her face was puffy, her nose red and pinched. She'd tried to cover it with makeup. Some sort of pink powder caked her nostril and a streak of mascara had left a dirty shadow on her cheek. He could scarcely believe this was his beautiful sister-in-law. Could it be she truly was in mourning?

"I knew you'd come," she whispered.

"I left right after you called."

"Thank you, Chase. I didn't know who else to turn to...." She stood back, looked at him. "Poor thing, you must be exhausted. Come in, I'll get you some coffee."

They stepped into the foyer. It was like stepping back into childhood, so little had changed. The same oak floors, the same light, the same smells. He almost thought that if he turned around and looked through the doorway into the parlor, he'd see his mother sitting there at her desk, madly scribbling away. The old girl never did take to the typewriter; she'd believed, and rightly so, that if a gossip column was juicy enough, an editor would accept it in Swahili. As it turned out, not only had the editor acquired her column, he'd acquired *her* as well. All in all, a practical marriage.

His mother never did learn to type.

"Hello, Uncle Chase."

Chase looked up to see a young man and woman standing at the top of the stairs. Those couldn't be the twins! He watched in astonishment as the pair came down the steps, Phillip in the lead. The last time he'd seen his niece and nephew they'd been gawky adolescents, not quite grown into their big feet. Both of them were tall and blond and lean, but there the resemblance ended. Phillip moved with the graceful assurance of a dancer, an elegant Fred Astaire partnered with—well, certainly not Ginger Rogers. The young woman who ambled down after him bore a closer resemblance to a horse.

"I can't believe this is Cassie and Phillip," said Chase.

"You've stayed away too long," Evelyn replied.

Phillip came forward and shook Chase's hand. It was the greeting of a stranger, not a nephew. His hand was slender, refined, the hand of a gentleman. He had his mother's stamp of aristocracy—straight nose, chiseled cheeks, green eyes. "Uncle Chase," he said somberly. "It's a terrible reason to come home, but I'm glad you're here."

Chase shifted his gaze to Cassie. When he'd last seen his niece she was a lively little monkey with a never-ending supply of questions. He could scarcely believe she'd grown into this sullen young woman. Could grief have wrought such changes? Her limp hair was pulled back so tightly it seemed to turn her face into a collection of jutting angles: large nose, rabbity overbite, a square forehead unsoftened by even a trace of bangs. Only her eyes held any trace of that distant ten-year-old. They were direct, sharply intelligent.

"Hello, Uncle Chase," she said. A strikingly businesslike tone for a girl who'd just lost her father.

"Cassie," said Evelyn. "Can't you give your uncle a kiss? He's come all this way to be with us."

Cassie moved forward and planted a wooden peck on Chase's cheek. Just as quickly she stepped back, as though embarrassed by this false ceremony of affection.

"You've certainly grown up," said Chase, the most charitable assessment he could offer.

"Yes. It happens."

"How old are you now?"

"Almost twenty."

"So you both must be in college."

Cassie nodded, the first trace of a smile touching her lips. "I'm at the University of Southern Maine. Studying journalism. I figured, one of these days the *Herald*'s going to need a—"

"Phillip's at Harvard," Evelyn cut in. "Just like his father."

Cassie's smile died before it was fully born. She shot a look of irritation at her mother, then turned and headed up the stairs.

"Cassie, where are you going?"

"I have to do my laundry."

"But your uncle just got here. Come back and sit with us."

"Why, Mother?" she shot back over her shoulder. "You can entertain him perfectly well on your own."

"Cassie!"

The girl turned and glared down at Evelyn. "What?"

"You are embarrassing me."

"Well, that's nothing new."

Evelyn, close to tears, turned to Chase. "You see how things are? I can't even count on my own children. Chase, I can't deal with this all alone. I just can't." Stifling a sob, she turned and walked into the parlor.

The twins looked at each other.

"You've done it again," said Phillip. "It's a lousy time to fight, Cassie. Can't you feel sorry for her? Can't you try and get along? Just for the next few days."

"It's not as if I *don't* try. But she drives me up a wall."

"Okay, then at least be civil." He paused, then added, "You know it's what Dad would want."

Cassie sighed. Then, resignedly, she came down the steps and headed into the parlor, after her mother. "I guess I owe him that much...."

Shaking his head, Phillip looked at Chase. "Just another episode of the delightful Tremain family."

"Has it been like this for a while?"

"Years, at least. You're just seeing them at their worst. You'd think, after last night, after losing Dad, we could pull together. Instead it seems to be driving us all apart."

They went into the parlor and found mother and daughter sitting at opposite ends of the room. Both had regained their composure. Phillip took a seat between them, reinforcing his role as perpetual human buffer. Chase settled into a corner armchair—his idea of neutral territory.

Sunshine washed in through the bay windows, onto the gleaming wood floor. The silence was filled by the ticking of the clock on the mantelpiece. It all looked the same, thought Chase. The same Hepplewhite tables, the same Queen Anne chairs. It was exactly the way he remembered it from childhood. Evelyn had not altered a single detail. For that he felt grateful.

Chase launched a foray into that dangerous silence. "I drove by the newspaper building, coming through town,'' he said. ''Hasn't changed a bit.''

''Neither has the town,'' said Phillip.

''Just as thrilling as ever,'' his sister deadpanned.

''What's the plan for the *Herald?*'' asked Chase.

''Phillip will be taking over,'' said Evelyn. ''It's about time, anyway. I need him home, now that Richard...'' She swallowed, looked down. ''He's ready for the job.''

''I'm not sure I am, Mom,'' said Phillip. ''I'm only in my second year at college. And there are other things I'd like to—''

''Your father was twenty when Grandpa Tremain made him an editor. Isn't that right, Chase?''

Chase nodded.

''So there's no reason you couldn't slip right onto the masthead.''

Phillip shrugged. ''Jill Vickery's managing things just fine.''

''She's just a hired hand, Phillip. The *Herald* needs a real captain.''

Cassie leaned forward, her eyes suddenly sharp. ''There are others who could do it,'' she said. ''Why does it have to be Phil?''

''Your father wanted Phillip. And Richard always knew what was best for the *Herald.*''

There was a silence, punctuated by the steady ticking of the clock on the mantelpiece.

Evelyn let out a shaky breath and dropped her head in her hands. ''Oh, God, it all seems so cold-blooded. I can't believe we're talking about this. About who's going to take his place....''

''Sooner or later,'' said Cassie, ''we have to talk about it. About a lot of things.''

Evelyn nodded and looked away.

In another room, the phone was ringing.

''I'll get it,'' said Phillip, and left to answer it.

''I just can't *think,*'' said Evelyn, pressing her hands to her head. ''If I could just get my mind working again....''

''It was only last night,'' said Chase gently. ''It takes time to get over the shock.''

"And there's the funeral to think of. They won't even tell me when they'll release the—" She winced. "I don't see why it takes so long. Why the state examiner has to go over and over it. I mean, can't they *see* what happened? Isn't it obvious?"

"The obvious isn't always the truth," said Cassie.

Evelyn looked at her daughter. "What's that supposed to mean?"

Phillip came back into the room. "Mom? That was Lorne Tibbetts on the phone."

"Oh, Lord." Evelyn rose unsteadily to her feet. "I'm coming."

"He wants to see you in person."

She frowned. "Right this minute? Can't it wait?"

"You might as well get it over with, Mom. He'll have to talk to you sooner or later."

Evelyn turned and looked at Chase. "I can't do this alone. Come with me, won't you?"

Chase didn't have the faintest idea where they were going or who Lorne Tibbetts was. At that moment what he really wanted was a hot shower and a bed to collapse onto. But that would have to wait.

"Of course, Evelyn," he said. Reluctantly he stood, shaking the stiffness from his legs, which felt permanently flexed by the long drive from Greenwich.

Evelyn was already reaching for her purse. She pulled out the car keys and handed them to Chase. "I—I'm too upset to drive. Could you?"

He took the keys. "Where are we going?"

With shaking hands Evelyn slipped on her sunglasses. The swollen eyes vanished behind twin dark lenses. "The police," she said.

CHAPTER TWO

The Shepherd's Island police station was housed in a converted general store that had, over the years, been chopped up into a series of hobbit-size rooms and offices. In Chase's memory, it had been a much more imposing structure, but it had been years since he'd been inside. He'd been only a boy then, and a rambunctious one at that, the sort of rascal to whom a police station represented a distinct threat. The day he'd been dragged in here for trampling Mrs. Gordimer's rose bed—entirely unintentional on his part—these ceilings had seemed taller, the rooms vaster, every door a gateway to some unknown terror.

Now he saw it for what it was—a tired old building in need of paint.

Lorne Tibbetts, the new chief of police, was built just right to inhabit this claustrophobic warren. If there was a height minimum for police work, Tibbetts had somehow slipped right under the requirement. He was just a chunk of a man, neatly decked out in official summer khaki, complete with height-enhancing cap to hide what Chase suspected was a bald spot. He reminded Chase of a little Napoleon in full dress uniform.

Though short on height, Chief Tibbetts was long on the social graces. He maneuvered through the clutter of desks and filing cabinets and greeted Evelyn with the overweening solicitousness due a woman of her local status.

"Evelyn! I'm so sorry to have to ask you down here like this." He reached for her arm and gave it a squeeze, an intended gesture of comfort that made Evelyn shrink away. "And it's been a terrible night for you, hasn't it? Just a terrible night."

Evelyn shrugged, partly in answer to his question, partly to free herself from his grasp.

"I know it's hard, dealing with this. And I didn't want to bother you, not today. But you know how it is. All those reports to be filed." He looked at Chase, a deceptively casual glance. The little Napoleon, Chase noted, had sharp eyes that saw everything.

"This is Chase," said Evelyn, brushing the sleeve of her blouse, as though to wipe away Chief Tibbetts's paw print. "Richard's brother. He drove in this morning from Connecticut."

"Oh, yeah," said Tibbetts, his eyes registering instant recognition of the name. "I've seen a picture of you hanging in the high school gym." He offered his hand. His grasp was crushing, the handshake of a man trying to compensate for his size. "You know, the one of you in the basketball uniform."

Chase blinked in surprise. "They still have that thing hanging up?"

"It's the local hall of fame. Let's see, you were class of '71. Star center, varsity basketball. Right?"

"I'm surprised you know all that."

"I was a basketball player myself. Madison High School, Wisconsin. Record holder in free throws. And points scored."

Yes, Chase saw it clearly. Lorne Tibbetts, rampaging midget of the basketball court. It would fit right in with that bone-crushing handshake.

The station door suddenly swung open. A woman called out, "Hey, Lorne?"

Tibbetts turned and wearily confronted the visitor, who looked as if she'd just blown in from the street. "You back again, Annie?"

"Like the proverbial bad penny." The woman shifted her battered shoulder bag to her other side. "So when am I gonna get a statement, huh?"

"When I have one to make. Now scram."

The woman, undaunted, turned to Evelyn. The pair of them could have posed for a magazine feature on fashion make-overs. Annie, blowsy haired and dressed in a lumpy sweatshirt and jeans, would have earned the label Before. "Mrs. Tremain?" she said politely. "I know this is a bad time, but I'm under deadline and I just need a short quote—"

"Oh, for Chrissakes, Annie!" snapped Tibbetts. He turned to the cop manning the front desk. "Ellis, get her out of here!"

Ellis popped up from his chair like a spindly jack-in-the-box. "C'mon, Annie. Get a move on, 'less you wanna write your story from the inside lookin' out."

"I'm going. I'm going." Annie yanked open the door. As she walked out they heard her mutter, "Geez, they won't let a gal do her job around here...."

Evelyn looked at Chase. "That's Annie Berenger. One of Richard's star reporters. Now a star pest."

"Can't exactly blame her," said Tibbetts. "That's what you pay her for, isn't it?" He took Evelyn's arm. "Come on, we'll get started. I'll take you into my office. It's the only private place in this whole fishbowl."

Lorne's office was at the far end of the hallway, past a series of closet-size rooms. Almost every square inch was crammed with furniture: a desk, two chairs, a bookcase, filing cabinets. A fern wilted, unnoticed, in a corner. Despite the cramped space, everything was tidy, the shelves dusted, all the papers stacked in the Out box. On the wall, prominently displayed, hung a plaque: *The smaller the dog, the bigger the fight.*

Tibbetts and Evelyn sat in the two chairs. A third chair was brought in for the secretary to take accessory notes. Chase stood off to the side. It felt good to stand, good to straighten those cramped legs.

At least, it felt good for about ten minutes. Then he found himself sagging, scarcely able to pay attention to what was being said. He felt like that wretched fern in the corner, wilting away.

Tibbetts asked the questions and Evelyn answered in her usual whispery voice, a voice that could induce hibernation. She gave a detailed summary of the night's events. A typical evening, she said. Supper at six o'clock, the whole family. Leg of lamb and asparagus, lemon soufflé for dessert. Richard had had a glass of wine; he always did. The conversation was routine, the latest gossip from the paper. Circulation down, cost of newsprint up. Worries about a possible libel suit. Tony Graffam upset about that last article. And then talk about Phillip's exams, Cassie's grades. The lilacs were lovely this year, the driveway needed resurfacing. Typical dialogue from a family dinner.

At nine o'clock Richard had left the house to do some work at the office—or so he'd said. And Evelyn?

"I went upstairs to bed," she said.

"What about Cassie and Phillip?"

"They went out. To a movie, I think."

"So everyone went their separate ways."

"Yes." Evelyn looked down at her lap. "And that's it. Until twelve-thirty, when I got the call...."

"Let's go back to that dinner conversation."

The account went into replay. A few extra details here and there, but essentially the same story. Chase, his last reserves of alertness wearing thin, began to drift into a state of semiconsciousness. Already his legs were going numb, sinking into a sleep that his brain longed to join. The floor began to look pretty good. At least it was horizontal. He felt himself sliding....

Suddenly he jerked awake and saw that everyone was looking at him.

"Are you all right, Chase?" asked Evelyn.

"Sorry," he muttered. "I guess I'm just more tired than I thought." He gave his head a shake. "Could I, uh, get a cup of coffee somewhere?"

"Down the hall," said Tibbetts. "There's a full pot on, plus a couch if you need it. Why don't you wait there?"

"Go ahead," said Evelyn. "I'll be done soon."

With a sense of relief Chase fled the office and went in search of the blessed coffeepot. Moving back down the hall, he poked his head into the first doorway and discovered a washroom. The next door was locked. He moved on and glanced into the third room. It was unlit. Through the shadows he saw a couch, a few chairs, a jumble of furniture off in a corner. In the sidewall there was a window. It was that window that drew his attention because, unlike a normal window, it didn't face the outside; it faced an adjoining room. Through the pane of glass he spied a woman, sitting alone at a small table.

She was oblivious to him. Her gaze was focused downward, on the table before her. Something drew him closer, something about her utter silence, her stillness. He felt like a hunter who has quite unexpectedly come upon a doe poised in the forest.

Quietly Chase slipped into the darkness and let the door close behind him. He moved to the window. A one-way mirror—that's what it was, of course. He was on the observing side, she on the blind side. She had no idea he was standing here, separated from her by only a half inch of glass. It made him feel somehow contemptible to be standing there, spying on her, but he couldn't help himself. He was drawn in by that old fantasy of invisibility, of being the fly on the wall, the unseen observer.

And it was the woman.

She was not particularly beautiful, and neither her clothes nor her hairstyle enhanced the assets she did have. She was wearing faded blue jeans and a Boston Red Sox T-shirt a few sizes too big. Her hair, a chestnut brown, was gathered into a careless braid. A few strands had escaped and drooped rebelliously about her temples. She wore little or no makeup, but she had the sort of face that needed none, the sort of face you saw on those Patagonia catalog models, the ones raking leaves or hugging lambs. Wholesome, with just a hint of sunburn. Her eyes, a light color, gray or blue, didn't quite fit the rest of the picture. He could see by the puffiness around the lids that she'd been crying. Even now, she reached up and swiped a tear from her cheek. She glanced around the table in search of something. Then, with a look of frustration, she tugged at the edge of her T-shirt and wiped her face with it. It seemed a helpless gesture, the sort of thing a child would do. It made her look all the more vulnerable. He wondered why she was in that room, sitting all alone, looking for all the world like an abandoned soul. A witness? A victim?

She looked straight ahead, right at him. He instinctively drew away from the window, but he knew she couldn't see him. All she saw was a reflection of herself staring back. She seemed to take in her own image with passive weariness. Indifference. As though she was thinking, *There I am, looking like hell. And I couldn't care less.*

A key grated in the lock. Suddenly the woman sat up straight, her whole body snapping to alertness. She wiped her face once more, raised her chin to a pugnacious angle. Her eyes might be swollen, her T-shirt damp with tears, but she had determinedly thrown off that cloak of vulnerability. She reminded Chase of a soldier girded for battle, but scared out of her wits.

The door opened. A man walked in—gray suit, no tie, all business. He took a chair. Chase was startled by the loud sound of the chair legs scraping the floor. He realized there must be a microphone in the next room, and that the sound was coming through a small speaker by the window.

"Ms. Wood?" asked the man. "Sorry to keep you waiting. I'm Lieutenant Merrifield, state police." He held out his hand and smiled. It said a lot, that smile. It said *I'm your buddy. Your best friend. I'm here to make everything right.*

The woman hesitated, then shook the offered hand.

Lieutenant Merrifield settled into the chair and gave the woman a long, sympathetic look. "You must be exhausted," he said, maintaining that best-friend voice. "Are you comfortable? Feel ready to proceed?"

She nodded.

"They've read you your rights?"

Again, a nod.

"I understand you've waived the right to have an attorney present."

"I don't have an attorney," she said.

Her voice was not what Chase expected. It was soft, husky. A bedroom voice with a heartbreaking quaver of grief.

"We can arrange for one, if you want," said Merrifield. "It may take some time, which means you'll have to be patient."

"Please. I just want to tell you what happened...."

A smile touched Lieutenant Merrifield's lips. It had the curve of triumph. "All right, then," he said. "Let's begin." He placed a cassette recorder on the table and pressed the button. "Tell me your name, your address, your occupation."

The woman sighed deeply, a breath for courage. "My name is Miranda Wood. I live at 18 Willow Street. I work as a copy editor for the *Island Herald*."

"That's Mr. Tremain's newspaper?"

"Yes."

"Let's go straight to last night. Tell me what happened. All the events leading up to the death of Mr. Richard Tremain."

Chase felt his whole body suddenly go numb. *The death of Mr. Richard Tremain.* He found himself pressing forward, against that cold glass, his gaze fixed on the face of Miranda Wood. Innocence. Softness. That's what he saw when he looked at her. What a lovely mask she wore, what a pure and perfect disguise.

My brother's mistress, he thought with sudden comprehension. *My brother's murderer.*

In terrible fascination he listened to her confession.

"Let's go back a few months, Ms. Wood. To when you first met Mr. Tremain. Tell me about your relationship."

Miranda stared down at her hands, knotted together on the table. The table itself was a typically ugly piece of institutional furniture. She noticed that someone had carved the initials JMK onto the surface. She wondered who JMK was, if he or she had sat there under similar circumstances, if he or she had been similarly innocent. She felt a sudden bond with this unknown predecessor, the one who had sat in the same hot seat, fighting for dear life.

"Ms. Wood? Please answer my question."

She looked up at Lieutenant Merrifield. The smiling destroyer. "I'm sorry," she said. "I wasn't listening."

"About Mr. Tremain. How did you meet him?"

"At the *Herald.* I was hired about a year ago. We got to know each other in the course of business."

"And?"

"And..." She took a deep breath. "We got involved."

"Who initiated it?"

"He did. He started asking me out to lunch. Purely business, he said. To talk about the *Herald*. About changes in the format."

"Isn't it unusual for a publisher to deal so closely with the copy editor?"

"Maybe on a big city paper it is. But the *Herald*'s a small-town paper. Everyone on the staff does a little of everything."

"So, in the course of business, you got to know Mr. Tremain."

"Yes."

"When did you start sleeping with him?"

The question was like a slap in the face. She sat up straight. "It wasn't like that!"

"You didn't sleep with him?"

"I didn't—I mean, yes, I did, but it happened over the course of months. It wasn't as if we—we went out to lunch and then fell into bed together!"

"I see. So it was a more, uh, *romantic* thing. Is that what you're trying to say?"

She swallowed. In silence she nodded. It all sounded so stupid, the way he'd phrased it. A more romantic thing. Now, hearing those words said aloud in that cold, bare room, it struck her how foolish it all had been. The whole disastrous affair.

"I thought I loved him," Miranda whispered.

"What was that, Ms. Wood?"

She said, louder, "I thought I loved him. I wouldn't have slept with him if I didn't. I don't *do* one-night stands. I don't even do affairs."

"You did this one."

"Richard was different."

"Different than what?"

"Than other men! He wasn't just—just cars and football. He cared about the same things I cared about. This island, for instance. Look at the articles he wrote—you could see how much he loved this place. We used to talk for hours about it! And it just seemed the most natural thing in the world to…" She gave a little shudder of grief and looked down. Softly she said, "I thought he was different. At least, he seemed to be…."

"He was also married. But you knew that."

She felt her shoulders droop. "Yes."

"And did you know he had two children?"

She nodded.

"Yet you had an affair with him. Did it mean so little to you, Ms. Wood, that three innocent people—"

"Don't you think I thought about that, every waking moment?" Her chin shot up in rage. "Don't you think I hated myself? I never *stopped* thinking about his family! About Evelyn and the twins. I felt evil, dirty. I felt—I don't know." She gave a sigh of helplessness. "Trapped."

"By what?"

"By my love for him. Or what I thought was love." She hesitated. "But maybe—maybe I never really *did* love him. At least, not the real Richard."

"And what led to this amazing revelation?"

"Things I learned about him."

"What things?"

"The way he used people. His employees, for instance. The way he treated them."

"So you saw the real Richard Tremain and you fell out of love."

"Yes. And I broke it off." She let out a deep breath, as though relieved that the most painful part of her confession was finished. "That was a month ago."

"Were you angry at him?"

"I felt more...betrayed. By all those false images."

"So you must have been angry."

"I guess I was."

"So for a month you walked around mad at Mr. Tremain."

"Sometimes. Mostly I felt stupid. And then he wouldn't leave me alone. He kept calling, wanting to get back together."

"And that made you angry, as well."

"Yes, of course."

"Angry enough to kill him?"

She looked up sharply. "No."

"Angry enough to grab a knife from your kitchen drawer?"

"No!"

"Angry enough to go into the bedroom—your bedroom, where he was lying naked—and stab him in the chest?"

"No! No, no, no." She was sobbing now, screaming out her denials. The sound of her own voice echoed like some alien cry in that stark box of a room. She dropped her head into her hands and leaned forward on the table. "No," she whispered. She had to get away from this terrible man with his terrible questions. She started to rise from the chair.

"Sit down, Ms. Wood. We're not finished."

Obediently she sank back into the chair. "I didn't kill him," she cried. "I told you, I found him on my bed. I came home and he was lying there...."

"Ms. Wood—"

"I was on the beach when it happened. Sitting on the beach. That's what I keep telling all of you! But no one listens. No one believes me...."

"Ms. Wood, I have more questions."

She was crying, not answering, not able to answer. The sound of her sobs was all that could be heard.

At last Merrifield flicked off the recorder. "All right, then. We'll take a break. One hour, then we'll resume."

Miranda didn't move. She heard the man's chair scrape back, heard Merrifield leave the room, then the door shut. A few moments later the door opened again.

"Ms. Wood? I'll take you back to your cell."

Slowly Miranda rose to her feet and turned to the door. A young cop stood waiting, nice face, friendly smile. His name tag said Officer Snipe. Vaguely she remembered him from some other time, from her life before jail. Oh, yes. Once, on a Christmas Eve, he'd torn up her parking ticket. It had been a kind gesture, gallantry offered to a lady. She wondered what he thought of the lady now, whether he saw *murderer* stamped on her face.

She let him lead her into the hall. At one end she saw Lieutenant Merrifield, huddled in conference with Chief Tibbetts. The polite

Officer Snipe guided her in the opposite direction, away from the pair. Miranda had gone only a short distance when her footsteps faltered, stopped.

A man was standing at the far end of the hall, watching her. She had never seen him before. If she had, she certainly would have remembered him. He stood like some unbreachable barrier, his hands jammed in his pockets, his shoulders looming before her in the cramped corridor. He didn't look like a cop. Cops had standards of appearance, and this man was on the far edge of rumpled—unshaven, dark hair uncombed, his shirt a map of wrinkles. What disturbed her the most was the way he looked at her. That wasn't the passive curiosity of a bystander. No, it was something far more hostile. Those dark eyes were like judge and jury, weighing the facts, pronouncing her guilty.

"Keep moving, Ms. Wood," said Officer Snipe. "It's right around the corner."

Miranda forced herself to move forward, toward that forbidding human barrier. The man moved aside to let her pass. As she did, she felt his gaze burning into her and heard his sharp intake of breath, as though he was trying not to breathe the same air she did, as if her very presence had somehow turned the atmosphere to poison.

For the past twelve hours she'd been treated like a criminal, handcuffed, fingerprinted, intimately searched. She'd had questions fired at her, humiliations heaped upon her. But never, until this man had looked at her, had she felt like a creature worthy of such disgust, such loathing. Rage suddenly flared inside her, a rage so fierce it threatened to consume her in its flames.

She halted and stared up at him. Their gazes locked. *There, damn you!* she thought. *Whoever you are, take a look at me! Take a good, long look at the murderess. Satisfied?*

The eyes staring down at her were dark as night, stony with condemnation. But as they took each other in, Miranda saw something else flicker in those depths, a hint of uncertainty, almost confusion. As if the picture he saw was all wrong, as if image and caption were terribly mismatched.

Just down the hall, a door swung open. Footsteps clicked out and stopped dead.

"Dear God," whispered a voice.

Miranda turned.

Evelyn Tremain stood frozen in the washroom doorway. "Chase," she whispered. "It's her...."

At once the man went to Evelyn and offered her his steadying arm. Evelyn gripped it with both hands, as if holding on to her only lifeline. "Oh, please," she murmured helplessly. "I can't stand to look at her."

Miranda didn't move. She felt paralyzed by guilt, by what she'd done to this woman, to the whole family. Though her crime might not be murder, still she had committed a sin against Evelyn Tremain and for that she would always be tormented.

"Mrs. Tremain," she said quietly. "I'm sorry...."

Evelyn buried her face against the man's shoulder. "Chase, please. Get her out of here."

"He loved you," said Miranda. "I want you to know that. I want you to know that he never stopped loving—"

"Get her out of here!" cried Evelyn.

"Officer," said Chase quietly. "Please. Take her away."

Officer Snipe reached for Miranda's arm. "Let's go."

As she was led away Miranda called over her shoulder, "I didn't kill him, Mrs. Tremain! You have to believe that—"

"You tramp!" shouted Evelyn. "You filthy whore! You ruined my life."

Miranda glanced back and saw the other woman had pulled away from Chase and was now facing her like some avenging angel. Strands of blond hair had fallen free and her face, always pale, was now a stark white.

"You ruined my life!" Evelyn screamed.

That accusing shriek echoed in Miranda's ears all the way down that long walk to the jail.

Drained of resistance, she quietly entered the cell. She stood there, frozen, as the door clanged shut. Officer Snipe's footsteps faded away. She was alone, trapped in this cage.

Suddenly she felt as if she were suffocating, as if she would smother without fresh air. She scrambled over to the one small window and tried to pull herself up by the bars, but it was too high. She ran to the cot, dragged it across the cell and climbed on top. Even then she was barely tall enough to peek over the sill, to gulp in a tantalizing taste of freedom. Outside the sun was shining. She could see maple trees beyond the fenced yard, a few rooftops, a sea gull soaring in the sky. If she breathed in deeply, she could almost smell the sea. Oh, Lord, how sweet it all seemed! How unattainable! She gripped the window bars so tightly they dug into her palms. Pressing her face against the sill, she closed her eyes and willed herself to stay in control, to keep panic at bay.

I am innocent. They have to believe me, she thought.

And then, *What if they don't?*

No, damn it. Don't think about that.

She forced herself to concentrate on something else, anything else. She thought of the man in the hallway, the man with Evelyn Tremain. What had Evelyn called him? Chase. The name stirred a memory; Miranda had heard it before. She snatched desperately at that irrelevant strand of thought, concentrated hard on dredging up the memory, anything to crowd the fears from her mind. Chase. Chase. Someone had said it. She tried to bring back the voice, to match it to the utterance of that name.

The memory hit her like a blow. It was Richard who'd said it. *I haven't seen my brother in years. We had a falling-out when my father died. But then, Chase was always the problem kid in the family....*

Miranda's eyes flew open with the revelation. Was it possible? There'd been no resemblance, no hint of familial ties in that face. Richard had had blue eyes, light brown hair, a weathered face always on the verge of sunburn. This man called Chase was all darkness, all shadow. It was hard to believe they were brothers. But that would explain the man's coldness, his look of condemnation. He thought she'd murdered Richard, and repulsion was exactly what he would feel, coming face-to-face with his brother's killer.

Slowly she sank onto the cot. Lying there beneath the window she could catch glimpses of blue sky and cloud. August. It would be a hot day. Already her T-shirt was damp with sweat.

She closed her eyes and tried to imagine soaring like a sea gull in that bright blue sky, tried to picture the island far below her.

But all she could see were the accusing eyes of Chase Tremain.

CHAPTER THREE

He truly was the ugliest dog on earth.

Miss Lila St. John regarded her pet with a mixture of affection and pity. Sir Oscar Henry San Angelo III, otherwise known as Ozzie, was a rare breed known as a Portuguese Water Dog. Miss St. John was not quite clear as to the attributes of this particular breed. She suspected it was some sort of geneticist's joke. Her niece had presented the dog to her—"to keep you company, Auntie"—and Miss St. John had been trying to remember ever since what that niece could hold against her. Not that Ozzie was entirely without redeeming value. He didn't bite, didn't bother the cat. He was a passable watchdog. But he ate like a horse, twitched like a mouse and was absolutely unforgiving if you neglected to take him on his twice-daily walk. He would stand by the door and whine.

The way he was doing now.

Oh, Miss St. John knew that look. Even if she couldn't actually see the beast's eyes under all that fur, she knew what the look meant. Sighing, she opened the door. The black bundle of fur practically shot down the porch steps and took off for the woods. Miss St. John had no choice but to follow him, and so off into the woods she went.

It was a warm evening, one of those still, sweet twilights that seem kissed with midsummer magic. She would not be surprised to see something extraordinary tonight. A doe and fawn, perhaps, or a fox cub, or even an owl.

She moved steadily through the trees in pursuit of the dog. She noticed they were headed in a direct line toward Rose Hill Cottage, the Tremains' summer camp. Such a tragedy, Richard Tremain's death. She hadn't particularly liked the man, but theirs were the last two cottages on this lonely road, and on her walks here she had occasionally seen him through his window, his head bent in concentration at his desk. He'd always been polite to her, and deferential, but she'd suspected much of it was automatic and not, in any sense, true respect. He'd had no use for elderly women; he simply tolerated them.

But as for young women, well, she'd heard that was a different story.

It troubled her, these recent revelations about his death. Not so much the fact of his murder, but the identity of the one accused. Miss St. John had met Miranda Wood, had spoken to her on several occasions. On this small island, in the dead of winter, only green thumb fanatics braved the icy roads to attend meetings of the local garden club. That's where Miss St. John had met Miranda. They'd sat together during a lecture on triploid marigolds, and again at the talk on gloxinia cultivation. Miranda was polite and deferential, but genuinely so. A lovely girl, not a hint of dishonesty in her eyes. It seemed to Miss St. John that any woman who cared so passionately about flowers, about living, growing things, could simply not be a murderess.

It bothered her, all that cruel talk flying about town these days. Miranda Wood, a killer? It went against Miss St. John's instincts, and her instincts were always, always good.

Ozzie bounded through the last stand of trees and shot off toward Rose Hill Cottage. Miss St. John resignedly followed suit. That's when she saw the light flickering through the trees. It came from the Tremain cottage. Just as quickly, it vanished.

At once she froze as an eerie thought flashed to mind. *Ghosts?* Richard was the only one who ever used that cottage. *But he's dead.*

The rational side of her brain, the side that normally guided Miss St. John's day-to-day existence, took control. It must be one of the family, of course. Evelyn, perhaps, come to wrap up her husband's affairs.

Still, Miss St. John couldn't shake off her uneasiness.

She crossed the driveway and went up the front porch steps.

"Hello?" she called. "Evelyn? Cassie?" There was no answer to her knock.

She tried to peer in the window, but it was dark inside. "Hello?" she called again, louder. She thought she heard, from somewhere in the cottage, a soft thud. Then—silence.

Ozzie began to bark. He danced around on the porch, his claws tip-tapping on the wood.

"Oh, hush!" snapped Miss St. John. "Sit!"

The dog whined, sat, and gave her a distinctly wounded look.

Miss St. John stood there a moment, listening for more sounds, but she heard nothing except the whap-whap of Ozzie's tail against the porch.

Perhaps she should call the police. She debated that move all the way back to her cottage. Once there, in her cheery little kitchen, the very idea seemed so silly, so alarmist. It was a good half-hour drive out here to the north shore. The local police would be reluctant to send a man all the way out here, and for what? A will-o'-the-wisp tale? Besides, what could there possibly be in Rose Hill Cottage that would interest any burglars?

"It's just my imagination. Or my failing eyesight. After all, when one's seventy-four, one has to expect the faculties to get a little screwy."

Ozzie walked in a tight circle, lay down and promptly went to sleep.

"Good Lord," said Miss St. John. "I'm talking to my dog now. What part of my brain will rot next?"

Ozzie, as usual, offered no opinion.

The courtroom was packed. Already, a dozen people had been turned away at the door, and this wasn't even a trial, just a bail review hearing, a formality required by law to be held forty-eight hours after arrest.

Chase, who sat in the second row with Evelyn and her father, suspected the proceedings would be brief. The facts were stark, the suspect's guilt indisputable. A few words by the judge, a bang of the gavel and they'd all be out of there.

And the murderess would slink back to her cell, where she belonged.

"Damned circus, that's what it is," growled Evelyn's father, Noah DeBolt. Silver haired and gravel throated, at sixty-six he was still as formidable as ever. Chase felt the automatic urge to sit up straight and mind his manners. One did not slouch in the presence of Noah DeBolt. One was always courteous and deferential, even if one was an adult.

Even if one was the chief of police, Chase noted, as Lorne Tibbetts stopped and politely tipped his hat at Noah.

The principals were settling in their places. The deputy D.A. from Bass Harbor was seated at his table, flipping through a sheaf of papers. Lorne and Ellis, representing half the local police force, sat off to the left, their uniformed spines ramrod straight, their hair neatly slicked down. They had even parted it on the same side. The defense attorney, a youngster wearing a suit that looked as if it cost twice his annual salary, was fussing with the catch on his leather briefcase.

"They should clear this place out," grunted Noah. "Who the hell let all these spectators in? Invasion of privacy, I call it."

"It's open to the public, Daddy," said Evelyn wearily.

"There's public, and then there's *public*. These people don't belong here. It's none of their damn business." Noah rose and waved for Lorne's attention, but the chief of police's brilliantined head was facing forward. Noah glanced around for the bailiff, but the man had disappeared through a side door. In frustration, Noah sat back down. "Don't know what this town's coming to," he muttered. "All these new people. No sense of what's proper anymore."

"Quiet, Daddy," murmured Evelyn. Then, fuming, she muttered, "Where are the twins? Why aren't they here? I want the judge to see them. Poor kids without a father."

Noah snorted. "They're full-grown adults. They won't impress anyone."

"There. I see them," said Chase, spotting Cassie and Phillip a few rows back. They must have slipped in later, with the other spectators.

So the audience is in place, he thought. *All we need now are the two main players. The judge. And the accused.*

As if on cue, a side door opened. The ape-size bailiff reappeared, his hand gripping the arm of the much smaller prisoner.

At his second glimpse of Miranda Wood, Chase was struck by how much paler she appeared than he remembered. And how much more fragile. The top of her head barely reached the bailiff's shoulder. She was dressed unobtrusively, in a blue skirt and a simple white blouse, an outfit no doubt chosen by her attorney to make her look innocent, which she did. Her hair was gathered back in a neat but trim ponytail. No wanton-woman looks here. Those lush chestnut highlights were carefully restrained by a plain rubber band. She wore no jewelry, no makeup. The pallor of those cheeks came without the artifice of face powder.

On her way to the defendant's table she looked once, and only once, at the crowd. Her gaze swept the room and came to rest on Chase. It was only a few seconds of eye contact, a glimpse of her brittle mask of composure. Pride, that's what he saw in her face. He could read it in her body language: the straight back, the chin held aloft. Everyone else in this room would see it, too, would resent that show of pride. The brazen murderess, they'd think. A woman without repentance, without shame. He wished *he* could feel that way about her. It would make her guilt seem all the more assured, her punishment all the more justified.

But he knew what lay beneath the mask. He'd seen it in those eyes two days before, when they'd gazed out at him through a one-way mirror. Fear, pure and simple. She was terrified.

And she was too proud to show it.

From the instant Miranda walked into the courtroom, none of it seemed real. Her feet, her legs felt numb. She was actually grateful for the firm grip of the bailiff's hand around her arm as they stepped in the side door. She caught a kaleidoscopic glimpse of all those faces in the audience—if that's what you called a courtroom full of spectators. What else could you call them? An audience here to watch her performance, an act in the theater of her life. Half of them had come to hang her; the other half were here to watch. As her gaze slowly swept the room she saw familiar faces. There were her colleagues from the *Herald:* Managing Editor Jill Vickery, looking every bit the sleek professional, and staff reporters Annie Berenger and Ty Weingardt, both of them dressed à la classic rumpled writer. It was hard to tell that they were—or had been—friends. They all wore such carefully neutral expressions.

As her gaze shifted, she took in a single friendly face in the crowd—old Mr. Lanzo, her next-door neighbor. He was mouthing the words *I'm with you, sweetie!* She found herself almost smiling back.

Then her gaze shifted again, to settle on Chase Tremain's stony face. The smile instantly died on her lips. Of all the faces in the room, his was the one that most made her feel like shrinking into some dark, unreachable crevice, anywhere to escape his gaze of judgment. The faces beside him were no less condemning. Evelyn Tremain, dressed in widow's black, looked like a pale death's mask. Next to Evelyn was her father, Noah DeBolt, town patriarch, a man who with one steely look could wither the spirit of any who dared offend him. He was now aiming that poisonous gaze at Miranda.

The tug of the bailiff's hand redirected Miranda toward the defendant's table. Meekly she sat beside her attorney, who greeted her with a stiff nod. Randall Pelham was Ivy League and impeccably dressed for the part, but all Miranda could think of when she saw his face was how young he looked. He made her feel, at twenty-nine, positively middle-aged. Still, she'd had little choice in the matter. There were only two attorneys in practice on Shepherd's Island. The other was Les Hardee, a man with experience, a fine reputation and a fee to match. Unfortunately, Hardee's client list happened to include the names DeBolt and Tremain.

Randall Pelham had no such conflict of interest. He didn't have many clients, either. As the new kid in town, he was ready and willing to represent anyone, even the local murderess.

She asked softly, "Are we okay, Mr. Pelham?"

"Just let me do the talking. You sit there and look innocent."

"I am innocent."

To which Randall Pelham offered no response.

"All rise for His Honor Herbert C. Klimenko," said the bailiff. Everyone stood.

The sound of shuffling feet announced the arrival of Judge Klimenko, who creaked behind the bench and sank like a bag of old bones into his chair. He fumbled around in his pockets and finally managed to perch a pair of bifocals on his nose.

"They brought him out of retirement," someone whispered in the front row. "You know, they say he's senile."

"They also say he's deaf!" shot back Judge Klimenko. With that, he slammed down the gavel. "Court is now in session."

The hearing convened. She followed her attorney's advice and let him do the talking. For forty-five minutes she didn't say a word as two men, one she barely knew, one she knew not at all, argued the question of her freedom. They weren't here to decide guilt or innocence. That was for the trial. The issue to be settled today was more immediate: should she be set free pending that trial?

The deputy D.A. ticked off a list of reasons the accused should remain incarcerated. Weight of evidence. Danger to the community. Undeniable flight risk. The savage nature of the crime, he declared, pointed to the defendant's brutal nature. Miranda could not believe that this monster he kept referring to was *her. Is that what they all think of me?* she wondered, feeling the gaze of the audience on her back. *That I'm evil? That I would kill again?*

Only when she was asked, twice, to stand for Judge Klimenko's decision did her attention shift back to the present. Trembling, she rose to her feet and gazed up at the pair of eyes peering down at her over bifocals.

"Bail is set at one hundred thousand dollars cash or two hundred thousand dollars secured property." The gavel slammed down. "Court dismissed."

Miranda was stunned. Even as the audience milled around behind her, she stood frozen in despair.

"It's the best I could do," Pelham whispered.

It might as well have been a million. She would never be able to raise it.

"Come on, Ms. Wood," said the bailiff. "Time to go back."

In silence she let herself be escorted across the room, past the gazes of all those prying eyes. Only for a second did she pause, to glance back over her shoulder at Chase Tremain. As their gazes locked she thought she saw, for an instant, a flicker of something she hadn't seen before. Compassion. Just as quickly, it was gone.

Fighting tears, she turned and followed the bailiff through the side door.

Back to jail.

"That will keep her locked away," said Evelyn.

"A hundred thousand?" Chase shook his head. "It doesn't seem out of reach."

"Not for us, maybe. But for someone like her?" Evelyn snorted. The look of satisfaction on her flawlessly made-up face was not becoming. "No. No, I think Ms. Miranda Wood will be staying right where she belongs. Behind bars."

"She hasn't budged an inch," said Lorne Tibbetts. "We've been questioning her for a week straight now and she sticks to that story like glue."

"It doesn't matter," said Evelyn. "Facts are facts. She can't refute them."

They were sitting outside, on Evelyn's veranda. At midmorning they'd been driven from the house by the heat; the sun streaming in the windows had turned the rooms into ovens. Chase had forgotten about these hot August days. In his memory, Maine was forever cool, forever immune to the miseries of summer. So much for childhood memories. He poured another glass of iced tea and handed the pitcher over to Tibbetts.

"So what do you think, Lorne?" asked Chase. "You have enough to convict?"

"Maybe. There are holes in the evidence."

"What holes?" demanded Evelyn.

Chase thought, *my sister-in-law is back to her old self again. No more hysterics since that day at the police station.* She looked cool and in control, which is how he'd always remembered her from their childhood. Evelyn the ice queen.

"There's the matter of the fingerprints," said Tibbetts.

"What do you mean?" asked Chase. "Weren't they on the knife?"

"That's the problem. The knife handle was wiped clean. Now, that doesn't make a lot of sense to me. Here's this crime of passion, see? She uses her own knife. Pure impulse. So why does she bother to wipe off the fingerprints?"

"She must be brighter than you think," Evelyn said, sniffing. "She's already got you confused."

"Anyway, it doesn't go along with an impulse killing."

"What other problems do you have with the case?" asked Chase.

"The suspect herself. She's a tough nut to crack."

"Of course she is. She's fighting for her life," said Evelyn.

"She passed the polygraph."

"She submitted to one?" asked Chase.

"She insisted on it. Not that it would've hurt her case if she flunked. It's not admissible evidence."

"So why should it change *your* mind?" asked Evelyn.

"It doesn't. It just bothers me."

Chase stared off toward the sea. He, too, was bothered. Not by the facts, but by his own instincts.

Logic, evidence, told him that Miranda Wood was the killer. Why did he have such a hard time believing it?

The doubts had started a week ago, in that police station hallway. He'd watched the whole interrogation. He'd heard her denials, her lame explanations. He hadn't been swayed. But when they'd come face-to-face in the hall, and she'd looked him straight in the eye, he'd felt the first stirrings of doubt. Would a murderess meet his gaze so unflinchingly? Would she face an accuser with such bald courage? Even when Evelyn had appeared, Miranda hadn't ducked for cover. Instead, she'd said the unexpected. *He loved you. I want you to know that.* Of all the things a murderess might have said, that was the most startling. It was an act of kindness, an honest attempt to comfort the widow. It earned her no points, no stars in court. She could simply have walked past, ignoring Evelyn, leaving her to her grief. Instead, Miranda had reached out in pity to the other woman.

Chase did not understand it.

"There's no question but that the weight of the evidence is against her," said Tibbetts. "Obviously, that's what the judge thought. Just look at the bail he set. He knew she'd never come up with that kind of cash. So she won't be walking out anytime soon. Unless she's been hiding a rich uncle somewhere."

"Hardly," said Evelyn. "A woman like that could only come from the wrong side of the tracks."

Wrong side of the tracks, thought Chase. Meaning poor. But not trash. He'd been able to see that through the one-way mirror. Trash was cheap, easily bent, easily bought. Miranda Wood was none of those.

A car marked Shepherd's Island Police pulled up in the driveway.

Tibbetts sighed. "Geez, they just won't leave me alone. Even on my day off."

Ellis Snipe, spindly in his cop's uniform, climbed out. His boots crunched toward them across the gravel. "Hey, Lorne," he called up to the veranda. "I figured you was here."

"It's Saturday, Ellis."

"Yeah, I know. But we sort of got us a problem."

"If it's that washroom again, just call the plumber. I'll okay the work order."

"No, it's that—" Ellis glanced uneasily at Evelyn. "It's that Miranda Wood woman."

Tibbetts rose to his feet and went over to the veranda railing. "What about her?"

"You know that hundred thousand bail they set?"

"Yeah."

"Well, someone paid it."

"*What?*"

"Someone's paid it. We just got the order to release her."

There was a long silence on the veranda. Then, in a low voice laced with venom, Evelyn said, "*Who* paid it?"

"Dunno," said Ellis. "Court says it was anonymous. Came through some Boston lawyer. So what do we do, huh, Lorne?"

Tibbetts let out a deep breath. He rubbed his neck, shifted his weight back and forth a few times. Then he said, "I'm sorry, Evelyn."

"Lorne, you can't do this!" she cried.

"I don't have a choice." He turned back to the other cop. "You got the court order, Ellis. Let her walk."

"I don't understand," said Miranda, staring in bewilderment at her attorney. "Who would do this for me?"

"A friend, obviously" was Randall Pelham's dry response. "A very *good* friend."

"But I don't have any friends with that kind of money. No one with a hundred thousand to spare."

"Well, someone's putting up the bail. My advice is, don't look a gift horse in the mouth."

"If I just knew who it was—"

"It's been handled through some Boston attorney who says his client wishes to stay anonymous."

"Why?"

"Maybe the donor's embarrassed."

To be helping a murderess, she thought.

"It's his—or her—right to remain anonymous. I say, take it. The alternative is to stay in jail. Not exactly the most comfortable spot to be in."

She let out a deep breath. "No, it isn't." In fact, it had been horribly bleak in that cell. She'd spent the past week staring at the window, longing for the simple pleasure of a walk by the sea. Or a decent meal. Or just the warmth of the sunshine on her face. Now it was all within reach.

"I wish I knew who to thank," she said softly.

"Not possible, Miranda. I say, just accept the favor." He snapped his briefcase shut.

Suddenly he irritated her, this kid barely out of braces, so smart and snazzy in his gray suit. Randall Pelham, Esquire.

"The arrangements are made. You can leave this afternoon. Will you be staying at your house?"

She paused, shuddering at the memory of Richard's body in her bed. The house had since been cleaned, courtesy of a housekeeping service. Her neighbor Mr. Lanzo had arranged it all, had told her the place looked fine now. It would be as if nothing had happened in that bedroom. There would be no signs of violence at all.

Except in her memory.

But where else could she go?

She nodded. "I—I suppose I'll go home."

"You know the drill, right? Don't leave the county. Bass Harbor's as far as you can go. Stay in touch at all times. And don't, I repeat don't, go around discussing the case. My job's tough enough as it is."

"And we wouldn't want to tax your abilities, would we?" she said under her breath.

He didn't seem to hear the comment. Or maybe he was ignoring her. He strode out of the cell, then turned to gaze at her. "We can still try a plea bargain."

She looked him in the eye. "No."

"That way we could limit the damage. You could walk out of here in ten years instead of twenty-five."

"I didn't kill him."

For a moment Pelham returned her gaze. With a shrug of impatience, he turned. "Plea bargain," he said. "That's my advice. Think about it."

She *did* think about it, all afternoon as she sat in that stark cell waiting for the release papers.

But as soon as she stepped out of the building and walked, as a free woman, into the sunshine, all thoughts of trading away even ten years of her life seemed unimaginable. She stood there on the sidewalk, gazing up at the sky, inhaling the sweetest air she'd ever breathed in her life.

She decided to walk the mile to her house.

By the time she came within sight of her front yard, her cheeks were flushed, her muscles pleasantly tired. The house looked the same as it always had, shingled cottage, trim lawn—which someone had obviously watered in her absence—brick walkway, a hedge of hydrangea bushes sprouting fluffy white clouds of flowers. Not a large house, but it was hers.

She started up the walkway.

Only when she'd mounted the porch steps did she see the vicious words someone had soaped on her front window. She halted, stung by the cruelty of the message.

Killer.

In sudden fury she swiped at the glass with her sleeve. The accusing words dissolved into soapy streaks. Who could have written such a horrible thing? Surely none of her neighbors. Kids. Yes, that's who it must have been. A bunch of punks. Or summer people.

As if that made it easier to dismiss. No one much cared what the summer people thought. The ones who lived on the island year round—those were the ones whose opinions counted. The ones you had to face every day.

She paused at the front door, almost afraid to go in. At last she reached for the knob and entered.

Inside, to her relief, everything seemed orderly, just the way things should be. A bill, made out by the Conscientious Cleaners Company, lay on the end table. "Complete cleaning," read the work order. "Special attention to the master bedroom. Remove stains." The work order was signed by her neighbor, Mr. Lanzo, bless him. Slowly she made a tour of inspection. She glanced in the kitchen, the bathroom, the spare bedroom. Her bedroom she left for last, because it was the most painful to confront. She stood in the doorway, taking in the neatly made bed, the waxed floor, the spotless area rug. No signs of murder, no signs of death. Just a sunny bedroom with plain farmhouse furniture. She stood there, taking it all in, not budging even when the phone rang in the living room. After a while the ringing stopped.

She went into the bedroom and sat on the bed. It seemed like a bad dream now, what she'd seen here. She thought, *If I just concentrate hard enough, I'll wake up. I'll find it was a nightmare.* Then she stared down at the floor and saw, by the foot of the bed, a brown stain in the oak planks.

At once she rose and left the room.

She walked into the living room just as the phone rang again. Automatically she picked up the receiver. "Hello?"

"Lizzie Borden took an ax and gave her mother forty whacks. When she saw what she had done, she gave her father forty-one!"

Miranda dropped the receiver. In horror she backed away, staring at the dangling earpiece. The caller was laughing now. She could hear the giggles, cruel and childlike, emanating from the receiver. She scrambled forward, grabbed the earpiece and slammed it down on the cradle.

The phone rang again.

She picked it up.

"Lizzie Borden took an ax—"

"Stop it!" she screamed. "Leave me alone!"

She hung up and again the phone rang.

This time she didn't answer it. In tears, she ran out the kitchen door and into the garden. There she sank into a heap on the lawn. Birds chirped overhead. The smell of warm soil and flowers drifted sweetly in the afternoon. She buried her face in the grass and cried.

Inside, the phone kept on ringing.

CHAPTER FOUR

Miranda stood alone and unnoticed outside the cemetery gates. Through the wrought-iron grillwork she could see the mourners grouped about the freshly dug grave. It was a large gathering, as befitted a respected member of the community. *Respected, perhaps,* she added to herself. *But was he beloved?* Did any among them, including his wife, truly love him? *I thought I did. Once....*

The voice of Reverend Marriner was barely a murmur. Much was lost in the rustle of the lilac branches overhead. She strained to hear the words. "Loving husband...always be missed...cruel tragedy...Lord, forgive..."

Forgive.

She whispered the word, as though it were a prayer that could somehow pull her from the jaws of guilt. But who would forgive her?

Certainly not anyone in that gathering of mourners.

She recognized almost every face there. Among them were her neighbors, her colleagues from the newspaper, her friends. *Make that former friends,* she thought with bitterness. Then there were those too lofty to have made her acquaintance, the ones who moved in social circles to which Miranda had never gained entrance.

She saw the grim but dry-eyed Noah DeBolt, Evelyn's father. There was Forrest Mayhew, president of the local bank, attired in his regulation gray suit and tie. In a category all to herself was Miss Lila St. John, the local flower and garden nut, looking freeze-dried at the eternal age of seventy-four. And then, of course, there were the Tremains. They formed a tragic tableau, poised beside the open grave. Evelyn stood between her son and Chase Tremain, as though she needed both men to steady her. Her daughter, Cassie, stood apart, almost defiantly so. Her flowered peach dress was in shocking contrast to the background of grays and blacks.

Yes, Miranda knew them all. And they knew her.

By all rights she should be standing there with them. She had once been Richard's friend; she owed it to him to say goodbye. She should follow her heart, consequences be damned.

But she lacked the courage.

So she remained on the periphery, a lone and voiceless exile, watching as they laid to rest the man who had once been her lover.

She was still there when it was over, when the mourners began to depart in a slow and steady procession through the gates. She saw their startled glances, heard the gasps, the murmurs of "Look, it's her." She met their gazes calmly. To flee would have seemed an act of cowardice. *I may not be brave,* she thought, *but I am not a coward.* Most of them quickly passed by, averting their eyes. Only Miss Lila St. John returned Miranda's gaze, and the look she gave her was neither friendly nor unfriendly. It was merely thoughtful. For an instant Miranda thought she saw a flicker of a smile in those searching eyes, and then Miss St. John, too, moved on.

A sharp intake of breath made Miranda turn.

The Tremains had halted by the gate. Slowly Evelyn raised her hand and pointed it at Miranda. "You have no right," she whispered. "No right to be here."

"Mom, forget it," said Phillip, tugging her arm. "Let's just go home."

"She doesn't belong here."

"Mom—"

"Get her away from here!" Evelyn lunged toward Miranda, her hands poised to claw.

At once Chase stepped between the two women. He pulled Evelyn against him, trapping her hands in his. "Evelyn, don't! I'll take care of it, okay? I'll talk to her. Just go home. Please." He glanced at the twins. "Phillip, Cassie! Come on, take your mother home. I'll be along later."

The twins each took an arm and Evelyn allowed herself to be

led away. But when they reached their car she turned and yelled, "Don't let the bitch fool you, Chase! She'll twist you around, the way she did Richard!"

Miranda stumbled back a step, physically reeling from the impact of those accusing words. She felt the gate against her back swing away, found herself grabbing at it for support. The cold wrought iron felt like the only solid thing she could cling to and she held on for dear life. The squeal of the gate hinges suddenly pierced her cloud of confusion. She found she was standing in a clump of daisies, that the others had gone, and that she and Chase Tremain were the only people remaining in the cemetery.

He was watching her. He stood a few feet away, as though wary of approaching her. As though she was some sort of dangerous animal. She could see the suspicion in his dark eyes, the tension of his pose. How aristocratic he looked today, so remote, so untouchable in that charcoal suit. The jacket showed off to perfection his wide shoulders and narrow waist. Tailored, of course. A real Tremain wouldn't consider any off-the-rack rag.

Still, she had trouble believing this man, with his Gypsy eyes and his jet black hair, was a Tremain.

For a year she had gazed up at those portraits in the newspaper building. They'd hung on the wall opposite her desk, five generations of Tremain men, all of them ruddy faced and blue eyed. Richard's portrait, just as blue eyed, had fit right in. Hang a portrait of Chase Tremain on that same wall and it would look like a mistake.

"Why did you come here, Ms. Wood?" he asked.

She raised her chin. "Why shouldn't I?"

"It's inappropriate, to say the least."

"It's very appropriate. I cared about him. We were—we were friends."

"*Friends?*" His voice rose in mocking disbelief. "Is that what you call it?"

"You don't know anything about it."

"I know that you were more than friends. What shall we call your relationship, Ms. Wood? An affair? A romance?"

"Stop it."

"A hot little tumble on the boss's couch?"

"Stop it, damn you! It wasn't like that!"

"No, of course not. You were just *friends*."

"All right! All right...." She looked away, so he wouldn't see her tears. Softly she said, "We were lovers."

"At last. A word for it."

"And friends. Most of all, friends. I wish to God it had stayed that way."

"So do I. At least he'd still be alive."

She stiffened. Turning back to him she said, "I didn't kill him."

He sighed. "Of course you didn't."

"He was already dead. I found him—"

"In your house. In your bed."

"Yes. In my bed."

"Look Ms. Wood. I'm not the judge and jury. Don't waste your breath with me. I'm just here to tell you to stay away from the family. Evelyn's gone though enough hell. She doesn't need constant reminders. If we need to, we'll get a restraining order to keep you away. One false move and you'll be back in jail. Right where you belong."

"You're all alike," she said. "You Tremains and DeBolts. All cut from the same fancy silk. Not like the rest of us, who can be shoved out of sight. Right where we belong."

"It's not a matter of which cloth we're cut from. It's a matter of cold-blooded murder." He took a step toward her. She didn't move. She couldn't; her back was against the gate. "What happened, exactly?" he said, moving closer. "Did Richard break some sacred promise? Refuse to leave his wife? Or did he just come to his senses and decide he was walking out on you?"

"That's not what happened."

"So what did happen?"

"I walked out on *him!*"

Chase gazed down at her, skepticism shadowing every line of his face. "Why?"

"Because it was over. Because it was all wrong, everything between us. I wanted to get away. I'd already left the paper."

"He fired you?"

"I quit. Look in the files, Mr. Tremain. You'll find my letter of resignation. Dated two weeks ago. I was going to leave the island. Head somewhere I wouldn't have to see him every day. Somewhere I wouldn't be constantly reminded of what a disaster I'd made of things."

"Where were you planning to go?"

"It didn't matter. Just away." She looked off, past the gravestones. Far beyond the cemetery lay the sea. She could catch glimpses of it through the trees. "I grew up just fifty miles from here. Right across the water. This bay is my home. I've always loved it. Yet all I could think about was getting away."

She turned to look at him. "I was already free of him. Halfway back to happiness. Why should I kill Richard?"

"Why was he in your house?"

"He insisted on meeting me. I didn't want to see him. So I left and went for a walk. When I came back, I found him."

"Yes, I've heard your version. At least your story's consistent."

"It's also the truth."

"Truth, fiction." He shrugged. "In your case it all blends together, doesn't it?" Abruptly he turned and headed up the cemetery drive.

"What if it's *all* truth?" she called after him.

"Stay away from the family, Ms. Wood!" he yelled over his shoulder. "Or I'll have to call in Lorne Tibbetts."

"Just for a moment, consider the possibility that I didn't kill him! That someone else did!"

He was still walking away.

"Maybe it's someone you know!" she shouted. "Think about it! Or do you already know and you want me to take the blame? Tell me, Mr. Tremain! Who *really* killed your brother?"

That brought Chase to a sudden halt. He knew he should keep walking. He knew it was a mistake to engage the woman in any more of this insane dialogue. It *was* insane. Or she was insane. Yet he couldn't break away, not yet. What she'd just said had opened up too many frightening possibilities.

Slowly he turned to face her. She stood absolutely still, her gaze fixed on him. The afternoon sun washed her head with a coppery glow. All that beautiful hair seemed to overwhelm her face. She looked surprisingly fragile in that black dress, as though a strong gust might blow her away.

Was it possible? he wondered. Could this woman really have picked up a knife? Raised the blade over Richard's body? Plunged it down with so much rage, so much strength, that the tip had pierced straight through to his spine?

Slowly he moved toward her. "If you didn't kill him," he said, "who did?"

"I don't know."

"That's a pretty disappointing answer."

"He had enemies—"

"Angry enough to kill him?"

"He ran a newspaper. He knew things about certain people in this town. And he wasn't afraid to print the truth."

"Which people? What sort of scandal are we talking about?"

He saw her hesitate, wondered if she was dredging up some new lie.

"Richard was writing an article," she said. "About a local developer named Tony Graffam. He runs a company called Stone Coast Trust. Richard said he had proof of fraud—"

"My brother had paid reporters on his staff. Why would he bother to do his own writing?"

"It was a personal crusade of his. He was set on ruining Stone Coast. He needed just one last piece of evidence. Then he was going to print."

"And did he?"

"No. The article was supposed to appear two weeks ago. It never did."

"Who stopped it?"

"I don't know. You'd have to talk to Jill Vickery."

"The managing editor?"

Miranda nodded. "She knew the article was in the works and she wasn't crazy about the idea. Richard was the driving force behind the story. He was even willing to risk a libel suit. In fact, Tony Graffam has already threatened to sue."

"So we have one convenient suspect. Tony Graffam. Anyone else?"

She hesitated. "Richard wasn't a popular man."

"*Richard?*" He shook his head. "I doubt that. I was the brother with the popularity problem."

"Two months ago he cut salaries at the *Herald*. Laid off a third of the staff."

"Ah. So we have more suspects."

"He hurt people. Families—"

"Including his own."

"You don't know how hard it is these days! How desperate people are for work. Oh, he talked a good story. About how sorry he was to be laying people off. How it hurt him just as much as it hurt everyone else. It was *garbage*. I heard him talking about it later, to his accountant. He said, 'I cut the deadwood, just as you advised.' Deadwood. Those employees had been with the *Herald* for years. Richard had the money. He could have carried the loss."

"He was a businessman."

"Right. That's exactly what he was." Her hair, tossed by the wind, was like flames dancing. She was a wild and blazing fire, full of anger at him, at Richard, at the Tremains.

"So we've added to the pool of suspects," he said. "All those poor souls who lost their jobs. And their families. Why don't we toss in Richard's children? His father-in-law? His wife?"

"Yes! Why not Evelyn?"

Chase snorted in disgust. "You're very good, you know that? All that smoke and mirrors. But you haven't convinced me. I hope the jury is just as smart. I hope to hell they see through you and make you pay."

She looked at him mutely, all the fire, all the spirit suddenly drained from her body.

"I've already paid," she whispered. "I'll pay for the rest of my life. Because I'm guilty. Not of killing him. I didn't kill him." She swallowed and looked away. He could no longer see her face, but he could hear the anguish in her voice. "I'm guilty of being stupid. And naive. Guilty of having faith in the wrong man. I really thought I loved your brother. But that was before I knew him. And then, when I did know him, I tried to walk away. I wanted to do it while we were still...friends."

He saw her hand come up and stroke quickly across her face. It suddenly struck him how very brave she was. Not brazen, as he'd first thought upon seeing her today, but truly, heartbreakingly courageous.

She raised her head again, her gaze drawing level to his. The tears she'd tried to wipe away were still glistening on her lashes. He had a sudden, crazy yearning to touch her face, to wipe away the wetness of those tears. And with that yearning came another, just as insane, a man's hunger to know the taste of her lips, the softness of her hair. At once he took a step back, as though retreating from some dangerous flame. He thought, *I can see why you fell for her, Richard. Under different circumstances I might have fallen for her myself.*

"Oh, hell," she muttered in disgust. "What does it matter now, what I felt? To you or to anyone else?" Without looking back she left him and started up the driveway. Her abrupt departure seemed to leave behind an unfillable vacuum.

"Ms. Wood!" he yelled. She kept walking. He called out, "Miranda!" She stopped. "I have one question for you," he said. "Who bailed you out?"

Slowly she turned and looked at him. "You tell me," she said. And then she walked away.

It was a long walk to the newspaper building. It took Miranda past familiar streets and storefronts, past people she knew. That was the worst part. She felt them staring at her through the shop windows. She saw them huddle in groups and whisper to each other. No one came right out and said anything to her face. They didn't have to. *All I lack,* she thought, *is a scarlet letter sewn on my chest.* M *for murderess.*

She kept her gaze fixed straight ahead and walked up Limerock Street. The *Herald* building stood before her, a brick-and-slate haven against all those watching eyes. She ducked through the double glass doors, into the newsroom.

Inside, all activity came to a dead halt.

She felt assaulted by all those startled looks.

"Hello, Miranda," said a cool voice.

Miranda turned. Jill Vickery, the managing editor, glided out of the executive office. She hadn't changed clothes since the funeral. On dark-haired, ivory-skinned Jill, the color black looked quite elegant. Her short skirt hissed against her stockings as she clipped across the floor.

"Is there something I can do for you?" Jill asked politely.

"I—I came to get my things."

"Yes, of course." Jill shot a disapproving glance at the other employees, who were still gawking. "Are we all so efficient that we've no more work to do?"

At once everyone redirected their attention to their jobs.

Jill looked at Miranda. "I've already taken the liberty of cleaning out your desk. It's all in a box downstairs."

Miranda was so grateful for Jill's simple civility she scarcely registered annoyance that her desk had been cold-bloodedly emptied of her belongings. She said, "I've also a few things in my locker."

"They should still be there. No one's touched it." There was a silence. "Well," said Jill, a prelude to escape from a socially awkward situation. "I wish you luck. Whatever happens." She started back toward her office.

"Jill?" called Miranda.

"Yes?"

"I was wondering about that article on Tony Graffam. Why it didn't run."

Jill looked at her with frank puzzlement. "Why does it matter?"

"It just does."

Jill shrugged. "It was Richard's decision. He pulled the story."

"Richard's? But he was working on it for months."

"I can't tell you his reasons. I don't know them. He just pulled it. And anyway, I don't think he ever wrote the story."

"But he told me it was nearly finished."

"I've checked his files." Jill turned and walked toward her office. "I doubt he ever got beyond the research stage. You know how he was, Miranda. The master of overstatement."

Miranda stared after her in bewilderment. The master of over-statement. It hurt to admit it, but yes, there was a lot of truth in that label.

People were staring at her again.

She headed down the stairwell and pushed into the women's lounge. There she found Annie Berenger, lacing up running shoes. Annie was dressed in her usual rumpled-reporter attire—baggy drawstring pants, wrinkled cotton shirt. The inside of her locker looked just as disorderly, a mound of wadded-up clothes, towels and books.

Annie glanced up and tossed her head of gray-streaked hair in greeting. "You're back."

"Just to clean out my things." Miranda found the cardboard box with her belongings stuffed under one of the benches. She dragged it out and carried it to her locker.

"I saw you at the funeral," said Annie. "That took guts, Mo."

"I'm not sure guts is the word for it."

Annie shoved her locker door shut and breathed a sigh of relief. "Comfortable at last. I just had to change out of that funeral getup. Can't think in those stupid high heels. Cuts the blood supply to my brain." She finished lacing up her running shoe. "So what's going to happen next? With you, I mean."

"I don't know. I refuse to think beyond a day or two." Miranda opened her locker and began to throw things into the box.

"Rumor has it you have friends in high places."

"What?"

"Someone bailed you out, right?"

"I don't know who it was."

"You must have an idea. Or is this your lawyer's advice, to plead ignorance?"

Miranda gripped the locker door. "Don't, Annie. Please."

Annie cocked her head, revealing all the lines and freckles of too many summers in the sun. "I'm being a jerk, aren't I? Sorry. It's just that Jill assigned me to the trial. I don't like having to drag an old colleague across the front page." She watched as Miranda emptied the locker and shut the door. "So. Can I get a statement from you?"

"I didn't do it."

"I've already heard that one."

"Want to earn a Pulitzer?" Miranda turned, squarely faced her. "Help me find out who killed him."

"You'll have to give me a lead, first."

"I don't have one."

Annie sighed. "That's the problem. Whether or not you did it, you're still the obvious suspect."

Miranda picked up the box and headed up the stairs. Annie trailed behind her.

"I thought real reporters went after the truth," said Miranda.

"This reporter," said Annie, "is basically lazy and angling for early retirement."

"At your age?"

"I turn forty-seven next month. I figure that's a good age to retire. If I can just get Irving to pop the question, it'll be a life of bonbons and TV soaps."

"You'd hate it."

"Oh, yeah." Annie laughed. "I'd be just miserable."

They walked into the newsroom. At once Miranda felt all those gazes turn her way. Annie, oblivious to their audience, went to her desk, threw her locker keys in her drawer and pulled out a pack of cigarettes. "You happen to have a light?" she asked Miranda.

"You always ask me, and I never have one."

Annie turned and yelled, "Miles!"

The summer intern sighed resignedly and tossed her a cigarette lighter. "Just give it back," he said.

"You're too young to smoke, anyway," snapped Annie.

"So were you once, Berenger."

Annie grinned at Miranda. "I love these boy wonders. They're so damn petulant."

Miranda couldn't help smiling. She sat on the desktop and looked at her ex-colleague. As always, Annie wore a wreath of cigarette smoke. It was part addiction, part prop, that cigarette. Annie had earned her reporter's stripes in a Boston newsroom where the floor was said to be an inch deep in cigarette butts.

"You do believe me, don't you?" asked Miranda softly. "You don't really think..."

Annie looked her straight in the eye. "No. I don't. And I was kidding about being lazy," said Annie. "I've been digging. I'll come up with something. It's not like I'm doing it out of friendship or anything. I mean, I could find out things that could hurt you. But it's what I have to do."

Miranda nodded. "Then start with this."

"What?"

"Find out who bailed me out."

Annie nodded. "A reasonable first step."

The back office door swung open. Jill Vickery came out and glanced around the newsroom. "Marine distress call. Sailboat's taking on water. Who wants the story?"

Annie slunk deep in her chair.

Miles sprang to his feet. "I'll take it."

"Coast Guard's already on the way. Hire a launch if you have to. Go on, get going. You don't want to miss the rescue." Jill turned and looked at Annie. "Are you busy at the moment?"

Annie shrugged. "I'm always busy."

Jill nodded toward Miles. "He'll need help. Go with the kid." She turned back to her office.

"I can't."

Jill stopped, turned to confront Annie. "Are you refusing my assignment?"

"Yeah. Sort of."

"On what grounds?"

Annie blew out a long, lazy puff of smoke. "Seasickness."

"I knew she'd confuse you, Chase. I just knew it. You don't understand her the way I do."

Chase looked up from the porch chair where he'd been brooding for the past hour. He saw that Evelyn had changed out of her black dress and was now wearing an obscenely bright lime green. He knew he should feel sorry for his sister-in-law, but at the moment Evelyn looked more in need of a stiff drink than of pity. He couldn't help comparing her to Miranda Wood. Miranda, with her ill-fitting black dress and her windblown hair, so alone on that cemetery hillside. He wondered if Richard ever knew how much damage he'd done to her, or if he'd ever cared.

"You haven't said a word since you got home," complained Evelyn. "What is going on with you?"

"Just how well did you know Miranda Wood?" he asked.

She sat down and fussily arranged the folds of her green dress. "I've heard things. I know she grew up in Bass Harbor. Went to some—some state university. Had to do it all on scholarship. Couldn't afford it otherwise. Really, not a very good family."

"Meaning what?"

"Mill workers."

"Ah. Dregs of the earth."

"What is the matter with you, Chase?"

He rose to his feet. "I need to take a walk."

"Oh. I'll go with you." She jumped to her feet, instantly wreaking havoc on all those nicely arranged folds of her dress.

"No. I'd like to be alone for a while. If you don't mind."

Evelyn looked as if she minded very much, but she managed to cover it gracefully. "I understand, Chase. We all need to mourn in our own way."

He felt a distinct sense of relief as he walked away from that front porch. The house had started to feel oppressive, as though the weight of all those memories had crowded out the breathable air. For a half hour he walked aimlessly. Only as his feet carried him closer to town did he begin to move with a new sense of purpose.

He headed straight for the newspaper building.

He was greeted by Jill Vickery, the sleekly attractive managing editor. It was just like Richard to surround himself with gorgeous women. Chase had met her earlier that day, at the funeral. Then, as now, she played the part of the professional to the hilt.

"Mr. Tremain," she said, offering her hand. "What a pleasure to see you again. May I show you around?"

"I was just wondering..." He glanced around the newsroom, which was currently occupied by only a bare-bones staff: the lay-out man arranging ads, another one staring at a computer screen, and that sloppy reporter puffing on a cigarette as she talked on the phone.

"Yes?" asked Jill.

"If I could go over some of my brother's files."

"Business or personal files?"

"Both."

She hesitated, then led him into the back office and through a door labeled Richard Tremain, Owner and Publisher. "These aren't all his files, you understand. He kept most of them here, but some he kept at home or at the cottage."

"You mean Rose Hill?"

"Yes. He liked to work out there, on occasion." She pointed to the desk. "The key's in the top drawer. Please let me know if you take anything."

"I wasn't planning to."

She paused, as though uncertain whether to trust him. But what choice did she have? He was, after all, the publisher's brother. At last she turned and left.

Chase waited for the door to shut, then he unlocked the file cabinet. He flipped immediately to the *W*'s.

He found a file on Miranda Wood.

Chase carried it to the desk and spread it open. It appeared to be a routine personnel record. The employment application was dated one year ago, when Miranda was twenty-eight. Her address was listed as 18 Willow Street. In the attached photograph she was smiling; it was the face of a confident young woman with her whole life ahead of her. It almost hurt to see how happy she looked. Her university record was outstanding. If anything, she was overqualified for her job as copy editor. Under the question "Why do you want this job?" she had written, "I grew up near Penobscot Bay. I want, more than anything, to live and work in the place I've always called home." He flipped through the pages and scanned the semiannual employee evaluation, filled out by Jill Vickery. It was excellent. He turned to the last page.

There was a letter of resignation, dated two weeks ago.

To: Richard Tremain, Publisher, *Island Herald.*
Dear Mr. Tremain,
I hereby notify you of my resignation from my position as copy editor. My reasons are personal. I would greatly appreciate a letter of reference, as I plan to seek employment elsewhere.

That was all. No explanations, no regrets. Not even a hint of recrimination.

So she told me the truth, he thought. *She really did walk off the job.*

"Mr. Tremain?" It was Jill Vickery, back again. "Are you looking for anything in particular? Maybe I can help you."

"Maybe you can."

She came in and gracefully settled into the chair across from him. Her gaze at once took in the file on the desk. "I see you have Miranda's employee record."

"Yes. I'm trying to understand what happened. Why she did it."

"I think you should know she was here just a short while ago."

"In the building?"

"She came to collect her things. I'm glad you two avoided a, uh...unexpected encounter."

He nodded. "So am I."

"Let me say this, Mr. Tremain. I'm very sorry about your

brother. He was a wonderful man, an exceptional writer. He truly believed in the power of the printed word. We're going to miss him.''

It was a canned speech, but she delivered it with such sincerity he was almost convinced she meant it. Jill Vickery certainly had the PR down flat.

"I understand Richard had a story in the pipeline," he said. "Something about a company called Stone Coast Trust. You familiar with it?"

Jill sighed. "Why does this particular article keep coming up?"

"Someone else interested?"

"Miranda Wood. She just asked about it. I told her that as far as I know, the story was never written. At least, I never saw it."

"But it was scheduled to run?"

"Until Richard canceled it."

"Why?"

She sat back and smoothly flicked her hair off her face. "I wouldn't know. I suspect he didn't have enough evidence to go to print."

"What, exactly, is the story on Stone Coast Trust?"

"Small-town stuff, really. Not very interesting to outsiders."

"Try me."

"It had to do with developers' rights. Stone Coast has been buying up property on the north shore. Near Rose Hill Cottage, as a matter of fact, so you know how lovely it is up there. Pristine coastline, trees. Tony Graffam—he's president of Stone Coast—claimed he was out to preserve the area. Then we heard rumors of a high-class development in the works. And then, a month ago, the zoning on those lots was abruptly changed from conservation to resort. It's now wide open to development."

"That's all there is to the article?"

"In a nutshell. May I ask the reason for your interest?"

"It was something Miranda Wood told me. About other people having motives to kill my brother."

"In this case, she's stretching the point." Jill rose to her feet.

"But one can hardly blame her for trying. She hasn't much else to grab onto."

"You think she'll be convicted?"

"I wouldn't want to hazard a guess. But from what my news staff tells me, it sounds likely."

"You mean that reporter? Annie something?"

"Annie Berenger. Yes, she's assigned to the story."

"Can I talk to her?"

Jill frowned. "Why?"

He shook his head. "I don't know. I guess I'm just trying to understand who this Miranda Wood really is. Why she would kill." He sat back, ran his hand through his hair. "I still can't quite fit the pieces together. I thought, maybe someone who's been watching the case—someone who knew her personally..."

"Of course. I understand." The words were sympathetic but her eyes were indifferent. "I'll send Annie in to talk to you."

She left. A moment later Annie Berenger appeared.

"Come in," said Chase. "Have a seat."

Annie shut the door and sat in the chair across from him. She looked like a reporter: frizzy red hair streaked with gray, sharp eyes, wrinkled slacks. She also reeked of cigarettes. It brought back memories of his father. All she needed was a splash of whiskey on her breath. A good old newsman's smell.

She was watching him with clear suspicion. "Boss lady says you want to talk about Miranda."

"You knew her pretty well?"

"The word is *know*. Present tense. Yes, I do."

"What do you think of her?"

Her mouth twitched into a smile. "This is your own private investigation?"

"Call it my quest for the truth. Miranda Wood denies killing my brother. What do you think?"

Annie lit a cigarette. "You know, I used to cover the police beat in Boston."

"So you're familiar with murder."

"In a manner of speaking." Leaning back, she thoughtfully

exhaled a cloud of smoke. "Miranda had the motive. Oh, we all knew about the affair. It's hard to hide something like that in this newsroom. I tried to, well, advise her against it. But she follows her heart, you know? And it got her into trouble. That's not to say she did it. Killed him." Annie flicked off an ash. "I don't think she did."

"Then who did?"

Annie shrugged.

"You think it's tied to the Tony Graffam story?"

Annie's eyebrow shot up. "You dig stuff up fast. Must run in the family, that newsman's nose."

"Miranda Wood says Richard had a story about to break. True?"

"He said he did. I know he was writing it. He had a few more details to check before it went to print."

"What details?"

"Financial data, about Stone Coast Trust. Richard had just got his hands on some account information."

"Why didn't the article get to print?"

"Honest opinion?" Annie snorted. "Because Jill Vickery didn't want to risk a libel suit."

Chase frowned. "But Jill says the article doesn't exist. That Richard never wrote it."

Annie blew out a last breath of smoke and stubbed out her cigarette in the ashtray. "Here's a piece of wisdom for you, Mr. T," she said. She looked him in the eye. "Never trust your editor."

Did the article exist or didn't it?

Chase spent the next hour searching the files in Richard's office. He found nothing under *G* for Graffam or *S* for Stone Coast Trust. He tried a few more headings, but none of them panned out. Did Richard keep the file at home?

It was late afternoon when he finally returned to the house. To his relief, Evelyn and the twins were out. He had the place to himself. He went straight into Richard's home office and continued his search for the Graffam file.

He didn't find it. Yet Miranda claimed it existed. So did Annie Berenger.

Something strange was going on, something that added to all his doubts about Miranda's guilt. He mentally played back all the holes in the prosecution's case. The lack of fingerprints on the murder weapon. The fact she had passed the polygraph test. And the woman herself—proud, unyielding in her protestations of innocence.

He gave up trying to talk himself out of his next move. There was no way around it. Not if he wanted to know more. Not if he wanted to shake these doubts.

He had to talk to Miranda Wood.

He pulled on his windbreaker and headed out into the dusk.

Five blocks later he turned onto Willow Street. It was just the way he'd remembered it, a tidy, middle-class neighborhood with inviting front porches and well-tended lawns. Through the fading light he could just make out the address numbers. A few more houses to go....

Farther up the street a screen door slammed shut. He saw a woman come down her porch steps and start toward him along the sidewalk. He recognized her silhouette, the thick cloud of hair, the slim figure clad in jeans. She'd taken only a few steps when she spotted him and stopped dead in her tracks.

"I have to talk to you," he said.

"I made a promise, remember?" she answered. "Not to go near you or your family. Well, I'm keeping that promise." She turned and started to walk away.

"This is different. I have to ask you about Richard."

She kept walking.

"Will you listen to me?"

"That's how I got into this mess!" she shot back over her shoulder. "Listening to a Tremain!"

He watched in frustration as she headed swiftly up the street. It was useless to pursue her. She was already a block away now, and by the set of her shoulders he could tell she wasn't going to change her mind. In fact, she had just stepped off the sidewalk and was crossing the street, as though to put the width of the road between them.

Forget her, he thought. *If she's too stubborn to listen, let her go to jail.*

Chase turned and had started in the opposite direction when a car drove past. He would scarcely have noticed it except for one detail: its headlights were off. A few paces was all it took for Chase to register that fact. He stopped, turned. Far ahead, Miranda's slender figure was crossing the street.

By then the car had moved halfway down the block.

The driver'll see her in time, he thought. *He has to see her.*

The car's engine suddenly revved up in a threatening growl of power. Tires screeched. The car leaped forward in a massive blur of steel and smoke, and roared ahead through the shadows.

It was aiming straight for Miranda.

CHAPTER FIVE

The headlights sprang on, trapping its insubstantial victim in a blaze of light.

"Look out!" Chase shouted.

Miranda whirled and found her eyes flooded with a terrible, blinding brightness. Even as the car shot closer and those lights threatened to engulf her, she was paralyzed by disbelief, by the detached sense of certainty that this was not really happening. She had no time to reason it out. An instant before that ton of steel could slam into her body, her reflexes took over. She flung herself sideways, out of the path of the onrushing headlights.

Suddenly she was flying, suspended for an eternity in the summer darkness as death rushed past her in a roar of wind and light.

And then she was lying on the grass.

She didn't know how long she had been there. She knew only that the grass was damp, that her head hurt and that gentle hands were stroking her face. Someone called her name, again and again. It was a voice she knew, a voice she thought, in that confused moment, she must have known all her life. Its very timbre seemed to blanket her with the warmth of safety.

Again he called her name, and this time she heard panic in his voice. *He's afraid. Why?*

She opened her eyes and dazedly focused on his face. That's when she registered exactly who he was. All illusion of safety fell away.

"Don't." She brushed his hand aside. "Don't touch me."

"Lie still."

"I don't need you!" She struggled to sit up, but found herself unable to move under his restraining hands. He had her pinned by her shoulders to the grass.

"Look," he said, his voice maddeningly reasonable. "You took a mean tumble. You might have broken something—"

"I said, don't touch me!" Defiantly she shoved him away and sat up. Pure rage propelled her to her knees. Then, as the night wavered before her eyes, she found herself sinking back to the grass. There she sat and clutched her spinning head. "Oh, God," she groaned. "Why can't you just—just go away and leave me alone."

"Not on your life," came the answer, grim and resolute.

To her amazement she was suddenly, magically lifted up into the air. Through her anger she had to admit it felt good to be carried, good to be held, even if the man holding her was Chase Tremain. She was floating, borne like a featherweight through the darkness. *Toward what?* she wondered with sudden apprehension.

"That's enough," she protested. "Let me down."

"Only a few more steps."

"I hope you get a hernia."

"Keep up the damn wiggling and I will."

He swept her up the porch steps and in the front door. With unerring instinct he carried her straight to the bedroom and managed to flick on the wall switch. The room—the bed—sprang into view. The bed where she'd found Richard. Though the blood was gone, the mattress new and unstained, this room would always remind her of death. She hadn't slept here since that night, would never sleep here again.

She shuddered against him. "Please," she whispered, turning her face against his chest. "Not here. Not this room."

For a moment he paused, not understanding. Then, gently he answered, "Whatever you say, Miranda."

He carried her back to the living room and lowered her onto the couch. She felt the cushions sag as he sat beside her. "Does anything hurt?" he asked. "Your back? Your neck?"

"My shoulder, a little. I think I fell on it."

She flinched at the touch of his hands. Carefully he maneuvered her arm, checking its range of motion. She was scarcely aware of the occasional twinges he evoked from her muscles. Her attention was too acutely focused on the face gazing down at her. Once again she was struck by how unlike Richard he was. It wasn't just the blackness of his hair and eyes. It was his calmness under fire, as though he held any emotions he might be feeling under tight rein. This was not a man who'd easily reveal himself, or his secrets, to anyone.

"It seems all right," he said, straightening. "Still, I'd better call a doctor. Who do you see?"

"Dr. Steiner."

"Steiner? Is that old goat still in practice?"

"Look, I'm okay. I don't need to see him."

"Let's just be on the safe side." He reached for the telephone.

"But Dr. Steiner doesn't make house calls," she protested. "He never has."

"Then tonight," Chase said grimly, dialing the phone, "I guess we're going to make history."

Lorne Tibbetts poured himself a cup of coffee and turned to look at Chase. "What I want to know is, what in blazes are you doing here?"

Chase, leaning over Miranda's kitchen table, wearily rubbed his face. "To tell you the truth, Lorne," he muttered, "I don't know."

"Oh."

"I guess I thought I could...figure things out. Make sense of what's happened."

"That's our job, Chase. Not yours."

"Yeah, I know. But—"

"You don't think I'm doing a good job?"

"I just get this feeling there's more than meets the eye. Now I know there is."

"You mean that car?" Lorne shrugged. "Doesn't prove a thing."

"He was *aiming* for her. I saw it. As soon as she stepped into the street he hit the gas."

"He?"

"He, she. It was dark. I didn't see the driver. Just the license plate. And the taillights. Big car, American. I'm pretty sure."

"Color?"

"Dark. Black, maybe blue."

Lorne nodded. "You're not a bad witness, Chase."

"What do you mean?"

"I had Ellis check on that license number. Matches a brown '88 Lincoln, registered to an island resident."

"Who?"

"Mr. Eddie Lanzo. Ms. Wood's next-door neighbor."

Chase stared at him. "Her neighbor? Have you brought him in yet?"

"The car was stolen, Chase. You know how it is around here. Folks leave their keys in the ignition. We found the car over by the pier."

Chase sat back, stunned. "So the driver's untraceable," he said. "That makes it even more likely he was trying to kill her."

"It just means it was some crazy kid out for a joyride. Got his hands on that wheel, got a little overwhelmed by all that power, pushed too hard on the gas pedal."

"Lorne, he was out to kill her."

Lorne sat down and looked him in the eye. "And what are you out to do?"

"Learn the truth."

"You don't believe she did it?"

"I've been hearing some things, Lorne. Other names, other motives. Tony Graffam, for instance."

"We've looked into that. Graffam was off the island when your brother was killed. I have half a dozen witnesses who'll say so."

"He could have hired someone."

"Graffam was in big enough trouble with that north shore development. Charges of bribing the land planning commission. That article would've simply been the last nail in the coffin. Anyway, how does this tie in with what happened tonight? Why would he go after Miranda Wood?"

Chase fell silent at that question. He couldn't see a motive, either. Other people in town might dislike Miranda, but who would go to the trouble of killing her?

"Maybe we're looking at this the wrong way," said Chase. "Let's ask a more basic question. Who put up the bail money? Someone wanted her out so badly he put up a hundred thousand dollars."

"A secret admirer?"

"In jail she's safe. Out here she's a sitting duck. You have any idea who bailed her out, Lorne?"

"No."

"The money could be traced."

"A lawyer handled the transfer of funds. All cash. Came from some Boston account. Only the bank knows the account holder's identity. And they aren't talking."

"Subpoena the bank. Get the name on that account."

"It'll take time."

"Do it, Lorne. Before something else happens."

Lorne went to the sink and rinsed his coffee cup. "I still don't see why you're getting into this," he said.

Chase himself didn't know the answer. Just this morning he'd wanted Miranda Wood put behind bars. Now he wasn't sure what he wanted. That innocent face, her heartfelt denials of guilt had him thoroughly confused.

He looked around the kitchen, thinking it didn't *look* like the kitchen of a murderess. Plants hung near the window, obviously well tended and well loved. The wallpaper had dainty wildflowers scattered across an eggshell background. Tacked to the refrigerator were snapshots of two little towheaded boys—nephews, maybe?— a schedule of the local garden club meetings and a shopping list. At the bottom of the list was written "cinnamon tea." Was that the sort of beverage a murderess would drink? He couldn't picture Miranda holding a knife in one hand and a cup of herbal tea in the other.

Chase looked around as Dr. Steiner shuffled into the kitchen. Some things on the island never changed, and this old grouch was one of them. He looked exactly the same as Chase remembered from his boyhood, right down to the wrinkled brown suit and the alligator medical bag. "All this to-do," the doctor said disapprovingly. "For nothin' but a muscle strain."

"You sure about that?" asked Chase. "She was sort of dazed for a minute. Right after it happened."

"I looked her over good. She's fine, neurologically speaking. You just keep an eye on her tonight, young man. Make sure she doesn't get into trouble. You know, headache, double vision, confusion—"

"I can't."

"Can't what?"

"I can't stay and watch her. It's awkward. Considering..."

"No kidding," muttered Lorne.

"She's not my responsibility," said Chase. "What do I do?"

Dr. Steiner grunted and turned for the kitchen door. "You figure it out. By the way," he said, pausing in the doorway, "I don't do house calls." The door slammed shut.

Chase turned to find Lorne looking at him. "What?"

"Nothing," said Lorne. He reached for his hat. "I'm going home."

"And what the hell am I supposed to do?"

"That," said Lorne with an I-told-you-so look, "is your problem."

Miranda lay on the living-room couch and stared at the ceiling. She could hear voices from the kitchen, the sound of the door opening and closing. She wondered what Chase had told them, whether Tibbetts believed any of it. She herself couldn't believe what had happened. But all she had to do was close her eyes and it came back to her: the roar of the car engine, the twin headlights rushing at her.

Who hates me so much they want me dead?

It wasn't hard to come up with an answer. The Tremain family. Evelyn and Phillip and Cassie....

And Chase.

No, that wasn't possible. His shout of warning had saved her life. If not for him, she would be lying right now on a slab in Ben LaPorte's Funeral Home.

That thought made her shudder. Hugging herself, she burrowed deeper into the couch cushions, seeking some safe little nook in which to hide. She heard the kitchen door open and shut again, then footsteps creaked into the living room and approached the couch. She looked up and saw Chase.

Weariness was what she read in his eyes, and uncertainty, as though he hadn't quite made up his mind what should be done next. Or what should be said next. He'd shed his windbreaker. His chambray shirt was the comfortably faded blue of a well-worn, well-loved garment. That shirt reminded her of her father, of how it used to feel to nestle her face against his shoulder, of those wondrous childhood scents of laundry soap and pipe tobacco and safety. That was what she saw in that faded blue shirt, what she longed for.

What she'd never find with this man.

Chase sat in the armchair. A prudent distance away, she noted. *Keeping me at arm's length.*

"Feeling better?" he asked.

"I'll be fine." She kept her voice like his—detached, neutral. She added, "You can leave if you want."

"No. Not yet. I'll wait here awhile, if that's okay. Until Annie gets here."

"Annie?"

"I didn't know who else to call. She said she'd be over to spend the night. You should have someone here to keep an eye on you. Make sure you don't slide into a coma or something."

She gave a tired laugh. "A coma would feel pretty good right now."

"That's not very funny."

She looked up at the ceiling. "You're right. It isn't."

There was a long silence.

Finally he said, "That wasn't an accident, Miranda. He was trying to kill you."

She didn't answer. She lay there fighting back the sob swelling in her throat. *Why should it matter to you?* she thought. *You, of all people.*

"Maybe you haven't heard," he said. "The car belonged to your neighbor. Mr. Lanzo."

She looked at him sharply. "Eddie Lanzo would never hurt me! He's the only one who's stood by me. My one friend in this town."

"I didn't say it was him. Lorne thinks the driver stole Mr. Lanzo's car. They found it abandoned by the pier."

"Poor Eddie," she murmured. "Guess that's the last time he leaves his keys in the car."

"So if it wasn't Eddie, who does want you dead?"

"I can make a wild guess." She looked at him. "So can you."

"Are you referring to Evelyn?"

"She hates me. She has every right to hate me. So do her children." She paused. "So do you."

He was silent.

"You still think I killed him. Don't you?"

Sighing, he raked his fingers through his hair. "I don't know what to think anymore. About you, about anyone. All I can be sure of is what I saw tonight. It's all tied in, this whole bloody mess. It has to be."

He looks so tired, so confused, she thought. *Almost as confused as I am.*

"Maybe you should move out of here for a few days," he said. "Until things get sorted out."

"Where would I go?"

"You must have friends."

"I did." She looked away. "At least, I thought I did. But everything's changed. I pass them on the street and they don't even say hello. Or they cross to the other side. Or they pretend they don't see me. That's the worst of all. Because I begin to think I don't exist." She looked at him. "It's a very small town, Chase. You either fit in, or you don't belong. And there's no way a murderess could ever fit in." She lay back against the cushions and stared at the ceiling. "Besides, this is my house. *My* house. I saved like crazy for the down payment. I won't leave it. It's not much, but at least it's mine.''

"I can understand that. It's a nice house.''

He sounded sincere enough, but his words struck her as patronizing. The lord of the manor extolling the charms of the shepherd's hovel.

Suddenly annoyed, she sat up. The abrupt movement made the room spin. She clutched her head for a moment, waiting for the spell to pass.

"Look, let's be straight with each other,'' she muttered through her hands. "It's only a two-bedroom cottage. The basement's damp, the water pipes screech and there's a leak in the kitchen roof. It's not Chestnut Street.''

"To be honest,'' he said quietly, "I never felt at home on Chestnut Street.''

"Why not? You were raised there.''

"But it wasn't really a home. Not like this house.''

Puzzled, she looked up at him. It struck her then how rough around the edges he seemed, a dark, rumpled stranger hulking in her mauve armchair. No, this man didn't quite fit on Chestnut Street. He belonged on the docks, or on the windswept deck of a schooner, not in some stuffy Victorian parlor.

"I'm supposed to believe you'd prefer a cottage on Willow Street to the family mansion?''

"I guess it does sound—I don't know. Phony. But it's true. Know where I spent most of my time as a kid? In the turret, playing around all the trunks and the old furniture. That was the only place in the house where I felt comfortable. The one room no one else cared to visit.''

"You sound like the family outcast.''

"In a way, I was.''

She laughed. "I thought all Tremains were, by definition, *in.*''

"One can have the family name and still not be part of the family. Or didn't you ever feel that way?''

"No, I was always very much part of my family. What there was of it.'' Her gaze drifted to the spinet piano, where the framed photo of her father was displayed. It was a grainy shot, one of the few she still had of him, taken with her old Kodak Brownie. He was grinning at her over the hood of his Chevy, a bald little gnome of a man dressed in blue overalls. She found herself smiling back at the image.

"Your father?" asked Chase.

"Yes. Stepfather, really. But he was every bit as wonderful as any real father."

"I hear he worked for the mill."

She frowned at him. It disturbed her that Chase was obviously acquainted with that detail of her life. A detail that was none of his business. "Yes," she said. "Both my parents did. What else have you heard about me?"

"It's not that I've been checking up on you."

"But you have, haven't you? You and your family have probably run my name through some computer. Criminal check. Family history. Credit report—"

"We've done no such thing."

"Personal life. All the hot and juicy details."

"Where would I find those?"

"Try my police record." In irritation she rose from the couch and moved to the fireplace. There she stood focused on the clock over the mantelpiece. "It's getting late, Mr. Tremain. Annie should be here any minute. You're free to leave, so why don't you?"

"Why don't you sit back down? It makes me nervous, having you up and about."

"I make *you* nervous?" She turned to him. "You hold all the cards. You know everything about me. What my parents did for a living. Where I went to school. Who I slept with. I don't like that."

"Were there that many?"

His retort struck her like a physical blow. She could think of no response to such a cruel question. She was reduced to staring at him in speechless fury.

"Don't answer," he said. "I don't want to know. Your love life's none of my business."

"You're right. It's none of your damn business." She turned away, angrily clutching the mantelpiece with both hands. "No matter what you learn about me, it'll all fit right in with your image of the mill worker's daughter, won't it? Well, I'm not ashamed of where I came from. My parents made an honest living. They didn't have some trust fund to keep them in caviar. Like some families I know," she added, leaving no doubt by the tone of her voice just which family she was referring to.

He acknowledged the insult with a brief silence.

"I'm surprised you fell for Richard," he said. "Considering your attitude toward trust-funders."

"Before I knew Richard, I didn't *have* an attitude problem." She turned to confront him. "Then I got to know him. I saw what the money did to him. For him. He never had to struggle. He always had that green buffer to protect him. It made him careless. Immune to other people's pain." Her jaw came up in a pose of proud disdain. "Just like you."

"Now you're making the assumptions about me."

"You're a Tremain."

"I'm like you. I have a job, Miranda. I work."

"So did Richard. It kept him amused."

"Okay, maybe you're right about Richard. He didn't need to work. The *Herald* was more of a hobby to him, a reason to get up in the morning. And he got a kick out of telling his friends in Boston that he was a publisher. But that was Richard. You can't slap that rich-boy label on me because it won't stick. I was booted out of the family years ago. I don't have a trust fund and I don't own a mansion. But I do have a job that pays the bills. And, yes, keeps me *amused.*"

His anger was tightly controlled but evident all the same. *I've touched a nerve,* she thought. An acutely sensitive one. Chastened, she sat in a chair by the fireplace. "I guess—I guess I assumed a few too many things."

He nodded. "We both did."

In silence they gazed at each other across the room. A truce, however uneasy, had at last settled between them.

"You said you were booted out of the family. Why?" she asked.

"Simple. I got married."

She looked at him in puzzlement. He had said the words without emotion, with the tone of voice one used to describe the weather. "I take it she wasn't a suitable bride."

"Not according to my father."

"The wrong side of the tracks?"

"In a manner of speaking. My father, he was attuned to that sort of thing."

Naturally, she thought. "And was your father right? About those girls from the wrong side of the tracks?"

"That wasn't why we got divorced."

"Why did you?"

"Christine was too…ambitious."

"Hardly a flaw."

"It is when I'm just the rung on the social ladder she's trying to climb."

"Oh."

"And then we had some lean years. I was working all the time, and…" He shrugged. Another silence stretched between them.

"Richard never told me what kind of work you do."

He leaned back, the tension easing away from his face. Unexpectedly he laughed. "Probably because what I do struck him as so damn boring. My partners and I design office buildings."

"You're an architect?"

"Structural engineer. My architect partners do the creative work. I make sure the walls don't come crashing down."

An engineer. Not exactly a fluff career, she thought, but a real, honest job. Like her father had.

She shook her head. "It's strange. When I look at you, I can't quite believe you're his brother. I always assumed…"

"That we'd be a matched set? No, we were definitely different. In more ways than you'll ever know."

Yes, the more she knew about Chase, the less he seemed like
a Tremain. And the more she thought she could like him.

"What did you ever see in my brother?" he asked.

His question, voiced so softly, was jarring all the same. It reminded her of the ghosts that still hovered in this house.

She sighed. "I saw what I wanted to see."

"Which was?"

"A man who needed me. A man I could play savior to."

"Richard?"

"Oh, it *seemed* as if he had everything going for him. But he
also had this…this vulnerability. This need to be saved. From
what, I don't know. Maybe himself."

"And you were going to save him."

She gave a bitter laugh. "I don't know. You don't think about
these things. You just feel. And you fall into it…."

"You mean you followed your heart."

She looked up at him. "Yes," she whispered.

"Didn't it seem wrong to you?"

"Of course it did!"

"But?"

Her whole body sagged with the weight of her unhappiness. "I
couldn't…see my way out of it. I cared about him. I wanted to
be there for him. And he'd string me along. He'd tell me things
would work out, as long as we both had faith." She looked down
at her hands, clasped together in her lap. "I guess I lost my faith
first."

"In him? Or the situation?"

"Him. I began to see the flaws. It came out, after a while. How
he manipulated people, used people. If he didn't need you, he'd
ignore you. A user, that's what he was. An expert at making people do what he wanted."

"Then you broke it off. How did he react?"

"He couldn't believe it. I don't think anyone ever left *him.* He
kept calling me, bothering me. And every day, at work, I'd have
to face him. Pretend nothing was going on between us."

"Everyone knew, though."

She shrugged. "Probably. I'm not very good at hiding things. Annie knew, because I told her. And everyone else must have guessed." She sighed. The truth was, she hadn't cared at the time. Love, and then pain, had made her indifferent to public opinion.

They said nothing for a moment. She wondered what he thought of her now, whether any of it made a difference. Suddenly it mattered what he *did* think of her. He was scarcely more than a stranger, and a hostile one, but it mattered very much.

"You're not the first one, you know," he said. "There were other women."

It was a cruel revelation to spring on her, and Chase didn't know why he did it. He only knew that he wanted to give her a good, hard shaking. To shatter any rose-colored illusions she might still harbor about Richard. She might say the feelings were gone, but deep inside, might a few warm memories still linger?

He saw, by the look in her eyes, that his words had had their intended effect. Instantly he regretted the wounds he'd inflicted. Still, shouldn't she know? Shouldn't she be told just how naive she'd been?

"Were there many?" she asked softly.

"Yes."

She looked away, as though to hide the pain from view. "I—I think I knew that. Yes, I must have known that."

"It's just the way he was," said Chase. "He liked being admired. He was like that as a boy, too."

She nodded. And he realized, yes, she did know that about Richard. On some level she must have sensed his unquenchable thirst for admiration. And tried to satisfy it.

Chase had done damage enough. Here she was, demoralized and wounded. *And I pour on the salt.*

I should get out of here, leave her alone.

Where the hell was Annie Berenger?

Miranda seemed to shake herself back to life. She brushed her hair off her face, sat up and looked at him. So much torment in those eyes, he thought. And, at the same time, so much courage.

"You never told me why you're here," she said.

"The doctor thought someone should watch you—"

"No. I mean, why did you come in the first place?"

"Oh." He sat back. "I was at the *Herald* this afternoon. Talked to Jill Vickery, about the Stone Coast Trust article you mentioned. She says it was never written. That Richard never got that far with it."

Miranda shook her head. "I don't understand. I know he had at least a few pages written. I saw them on his desk, at the *Herald*."

"Well, I couldn't find any article. I thought maybe you'd know where to look. Or maybe you'd have it."

She looked at him in bewilderment. "Why would I?"

"I assume Richard was a frequent visitor here."

"But he didn't bring his work. Have you checked the house?"

"It's not there."

She thought about it a moment. "Sometimes," she said, "he'd drive up to the north shore, to write. He had a cottage…"

"You mean Rose Hill. Yes, I suppose I should check there tomorrow."

Their gazes intersected, held. She said, "You're starting to believe me. Aren't you?"

He heard, in her voice, the stirring of hope—however faint. He found himself wanting to respond, to offer her some small scrap of a chance that he might believe her. It was hard *not* to believe her, especially when she looked at him that way, her gaze unwavering, those gray eyes bright and moist. They could rob a man of his common sense, those eyes, could sweep self-control right out from under him. They awakened other sensations as well, disturbing ones. She was sitting more than half a room away, but even at that distance her presence was like some heady perfume, impossible to ignore.

She asked again, softly, "Do you believe me?"

Abruptly he rose to his feet, determined to shake off the dangerous spell she was weaving around him. "No," he said. "I can't say that I do."

"But don't you see there's something more to this than just a—a crime of passion?"

"I admit, things don't feel quite right. But I'm not ready to believe you. Not by a long shot."

There was a knock on the door. Startled, Chase turned to see the door swing open and Annie Berenger poke her head in.

"Hello, cavalry's here," she called. She came in dressed in an old T-shirt and sweatpants. Blades of wet grass clung to her running shoes. "What's the situation?"

"I'm fine," said Miranda.

"But she needs watching," said Chase. "If there are any problems, Dr. Steiner's number is by the phone."

"Leaving already?" asked Annie.

"They'll be expecting me at home." He went to the door. There he paused and glanced back at Miranda.

She hadn't moved. She just sat there. He had the urge to say something comforting. To tell her that what he'd said earlier wasn't quite true. That he *was* starting to believe her. But he couldn't admit it to her; he could scarcely admit it to himself. And there was Annie, watching everything with her sharp reporter's eyes.

So he merely said, "Good night, Miranda. I hope you're feeling better. And Annie, thanks for the favor." Then he turned and walked out the door.

Outside, it took him a few seconds to accustom his eyes to the darkness. By the time he'd reached the edge of the front yard he could finally make out the walkway under his feet.

He could also see the silhouette of a man standing stoop-shouldered before him on the sidewalk.

Chase halted, instantly tense.

"She okay?" asked the man.

"Who are you?" demanded Chase.

"I could ask the same o' you," came the cranky reply.

"I'm...visiting," said Chase.

"So, is Mo gonna be all right, or what?"

"Mo? Oh, you mean Miranda. Yes, she'll be fine, Mr...."

"Eddie Lanzo. Live next door. Like to keep an eye on her, y'know? Not good, a nice young woman livin' all by herself. And all these crazies runnin' around here, peekin' in windows. Not safe to be female these days."

"Someone's staying with her tonight, so you needn't worry."

"Yeah. Okay. Well, I won't bother her none, then." Eddie Lanzo turned to go back to his house. "Whole island's going to pot, I tell ya," he muttered. "Too many crazies. Last time I leave my keys in the car."

"Mr. Lanzo?" called Chase.

"Yeah?"

"Just a question. I was wondering if you were home the night Richard Tremain was killed?"

"Me?" Eddie snorted. "I'm always home."

"Did you happen to see or hear anything?"

"I already tol' Lorne Tibbetts. I go to bed at nine o'clock sharp, and that's it till morning."

"Then you're a sound sleeper? You didn't hear anything?"

"How can I with my hearing aid turned off?"

"Oh." Chase watched as the man shuffled back to his house, still muttering about Peeping Toms and car thieves. It somehow surprised Chase that a grouchy old geezer like Lanzo would show such concern about Miranda Wood. *A nice young woman,* Lanzo had called her.

What the hell does he know? thought Chase. *What do we ever know about anyone? People have their secrets. I have mine, Miranda Wood has hers.*

He turned and headed for Chestnut Street.

It was a twenty-minute walk, made invigorating by the brisk night air. When at last he stepped in the front door he found that, except for the lamp in the foyer, all the lights were out. Had no one else come home?

Then he heard Evelyn call out his name.

He found her sitting all alone in the darkened parlor. He could barely make out her shadow in the rocking chair. The dim glow of the street lamp through the window framed her silhouette.

"At last you're home," she said.

He started toward one of the lamps. "You need some light in here, Evelyn."

"No, Chase. Don't. I like the dark. I always have."

He paused, uncertain of what to say, what to do. He lingered in the shadows, watching her.

"I've been waiting for you," she murmured. "Where did you go, Chase?"

He paused. "To see Miranda Wood."

Her reaction was cold, dead silence. Even the creak of her rocking chair had stilled.

"She has you in her spell. Doesn't she?" Evelyn whispered.

"There's no spell. I just had some questions to ask her, about Richard." He sighed. "Look, Evelyn, it's been a long day for you. Why don't you go up and get some sleep?"

Still the figure did not move. She sat like a black statue against the window. "That night I called you," she said, "the night he died—I was hoping..."

"Yes?"

Another silence. Then, "I've always liked you, Chase. Since we were kids. I always hoped you'd be the one to propose. Not Richard, but you." The rocking chair began to creak again, softly. "But you never did."

"I was in love with Christine. Remember?"

"Oh, Christine." She hissed out the name in disgust. "She wasn't good enough for you. But you found that out."

"We were mismatched, that's all."

"So were Richard and I."

He didn't know what to say. He knew what she was leading up to, and he wanted to avoid that particular path of conversation. In all those years of growing up together he had never been able to picture himself and Evelyn DeBolt as a couple. Certainly she was attractive enough. And she was closer to his age than she was to Richard's. But he had seen, early on, that she had a talent for manipulating people, for twisting minds and hearts. The same talent Richard had possessed.

And yet, he felt so very sorry for her.

He said gently, "You're just tired, Evelyn. You've had a terrible week. But the worst of it's over now."

"No. The worst part is just beginning. The loneliness."

"You have your children—"

"You'll be leaving soon, won't you?"

"A few more days. I have to. I have a job in Greenwich."

"You could stay. Take over the *Herald*. Phillip's still too young to run it."

"I'd be a lousy publisher. You know that. And I don't belong here anymore. Not on this island."

For a moment they regarded each other through the shadows.

"So that's it, then," she whispered. "For us."

"I'm afraid so."

He saw the silhouette nod sadly.

"Will you be all right?"

"Fine." She gave a soft laugh. "I'll be just fine."

"Good night, Evelyn."

"Good night."

He left her sitting there by the window. Only as he moved toward the stairwell did he suddenly notice the sour odor lingering in the hall. An empty glass sat on the foyer table, near the telephone. He picked up the glass and sniffed it.

Whiskey.

We all have our secrets. Evelyn does, too.

He set the glass back down. Then, deep in thought, he climbed the stairs to bed.

CHAPTER SIX

"So where were you two last night?" Chase asked.

The twins, busy attacking sausage and eggs, simultaneously looked up at their uncle.

"I was over at Zach Brewer's," said Phillip. "You remember the Brewers, don't you? Over on Pearl Street."

"What little Phil really means is, he was checking out Zach's sister," said Cassie.

"At least I wasn't holed up in some cave, pining for a date."

"I wasn't pining for a date. I was busy."

"Oh, sure," snorted Phillip.

"Busy? Doing what?" asked Chase.

"I was over at the *Herald*, trying to get a handle on things," said Cassie. "You know, Dad left things such a mess. No written plans for succession. Not a clue as to which direction he wanted the paper to go. Editorially speaking."

"Let Jill Vickery take care of it," said Phillip with a shrug. "That's what we pay her for."

"I'd think at least you'd care, Phil. Seeing as you're the heir apparent."

"These transitions need to be handled gradually." Phil non-chalantly shoveled another forkful of eggs into his mouth.

"In the meantime, the *Herald* drifts around rudderless. I don't want it to be just another church and social rag. We should turn it into a muckraking journal. Shake things up along the coast, get people mad. The way Dad got 'em mad a few months ago."

"Got who mad?" asked Chase.

"Those stooges on the planning board. The ones who voted to rezone the north shore. Dad made 'em out to look pretty greasy.

I bet Jill was quaking in her shiny Italian shoes, waiting for that libel suit to pop.''

"You seem to know a lot about what goes on at the *Herald*," said Chase.

"Of course. Second best tries harder."

She said it lightly, but Chase couldn't miss the note of resentment in her voice. He understood exactly how she felt. He, too, had been the second-best sibling, had spent his childhood trying harder, to no avail. Richard had been the anointed one. Just as Phillip was now.

The doorbell rang. "That'll be Granddad," said Phillip. "He's early."

Chase stood. "I'll get it."

Noah DeBolt was standing on the front porch. "Good morning, Chase. Is Evelyn ready for her appointment?"

"I think so. Come in, sir."

That "sir" was automatic. One simply didn't call this man by his first name. As Noah walked in the door, Chase marveled at the fact that the years hadn't stooped the shoulders in that tailored suit, nor softened the glare of those ice blue eyes.

Noah paused in the foyer and glanced critically around the house. "It's about time we made some changes in here. A new couch, new chairs. Evelyn's put up with this old furniture long enough."

"They're my mother's favorites," said Chase. "Antiques—"

"I know what the hell they are! Junk." Noah's gaze focused on the twins, who were staring at him through the doorway. "What, are you two still eating breakfast? Come on, it's eight-thirty! With the fees lawyers charge, we don't want to be late."

"Really, Mr. DeBolt," said Chase. "I can drive us all to the lawyer. You didn't have to bother—"

"Evelyn asked me to come," said Noah. "What my girl asks for, I deliver." He glanced up the stairs. Evelyn had just appeared on the landing. "Right, sweetheart?"

Head held high, Evelyn came down the stairs. It was the first Chase had seen of her since the night before. No tremor, no effects of whiskey were apparent this morning. She looked cool as aspic. "Hello, Daddy," she said.

Noah gave her a hug. "Now," he said softly, "let's go finish this unpleasant business."

They drove in Noah's Mercedes, Evelyn and her father in the front seat, Chase crammed in the back with the twins. How had Richard tolerated it all these years, he wondered, living in the same town with this bully of a father-in-law? But that was the price one paid for marrying Noah DeBolt's only daughter: eternal criticism, eternal scrutiny.

Now that Richard was dead, Noah was back in control of his daughter's life. He drove them to Les Hardee's office. He escorted Evelyn through the front door. He led her by the arm right up to the reception desk.

"Mrs. Tremain to see Les," said Noah. "We're here to review the will."

The receptionist gave them a strange look—something Chase could only read as panic—and pressed the intercom button. "Mr. Hardee," she said. "They're here."

Instantly Les Hardee popped out of his office. His suit and tie marked him as a dapper man; his sweating brow did not match the image. "Mr. DeBolt, Mrs. Tremain," he said, almost painfully. "I would have called you earlier, but I only just— That is to say, we..." He swallowed. "There seems to be a problem with the will."

"Nothing that can't be fixed," said Noah.

"Actually..." Hardee opened the conference-room door. "I think we should all sit down."

There was another man in the room. Hardee introduced them to Vernon FitzHugh, an attorney from Bass Harbor. FitzHugh looked like a working-class version of Hardee, articulate enough, but rough around the edges, the sort of guy who probably had had to sling hash to pay his way through law school. They all sat at the conference table, Hardee and FitzHugh at opposite ends.

"So what's this little problem with Richard's will?" asked Noah. "And what do you have to do with all this, Mr. FitzHugh?"

FitzHugh cleared his throat. "I'm afraid I'm the bearer of bad news. Or, in this case, a new will."

"What?" Noah turned to Hardee. "What's this garbage, Les? *You* were Richard's attorney."

"That's what I thought," said Hardee morosely.

"Then where did this other will come from?"

Everyone looked at FitzHugh.

"A few weeks ago," explained FitzHugh, "Mr. Tremain came to my office. He said he wanted to draw up a new will, superseding the will drawn up previously by Mr. Hardee. I advised him that Mr. Hardee was the one who should do it, but Mr. Tremain insisted I draw it up. So I honored his request. I would have brought it to your attention earlier, but I've been out of town for a few weeks. I didn't hear of Mr. Tremain's death until last night."

"This is bizarre," said Evelyn. "Why would Richard draw up a new will? How do we even know it was really him?"

"It was him," confirmed Hardee. "I recognize his signature."

There was a long silence.

"Well," said Evelyn. "Let's hear it, Les. What's been changed."

Hardee slipped on his glasses and began to read aloud. "I, Richard D. Tremain, being of sound mind and body—"

"Oh, skip the legal gobbledygook!" snapped Noah. "Get to the basics. What's different about the new will?"

Hardee looked up. "Most of it is unchanged. The house, joint accounts, contents therein, all go to Mrs. Tremain. There are generous trust accounts for the children, and a few personal items left to his brother."

"What about Rose Hill Cottage?" asked Noah.

Here Hardee shifted in his chair. "Perhaps I should just read it." He flipped ahead six pages and cleared his throat. "That parcel of land on the north shore comprising approximately forty acres, inclusive of the access road, as well as the structure known as Rose Hill Cottage, I bequeath to..." Here Hardee paused.

"What about Rose Hill?" pressed Evelyn.

Hardee took a deep breath. "I bequeath to my dear friend and companion, Miranda Wood."

"Like hell," said Noah.

On the street outside Hardee's office, Noah and Evelyn sat side by side in the car. Neither one spoke. Neither was comfortable with the silence. The others had chosen to walk home, much to Noah's relief. He needed this time alone with Evelyn.

Noah said softly, "Is there anything you want to tell me, Evelyn?"

"What do you mean, Daddy?"

"Anything at all. About Richard."

She looked at her father. "Am I supposed to say something?"

"You can tell me, you know. We're family, that's what matters. And family stick together. Against the whole world, if they have to."

"I don't know what you're talking about."

Noah looked into his daughter's eyes. They were the same shade of green as his wife's eyes had been. Here was the one link he had left to his darling Susannah. Here was the one person in the world he still cared about. She returned his gaze calmly, without even the tiniest flicker of uneasiness. Good. Good. She could hold her own against anyone. In that way, she truly was a DeBolt.

He said, "I'd do anything for you, Evelyn. Anything. All you have to do is ask."

She looked straight ahead. "Then take me home, Daddy."

He started the engine and turned the car toward Chestnut Street. She didn't say a word during the entire drive. She was a proud girl, his daughter. Though she'd never ask for it, she needed his help. And she'd get it.

Whatever it takes, he thought. *It'll be done.*

After all, Evelyn was his flesh and blood, and he couldn't let flesh and blood go to prison.

Even if she was guilty.

Her garden had always been her sanctuary. Here Miranda had planted hollyhocks and delphiniums, baby's breath and columbine.

She hadn't bothered with color schemes or landscape drawings. She'd simply sunk plants into the earth, scattered seeds and let the jungle of vines and flowers take over her backyard. They'd been neglected this past week, poor things. A few days of no watering had left the blooms bedraggled. But now she was home and her babies looked happier. Strangely enough, *she* was happy, as well. Her back was warmed by the sun, her hands were working the rich loam. This was all she needed. Fresh air and freedom. *How long will I have it?*

She put that thought firmly aside and swung the pickax into the hardened earth. She'd turn a little more soil, expand the perennial bed another two feet. She leaned the pickax against the house and knelt to loosen up the clods, sift out the stones.

The sun was making her drowsy.

At last, unable to resist the promise of a nap, she stretched out on the lawn. There she lay, her hands and knees caked with soil, the grass cushioning her bare legs. A perfect summer day, just like the days she remembered from her childhood. She closed her eyes and thought about all those afternoons when her mother was still alive, when her father would stand at the barbecue, singing as he grilled hamburgers....

"What a sharp game you play," said a voice.

Miranda sat up with a start and saw Chase standing at her white picket fence. He shoved open the gate and came into the yard. As he approached, it occurred to her how filthy she must look in her gardening shorts and T-shirt. Framed against the glare of sun and blue sky, Chase looked immaculate, untouchable. She squinted to see his expression, but all she could make out was a dark oval, the flutter of his windblown hair.

"You knew, didn't you?" he said.

She rose to her feet and clapped the dirt from her hands. "Knew what?"

"How did you manage it, Miranda? A few sweet whispers? Write me into the will and I'll be yours forever?"

"I don't know what you're talking about."

"I just came from our family attorney. We found a nasty surprise waiting for us. Two weeks ago Richard made out a new will. He left Rose Hill Cottage to you."

Her immediate reaction was stunned silence. In disbelief she stared at him.

"Nothing to say? No denials?"

"I never expected—"

"I think it's exactly what you expected."

"No!" She turned away, confused. "I never wanted a thing—"

"Oh, come on!" He reached for her arm and pulled her around to face him. "What was it, blackmail? A way to keep you quiet about the affair?"

"I don't know anything about a will! Or the cottage! Besides, how could he leave it to me? Doesn't it go to his wife? Evelyn owns half—"

"No, she doesn't."

"Why not?"

"Rose Hill came through my mother's family. An inheritance that went directly to Richard, so Evelyn had no claim on it. It was Richard's to pass on any way he chose. And he chose to give it to you."

She shook her head. "I don't know why."

"That cottage was the one place on this island he really cared about. The one place we both cared about."

"All right, then!" she cried. "*You* take it! It's yours. I'll sign a statement today, handing it over. I don't want it. All I want is to be left *alone*." She stared straight up at his coldly immobile face. "And to never, ever see another Tremain for as long as I live."

She broke away and ran up the back porch steps, into the house. The screen door slammed shut behind her. She headed straight into the kitchen, where she suddenly halted. There was nowhere else to run. In agitation she went to the sink and turned on the faucet. There, surrounded by her beloved ferns, she scrubbed furiously at the dirt caked on her hands.

She was still scrubbing when the screen door opened, then

softly swung shut again. For a long time he didn't say a word. She knew he was standing behind her, watching her.

"Miranda," he said.

Angrily she turned off the faucet. "Go away."

"I want to hear your side of it."

"Why? You wouldn't believe me. You don't *want* to believe me. But you know what? I don't care anymore." She grabbed a dish towel and blotted her hands. "I'll go to the lawyer's this afternoon. Sign a statement of refusal, or whatever it's called. I would never accept it. Anything I received from him would be tainted. Just like I'm tainted."

"You're wrong, Miranda. I do want to believe you."

She stood very still, afraid to turn, to look at him. She sensed his approach as he moved toward her across the kitchen. And still she couldn't turn, couldn't face him. She could only stare down at the clumps of wet garden dirt in the sink.

"But you can't, can you?" she said.

"The facts argue against it."

"And if I tell you the facts are misleading?" Slowly she turned and found he was right there, so close she could reach up and touch his face. "What then?"

"Then I'd be forced to trust my instincts. But in this particular case, my instincts are shot all to hell."

She stared at him, suddenly confused by the signals he was sending. By the signals her body was sending. He had her closed off from all retreat, her back pinned against the kitchen sink. She had to tilt her head up just to meet his gaze, and the view she had of him, towering above her, was more than a little frightening. Yet it wasn't fear that seemed to be pumping through her veins. It was the warm and unexpected pulse of desire.

She slid away and paced across the kitchen, as far as she could get from him and still be in the same room. "I meant what I said. About refusing all rights to Rose Hill Cottage. In fact, I think we should do it right now. Go to the lawyer."

"Is that really what you want?"

"I know I don't want anything of his. Anything to remind me of him."

"You'd give up the cottage, just like that?"

"It doesn't mean a thing to me. I've never even seen the place."

Chase looked surprised. "He never took you to Rose Hill?"

"No. Oh, he told me about it. But it was his own private retreat. Not the sort of place he'd share with me."

"You could be handing back a fortune in real estate, sight unseen."

"It's not my fortune. It never was."

He regarded her with narrowed eyes. "I can't figure you out. Every time I think I have, you throw me a curve ball."

"I'm not all that complicated."

"You managed to intrigue Richard."

"I was hardly the first woman to do that."

"But you're the first one who ever left him."

"And look where it got me." She gave a bitter laugh. "You may not believe this, but I used to think of myself as a person with high morals. I paid my taxes. Stopped at every red light. Followed all the rules." She turned and stared out the window. Softly she said, "Then I fell for your brother. Suddenly I didn't know what the rules were anymore. I was slipping around in strange territory. God, it scared me. At the same time I felt...exhilarated. And that scared me even more." She turned to him. "I'd give anything to turn back the clock. To feel...innocent again."

Slowly he came toward her. "Some things we can't recapture, Miranda."

"No." She stared down, her cheeks flushed with guilt. "Some things we lose forever."

His touch, so unexpected, made her flinch. It was the gentlest of strokes, just his hand tracing the curve of her cheek. Startled, she looked up to find a gaze so searching it left her nowhere to hide. She hated feeling so nakedly exposed but she found she could not break away. The hand cupping her face was warm and so very compelling.

Here I am, falling into the same old trap, she thought. *With Richard I lost my innocence. What will I lose to this man? My soul?*

She said, "I learned my lesson from your brother, Chase. I'm no longer fair game." She turned and walked away, into the living room.

"I'm not Richard."

She looked back. "It doesn't matter who you are. What matters is that I'm not the same dumb, trusting soul I used to be."

"He really hurt you, didn't he?" He was watching her from the kitchen threshold. His shoulders seemed to fill the doorway.

She didn't answer. She sank into an armchair and stared at her dirt-stained knees.

Chase studied her from across the room. All his anger toward her, which had built up since that morning in Les Hardee's office, suddenly evaporated. In its place was a fury toward Richard. Golden boy Richard, who had always gotten what he wanted. Richard the firstborn, the one with the classic Tremain fair hair and blue eyes, had bought everything he ever coveted with the coin of wit and charm. But once he'd attained his goal, he'd lose interest.

That was his pattern with women. Once, Richard had wanted Evelyn DeBolt, and he'd won her. He'd had to marry her, of course. You didn't play games with the only child of Noah DeBolt. But after the prize was his he'd grown bored with his wife. That was Richard, always coveting, never satisfied.

And here was the one woman, the one prize, he hadn't been able to keep. Such an unassuming female, thought Chase, feeling a strange ache in his throat. Was it pity or sympathy? He couldn't tell the difference.

He sat in the chair across from her. "You...seem to have recovered from last night."

"Just some sore muscles. That's all." She shrugged, as though she knew he couldn't possibly be interested. Whatever turmoil was swirling in her head, she kept it carefully concealed. "I sent Annie home this morning. I couldn't see the point of her staying."

"Safety's sake?"

"Safety from what?"

"What if it wasn't an accident?"

She looked up. "At the moment I'm not terrifically popular in this town. But I can't see one of our upstanding citizens turning hit-and-run driver."

"Still, one of our upstanding citizens did steal Mr. Lanzo's car."

"Poor Eddie." She shook her head. "It'll just reinforce his paranoia. Now he'll add car thieves to that list of crazies he imagines cruising the street."

"Yes, he mentioned that last night. Something about Peeping Toms."

She smiled. "Eddie grew up in Chicago. He never did shake those big-city jitters. He swears he spotted some mob car watching my…" She suddenly paused, frowning. "You know, I never paid much attention to his stories. But now that I think about it…"

"When did he tell you about that car?"

"Maybe a month or two ago."

"Before Richard's murder, then."

"Yes. So it's probably not related." She sighed. "It's just poor, crazy Eddie." She stood. "I'll change clothes. I can't go to the lawyer looking like this."

"You really want to go right now?"

"I have to. Until I do, I won't feel clean. Or free of him."

"I'll call ahead, then." He glanced at his watch. "We can just make the ferry to Bass Harbor."

"Bass Harbor? I thought Les Hardee was Richard's lawyer."

"He is. But this last will was drawn up by some lawyer named Vernon FitzHugh. Do you know him?"

"No, thank God." She turned and headed up the hall. "Or you'd probably accuse Mr. FitzHugh and me of fraud." She vanished into the bedroom.

Chase watched the door swing shut behind her. "As a matter of fact," he muttered, "the thought did cross my mind."

Vernon FitzHugh was expecting them. What he didn't anticipate was the purpose of their visit.

"Have you really thought this through, Ms. Wood? This is prime real estate we're talking about. The north shore has just been rezoned for development. I expect your piece of property, in a few years, will be worth well over—"

"It should never have come to me," said Miranda. "It belongs to the Tremain family."

FitzHugh glanced uneasily at Chase, one of those sidelong looks that reveal so much. "Perhaps we should discuss this in private, Ms. Wood. If Mr. Tremain would care to wait outside…"

"No, I want him to stay. I want him to hear every word." She looked meaningfully at FitzHugh. "So he can't accuse us of collusion."

"Collusion?" FitzHugh, alarmed, sat up straight. "Mr. Tremain, you don't think I wanted to get involved in this, do you? It's a messy situation. Two lawyers, two wills. And then, the complicating circumstances of the client's death." He assiduously avoided looking at Miranda. "I'm just trying to carry out Mr. Tremain's instructions. Which are to ensure that Rose Hill Cottage goes to Ms. Wood."

"I don't want it," said Miranda. "I want to give it back."

FitzHugh looked troubled. He removed his glasses and set them on the desk. It seemed, with that one gesture, he simultaneously shed the role of the detached professional. Now he was speaking to her as a friend, an adviser. The flat accent of a working-class Mainer slipped into his voice. This man knew only too well what it was like to be poor. And here was this stubborn young woman, throwing away the promise of security.

"Richard Tremain," he began, "came to me with a request. I'm bound to honor it. It's not my job to decide whether you're innocent or guilty. I just want to see that the intent of the will is carried out. I made very sure that this was what he wanted, and he wanted that land to go to you. If you're convicted, then the point will be moot—you can't inherit. But let's say you're found innocent. Then Rose Hill goes to you, no question about it. Wait a few days, Ms. Wood. If this is really what you want, come back and I'll draw up the papers. But I won't do it today. I have to think of Mr. Tremain's last request. After all, he was my client.''

"Why *did* he come to you?'' Chase asked. ''Mr. Hardee has been Richard's attorney for years.''

FitzHugh studied Chase for a moment, weighing the man's motives. Coercion was what he suspected, the wealthy Tremain family putting pressure on this woman, this outsider, to surrender her inheritance. It wasn't right. Someone had to take the woman's side, even if she refused to stand up for herself.

"Richard Tremain came to me,'' FitzHugh said, ''because he *didn't* want Les Hardee involved.''

"Why not?''

"Mr. Hardee is also Noah DeBolt's attorney. I think Mr. Tremain was worried this would leak out to his father-in-law.''

"And what a riot that would have caused,'' said Chase.

"Having met Mr. DeBolt this morning, yes, I can imagine there would've been fireworks.''

Chase leaned forward, his gaze narrowing on the attorney. ''The day Richard was here to change his will, how did he seem to you? I mean, his state of mind. People don't just walk in and change their wills for no good reason.''

FitzHugh frowned. ''Well, he seemed...upset. He didn't mention any fear of dying. Said he just wanted to straighten out his affairs....'' He glanced at Miranda and reddened at the unintentional double entendre.

Miranda flushed, as well, but she refused to shrink from his gaze. *I'm through with being punished,* she thought. *Through with cringing at the looks people give me.*

"You said he was upset. What do you mean?'' asked Chase.

"He seemed angry.''

"At whom?''

"We didn't discuss it. He just came in and said he didn't want the cottage to go to Mrs. Tremain.''

"He was specific about Evelyn?"

"Yes. And he was concerned only about Rose Hill Cottage. Not the bank account or the other assets. I assumed it was because those other assets were joint marital property, and he couldn't redirect those. But Rose Hill was his, through inheritance. He could dispose of it as he wished." FitzHugh looked at Miranda. "And he wanted you to have it."

She shook her head. "Why?"

"I assume, because he cared about you. Giving you Rose Hill was his way of telling you how much."

In silence Miranda bowed her head. She knew both men were watching her. She wondered what expression she'd see in Chase's eyes. Cynicism? Disbelief? *You can't imagine that your brother would feel love, not just lust, for a woman like me?*

"So, Ms. Wood?" asked FitzHugh. "You agree this isn't a move you should make?"

She raised her head and looked across the desk at the attorney. "Draw up the papers. I want to do it now."

"Maybe you don't," said Chase quietly.

Miranda looked at him in disbelief. "What?"

"Mr. FitzHugh has brought up some points I hadn't considered. You should think about it, just for a few days." His gaze met Miranda's. She could see that he was baffled by something he'd heard here today.

"Are you saying I should keep Rose Hill Cottage?"

"All I'm saying is this. Richard had a reason for changing the will. Before we go changing things back, let's find out why he did it."

Vernon FitzHugh nodded. "My thoughts exactly," he said.

They exchanged scarcely a word on the ferry back to Shepherd's Island. Only when they'd driven off the pier and turned onto Shore Circle Road did Miranda stir from her silence. "Where are we going?" she asked.

"The north shore."

"Why?"

"I want you to see Rose Hill. It's only fair you know exactly what you're handing back to Evelyn."

"You enjoy this, don't you?" she said. "Running me around in circles. Playing your little mind games. One minute you say I'm stealing Tremain property. The next, you're trying to talk me into playing thief. What's the point of it all, Chase?"

"I'm bothered by what FitzHugh told us. That Richard wanted to keep the cottage away from Evelyn."

"But it *should* go to her."

"Rose Hill came from my mother's side. The Pruitts. Evelyn has no claim to it."

"He could have left it to you."

Chase laughed. "Not likely."

"Why not?"

"We weren't exactly the closest of brothers. I was lucky just to get his collection of rusty Civil War swords. No, he wanted Rose Hill to go to someone he loved. You were his first choice. Maybe his only choice."

"He didn't love me, Chase," she said softly. "Not really."

They drove north, winding past summer cottages, past granite cliffs jagged with pines, past stony beaches where waves broke into white foam. Gulls circled and swooped at the blue-gray sea.

"Why did you say that?" he asked. "About Richard not loving you?"

"Because I knew. I think I always knew. Oh, maybe he *thought* he loved me. But for Richard, love was a lot of moonlight and madness. A fever that eventually breaks. It was just a matter of time."

"That sounds like Richard. As a kid, he was always in pursuit of the never-ending high."

"Are all you Tremains like that?"

"Hardly. My father was married to his work."

"And what are you married to?"

He glanced at her. She was struck by the intensity of his gaze, the gaze of a man who's not afraid to tell the truth. "Nothing and no one. At least, not anymore. Not since Christine."

"Your wife?"

He nodded. "It didn't last very long. I was just a kid, really, only twenty. Doing my share of wild and crazy things. It was a handy way to get back at my father, and it worked."

"What happened to Christine?"

"She found out I wasn't going to inherit the Tremain fortune and she walked out. Smart girl. She, at least, was using her head."

He focused on the road, which he obviously knew well. Miranda noticed how easily he handled the curves, guiding the car skillfully around each treacherous bend. Whatever wildness he'd displayed in his youth had since been reined in. Here was a man in tight control of his life, his emotions, not a man in pursuit of the ephemeral moonlight and madness.

A twenty-minute drive brought them to the last stretch of paved road. The asphalt gave way to a dirt access road flanked by birch and pine. Rustic signs proclaimed the different camps hidden among the tress. Mom and Pop's. Brandywine Cottage. Sanity Camp. Here and there, dirt tracks led off to the dozen or so summer retreats of prominent island families, most of whom had held their cottages for generations.

The access road began to climb, winding a half mile up the contours of the hillside. They passed a stone marker labeled St. John's Wood. Then they came to the last sign, every bit as rustic as the others: Rose Hill. A final bend in the road took them through the last stand of trees, and then a broad, sloping field lay before them. It sat at the very crest of the hill—a weathered cottage facing north, to the sea. Vines of purple clematis clung lovingly about the veranda railings. Rosebushes, overgrown with weeds but still valiantly blooming, crouched like thorny sentinels beside the porch steps.

They parked in the gravel turnaround and stepped out into an afternoon fragrant with the scent of flowers and sun-warmed grass. For a moment Miranda stood motionless, her face turned to the sky. Not a cloud marred that perfect blue. A single gull, riding the wind off the hillside, drifted overhead.

"Come on," said Chase. "Let me show you inside."

He led her up the porch steps. "I haven't seen the place in at least ten years. I'm almost afraid to go in."

"Afraid of what?"

"The changes. Of what they might've done to it. But I guess that's how it is with your childhood home."

"Especially if you were happy there."

He smiled. "Exactly."

For a moment they stood and regarded the old porch swing, creaking back and forth in the breeze.

"Do you have a key?" she asked.

"There should be one under here." He crouched down beneath one of the windowsills. "There's this little crack in the wood where Mom always kept a spare key...." He sighed and straightened. "Not anymore. Well, if the door's locked, maybe we can find a window open somewhere." Tentatively he reached for the knob. "How do you like that?" He laughed, pushing open the door. "It's not even locked."

As the door creaked open, the front room swung into view—a faded Oriental carpet stretched across the threshold, a stone fireplace, wide pine floors. Miranda stepped inside and suddenly halted in surprise.

At her feet lay a jumble of papers. A rolltop desk stood in the corner, its drawers wide open, their contents strewn across the floor. Books had been pulled off a nearby shelf and tossed haphazardly among the papers.

Chase stepped inside and came to a halt beside her. The screen door slammed shut.

"What the hell?" he said.

CHAPTER SEVEN

In silence they took in the ransacked desk, the scattered papers. Without a word Chase moved quickly toward the next room.

Miranda followed him into the kitchen. There were no signs of disturbance here. The pots and pans were hung on a beam rack, the flour and sugar canisters lined up neatly on the butcher block counters.

She was right on his heels as he headed for the stairs. They ran up the steps and looked first in the small guest bedroom. Everything appeared in order. Quickly Chase circled the room, opening closets, glancing in drawers.

"What are you looking for?" she asked.

He didn't answer. He moved across the hall, into the master bedroom.

Here double windows, flanked by lace curtains, faced the sea. A cream coverlet draped the four-poster bed. Motes of dust drifted in the sun-warmed stillness.

"Doesn't look like they touched this room, either," said Miranda.

Chase went to the dresser, picked up a silver hairbrush, and set it back down. "Obviously not."

"What on earth is going on here, Chase?"

He turned and glanced in frustration about the room. "This is crazy. They left the paintings on the walls. The furniture..."

"Nothing's missing?"

"Nothing valuable. At least, nothing your ordinary thief would go after." He opened a dresser drawer and glanced through the contents. He opened a second drawer and paused, staring inside. Slowly he withdrew a pair of women's panties. It was scarcely more than a few strips of black lace and silk. He pulled out a matching bra, equally skimpy, equally seductive.

He looked at Miranda, his gaze flat and unreadable. "Yours?" he asked quietly.

"I told you, I've never been here. They must belong to Evelyn."

He shook his head. "I don't think so."

"How would you know?"

"She never comes out here. Despises the rustic life, or so she claims."

"Well, they're not mine. I don't own anything like—like that."

"There's more inside here. Maybe you'll recognize something else."

She went to the dresser and pulled out an emerald-and-cream bra. "Well, it's obvious this isn't mine."

"How so?"

"This is a 36C. I'm..." She cleared her throat. "Not that big."

"Oh."

Quickly she turned away, before he could confirm her statement. Not that he hadn't had the chance to look. He had eyes, didn't he?

And he sees too damn much, she thought. She turned toward the window and stood with her back to Chase, all the while struggling to regain her composure. Outside, the fading light of day slanted across the treetops. A long summer dusk. In the field below there would be fireflies and the hum of insects in the grass. And the chill. Even on these August evenings there was always the chill that rose from the sea. She hugged herself and shivered.

His approach was gentle, silent. She couldn't hear him, but she knew, without looking, that he was right behind her.

Chase was standing so close, in fact, that he could smell the scent of her hair—clean and sweet and intoxicating. The fading daylight from the window brought out its glorious chestnut hues. He wanted to reach out and run his fingers through those shimmering strands, to bury his face in the tangled silk. A mistake, a mistake. He knew it before it happened, and yet he couldn't help himself.

She shivered at his touch. Just the tiniest tremble, the softest sigh. He ran his hands down her shoulders, down the cool smoothness of her bare arms. She didn't pull away. No, she leaned back, as though melting against him. He wrapped his arms around her, enfolding her in their warmth.

"When I was a boy," he whispered, "I used to think there were magical creatures in that field down there. Elves and fairies hiding among the toadstools. I'd see their lights flitting about at night. It was only fireflies, of course. But to a kid, they might have been anything. Elvish lanterns, Dragon lights. I wish..."

"What do you wish, Chase?"

He sighed. "That I still had some of that child inside me. That we could have known each other then. Before all this happened. Before..."

"Richard."

Chase fell silent. His brother would always be there, his life and his death like a darkness hovering over them. What could possibly thrive in such shadow? Not friendship; certainly not love. *Love?* No, what Chase felt, standing there behind her, hugging her slim, warm body to his, had far more to do with lust. *Well, what the hell. Maybe it runs in my family,* he thought, *in my tainted bloodline. This propensity for reckless, hopeless affairs. Richard had it. My mother had it. Is it my turn to succumb?*

Miranda shifted in his embrace, turned to face him. One look at that soft, upturned mouth and he was lost.

She tasted of summer and warmth and sweet amber honey. At the first touch of their lips he wanted more, more. He felt like a man who has fallen drunk at his first sip of nectar and now craves nothing else. His hands found their way into that silken mass of hair, were buried in it, lost in it. He heard her murmur, "please," and was too fevered to think it anything but a request for more. Only when she said it again, and then, "Chase, no," did he finally pull away.

They stared at each other. The confusion he felt was mirrored in her eyes. She retreated a step, nervously shoving back her hair.

"I shouldn't have let you do that," she said. "It was a mistake."

"Why?"

"Because you—you'll say I led you on. That's what you'll tell Evelyn, isn't it? You think it's how I got hold of Richard. Temptation. Seduction. It's what everyone else believes."

"But is it true?"

"You've just proved it. Get me alone in a room and look what happens! Another Tremain male bites the dust." Her voice took on a cold edge. "What I want to know is, who's really seducing whom?"

She's all motion, all skittishness, he thought. In another moment she would shatter and fly into pieces.

"Neither of us did any seducing, any tempting. It just happened, Miranda. The way it usually happens. Nature tugs on our strings and we can't always resist."

"This time I will. This time I know better. Your brother taught me a few things. The most important thing is not to be so damn gullible when it comes to men."

That last word was still hanging in the air between them when they heard footsteps thump onto the porch below. Someone rapped on the front door.

Chase turned and left the room.

Miranda, suddenly weak, leaned against the windowsill. She clutched it tightly, as though drawing strength from the wood. *Too close,* she thought. *I let down my guard, let him slip right past my defenses.*

She would have to be more careful. She would have to remind herself that Chase and Richard were variations on a theme, a theme that had already wreaked havoc on her life. She took a deep breath and slowly let it out, willing the turmoil, the confusion, to flow out of her body. *Back in control,* she thought. She released the sill. She stood straight. Then, with a new semblance of calmness, she followed Chase down the stairs.

He was in the front room with the visitor. Miranda recognized her old acquaintance from the garden club, Miss Lila St. John, local expert on flowering perennials. Miss St. John was dressed in her signature black dress. Summer or winter, she always wore black, set off with a touch of white lace here and there. Today it was a black walking dress of crinkled linen. It did not quite match her brown boots or her straw hat, but on Miss St. John it all seemed to look just right.

She turned at the sound of Miranda's footsteps. If she was surprised to see Miranda she didn't show it. She simply nodded, then turned her sharp gray eyes back to the ransacked desk. On the front porch a dog whined. Through the screen door Miranda saw what looked like a large black fur ball with a red tongue.

"It's all my fault, you know," said Miss St. John. "I can't believe I was such an imbecile."

"How is it your fault?" asked Chase.

"I sensed something was wrong last week. We were taking our walk, you see, Ozzie and I. We walk every evening around dusk. That's when the deer come out, the pests, though I do love to see them. Anyway, I saw a light through the trees, somewhere in this direction. I came up to the cottage and knocked on the door. No one answered, so I left." She shook her head. "I shouldn't have, you know. I should have looked into it. I *knew* it didn't feel right."

"Did you see a car?"

"If you were coming to loot the joint, would *you* park your car out front? Of course not. I know I'd park down the road a bit, in the trees. Then I'd sneak up here on foot."

It was hard to imagine Miss St. John doing any such thing.

"It's a good thing you didn't get involved," said Chase. "You could have gotten yourself killed."

"At my age, Chase, getting killed is not a major concern." She used her walking stick, a knobby affair with a duck's head handle, to prod among the papers on the floor. "Any idea what he was after?"

"Not a clue."

"Not valuables, obviously. That's a Limoges on that shelf over there, isn't it?"

Chase glanced sheepishly at the hand-painted vase. "If you say so."

Miss St. John turned to Miranda. "Have you any thoughts on the matter?"

Miranda found herself under the gaze of two very intense gray eyes. Miss St. John might be dismissed by many as little more than a charming eccentric, but Miranda could see the intelligence in that gaze. While their previous conversations had tended more toward delphiniums and daffodils, even then, Miss St. John had made her feel like some sort of new plant species under a magnifying glass. "I'm not sure I know what to think, Miss St. John," she said.

"Take a look at the mess. What does it tell you?"

Miranda glanced at the papers, the scattered books. Then her gaze shifted to the bookcases. Only a top shelf had been emptied. Two full bookcases were undisturbed. "He didn't look through all the books. So whoever broke in here must have been interrupted. By you, maybe."

"Or he found what he was looking for," said Chase.

Miss St. John turned to him. "And what might that be?"

"A guess?" Chase and Miranda glanced at each other. "The file on Stone Coast Trust," Chase ventured.

"Ah." Miss St. John's eyes took on a gleam of interest. "Your brother's little campaign against Tony Graffam. Yes, Richard seemed to do quite a bit of writing out here. At that desk, in fact. On my evening walks I'd see him through the window."

"Did you ever stop to talk to him? About what he was working on?"

"Oh, no. That's why we come out here, isn't it? To get away from all those prying townies." She glanced at Miranda. "I never saw *you* out here."

"I've never been here," she said, shifting uneasily under that thoughtful gaze. This matter-of-fact reference to her link with Richard had taken her by surprise. And yet, Miss St. John's bluntness was far preferable to the delicate avoidance with which so many others treated the subject.

Miss St. John bent down for a closer look at the papers. "He must have done a prodigious amount of work here, judging by this mess. What is all this, anyway?"

Chase bent and sifted through the papers. "Looks like a lot of old article files.... Financial records from the *Herald*... And here we've got a collection of local personality profiles. Why, here's one of you, Miss St. John."

"Me? But I was never interviewed for anything."

Chase grinned. "Must be the unauthorized version, then."

"Does it mention all my sexy secrets?"

"Well, let's just take a good look here—"

"Oh, *give* me the damn thing." Miss St. John snatched the page out of his hands and scanned the typewritten notes. She read them aloud. "Age seventy-four...holds title to lot number two, St. John's Wood, and cottage thereon...rabid member of local garden club." Here she glanced up huffily. *"Rabid?"* She continued reading. "Eccentric recluse, never married. Engaged once, to an Arthur Simoneau, killed in action...Normandy...." Her voice trailed off. Slowly she sat down, still clutching the piece of paper in both hands.

"Oh, Miss St. John," said Miranda. "I'm sorry."

The elderly woman looked up, still shaken. "It...was a very long time ago."

"I can't believe he went digging into your personal life, without you even knowing about it. Why would he do that?"

"You're saying it was Richard?" asked Miss St. John.

"Well, these are his papers."

Miss St. John frowned at the page for a moment. "No," she said slowly. "I don't believe he wrote this. There's an error in here. It says my cottage lies in St. John's Wood. But it lies three feet over the line, on Tremain property. A surveyor's mistake from seventy years past. Richard knew that."

Chase frowned. "I never heard that, about your cottage."

"Yes, your family land goes past the second stone wall. It includes the entire access road. So, technically, all the rest of us are trespassers on your private road. Not that it ever mattered. It always felt like a giant family out here. But now...'' She shook her head. ''So many strangers on the island. All those tourists from *Massachusetts.*'' She made it sound like an invasion from hell.

''Did Stone Coast Trust approach you?'' Miranda asked her. ''About selling St. John's Wood?''

''They approached everyone on this road. I, of course, refused. So did Richard. That effectively squelched the project. Without Rose Hill, Stone Coast would own a disconnected patchwork of little lots. But now...'' Sadly she sighed. ''I imagine Evelyn, at this very moment, has her pen poised over the sales contract.''

''Actually, she does not,'' said Chase. ''Rose Hill didn't go to Evelyn. Richard left the property to Miranda.''

Miss St. John stared at them. ''Now that,'' she said after a long pause, ''is an entirely unexpected development.''

''For me, as well,'' said Miranda.

While Miss St. John sat back in thought, Miranda and Chase gathered up the rest of the papers. They found more article files, a few miscellaneous clippings, an old financial report from the *Herald.* Obviously Richard had used the cottage as another office. Was this where he had stored his most sensitive papers? Miranda wondered about this when she came across a whole bundle of personality profiles. Like the page on Miss St. John, the information contained in these files was highly private.

In some cases it was downright shocking. She was startled to read that Forrest Mayhew, the local bank president, had been arrested for drunk driving in Boston. That town selectman George LaPierre, married thirty years, had been treated last year for syphilis. That Dr. Steiner—*her* doctor—was under investigation for medicare fraud.

She handed the papers to Chase. ''Look at these! Richard was collecting dirt on everyone in town!''

''Here, what's this?'' he asked. There was a yellow adhesive note attached to the back cover of the folder. On it was the handwritten scrawl, "Mr. T., do you want more? Let me know." It was signed "W.B.R."

"So Richard *didn't* write these," said Miranda. "This person W.B.R.—whoever he was—must've done the reporting."

"You have anyone on staff with those initials?"

"No. At least, not at the moment." She reached for a manila folder lying on the floor. "Look, there's another note from W.B.R." This time the note was paper-clipped to the top cover. "All I could get. Sorry—W.B.R."

"What's inside?" asked Miss St. John.

Miranda opened the file and stared. "This is it! The file on Stone Coast Trust!"

"Jackpot," said Chase.

"There's no profile of Tony Graffam. But here's his tax return. A list of bank account numbers and assets…" She nodded. "We hit pay dirt."

"I think not," said Miss St. John.

They both looked at her.

"If that file is so important, why did the burglar leave it here?"

In silence they considered that question.

"Maybe our burglar wasn't interested in Stone Coast Trust at all," said Miss St. John. "I mean, look at all this nasty information Richard's been gathering. Snoopy reports on drunk driving. Medicare fraud. Syphilis. George LaPierre, of all people! And at his age, too. These files could destroy some fine reputations. Now, I tell you, isn't that a motive for burglary?"

Or murder, thought Miranda. Why had Richard gathered such information in the first place? Was he planning an exposé on island residents? Or was there some darker reason? Coercion, for instance. Blackmail.

"If someone broke in to steal his own file, then we can assume it's now gone," said Chase. "Which means George LaPierre, Dr. Steiner, all the others in this pile didn't do it."

"Not necessarily," said Miss St. John. "What if he broke in and simply substituted a milder version? Mine, for instance. There's not a thing in my profile that qualifies as scandalous. How do you know I didn't come in here and destroy a far more venomous version?''

Chase smiled. "I will duly place you on the list of suspects, Miss St. John.''

"Don't you discount me, Chase Tremain. Age alone does not take one out of the running. I have more up here—'' she tapped her head ''—than that imbecile George LaPierre had in his prime. If he ever *had* a prime.''

"What you're saying, Miss St. John,'' said Miranda, "is that we can't count out any name in this pile. Or any name *not* in this pile.''

"Correct.''

Miranda frowned at the books. "One thing doesn't make sense. First, our burglar searches the desk. He throws around some papers, looking for some incriminating file. Why would he then search the bookcase? That's not the sort of place Richard would keep papers.''

After a pause Miss St. John said, "You're right, of course. That doesn't make sense.''

"Well," said Chase, "I guess we should call Lorne. Though I'm not sure he'd be much help at this point.'' He turned to the phone.

He'd already picked up the receiver when Miss St. John suddenly said, "Wait. Perhaps you should hold off on that call.'' She was staring at a loose page near her feet. Thoughtfully she picked up the paper and smoothed it across her knee.

Frowning, Chase hung up the receiver. "Why?''

"This is a profile of Valerie Everhard. You remember her, Chase. Our local librarian. And a married lady. According to this, Valerie has taken on a lover.''

"So?''

"The man she's seeing is our chief of police.'' Miss St. John looked up and her eyes had lost all trace of humor. "Lorne Tibbetts.''

"Why did he have these awful reports?" asked Miranda. "What was he planning to do with them?''

They were driving through darkness back to town. The fog had rolled in from the sea and curtained off all view beyond the dim haze of their headlights. Nothing seemed real in this mist, nothing seemed familiar. They were driving through a strange land, through a swirling cloud that seemed as if it would never lift.

"It doesn't sound like Richard," said Chase. "Snooping around in his neighbors' private lives. He committed enough sins of his own. If anyone was vulnerable to blackmail, it was Richard. Besides, who cares if Lorne is having a little fling with the librarian?"

"The librarian's husband?"

"Okay, but why would Richard care?"

She shook her head, unable to come up with an answer. "I wonder if any of these people knew about these files. Miss St. John didn't." She looked down at the papers on her lap and thought of the terrible secrets they contained. She had the sudden urge to shove the pile away, to throw off that unclean burden. "Chase?" she asked. "How do we know any of this is true?"

"We don't." He gave a short laugh. "And we can't exactly knock on George LaPierre's door and ask if he's had syphilis."

Miranda frowned at the note clipped to the folder. "I wonder who this is. This W.B.R. who got the information."

"The initials don't ring any bells?"

"None at all."

As the darkness flew past their windshield, Miranda thought of all the secrets revealed in these files. The banker's weakness for whiskey. The doctor's white-collar fraud. The husband and wife who conversed with their fists. All of it concealed beneath the glaze of respectability. *What private pains we nurse in silence.*

"Why *these* particular people?" she asked suddenly.

"Because they have the most to lose?" Chase suggested. "We're talking old island families here. LaPierre, Everhard, St. John. All of them respected names."

"Except for Tony Graffam."

"That's true. I guess he has a file in there, too…" He paused. "Wait. There's our link."

"What?"

"The north shore. You haven't lived here long enough to know all these families. But I grew up with them. I remember the summers I used to play with Toby LaPierre. And Daniel Steiner. And Valerie Everhard. Their families all have summer cottages out there."

"It could be coincidental."

"Or it could mean everything."

Chase frowned at the highway. The fog was thinning. "When we get back to your house," he said, "let's take a good look at those names. See if my hunch holds up."

An hour and a half later they sat at Miranda's dining table, the pages spread out before them. The remains of a hastily prepared supper—mushroom omelets and toast—had been pushed aside and they were now on their second cup of coffee. It was such a domestic scene, she thought with a twinge of longing, almost like newlyweds lingering at the dinner table. Except that the man sitting across from her could never, would never, fit into the picture. He was a temporary apparition, a visitor passing through her dining room.

She forced herself to focus on the sheet of paper, where he'd just checked off the final name.

"Okay, here's the list," said Chase. "Everyone in Richard's file. I'm almost certain they all own property on the north shore."

"Are any names missing?"

Chase sat back and mentally ticked off the camps along the access road. "There's Richard, of course. Then there's old man Sulaway's property, down the road. He's a retired lobsterman, sort of a recluse. And then there's Frenchman's Cottage. I think it was sold some years back. To hippies, I heard. They come up for the summers."

"So they'd be living there now."

"If they still own the place. But they're not from this area. I can't see Richard bothering to dig up information on them. And as for old Sully, well, an eighty-five-year-old sounds like a pretty unlikely victim for blackmail."

Blackmail. Miranda gazed at the papers on the table. "What was Richard thinking of?" she wondered. "What did he have against these people?"

"Something to do with the rezoning? Were any of these names on the land commission?"

"They couldn't have voted, anyway. They would've been disqualified. You know, conflict of interest." She sat back. "Maybe our burglar was looking for something entirely different."

"Then the question is, did he—or she—find it?"

From somewhere in the house came a sound that made them both glance up. It was the soft tinkle of breaking glass.

Miranda jerked to her feet in alarm. At once Chase grabbed her hand, signaled her to be silent. Together they moved from the dining room into the living room. A quick glance around told them the windows were all intact. They paused for a moment, listening, but heard no other sounds. Chase started toward the bedrooms.

They were moving up the hall when they heard, louder this time, the distinct crash of shattering glass.

"That came from the cellar!" said Miranda.

Chase wheeled and headed back into the kitchen. He flicked on a wall switch and yanked open the cellar door. A single bare bulb shone over the narrow stairway. A strange mist seemed to swirl in the shadows, obscuring the bottom of the stairs. They had taken only two steps down when they both smelled smoke.

"You've got a fire in here!" said Chase, moving down the steps. "Where's your extinguisher?"

"I'll get it!" Miranda scrambled into the kitchen, pulled the extinguisher from the pantry shelf and dashed back down the cellar steps.

By now the smoke was thick enough to make her eyes burn. Through the whirling haze she saw the source: a bundle of flaming rags. Nearby, just beneath a shattered basement window, lay a red brick. At once she understood what had happened, and her panic gave way to fury. *How dare they smash my window? How dare they attack me in my own home?*

"Stay back!" Chase yelled, plunging forward through the

smoke. His shoes crunched over broken glass as he crossed the concrete floor. He aimed the extinguisher; a stream of white shot out and hissed over the flames. A few sweeps of the nozzle and the fire faltered and died under a smothering blanket of powder. Only the smoke remained, a stinking pall that hung like a cloud around the bare light bulb.

"It's out!" said Chase. He was prowling the basement now, searching for new flames. He didn't notice that Miranda had gone rigid with fury, didn't see that she was staring, white-faced, at the broken glass on the floor.

"Why can't they leave me *alone?*" she cried.

Chase turned and looked at her with sudden intensity. He said, dead quiet, "You mean this has happened before?"

"Not—not this. But phone calls, really cruel ones. Again and again. And messages, written on my window."

"What sort of messages?"

"What you'd expect." She swallowed and looked away. "You know, to the local murderess."

He took a step toward her. "You know who's doing it?"

"I told myself it was just—just some kids. But kids, they wouldn't set fire to my house...."

Chase glanced down at the brick, then up at the shattered window. "It's a crazy way to burn down a house," he said. He went to her, took her by the shoulders, gently rubbed her arms. She felt warmth in his touch, and strength. Courage. He framed her face with his hands and said quietly, "I'm going to call the police."

She nodded. Together they started up the steps to the kitchen. They were halfway up the stairs when the door above them suddenly slammed shut. An instant later the bolt squealed home.

"They've shut us in!" cried Miranda.

He dashed past her up the stairs and began pounding on the door. In frustration he threw himself against it. His shoulder slammed into the wood.

"It's solid!" said Miranda. "You can't break it down."

Chase groaned. "I think I just found that out."

Footsteps creaked across the floor overhead. Miranda froze, tracing with her gaze the intruder's movements.

"What's he doing?" she whispered.

As if in answer to her question, the single light bulb suddenly went out. The basement was plunged into darkness.

"Chase?" she cried.

"I'm here! Right here. Give me your hand."

She reached up blindly toward him; at once he found her wrist. "It's all right," he murmured, pulling her toward him, gathering her tightly against his chest. Just the unyielding support of that embrace was enough to take the edge off her panic. "We'll be okay," he murmured. "We just have to find a way out. We can't make it through the window. You have a cellar door? A coal hatch?"

"There's—there's an old loading hatch near the furnace. It opens to the side yard."

"All right. Let's see if we can get it open. Just move us in the right direction."

Together they felt their way down the steps, to the cellar floor. Shards of glass skittered before their feet as they inched their way through the darkness. It seemed like a journey across eternity, through a blackness so thick it might have been firm to the touch. At last Miranda's extended hand touched pipes, then the cold, damp granite of the cellar wall.

"Which way to the hatch?" asked Chase.

"I think it's to the left."

Upstairs, the creaking moved across the floor, then a door slammed shut. *They've left the house,* Miranda thought in relief. *They're not going to hurt us.*

"I found the oil tank!" said Chase.

"Then the coal hatch should be just above. There are some steps—"

"Right here." He released her hand. Though she knew he was right beside her, that break in contact left her hovering at the edge of panic. If only she could see something, anything! She could hear Chase shoving up against the wood, could hear the crack and groan of the hatch as he struggled to swing it open. Straining to see through the darkness, she could make out, little by little, the vague outline of his head, then the gleam of sweat on his face. More details seemed to emerge out of darkness: the hulking shadow of the furnace, the oil tank, the reddish glint of the copper pipes. It was all visible now.

Too visible. Where was the light coming from?

With new apprehension she turned and stared up at the basement window. Reflected in the shattered glass was a flickering dance of orange light. Firelight. "Oh, my God," she whispered. "Chase…"

He turned and stared.

Even as they watched, the glow in the window shards leaped to a new and horrifying brilliance.

"We have to get out of here!" she cried.

He shoved against the hatch. "I can't get it open!"

"Here, let me help you!"

They both pushed up against the wood, pounded it with their bare fists. Already, smoke was swirling in through the broken window. Overhead, through the cracks in the floorboards, they could see the terrible glow of flames consuming the house above. Most of the heat was funneled up, toward the roof, but soon the timbers would give way. They would be trapped beneath falling debris.

The hatch was immovable.

Chase snatched up the fire extinguisher and began to pound it against the wood. "I'll keep trying to break through!" he yelled. "You get to the window—yell for help!"

Miranda scrambled over to the window. Smoke was billowing in, a thick, suffocating black cloud. She could barely reach the opening. She glanced around in panic for a crate, a chair, something to stand on. Nothing was in sight.

She screamed louder than she had ever screamed in her life.

Even then, she knew help wouldn't reach them in time. The basement window faced the back of the house, toward the garden. She was too far below the opening for her voice to carry any distance. She glanced up, at the floor beams. Already, the evil glow of heat shone through. She could hear the groan of the wood as it sagged. How long before those beams gave way? How long before she and Chase collapsed under that smothering blackness of smoke? The air had grown unbearably close.

It's already an oven, she thought. *And it will only get hotter....*

CHAPTER EIGHT

Chase pounded desperately at the hatch. A board splintered, but the barrier held. "Someone's nailed it shut!" he yelled. "Keep calling for help!"

She screamed, again and again, until her voice cracked, until she had almost no voice left.

She heard, in the distance, the sound of a dog barking, and Mr. Lanzo's far-off shouts. She tried to shout back. All she could manage was a pitifully weak cry. There was no answering call. Had she imagined the voice? Or couldn't he hear her?

Even if he did, would he track her screams to this small opening facing the garden? Safety lay so close, yet was so unreachable. If she stood on tiptoe she could actually poke her hand through the shards of broken glass, could feel the soil beneath her fingertips. Just inches away would be her beloved delphiniums, her newly planted violas....

An image of her garden, of rich, moist earth and a freshly tilled flower bed suddenly flashed into her mind. Hadn't she just expanded that bed? Hadn't she used a pickax to break up the sod? The pickax—where did she leave it? She remembered laying it against the side of the house—

Near the cellar window.

With her bare fist she broke away the last shards of glass. Something warm ran down her arm. Blood, she thought with a strange sense of detachment. But no pain—she was too panicked to feel anything but the desperate need to escape the flames. She reached through the open window and ran her fingers along the outside wall. Nothing on the right, just the rough clapboard shingles above a granite foundation. She shifted to the left side of the window, swept her hand along the outside frame and touched warm metal. The pickax head!

She gripped it so tightly her fingers cramped. Painfully she managed to slide the heavy iron head sideways, in front of the window. With a little wriggling she maneuvered first the sharp point, then the blade end, through the window opening.

The pick landed with a hard clang on the concrete floor.

Coughing and gasping, she dragged the tool into the blinding smoke. Already, flames were engulfing the floorboards above her head. "Chase!" she cried. "Where are you?"

"I'm here!"

She started toward the sound of Chase's voice but halfway across she lost her bearings. The whole room seemed to be moving around her like some crazy circus ride. *I can't faint now,* she thought. *If I do, I'll never wake up.* Already her knees were giving way. How she needed a breath of fresh air, just one! She sank to the floor. The concrete felt blessedly damp and cool against her face.

"Miranda!"

The sound of Chase's voice seemed to jump-start some last internal surge of strength. She struggled back to her knees. "I can't—can't see you...."

"I'll find you! Keep talking!"

"No, we'll both get lost! Stay by the hatch!" She began to crawl, moving in the direction of his voice, dragging the pickax behind her. The sound of the fire above them had grown to a roar. Fallen embers lay scattered and glowing on the concrete. Blinded by smoke, she put her hand on one and the pain that seared her skin brought a sob to her throat.

"I'm coming for you!" Chase shouted.

His voice seemed far away, as though he were calling from some distant room. She realized she was fading, and that the room had grown dark, and that this inferno was where she would die. She clawed her way forward, dragging herself and the pickax a few more precious inches.

"Miranda!" His voice seemed even more distant now, another

world, another universe. And that seemed most terrible of all—
that she would die without the comfort of his touch.

She reached out to drag herself one last time—

And found his hand. Instantly his fingers closed around her
wrist and he hauled her close. His touch was like some wondrous
restorative. She found the strength to rise once again to her knees.

"Here," she said with a cough, dragging the pickax toward
him. "Will this work?"

"It has to!" He staggered to his feet. "Stay low," he commanded. "Keep your head down!"

She heard him grunt as he swung the pickax, heard the thunk
of the metal slamming into the wood. Another swing, another
blow. Splinters flew, raining into her hair. He was coughing,
weaving. Against the backlight of flames she could see him struggle to stay on his feet.

He swung again.

The hatch gave way. A blast of cool air flew in through the
jagged opening. The inrush of fresh oxygen was like throwing
fuel on the fire. Everywhere, timbers seemed to explode into
flame. Miranda dropped to the ground, her face buried in her arms.
An ember fell hissing onto her head. She brushed it away, shuddering at the smell of her own burning hair.

Chase gasped in one last breath of air, then, grunting from the
effort, he heaved the pickax against the wood.

The hatch flew apart.

Miranda felt herself yanked upward, through some long, dark
tunnel. She could see no light at the other end, could see no end
at all. There was just that black passage, the dizzying sense of
motion, the clawlike grasp of fingers against her flesh.

Then, suddenly, there was the grass.

And there was Chase, cradling her in his arms, stroking her
face, her hair.

She took in a breath. The rush of air into her lungs was almost
painful. She coughed, drew in more air, more! She felt drunk on
its sweetness.

The night was a whirlwind of noise, sirens, shouting voices and the crackle of fire. She gazed up in horror at the flames; they seemed to fill the heavens.

"Oh, God," she whispered. "My house..."

"We made it out," said Chase. "That's all that matters. We're alive."

She focused on his face. It was a mask of soot, lit by the hellish glow of the fire. They stared at each other, a look of shared wonder that they were both still breathing.

"Miranda," he murmured. He bent and pressed his lips to her forehead, her eyelids, her mouth. He tasted of smoke and sweat and desperation. All at once, they were both shaking and clutching each other in wild relief.

"Mo! Honey! You all right?"

Mr. Lanzo, dressed in his pajamas, scuttled toward them across the lawn. "I was afraid you were inside! Kept tellin' those idiot firemen I heard you screaming!"

"We're okay," Chase said. He took Miranda's face in his hands and kissed her. "We're fine."

Somewhere, a window shattered in the heat of the flames.

"Hey! You people move back!" a fireman yelled. "Everyone get back!"

Chase pulled Miranda to her feet. Together they retreated across Mr. Lanzo's lawn and onto the street. They watched as the fire hoses unleashed a torrent of spray. Water hissed onto the flames.

"Aw, honey," said Mr. Lanzo sadly. "It's too late. She's gone."

Even as he said it, the roof collapsed. Miranda watched in despair as a sheet of flame shot up, turning the night sky into a blazing dawn. *It's all gone,* she thought. *Everything I owned. I've lost it all.*

She wanted to scream out her fury, her anguish, but the violence of those flames held her in a trance. She could only watch as a strange numbness took hold.

"Ms. Wood?"

Slowly she turned.

Lorne Tibbetts was standing beside her. "What happened here?" he asked.

"What the hell do you *think* happened?" Chase shot back. "Someone torched her house. While we were in it."

Lorne looked at Miranda, who stared back at him with dazed eyes. He looked at the burning house, which had already collapsed into little more than a heap of firewood.

"You'd better come with me," he said. "I'll need a statement. From both of you."

"Now do you believe it?" asked Chase. "Someone's trying to kill her."

Lorne Tibbetts's gaze, in the best poker player tradition, revealed absolutely nothing. He began to doodle in the margin of his notepad. Nothing artistic there, not even a few healthy free-form loops. These were tight little triangles linked together like crystals. The geometric creation of a geometric mind. He clicked his pen a few times, then he turned and yelled, "Ellis?"

Ellis poked his head in the door. "Yo, Lorne."

"You finished with Ms. Wood?"

"Got it all down."

"Okay." Lorne rose to his feet and started out of the room.

"Wait," said Chase. "What happens now?"

"I talk to her. Ellis talks to you."

"You mean I have to tell it all over again?"

"It's the way we do things around here. Independent questioning. Routine police procedure." He tucked his shirt into his trousers, smoothed back his hair and walked out the door.

Ellis Snipe sat in Lorne's vacated seat and grinned at Chase. "Hey, Mr. T. How ya doing?"

Chase looked at that moronic, gap-toothed smile and wondered, *Was Mayberry ever this bad?*

"Why don't we start at the beginning," said Ellis.

"Which beginning?" Chase shot back.

Ellis looked confused. "Uh, you choose."

Chase sighed. He glanced at the door, wondering how Miranda was holding up. No matter what Dr. Steiner had said, a hospital bed was where she belonged. But the old quack had simply dressed her glass cuts, examined her lungs and declared hospitalization unnecessary. What Dr. Steiner had neglected to consider was her emotional state. She'd lost her house, her possessions; she was left with no sense of order to her life. What she needed was a safe place, a cocoon where no one could hurt her....

"Uh, Mr. Tremain? You think you could maybe try and cooperate?"

Chase looked at Ellis. What was the point of fighting? he thought wearily. Ellis Snipe looked like the kind of robot who'd follow orders to the letter. If he had to, he'd sit there all night, waiting for Chase to talk.

For the second time that night Chase told the story. He took it back to the cottage, the evidence of a break-in, the secret files. This time he left out the information about Lorne Tibbetts and his fling with the librarian. Some things, he thought, should remain private.

Ellis wrote it all down in a weird, spidery script that couldn't possibly be produced by a normal personality.

When Chase was finished, Ellis asked one and only one question. "Was there anything in those secret files about me?"

"Not a thing," said Chase.

Ellis looked disappointed.

After Ellis had left, Chase sat alone at the table, wondering what came next. A third cop, another go-around with the story? The whole affair had taken on a surreal quality, like some never-ending nightmare. For ten minutes he waited for something to happen. Then, fed up with being ignored, he shoved his chair back and went in search of Miranda.

He found her in the same interrogation room where he'd first laid eyes on her over a week before. She was sitting alone. A smudge of soot blackened her cheek, and her hair was dusted with ash.

She gazed at him with a look of utter exhaustion. "The cop station from hell," she murmured.

He smiled. Then he saw her hand. It was encased in bandages. "Is it as serious as it looks?"

"The doctor just believes in doing a thorough job." She looked in wonder at the free-form sculpture of surgical gauze and tape. "I was afraid he'd amputate."

"A hand as nice as yours? I wouldn't have let him."

She tried to return the smile, but couldn't quite manage it.

"You have to leave the island," he said.

"I can't. The terms of my bail—"

"To hell with the bail terms! You can't wait around for the next accident, the next fire."

"I can't leave the county."

"This time you were lucky. Next time—"

"What am I *supposed* to do?" She looked at him in sudden anger. "Run and hide?"

"Yes."

"From *what?* I don't even know who's trying to kill me!" Her cry echoed in the stark room. At once she flushed, as though shamed by the sound of her own hysteria.

"If I leave, I'll never know what I'm running from," she said quietly. "Or if I'm still being hunted. What kind of life is that, Chase? Never knowing if I'm safe. Always waking up at night, listening for footsteps. Wondering if that creak on the stairs is someone coming for me...." She shuddered and stared down at the table.

Lord, he thought. *How did I ever get involved with this woman? She's not my problem. I'm not her white knight. I should get up and walk right out of this room. Who would blame me?*

And then a voice inside him said, *I would.*

He pulled out a chair and sat across from her. She didn't look up. She just kept staring at the ugly tabletop.

"If you won't leave, then what are you going to do?"

She shrugged. It hurt him to see the hopelessness in that gesture. "Does it matter?"

"It matters to me."

"Why?" The look she gave him made him want to say things

he knew he'd regret. That he cared whether she lived or died. He cared what happened to her. He cared too much.

He said, with unassailable logic, "Because what happened tonight is somehow tied in with Richard. The break-in at Rose Hill. The fire. And you."

She gave a dispirited laugh. "Yes, somewhere in all this mess, I seem to fit in. And I haven't the faintest idea why."

The door opened. Ellis said, "There you are, Mr. T. Lorne says you both can go. Says he can't think of any more questions."

I hope I never see this place again, thought Chase as they followed Ellis down the hall, into the front office. Lorne was sitting at one of the desks, talking on the phone. He glanced up as Chase and Miranda walked past, and motioned to them to wait.

"Oh, hell." Chase sighed. "He just thought of another question."

Lorne hung up and said to Ellis, "Bring the car around. We got us another call."

"Man, oh, man," Ellis whined as he headed out to the garage. "This is one heck of a Thursday night."

Lorne looked at Miranda. "You got a place to stay?"

"I'll drive her to the hotel," said Chase.

"I was thinking along the lines of someplace safer," Lorne said. "A friend's house, maybe?"

"There's always Mr. Lanzo," said Miranda.

"No, I'll take you over to Annie's house," said Chase. "At least *her* faculties are still intact."

"Yeah, that'd be better," said Lorne, reaching for his hat. "Considering."

"Considering what?" said Chase.

"The two empty gas cans we found over by Ms. Wood's house. Plus the two-by-fours nailed over the cellar hatch."

Miranda stared at him. There it was. Undeniable proof someone was trying to kill her. Her body seemed to sag against Chase. "Then you believe me," she whispered.

Lorne reached for his hat. "Well, I'll tell you what I believe,

Ms. Wood. I do believe this is one of the weirdest nights we've ever had here on this island. And I do not like the trend.''

"What else is going on?'' asked Chase.

"An assault. On Miss Lila St. John, if you can believe it. She just called in the report.''

"Someone attacked her?'' said Chase, shocked. "Why?''

"She claims she tried to stop a break-in.'' Lorne, obviously skeptical, started for the door. "At Rose Hill Cottage.''

"So,'' said Annie Berenger, pouring out three tall whiskeys. "Do I get to write all about the juicy details? Or is this baby-sitting job another gratis deal?''

"I thought you and Miranda were friends,'' said Chase.

"Oh, we are. But I'm a reporter, too.'' She handed Chase a glass. "It's my job to take advantage of the situation.'' She glanced at the closed door to the bathroom, where Miranda was showering. "You know, Chase, she looked pretty beat-up. Shouldn't she be in a hospital or something?''

"She'll be fine right here, Annie. As long as you keep your eagle eye on her.''

"Terrific. What I always wanted to be. A mommy.'' She tossed back a quick slug of whiskey. "Oh, don't get me wrong. I like Miranda. I used to be a lot like her. About a century ago.'' She poured herself a second glass. "But women grow up fast these days. We have to. It's the men who age us. Take my boyfriend, Irving. Please. I've been waiting a year for him to pop the ques-tion. It's giving me gray hairs.'' She took a sip of whiskey, then turned and looked at Chase. "So how much trouble is she in?''

"It could get dangerous. Are you ready for that?''

"Ready?'' She went to an end table and opened the drawer. Casually she pulled out a revolver. "Little souvenir I picked up in Boston. I'm a lousy shot, but sometimes I get lucky.'' She tossed the gun back into the drawer. "Good enough?''

"I'm impressed.''

Annie laughed. "Men always are when they see my pistol's bigger than theirs.'' She glanced over her shoulder as the bath-room door opened. "Hi. Feeling better?''

"Just cleaner," said Miranda, walking barefoot into the living room. She was wearing one of Annie's huge T-shirts. It hung like a dress over her slim hips.

Annie held out a glass of whiskey. "Join us in a toast."

"To what?"

"Just drink it. We'll think of something."

Miranda came toward them and took the glass. She brought with her those fresh shower smells, the scent of flowers and soap and feminine warmth. Her hair, still damp, was a mass of unruly waves. The sight of her sent Chase's head swimming. Or was it the whiskey?

"So what happens now?" asked Annie.

Chase turned away and set his glass on the nearest table. "The police are handling it."

"Look, I've been covering that beat for five years. I wouldn't be too optimistic."

"Lorne's a bright guy. He can figure it out."

"But whose side is he on? I'm not saying Lorne's corrupt, or anything. But you did find that page about him and Valerie Everhard."

"A fling with the local librarian?" Chase shrugged. "I'd consider that only a minor scandal."

"Did you ask Lorne about it?"

"Yes. He didn't deny it. And he didn't seem bothered by it."

"Annie, did you know Richard had those files?" Miranda asked.

Annie shrugged. "We had a number of files on local personalities. Jill did the interviews, wrote the pieces. Every summer we'd run a few profiles. But nothing that'd make tongues twitter." She set her glass down. "Well, whatever was in those files, it's all up in smoke now. A pity you didn't have copies. You've lost your only clues."

"I don't think so," said Chase. "Those were the papers the burglar left behind. Whatever he's really after is still at Rose Hill."

"How do you know?"

"Because he went back there tonight."

"What he didn't count on," said Miranda, "was tangling with Miss Lila St. John. Again."

Annie shook her head and laughed. "That is one poor, unfortunate burglar."

Miss Lila St. John was, at that moment, holding a bag of ice to a nasty-looking goose egg on the back of her head. "What do you mean, did I get a good look at him?" she snapped. "Does it seem likely I got a look at him? Considering where he whacked me?"

"It was just a routine question, ma'am," whimpered Ellis.

"That is the problem with you police people. You are so tied up with your routine questions you never bother to think."

"Miss St. John," Lorne politely interjected, "allow me to rephrase Ellis's question. What, exactly, *did* you see?"

"Precious little."

"A figure? A face?"

"Just a light. I told you, I was sitting here reading. *Death Becomes You.*

"Excuse me?"

"The name of the book. It features a police detective with a genius IQ." She paused. "Obviously, a novel with no basis in reality."

Lorne let that one slide by. Miss St. John deserved a little leeway tonight. After all, a blow on the head—even a head as hard as hers—would make anyone cranky. "Go on," he said.

"Well, I put the book aside to make tea. And as I did, I happened to look out that window. It faces south, toward Rose Hill Cottage. That's when I saw the light."

"A car headlight?"

"No, much dimmer. A flashlight, I think. Moving through the woods. I knew it was headed for Rose Hill. That's all that lies in that direction. So I decided to check on it."

"Why didn't you call us?"

"Because it might simply have been one of the Tremains. Now, how would it look if I dragged you men all the way out here, just to confront the rightful owner?''

"The rightful owner seems to be in doubt.''

"Let's not confuse ourselves with that issue. Anyway, I went out—''

"Alone?''

"If only! I would have been just fine if Ozzie hadn't followed me.''

"Ozzie?'' inquired Ellis.

As if on cue, an enormous black dog sauntered across the room and eyed Ellis.

"Yes, you certainly made a racket,'' said Miss St. John to the dog. "All that yowling and thrashing in the bushes. No wonder you never catch anything.'' She looked at Lorne. "It's *his* fault. He followed me up the road. Somewhere along the way I lost track of the light. I was trying to see through the dark and shoo off Ozzie at the same time. He was making such unattractive noises. I turned around and gave him a slap. And that's when he whacked me.''

"Ozzie?'' asked Ellis.

"No! The man. Or woman. It was dark, so I couldn't tell you which.''

"Did you black out?''

"I'm not sure. Things got a little confused at that point. I remember being on my knees in the bushes. Hearing footsteps run away. And feeling mad as hell.'' She glared at Ozzie. "Yes, and I do mean at *you*.''

The dog, unperturbed, began to lick Lorne's brand-new boot. Gingerly, Lorne gave the dog a little shove. Ozzie, looking insulted, redirected his affectionate overtures toward a more agreeable target—Ellis's leg.

"Then you never saw your attacker?'' Lorne asked.

"No, I can't say I did.''

"What happened then?''

"I came back here. Oh, I got a little turned around in the dark, but I found my way back, eventually. And I called you.''

"So the attack happened—when?"

"It would be about two hours ago."

About the same time the flames were consuming the last of Miranda Wood's house, thought Lorne. It seemed unlikely that the same culprit could have set fire to the house, then raced out here in time to knock Miss St. John on the head. Two crimes, two criminals. Too bad.

Lorne preferred simple solutions.

"Are you certain your attacker was headed for Rose Hill?" he asked.

"I know he was. And he'll be back."

"Why?"

"Because he didn't get what he wanted."

"You're referring to the scandal sheets?"

Miss St. John gave him a look of pure innocence. "Oh. You know about that?"

"Yes. And for your information, Miss St. John, I didn't come on to Valerie Everhard. She came on to me."

Ellis looked up from the dog now nuzzling his knee. "What was that about Valerie Everhard?"

"Never mind," snapped Lorne and Miss St. John simultaneously.

"There was a report on me, too," said Miss St. John with a faint note of pride. "As well as almost everyone on this road. I had no idea Richard Tremain was such a busybody."

"Any idea why?"

"I'll give the man the benefit of the doubt and attribute it to mere curiosity. As opposed to less benign motives."

Blackmail was what she meant. Lorne couldn't see that such a scheme made much sense. First of all, none of those secrets was particularly nasty. Embarrassing, perhaps, but nothing that couldn't be lived down. And that included his own penchant for married librarians. Second, the would-be victims ranged from the moderately well-to-do Forrest Mayhew to the outright cash-strapped Gordimers. Why blackmail a family that can scarcely pay their grocery bills?

Unless money was not the sought-after payment.

He wondered about this all the way back to town. Wondered why Richard Tremain would want those secrets. Wondered if he was even the one who'd collected them in the first place. The cottage, after all, had been open to others in the family. Cassie. Phillip.

Evelyn.

No, not Evelyn, he thought. She wouldn't dirty her hands in this filth.

"You and Valerie Everhard," Ellis muttered as he drove. "I never woulda guessed."

"Look, I felt sorry for her," said Lorne. "She needed some male attention."

"Oh." Ellis kept staring straight ahead at the road and nodding to himself.

"What the hell's that supposed to mean?" Lorne demanded.

"Oh, I was just thinking."

"About what?"

"How awful sorry you must be feeling for that woman right now."

"Valerie Everhard?"

"No." said Ellis. "The widow Tremain."

"It's a matter of loyalty, Chase," said Noah. "To the family. To your brother. To the people who *matter*."

Chase said nothing. He simply continued slicing his ham, albeit with more concentrated vigor than usual. He knew they were all watching him. Noah and Evelyn. The twins. They were waiting for him to respond. But he kept on slicing that meat, mangling it, really, into smaller and smaller pieces.

"Never mind, Daddy," said Evelyn. "Can't you see? He's so wrapped up with that witch, he can't see the trap he's—"

"Please, Evelyn." Chase set down his knife.

"She's twisted you around, Chase! She has a talent for that! Among other things. But you can't be bothered with the facts anymore. No, all you want to believe are her lies."

"I want to believe the truth," he said quietly.

"The truth is, she's a whore."

"Evelyn," cut in Noah. "That is quite enough."

Evelyn turned on her father. "Whose side are you on?"

"You know damn well I'm on your side. I always have been."

"Then why don't you back me up?"

"Because this conversation doesn't become you. You've forgotten all I taught you about dignity. Pride."

"Well, *excuse me,* Daddy. It's not every day one's husband gets murdered." She glanced around at the sideboard. "Where's that wine? It's not too early for a drink."

"You will get over the murder. You'll get beyond it. And you will remember who you are."

"Who I am?" She rose to her feet. "Who I am is more of an embarrassment every day." She shoved her chair back against the table and left the room.

There was a long silence.

"She does have a point, Chase," said Noah, sounding quite reasonable. "The family should stick together. No matter what attractions this Miranda Wood person offers, don't you think it's best you stand by us?"

"What attraction *does* she offer?" asked Cassie.

"That's irrelevant," snapped Chase.

Noah raised an eyebrow. "Is it?"

Chase met Noah's gaze with a look of sheer indifference. Which, at that moment, wasn't at all what he was feeling. He had plenty of feelings when it came to Miranda Wood, and indifference wasn't one of them. All night he'd dreamt about her. He'd awakened sweating, remembering the fire, feeling once again the panic of not being able to find her in that well of smoke and flames. He'd drop back to sleep, only to sink yet again into the same nightmare. Some time during his fitful tossing and turning, he'd come to several realizations. That he was incapable of logical thought where Miranda Wood was concerned. That the attraction he felt for her was growing more dangerous every day.

And that, no matter what his instincts told him, the weight of evidence still pointed to her guilt.

This morning he'd risen from bed exhausted but absolutely clearheaded. He knew what he had to do. He had to put some distance between them. As he should have done from the very beginning.

He said, "You don't have to worry, Noah. I don't plan to see her again."

"I always thought you were the smarter Tremain," said Noah. "I was right."

Chase shrugged. "Not really a flattering comment. Considering how little you thought of Richard."

Noah glanced at the twins. "You two! Don't you have something better to do?"

"Not really," said Phillip.

"Well, clear the table, then. Go on."

"It's not as if we didn't know," said Cassie.

Noah frowned at her. "Know what?"

"That you and Dad didn't get along."

"For that matter, young lady, he didn't get along with you, either."

"Normal father-daughter disagreements. Not like you two, always at each other's throats. All that yelling and name-calling—"

"That's enough!" Noah's face had turned an ugly red. He rose partway out of his chair, his gaze targeted on his insolent granddaughter. "The day you were born, Cassandra, I took one look at you and I said, 'Watch out for that one. She's going to be trouble.'"

"Yes, it runs in our family, doesn't it?"

Instantly Phillip was on his feet, tugging at Noah's arm. "Come on, Granddad. Let's go outside, you and me. Walk around the block. I wanted to tell you about my year at Harvard—"

"Damn nursery for snooty rich boys."

"Just a walk, Granddad. It'll do you good."

Noah harrumphed and shoved his chair against the table. "Let's go, then. Hell, I could use the fresh air."

The two men walked out, slamming the front door behind them.

Cassie looked at Chase and smiled ironically. "One big happy family."

"What was that you said? About Noah and Richard."

"They despised each other. You knew that."

"*Despised* wasn't the word that came to mind. Disliked, maybe. You know, the usual rivalry between father and son-in-law."

"This wasn't just your usual rivalry." Cassie began to slice her ham into dainty pieces. For the first time Chase found himself actually seeing his niece. Before, she'd always seemed lost from view, the colorless sister skulking in the shadow of her brother. Now he took a new and closer look, and what he saw was a young woman with a square jaw and eyes like a ferret's. The resemblance to Noah was startling. No wonder the old man didn't get along with her. He probably saw too much of himself in that face. She looked him straight in the eye. No squirming, no discomfort, just that steady gaze.

"What did they argue about? Noah and your father?"

"Anything. Everything. Oh, they never let it get beyond these walls. Dad was weird that way. We could all be screaming at each other in this house, but once we stepped out the door he insisted we look like the perfect family. It was so phony. In public Dad and Noah would make like old buddies. And all the time there was that rivalry between them."

"Over your mother?"

"Of course. Noah's darling. And Dad could never be a good enough husband." She snorted. "Not that he tried very hard."

Chase paused, wondering how to phrase his next question. "Did you know your father was having...affairs?"

"He's been at it for years," Cassie said with a wave of her hand. "Lots of women."

"Which ones?"

She shrugged. "I figured that was his business."

"You two weren't very close, were you?"

"Daughters just weren't his thing, Uncle Chase. While I was working my butt off, getting straight A's, he was planning for

Phillip's Harvard education. Grooming him to take over the *Herald*."

"Phillip doesn't seem exactly thrilled by the prospect."

"You noticed that? Dad never did." She took a few bites of ham, then gave Chase a thoughtful look. "And what was the problem between *you* two?"

"Problem?" He resisted the urge to look away, to avoid her gaze. She would probably know immediately that he was hiding something. As it was, she'd probably already detected the flicker of discomfort in his eyes.

"The last time I saw you, Uncle Chase, I was ten years old. That was at Grandpa Tremain's funeral. Now, Greenwich isn't that far away. But you never came back for a visit, not once."

"Lives get complicated. You know how it is, Cassie."

She gave him a searching look, then said, "It's not easy, is it? Being the ignored sibling in the family?"

Damn this sharp-eyed brat, he thought. He gathered up his empty dishes and rose to his feet.

"You don't think she did it. Do you?" Cassie asked. They didn't have to mention names. They both knew exactly what they were talking about.

"I haven't decided," he said. He carried the dishes toward the kitchen. In the doorway he stopped. "By the way, Cassie," he said. "I called here last night about seven, to say I wouldn't be home for dinner. No one answered the phone. Where was your mother?"

"I really wouldn't know." Cassie picked up a slice of toast and calmly began to spread marmalade on it. "You'd have to ask her."

Chase drove directly to Rose Hill. No detours, no little side trips to pick up suspected murderesses. He had no intention of being distracted by Miranda Wood today. What he needed was a dose of coolheaded logic, and that meant keeping his distance. Today he had other things on his mind, the first item being: Who kept trying to break in to the cottage, and what was he searching for?

The answer lay somewhere in Rose Hill.

So that was where he headed. He drove with the window rolled down, the salt air whistling past his cheek. It brought back all those summer days of his childhood, riding with his mother along this very road, the smell of the sea in his face, the cry of the gulls echoing off the cliffs. How she had loved this drive! His mother had been a daredevil behind the wheel, screeching around these curves, laughing as the wind tangled her dark hair. They'd both laughed a lot those days, and he'd wondered if anyone else in the world had a mother so wild, so beautiful. So free.

Her death had left him devastated.

If only, before she'd died, she'd told him the truth.

He turned onto the access road and bumped along past all the old camp signs, past the cottages of families whose kids he'd once played with. Good memories, bad memories—they all returned as he drove up that road. He remembered twirling in the tire swing until he was so dizzy he threw up. Kissing buck-toothed Lucy Baylor behind the water tower. Hearing that awful crash of a breaking window and knowing it was *his* baseball they'd find lying in the shattered glass. The memories were so vivid he didn't notice that he'd already rounded the last bend and was just now turning onto the gravel driveway.

There was a car parked in front of the cottage.

He pulled up beside it and climbed out. He saw no sign of the driver. Could their burglar have turned desperate enough to pay a visit in broad daylight?

He hurried up the porch steps and was startled to hear the whistling of a kettle from the kitchen. Who the hell would be brazen enough to not only break in, but also make himself right at home? He shoved open the door and came face-to-face with the guilty party.

"I've just made some tea," said Miranda. She gave him a tight smile, not unfriendly, just nervous. Perhaps afraid. She nodded down at the tea tray she was carrying. "Would you like some?"

Chase glanced around the room, at the books arranged in neat piles on the floor. The desk had been cleared, the drawers' contents emptied into a series of cardboard boxes. Slowly his gaze shifted and took in the three bookcases. One was already two-thirds empty.

"We spent the morning going through Richard's papers," Miranda explained. "I'm afraid we haven't turned up anything yet, but—"

He shook his head. "We?"

"Miss St. John and I."

"Is she here?"

"She went back to her house, to feed Ozzie."

Their gazes met. *I try to stay away from you,* he thought, *and damn it, here you are. Here we are, alone in this house.*

The possibilities flooded his mind. Temptation, enemy of reason, danced its devil dance, the way it did every time he was in the same room with her. He thought of Richard, thought of her, thought of the two of them together. It hurt. Maybe that's why he chose to think of it. To quell the rising need he felt when he looked at her now.

"She—Miss St. John—thought it made sense to get started without you," Miranda said in a rush, as though suddenly frantic to fill the silence. "We didn't know when you'd get here, and we didn't want to call the house. I suppose we're trespassing, in a way, but..." Her voice trailed off.

"Technically speaking," he said after a pause, "you are."

She set down the tea tray, then straightened to face him. Her nervousness was gone. In its place was calm determination. "Maybe so. But it's what I have to do. We can search together. Or we can search separately. But I am going to search." She raised her chin, met his gaze without flinching. "So, Chase. Which way shall it be?"

CHAPTER NINE

His gaze was neutral, as unrevealing as that blank wall behind him. More revealing to Miranda was her acute sense of disappointment. She'd hoped to see at least a trace of gladness in his eyes, that he'd be pleased to find her here today. What she hadn't expected was this...indifference. *So that's how it is between us,* she thought. *What's happened since I saw you last? What did Evelyn say to you? That's it, isn't it? They've gotten to you. Richard's family. Your family.*

He shrugged. "It does make sense, I suppose. Working together."

"Of course it does."

"And you've already gotten off to a good start, I see."

In silence she poured a cup of tea, then carried it to the bookcase. There she calmly continued the task she'd been working on earlier—pulling down the books, riffling through the pages for any loose papers. She felt him watching her, sensed his gaze like a prickling in her back. "You can start on the other bookcase," she said without looking at him.

"What have you found so far?"

"No surprises." She reached for another book. "Unless you count Richard's rather weird taste in reading material." She looked at a book jacket. *The Advanced Physics of Ocean Waves.* "This one, for instance. I never knew he was interested in physics."

"He wasn't. When it came to science, he was functionally illiterate."

She opened the cover. "Well, this *is* his book. I see someone's written him a dedication in the front...." Glancing at the title page, she suddenly flushed.

"What is it?"

"You know the old saying?" Miranda murmured. "About not judging a book by its cover?"

Chase moved behind her and read over her shoulder. "*One Hundred and One Sexual Positions*. Fully illustrated?"

Miranda flipped open to a random page and instantly flushed. "They meant what they said about fully illustrated."

He reached around her to take the book. His breath grazed her neck; it left her skin tingling.

"Obviously a dummy jacket," said Chase. "I wonder how many other disguised books are in that stack?"

"I didn't really check," Miranda admitted. "I was looking for loose papers. I wasn't paying much attention to the books themselves."

Chase flipped to the title page and read aloud the handwritten dedication. "To my darling Richard. Can we try number forty-eight again? Love, M." Chase glanced at Miranda.

"I didn't give him that thing!" she protested.

"Then who's M?"

"Someone else. Not me."

He frowned at the dedication. "I wonder what number forty-eight is." He flipped to the page.

"Well?"

Chase took a discreet peek. "You don't want to know," he muttered and let the page riffle shut.

A slip of paper flew out and landed on the floor. They both stared at it in surprise. Chase was the first to snatch it up.

"Dearest love," he read aloud. "I'm thinking of you every day, every hour. I've given up caring about propriety or reputation or hellfire. There's only you and me and the time we have together. That, my darling, is my new definition of heaven." Chase glanced at her, one eyebrow raised in a cynical slant.

Miranda looked straight at him. "In case you're wondering," she said evenly, "I didn't write that note, either." In irritation she took the book and set it down on the nearest pile.

"Then I guess we'll just file it under 'interesting stuff,'" said Chase. "And continue with the rest of these books."

Miranda settled onto the rug. Chase sat in front of the other bookcase. They didn't touch, didn't look at each other. *Safer that way,* she thought. *For both of us.*

For half an hour they flipped through books, slapped them shut, threw clouds of dust in the air. Miranda was the one who found the next piece of the puzzle. It was tucked away in a financial ledger, in an envelope labeled Deductible Expenses.

"It's a receipt," she said, frowning at the slip of paper. "A month ago Richard paid four hundred dollars to this company."

"For what services?" asked Chase.

"It doesn't say. It's just made out to the Alamo Detective Agency in Bass Harbor."

"A detective agency? I wonder what Richard was after."

"Chase." She handed him the slip of paper. "Look at the name of the payee."

"William B. Rodell?" He glanced at her quizzically.

At least you're looking at me again, she thought. *At least we're connecting.* "Don't you remember?" she said. "That note attached to Richard's files."

Chase stared at the receipt, revelation suddenly brightening his dark features.

"Of course," he said softly. "William B. Rodell..."

W.B.R.

It was easy to see how the Alamo Detective Agency got its name. Willie Rodell was a good ol' boy transplant from San Antonio who split his time between Maine and Florida. Summertime was for Maine, and here he was, sitting behind his old steel desk, books and papers piled up in front of him like the battlements of a fort. The office was strictly a solo affair—one phone, one desk, one man. But what a man. Willie Rodell had enough flesh on his bones to fill the suits of two six-footers. *This must be what they mean by Texas-size,* thought Miranda.

"Yeah, I mighta done some work for Mr. Tremain now and again," said Rodell, leaning back in his equally Texas-size chair.

"Meaning you did or you didn't?" asked Chase.

"Well, you're holdin' one of my receipts there, so I guess it means I did."

"What sort of job?"

Willie shrugged. "Routine stuff."

"What *is* your routine stuff?"

"Mostly I do domestic affairs, if you catch my drift. Who's doin' what to whom, that sorta thing." His smirk rearranged the folds of his face into something vaguely obscene.

"But that's not the sort of thing you did for Richard, was it?"

"Nope. Though I hear tell there was more than enough dirt to dig in his particular case."

Cheeks burning, Miranda stared down fixedly at Willie's desk, a battle zone of broken pencils and twisted paper clips scattered among a bizarre assortment of magazines. *Hot Ladies. National Locksmith. Car and Driver.*

Chase got right to the point. "He hired you to compile files on his neighbors. Didn't he?"

Willie looked at him blandly. "Files?"

"We saw them, Mr. Rodell. They were among Richard's papers. Detailed reports on almost every resident along the access road. Each one containing sensitive information."

"Dirt sheets."

"That's right."

Willie shrugged. "I didn't write 'em."

"There was a note attached to one of the reports. It said, 'Want more? Let me know.' It was signed with the initials W.B.R." Chase reached over and plucked one of Willie's business cards from the desk. "Which just happens to be your initials."

"Helluva coincidence, hey?"

"He wanted dirt on his neighbors. Why?"

"He was snoopy?"

"So he paid you to write those reports."

"I told you, I didn't write 'em." Willie held up one fat hand. "Scout's honor."

"Then who did?"

"Dunno. But I admire his work."

Miranda, who'd been sitting quietly, focused on one of the magazines on the desk. *National Locksmith.* "You stole them," she said. She looked up at Willie's moonlike face. "That's what Richard hired you for. To steal those files from someone else."

Willie reached up and smoothed back a nonexistent strand of hair.

"You were paid to be a burglar," said Miranda. "What else were you paid for?"

"Look," said Willie, holding up both fat hands in a gesture of mock surrender. "Folks pay me to gather info, okay? That's all I do. Clients don't care how I get it, long as I get it."

"And where did you get those dirt sheets?" asked Chase.

"They were part of a bunch o' papers I sorta picked up."

"What else did you sort of pick up?"

"Financial records, bank statements. Hey, I didn't exactly *steal* 'em. I just, well, borrowed 'em for a few minutes. Long enough to run 'em through ol' man Xerox. Then I put 'em right back where I found 'em."

"The office of Stone Coast Trust," said Miranda.

Willie gave her a man-in-the-moon grin. "Betcha you're real good at Twenty Questions."

"So those were Tony Graffam's files," said Chase. "Not Richard's."

"Mr. T. didn't even know they existed till I handed 'em over. Thought for sure he was gonna want more. You know how it is. Get a taste of appetizer, you want the main course. Well, those papers were just the appetizer. I coulda got more."

"Why didn't you?"

"He fired me."

They frowned at him. "What?" said Miranda.

"That's right," said Willie. "Two days after I hand him those papers, he calls and says, thanks, he won't be needin' my services no more and how much do I owe you? That was that."

"Did he say why he fired you?"

"Nope. Just told me to keep it under my hat, and that he wasn't interested in Stone Coast no more."

"When was this?"

"Oh, about a week before he died."

"The same time he told Jill to kill the article," said Miranda. She looked at Chase. "Maybe he saw what Tony Graffam had on him. And decided to drop the whole investigation."

"But I looked over those papers, 'fore I handed 'em over," said Willie. "There wasn't any report on Tremain. Far as I could tell, wasn't nothin' in there to blackmail him with."

"Did you keep copies?"

"Mr. T. took it all. Didn't want loose papers floatin' around." Willie folded his hands behind his neck and stretched. Blots of sweat showed in his cavernous armpits. "Naw, I don't think it was the files. I think someone went and offered him a little, you know, incentive payment to forget the whole thing. So that's what he did."

"But Richard didn't need the money," said Miranda. "They couldn't bribe him."

"Sweetie, you can bribe just about anyone," said Willie, obviously an authority on such matters. "All it takes is the right price. And even a fella as rich as Tremain had his price."

"The lazy man's method of investigative journalism," said Chase. "Hire a thug to steal the evidence."

"I had no idea he'd do such a thing," said Miranda, gazing ahead in quiet disbelief. It was just after noon, a time when Main Street in Bass Harbor should have been bustling with tourists. Today, though, a cold summer drizzle had cooled the ardor of even the most inveterate sightseers. Miranda and Chase, hunched in their jackets, walked alone.

"And I thought it was just talent," she said softly. "The way he could pull a story together. Come up with evidence that surprised everyone. All that time he was paying someone to do the dirty work."

"It was just Richard's way," said Chase. "Meaning the easy way."

She looked at him. His hair, dampened by mist, was a cap of black, unruly waves. He stared straight ahead, his profile unrevealing. "Is that how he was as a boy?" she asked.

"He was good at finding shortcuts. For a few bucks he'd get someone to write his book report. Or help him cram for tests. He even found some idiot to finish his math homework for him." Chase grinned sheepishly. "Me."

"He bribed you into doing his homework?"

"It was more like, well, blackmail."

"What did he have on you?"

"Lots. Broken windows. Trampled flower beds. I was a pretty bad kid."

"But good at math, obviously."

Chase laughed. "When someone threatened exposure, I was good at a lot of things."

"And Richard took advantage of it."

"He was older. In a lot of ways, smarter. Everyone liked him, wanted to believe the best of him. And the worst of me." He shook his head. "I can see the same thing happening with his kids now. Phillip's the golden boy. And Cassie, she'll be trying all her life to match up."

"Will you be trying all *your* life to match up?"

He looked at her, then looked away. "No. I don't particularly care to make the same mistakes Richard did."

Meaning me, she thought.

The day suddenly seemed colder, darker. It was more than just her sagging spirits. The drizzle had turned to rain.

"Let's duck in someplace and get lunch," said Chase. "We've got another hour and a half till the ferry leaves."

They found a café tucked into an alley off Main Street. From the outside it seemed an unassuming little place with a name to match: Mary Jane's. It was the whiff of rich coffee and grilled meat that finally drew them in. Nothing fancy served here, just good plain food, roast chicken and red potatoes and crisp green beans, accompanied by freshly brewed coffee. Miranda's spirits might be sagging, but her appetite was in fine shape. She moved on to a slice of peach pie and a third round of coffee. A good thing she didn't normally react to stress by overeating. By now she'd be twenty pounds overweight.

"In a way," said Chase, "I'm relieved to learn the truth about those files."

"Relieved to learn Richard paid for an out-and-out burglary?"

"At least he wasn't the one snooping on his neighbors. The one planning blackmail."

She set down her fork. "Yes, I suppose you could talk yourself into thinking that breaking into Stone Coast Trust was somehow, well, morally correct."

"I'm not saying it was. But I can see how Richard might justify it. He's seen the coast eaten away by development. Then it hits close to home and he figures it's time to play dirty. Find out what you can about the developer. Steal a few files, financial records. Throw it back in the other guy's face."

"But he didn't. That's the strange part. He paid Rodell to steal those files. Then, after he gets hold of them, he drops the whole crusade. Kills the article, fires Rodell." She paused, and added softly, "And changes his will."

Chase frowned. "I don't see how that's related."

"The timing fits. Maybe he found something in those papers that got him angry at Evelyn. Made him decide to keep her from ever getting Rose Hill."

"You think there was a file on Evelyn? We didn't see one."

"He might've destroyed it. Or it could have been taken from the cottage. After his death."

They both fell silent at the implications of that statement. Who but Evelyn herself would bother to take such a file?

"This is crazy," said Chase. "Why would Evelyn steal it? It was her own damn cottage. She could walk in and out without anyone raising an eyebrow." He reached for his coffee cup, took a deliberate sip. "I can't see her breaking in and trashing the place."

You can't see her killing anyone, either. Can you? she thought. She wondered about Chase and his sister-in-law. Was their relationship merely cordial? Or did it run deeper than that? He'd stubbornly resisted the possibility that Evelyn might be guilty of wrongdoing, be it theft or murder. Miranda could understand why. Evelyn was a beautiful woman.

Now a free woman.

There was, after all, an appealing tidiness to a match between Chase and Evelyn. It would keep the money in the family, the same last name on the checkbook. Everyone would slip into their new roles with a minimum of muss and fuss. Chase had spent his boyhood trying to live up to his brother's image. Now he could slip right into Richard's place. Much as Miranda hated to admit it, such a mating would have a certain symmetry, a social correctness.

Something I'd never be able to give him.

The waitress came by with the check. Miranda reached for it, but Chase snatched it up first. "I'll take care of it," he said.

Miranda took a few bills from her pocket and laid them on the table.

"What's that for?" asked Chase.

"Call it pride," she said, rising to her feet, "but I always pay my way."

"With me you don't have to."

"I have to," she said flatly. "Especially with you." She grabbed her jacket and headed out the door.

He caught up with her outside. The rain had stopped but the sun had not yet emerged and the sky was a cold monochrome of gray. They walked side by side for a moment, not quite friends, not quite strangers.

"I'll be honest," he said. "I wasn't planning to see you today. Or ever again."

"It's a small town, Chase. It's hard to avoid a person here."

"I was going to drive back to Greenwich tomorrow."

"Oh." She lowered her eyes, willing herself not to feel disappointment. Or hurt. All those emotions she'd vowed never to feel for another Tremain. The emotions she was feeling now.

"But I've been thinking," he said.

Those four words made her halt and look up at him. *He's watching me, waiting for me to reveal myself. Give myself away as beguiled and bedazzled.*

Which, damn it, I am.

"I've been thinking," he said, "of staying a few more days. Just to clear up those questions about Richard."

She said nothing.

"Anyway, that's why I'm staying in town. It's the only reason."

Her chin came up. "Did I imply otherwise?"

"No." He let out a breath. "No, you didn't."

They walked on, another block, another silence.

"You'll be looking for the same answers, I expect," he said.

"I don't have much choice, do I? It's my future. My freedom."

"Look, I know it makes sense, in a way, for you and I to work together. But it's not exactly..."

"Seemly," she finished for him. "That's what you mean, isn't it? That it's embarrassing for you to be consorting with a woman like me."

"I didn't say that."

"Never mind, Chase." In irritation she turned and continued walking. "You're right, of course. We can't work together. Because we don't really trust each other. Do we?"

He didn't answer. He simply walked beside her, his hands thrust deep in his pockets. And that, more than anything he could have said, was what hurt her most.

They might not trust each other. They might not want anything to do with each other. But the simple fact was, if they wanted answers, the cottage was where they both had to look. So when Miranda pulled into the gravel driveway of Rose Hill the next morning she was not surprised to see Chase's car already parked there. Ozzie was sprawled on the front porch, looking dejected. He managed a few halfhearted wags of his tail as she came up the steps, but when he saw she wasn't going to invite him inside he flopped back down into a whimpering imitation of a shag rug.

Miss St. John and Chase had already gone through the second

bookcase. The place was looking more and more like a disaster zone, with cardboard boxes filled with papers, books precariously stacked in towers, empty coffee cups and dirty spoons littering the end tables.

"I see you started without me," said Miranda, careful to avoid looking at Chase. He was just as carefully avoiding her gaze. "What have you found?"

"Odds and ends," said Miss St. John, thoughtfully eyeing them both. "Shopping lists, receipts. Another love note from M. And a few quite literate college term papers."

"Phillip's?"

"Cassandra's. She must have done some writing out here. A few of the books are hers, as well."

Miranda picked up a bundle of papers and glanced through the titles. "A political analysis of the Boer conflict." "Doom foretold: the French colonialists in Vietnam." "The media and presidential politics." All were authored by Cassandra Tremain.

"A smart cookie," said Miss St. John. "A pity that slick brother of hers always steals the spotlight."

Miranda dug deeper in the box and pulled out the latest note from M. It was typewritten.

I waited till midnight—you never came. Did you forget? I wanted to call, but I'm always afraid she'll pick up the phone. She has you every weekend, every night, every holiday. I get the dregs.

How can you say you love me, when you leave me here, waiting for you? I'm worth more than this. I really am.

Quietly Miranda let the note flutter back into the box. Then she went to the window and stood staring out, toward the sea. Pity stirred inside her, for the woman who had written that note, for the pain she'd suffered. *The price we both paid for loving the wrong man.*

"Miranda?" Chase asked. "Is something wrong?"

"No." She cleared her throat and turned to him. "I'm fine. So...where should I start looking?"

"You could help me finish with this shelf. I'm finding papers here and there, so it's going slower than I expected."

"Yes, of course." She went to the shelf, pulled out a book and sat on the floor beside him. Not too close, not too far. *Neither friends nor enemies,* she thought. Just two people sharing the same rug, the same purpose. *For that, we don't even have to like each other.*

For an hour they flipped through pages, brushed away dust. Most of the books, it seemed, hadn't been opened in ages. There were old postcards dated twenty years earlier, addressed to Chase's mother. There was a hand-scrawled list of bird species sighted at Rose Hill, and a library notice from twelve years before, still stuck in the overdue book. Over the years, so many bits and pieces of the Tremain and Pruitt families had ended up on these shelves. It took time to sort out the vital from the trivial.

An oversize atlas of the state of Maine provided the next clue. Chase pulled it off the shelf and glanced in the front cover. Then he turned and called, "Miss St. John? You ever heard of a place called Hemlock Heights?"

"No. Why?"

"There's a map of it tucked in here." Chase pulled the document out of the atlas and spread it out on the rug. It was a collection of six photocopied pages taped together to form a site map. The pages looked fairly fresh. Property lines had been sketched in, and the lots were labeled by number. At the top was the development's name: Hemlock Heights. "I wonder if Richard was thinking of investing in real estate."

Miss St. John crouched down for a closer look. "Wait. This looks rather familiar. Isn't this our access road? And this lot at the end—lot number one. That's Rose Hill. I recognized that little jag up the mountain."

Chase nodded. "You're right. That's exactly what this is. Here's St. John's Wood. And the stone wall."

"It's the Stone Coast Trust map," said Miranda. "See? Most of the lots are labeled Sold."

"Good heavens," said Miss St. John. "I had no idea so many

of the camps have changed hands. There are only four of us who haven't sold out to Tony Graffam.''

"What kind of offer did he make for St. John's Wood?'' asked Miranda.

"It was a very good price at the time. When I refused to sell he bumped it up even higher. That was a year ago. I couldn't understand why the offer was so generous. You see, this was all conservation land. These old camps were grandfathered in, built before the days of land commissions. The cottages were allowed to stand, but you couldn't develop any of it. From a commercial standpoint the land was worthless. Then suddenly it's all been rezoned for development. And now I'm sitting on a gold mine.'' She looked at the other unsold lots on the map. "So is old Sulaway. And the hippies in Frenchman's Cottage.''

"And Tony Graffam,'' said Miranda.

"But what if the zoning decision was a sham?'' said Chase. "What if there were payoffs? If that fact became public knowledge...''

"My guess is, there'd be such protest, the zoning would be reversed,'' said Miss St. John. "And Mr. Graffam would be the proud owner of a lot of worthless property.''

"But it's worthless to him right now, Miss St. John,'' said Miranda, studying the map. "Graffam needs that access road to get to his lots. And you said the road belongs—belonged—to Richard.''

"Yes, we keep coming back to that, don't we?'' said Chase softly. "That link between Richard and Stone Coast Trust. The link that refuses to go away....'' He stood, clapping the dust from his trousers. "Maybe it's time we paid a visit to our neighbors.''

"Which ones?'' asked Miranda.

"Sulaway and the hippies. The other two on this road who didn't sell. Let's find out if Graffam put any pressure to bear. Like a blackmail note or two.''

"He didn't try to blackmail Miss St. John,'' pointed out Miranda. "And she didn't sell.''

"Ah, but my property's scarcely worth the effort,'' said Miss

St. John. "I'm just a tiny patch off to the side. And as for trying to blackmail me, well, you saw for yourself he doesn't have a thing on me worth mentioning. Not that I wouldn't mind generating a whiff of scandal at my age."

"The others could be more vulnerable," said Chase. "Old Sulaway, for instance. We should at least talk to him."

"A good idea," said Miss St. John. "Since you thought of it, Chase, *you* do it."

Chase laughed. "You are a coward, Miss St. John."

"No, I'm just too old for the aggravation."

Without warning, Chase reached for Miranda's hand and with one smooth motion pulled her up in an arc that almost, but not quite, ended in his arms. She reached out to steady herself and found her palms pressing against his chest. At once she stepped back.

"Is this a request for me to come along?" she said.

"It's more along the lines of a plea. To help me soften up old Sulaway."

"Does he need softening up?"

"Let's just say he hasn't taken kindly to me since I batted a baseball through his window. And that was twenty-five years ago."

Miranda laughed in disbelief. "You sound like you're afraid of him. Both of you."

"Obviously she's never met old Sulaway," said Miss St. John.

"Is there something I should know about him?"

Chase and Miss St. John glanced at each other.

"Just be careful when you walk into his front yard," said Miss St. John. "Give him lots of warning. And be ready to get out of there fast."

"Why? Does he have a dog or something?"

"No. But he does have a shotgun."

CHAPTER TEN

"You're that boy who broke my window!" yelled Homer Sulaway. "Yeah, I recognize you." He stood on the front porch, his skinny arms looped around a rifle, his lobsterman's dungarees rolled up at the ankles. Chase had told Miranda the man was eighty-five. The toothless, prune-faced apparition on that porch looked about a century older. "You two go on, now! Leave me alone. Can't afford to fix no more broken windows."

"But I paid for it, remember?" said Chase. "Had to mow lawns for six months, but I did pay for it."

"Damn right," said Sully. "Or I'd 'a got it outta your old man's hide."

"Can we talk to you, Mr. Sulaway?"

"What about?"

"Stone Coast Trust. I wanted to know if—"

"Not interested." Sully turned and shuffled back across the porch.

"Mr. Sulaway, I have a young lady here who'd like to ask—"

"Don't have no use for young ladies. Or old ladies, either." The screen door slammed shut behind him.

There was a silence. "Well," muttered Chase. "The old boy's definitely mellowed."

"I think he's afraid," said Miranda. "That's why he's not talking to us."

"Afraid of what?"

"Let's find out." She approached the cottage and called, "Mr. Sulaway? All we want to know is, are they trying to blackmail you? Has Stone Coast threatened you in some way?"

"Those are lies they're spreading!" Sulaway yelled through the screen door. "Vicious lies! Not true, any of it!"

"That's not what Tony Graffam says."

The door flew open and Sully stormed out onto the porch. "What's Graffam got to say about me? What's he tellin' people now?"

"We could stand out here and yell about it. Or we could talk in private. Which do you prefer?"

Sulaway glanced around, as though searching for watchers in the woods. Then he snapped, "Well? You two need an engraved invitation, or what?"

They followed him inside. Sully's kitchen was a dark little space, the windows closed in by trees, every shelf and countertop crammed full with junk and knickknacks. Newspapers were stacked in piles about the floor. The kitchen table was about the only unoccupied surface. They sat around it, in old ladder-back chairs that look dangerously close to collapse.

"Your brother's the one they was really pressurin'," Sully told Chase. "But Richard, he wasn't about to give in, no sir. He tells us, we gotta stick together. Says we can't sell, no matter how many letters they send us, how many lies they tell." Sully shook his head. "Didn't do no good. Just about everybody on this road went and signed on Graffam's dotted line, just like that. And Richard, look what went and happened to him. Hear he got himself poked with a knife."

Miranda saw Chase glance in her direction. Old Sully was so out of touch he didn't realize he was sitting with the very woman accused of plunging that knife into Richard Tremain.

"You said something about a letter," said Chase. "Telling you to sell. Did Graffam send it?"

"Wasn't signed. I hear none of 'em were."

"So Richard got a letter, as well?"

"I figure. So did Barretts down the way. Maybe everyone did. People wouldn't talk about 'em."

"What did the letter say? The one you got?"

"Lies. Mean, wicked lies...."

"And the one they sent Richard?"

Sully shrugged. "I wasn't privy to that."

Miranda glanced around the kitchen with its overflowing shelves. A pack rat, this Mr. Sulaway was. He kept things, junk and treasure both. She said, "Do you still have that letter?"

Sully hunched his shoulders, like a hermit crab about to retreat into its shell. He grunted. "Maybe."

"May we see it?"

"I dunno." He sighed, rubbed his face. "I dunno."

"We know they're lies, Mr. Sulaway. We just want to see what tactics they're using. We have to stop Graffam before he does any more damage."

For a moment Sully sat hunched and silent. Miranda thought he might not have heard what she said. But then he creaked to his feet and shuffled over to the kitchen counter. From the flour canister he pulled out a folded sheet of paper. He handed it to Miranda.

She laid it flat on the table.

"What really happened to Stanley? The Lula M knows. So do we."

Below those cryptic words was a handwritten note, penciled in. "Sell, Sully."

"Who's Stanley?" asked Miranda.

Sully had shrunk into his chair and was staring down at his leathery hands.

"Mr. Sulaway?"

The answer came out in a whisper. "My brother."

"What does that note refer to?"

"It was a long time ago...." Sully wiped his eyes, as though to clear away some mist clouding his vision. "Just an accident," he murmured. "Happens all the time out there. The sea, you can't trust her. Can't turn yer back on her...."

"What happened to Stanley?" asked Miranda gently.

"Got...got his boot caught in the trap line. Pulled him clean over the side. Water's cold in December. It'll freeze yer blood. I was aboard the *Sally M,* didn't see it." He turned, stared at the window. The trees outside seemed to close in upon the house, shutting it off from light, from warmth.

They waited.

He said softly. "I was the one found him. Draggin' in the water off *Lula*'s stern. I cut him loose…hauled him aboard…brought him to port." He shuddered. "That was it. Long time ago, fifty years. Maybe more.…"

"And this note?"

"It's a lie, got spread around after…"

"After what?"

"After I married Jessie." He paused. "Stanley's wife."

There it is, thought Miranda. The secret. The shame.

"Mr. Sulaway?" asked Chase quietly. "What did they have on Richard?"

Sully shook his head. "Didn't tell me."

"But they did have something?"

"Whatever it was, it didn't make him sell. Had a hard head, your brother. That's what got him in the end."

"Why didn't *you* sell, Mr. Sulaway?" Miranda asked.

The old man turned to her. "Because I won't," he said. She saw in his eyes the look of a man who's been backed into the last corner of his life. "Ain't no way they can scare me. Not now."

"Can't they?"

He shook his head. "I got cancer."

"Do you think he killed his brother?" asked Miranda.

They were walking along the road, through the dappled shade of pine and birch. Chase had his hands in his pockets, a frown on his brow. "What does it matter now, whether he did it or not?"

Yes, what did it matter? she wondered. The old man was about to face his final judgment. Innocent or guilty, he'd already lived fifty years with the consequences.

"It's hard to believe Graffam was able to dig up that story," said Miranda. "He's a newcomer to the island. What he had on Sully was fifty years old. How did Graffam find out about it?"

"Hired investigator?"

"And he used the name 'Sully' in that note. Remember? Only a local person would use that nickname."

"So he had a local informant. Someone with his finger on the island's pulse."

"Or someone in the business of knowing what goes on in this town," she added, thinking of Willie B. Rodell and the Alamo Detective Agency.

They came to a sign that read Harmony House.

"Used to be called Frenchman's Cottage," said Chase. "Until the hippies bought it." Down a rutted road they walked. They heard the tinkle of wind chimes before they saw the cottage. The sound floated through the trees, dancing on the breeze. The chimes were of iridescent glass, sparkling as they swayed from the porch overhang. The cottage door hung wide open.

"Anyone home?" called Chase.

At first only the wind chimes answered. Then, faintly, they heard the sound of laughter, approaching voices. Through the trees they saw them—two men and a woman, walking toward them.

None of the three was wearing a stitch.

The trio, spotting unexpected visitors, didn't seem in the least perturbed. The woman had wild hair generously streaked with gray, and an expression of placid indifference. The two men flanking her were equally shaggy and serene. One of the men, silver haired and weathered, seemed to be the official spokesperson. As his two companions went into the cottage, he came forward with his hand held out in greeting.

"You've found Harmony House," he said. "Or is this just a fortunate accident?"

"It's on purpose," said Chase, shaking the man's hand. "I'm Chase Tremain, Richard's brother. He owned Rose Hill Cottage, up the road."

"Ah, yes. The place with the weird vibes."

"Weird?"

"Vanna feels it whenever she gets close. Disharmonic waves. Tremors of dissonance."

"I must have missed it."

"Meat eaters usually do." The man looked at Miranda. He had

pale blue eyes and a gaze that was far too direct for comfort. "Does my natural state bother you?"

"No," she said. "It's just that I'm not used to..." Her gaze drifted downward, then snapped back to his face.

The man looked at her as though she were a creature to be pitied. "How far we've fallen from Eden," he said, sighing. He went to the porch railing and grabbed a sarong that had been hanging out to dry. "But the first rule of hospitality," he said, wrapping the cloth around his waist, "is to make your guests comfortable. So we'll just cover the family jewels." He motioned them into the cottage.

Inside, the woman, Vanna, now also draped in a sarong, sat cross-legged beneath a stained glass window. Her eyes were closed; her hands lay palm up on her knees. The other man knelt at a low table, rolling what appeared to be brown rice sushi. Potted plans were everywhere, thick as weeds. They blended right in with the Indonesian hangings, the dangling crystals, the smell of incense. The whole effect was jarred only by the fax machine in the corner.

Their host, who went by the surprisingly mundane name of Fred, poured rose hip tea and offered them carob cookies. They came to Maine every summer, he said, to reconnect with the earth. New York was purgatory, a place with one foot in hell. False people, false values. They worked there only because it kept them in touch with the common folk. Plus, they needed the income. For most of the year they tolerated the sickness of city life, breathing in the toxins, poisoning their bodies with refined sugars. Summers were for cleansing. And that was why they came here, why they left their jobs for two months every year.

"What *are* your jobs?" asked Miranda.

"We own the accounting firm of Nickels, Fay and Bledsoe. I'm Nickels."

"I'm Fay," said the man rolling sushi.

The woman, undoubtedly Bledsoe, continued to meditate in silence.

"So you see," said Fred Nickels, "there is no way we can be persuaded to sell. This land is a connection to our mother."

"Was it hers?" asked Chase.

"Mother Earth owns everything."

Chase cleared his throat. "Oh."

"We refuse to sell. No matter how many of those ridiculous letters they send us—"

Both Miranda and Chase sat up straight. "Letters?" they said simultaneously.

"We three have lived together for fifteen years. Perfect sexual harmony. No jealousy, no friction. All our friends know it. So it would hardly upset us to have our arrangement announced to the world."

"Is that what the letters threatened to do?" asked Miranda.

"Yes. 'Expose your deviant life-style' was the phrase, I think."

"You're not the only ones to get a letter," said Chase. "My hunch is, everyone on this road—everyone who didn't want to sell—got one in the mail."

"Well, they threatened the wrong people here. Deviant life-styles are exactly what we wish to promote. Am I right, friends?"

The man with the sushi looked up and said, "Ho."

"He agrees," said Fred.

"Was the letter signed?" asked Miranda.

"No. It was postmarked Bass Harbor, and it came to our house in New York."

"When?"

"Three, four months ago. It advised us to sell the camp. It didn't say to whom, specifically. But then we got the offer from Mr. Graffam, so I assumed he was behind it. I had Stone Coast Trust checked out. A few inquiries here and there, just to find out what I was dealing with. My sources say there's money involved. Graffam's just a front for a silent investor. My bet is it's organized crime."

"What would they want with Shepherd's Island?" asked Chase.

"New York's getting uncomfortable for 'em. Hotdog D.A.'s and all that. I think they're moving up the coast. And the north shore's just the foothold they'd want. Tourist industry's already booming up here. And look at this place! Ocean. Forest. No crime. Tell me some poor schlump from the city wouldn't pay good money to stay at a resort right here.''

"Did you ever meet Graffam?"

"He paid us a visit, to talk land deal. And we told him, in no uncertain terms, to—" Fred stopped, grinned "—fornicate with himself. I'm not sure he knew the meaning of the word."

"What kind of man is he?" asked Miranda.

Fred snorted. "Slick. Dumb. I mean, we're talking *really* stupid. The IQ of an eggplant. What idiot names a development Hemlock Heights? Might as well call it Poison Oak Estates." He shook his head. "I can't believe he got those other suckers to sell." He laughed. "You should meet him, Tremain. Tell me if you don't agree he's a throwback to our paramecium ancestors."

"A paramecium," said the woman, Bledsoe, briefly opening her eyes, "is far more advanced."

"Unfortunately," said Fred, "I'm afraid the rezoning is a fait accompli. Soon we'll be surrounded. Condos here, a Dunkin' Donuts there. The Cape Codification of Shepherd's Island." He paused. "And you know what? *That's* when we'll sell! My God, what a profit! We could buy a whole damn county up in the Allagash."

"The project could still be stopped," said Miranda. "They won't get their hands on Rose Hill. And the zoning could be reversed."

"Not a chance," said Fred. "We're talking tax income here. Conservation land brings in zilch for the island. But a nice little tourist resort? Hey, I'm a CPA. I know the powers of the almighty buck."

"There are people who'll fight it."

"Makes no difference." Fred sniffed appreciatively at his rose hip tea. The edges of his sarong had slipped apart and he sat with thighs naked. Incense smoke wafted about his grizzled head. "They can scream, protest. Lay their bodies before the bulldozers. But it's hopeless. There are things people just can't stop."

"A cynical answer," said Miranda.

"For cynical times."

"Well, they can't buy Rose Hill," said Miranda, rising to her feet. "And if organized crime's behind these purchases, you can bet the island will fight back. People here don't take well to mobsters. They don't take to outsiders, period."

Fred gazed up at her with a smile. "But *you* are an outsider, aren't you, Ms. Wood?"

"I'm not from this island. I came here a year ago."

"Yet they accepted *you*."

"No, they didn't." Miranda turned toward the door. She stood there for a moment, staring through the screen. Outside, the trees were swaying under a canopy of blue sky. "They never accepted me," she said softly. "And you know what?" She let out a long sigh of resignation. "I've only now come to realize it. They never will."

There was a third car parked in the driveway at Rose Hill.

They saw it as they walked up the last bend of the road—a late-model Saab with a gleaming burgundy finish. A glance through the car window revealed a spotless interior, not even a loose business card or candy wrapper on the leather upholstery.

The screen door squealed open and Miss St. John came out on the porch. "There you are," she said. "We have a visitor. Jill Vickery."

Of course, thought Miranda. Who else would manage to keep such an immaculate car?

Jill was standing amidst all the books, holding a box in her arms. She glanced at Miranda with a look of obvious surprise, but made no comment about her presence. "Sorry to pop in unannounced," she said. "I had to get a few records. Phillip and I are meeting the accountant tomorrow. You know, working out any tax problems for the transfer of the *Herald*."

Chase frowned. "You found the financial records here?"

"Just last month's worth. I couldn't find them back in the office, so I figured he'd brought them out here to work on. I was right."

"Where were they?" asked Chase. "We've combed all through his files. I never saw them."

"They were upstairs. The nightstand drawer." How she knew where to look was something she didn't bother to explain. She glanced around the front room. "You've certainly torn the place apart. What are you looking for? Hidden treasure?"

"Any and all files on Stone Coast Trust," said Chase.

"Yes, Annie mentioned you were dogging that angle. Personally, I think it's a dead end." Coolly she turned to look at Miranda. "And how are things going for you?" It was merely a polite question, carrying neither warmth nor concern.

"Things are...difficult," said Miranda.

"I can imagine. I hear you're staying with Annie these days."

"Only temporarily."

Jill flashed her one of those ironic smiles. "It's rather inconvenient, actually. The trial was going to be Annie's story. And now you're living with her. I'll have to pull her off it. Objective reporting and all."

"No one at the *Herald* could possibly be objective," Chase pointed out.

"I suppose not." Jill shifted the box in her arms. "Well, I'd better be going. Let you get on with your search."

"Ms. Vickery?" called Miss St. John. "I wonder if you could shed some light on an item we found here."

"Yes?"

"It's a note, from someone named M." Miss St. John handed her the slip of paper. "Miranda here didn't write it. Do you know who did?"

Jill read the note without any apparent emotion, not even a twitch of her perfect eyebrow. Miranda thought, *If only I had an ounce of her style, her poise.*

"It's not dated. So..." Jill looked up. "I can think of several possibilities. None of them had that particular initial. But M could stand for a nickname. Or just the word *me.*"

"Several possibilities?"

"Yes." Jill glanced uneasily at Miranda. "Richard, he...had

his attractions. Especially for the female summer interns. There
was that one we had last year. Before you were hired, Miranda.
Her name was Chloe something or other. Couldn't write worth a
damn, but she was good decoration. And she picked up interviews
no one else could get, which drove poor Annie up a wall." Jill
looked again at the note. "This was typed on a manual typewriter.
See? The *e* loop's smudged, key needs to be cleaned. If I remember right, Chloe always worked on an old manual. The only one
in the office who couldn't compose on a computer keyboard."
She gave the note back to Miss St. John. "It could have been
her."

"Whatever happened to Chloe?" asked Chase.

"What you'd expect to happen. Some hot and heavy flirting. A
few fireworks. And then, just another broken heart."

Miranda felt her throat tighten, her face flush. None of them
was looking directly at her, but she knew she was the focus of
their attention, as surely as if they were staring. She went to the
window and found herself gripping the curtain, fighting to keep
her head erect, her spine straight. Another broken heart. It made
her feel like some object on an assembly line, just another stupid,
gullible woman. It's what they thought of her.

It's what she thought of herself.

Jill again shifted her box of papers. "I'd better get back to the
office or the mice will play." She went to the door, then stopped.
"Oh, I almost forgot to tell you, Chase. Annie just heard the
news."

"What news?" asked Chase.

"Tony Graffam's back in town."

Miranda didn't react. She heard Jill go down the porch steps,
heard the Saab's engine roar to life, the tires crunch away across
the gravel. She felt Chase and Miss St. John's gaze on her back.
They were watching her in silence, an unbearable, pitying silence.

She pushed open the screen door and fled from the cottage.

Halfway across the field Chase caught up to her. He grabbed
her arm and pulled her around to face him. "Miranda—"

"Leave me alone!"

"You can't run away from it—"

"If only I could!" she cried. "Jill said it! I'm just another broken heart. Another dumb woman who got exactly what she deserved."

"You didn't deserve it."

"Damn you, Chase, don't feel sorry for me! I can't stand that, either." She broke free and started to turn away. He pulled her back. This time he held on, got a tight grip on each wrist. She found herself staring into his dark, inescapable eyes.

"I don't feel sorry for you," he shot back. "You don't get my pity, Miranda. Because you're too good for it. You've got more going for you than any woman I've met. Okay, you're naive. And gullible. We all start out that way. You've learned from it, fine. You should. You want to kick yourself, and maybe it's well deserved. But don't overdo it. Because I think Richard fell just as hard for you as you fell for him."

"Is that supposed to make me feel better?"

"I'm not trying to make you feel better. I'm just telling you what I think."

"Right." Her laughter was self-mocking. "That I'm one notch above a bimbo?" Again she tried to pull free. Again he held her tight.

"No," he said quietly. "What I'm saying is this. I know you're not the first. I know Richard had a lot of women. I've met a few of them through the years. Some of them were gorgeous. Some of them were talented, even brilliant. But out of all those women—and they were, each and every one of them, exceptional—you're the only one I could see him really falling for."

"Out of all those *gorgeous* women?" She shook her head and laughed. "Why me?"

Quietly he said, "Because you're the one *I'd* fall for."

At once she went still. He stared down at her, his dark hair stirring in the wind, his face awash in sunlight. She heard her own quick breaths, heard her heartbeat pounding in her ears. He released her wrists. She didn't move, even when his arms circled behind her, even as he drew her hard against him. She scarcely had the breath to whimper before he settled his mouth firmly on hers.

At the first touch of his lips she was lost. The sun seemed to spin overhead, a dizzying view of brightness against a field of blue. And then there was only him, all rough edges and shadows, his dark head blotting out the sky, his mouth stealing away her breath. She wavered for an instant between resistance and surrender. Then she found herself reaching up and around his neck, opening her lips to his eager assault, pressing more eagerly against the bite of his teeth. She drank him in, his taste, his warmth. Through the roaring in her ears she heard his low groans of satisfaction and need, ever more need. How quickly she had yielded, how easily she had fallen—the woman mastered first by one brother, and now the other.

The day's unbearable brightness seemed to flood her eyes as she pulled away. Her cheeks were blazing. The buzz of insects in the field and the rustle of grass in the wind were almost lost in the harsh sound of her own breathing.

"I won't be passed around, Chase," she said. "I won't."

Then she turned and stalked across the field. She headed back to the cottage, her feet stirring the perfume of sun-warmed grass. She knew he was following somewhere behind, but this time he made no attempt to catch up. She walked alone, and the brightness of the afternoon, the dancing wildflowers, the floating haze of dandelion fuzz only seemed to emphasize her own wretchedness.

Miss St. John was standing on the porch. With scarcely a nod to the other woman, Miranda walked right past her and into the cottage. Inside, she went straight to the bookcase, grabbed another armful of books from the shelf and sat on the floor. She was single-mindedly flipping through the pages when she heard footsteps come up the porch.

"It's not a good time for an argument, Chase," she heard Miss St. John say.

"I'm not planning to argue."

"You have that look in your eye. For heaven's sake, cool down. Stop. Take a deep breath."

"With all due respect, Miss St. John, you're *not* my mother."

"All right, I'm not your mother!" Miss St. John snapped. As she stomped away down the steps, she muttered, "But I can see when a man sorely needs my advice!"

The screen door slapped shut. Chase stood just inside the threshold, gazing at Miranda. "You took it the wrong way," he said.

Miranda looked up at him. "Did I?"

"What happened between you and Richard is a separate issue. A dead issue. It has nothing to do with you and me."

She snapped the book shut. "It has everything to do with you and me."

"But you make it sound like I'm just—just picking up the affair where he left off."

"Okay, maybe it's not that bald. Maybe you're not even aware you're doing it." She reached for another book and stubbornly focused on the pages as she flipped through it. "But we both know Richard was the golden boy of the family. The one who had it all, inherited everything. You were the Tremain who didn't even get a decent trust fund. Well, if you can't inherit a newspaper or a fortune, at least you can inherit your brother's cast-off mistress. Or, gee, maybe even his wife. Just think. Evelyn wouldn't even have to go to the trouble of changing her last name."

"Are you finished?"

"Definitely."

"Good. Because I don't think I can stand here and listen to that garbage any longer. First of all, I'm not in the least bit interested in my sister-in-law. I never was. When Richard married her, I had to stop myself from sending him my condolences. Second, I don't give a damn who gets the *Herald.* I sure as hell never wanted the job. The paper was Richard's baby, from the start. And third—" He paused and took a deep breath, as though drawing the courage to say what had to be said. "Third," he said quietly, "I'm not a Tremain."

She looked up at him sharply. "What are you saying? You're Richard's brother, aren't you?"

"His half brother."

"You mean…" She stared into those Gypsy eyes, saw herself reflected in irises dark as coals.

Chase nodded. "My father knew. I don't think Mother ever told him, exactly. She didn't have to. He could just look at me and see it." He smiled, a bitter, ironic smile. "Funny that I myself never did. All the time I was growing up, I didn't understand why I couldn't match up to Richard. No matter how hard I tried, he was the one who got Dad's attention. My mother tried to make up for it. She was my very best friend, right up until she died. And then it was just the three of us." He sank into a chair and rubbed his forehead, as though trying to massage away the memories.

"When did you learn?" Miranda asked softly. "That he wasn't your father?"

"Not until years later, when Dad was dying. He had one of those cliché deathbed confessions. Only he didn't tell *me*. He told Richard. Even at the very end, Richard was the privileged one." Wearily Chase leaned back, his head pressed against the cushions, his gaze focused on the ceiling. "Later they read the will. I couldn't understand why I'd been essentially cut out. Oh, he left me enough to get me started in business. But that was it. I thought it had to do with my marriage, the fact Dad had opposed it from the start. I was hurt, but I accepted it. My wife didn't. She got in a shouting match with Richard, started yelling that it wasn't fair. Richard lost his cool and let it all out. The big secret. The fact his brother was a bastard."

"Is that when you left the island?"

He nodded. "I came back once or twice, to humor my wife. After we got divorced it seemed like my last link to this place had been cut. So I stayed away. Until now."

They fell silent. He seemed lost in bad memories, old hurts. *No wonder I could never find any hint of Richard in his face,* she thought. *He's not a Tremain at all. He's his own man, the sort of man Richard could never be.*

The sort of man I could love.

He felt her studying him, sensed she was reaching out to him. Abruptly he rose to his feet and moved with studied indifference toward the screen door. There he stood looking out at the field. "Maybe you were right," he said.

"About what?"

"That what happened between you and Richard is still hanging over us."

"And if it is?"

"Then this is a mistake. You, me. It's the wrong reason to get involved."

She looked down, unwilling to reveal, even to the stiffly turned back, the hurt in her eyes. "Then we shouldn't, should we?" she murmured.

"No." He turned to face her. She found her gaze drawn, almost against her will, to meet his. "The truth is, Miranda, we have too many reasons not to. What's happened between us has been..." He shrugged. "It was an attraction, that's all."

That's all. Nothing, really, in the larger context of life. Not something you risked your heart on.

"Still..." he said.

"Yes?" She looked up with a sudden, insane leap of hope.

"We can't walk away from each other. Not with all that's happened. Richard's death. The fire." He gestured about the book-strewn room. "And this."

"You don't trust me. Yet you want my help?"

"You're the only one with stakes high enough to see this through."

She gave a tired laugh. "You got that part right." She wrapped her arms around herself. "So, what comes next?"

"I'll go have a talk with Tony Graffam."

"Shall I come?"

"No. I want to check him out on my own. In the meantime, you can finish up here. There's still the upstairs."

Miranda gazed around the room, at the dusty piles of books, the stacks of papers, and she shook her head. "If I just knew what I was looking for. What the burglar was looking for."

"I have a hunch it's still here somewhere."

"Whatever *it* is."

Turning, Chase pushed open the door. "When you find it, you'll know."

CHAPTER ELEVEN

Fred Nickels had said Tony Graffam was slick and dumb. He was right on both counts. Graffam wore a silk suit, a tie in blinding red paisley and a gold pinkie ring. The office, like the man, was all flash, little substance: plush carpet, spanking new leather chairs, but no secretary, no books on the shelves, no papers on the desk. The wall had only one decoration—a map of the north shore of Shepherd's Island. It was not labeled as such, but Chase needed only a glance at the broad, curving bay to recognize the coastline.

"I tell you, it's a witch-hunt!" Graffam complained. "First the police, now you." He stayed behind his desk, refusing to emerge even to shake hands, as though clinging to the polished barrier for protection. In agitation he slid his fingers through his tightly permed hair. "You think I'd go and waste someone? Just like that? And for what, a piece of property? Do I look dumb?"

Chase politely declined to answer that question. He said, "You were pressing an offer for Rose Hill Cottage, weren't you?"

"Well, of course. It's the prime lot up there."

"And my brother refused to sell."

"Look, I'm sorry about your brother. Tragedy, a real tragedy. Not that he and I were on good terms, you understand. I couldn't deal with him. He had a closed mind when it came to the project. I mean, he actually went and got hostile. I don't know why. It's only business, right?"

"But I was under the impression this wasn't a business deal, at all. Stone Coast Trust is billed as a conservation project."

"And that's exactly what it is. I offered your brother top dollar for that land, more than Nature Conservancy would've paid. Plus, he would've retained lifetime use of the family cottage. An incredible deal.''

"Incredible."

"With the addition of Rose Hill, we could extend the park all the way back to the hillside. It would add elevation. Views. Access.''

"Access?"

"For maintenance, of course. You know, for the hiking trails. Decent footpaths, so everyone could enjoy a taste of nature. Even the handicapped. I mean, mobility impaired.''

"You thought of everything."

Graffam smiled. "Yes. We did."

"Where does Hemlock Heights come in?"

Graffam paused. "Excuse me?"

"Hemlock Heights. That is, I believe, the name of your planned development.''

"Well, nothing was *planned*—"

"Then why did you apply for rezoning? And how much did you pay to bribe the land commission?''

Graffam's face had gone rigid. "Let me repeat myself, Mr. Tremain. Stone Coast Trust was formed to protect the north shore. I admit, we might have to develop a parcel here and there, just to maintain the trust. But sometimes we have to compromise. We have to do things we'd rather not.''

"Does that include blackmail?"

Graffam sat up sharply. "What?"

"I'm talking about Fred Nickels. And Homer Sulaway. The names should be familiar to you.''

"Yes, of course. Two of the property owners. They declined my offer.''

"Someone sent them nasty letters, telling them to sell."

"You think I sent them?"

"Who else? Four people turned you down. Two of them got threatening letters. And a third—my brother—winds up dead.''

"That's what you're leading up to, isn't it? Trying to make it look like I had something to do with his death.''

"Is that what I said?"

"Look, I've taken enough heat on this deal. A year of putting up with this—this small-town crap. I've turned handsprings to make this project work, but I'm not going to be his fall guy."

Chase stared at Graffam in confusion. What was the man babbling about? Whose fall guy?

"I was out of state when it happened. I have witnesses who'll swear to that."

"Who are you working for?" Chase cut in.

Graffam's jaw suddenly snapped shut. Slowly he sat back, his expression hardening to stone.

"So you have a backer," said Chase. "Someone who's put up the money. Someone who's doing the dirty work. Who are you fronting for? The mob?"

Graffam said nothing.

"You're scared, Graffam. I can tell."

"I don't have to answer any of your questions."

Chase pressed the attack. "My brother was set to blow the whistle on Stone Coast, wasn't he? So you sent him one of your threatening letters. But then you found out he couldn't be blackmailed. Or bought off. So what did you do? Pay someone to take care of the problem?"

"Meaning murder?" Graffam burst out laughing. "Come on, Tremain. A broad killed him. We both know that. Dangerous creatures, broads. Tick 'em off and they get ideas. They see red, grab a kitchen knife and that's it. Even the cops agree. It was a broad. She had the motive."

"And you had a lot of money to lose. So did your backer. Richard already had his hands on your account numbers. He traced your invisible partner. He could have exposed the deal—"

"But he didn't. He killed the article, remember? I had it on good authority it was gonna stay dead. So why should we go after him?"

Chase fell silent. That's what Jill had said, that Richard was the one who'd canceled the article, called off the crusade. It was the one detail that didn't make sense. Why had Richard backed down?

Did he back down? Or had Jill Vickery lied?

He brooded over that last possibility as he left Graffam's office and walked to the car. What did he know about Jill, really? Only that she'd been with the *Herald* for five years, that she kept it running smoothly. That she was bright, stylish and underpaid. She could land a better job anywhere on the East Coast. Why had she chosen to stay with this Podunk paper and work for slave wages?

He'd planned to return at once to Rose Hill Cottage. Instead, he drove to the *Herald.*

He found the office manned only by a skeleton crew: the summer intern, tapping at a computer keyboard, and the layout tech, stooped over a drawing table. Chase walked past them, into Richard's office, and went straight to the file cabinet.

He found Jill Vickery's employment file right where it should be. He sat at the desk and opened the folder.

Inside was a neatly typed résumé, three pages, all the right names and jobs. B.A., Bowdoin, 1977. Masters, Columbia, 1979. Stints on the city desk, *San Francisco Chronicle;* then obits, *San Diego Union;* police beat, *San Jose Times;* op-ed editor, *Portland Press Herald.* A solid résumé.

So why does she end up here?

Something about that résumé bothered him. Something that didn't seem quite right. It was enough to make him reach for the phone and dial the *Portland Press Herald,* her previous employer. He spoke to the current op-ed editor, a woman who vaguely recalled a Jill Vickery. It had been a while back, though.

Chase next called the *San Jose Times.* This time there was some uncertainty, a lot of yelling around the city room, asking if anyone remembered a reporter named Jill Vickery from seven years before. Someone yelled, wasn't there a Jill on the police beat years back? That was good enough for Chase. He hung up and considered letting it drop.

Still, that résumé. What was it that bothered him?

The obits. *San Diego Union.* That didn't make sense. Obits was the coal mine equivalent of the newspaper business. You worked your way up from there. Why had she gone from the city desk in San Francisco to a bottom-of-the-barrel position?

He dialed the *San Diego Union*. No one named Jill Vickery had ever worked there.

Ditto for San Francisco.

Half the résumé was a fraud. Was it just a case of padding a thin work history? And what was she doing during those eight years between college and her job with the *San Jose Times?*

Once again he reached for the phone. This time he called Columbia University, Department of Journalism. In any given year, how many students could possibly graduate with a master's degree? And how many of these students would have the first name Jill?

There was only one in 1979, they told him. But it wasn't a Jill Vickery who'd graduated. It was a Jill Westcott.

Once again, he called the *San Diego Union*. This time he asked about a Jill Westcott. This time they remembered the name. We'll fax you the article, they said.

A few minutes later it slid out of the fax machine, sharp and clear.

A photo of Jill Westcott, now named Jill Vickery. And with it was a tale of cold-blooded murder.

Miranda sat in the fading light of day and stared listlessly at her surroundings. She'd spent the afternoon rummaging through the bathroom and two bedrooms. Now she was hot, dusty and discouraged. Nothing of substance had turned up, only innocuous bits of paper—store receipts, a ten-year-old postcard from Spain, another typewritten note from M.

...I am not the weak little nothing I used to be. I can live without you quite nicely, and I intend to do so. I don't need your pity. I am not like the others, those women with minds the size of walnut shells. What I want to know, what I don't understand, is what attracts you to creatures like that? Is it the jiggling flesh? The cow-eyed worship? Well, it doesn't mean a thing. It's empty devotion. Without your money, you wouldn't rate a second glance from those bimbos. I'm the only one who doesn't give a damn how much you have in the bank. And now you've lost me.

The bitterness, the pain of that letter seemed to rub off on her own mood. She put it back in the drawer, buried it among the silky underclothes. Another woman's lingerie. Another woman's anguish.

By the time she'd straightened up the room again the afternoon had slid toward twilight. She didn't turn on the lamp. It was soothing, the veil of semidarkness, the chirp of crickets through the open window. From the field came that indefinable scent of evening—the mist from the sea, the cooling grasses. She went to a chair by the window, sat down and leaned her head back to rest. So many doubts, so many worries weighed upon her. Always, looming over every tentative moment of joy, was that threat of prison. There were times, during these past few days of freedom, that she had almost been able to push the thought from mind. But in the moments like this, when the silence was deep and she was alone in her fears, the image of prison bars seemed to close around her. *How many years will they keep me? Ten, twenty, a lifetime? I would rather die.*

She shuddered back to alertness.

Downstairs, the screen door had softly squealed open.

"Chase?" she called. "Is that you?" There was silence. She rose from the chair and went to the top of the stairs. "Chase?"

She heard the screen door softly tap shut, then there was nothing, only the distant chirp of crickets from the fields.

Her first instinct was to reach for the light switch. Just in time she stopped herself. Darkness was her friend. It would hide her, protect her.

She shrank away from the stairs. Trembling, she stood with her back pressed against the wall and listened. No new sounds drifted up from the first floor. All she heard was the hammering of her own heartbeat. Her palms were slick. Every nerve ending was scraped raw with fear.

There it was—a footstep. In the kitchen. An image shot through her mind. The cabinets, the drawers. The knives.

Her breath was coming in tight gasps. She shrank farther from the stairs, her thoughts flying frantically toward escape. Two upstairs bedrooms, plus a bathroom. 'And screens on all the windows. Could she make it through in time?

From below came more footsteps. The intruder had moved out of the kitchen. He was approaching the stairs.

Miranda fled into the master bedroom. Darkness obscured her path; she collided with a nightstand. A lamp wobbled, fell over. The clatter as it crashed to the floor was all the intruder needed to direct him toward this bedroom.

In panic she dashed to the window. Through the darkness she saw a portion of gently sloping roof. From there it would be a twenty-foot drop to the ground. The sash was already up. Only the screen stood between her and freedom. She shoved at it—and it refused to push free. Only then did she see that the screen had been nailed to the window frame.

Frantic now, she began to kick at the steel mesh, sobbing as each blow met resistance. Again and again she kicked, and each time the wire sagged outward, but held.

A footstep creaked on the stairway.

She aimed a last desperate kick at the mesh.

The window frame splintered, and the whole screen fell away and thudded to the ground. At once she scrambled over the sill and dropped down onto the ledge of roof. There she hesitated, torn between the solid comfort of shingles beneath her feet and the free-fall of escape. She couldn't see what lay directly below. The rosebushes? She grabbed hold of the roof and lowered her body over the edge. For a few seconds she clung there, steeling herself for the impact.

She let go.

The night air rushed up at her. The fall seemed endless, a hurtling downward through space and darkness.

Her feet slammed into the ground. Instantly her legs buckled, and she fell sprawling to the gravel. For a moment she lay there as the sky whirled overhead like a kaleidoscope of stars. A frantic burst of adrenaline had masked all the sensation of pain. Her legs could be shattered. She wouldn't have felt it. She knew only that she had to escape, had to run.

She staggered to her feet and began to stumble down the road. She rounded the bend of the driveway—

And was instantly blinded by a pair of headlights leaping at her from the darkness. Instinctively she raised her arms to shield her eyes against the onslaught. She heard the car's brakes lock, heard gravel fly under the skidding tires. The door swung open.

"Miranda?"

With a sob of joy she stumbled forward into Chase's arms. "It's you," she cried. "Thank God it's you."

"What is it?" he whispered, pulling her close against him. "Miranda, what's happened?"

She clung to the solid anchor of his chest. "He's there—in the cottage—"

"Who?"

Suddenly, through the darkness, they both heard it: the slam of the back door, the thrash of running footsteps through the brush.

"Get in the car!" ordered Chase. "Lock the doors!"

"What?"

He gave her a push. "Just do it!"

"Chase!" she yelled.

"I'll be back!"

Stunned, she watched him melt into the night, heard his footsteps thud away. Her instinct was to follow him, to stay close in case he needed her. But already she'd lost sight of him and could make out nothing but the towering shadows of trees against the starry sky, and beneath them, a darkness so thick it seemed impenetrable.

Do what he says!

She climbed into the car, locked the doors and felt instantly useless. While she sat here in safety Chase could be fighting for his life.

And what good will I do him?

She pushed open the door and scrambled out of the car, around to the rear.

In the trunk she found a tire iron. It felt heavy and solid in her grasp. It would even the odds against any opponent. Any unarmed opponent, she was forced to amend.

She turned, faced the forest. It loomed before her, a wall of shadow and formless threat.

Somewhere in that darkness Chase was in danger.

She gripped the tire iron more tightly and started off into the night.

The crash of footsteps through the underbrush alerted Chase that his quarry had shifted direction. Chase veered right, in pursuit of the sound. Branches thrashed his face, bushes clawed at his trousers. The darkness was so dense under the trees that he felt like a blind man stumbling through a landscape of booby traps.

At least his quarry would be just as blind. *But maybe not as helpless,* he thought, ducking under a pine branch. *What if he's armed? What if I'm being led into a trap?*

It's a risk I have to take.

The footsteps moved to the left of him. By slivers of starlight filtering through the trees Chase caught a glimpse of movement. That was all he could make out, shadow moving through shadow. Heedless of the branches whipping his face he plunged ahead and found himself snagged in brambles. The shadow zigzagged, flitting in and out of the cover of trees. Chase pulled free of the thicket and resumed his pursuit. He was gaining. He could hear, through the pounding of his heart, the hard breathing of his quarry. The shadow was just ahead, just beyond the next curtain of branches.

Chase mustered a last burst of speed and broke through, into a clearing. There he came to a halt.

His quarry had vanished. There was no movement, no sound, only the whisper of wind through the treetops. A flutter of shadow off to his right made him whirl around. Nothing there. He halted in confusion as he heard the crackle of underbrush to his left. He turned, listening for footsteps, trying to locate his quarry. Was that breathing, somewhere close by? No, the wind....

Again, that crackle of twigs. He moved forward, one step, then another.

Too late he felt the rush of air, the hiss of the branch as it swung its arc toward his head.

The blow pitched him forward. He reached out to cushion the fall, felt the bite of pine needles, the slap of wet leaves as he scraped across the forest floor. He tried to cling to consciousness, to order his body to rise to its feet and face the enemy. It refused to obey. Already he saw the darkness thicken before his eyes. He wanted to curse, to rail in fury at his own helplessness. But all he could manage was a groan.

Pain. The pounding of a jackhammer in his head. Chase ordered it to stop, demanded it stop, but it kept beating away at his brain.

"He's coming around," said a voice.

Then another voice, softer, fearful. "Chase? Chase?"

He opened his eyes and saw Miranda gazing down at him. The lamplight shimmered in her tumbled hair, washed like liquid gold across her cheek. Just the sight of her seemed to quiet the aching in his head. He struggled to remember where he was, how he had gotten there. An image of darkness, the shadow of trees, still lingered.

Abruptly he tried to sit up, and caught a spinning view of other people, other faces in the room.

"No," said Miranda. "Don't move. Just lie still."

"Someone—someone out there—"

"He's gone. We've already searched the woods," said Lorne Tibbetts.

Chase settled back on the couch. He knew where he was now. Miss St. John's cottage. He recognized the chintz fabric, the jungle of plants. And the dog. The panting black mop sat near one end of the couch, watching him. Or was it? With all that hair, who could say if the beast even had eyes? Slowly Chase's gaze shifted to the others in the room. Lorne. Ellis. Miss St. John. And Dr. Steiner, wielding his trusty penlight.

"Pupils look fine. Equal and reactive," said Dr. Steiner.

"Take that blasted thing away," Chase groaned, batting at the penlight.

Dr. Steiner snorted. "Can't do much damage to a head as hard as his." He set a bottle of pills on the end table. "For the headache. May make you a little drowsy, but it'll cut the pain." He snapped his bag shut and headed for the door. "Call me in the morning. But not too early. And may I remind you—all of you— I do not, repeat, do *not* make house calls!" The door slammed shut behind him.

"What wonderful bedside manner," moaned Chase.

"You remember anything?" asked Lorne.

Chase managed to sit up. The effort sent a bolt of pain into his skull. At once he dropped his head into his hands. "Not a damn thing," he mumbled.

"Didn't see his face?"

"Just a shadow."

Lorne paused. "You sure there was someone there?"

"Hey, I didn't imagine the headache." Chase grabbed the pill bottle, fumbled the cap off and gulped two tablets down, dry. "Someone hit me."

"A man? Woman?" pressed Lorne.

"I never saw him. Her. Whatever."

Lorne turned to Miranda. "He was unconscious when you found him?"

"Coming around. I heard his groans."

"Pardon me for asking, Ms. Wood. But can I see that tire iron you were carrying?"

"What?"

"The tire iron. You had it earlier."

Miss St. John sighed. "Don't be ridiculous, Lorne."

"I'm just being thorough. I have to look at it."

Without a word Miranda fetched the tire iron from the porch and brought it back to Lorne. "No blood, no hair," she said tightly. "I wasn't the one who hit him."

"No, I guess not," said Lorne.

"Jill Vickery," Chase muttered.

Lorne glanced at him. "Who?"

The pain in Chase's head suddenly gave way to a clear memory of that afternoon. "It's not her real name. Check with the San Diego police, Lorne. It may or may not tie in. But you'll find she has an arrest record."

"For what?"

Chase raised her head. "She killed her lover."

They all stared at him.

"*Jill?*" said Miranda. "When did you find this out?"

"This afternoon. It happened ten, eleven years ago. She was acquitted. Justifiable homicide. She claimed he'd threatened her life."

"How does this fit in with anything else?" asked Lorne.

"I'm not sure. All I know is, half her job résumé was pure fiction. Maybe Richard found out. If he did—and confronted her…"

Lorne turned to Miss St. John. "I need to use your telephone."

"In the kitchen."

Lorne spent only a few minutes on the phone. He emerged from the kitchen shaking his head. "Jill Vickery's at home. Says she was home all evening."

"It's only a half-hour drive to town," said Miss St. John. "She could have made it, barely."

"Assuming her car was right nearby. Assuming she could slip right behind the wheel and take off." He looked at Ellis. "You checked up and down the road?"

Ellis nodded. "No strange cars. No one saw nothin'."

"Well," said Lorne, "whoever it was, I don't think he'll be back." He reached for his hat. "Take my advice, Chase. Don't drive anywhere tonight. You're in no shape to get behind a wheel."

Chase gave a tired laugh. "I wasn't planning to."

"I can take him up to the cottage," said Miranda. "I'll keep an eye on him."

Lorne paused and looked first at Miranda, then at Chase. If he had doubts about the arrangement, he didn't express them. He simply said, "You do that, Ms. Wood. You keep a *good* eye on him." Motioning to Ellis, he opened the door. "We'll be in touch."

CHAPTER TWELVE

Light spilled from the hallway across the pine floor of the bedroom. Miranda pulled down the coverlet and said, "Come on, lie down. Doctor's orders."

"To hell with doctors. That doctor, anyway," growled Chase. He sat on the side of the bed and gave his head a shake, as though to clear it. "I'm okay. I feel fine."

She regarded his battered, unshaven face. "You look like a truck ran over you."

"The brutal truth!" He laughed. "Are you always so damn honest?"

There was a silence. "Yes," she said quietly. "As a matter of fact, I am."

He looked up at her. *What do you see in my eyes?* she wondered. *Sincerity? Or lies, bald, dangerous lies?*

It's still not there, is it? Trust. There'll always be that doubt between us.

She sat beside him on the bed. "Tell me everything you learned today. About Jill."

"Only what I read in the press file from San Diego." He reached down and began to pull off his shoes. "The trial got a fair amount of coverage. You know, sex, violence. Circulation boosters."

"What happened?"

"The defense claimed she was an emotionally battered woman. That she was young, naive, vulnerable. That her boyfriend was an abusive alcoholic who regularly beat her up. The jury believed it."

"What did the prosecution say?"

"That Jill had a lifelong hatred of men. That she used them, manipulated them. And when her lover tried to leave her, she flew into a rage. Both sides agreed on the facts of the killing. That while her lover was passed out drunk she picked up a gun, put it to his head and pulled the trigger.'' Exhausted, Chase lay back on the pillows. The pills were taking effect. His eyelids were already drifting shut. ''That was ten years ago,'' he said. ''An era Jill conveniently left behind when she came to Maine.''

''Did Richard know all this?''

''If he bothered to check, he did. Only the last half of her résumé was true. Richard may have been so dazzled by the whole package he didn't bother to confirm much beyond the last job or two. Or he may have found out the truth only recently. Who knows?''

Miranda sat thinking, trying to picture Jill as she must have been ten years ago. Young, vulnerable. Afraid.

Like me.

Or was the prosecution's description a more accurate image? A man hater, a woman of twisted passions?

That's how they'll try to portray me. As a killer. And some people will believe it.

Chase had fallen asleep.

For a moment she sat beside him, listening to his slow and even breaths, wondering if he could ever learn to trust her. If she could ever be more to him than just a piece of the puzzle—the puzzle of his brother's death.

She rose and pulled the coverlet over his sleeping form. He didn't move. Gently she smoothed back his hair, stroked the beard-roughened cheek. Still he didn't move.

She left him and went downstairs. The boxes of papers confronted her, other bits and pieces of that puzzle. She separated them into files. Article files. Financial records. Personal notes from M, as well as from other, unidentified women. The miscellaneous debris of a man's life. How little she had known Richard! What a vast part of him he had kept private, even from his family. That's why he had so jealously guarded this north shore retreat.

In the fabric of his life, I was just a single, unimportant thread. Will I ever stop hurting from that?

She rose and checked the doors, the windows. Then she went back upstairs, to the master bedroom.

Chase was still asleep. She knew she should use the other room, the other bed, but tonight she didn't want to lie alone in the darkness. She wanted warmth and safety and the comfort of knowing Chase was nearby.

She had promised to look after him tonight. What better place to watch over him than in the same bed?

She lay down beside him, not close but near enough to imagine his warmth seeping toward her through the sheets.

Sometime during the night the dreams came.

A man, a lover, was holding her. Protecting her. Then she looked up at his face and saw he was a stranger. She pulled away, began to run. She found she was in a crowd of people. She began to search for a familiar face, a pair of arms she could reach out to, but they were all strangers, all strangers.

And then there he was, standing far beyond her reach. She cried out to him, held her hands out for him to grab. He moved toward her and her hands connected with warm and solid flesh. She heard him say, "I'm here, Miranda. Right here...."

And he was.

Through the semidarkness she saw the gleam of his face, the twin shadows of his eyes. His gaze was so still, so very quiet. Her breath caught as he took her face in his hands. Slowly he pressed his lips to hers. That one touch sent a shudder of pleasure through her body. They stared at each other and the night seemed filled with the sounds of their breathing.

Again, he kissed her.

Again, that wave of pleasure. It crested to a wanting for more, more. Her sleep-drugged body awoke, alive with hunger. She pressed hard against him, willing their bodies to meld, their warmth to mingle, but that frustrating barrier of clothes still lay between them.

He reached for her T-shirt. Slowly he pulled it up and over her head, let it drop from the bed. She was not so patient. Already she was undoing his buttons, sliding back his shirt, fumbling at his belt buckle. No words were spoken; none were needed. The soft whispers, the whimpers, the moans said more than any words could have.

So did his hands. His fingers slid across, between, inside all the warm and secret places of her body. They teased her, inflamed her, brought her to the very edge of release. Then, with knowing cruelty, they abandoned her, leaving her unsatisfied. She reached out to him, silently pleading for more.

He grasped her hips and willingly thrust into her again, but this time not with his fingers.

She cried out, a sound of joy, of delight.

At the first ripple of her climax he let his own needs take over. Needs that made him drive deep inside her, again and again. As her last wave of pleasure washed through her, he found his own cresting, breaking. He rode it to the very end and collapsed, sweating and triumphant, into her welcoming arms.

And so they fell asleep.

Chase was the first to awaken. He found his arms looped around her, his face buried in the sweet-smelling strands of her hair. She was curled up on her side, facing away from him, the silky skin of her back pressed against his chest. The memory of their love-making was at once so vivid he felt his body respond with automatic desire. And why not, with this woman in his arms? She was life and lust and honeyed warmth. She was everything a woman should be.

And I'm treading on dangerous ground.

He pulled away and sat up. Morning light shone through the window, onto her pillow. So innocent she looked, so untouched by evil. It occurred to him that Jill Vickery once must have looked as pure.

Before she shot her lover.

Dangerous women. How could you tell them from the innocents?

He left the bed and went straight to the shower. Wash the magical spell away, he thought. Wash away the desire, the craving for Miranda Wood. She was like a sickness in his blood, making him do insane things.

Last night, for instance.

They had simply fallen into it, he told himself. A physical act, that was all, a chance collision of two warm bodies.

He watched her sleep as he dressed. With each layer of clothes he felt more protected, more invulnerable. But when she stirred and opened her eyes and smiled at him, he realized how thin his emotional armor really was.

"How are you feeling this morning?" she asked softly.

"Much better, thanks. I think I can drive myself back to town."

There was a silence. Her smile faded as she took in the fact he was already dressed. "You're leaving?"

"Yes. I just wanted to make sure you got out of here safely."

She sat up. Hugging the sheets to her chest, she watched him for a moment, as though trying to understand what had gone wrong between them. At last she said, "I'll be fine. You don't have to wait around."

"I'll stay. Until you get dressed."

A shrug was her response, as if it didn't matter to her one way or the other. *Good,* he thought. *No sticky emotions over last night. We're both too smart for that.*

He started to leave, then stopped. "Miranda?"

"Yes?"

He turned to look at her. She was still hugging her knees, still every bit as bewitching. To see her there could break any man's heart. He said, "It's not that I don't think you're a wonderful woman. It's just that…"

"Don't worry about it, Chase," she said flatly. "We both know it won't work."

He wanted to say, "I'm sorry," but somehow it seemed too lame, too easy. They were both adults. They had both made a mistake.

There was nothing more to be said.

"It's not as if any of this is incriminating," said Annie, flipping through the notes from M that were arrayed on her kitchen table. "Just your routine desperate-woman language. Darling. If you'd only see me. If only this, if only that. It's pathetic, but it's not murderous. It doesn't tell us that M—whoever she is—killed him."

"You're right." Miranda sighed, leaning back in the kitchen chair. "And it doesn't seem to tie in with Jill at all."

"Sorry. The only M around here is you. I'd say these letters could cause you more damage than good."

"Jill said there was a summer intern a year ago. A woman who got involved with Richard."

"Chloe? Ancient history. I can't imagine she'd sneak back to town just to kill an ex-lover. Besides, there's no *M* in her name."

"The *M* could stand for a nickname. A name only Richard used for her."

"Muffin? Marvelous?" Laughing, Annie rose to her feet. "I think we're beating a dead horse. And I'm going to be late." She went to the closet and pulled out a warm-up jacket. "Irving hates to be kept waiting."

Miranda glanced with amusement at Annie's attire: a torn T-shirt, scruffy running shoes and sweatpants. "Irving likes the casual look?"

"Irving *is* the casual look." Annie slung her purse over her shoulder. "We're sanding the deck this week. Loads of fun."

"Will I ever get to meet this boat bum of yours?"

Annie grinned. "Soon as I can drag him to shore. I mean, the yachting season's gotta end one of these days." She waved. "See ya."

After Annie had left, Miranda scrounged together a salad and sat down at the kitchen table for a melancholy dinner. Irving and his boat didn't sound like much in the way of companionship, but at least Annie had someone to keep her company. Someone to keep away the loneliness.

Once, Miranda hadn't minded being alone. She'd even enjoyed the silence, the peace of a house all to herself. Now she craved the simple presence of another human being. Even a dog would be nice. She'd have to think about getting one, a large one. A dog wouldn't desert her the way most of her friends had. The way Chase had.

She set down her fork, her appetite instantly gone. Where was he now? Probably sitting in that house on Chestnut Street, surrounded by all the other Tremains. He'd have Evelyn and the twins to keep him company. He wouldn't be alone or lonely. He would be just fine without her.

In anger she rose to her feet and slid the remains of her salad into the trash. Then she started for the door, determined to get outside, to run around the block, anything to escape the house.

At the front door she halted. A visitor stood on the porch, hand poised to ring the bell.

"Jill," whispered Miranda.

This was not the cool, unflappable Jill she knew. This Jill was white-faced and brittle.

"Annie's not here right now," said Miranda. "She...should be back any minute."

"You're the one I came to see." Without warning Jill slipped right past into the living room and shut the door behind her.

"I—I was just on my way out." Miranda edged slowly for the door.

Jill took a sidestep, blocking her way. For a moment she stood there, regarding Miranda. "It's not as if I haven't been punished," she said softly. "I've done everything I could to put it behind me. Everything. I've worked like a madwoman these last five years. Built the *Herald* into a real newspaper. You think Richard knew what he was doing? Of course not! He relied on me. *Me.* Oh, he never admitted it, but he let me run the show. Five years. And now you've ruined it for me. You've already got the police shoveling up old dirt. You think the Tremains will keep me on? Now that they know? Now that everyone knows?"

"I wasn't the one. I didn't tell Lorne."

"*You're* the reason it's all come up! You and your pathetic denials! Why don't you just admit you killed him? And leave the rest of us out of it."

"But I didn't kill him."

Jill began to pace the room. "I've sinned, you've sinned. Everyone has. We're all equal. What sets us apart is how we live with our sins. I've done the best I could. And now I find it's not good enough. Not good enough to erase what happened...."

"Did Richard know? About San Diego?"

"No. I mean, yes, in the end. He found out. But it didn't matter to him—"

"It didn't matter that you killed a man?"

"He understood the circumstances. Richard was good that way." She let out a shaky laugh. "After all, he himself wasn't above a little sinning."

Miranda paused, gathered the courage for her next question. "You had an affair with him, didn't you?"

Jill's response was a careless shrug. "It didn't mean anything. It was years ago. You know, the new girl on the block. He got over it." She snapped her fingers. "Just like that. We stayed friends. We understood each other." She stopped pacing and turned to look at Miranda. "Now Lorne wants to know where I was the night Richard was killed. He's asking *me* to come up with an alibi! You're casting the blame all around, aren't you? To hell with who gets hurt. You just want off the hook. Well, sometimes that's not possible." She moved closer, her gaze fixed on Miranda, like a cat's on a bird. Softly she said, "Sometimes we have to pay for our sins. Whether it's an indiscreet affair. Or murder. We pay for it. I did. Why can't you?"

They stared at each other, caught in a binding fascination for each other's transgressions, each other's pain. *Killer and victim,* thought Miranda. *That's what I see in her eyes. Is that what you see in mine?*

The telephone rang, shattering the silence.

The sound seemed to rattle Jill. At once she turned and reached for the door. There she stopped. "You think you're the exception, Miranda. You think you're untouchable. Just wait. In a few years, when you're my age, you'll know just how vulnerable you are. We all are."

She walked out, closing the door behind her.

At once Miranda slid the bolt home.

The phone had stopped ringing. Miranda stared at it, wondering if it had been Chase, praying that he would call again.

The phone remained silent.

She began to pace the living room, hoping Chase, Annie, *anyone* would call. Starved for the sound of a human voice, she turned on the TV. Mindless entertainment, that's what she needed. For a half hour she sat on the couch among Annie's discarded socks and sweatshirts, flicking nervously between channels. Opera. Basketball. Game show. Opera again. In frustration she flicked it back to basketball.

Something clattered in the next room.

Startled, she left the couch and went into the kitchen. There she found herself staring down at a plastic saucer rolling around and around on its side across the linoleum floor. It collapsed, shuddered and fell still. Had it tumbled off the drainboard? She looked up at the sink and noticed, for the first time, that the window was wide open.

That's not the way I left it.

Slowly she backed away. The gun—Annie's gun. She had to get it.

In panic she turned to make a dash for the living room—

And found her head brutally trapped, her mouth covered by a wad of cloth. She flailed blindly against her captor, against the fumes burning her nose, her throat, but found her arms wouldn't work right. Her legs seemed to slide away from her, dissolving into some bottomless hole. She felt herself falling, caught a glimpse of the light as it receded into an impossibly high place. She tried to reach out for it but found her arms had gone numb.

The light wavered, shrank.

And then it winked out, leaving only the darkness.

Phillip was banging away at the piano. Rachmaninoff, Chase thought wearily. Couldn't the boy choose something a little more sedate? Mozart, for instance, or Haydn. Anything but this Russian thunder.

Chase headed out to the veranda, hoping to escape the racket, but the sound of the piano seemed to pound right through the walls. Resignedly he stood at the railing and stared toward the harbor. Already sunset. The sea had turned to red flame.

He wondered what Miranda was doing.

Wondered if he'd ever stop wondering.

This morning, when they'd driven off in their separate cars, their separate ways, he'd known their relationship had gone as far as it could. To go any further would require a level of trust he wasn't ready to give her. Their amateur detective work had come to a dead end; for now they had no reason to see each other. It was time to let the pros take over. The police, at least, would be objective. They wouldn't be swayed by emotions or hormones.

They still believed Miranda was guilty.

"Uncle Chase?" Cassie pushed through the screen door and came out to join him. "You can't stand the music, either, I see."

He smiled. "Don't tell your brother."

"It's not that he's a bad musician. He's just…loud." She leaned against one of the posts and looked up at the sky, at the first stars winking in the gathering darkness. "Think you could do me a favor?" she asked.

"What's that?"

"When Mom gets home, will you talk to her? About the *Herald.*"

"What about it?"

"Well, with all that's come up—about Jill Vickery, I mean— it's beginning to look like we'll need a strong hand on the helm. We all know Dad groomed Phillip to be the designated heir. And he's a bright kid—I'm not putting him down or anything. But the fact is, Phillip's just not that interested."

"He hasn't said much about it, one way or the other."

"Oh, he won't say anything. He'll never admit the truth. That he's not crazy about the job." She paused, then said with steel in her voice, "But I am."

Chase frowned at his niece. Not yet twenty, and she had the

look of a woman who knew exactly what she wanted in life. "You think you have what it takes?"

"It's in my blood! I've been involved from the time I could put pen to paper. Or fingers to keyboard. I know how that office works. I can write, edit, lay out ads, drive the damn delivery truck. I can *run* that paper. Phillip can't."

Chase remembered Cassie's term papers, the ones he'd glanced through at the cottage. They weren't just the chewing up and spitting out of textbook facts, but thoughtful, critical analyses.

"I think you'd do a terrific job," he said. "I'll talk to your mother."

"Thanks, Uncle Chase. I'll remember to mention your name when I get my Pulitzer." Grinning, she turned to go back into the house.

"Cassie?"

"Yes?"

"What do you think of Jill Vickery?"

Cassie frowned at the change of subject. "You mean as a managing editor? She was okay. Considering what she got paid, we were lucky to keep her."

"I mean, on a personal level."

"Well, that's hard to say. You never really get to know Jill. She's like a closed book. I never had any idea about that stuff in San Diego."

"Do you think she had an affair with your father?"

Cassie shrugged. "Didn't they all?"

"Do you think she was hurt by it?"

Cassie thought this over for a moment. "I think, if she was, she got over it. Jill's a tough cookie. That's the way I'd like to be." She turned and went into the house.

Phillip was still playing Rachmaninoff.

Chase stood and watched the last glow of sunset fade from the sea. He thought about Jill Vickery, about Miranda, about all the women Richard had hurt, including his own wife, Evelyn.

We're lousy, we Tremain men, he thought. *We use women, then we hurt them.*

Am I any different?

In frustration he slapped the porch railing. *Yes, I am. I would be. If only I could trust her.*

Phillip's pounding on the piano had become unbearable.

Chase left the porch, walked down the steps and headed for his car.

He would talk to her one last time. He would look her in the eye and ask her if she was guilty. Tonight he would get his answer. Tonight he would decide, once and for all, if Miranda Wood was telling the truth.

No one answered Annie's front door.

The lights were on inside, and Chase could hear the TV. He rang the bell, knocked, called out Miranda's name. Still there was no answer. At last he tried the knob and found the door was unlocked. He poked his head inside.

''Miranda? Annie?''

The living room was deserted. A basketball game, unwatched, was playing out its last minute on the TV. A pair of Annie's socks lay draped over the back of the sofa. Everything seemed perfectly normal, yet not quite right. He stood there for a moment, as though expecting the former occupants of the room to magically reappear and confront him.

The basketball game went into its fifteen-second countdown. A last-ditch throw, across the court. Basket. The crowd cheered.

Chase crossed the room, into the kitchen, and halted.

Here things were definitely not right. A chair lay toppled on its side. On the floor a saucer lay upside down. Though the kitchen window was wide open, an odor hung in the room, something vaguely sharp, medicinal.

Quickly he searched the rest of the house. He found neither Miranda nor Annie.

With growing panic he hurried outside and glanced up and down the street. Except for the far-off barking of a dog, the evening was still.

No, not quite. Was that the sound of a car engine running? If seemed muffled or distant. He circled around the house and saw a small detached garage in back. The door was shut. The sound of the car engine, though still muffled, seemed closer.

He started toward the garage. Then, out of the corner of his eye, he sighted a flicker of movement. He turned just in time to spy a shadow slipping away, blending into the darkness.

This time, you bastard, Chase thought, *you don't get away from me.*

Chase sprinted off in pursuit.

He heard his quarry dodge left, toward a thick hedge of bushes. Chase, too, veered left, scrambled over a low stone wall and broke into a sprint.

The fleeing shadow burst through the hedge and made a sharp right, into a neighboring yard littered with garden tools. Chase, intent on capture, didn't notice his quarry had swept up a rake. It came flying at him through the darkness.

Chase ducked. Tines first, it flew over his head, then clattered into a wheelbarrow behind him. Chase leaped back to his feet.

His quarry grabbed a pickax, flung it.

Again Chase dodged. He heard the whoosh of air as the lethal weapon looped past. By the time he'd recovered his balance the figure was off and running again, toward a stand of trees.

He'll be lost in the shadows! thought Chase. He mustered a final burst of speed, drew within reach. His quarry was tired. He could hear the other man's ragged breaths. Chase launched himself forward, grabbed a handful of shirt and held on.

His quarry, instead of trying to pull free, spun around and charged like a bull.

Chase was flung backward, into a tree. The shock lasted only an instant. Rage, not pain, was his first response. Shoving away from the tree, he flung himself at his attacker. Both men fell off balance, went skidding across the wet leaves. The attacker punched, and the blow caught Chase in the belly. With a new strength born of fury, Chase slammed his fist blindly at the squirming shadow. The man groaned, tried to lash out. Chase hit him again. And again.

The man went limp.

Chase rolled away from the body. For a moment he sat there, catching his breath, wincing at the pain in his knuckles. The other man was still alive—he could hear him breathing. Chase grabbed the inert figure by the legs and dragged him across the leaf-strewn lawn, toward a faint pool of light from a distant porch lamp. There he knelt to see who his prisoner was. In disbelief he stared at the face, now revealed.

It was Noah DeBolt. Evelyn's father.

CHAPTER THIRTEEN

The steady growl of an engine slowly penetrated Chase's numbed awareness. The car in the garage...the closed door...

That's when the realization hit him. He lurched to his feet.

Miranda.

He sprinted across the yard to the garage. A cloud of fumes assailed him as he pushed through the door. Miranda's car was parked inside, its engine still running. In panic, he flung open the car door.

Miranda lay sprawled across the front seat.

He switched off the ignition. Coughing, choking, he dragged her roughly out of the car, out of the garage. It terrified him how lifeless she felt in his arms. He carried her to the lawn and laid her down on the grass.

"Miranda!" he yelled. He shook her hard, so hard her whole body shuddered. "Wake up," he pleaded. "Damn you, Miranda. Don't you give up on me. Wake up!"

Still she didn't move.

In panic he slapped her face. The brutality of that blow, the sting of her flesh against his, shocked him. He laid his ear to her breast. Her heart was beating. And there it was—a breath!

She groaned, moved her head.

"Yes!" he shouted. "Come on. Come on." She sank back into unconsciousness. He didn't want to do it, but he had no choice. He slapped her again.

This time she moved her hand, a reflexive gesture to ward off the savage blows. "No," she moaned.

"Miranda, it's me! Wake up." He brushed back her hair, gently took her face in his hands and kissed her forehead, her temples. "Please, Miranda," he whispered. "Look at me."

Slowly she opened her eyes. They were dazed and full of confusion. At once she lashed out blindly, as though still fighting for her life.

"No, it's me!" he cried. He held her, hugged her tightly against him. Her frantic thrashing grew weaker. He felt the panic melt from her body until she lay quietly in his arms.

"It's all over," he whispered. "All over."

She pulled away and stared up at him with a look of bewilderment. "Who..."

"It was Noah."

"Evelyn's *father?*"

Chase nodded. "He's the one who's been trying to kill you."

"You have no right to hold me, Lorne. You understand? *No right.*" Noah, his face bruised an ugly purple, stared at his accusers. Through the closed door came the sounds of the police station: the clack of a typewriter, the ringing phone, the voices of patrolmen headed out for night duty. But here, in the back room, there was dead silence.

Quietly Lorne said, "You're not in any position to pull rank, Noah. So talk to us."

"I don't have to say a thing," said Noah. "Not until Les Hardee gets here."

Lorne sighed. "Legally speaking, yeah, you're right. But it would sure make things easy if you'd just tell us why you tried to kill her."

"I didn't. I went to her house to talk to her. I heard the car running in the garage. I thought maybe she was trying to kill herself. I started to go in, to check on it. Then Chase showed up. I guess I panicked. That's why I ran."

"That's all you were doing there? Just paying Ms. Wood a visit?"

Noah gave him an icy nod.

"In a getup like that?" Lorne nodded at Noah's black shirt and trousers.

"What I wear happens to be my concern."

"Chase says differently. He says you dragged her in the garage, left her there and started the car."

Noah snorted. "Chase has a little trouble being objective. Especially where Miranda Wood is concerned. Besides, *he* attacked *me.* Who the hell's got the bruises, anyway? Look at my face. Look at it!"

"Seems to me you both got some pretty good bruises," said Lorne.

"Self-defense," claimed Noah. "I had to fight back."

"Chase thinks you're the one who's been going after her. That you set fire to her house. Drove at her with a stolen car. And what about tonight? Was that supposed to be a convenient little suicide?"

"She's got him all twisted around. Got him taking her side. The side of a murderer—"

"Who's the guilty party here, Noah?"

Noah, sensing he'd said too much already, said abruptly, "I'm not going to talk till Les gets here."

In frustration Lorne crumpled his paper coffee cup in his fist. "Okay," he said, dropping into a chair. "We can wait. As long as it takes, Noah. As long as it takes."

"It's not going to stick," said Miranda. "I know it won't."

They sat huddled together on a bench in the intake area. Ellis Snipe had brought them coffee and cookies. Perhaps it was his way of personally atoning for the ordeal the police had put them through. So many questions, so many reports to be filed. And then, halfway through the interrogation, Dr. Steiner had shown up, called in by Lorne to check on her condition. In the guise of a medical exam, he had practically assaulted her with his stethoscope. *Breathe deep, damn it! Gotta check your lungs. You think I like making all these house calls? This keeps up, you two will have to put me on retainer!*

The questions, the demands, had left her exhausted. It was all she could manage, to sit propped up against Chase's shoulder. Waiting—for what? For Noah to confess? For the police to tell her the nightmare was over?

She knew better than that.

"He'll get out of it," she said. "He'll find a way."

"This time he won't," said Chase.

"But I never saw his face. I can barely remember what happened. What can they charge him with? Trespassing?" Miranda shook her head. "This is Noah DeBolt we're talking about. In this town, a DeBolt can get away with murder."

"Not Richard's murder."

She stared at him. "You think he killed Richard? His own son-in-law?"

"It's starting to fall together, Miranda. Remember what that lawyer FitzHugh told us? The real reason Richard gave Rose Hill to you? It was to keep the land out of Evelyn's control."

"I don't see what you're getting at."

"Who's the one person in the world Evelyn listens to? Trusts? Her *father.* Noah could have talked her into selling the land."

"You think this is all for control of Rose Hill? That's not much of a motive for murder."

"But the threat of bankruptcy is. If his investment collapsed, Noah would be left holding acres of land he could never develop. Worthless land."

"The north shore? Then you think Noah was the money behind Stone Coast Trust."

"Which makes Tony Graffam nothing but a front man. A patsy, really. My guess is, Richard found out. He had those financial records from Stone Coast, remember? The account numbers, the tax returns. I think he matched one of those accounts to Noah."

"Richard could have ruined him right then and there," she pointed out. "All he had to do was run the story in the *Herald.* But he canceled it."

"It's the way their relationship worked, Richard and Noah. They were always out to cut each other down. But not in public, *never* in public. It was a private rivalry, just between them. That's why Richard didn't print the article. It would've exposed his own father-in-law. And brought the family's dirty linen out into the public eye."

Miranda shook her head. "We'll never prove it. Not after Noah's lawyer gets through with the smoke and mirrors. You've been away from this island too long, Chase. You've forgotten how it is. The DeBolts, they're the equivalent of gods in this town."

"Not any longer."

"Then there's the matter of evidence. How do you prove he killed Richard?" She sighed, an admission of defeat. "No, *I'm* the convenient suspect. The one they'll convict." She sat back wearily. "The one they'll put away."

"That won't happen, Miranda. I won't let it happen."

Their gazes met. For the first time she saw what she'd been longing to see in his eyes. Trust. "Then you think I'm telling the truth."

"I know you're telling the truth." He touched her face. As his hand stroked down the curve of her cheek she closed her eyes and felt herself melting, flowing like warm liquid against him. "I think I've known it all along. But I was afraid to admit it. Afraid to consider the other possibilities...."

"It wasn't me, Chase. It wasn't." She slid into his arms and there she found warmth and courage, all the courage she'd somehow lost in these past soul-battering days. *Believe me,* she thought. *Never stop believing me.*

They were still locked in that embrace when Evelyn Tremain walked in the station door.

Miranda felt Chase stiffen against her, heard his sharp intake of breath. Slowly she raised her head and turned to see Evelyn and the DeBolt family attorney, Les Hardee, standing a few feet away.

"So it's come to this, has it?" Evelyn said quietly.

Chase said nothing.

"Where is my father?" said Evelyn.

"In the room down the hall," said Chase. "He's talking to Lorne."

"Without me?" cut in the attorney. He headed swiftly down the hall, muttering, "A clear violation of rights...."

Evelyn hadn't moved. She was still staring at them. "What sort of lies are you spreading about my father, Chase?"

Slowly Chase stood to face her. "Only the truth, Evelyn. It may be hard to take, but you'll have to accept it."

"The *truth?*" Evelyn let out a disbelieving laugh. "An officer calls me, tells me my father's been arrested for assault. Assault? *Noah DeBolt?* Who's lying, Chase? My father? You?" She looked at Miranda. "Or someone else?"

"Lorne will explain the charges. You'd better talk to him."

"Because you won't? Is that it? Oh, Chase." She shook her head. "You've turned your back on your own family. We love you. And look how you hurt us." She turned, faced the corridor. Softly she said, "I just hope Lorne has the good sense to know the truth when he hears it." Taking a deep breath, she started down the hall.

"Wait here," Chase said to Miranda.

"What are you going to do?"

He didn't answer. He just kept walking away, in pursuit of Evelyn.

Stunned, Miranda watched him vanish around the corner. She heard a door open, then close behind him, shutting her out. She wondered what was going on in that room, what words were being exchanged, what deals forged. She had no doubt there *would* be deals, declarations of Noah's innocence. His attorney would do his best to twist the story around, make it seem like some crazy misunderstanding. Somehow they'd manage to make Miranda look like the guilty party.

Please, Chase, she thought. *Don't let them sway you. Don't start doubting me again.*

She stared down the hall and waited.

And she feared the worst.

"The charges are preposterous," said Evelyn. "My father's never broken a law in his life. Why, if he gets too much change back from a clerk, he'll go across town to return it. How can you accuse him of assault, much less attempted murder?"

"Mr. Tremain here has the bruises to prove it," said Lorne.

"So does my client!" cut in Les Hardee. "All that proves is, they traded blows in the dark. A case of mistaken identity. Two men blindly duking it out. At the very worst, you can accuse my client of idiotic behavior."

"Thanks a lot, Les," grunted Noah.

"The point is," said Hardee, "you can't hold him. The damage—" he glanced at Chase's bruised face, then at Noah's face, even more bruised "—appears to be mutual. And as for that nonsense about trying to kill Miranda Wood, well, where's your evidence? She was facing a jail term. Of course she was depressed. Of course she'd consider suicide."

"What about the fire?" pointed out Chase. "The car that almost ran her down? I was there, I saw it. *Someone*'s trying to kill her."

"Not Mr. DeBolt."

"Does he have alibis?"

"Do *you* have evidence?" Hardee shot back. He turned to Lorne. "Look, let's call a halt to this farce. I'll take the responsibility. Release Mr. DeBolt."

Lorne sighed. "I can't."

Evelyn and Hardee stared at the diminutive chief of police.

"I'm afraid there *is* evidence," said Lorne, almost apologetically. "Ellis found a bottle of chloroform behind the garage. That kind of argues against suicide, doesn't it?"

"Nothing to do with me," said Noah.

"Then here's some more evidence," cut in Chase. It was time to gamble, time to shoot the wad. He was going to make a guess here; he only hoped it was the right one. "You know that money from the Bank of Boston? That hundred thousand dollars used to bail out Miranda Wood? Well, I had a banker friend of mine slip into the computer. Match that money transfer to an account."

"What?" Lorne turned to Chase in surprise. "You know who paid the bail?"

"Yes." *Here goes,* thought Chase. "Noah DeBolt."

It was Evelyn who reacted first, with a rage that transformed her face into an ugly mask. The look was directed at her father. "You did *what?*"

Noah said nothing. His silence was all Chase needed to back up his hunch. Right on target.

"It can be officially confirmed," said Chase. "Yes, it was your father who paid the bail."

Evelyn was still staring at Noah. "You let her out?"

Noah's head drooped. In an instant he'd been transformed into a very old, very tired-looking man. "I did it for you," he whispered.

"For me? For *me?*" Evelyn laughed. "What other favors have you done for me, Daddy?"

"It was for you. Everything was for you—"

"You crazy old man," muttered Evelyn. "You must be going senile."

"*No.*" Noah's head shot up. "I would've done anything, don't you see? I was protecting you! My little girl—"

"Protecting me from what?"

"From yourself. From what you did...."

Evelyn turned away in disgust. "I don't know what the hell he's raving about."

"Don't turn your back on me, young lady!"

"You can see he needs a doctor, Lorne. Try a psychiatrist."

"This is the thanks I get!" Noah roared. "For keeping you out of *prison?*"

Instant silence. Evelyn, white-faced, turned to confront her father. "Prison? For what?"

"Richard." Noah, his rage suddenly spent, sank slowly back against the chair. Softly he said, "For Richard."

"You thought...that I—" Evelyn shook her head. "Why? You knew it was that—that bitch!"

Noah merely looked away. With that one gesture he gave his answer. An answer that lifted a weight so heavy from Chase's soul he felt he was floating. It was a burden he could only now acknowledge had been there all along, the burden of proof. With that one gesture, the last blot of suspicion was washed away.

"You know Miranda's innocent," said Chase.

Noah dropped his head in his hands. "Yes," he whispered.

"How?" cut in Lorne.

"Because I had her followed. Oh, I knew about the affair. I knew what he was up to. I'd had enough of it! I wasn't going to see him hurt Evelyn again. So I hired a man, told him to watch her. To follow her, take photos. Catch 'em in the act. I wanted Evelyn to know, once and for all, what a bastard she'd married."

"And the night he was killed, you had Miranda under surveillance?" asked Lorne.

Noah nodded.

"What did your man see?"

"Of the murder? Nothing. He was busy following the woman. She left the house, walked to the beach. Sat there for an hour or so. Then she went home. By then my son-in-law was already dead."

Exactly what she said, thought Chase. *It was all the truth, right down to the last detail.*

"Then your man never saw the killer?" said Lorne.

"No."

"But you assumed your daughter..."

Noah shrugged. "It seemed...a logical guess. He had it coming. All these years of hurting her. You think he didn't deserve it? You think she wasn't justified?"

"But I didn't do it," said Evelyn.

Her words went ignored.

"Why did you bail out Miranda Wood?" asked Lorne.

"I thought if she went to trial, if her story held together, there was a chance they'd start to look at other suspects."

"You mean Evelyn."

"Better to have it over and done with!" blurted out Noah. "If there was an accident, that would end it. No more questions. No more suspects."

"So you wanted her out of jail," said Chase. "Out on the street, where you could reach her."

"That's enough, Noah!" cut in Hardee. "You don't have to answer these questions."

"Damn you, Les!" snapped Evelyn. "You should have told

him that earlier!'' She looked at her father, her expression a mixture of pity and disgust. ''Let me set your mind at rest, Daddy. I didn't kill Richard. The fact you thought I did only shows how little you know me. Or I you.''

''I'm sorry about this, Evelyn,'' said Lorne quietly. ''But now I'm going to have to ask you a few questions.''

Evelyn turned to him. Her chin came up, a gesture of stubborn pride, newfound strength. For the first time in all the years he'd known her Chase felt a spark of admiration for his sister-in-law.

''Ask away, Lorne,'' she said. ''You're the cop. And I guess I'm now your prime suspect.''

Chase didn't stay to hear the rest. He left the room and headed down the hall to find Miranda. *Now it can be proved. It was true, every word you said.* They could start from the beginning, he thought. He suddenly strode ahead with new hope, new anticipation. The shadow of murder was gone, and they had a chance to do it over, to do it right.

He rounded the corner eagerly, expecting to see her sitting on the bench.

The bench was empty.

He went over to the clerk, who was typing out Noah's arrest report. ''Did you see where she went?''

The clerk glanced up. ''You mean Ms. Wood?''

''Yes.''

''She left the station. About, oh, twenty minutes ago.''

''Did she say where she was going?''

''Nope. Just got up and walked out.''

In frustration Chase turned to the door. *You never make it easy for me, do you?* he thought. Then he pushed through the door and headed out into the night.

All day Ozzie had been restless. Last night, all that frantic running around and police activity had driven the beast nearly mad with excitement. A day later and the agitation still hadn't worn off. He was all nerved up, clawing at the door, whining and tip-tapping back and forth across the wood floor.

Maybe it's my fault, Miss St. John thought, gazing in disgust at her hysterical dog. *Maybe my mood has simply rubbed off on him.*

Ozzie crouched at the front door like a discarded fur coat, staring pitifully at his mistress.

"You," said Miss St. John, "are a tyrant."

Ozzie merely whimpered.

"Oh, all right," said Miss St. John. "Out, out!" She opened the door. The dog bounded out into the twilight.

Miss St. John followed the beast down the gravel driveway. Ozzie was dancing along, his fur bouncing like black corkscrews. Truly an ugly animal, thought Miss St. John, the same thought that occurred to her on every walk. That he was worth several thousand dollars for his pedigree alone only went to show you the worthlessness of pedigrees, be they for dogs or people. But what Ozzie lacked in beauty he made up in energy. Already he was trotting far ahead and veering up the path, toward Rose Hill.

Miss St. John, feeling more like dog than mistress, followed him.

The cottage was dark. Chase and Miranda had left that morning and now the place stood deserted and forlorn. A pity. Such charming cottages should not go empty, especially not in the summertime.

She climbed the steps and peered through the window. Shadows of furniture huddled within. The books were back in the shelves. She could see the gleam of their spines lined up against the wall. Though they'd combed those books and papers thoroughly, she still wondered whether they had missed something. Some small, easily overlooked item that held the answers to Richard Tremain's death.

The door was locked, but she knew where the key was kept. What harm would there be in another little visit? She'd always felt just a bit proprietary when it came to Rose Hill. After all, she'd played near here almost every day as a child. And as an adult she'd made a point of keeping an eye on the cottage, as a favor to the Tremains.

Ozzie seemed happy enough, padding about in the yard.

Miss St. John retrieved the key from the planter, unlocked the door and went inside.

It seemed very still, very sad in that living room. She turned on all the lamps and wandered about, her gaze combing the nooks and crannies of the furniture. They'd already made a search of those places. There was no point repeating it.

She went through the kitchen, through the upstairs bedrooms, came back down again. No hunches, no revelations.

She was turning to leave when her gaze swept past the area rug, set right in front of the door. That's when a memory struck her, of a scene from *Tess of the D'Urbervilles*. A confessional note, slipped under the closed door, only to be pushed accidentally under the adjacent rug. A note that was never found because it lay hidden from view.

So vivid was that image that when she bent and pulled up the edge of the rug she was not at all startled to see a sealed envelope lying there.

The note was from M. The intended recipient had never found it, never read it.

...This pain is alive, like a creature gnawing at my organs. It won't die. It refuses to die. You put it there, you planted it, you gave the embryo all those years of nourishment.

And then you walked away.

You say you are doing me a kindness. You say it is better to break off now, because, if it goes on longer, it will only hurt more. You don't know what it is to hurt. Once you claimed to be love's walking wounded. Once, I thought to save you.

You were the serpent I hugged to my breast.

Now you say you've found a new savior. You think she'll make you happy. But she won't. It will be the same with her as it was with the others. You'll decide she isn't perfect. No one who's ever loved you, really loved you, has ever been good enough for you.

But you're getting old, flabby, and still you think that

somewhere there's a young and perfect woman just longing to make love to your wrinkled old carcass.

She doesn't know you the way I do. I've had years to learn all your dirty little secrets. Your conceits and lies and cruelty. You'll use her, the way you've used all the others. And then she'll be tossed on the heap with the rest of us, another woman terribly hurt.

You should suffer where you've sinned. A good clean slice—

Miss St. John, still clutching the letter, abruptly left Rose Hill and hurried home.

With shaking hands she made two phone calls. The first was to Lorne Tibbetts.

The second was to Miranda Wood.

CHAPTER FOURTEEN

Miranda was near the point of exhaustion by the time she climbed up Annie's porch steps. It had been only a ten-minute walk from the police station, but the distance she had traveled had been emotional, not physical. Sitting alone on that bench, shut out from the fancy deal-making between attorneys and cops, she'd come to the sad realization that Noah DeBolt would never be charged with any crime worse than trespassing. That she, Miranda, was too convenient a suspect to be let off the hook. And that Chase, by walking down the corridor, by joining Evelyn and Noah behind that closed door, had made his choice.

Didn't they say that crisis brought families together? Well, the arrest of patriarch Noah DeBolt was one hell of a crisis. The family would rally.

Miranda was not, could never be, part of that family.

She stepped in the front door. Annie was still not home. Silence hung like a shroud over the house. When the phone suddenly rang, the sound was almost shocking to her ears.

She picked up the receiver.

"Miranda?" came a breathless voice.

"Miss St. John? Is something wrong?"

"Are you home alone?" was Miss St. John's bizarre reply.

"Well, yes, at the moment—"

"I want you to lock the door. Do it now."

"No, everything's all right. They've arrested Noah DeBolt—"

"Listen to me! I found another letter, at Rose Hill. That's what she was after, don't you see? The reason she kept going to the cottage! To get back all her letters!"

"Whose letters?"

"M."

"But Noah DeBolt—"

"This has nothing to do with Noah! It was a crime of passion, Miranda. The classic motive. Let me read you the letter...."

Miranda listened.

By the time Miss St. John had finished, Miranda's hands were numb from clutching the receiver.

"I've already called the police," said Miss St. John. "They've sent a man to pick up Jill Vickery. Until then, keep your doors locked. It's a sick letter, Miranda, written by a sick woman. If she comes to the house, *don't let her in.*"

Miranda hung up.

At once she missed the sound of a human voice, any voice, even one transmitted through telephone wires. *Annie, come home. Please.*

She stared at the phone, wondering if she should call someone. But who? It was only as she stood there, thinking, that she noticed several days' mail mounded haphazardly by the telephone, some of it threatening to spill over onto the floor. A half-dozen household bills mingled with ad circulars and magazines. Annie's bookkeeping must be as sloppy as her housekeeping, she thought, straightening the pile. Only then did she notice the newsletter from the alumni association of Tufts University—Annie's old alma mater. It lay at the edge of the table, four photocopied pages stapled together, personal notes from the class of '68, with a mass-mailing label on front. Of no particular interest to Miranda—except for one detail.

It was addressed to Margaret Ann Berenger.

You're the only M I know, Annie had said.

And all the time, she'd known another.

It doesn't mean she's the one.

Miranda stood staring at that label. Margaret Ann Berenger. Where was the proof, where was the link between Annie and all those letters from M?

It suddenly occurred to her. *A typewriter.*

A manual model, Jill had said, with an *e* hammer in need of cleaning. It would be a large item, difficult to hide. A quick check of all the closets, all the cabinets, confirmed that there was no manual typewriter in the house. Could it be in the garage?

No, she'd been in the garage. It was barely large enough to hold a car, much less store household items.

She checked, anyway. No typewriter.

She went back into the house, her mind racing. By now Jill might already be under arrest. Annie would hear of it in no time, would know the search for the real M was on. Her first move would be to get rid of the incriminating typewriter, if she hadn't already done so. It was the one piece of evidence that could link Annie to Richard's murder.

It could prove my innocence. I have to find it, before she destroys it. I have to get it to the police.

There was one more place she had to look.

She ran from the house and got into her car.

Moments later she pulled up in front of the *Herald* building. It was dark inside. The latest issue had just been put to bed. No one would be working late tonight, so she'd have the building to herself.

She let herself in the front door with her key—the key she'd never gotten around to turning in. With a twinge of irony she remembered that it was Richard who'd told her to keep it. He was certain he could talk her into returning to the job.

Well, here she was, back again.

She moved up the aisle of desks and went straight to Annie's. She flicked on the lamp. The top drawer was unlocked. Among the jumble of pens and paper clips she found some loose keys. Which one would open Annie's locker? She gathered them all up and headed down the stairwell and into the women's room.

She turned on the light. A flowered couch, mauve wallpaper, Victorian prints sprang into view. Jill's decorative touch couldn't disguise the fact it was a closed-in dungeon of a room, without a single window. Miranda moved to the bank of lockers. There were six of them, extra wide to accommodate employees' heavy coats and boots during the winter months. She knew which one belonged to Annie. It had the sticker that said I've Got PMS. What's Your Excuse?

She inserted the first key into the lock. It didn't turn.

She tried the second key, then the third. The lock popped open.

She swung open the door and frowned at the contents. On the top shelf were mittens, a pair of old running shoes, a wool scarf.

On the bottom shelf a sweater lay draped over a towel-wrapped bundle. Miranda took out the bundle. The object inside was heavy. She unwrapped the towel, revealed the contents.

It was an old blue-green Olivetti with pica type.

She slid in a scrap of paper and with shaking hands typed the name Margaret Ann Berenger. The *e* loop was smudged.

An overwhelming sense of relief, almost euphoria, at once washed over her. Quickly she shut the locker and rewrapped the typewriter. As she gathered it up in her arms, a puff of air blew past her cheek. That was all the warning she had, that soft whisper of wind through the door as it opened and shut behind her.

Miranda turned.

The intruder stood in the doorway, her hair a mass of wind-blown waves, her face utterly devoid of emotion.

Miranda said softly, "Annie."

In silence Annie's gaze settled on the typewriter in Miranda's arms.

"I thought you were with Irving," said Miranda.

Annie's gaze slowly rose once again to meet Miranda's. Sadness now filled those eyes, a look of pain that seemed to spill from her very soul. *Why did I never see it before?* thought Miranda.

"There is no Irving," said Annie.

Miranda shook her head in confusion.

"There never was an Irving. I made him up. All the dates, all those evenings out. You see, I'd drive to the harbor. Park there and just sit. Hours, sometimes." Annie took a deep breath and, shuddering, let it out. "I couldn't take the pity, Miranda. All that sympathy for an old maid."

"I never thought that—"

"Of course you did. You all did. Then there was Richard. I wouldn't give him the satisfaction of knowing that—" Her voice broke. She wiped her hand across her eyes.

Slowly Miranda set the typewriter down on the bench. "Knowing what, Annie?" she asked softly. "How badly he hurt you? How alone you really were?"

A shudder racked Annie's body.

"He hurt us both," said Miranda. "Every woman he ever touched. Every woman who ever loved him. He hurt us all."

"Not the way he hurt me!" Annie cried. The echo of her pain seemed to reverberate endlessly against those stark walls. "Five years of my life, Miranda. That's what I gave him. Five years of secrets. I was forty-two when we met. I still had time for a baby. A few short years left. I kept hoping, waiting for him to make up his mind. To leave Evelyn." She wiped her eyes again, smearing a streak of mascara and tears across her cheek. "Now it's too late for me. It was my last chance and he took it from me. He *stole* it from me. And then he ended it." She shook her head, laughing through her tears. "He said he was only trying to be kind. That he didn't want me to waste any more years on him. Then he said the thing that hurt me most of all. He said, 'It was just your fantasy, Annie. I never really loved you the way you thought I did.'" The look she gave Miranda was the gaze of a tortured animal's. "Five years, and he tells me that. What he didn't tell me was the truth. He'd found someone younger. You." There was no hostility, no anger in her voice, only quiet resignation. "I never blamed you, Miranda. You didn't know. You were just another victim. He would have left you, the way he left us all."

"You're right, Annie. We were all his victims."

"I'm sorry. I'm so sorry, Miranda." Annie slid her hand into her jacket pocket. "But someone has to suffer for it." Slowly she withdrew the gun.

Miranda stared at the barrel, now pointed at her chest. She wanted to argue, to plead, anything to make Annie lower the gun. But her voice had frozen in her throat. She could only stare at the black circle of the barrel and wonder if she would feel the bullet.

"Come, Miranda. Let's go."

Miranda shook her head. "Where—where are we going?"

Annie opened the door and gestured for Miranda to move first. "Up the stairs. To the roof."

No one was home.

Chase circled around Annie's house to the garage and found that the car was gone. Miranda must have returned, then left again. He was standing in the driveway, wondering where to look next, when he heard the phone ringing inside the house. He ran up the porch steps and into the living room to answer the call.

It was Lorne Tibbetts. "Is Miranda there?" he asked.

"No, I'm looking for her."

"What about Annie Berenger?"

"Not here, either."

"Okay," said Lorne. "I want you to leave the house, Chase. Do it right now."

Chase was stunned by the unexpected command. He said, "I'm waiting for Miranda to show up."

He heard Lorne turn and say something to Ellis. Then, "Look, we got evidence snowballing down here. If Annie Berenger shows up first, you keep things nice and casual, okay? Don't rattle her. Just calmly leave the house. Ellis is on his way over."

"What the hell's going on?"

"We think we know who M is. And it's not Jill Vickery. Now get out of there." Lorne hung up.

If it isn't Jill Vickery...

Chase went to the end table and opened the drawer. Annie's gun was missing.

He slammed the drawer shut.

Where are you, Miranda?

The next thought sent him running outside to his car. There might still be time to find them. He'd missed Miranda by only five, maybe ten minutes. They couldn't have gone far, not yet. If he circled around town, kept his eyes open, he might be able to find her car.

If they were still in the area.

I can't lose you. Now that we can prove your innocence. Now that we have a chance together.

He swung the car around. With tires screeching, he raced back toward town.

"Go on. Up the last flight."

Miranda paused, her foot on the next step. "Please, Annie..."

"Keep moving."

Miranda turned to face her. They were already on the third-floor landing. One more flight and then the door to the roof. Once she'd marveled at the beauty of this stairwell, at the carved mahogany banister, the gleaming wood finish. Now it had become a spiral death trap. She gripped the railing, drawing strength from the unyielding support of solid wood.

"Why are you doing this?" she asked.

"Go on. Go!"

"We were friends once—"

"Until Richard."

"But I didn't know! I had no idea you were in love with him! If only you'd told me."

"I never told anyone. I couldn't. It was his idea, you see. Keep it quiet, keep it our little secret. He said he wanted to protect me."

Then I'm the only one left who knows, thought Miranda. *The only one still alive.*

"Move," said Annie. "Up the stairs."

Miranda didn't budge. She looked Annie in the eye. Quietly she said, "Why don't you just shoot me now? Right here. If that's what you're going to do anyway."

"It's your choice." Calmly Annie raised the gun. "I'm not afraid of killing. They say that it's hardest the first time you do it. And you know what? It wasn't really hard at all. All I had to do was think about how much he hurt me. The knife seemed to move all by itself. I was just a witness."

"I'm not Richard. I never meant to hurt you."

"But you will, Miranda. You know the truth."

"So do the police. They found that letter, Annie. The last one you wrote."

Annie shook her head. "They arrested Jill tonight. But you're still the one they'll blame. Because they'll find the typewriter in your car. What a clever girl you'll seem, making up all those letters, planting them in the cottage. Throwing suspicion on poor innocent Jill. But then the guilt caught up with you. You got depressed. You knew jail was inevitable. So you chose the easy way out. You climbed to the roof of the newspaper building. And you jumped."

"I won't do it."

Annie gripped the gun with both hands and pointed it at Miranda's chest. "Then you'll die here. I had to kill you, you see. I found you planting the typewriter in Jill's office. You had a gun. You ordered me into the stairwell. I tried to grab the gun and it went off. A tidy end for everyone involved." Slowly she cocked back the pistol hammer. "Or would you rather it be the roof?"

I have to buy time, thought Miranda. *Have to wait for a chance, any chance, to escape.*

She turned and gazed up at the last flight of stairs.

"Go on," said Annie.

Miranda began to climb.

Fourteen steps, each one a fleeting eternity. Fourteen lifetimes, passing, gone. Frantically she tried to visualize the roof, the layout, the avenues of escape. She'd been up there only once, when the news staff had gathered for a group photo. She recalled a flat stretch of asphalt, punctuated by three chimneys, a heating duct, a transformer shed. Four stories down—that would be the drop. Would it kill her? Or was it just high enough to leave her crippled on the sidewalk, a helpless mound of broken bones, to be dispatched with a few blows by Annie?

The door to the roof loomed just above. If she could just get through that door and barricade it, she might be able to buy time, to scream for help.

Only a few steps more.

She stumbled and fell forward, catching herself on the stairs.

"Get up," said Annie.

"My ankle—"

"I said, get up!"

Miranda sat on the step and reached down to massage her foot. "I think I sprained it."

Annie took a step closer. "Then crawl if you have to! But get up those stairs!"

Miranda, her back braced firmly against the step, her legs wound up tight, calmly kept rubbing her ankle. And all the time she thought, *Closer, Annie. Come closer....*

Annie moved up another step. She was standing just below Miranda now, the gun frighteningly close. "I can't wait. Your time's run out." She raised the gun to Miranda's face.

That's when Miranda raised her foot—in a vicious, straight-out kick that thudded right into Annie's stomach. It sent Annie toppling backward down the stairs, to sprawl on the third-floor landing. But even as she fell she never released the gun. There was no opportunity to wrestle away the weapon. Annie was already rising to her knees, gun in hand. Her aim swept up toward her prey.

Miranda yanked open the rooftop door and dashed through just as Annie fired. She heard the bullet splinter the door, felt wood chips fly, sting her face. There was no latch, no way to bolt the door shut. So little time, so little time! Fourteen steps and Annie would be on the roof.

Miranda glanced wildly about her, could make out in the darkness the silhouette of chimneys, crates, other unidentifiable shapes.

Footsteps thudded up the stairs.

In panic Miranda took off into the shadows and slipped behind a transformer shed. She heard the door fly open, heard it bang shut again.

Then she heard Annie's voice, calling through the darkness. "There's nowhere to run, Miranda. Nowhere to go but straight down. Wherever you are, I'll find you...."

Chase spotted it from a block away: Miranda's old Dodge, parked in front of the *Herald* building. He pulled up behind it and climbed out. A glance through the window told him the car was unoccupied. Miranda—or whoever had driven it here—must be in the building.

He rattled the front door to the *Herald*. It was locked. Through the glass he saw a lamp burning on one of the desks. Someone had to be inside. He banged on the door and called, "Miranda?" There was no answer.

He rattled the door again, then started around to the back of the building. There had to be another way in, an unlocked window or a loading door. He had circled the corner and was moving down one of the alleys when he heard it. Gunfire.

It came from somewhere inside the building.

"Miranda?" he yelled.

He wasted no more time searching for unlocked entrances. He grabbed a trash can from the alley, carried it around to the front of the building and hurled it through the window. Glass shattered, flying like hail across the desks inside. He kicked in the last jagged fragments, scrambled over the sill and dropped onto a carpet littered with razorlike shards. At once he was running past the desks, moving straight for the back of the building. With every step he took he grew more terrified of what he might find. Images of Miranda raced through his head. He shoved through the first door and confronted the deserted print shop. Newspapers—the next issue—were bundled and stacked against the walls. No Miranda.

He turned, moved down the hall to the women's lounge. Again, that surge of terror as he pushed through the door.

Again, no Miranda.

He turned and headed straight into the women's rest room, pushing open stall doors. No one there.

Ditto for the men's room.

Where the hell had that gunshot come from?

He ran back into the hall and started up the stairwell. Two more floors to search. Offices on the second floor, storage and news file rooms on the third. Somewhere up there he'd find her.

Just let me find you alive.

Miranda hugged the side of the transformer shed and listened for the sound of footsteps. Except for the hammering of her own heart she heard nothing, not even the softest crunch of shoes on asphalt. *Where is she? Which way is she moving?*

Quickly Miranda glanced to either side of her. Her eyes had began to adjust to the darkness. She could make out, to the left, a jumble of crates. Right beside them were the handrails of a fire escape. A way off the roof! If she could just make it to that edge, without being seen.

Where was Annie?

She had to risk a look. She crouched down and slowly inched toward the corner. What she saw made her pull back at once in panic.

Annie was moving straight toward the transformer shed.

Miranda's instinct told her to run, to attempt a final dash for freedom. Logic told her she'd never make it. Annie was already too close.

In desperation she scrabbled for a few bits of gravel near her feet. She flung it high overhead, aiming blindly for the opposite end of the roof. She heard it clatter somewhere off in the darkness.

For a few terrifying seconds she listened for sounds—any sounds. Nothing.

Again she edged around the corner of the transformer. Annie was following the sound, toward the opposite edge of the roof, stalking slowly toward one of the chimneys. A few steps farther. One more…

Now was her chance—her only one! Miranda ran.

Her footsteps sounded like drumbeats across the asphalt roof. Even before she reached the fire escape she heard the first gunshot, heard the whine of the bullet as it hurtled past. No time to think, only move! She scrambled for the fire escape, swung her leg over onto the first metal rung.

Another gunshot exploded.

The bullet's impact was like a punch in the shoulder. Its force sent her toppling sideways, over the roof's edge. She caught a dizzying view of the night sky, then felt herself falling, falling. Instinctively she reach up, clawed blindly for a handhold. As she tumbled over the edge of the fire escape landing, her left hand closed around cold steel—the railing. Even as her legs slipped away, dangling beneath her like dead weights, her grip held. She tried to reach up with the other arm but it wouldn't seem to obey her commands. She could only raise it to shoulder height, and then her hand closed only weakly around the outside edge of the landing. For a second she clung there, her feet hanging uselessly. Then she managed to brace one foot against the brick face of the building. *Still alive, still here!* she thought. *If I can just pull myself over the rail—get back onto the landing...*

The flicker of a shadow moving just above made her freeze. Slowly she lifted her gaze and stared into the gun barrel. Annie was standing at the roof's edge, aiming directly at Miranda's head.

"Now," said Annie softly. "Let go of the fire escape."

"No. No—"

"Just open your fingers. Lean back. A fast and easy way to die."

"It won't work. They'll find out! They'll know you did it!"

"Jump, Miranda. *Jump.*"

Miranda stared down at the ground. It was so far away, so very far.

Annie swung one leg over the roof's edge, aimed her heel at Miranda's hand gripping the rail and stamped down.

Miranda screamed. Still she held on.

Annie raised her heel, stamped again, then again, each blow crushing Miranda's left hand.

The pain was unbearable. Miranda's grip loosened. She lost her foothold, was left dangling free. Her left hand, throbbing in agony, could stand the abuse no longer. Her right hand, already weak and growing numb from the bullet wound, didn't have the strength to hold her weight. She gazed up in despair as Annie raised her heel and prepared to stamp down one last time.

The blow never fell.

Instead, Annie's body was jerked up and backward, like a puppet whose strings have been yanked all at once. She let out an unearthly screech of rage, of disbelief. And then there was a thud as her body, hurled aside, slammed onto the rooftop.

An instant later Chase appeared at the roof's edge. He leaned over and grabbed her left wrist. "Take my other hand! Take it!" he yelled.

Bracing her feet against the brick wall, Miranda managed to raise her right arm. "I can't...can't reach you...."

"Come on, Miranda!" He leaned farther, his body stretching over the edge. "You have to do it! I need both your hands! Just reach up, that's all! I'll grab it, darling. Please!"

Darling. That single word, one she'd never heard before on his lips, seemed to spark some new source of strength deep inside her. She took a breath and strained toward the heavens. *That's as far as I can go,* she thought in despair. *No farther.*

That's when his hand closed around her wrist. At once she was held in a grip so tight she never feared, even for an instant, that she would fall. He dragged her up and up, over the roof's edge.

Only then did her strength give out. She had no need of it now, not when Chase was here to lend her his. She tumbled into his arms.

No tree had ever felt so solid, so unbendable. Nothing, no one could hurt her in the fortress of those arms. He said, "My God, Miranda, I thought—"

Instantly he fell silent.

A pistol hammer clicked back.

They both spun around to see Annie standing a few feet away. She wobbled on unsteady legs. With both hands she clutched the gun.

"It's too late, Annie," said Chase. "The police know. They have your final letter. They know you killed Richard. Even now they're looking for you. It's over."

Annie slowly lowered the gun. "I know," she whispered. She took a deep breath and looked up at the sky. "I loved you," she said to the heavens. "Damn you, Richard. *I loved you!*" she screamed.

Then she raised the gun, put the barrel in her mouth and calmly pulled the trigger.

CHAPTER FIFTEEN

This time the ministrations of cranky Dr. Steiner were insufficient. Only a hospital—and a surgeon—would do. An emergency ferry run was ordered and Miranda was loaded aboard the *Jenny B* with Dr. Steiner in attendance. The hospital in Bass Harbor was alerted to an incoming patient: gunshot wound to the right shoulder, patient conscious and oriented, blood pressure stable, bleeding under control. The *Jenny B* pulled away from the dock with two passengers, a crew of three and a corpse.

Chase wasn't aboard.

He was at that moment fidgeting in a chair in Lorne Tibbetts's back office, answering a thousand and one questions. A command performance. A woman, after all, was dead; an investigation was called for; and as Lorne so succinctly put it, the choice was between talk or jail. All the time Chase sat there, he was wondering about the *Jenny B*. Had it reached Bass Harbor yet? Was Miranda stable?

Would Lorne ever finish with the damn questions?

It was two in the morning when Chase finally walked out of the police station. The night was warm, warm for Maine, anyway, but he felt chilled as he walked to his car. No more ferries to Bass Harbor tonight. He was stranded on the island until morning. At least he knew that Miranda was out of danger. A phone call to the hospital had told him she was resting comfortably, and was expected to recover.

Now he wondered where to go, where to sleep.

Not Chestnut Street. He could never sleep under Evelyn's roof again, not after the damage he'd done to the DeBolt family. No, tonight he felt rootless, cut off from the DeBolts, from the Tremains, from the legacy of his rich and haughty past. He felt born anew. Cleansed.

He got in the car and drove to Rose Hill.

The cottage felt cold, devoid of life or spirit, as if any joy that had ever existed within had long since fled. Only the bedroom held any warmth. This was where he and Miranda had made love. Here the memory of that night, that one night, still lingered.

He lay on the bed and tried to conjure up the memory of her scent, her softness, but it was like trying to catch your own reflection in water. Every time you reach out to hold it, it slips from your grasp.

The way Miranda had slipped from his grasp.

She's not one of us, Evelyn had once said. *She's not our kind of people.*

Chase thought of Noah, of Richard, of Evelyn. Of his own father. And he thought, *Evelyn's right. Miranda's not our kind of people.*

She's far better.

"Happy endings," said Miss St. John, "are not automatic. Sometimes one has to work for them."

Chase took the advice, and the cup of coffee she handed him, in silence. The advice was something he already knew. Hadn't experience taught him that happy endings were what you found in fairy tales, not real life? Hadn't his own marriage proved the point?

But this time it will be different. I'll make it different. If only I could be certain I'm the one she wants.

He sipped his cup of coffee and absentmindedly scratched Ozzie's wild black mop of hair. He didn't know why he was petting the beast, except that Ozzie seemed so damn appreciative. A glance at his watch told Chase he had plenty of time to catch the twelve-o'clock ferry to Bass Harbor. To Miranda.

All night he'd lain sleepless in bed, wondering about their chances, their future. The specter of his brother couldn't be so easily dispelled. Just a few short weeks ago Richard had been the man she loved, or thought she loved. Richard had taken her innocence, used her, nearly destroyed her. *And now here I am, another Tremain. After what Richard did to her, why should she trust me?*

Events, emotions had moved at lightning speed these past few days. A week ago he had called her a murderess. Only hours ago he had come to accept her innocence as gospel truth. She had every right to resent him, to never forgive him for the things he'd once said to her. So many cruel and terrible words had passed between them. Could love, real love, grow from such poisoned beginnings?

He wanted to believe it could. He had to believe it could.

But those doubts kept tormenting him.

When Miss St. John had come knocking at the cottage door at ten o'clock with an offer of coffee and a morning chat, he'd almost welcomed the intrusion, though he suspected her invitation was inspired by more than neighborly kindness. Word of the night's goings-on must already be buzzing about town. Miss St. John, with her mile-long antennae, had no doubt picked up the signals and was probably curious as hell.

Now that she'd been brought up to date, she was going to offer an opinion, whether he wanted to hear it or not.

"Miranda's a lovely woman, Chase," she said. "A very kind woman."

"I know" was all he could answer.

"But you have doubts."

He sighed, a breath that seemed weighted with pain and uncertainty. "After all that's happened..."

"People are entitled to make mistakes, Chase. Miranda made one with your brother. It wasn't a terrible sort of mistake. It had nothing to do with cruelty or bad intentions. It had only to do with love. With misjudgment. The mistake was real. But the emotions were the right ones."

"But you don't understand," he said, looking up at her. "My doubts have nothing to do with her. It's *me,* whether she can forgive me. For being a Tremain. For being this symbol of everything, everyone who's ever hurt her."

"I think Miranda's the one who's searching for forgiveness."
He shook his head. "What should I forgive *her* for?"

"You have to answer that."

He sat in silence for a moment, rubbing the ugly head of that ugly dog. *What do I forgive you for? For showing me the real meaning of innocence. For making me question every stuffy notion I was brought up to believe in. For making me realize I've been an idiot.*

For making me fall in love with you.

With sudden determination he put down his coffee cup and rose to his feet. "I'd better get going," he said. "I've got a ferry to catch."

"And then what happens?" asked Miss St. John, walking him to the door.

Smiling, he took her hand—the hand of a very wise woman. "Miss St. John," he said, "when I find out, you'll be the first to know."

She waved as he headed out to his car. "I'll count on it!" she yelled.

Chase drove like a crazy man to the ferry landing. He arrived an hour early, only to find a long line of cars already waiting to board. Rather than risk missing the sail, he decided to leave his car and board as a foot passenger.

Two hours later he walked off onto the dock in Bass Harbor. No taxis here; he had to hitch a ride to the hospital. By the time he strode up to the patient information desk, it was already two-thirty.

"Miranda Wood," said the volunteer, setting down the phone receiver, "was discharged an hour ago."

"What?"

"That's what the floor nurse said. The patient left with Dr. Steiner."

Chase felt ready to punch the desk in frustration. "Where did they go?" he snapped.

"I wouldn't know, sir. You could ask upstairs, at the nurses' station, second floor."

Chase was about to head for the stairwell when he suddenly glanced up at the wall clock. "Miss—what time does the ferry return to Shepherd's Island?" he asked.

"I think the last one leaves at three o'clock."

Twenty minutes.

He hurried outside and glanced up and down the street for a taxi, a bus, anything on wheels that might take him to the landing. They *had* to be at the landing. Where else would she and Dr. Steiner go, except back to the island?

It was the last ferry of the day and he'd never catch it in time.

Happy endings are not automatic. Sometimes one has to work for them.

Okay, damn it, he thought. *I'm ready to work. I'm ready to do anything it takes to make this turn out right.*

He took off at a sprint down the street. It was two miles to the ferry landing.

He ran every step of the way.

The deckhand yelled, "All aboard!" and the engines of the *Jenny B* growled to life.

Standing at the rail, Miranda stared out over the gray-green expanse of Penobscot Bay. So many islands in the distance, so many places in the world to run to. Soon she'd be on her way, leaving memories, good and bad, behind her. There was just this one last journey to Shepherd's Island, to tie up all those loose ends, and then she could turn her back on this place forever. It was a departure she'd planned weeks ago, before Richard's murder, before the horrors of her arrest.

Before Chase.

"I still say it was an idiotic idea, young lady," said Dr. Steiner, hunched irritably on a bench beside her. "Checking out just like that. What if you start to bleed again? What if you get an infection? I can't handle those complications! I tell you, I'm getting too old for this business. Too old!"

"I'll be just fine, Doc," she said, her gaze focused on the bay. "Really," she said softly, "I'll be just fine...."

Dr. Steiner began to mutter to himself, a grumpy monologue

about disobedient patients and how hard it was to be a doctor these days. Miranda scarcely listened. She had too many other things on her mind.

A quiet exit, some time alone—yes, all in all, it was better this way. Seeing Chase again would be too confusing. What she needed was escape, a chance to analyze what she really felt for him. Love? She thought so. Yes, she was *sure* of it. But she'd been wrong before, terribly wrong. *I don't want to make the same mistake, suffer the same consequences.*

And yet...

She gripped the railing and gazed off moodily at the islands. The wind had come up and it whistled across the water, blew its cold salt breath against her face.

I do love him, she thought. *I know I do.*

But it's not enough to make a future. Too much stood in the way. The ghost of Richard. The shadow of mistrust. And always, always, those metaphorical train tracks on whose wrong side she'd grown up. It shouldn't make a difference, but then, she was merely Miranda Wood. Perhaps, to a Tremain, it made *all* the difference.

"Bow line's free!" called the deckhand.

The engines of the *Jenny B* throttled up. Slowly she pivoted to starboard, to face the far-off green hillock that was Shepherd's Island. The deckhand strode the length of the boat and released the stern line. Just as it slipped free there came a shout from the dock.

"Wait! Hold the boat!"

"We're full up!" yelled the deckhand. "Catch the next one."

"I said *hold up!*"

"Too late!" barked the deckhand. Already the *Jenny B* was pulling away from the dock.

It was the deckhand's sharp and sudden oath that made Miranda turn to look. She saw, far astern, a figure racing toward the end of the pier. He took a flying leap across the growing gap of water and landed with only inches to spare on the deck of the *Jenny B*.

"Son of a gun," marveled the deckhand. "Are you nuts?"

Chase scrambled to his feet. "Have to talk to someone—one of your passengers—"

"Man, you must want to talk *real* bad."

Chase took a calming breath and glanced around the deck. His gaze stopped at Miranda. "Yeah," he said softly. "Real bad."

Miranda, caught standing against the rail, could only stare in astonishment as Chase walked toward her. The other passengers were all watching, waiting to see what would happen next.

"Young man," snapped Dr. Steiner. "If you sprained your ankle, don't expect me to fix it. You two and all your damn fool stunts."

"My ankle's fine," said Chase, his gaze never leaving Miranda. "I just want to talk to your patient. If it's all right with her."

Miranda gave a laugh of disbelief. "After a leap like that, how could I refuse?"

"Let's go up front." Chase reached for her hand. "For this, I don't need an audience."

They walked to the bow and stood by the rail. Here the salt wind flew at them unremittingly, whipping at their clothes, their hair. Above, gulls swooped and circled, airborne companions of the plodding *Jenny B.*

Chase said, "They told me you checked out early. You should have stayed in the hospital."

Miranda hugged herself against the wind and stared down at the water. "I couldn't lie in that bed another day. Not with so many things hanging over me."

"But it's over, Miranda."

"Not yet. There's still that business with the police. And I have to settle with my lawyer."

"That can wait."

"But I can't." She raised her head and faced the wind. "I want to leave this place. As soon as I can. Any way I can."

"Where are you going?"

"I don't know. I've thought about heading west. Jill Vickery walked away from her past. Maybe I can, too."

There was a long silence. "Then you're not staying on the island," he said.

"No. There's nothing here for me now. I'll be getting the insurance money from the house. It will be enough to get me out of here. To go some place where they don't know me, or Richard, or anything that happened."

The water broke before the bow of the *Jenny B* and the spray flew up, misting their faces.

"It's not an easy thing," she said, "living in a town where they'll always wonder about you. I understand now why Jill Vickery left San Diego. She wanted to wash away the guilt. She wanted to get back her innocence. That's what I want back, Chase. My innocence."

"You never lost it."

"Yes, I did. That's what you thought. What you'll always think of me."

"I know better now. I have no more questions, Miranda. No more doubts."

She shook her head. Sadly she turned away. "It's not as easy as that, to bury the past."

"Okay, so it's not." He pulled her around to face him. "It's never easy, Miranda. Love. Life. You know, just this morning, Miss St. John said a very wise thing to me. She said happy endings aren't automatic. You have to work for them." He reached up and framed her face in his hands. "Don't you think this happy ending is worth working for?"

"But I don't know if I believe in them anymore. Happy endings."

"Neither did I. But I'm beginning to change my mind."

"You'll always be wondering about me, Chase. About whether you can trust me—"

"No, Miranda. That's the one thing I'll *never* wonder about."

He kissed her then, a sweet and gentle joining that spoke not of passion but of hope. That one touch of his lips seemed to rinse away the terrible grime of guilt, of remorse, that had stained her soul.

The renewal of innocence. That's what he offered; that's what she found in his arms.

It seemed only a short time later when the gulls suddenly burst forth into a wild keening, a raucous announcement that land was close at hand. The couple standing at the bow did not stir from each other's arms. Even when the boat's whistle blew, even when the *Jenny B* glided into the harbor, they would still be standing there.

Together.

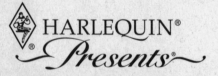

**Two sexy Randall brothers have yet to find brides...
and spring may be giving way to their last long,
hot summer of bachelorhood!**

Join bestselling author

Judy Christenberry

for

SUMMER SKIES

The eldest Randall brother continues his attempts to find
wives for his bachelor brothers in this captivating volume.
Containing the final two stories in Judy's famous
4 Brides for 4 Brothers miniseries, *Summer Skies* has
plenty of lighthearted family dynamics and irresistibly
sexy cowboys for perfect summer reading!

Look for SUMMER SKIES in May 2002.

HARLEQUIN®
Makes any time special®

COOPER'S CORNER

In April 2002 you are invited to three wonderful weddings in a very special town…

A Wedding at Cooper's Corner

USA Today bestselling author

Kristine Rolofson
Muriel Jensen
Bobby Hutchinson

Ailing Warren Cooper has asked private investigator David Solomon to deliver three precious envelopes to each of his grandchildren. Inside each is something that will bring surprise, betrayal…and unexpected romance!

And look for the exciting launch of *Cooper's Corner*, a NEW 12-book continuity from Harlequin— launching in August 2002.

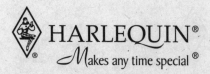